Man Plus
&
Jem

Man Plus
&
Jem

Two Volumes in One

Frederik Pohl

BARNES
&NOBLE
BOOKS
NEW YORK

Contents

Introduction   *vii*

Man Plus   1

Jem   187

Introduction

To most writers, literary awards are a sort of chronic, dull ache punctuated by rare flashes of startlingly intense pleasure. The pleasure, of course, comes when the writer happens to win one of the things, but that doesn't happen every day, and the chronic ache is, well, chronic.

You see, there's something basically unfair about awards—the assumption that all the books ever written can be ranked in some sort of order, best on top, the less-good ones dwindling down in quantity until, perhaps, you reach the point where they haven't managed to get published at all. (To see how silly it is to try to rank all books on the same scale, simply ask yourself which is better: *War and Peace* or *Huckleberry Finn?*)

Still, awards exist, and writers must deal with them. When *Man Plus* was first published in 1976, I had never won an award for any novel (and not that many for any other variety of writing, either). The awards ceremony for the Nebula, which is arguably the most prestigious award for science fiction novels, involves a banquet where nearly all your friendliest colleagues and deadliest competitors are sitting right there. I happen to be a realistic person who is pretty good at math. When I calculated the likelihood of a win for *Man Plus,* the numbers were so unconvincing that I didn't even run through a possible acceptance speech in my mind. The book did win, though. So there I was in front of all those colleagues and friends and, after a rather long moment of silence, managed to say only "Gee, thanks."

I was even less optimistic, if possible, about the chance that *Jem* might win the American Book Award when it was nominated in 1980. In fact, when my editor called to ask if I wanted a lift to the awards event, held in an armory a good distance uptown from my little apartment in New York City, I asked in what I am sure was a whiny voice, "Oh, hell, Tom, do I really *have* to go?" His expectations evidently being no greater than mine, he said I didn't absolutely have to, so I didn't. I later learned that when *Jem* was called as the winner, there was dead silence for some moments until Bill Buckley, out of the generosity of his right-wing but kindly heart, got up and accepted the trophy for me so they could get on with the meeting.

There is definitely one great value to awards. When I am asked, as I all too often am, whether some book of mine is really good, I don't have to appear immodest by saying it is or tamper with the truth by saying it isn't. All I need do is mention what awards it has won. Those are the ones for these two novels. I hope you'll agree they were fairly earned.

—Frederik Pohl

2002

Man Plus

One

An Astronaut and His World

It is necessary to tell you about Roger Torraway. One human being does not seem particularly important, when there are eight billion alive. Not more important than, for example, a single microchip in a memory store. But a single chip can be decisive when it carries an essential bit, and Torraway was important in just that way.

He was a good-looking man, as people go. Famous, too. Or had been.

There had been a time when Roger Torraway hung in the sky for two months and three weeks, along with five other astronauts. They were all dirty, horny and mostly bored. That wasn't what made him famous. That was just "people in the news" stuff, fit for two sentences on the seven o'clock wrap-up on a dull night.

But he did get famous. In Bechuanaland and Baluchistan and Buffalo, people knew his name. *Time* gave him its cover. He didn't have it all to himself. He had to share it with the rest of his team in the orbiting lab, because they were the ones who got lucky and rescued the Soviet bunch that came back to Earth with no steering jets.

So they were all famous men overnight. Torraway was twenty-eight years old when that happened, and had just married a green-eyed, black-haired teacher of ceramic sculpture. Dorrie on Earth was what made him yearn, and Rog in orbit was what made Dorrie a celebrity herself, which she loved.

It took something special to make an astronaut's wife newsworthy. There were so many of them. They looked so much alike. The newspersons used to think that NASA picked the astronauts' wives out of the entries in Miss Georgia contests. They all had that look, as though as soon as they changed out of their bathing suits they would show you some baton-twirling or would recite "The Female of the Species." Dorrie Torraway was a little too intelligent-looking for that, although she was also definitely pretty enough for that. She was the only one of the astronaut wives to get major space in both *Ladies' Home Journal* ("Twelve Christmas Gifts You Can Bake in Your Kiln") and *Ms.* ("Children Would Spoil My Marriage").

Rog was all for the nonfamily. He was all for everything Dorrie wanted, because he was for Dorrie very much.

In that respect, he was a little less like his fellows, who had mostly discovered fine female fringe benefits from the space program. In other ways he was just like them. Bright, healthy, smart, personable, technically trained. The newspersons thought for a while that the astronauts themselves also came from an assembly line somewhere. They were available in a range of twenty centimeters in height and about a dozen years in age, and came in a choice of four shades of skin color, from milk chocolate to Viking. Their hobbies were chess, swimming, hunting, flying, skydiving, fishing and golf. They mingled easily with senators and ambassadors. When they retired from the space program, they found jobs with aerospace companies or with lost causes needing a new publicity image. These jobs paid very well. Astronauts were valuable products. They were not only prized by the publicity media and the Man in the Street. We valued them very highly too.

What the astronauts represented was a dream. The dream was priceless to the Man in the Street, especially if it was a dank, stinking Calcutta street where families slept on the sidewalk and roused themselves at dawn to queue for the one free bowl of food. It was a gritty, grimy world, and space gave it a little bit of beauty and excitement. Not much, but better than none at all.

The astronauts formed a tight little community, all around Tonka, Oklahoma, like baseball families. When each man flew his first mission he joined the major leagues. From then on they were rivals and teammates. They fought one another to get into the line-up, and coached one another from the baselines. It was the dichotomy of the professional athlete. No aging knuckle-baller sitting on the bench and staring at the latest rifle-armed kid felt more sick and angry envy than the back-up man to a planetary landing felt when he watched his Number One suit up.

Rog and Dorrie fit nicely into that community. They made friends easily. They were just oddball enough to be distinctive, not odd enough to worry anyone. If Dorrie didn't want to have children herself, she was nice to the children of the other wives. When Vic Samuelson was out of radio contact for five days on the far side of the sun and Verna Samuelson came taken down with early labor pains, Dorrie took Verna's three infants into her own home. None of them was over five years old. Two of them were still in diapers, and she changed them uncomplainingly while other wives took care of Verna's house and Verna took care of giving birth to her fourth in the NASA hospital. At the Christmas parties Rog and Dorrie never got the drunkest, nor were they ever the first to leave.

They were a nice couple.

They lived in a nice world.

In that they were, they knew, lucky. The rest of the world wasn't all that nice. The little wars chased themselves all over Asia and Africa and Latin America. Western Europe was sometimes strangled by strikes and often crippled by shortages, and when winter came it usually shivered. People were hungry, and a lot of them were angry, and there were very few cities a person would want to walk in alone at night. But Tonka kept itself unpermissive and pretty safe, and astronauts (and cosmonauts and sinonauts) visited Mercury and Mars as well as the moon, swam into the halos of comets and hung in orbit around gas giants.

Torraway himself had flown five major missions. First he flew in one of the shuttle flights to replenish Spacelab, back in the early days after the freeze, when the space program was just getting on its feet again.

Then he spent eighty-one days in the second-generation space station. This was his big moment, the one that got him the cover of *Time*. The Russkis had fired off a manned mission to Mercury, and it had got there all right and landed all right and taken off for the return trip all right; but nothing after that was all right. The Russians had always had trouble with their stabilizing thrusters—several of the early cosmonauts had set themselves spinning, had not been able to stop, and had vomited helplessly all over the insides of their spacecrafts. This time they had trouble again and used up their attitude-correction reserves.

So they managed to get themselves into a wide-assed elliptical orbit around Earth, but they had no way to get out of it safely. Or to stay in it safely, either. Their control was only approximate by then, and the periterran point was low enough inside the ionosphere of Earth's atmosphere to heat them up pretty badly.

But Roger and the other five Americans were sitting there in a spacecraft designed for tug duty, with fuel hoarded for half a dozen more missions. That wasn't any too much, but they made it do: they matched course and velocity with the *Avrora Dva*, linked up and got the cosmonauts out. What a spectacle of free-fall bear hugs and bristly kisses! Back in the space tug with what the Russians had grabbed up to bring with them, they had a party—currant juice toasting Tang, pâté traded for cheeseburgers. And two orbits later the *Avrora* meteored in. "Like a bright exhalation in the evening," said Yuli Bronin, the cosmonaut who had gone to Oxford, and kissed his rescuers again.

When they got back down to Earth, belted in two to a hammock, closer than lovers, they were all heroes, and they were all adored, even Roger, even by Dorrie.

But that was long ago.

Since then Roger Torraway had done two circumlunar flights, tending ship while the radio-telescope crews conducted their orbital tests on the big new hundred-kilometer radio mirror on the farside. And finally he was on the aborted Mars lander, another time when they were lucky to get everyone back on Earth in one piece. But by then the glamour was gone once more. It had just been bad luck and mechanical failures, nothing dramatic.

So most of Roger's work since then had been, well, diplomatic. He played golf with senators on the space committee and commuted to the Eurospace installations in Zurich and Munich and Trieste. He had a modest sale with his memoirs. He served as back-up on an occasional mission. As the space program declined rapidly from national priority to contingency-planning exercises, he had less and less that mattered to do.

Still, he was backing up a mission now, although he didn't talk about it when he was wooing political support for the agency. He wasn't allowed to. This new manned mission, which looked as though it would actually be approved sooner or later, was the first one in the space program that had been classified Top Secret.

We expected a great deal from Roger Torraway, although he was not much different from any of the other astronauts: a little overtrained, a lot underemployed, a good deal discontented with what was happening in their jobs, but very much unwilling to trade them for any others as long as there was still a chance to be great again. They were all like that, even the one that was a monster.

Two
What the President Wanted

The man who was a monster was on Torraway's mind a lot. Roger had a special interest.

He was sitting in the co-pilot's seat at twenty-four thousand meters over Kansas, watching a blip on the IDF radar slide smoothly off the screen. "Shit," said the pilot. The blip was a Soviet Concordski III; their CB-5 had been racing it ever since they had picked it up over the Garrison Dam Reservoir.

Torraway grinned and throttled back another tiny increment. With the boost in relative speed, the Concordski blip picked up a momentum. "We were losing him," the pilot said glumly. "Where do you reckon he's going? Venezuela, maybe?"

"He better be," said Torraway, "considering how much fuel the both of you were burning up."

"Yeah, well," said the pilot, not at all embarrassed at the fact that he had been well over the international treaty limit of 1.5 Mach, "what's happening at Tulsa? Usually they let us come straight in, with a V.I.P. like you."

"Probably some bigger V.I.P. landing now," said Roger. It wasn't a guess, because he knew who the V.I.P. was, and they didn't come any bigger than the President of the United States.

"You fly this thing pretty good," offered the pilot generously. "Want to land it—I mean, when they let us do that thing?"

"Thanks, no. I'd better go back and sort out my junk." But he stayed in the seat, looking down. They had begun the descent, and the patchy field of L-1 cumulus was just below them; they could feel the bumps from the updrafts over the clouds. Torraway took his hands off the controls as the pilot took over. They would be passing over Tonka pretty soon, off to the right. He wondered how the monster was getting along.

The pilot was still feeling generous. "You don't do much flying any more, do you?"

"Only when somebody like you lets me."

"No sweat. What do you do, anyway, if you don't mind my asking? I mean, besides V.I.P.ing it around."

Torraway had an answer all ready for that. "Administration," he said. He always said that, when people asked what he did. Sometimes the people who asked had proper security clearance, not only with the government but with the private radar in his own mind that told him to trust one person and not another. Then he said, "I make monsters." If what they said next indicated that they too were in the know, he might go a sentence or two farther.

There was no secret about the Exomedicine Project. Everyone knew that what they did in Tonka was prepare astronauts to live on Mars. What was secret was how they did it: the monster. If Torraway had said too much he would have jeopardized both his freedom and his job. And Roger liked his job. It supported his pretty wife in her pottery shop. It gave him the feeling of doing something that people would remember, and it took him to interesting places. Back when he was an active astronaut he had been to even more interesting places, but they were out in space and kind of lonely. He liked better the places he went to in private jets, with flattering diplomats and impressionable cocktail-party women to greet him when he got there. Of course, there was the monster to think about, but he didn't really worry about that. Much.

They came in over the Cimarron River, or the crooked red gully that would be the river when it rained again, bent the jet flow to almost straight down, cut back on the power and eased gently in.

"Thanks," Roger said to the pilot, and went back to collect his gear from the V.I.P. cabin.

This time it had been Beirut, Rome, Seville and Saskatoon before he got back to Oklahoma, each place hotter than the place before. Because they were expected at the ceremonial briefing for the President, Dorrie met him at the airport motel. He changed swiftly into the clothes she had brought him. He was glad to be home, glad to be getting back to making monsters and glad to be back with his wife. While he was getting out of the shower he had a swift and powerful erotic impulse. He had a clock inside his head that kept track of what pieces of time were available, so he did not need to check his watch: there was time.

It would not matter if they were a few minutes late. But Dorrie wasn't in the chair where he had left her; the TV was going, her cigarette was burning out in the ashtray, but she was gone. Roger sat on the edge of the bed with a towel wrapped around him until the clock in his head said there was not enough time left to matter. Then he began to dress. He was tying his tie when Dorrie rapped on the door. "Sorry," she said when he opened for her. "I couldn't find the coke machine. One for you and one for me."

Dorrie was almost as tall as Roger, brunette by choice, green-eyed by nature. She took a brush from her bag and touched up the back and sleeves of his jacket, then touched coke cans with him and drank. "We'd better go," she said. "You look gorgeous."

"You look screwable," he said, putting his hand on her shoulder.

"I just put lipstick on," she said, turning her lips away and allowing him to kiss her cheek. "But I'm glad to see the señoritas didn't use you all up."

He chuckled good-humoredly; it was their joke that he slept with a different girl in every city. He liked the joke. It wasn't true. His couple of generally unsatisfactory experiments at adultery had been more shabby and troublesome than rewarding, but he liked thinking of himself as the sort of man whose wife had to worry about the attentions of other women. "Let's not keep the President waiting," he said. "I'll check out while you get the car."

They did not in fact keep the President waiting; they had more than two hours to get through before they even saw him.

Roger was familiar with the general process of being screened, since it had happened to him before. It wasn't just the President of the United States who was taking 200 percent overlap precautions against assassins these days. Roger had been a whole day getting to see the Pope, and even so there had been a Swiss guard holding a Biretta standing right behind him every minute he was in the papal chamber.

Half of the top brass of the lab was here for the briefing. The senior lounge had been cleaned and polished for the occasion and did not look like its familiar coffee-drinking self. Even the blackboards and the paper napkins that were used for scratch paper were tucked away out of sight. Folding screens had been set up in the corners and the shades of the nearest windows discreetly pulled down; that was for the physical search, Roger knew. After that, they would have their interviews with the psychiatrists. Then if everyone passed, if no lethal hypodermic turned up in a hatpin or murderous obsession turned up in a head, they would all go to the auditorium, and there the President would join them.

Four Secret Service men participated in the process of searching, frisking, magnetometering and identifying the male guests, though only two of the men physically took part. The other two just stood there, presumably ready to draw and fire at need. Female Secret Service personnel (they were called "secretaries," but Roger could see that they carried guns) searched the wives and Kathleen Doughty. The women were searched behind one of the shoulder-high screens, but Roger could read from the expressions on his wife's face the progress of the patting, probing hands. Dorrie did not like being touched by strangers. There were times when she did not like being touched at all, but above all not by strangers.

When Roger's own turn came, he understood some of the cold anger he had seen on his wife's face. They were being unusually thorough. His armpits were investigated. His belt was loosened and the cleft of his buttocks probed. His testicles were palpated. Everything in his pockets came out; the handkerchief at his breast was shaken open and swiftly refolded, neater than before. His belt buckle and watchband were studied through a loupe.

Everyone had the same treatment, even the director, who gazed around the room with good-natured resignation while fingers combed the kinky hair under his arms. The only exception was Don Kayman, who had worn his cassock in view of the formality of the occasion, and after some whispered discussion, was escorted into another room to take it off. "Sorry, Father," said the guard, "but you know how it is."

Don shrugged, left with the man, and came back looking annoyed. Roger was beginning to feel annoyed too. It would have been sensible, he thought, for them to have passed some of the people on to the shrinks as soon as they had had their search completed. After all, these were high-powered types, and their time was worth money. But the Secret Service had its own system and operated by stages. It was not until everyone had been searched that the first group of three was conducted to the typist rooms, evacuated specially to make room for the interviews.

Roger's shrink was black by courtesy, actually a sort of coffee-cream color by complexion. They sat in facing straight-backed chairs, with eighteen inches between their knees. The psychiatrist said, "I'll make this as short and painless as I can. Are your parents both alive?"

"No, actually neither of them is. My father died two years ago, my mother when I was in college."

"What sort of work did your father do?"

"Rented fishing boats in Florida." With half his mind Roger described the old man's Key Largo boat livery, while with the other half he maintained his twenty-four-hour-a-day surveillance of himself. Was he showing enough annoyance at being questioned like this? Not too much? Was he relaxed enough? More relaxed than enough?

"I've seen your wife," said the psychiatrist. "A very sexy-looking woman. Do you mind my saying that?"

"Not at all," said Roger, bristling.

"Some white people would not like to hear that from me. How do you feel about it?"

"I know she's sexy," Roger snapped. "That's what made me want to marry her."

"Would you mind if I went a step further and asked how the screwing is?"

"No, of course not—well, hell. Yes, I mind," said Roger savagely. "It's about like anybody else's, I guess. After being married a few years."

The psychiatrist leaned back, looking thoughtfully at Roger. He said, "In your case, Dr. Torraway, this interview is pretty much a formality. You've had quarterly checks for the last seven years and profiled well within the normal range every time. There's nothing violent or unstable in your history. Let me just ask you if you feel uneasy about meeting the President."

"A little awed, maybe," said Roger, shifting gears.

"That's natural enough. Did you vote for Dash?"

"Sure—wait the hell a minute. That's none of your business!"

"Right, Dr. Torraway. You can go back to the briefing room now."

They didn't actually let him go back in the same room, but in one of the smaller conference chambers. Kathleen Doughty joined him almost at once. They had worked together for two and a half years, but she was still formal. "Looks like we've passed, Mr. Dr. Colonel Torraway, sir," she said, her eyes focused as usual on a point over his left shoulder, the cigarette held between her face and him. "Ah, good, a little libation," she said, and reached out past him.

A liveried waiter—no, Roger reminded himself, a Secret Service man wearing a waiter's uniform—was standing there with a tray of drinks. Roger took a whiskey and soda, the big prosthesiologist accepted a small glass of dry sherry. "Be sure you drink it all," she whispered to his shoulder. "They put something in it, I think."

"Something what?"

"To calm you down. If you don't drink it all, they put an armed guard behind you."

To humor her Roger drank his whiskey straight down, but he wondered how someone with her delusions and fears had passed the psychiatric clearance so readily. His five minutes with the shrink had reinforced his self-observing stance, and he was busily analyzing with one part of his mind. Why did he feel uneasy in this woman's presence? Not just because she was wiggy in her mannerisms. He wondered if the trouble was that she admired his courage so much. He had tried to explain to her that being an astronaut no longer took much courage, no more than flying a transport, probably less than driving a cab. Of course, as a back-up for Man Plus there was a very real danger. But only if the men ahead of him in line all dropped out, and that was not a chance to cause much worry. Nevertheless, she went on regarding him with that intensity that in some lights seemed to be admiration, and in others pity.

With the other part of his mind, as always, he was alert for his wife. When she finally came in she was angry, and, for her, disheveled. The hair she had spent an hour putting up was now down. It hung waist-length, a fine frothy fall of black that made her look like a Tenniel drawing of Alice, if Tenniel had been working for *Playboy* at the time. Roger hurried over to soothe her, a job which took so much of his attention that he was caught off-guard when he felt a sudden stir and heard someone say, not very loud or formally, "Ladies and gentlemen, the President of the United States."

Fitz-James Deshatine came grinning and nodding into the room, looking exactly like himself on television, only shorter. Without prompting the lab people sorted themselves into a semicircle, and the President went around it, shaking every hand, with the project director at his side making the introductions. Deshatine had been beautifully briefed. He had the politician's trick of catching every name and making some sort of personal response. To Kathleen Doughty it was "Glad to see some Irish in this crew, Dr. Doughty." To Roger it was "We met once before, Colonel Torraway. After that fine job with the Russians. Let's see, that must be seven years ago, when I was chairman of the Senate committee. Perhaps you remember." Certainly Roger remembered—and was flattered, and knew he was being flattered, that the President remembered. To Dorrie it was "Good heavens, Mrs. Torraway, how come a pretty girl like you wastes herself on one of these scientific Johnnies?" Roger stiffened a little when he heard that. It was not so much that it was down-putting to him, it was the kind of empty compliment Dorrie always disdained. But she was not disdaining it. Coming from the President of the United States, it brought a sparkle to her eyes. "What a beautiful man," she whispered, following his progress as he made the circle.

When he had finished going around the semicircle, he hopped to the
little platform and said, "Well, friends, I came here to look and listen,
not to talk. But I do want to thank every one of you for putting up
with the nonsense they make you go through to have me around. I'm
sorry about that. It isn't my idea. They just tell me it's necessary, as
long as there are so many wacks around. And as long as the enemies of
the Free World are what they are, and we're the kind of open, trusting
people *we* are." He grinned directly at Dorrie. "Tell me, did they make
you soak your fingernails before they let you in?"

Dorrie laughed musically, startling her husband. (She had been complaining with vicious anger that her nail polish had been ruined.)
"They certainly did, Mr. President. Just like my manicurist," she
called.

"Sorry about that. They say that's to make sure that you don't have
any secret bio-chem-i-cal poisons to scratch me with when we shake
hands. Well, you got to do what the man says, I guess. Anyway"—he
chuckled—"if you think it's a nuisance for you pretty ladies, you should
see how my old cat acts when they do it to her. Good thing she didn't
really have poison on her claws last time they did it. She scored on
three Secret Service men, my nephew and two of her own kittens before she was through." He laughed, and Roger was a little surprised to
find that he and Dorrie and the rest were joining in.

"Anyway," said the President, coming to the point, "I'm grateful for
your courtesy. And I am one thousand times more grateful for the way
you're pushing the Man Plus project through. I don't have to tell you
what it means to the Free World. There's Mars out there, the only
piece of real estate around that's worth having, apart from the one
we're all standing on right now. By the end of this decade it's going to
belong to somebody. There are only two choices. It will belong to them,
or it will belong to us. And I want it to be us. You people are the ones
that are going to make sure that happens, because you're going to give
us the Man Plus that will live on Mars. I want to thank you deeply
and sincerely, from the bottom of my heart, in the name of every living
human being in the Free World democratic lands, for making this
dream possible. And now," he said, smothering an attempt at a round
of polite applause, "I think it's time I stopped talking and started listening. I want to see what's happening with our Man Plus. General
Scanyon, it's all yours."

"Right, Mr. President."

Vern Scanyon was director of the laboratory division of the Grissom

Memorial Institute of Space Medicine. He was also a retired two-star general and acted it. He checked his watch, glanced at his executive assistant (he sometimes called him his executive officer) for confirmation and said, "We have a few minutes before Commander Hartnett finishes his warm-up tests. Suppose we look in on him on the closed circuit for a minute. Then I'll try to tell you what's going to happen today."

The room darkened.

A TV projection screen lighted up behind the platform. There was a scrape as one of the "waiters" moved a chair for the President to sit in. He muttered something. The chair was moved back, and the President nodded, shadowy in the flicker from the projection screen, and looked up.

The screen showed a man.

He did not look like a man. His name was Will Hartnett. He was an astronaut, a Democrat, a Methodist, a husband, a father, an amateur tympanist, a beautifully smooth ballroom dancer; but to the eye he was none of those things. To the eye he was a monster.

He did not look human at all. His eyes were glowing, red-faceted globes. His nostrils flared in flesh folds, like the snout of a star-nosed mole. His skin was artificial; its color was normal heavy sun tan, but its texture was that of a rhinoceros's hide. Nothing that could be seen about him was of the appearance he had been born with. Eyes, ears, lungs, nose, mouth, circulatory system, perceptual centers, heart, skin—all had been replaced or augmented. The changes that were visible were only the iceberg's tip. What had been done inside him was far more complex and far more important. He had been rebuilt for the single purpose of fitting him to stay alive, without external artificial aids, on the surface of the planet Mars.

He was a cyborg—a cybernetic organism. He was part man and part machine, the two disparate sections fused together so that even Will Hartnett, looking at himself in the mirror on the occasions when he was permitted to see a mirror, did not know what of him was him and what had been added.

In spite of the fact that nearly everyone in the room had actually played a part in creating the cyborg, in spite of the familiarity all of them had had with his photos, TV image and his person itself, there was a muffled gasp. As the TV camera caught him he was doing endless effortless push-ups. The view was from a yard or so from the top of his strangely formed head, and as Hartnett locked himself up on his arms his eyes came level with the camera, glinting from the facets that gave him multiple scanning of the environment.

He looked very strange. Roger, remembering the old movies of his childhood hours before the TV, thought that his good old buddy looked a lot weirder than any animated carrot or magnified beetle on the horror shows. Hartnett had been born in Danbury, Connecticut. Every visible artifact he wore had been manufactured in California, Oklahoma, Alabama or New York. But none of it looked human or even terrestrial. He looked *Martian*.

In the sense that form follows function, Martian he was. He was shaped for Mars. In a sense, too, he was there already. Grissom Labs had the finest Mars-normal tanks in the world, and Hartnett's push-ups were on iron oxide sands, in a pressure chamber where the weight of gas had been dropped to ten millibars, only 1 percent of the thrust on the outside of the double glass walls. The temperature of the sparse gas molecules around him was held at forty-five degrees below zero, Celsius. Batteries of high-ultraviolet lamps flooded the scene with the exact spectrum of sunlight on a Martian winter day.

If the place where Hartnett was was not truly Mars, it was close enough to fool even a Martian—if there had ever been such things as Martians—in every respect but one. In all but that one respect, a Ras Thavas or a Wellsian mollusk might have emerged from sleep, looked about him and decided that he was indeed on Mars, on a late fall day in the middle latitudes, shortly after sunrise.

The one anomaly simply could not be helped. He was subject to standard Earth gravity instead of the fractional attraction that would be proper for the surface of Mars. The engineers had gone so far as to calculate the cost of flying the entire Mars-normal tank in a jet conversion, dropping it along a calculated parabola to simulate, at least for ten or twenty minutes at a time, the proper Martian weights. They had decided against it on the grounds of cost, and pondering, they had estimated, allowed for and finally dismissed the effects of the one anomaly.

The one thing no one feared might go wrong with Hartnett's new body was that it might be too weak for any stresses that might be placed on it. He was already lifting five-hundred-pound weights. When he really reached Mars, he would be able to carry more than half a ton.

In a sense Hartnett on Earth was more hideous than he would be on Mars, because his telemetry equipment was as monstrous as himself. Pulse, temperature and skin resistance sensor pads clung to his shoulders and head. Probes reached under the tough artificial skin to measure his internal flows and resistances. Transmitter antennae fanned out like a peasant's broom from his backpack. Everything that was going on in his system was being continually measured, encoded and transmitted to the 100-meter-per-second broad-band recording tapes.

The President was whispering something. Roger Torraway found himself leaning forward to catch the end of it: ". . . he hear what we say in here?"

"Not until I cycle us through his communications net," said General Scanyon.

"Uh-huh," said the President slowly, but whatever it had been that he intended to say if the cyborg couldn't hear him, he didn't say it. Roger felt a twinge of sympathy. He himself still had to select what he said when the cyborg could hear, and censored what he said even when old Hartnett wasn't around. It was simply not right that anything that had drunk a beer and fathered a child should be so ugly. All the words that were relevant were invidious.

The cyborg appeared willing to keep up his metronome exercising forever, but someone who had been counting cadence—"one and two, one and two"—came to a halt, and the cyborg stopped too. He stood up, methodically and rather slowly, as though it were a new dance step he was practicing. With a reflex action that no longer had a function, he rubbed the back of a thick-skinned hand against his plastic-smooth and browless forehead.

In the darkness Roger Torraway shifted position so that he could see better, past the famous craggy profile of the President. Even in outline Roger could see that the President was frowning slightly. Roger put his arm around his wife's waist and thought about what it must be like to be the President of three hundred million Americans in a touchy and treacherous world. The power that flowed through the man in the darkness ahead of him could throw fusion bombs into every hidden corner of the world in ninety minutes' time. It was power of war, power of punishment, power of money. Presidential power had brought the Man Plus project into being in the first place. Congress had never debated the funding, knew only in the most general terms what was going on: the enabling act had been called "A Bill to Provide Supplementary Space Exploration Facilities at Presidential Discretion."

General Scanyon said, "Mr. President, Commander Hartnett would be glad to show you some of the capacities of his prostheses. Weight-lifting, high jump. Whatever you like."

"Oh, he's worked hard enough for one day," smiled the President.

"Right. Then we'll go ahead, sir." He spoke softly into the communicator microphone and then turned back to the President. "Today's test is to disassemble and repair a short in the com unit under field conditions. We'll estimate seven minutes for the job. A panel of our own shop repairmen, operating with all their tools in their own workshops, averaged about five minutes, so if Commander Hartnett makes it in the optimal time that is pretty good evidence of close motor control."

"Yes, I see that," said the President. "What's he doing now?"

"Just waiting, sir. We're going to cycle him up to one hundred and fifty millibars so he can hear and talk a little more easily."

The President said acutely, "I thought you had equipment to talk to him in total vacuum."

"Well, ah, yes, sir, we do. We've had a little trouble with that. At present our basic communication facility at Mars-normal conditions is visual, but we expect to have the voice system functioning shortly."

"Yes, I hope so," said the President.

At the level of the tank, thirty meters into the ground under the room they were in, a graduate student functioning as a lab assistant responded to a cue and opened a valve—not to the external atmosphere, but to the tanks of Mars-normal gas that were mixed and ready in the pressure sink. Gradually the pressure built up to a thin, deepening whistle. The adding on of pressure to the 150-millibar level did not benefit Hartnett's functioning in any way. His redesigned body ignored most environmental factors. It could equally well tolerate Arctic winds, total vacuum or a muggy day at the Earth's equator, with the air at 1,080 millibars and soggy with damp. One was as comfortable to him as another. Or as uncomfortable, for Hartnett had reported that his new body ached, tweaked and chafed. They could just as easily have opened the valves and let the ambient air rush in, but then it would all have had to be pumped out again for the next test.

At last the whistle stopped and they heard the cyborg's voice. It was doll-shrill. "Thanksss. Hold eet dere, weel you?" The low pressure played tricks with his diction, especially as he no longer had a proper trachea and larynx to work with. After a month as a cyborg, speaking was becoming strange to him, for he was getting out of the habit of breathing anyway.

From behind Roger, the lab's expert in vision systems said glumly, "They know those eyes aren't made to stand sudden pressure changes. Serve them right if one of them cracks on them." Roger winced, with the fantasied pain of a faceted crystalline eyeball splintering in his socket. His wife laughed.

"Have a seat, Brad," she said, pulling away from Roger's arm. Absently Roger made room, staring up at the screen. The cadence-counting voice was saying, "On the tick. Five. Four. Three. Two. One. Start sequence."

The cyborg squatted clumsily over the entry plate of a black-finished metal canister. Without haste he slid a blade-thin screwdriver into a nearly invisible slot, made a precise quarter turn, repeated the movement again in another place and lifted off the plate. The thick fingers sorted carefully through the multicolored spaghetti of the internal wiring, found a charred red-and-white-candy-striped strand, detached it, shortened it to remove the burned insulation, stripped it down by simply pinching it through the nails, and held it to a terminal. The longest part of the operation was waiting for the fluxing iron to heat; that took more than a minute. Then the new joint was brazed, the spaghetti stuffed back inside, the plate replaced, and the cyborg stood up.

"Six minutes, eleven and two-fifths seconds," reported the counting voice.

The project director led a round of applause. He then stood up and delivered a short address. He told the President that the purpose of the Man Plus project was to so modify a human body that it could survive on the surface of Mars as readily and safely as a normal man could walk across a Kansas wheat field. He reviewed the manned space program from suborbital flight through space station and deep probe. He listed some of the significant data about Mars: land area actually greater than Earth's, in spite of its smaller diameter, because there were no seas to waste surface. Temperature range, suitable for life—suitably modified, to be sure. Potential wealth, incalculable. The President listened attentively, although, to be sure, he knew every word.

Then he said, "Thanks, General Scanyon. Just let me say one thing."

He climbed nimbly up to the platform and smiled thoughtfully down at the scientists. "When I was a boy," he began, "the world was simpler. The big problem was how to help the emerging free nations of Earth enter the community of civilized countries. Those were the Iron Curtain days. It was them on their side, locked in, quarantined. And all the rest of us on ours.

"Well," he went on, "things have changed. The Free World has had bad times. Once you get off our own North American continent, what have you got? Collectivist dictatorships everywhere you look, bar one or two holdouts like Sweden and Israel. I'm not here to rake up ancient history. What's done is done, and there's no point blaming anybody. Everybody knows who lost China and gave Cuba to the other side. We know what administration let England and Pakistan fall. We don't have to talk about those things. We're just looking toward the future.

"And I tell you, ladies and gentlemen," he said earnestly, "the future of the free human race lies with you. Maybe we've had some setbacks here on our own planet. That's over and done with. We can look out into space. We look, and what do we see? We see another Earth. The planet Mars. As the distinguished director of your project, General Scanyon, just said, it's a bigger planet than the one we were born on, in the ways that are important. And it can be ours.

"That's where the future of freedom is, and it's up to you to give it to us. I know you will. I'm counting on every one of you."

He looked thoughtfully around the room, meeting every eye. The old Dash charisma was making itself felt all over the room.

Then he smiled suddenly, said "Thank you," and was gone in a wave of Secret Service men.

Three
Man Becoming Martian

Time was when the planet Mars looked like another Earth. The astronomer Schiaparelli, peering through his Milanese telescope at the celebrated conjunction of 1877, saw what he thought were "channels," announced them as "canali" and had them understood as "canals" by half the literate population of Earth. Including nearly all the astronomers, who promptly turned their telescopes in the same direction and discovered more.

Canals? Then they must have been dug for a purpose. What purpose? To hold water—there was no other explanation that saved the facts.

The logic of the syllogism was compelling, and by the turn of the century there was hardly a doubter in the world. It was accepted as lore that Mars held an older, wiser culture than our own. If only we could somehow speak to them, what marvels we would learn! Percival Lowell mused over a sketching pad and came up with a first attempt. Draw great Euclidean shapes on the Sahara Desert, he said. Line them with brushwood, or dig them as trenches and fill them with oil. Then on some moonless night when Mars is high in the African heavens, set them afire. Those alien Martian eyes that he took to be fixed firmly to their alien Martian telescopes would see. They would recognize the squares and triangles. They would understand that communication was intended, and out of their older wisdom they would find a way to respond.

Not everybody believed quite as much quite so firmly as Lowell. Some said that Mars was too small and too cold ever to harbor a hugely intelligent race. Dig canals? Oh, yes, that was a simple enough peasant skill, and a race that was dying of thirst could well manage to scratch out ditches, even enormous ditches visible across interplanetary space, to keep itself alive. But beyond that, the environment was simply too harsh. A race living there would be like the Eskimos, forever trapped on the threshold of civilization because the world outside their ice huts was too hostile to grant them leisure to learn abstractions. No doubt when our telescopes were able to resolve the individual Martian face we would see only a brutish mask, stolid and stunned, brother to the ox; able to move soil and to plant crops, yes, but not to aspire to a life of the mind.

But, wise or brutal, Martians were there—or so thought the best opinion of the times.

Then better telescopes were built, and better ways were found to understand what they disclosed. To the lens and the mirror was added the spectroscope and the camera. In the eyes and understanding of astronomers Mars swam a little closer every day. At every step, as the image of the planet itself grew more sharp and clear, the vision of its putative inhabitants became more cloudy and less real. There was too little air. There was too little water. It was too cold. The canals broke up, under better resolution, into irregular blotches of surface markings. The cities that should have marked their junctions were not there.

By the time of the first Mariner fly-bys the Martian race, which had never lived except in the imagination of human beings, was irrevocably dead.

It still seemed that life of a sort could exist, perhaps lowly plants, even a rude sort of amphibian. But nothing like a man. On the surface of Mars an air-breathing, water-based creature like a human being could not survive for a quarter of an hour.

It would be the lack of air that would kill him most quickly. His death would not be from simple strangulation. He would not live long enough for that to happen. In the 10-millibar pressure of the surface of Mars his blood would boil away and he would die in agony of something like the bends. If he somehow survived that, then he would die of lack of air to breathe. If he survived both of those—given air in a backpack, and a face mask fed with a mixture of gases that did not contain nitrogen, at some intermediate pressure level between Earth- and Mars-normal—he would still die. He would die from exposure to unshielded solar radiation. He would die from the extremes of Martian temperature—at its best, a warmish spring day; at its coldest, worse than Antarctic polar night. He would die from thirst. And if he could somehow survive all of those, he would die more slowly, but surely, from hunger, since there was nowhere on the surface of Mars one morsel that a human being could eat. ·

But there is another kind of argument that contradicts the conclusions drawn from objective facts. Man is not bound by objective facts. If they inconvenience him, he changes them, or makes an end run around them.

Man cannot survive on Mars. However, man cannot survive in the Antarctic, either. But he does.

Man survives in places where he ought to die, by bringing a kinder environment with him. He carries what he needs. His first invention along those lines was clothing. His second, storable food, like dried meat and parched grain. His third, fire. His most recent, the whole series of devices and systems that gave him access to the sea bottoms and to space.

The first alien planet men walked on was the moon. It was even more hostile than Mars, in that the vital supplies of which Mars had very little—air, water and food—did not, on the moon, exist at all. Yet as early as the 1960s men visited the moon, carrying with them air and water and everything else they needed in life-support systems mounted on their spacesuits or built into their landing modules. From there it was no trick to build the systems bigger. It was not easy because of the magnitudes involved. But it was straightforward scaling up, to the point of semi-permanent and not far from self-sustaining closed-cycle colonies. The first problem of support was purely logistic. For each man you needed tons of supplies; for each pound of cargo blasted into space you spent a million dollars' worth of fuel and hardware. But it could be done.

Mars is orders of magnitude more remote. The moon circles the Earth only a quarter of a million miles out. At its very closest, a few times in a century, Mars is more than a hundred times as far.

Mars is not only distant from the Earth, it is farther than Earth from the sun. Whereas the moon receives as much energy per square inch as the Earth does, Mars, by the law of inverse squares, gets only half as much.

From some point on Earth, a rocket can be sent to the moon at any hour of any day. But Mars and Earth do not circle each other; both circle the sun, and as they do so at different speeds they are sometimes not very close and sometimes very far. It is only when they are at minimal travel distances that a rocket can efficiently be sent from one to another, and those times occur only once in every period of two years, for one month and some weeks.

Even the factors in Mars's makeup which make it more like the Earth work against maintaining a colony there. It is bigger than the moon, and thus its gravity is more like Earth's. But because it is bigger and pulls harder a rocket needs more fuel to land on it, and more fuel to take off again.

What it all comes down to is that a colony on the moon can be supported from Earth. A colony on Mars cannot.

At least a colony of human beings cannot.

But what if one reshapes a human being?

Suppose one takes the standard human frame and alters some of the optional equipment. There's nothing to breathe on Mars. So take the lungs out of the human frame, replace them with micro-miniaturized oxygen regeneration cat-cracking systems. One needs power for that, but power flows down from the distant sun.

The blood in the standard human frame would boil; all right, eliminate the blood, at least from the extremities and the surface areas—build arms and legs that are served by motors instead of muscles—and reserve the blood supply only for the warm, protected brain. A normal human body needs food, but if the major musculature is replaced by machines, the food requirement drops. It is only the brain that must be fed every minute of every day, and fortunately, in terms of energy requirements the brain is the least demanding of human accessories. A slice of toast a day will keep it fed.

Water? It is no longer necessary, except for engineering losses—like adding hydraulic fluid to a car's braking system every few thousand miles. Once the body has become a closed system, no water needs to be flushed through it in the cycle of drink, circulate, excrete or perspire.

Radiation? A two-edged problem. At unpredictable times there are solar flares, and then even on Mars there is too much of it for health; the body must therefore be clothed with an artificial skin. The rest of the time there is only the normal visible and ultraviolet light from the sun. It is not enough to maintain heat, and not quite enough even for good vision; so more surface must be provided to gather energy—hence the great bat-eared receptors on the cyborg—and, to make vision as good as it can be made, the eyes are replaced with mechanical structures.

If one does all these things to a human being, what is left is no longer precisely a human being. It is a man plus large elements of hardware.

The man has become a cybernetic organism: a cyborg.

The first man to be made into a cyborg was probably Willy Hartnett. There was some doubt. There were persistent rumors of a Chicom experiment that had succeeded for a while and then failed. But it was pretty clear that Hartnett was at least the only one alive at this particular moment. He had been born in the regular human way and had worn the regular human shape for thirty-seven years. It was only in the last eighteen months that he had begun to change.

At first the changes were minor and temporary.

His heart was not removed. It was only bypassed now and then by a swift soft-plastic impeller that he wore for a week at a time strapped on a shoulder.

His eyes were not removed either . . . then. They were only sealed closed with a sort of gummy blindfold, while he practiced recognizing the perplexing shapes of the world as they were revealed to him through a shrilly buzzing electronic camera that was surgically linked to his optic nerve.

One by one the separate systems that would make him a Martian were tested. It was only when each component had been tested and adjusted and found satisfactory that the first permanent changes had been made.

They were not *really* permanent. That was a promise that Hartnett clung to. The surgeons had made it to Hartnett, and Hartnett had made it to his wife. All the changes could be reversed and would be. When the mission was over and he was safely back, they would remove the hardware and replace it with soft human tissues again, and he would be returned to purely human shape.

It would not, he understood, be exactly the shape he had started out with. They could not preserve his own organs and tissues. They could only replace them with equivalents. Organ transplants and plastic surgery would do all they could to make him look like himself again, but there was small chance he would ever again be able to travel on his old passport photo.

He did not greatly mind that. He had never considered himself a handsome man. He was content to know that he would have human eyes again—not his own, of course. But the doctors had promised they would be blue, and that lids and lashes would cover them again, and with any luck at all, they thought, the eyes could even weep. (With joy, he foresaw.) His heart would again be a lump of muscle the size of a fist. It would pump red human blood to all the ends of limb and body. His lung muscles would take air into his chest, and there natural human alveoli would absorb oxygen and release CO_2. The great photoreceptor bat-ears (that gave so much trouble, because their support strength was up to the demands of Martian gravitation but not terrestrial, so that they were constantly being detached and returned to the shop) would be dismantled and gone. The skin that had been so painfully constructed and fitted to him would be equally painfully flayed off again, and replaced with human skin that sweated and grew hair. (His own skin was still there under the skin-tight artificial covering, but he did not expect it would survive the experiment. It had had to be discouraged from carrying on its normal functions during the time it was buried under the artificial hide. Almost surely it would have lost the capacity for them and would have to be replaced.)

Hartnett's wife had exacted one promise from him. She had made him swear that as long as he wore the Halloween mask of the cyborg, he would keep out of the sight of his children. Fortunately the children were little enough to be biddable, and teachers, friends, neighbors, parents of schoolmates and all had been made cooperative by hints of stories of jungle rot and skin ailments. They had been curious, but the story had worked, and no one had urged Terry's father to come to a PTA meeting or Brenda's husband to join her at their backyard barbecue.

Brenda Hartnett herself had tried not to see her husband, but in the long run curiosity drove out fear. She had herself smuggled into the tank room one day while Willy was practicing a coordination test, riding a bicycle around the reddish sands with a basin of water balanced on the handlebars. Don Kayman had stayed with her, fully expecting her to faint or scream or perhaps be sick to her stomach. She did none of those things, surprising herself as much as the priest. The cyborg looked too much like a Japanese horror film to be taken seriously. It was only that night that she really related the bat-eared, crystal-eyed creature on the bike with the father of her children. The next day she went to the project's medical director and told him that Willy must be getting starved for screwing by then and she didn't see why she couldn't accommodate him. The doctor had to explain to her what Willy had not been able to bring himself to say, that in the present state of the art those functions had had to be regarded as superfluous and therefore had been temporarily, uh, disconnected.

Meanwhile the cyborg toiled away at his tests and awaited each next installment of pain.

His world was in three parts. The first part was a suite of rooms kept at a pressure equivalent to about 7,500 feet of altitude so that the project staff could go in and out with only mild inconvenience when they had to. This was where he slept, when he could, and ate what little he was given. He was always hungry, always. They'd tried, but they hadn't been able to disconnect the cravings of his senses. The second part was the Mars-normal tank in which he did his gymnastics and performed his tests so that the architects of his new body could observe their creation at work. And the third part was a low-pressure chamber on wheels that rolled him from his private suite to his public test arena, or wherever else he, rarely, had any occasion to go.

The Mars-normal tank was like a zoo cage in which he was always on display. The rolling tank offered him nothing but waiting to be moved into something else.

It was only the little two-room suite that was officially his home that gave him any comfort at all. There he had his TV set, his stereo, his telephone, his books. Sometimes one of the graduate students or a fellow astronaut would visit with him there, playing chess or trying to talk a conversation while their chests labored and lungs pumped fruitlessly at the 7,500-foot pressure. These visits he looked forward to and tried to prolong. When no one was with him he was on his own resources. Infrequently he read. Sometimes he sat before the TV, regardless of what was being shown on it. Most often he "rested." That was how he described it to his overseers, by which he meant sitting or lying with his vision system in stand-by. It was like having one's eyes closed but remaining awake. A bright enough light would register on his senses, as it will even through a sleeper's closed lids; a sound would penetrate at once. In those times his brain raced, conjuring up thoughts of sex, food, jealousy, sex, anger, children, nostalgia, love . . . until he pleaded for relief and was given a course in self-hypnosis which let him wash his mind empty. After that in "rest" mode he did almost nothing that was conscious, while his nervous system groomed and prepared itself for the next sensations of pain and his brain counted the seconds until his flight would be over and his normal human body given back to him.

There were a lot of those seconds. He had multiplied them out often enough. Seven months in orbit to Mars. Seven months coming back. A few weeks at both ends, getting ready for the launch and then debriefing before they would start the process of restoring him to his own body. A few months—no one would tell him exactly how many—while the surgery took place and the replaced parts healed.

The number of seconds, close as he could guess it, was some forty-five million. Give or take as much as ten million. He felt each one of them arrive and linger and reluctantly slip past.

The psychologists had tried to avoid all this by planning every moment for him. He refused the plans. They tried to understand him with devious tests and pattern-scanning. He let them pry, but inside himself he kept a citadel of privacy that he would not let them invade.

Hartnett had never thought of himself as an introspective man; he knew that he was a mile wide and an inch deep, and that he led an unexamined life. He liked it that way. But now that he had nothing left but the interior of his mind that was his own, he guarded that.

He wished sometimes that he did know how to examine his life. He wished he could understand his reasons for doing what he did.

Why had he volunteered for the mission? Sometimes he tried to remember, and then decided he had never known. Was it because the free world needed Martian living space? Because he wanted the glamour of being the first Martian? For the money? For the scholarships and favors it would mean for the kids? To make Brenda love him?

It probably was in among those reasons somewhere, but he couldn't remember. If he had ever known.

In any case he was committed. The thing he *was* sure of was that he had no way to back out now.

He would let them do whatever savage, sadistic torturing they wanted of his body. He would board the spaceship that would take him to Mars. He would endure the seven endless months in orbit. He would go down to the surface, explore, stake claims, take samples, photograph, test. He would rise up again from the Martian surface and live somehow through the seven-month return, and he would give them all the information they wanted. He would accept the medals and the applause and the lecture tours and the television interviews and the contracts for books.

And then he would present himself to the surgeons to be put back the way he was supposed to be.

All of those things he had made his mind up to, and he was sure he would carry them out.

There was only one question in his mind to which he had not yet worked out an answer. It had to do with a contingency he was not prepared to meet. When he first volunteered for the program, they had told him very openly and honestly that the medical problems were complex and not fully understood. They would have to learn how to deal with some of them on him. It was possible that some of the answers would be hard to find or wrong. It was possible that returning him to his own shape would be, well, difficult. They told him that very clearly, at the very beginning, and then they never said it again.

But he remembered. The problem he had not resolved was what he would do if for any reason, when the whole mission was over, they could not put him back together right away. What he couldn't decide was whether he would then simply kill himself or at the same time kill as many as possible of his friends, superiors and colleagues as well.

Four
Group of Probable Pallbearers

Roger Torraway, Col. (Ret.) USAF, B.A., M.A., D.Sc. (Hon.). At the time he woke up in the morning, the night shift finished bench-running the cyborg's photoreceptors. There had been an unidentified voltage drop caught on the monitors when they were last in use on the cyborg, but nothing showed in the bench test, and nothing had been visible when they were stripped. They were certified serviceable.

Roger had slept badly. It was a terrible responsibility, being custodian of mankind's last forlorn hope for freedom and decency. When he woke up it was with that thought in mind; there was a part of Roger Torraway—it showed itself most commonly in dreams—that was about nine years old. It took all the things the President said at face value, although Roger himself, doubling as diplomat and mission head, world traveler, familiar of a dozen capitals, really did not think in his conscious mind that the "Free World" existed.

He dressed, his mind in the familiar occupation of resolving a dichotomy. Let's assume Dash is on the level, and occupying Mars means salvation for humanity, he thought. Can we cut it? He thought of Willy Hartnett—good-looking (or he had been, till the prosthesiologists got at him). Amiable. Good with his hands. But also a little bit of a lightweight, when you came to look at him honestly. Likely to take a drink too many at the club on a Saturday night. Not to be trusted in the kitchen with another man's wife at a party.

He was not a hero, by any measure Roger could find. But who was? He cast his mind down the list of back-ups to the cyborg. Number One, Vic Freibart, currently off on a ceremonial tour with the Vice

President and temporarily removed from the order of succession. Number Two, Carl Mazzini, on sick leave while the leg he had broken at Mount Snow healed up. Number Three: Him.

There was no Valley Forge quality in any of them.

He made his breakfast without waking Dorrie, got the car out and left it puffing on its skirts while he picked up the morning paper, threw it into the garage and closed the door. His next-door neighbor, walking toward his car pool, hailed him. "See the news this morning? I see Dash was in town last night. Some high-level conference."

Roger said automatically, "No, I haven't put on the TV this morning." But I did see Dash, he thought, and I could take the wind out of *your* sails. It annoyed him not to be able to say it. Security was a confounded nuisance. Half of his recent trouble with Dorrie, he was sure, came from the fact that in the neighborhood wives' morning block conference and coffee binge she was allowed to mention her husband only as a formerly active astronaut, now in administrative work. Even his trips abroad had to be played down—"out of town," "business trip," anything but "Well, *my* husband is meeting with the Chiefs of Staff of the Basutoland Air Force this week." She had resisted. She still resisted, or at least complained to Roger about it often enough. But as far as he knew, she had not broken security. Since at least three of the wives were known to report to the Lab intelligence officer, he undoubtedly would have known.

As Roger got into the car he remembered that he had not kissed Dorrie goodbye.

He told himself that it did not matter. She would not wake up and therefore would not know; if by any chance she did wake up, she would complain at being wakened. But he did not like to give up a ritual. While he thought about it, however, he was automatically putting the car into Drive and keying his code number for the Lab; the car began to move. He sighed, snapped on the TV and watched the *Today Show* all the way to work.

Fr. Donnelly S. Kayman, A.B., M.A., Ph.D., S.J. As he began celebrating the Mass in the Lady Chapel of St. Jude's, three miles away, on the other side of Tonka, the cyborg was greedily swallowing the one meal he would get that day. Chewing was difficult because lack of practice had made his gums sore, and the saliva didn't seem to flow as freely as it should any more. But the cyborg ate with enthusiasm, not even thinking about the test program for the day, and when he had finished he gazed sadly at the empty plate.

Don Kayman was thirty-one years old and the world's most authoritative areologist (which is to say, specialist in the planet Mars)—at least in the Free World. (Kayman would have admitted that old Parnov at the Shklovskii Institute in Novosibirsk also knew a thing or two.) He was also a Jesuit priest. He did not think of himself as being one thing first and the other with what part of him was left over; his work was areology, his person was the priesthood. Meticulously and with joy he elevated the Host, drank the wine, said the final *redempit*, glanced at his watch and whistled. He was running late. He shed his robes in record time. He aimed a slap at the Chicano altar boy, who grinned and opened the door for him. They liked each other; Kayman even thought that the boy might himself become both priest and scientist one day.

Now in sports shirt and slacks, Kayman jumped into his convertible. It was a classic, wheels instead of hoverskirts; it could even be driven off the guided highways. But where was there to go off the highways? He dialed the laboratories, switched on the main batteries and opened his newspaper. Without attention the little car nosed into the freeway, found a gap in the traffic, leaped to fill it and bore him at eighty miles an hour to his job.

The news in the newspaper was, as usual, mostly bad.

In Paris the MFP had issued another blast at the Chandrigar peace talks. Israel had refused to vacate Cairo and Damascus. New York City's martial law, now in its fifteenth month, had failed to prevent the ambush of a Tenth Mountain Division convoy trying to sneak across the Bronx-Whitestone Bridge to the relief of the garrison in Shea Stadium; fifteen soldiers were dead, and the convoy had returned to the Bronx.

Kayman dropped the paper sadly. He tilted the rear-view mirror back, raised the side windows to deflect some of the wind and began to brush his shoulder-length hair. Twenty-five strokes on each side—it was almost as much a ritual with him as the Mass. He would brush it again that day, because he had a lunch date with Sister Clotilda. She was already half convinced that she wanted to apply for relief from certain of her vows, and Kayman wanted to resume the discussion with her as soon, and as often and as long, as suitable.

Because he had less distance to travel, Kayman arrived at the laboratories just behind Roger Torraway. They got out together, turned their cars over to the parking system and went up to the briefing room in the same elevator.

Deputy Director T. Gamble de Bell. As he prepared to juice up key personnel at the morning briefing, the cyborg was thirty meters away, spread-eagled face down and nude. On Mars he would eat only low-residue food and not much of that. On Earth it was thought necessary to keep his eliminatory system at least minimally functional, in spite of the difficulties the changes in skin and metabolism produced. Hartnett was glad for the food, but hated the enemas.

The project director was a general. The science chief was a distinguished biophysicist who had worked with Wilkins and Pauling; twenty years back he had stopped doing science and started doing figureheading, because that was where the rewards were. Neither had much to do with the work of the labs themselves, only with liaison between the operating people and those shadowy outside figures who worked the money switch.

For the nitty-gritty of daily routine, it was the deputy director who did the work. This early in the morning, he already had a sheaf of notes and reports, and he had read them.

"Scramble the picture," he ordered from the lectern, not looking up. On the monitor above him Willy Hartnett's grotesque profile broke up into a jackstraw bundle of lines, then turned into snow, then rebuilt itself into its proper features. (Only the head showed. The people in the briefing room could not see what indignity Willy was suffering, though most of them knew well enough. It was on the daily sked sheet.) The picture was no longer in color. The scan was coarser now, and the image less steady. But it was now security-safe (on the chance that some spy had tapped the closed circuit), and in portraying Hartnett the quality of the picture made, after all, very little difference.

"All right," said the deputy director harshly, "you heard Dash last night. He didn't come here to get your votes, he wants action. So do I. I don't want any more screw-ups like the photoreceptor crap."

He turned a page. "Morning progress report," he read. "Commander Hartnett is functioning well in all systems, with three exceptions. First, the artificial heart does not respond well to prolonged exercise at low temperatures. Second, the CAV system receives poorly in frequencies higher than medium blue—I'm disappointed in that one, Brad," he interpolated, looking up at Alexander Bradley, the expert in the perceptual systems of the eye. "You know we're locked into UV capability on that. Third, communications links. We had to admit to that one in front of the President last night. He didn't like it, and I didn't like it. That throat mike doesn't work. Effectively we don't have voice link at Mars-normal pressure, and if we don't come up with a solve we'll have to go back to plain visual systems. Eighteen months down the drain."

He glanced around the room and settled on the heart man. "All right. What about the circulation?"

"It's the heat build-up," Fineman said defensively. "The heart is functioning perfectly. You want me to design it for ridiculous conditions? I could, but it would be eight feet high. Fix up the thermal balance. The skin closes up at low temperatures and won't transmit. Naturally the oxygen level in the blood drops, and naturally the heart speeds up. That's what it's supposed to do. What do you want? Otherwise he'll go into syncope, maybe short-change the brain on O_2. Then what've you got?"

From high on the wall of the room the cyborg's face looked on impassively. He had changed position (the enema was over, the bedpan had been removed, he was now sitting). Roger Torraway, not very interested in a discussion that did not in any way involve his specialty, was gazing at the cyborg thoughtfully. He wondered what old Willy thought, hearing himself talked about that way. Roger had gone to the trouble of requisitioning the private psychological studies on Hartnett because of curiosity on that point, but they hadn't been very informative. Roger was pretty sure he knew why. All of them had been so tested and retested that they had acquired considerable skill in answering test questions the way the examiners wanted them answered. By now nearly everyone in the labs must have come to do that, either by design or simply as a trained-in reflex. They would make marvelous poker players, he thought; smiling, he remembered poker games with Willy. Covertly he winked at the cyborg and gave him a thumbs-up. Hartnett did not respond. It was impossible to tell, from those faceted ruby eyes, what he saw.

"—we can't change the skin again," the integuments man was arguing. "There's already a weight penalty. If we put in any more sensor-actors he'll feel like he's wearing a wet-suit all the time."

Surprisingly, a rumble from the monitor. The cyborg spoke: "What theee hell do you think it feeeelsss layk now?"

A beat of silence, as everyone in the room remembered it was a living person they were talking about. Then the skin man insisted: "All the more reason. We'd like to fine it down, simplify it, get some of the weight off. Not complicate it."

The deputy director raised his hand. "You two get together," he ordered the opponents. "Don't tell me what you can't do—I'm telling you what we have to do. Now you, Brad. What about that vision cutoff?"

Alex Bradley said cheerily, "Under control. I can fix. But listen, Will, I'm sorry, but it means another implant. I see what's wrong. It's in the retinal mediation system; it's filtering the extra frequencies. The system's all right, but—"

"Then make it work," said the deputy director, glancing at the clock. "How about the communications foul-up?"

"Talk to respiration," said the hardware man. "If they give us a little more retained air, Hartnett can get some voice. The electronics systems are fine, there's just nothing for them to carry."

"Impossible!" shouted the lung man. "You've only left us five hundred cc's of space now! He uses that in ten minutes. I've gone over the drill with him a hundred times to practice conserving it—"

"Can't he just whisper?" asked the deputy director. Then, as the communications man began hauling out frequency-response curves, he added, "Work it out, will you? All the rest of you, looks good. But don't let up." He closed the notes into their plastic folder and handed it to his assistant. "That's that," he said. "Now let me get to the important part."

He waited for them to settle down. "The reason the President was here last night is that a launch target has been approved. Friends, we are now on real time."

"When?" cried a voice.

The deputy went on: "A.S.A.P. We've got to complete this job—and by that, friends, I mean complete it: get Hartnett up to optimum performance so that he can actually live on Mars—no back to the workshops if something goes wrong—in time for the launch window next month. Launch time is set for oh eight hundred hours on twelve November. That gives us forty-three days, twenty-two hours and some odd minutes. No more."

There was a second's pause, then a rush of voices. Even the cyborg's expression visibly changed, though no one could have said in what direction.

The deputy director continued: "That's only part of it. The date is fixed, it can't be changed, we have to meet it; now I want to tell you why. Lights, please."

The chamber lights dimmed down, and the deputy's deputy, without waiting for a signal, projected a slide on the end wall of the room where all could see it, even the cyborg in his distant cell. It displayed a crosshatched chart, with a broad black line growing diagonally upward toward a red bar. In bright orange letters at the top it was marked MOST SECRET. EYES ONLY.

"Let me explain what you're looking at," said the deputy director. "The black diagonal is a composite of twenty-two trends and indices, ranging from the international credit balance to the incidence of harassment of American tourists by government officials abroad. The measure is of probability of war. The red bar at the top is marked 'O.H.,' which I can tell you stands for 'Outbreak of Hostilities.' It is not certainty. But the statistics people tell us that when the upper limit is reached there is a point-nine probability of war within six hours, and as you can see, we are moving toward it."

The noise had stopped. The room was crypt-still. Finally one voice inquired, "What's the time scale?"

"The back data covers thirty-five years," said the deputy director. There was some easing—at least the white space at the top would have to be some months, not minutes.

Then Kathleen Doughty asked, "Does it say anywhere in there who it is we're going to be at war with?"

The deputy director hesitated, then said carefully, "No, that is not included in the chart, but I think we can all form our own guesses. I don't mind giving you mine. If you've been reading the papers you know that the Chicoms have been talking about the wonders of increased food production they could bring the world by applying Sinkiang Province farming techniques to the Australian outback. Well, no matter what that quisling bunch in Canberra are willing to agree to, I feel pretty sure that this administration is not going to let the Chinks move in. Not if they want to keep my vote, anyway." After a moment, he added, "That's just personal opinion, off the record; do not include it in the minutes of this meeting. I don't know any official answer, and I wouldn't tell you if I did. All I know is what you know now. The trendline forecasts look pretty sour. Now they show nuclear escalation probabilities peaking pretty fast. We've got a date for it. The curve continued shows the point-nine probability in less than seven years.

"Which means," he added, "that if we don't have a viable Mars colony by then, we may not live to have it ever."

Alexander Bradley, B.Sc., E.E., M.D., D.Sc., Lt. Col. USMCR (Ret.). While Bradley was leaving the conference and changing from the expression of concern he had worn for the briefing to the more natural open-faced jollity he showed the world, the cyborg was down-pressuring for the Mars-normal tank. His monitors were somewhat concerned. Although they could not read emotion from his face, they could from his heart, breath and vital signs, as telemetered constantly to them, and it appeared to them that he was in some sort of up-tight state. They proposed delaying the test, but he refused angrily. "Don't you know there'sss a war on, almosssst?" he demanded in shrill tones, and would not answer when they spoke to him again. They decided to continue with the tests, but to recheck his psych profile as soon as they were completed.

When Alexander Bradley was ten years old he lost his father and his left eye. The Sunday after Thanksgiving, the family was driving back from church. It had turned cold. The morning dew had frozen, impalpably thin and slick, in a film on the road. Brad's father was driving with great care, but there were cars in front of him, cars behind him, cars in the other half of the two-lane road going in the other direction; he was constrained to keep to a certain speed, and he was short in his answers when the rest of the family said anything to him. He was concerned, but he was not concerned enough. When the disaster came he could do nothing to avert it. To Brad, sitting beside his father in the front seat, it looked as though a station wagon coming toward them a hundred yards away turned out, slowly and calmly, as though it were making a left turn. But there was no road there for it to turn into. Brad's father stepped on the brake and held it. Their car slowed and slid. And for some seconds the boy sat watching the other car sliding sidewise toward them, themselves skidding gently and inevitably toward it. It was stately and deliberate, and inevitable. No one said anything, not Brad, not his father, not Brad's mother in the back seat. No one did anything, except to hold their rigid poses as though they were actors in a National Traffic Council tableau. The father sat silent and erect at the wheel, staring concentratedly at the other car. The driver of the other vehicle looked wide-eyed and inquiringly toward them over his shoulder. Neither moved until they hit. Even on the ice the friction was slowing them, and they could not have been moving at a combined velocity of much more than twenty-five miles an hour. It was enough. Both drivers were killed—Brad's father impaled, the other man decapitated. Brad and his mother, though they were wearing their safety belts, suffered fractures, cuts and bruises as well as internal injuries; and she lost the flexure of her left wrist forever, while her son lost his eye.

Twenty-three years later Brad still dreamed about it as though it had just happened. In his sleep it scared him witless, and he awakened sweaty and crying and gasping for breath.

It was not all loss. He had discovered that considerable advantages had been bought at the cost of an eye. Item, there was the insurance, on the life of his father and on the maiming of everyone concerned. Item, the injury had kept him out of the Army, and had permitted him to join the Marine Corps in an essentially civilian capacity when he wanted field experience in his specialty. Item, it had given him an acceptable excuse for avoiding the stupider risks and more tiresome obligations of adolescence. He never had to prove his courage in violent sports and always was excused from whatever parts of gym he most detested.

Biggest item of all, it gave him an education. Under the Aid to

Handicapped Children provisions of his state's welfare system, it had paid his way through school, college and graduate school. It had given him four degrees and turned him into one of the world's greatest experts on the perceptual systems of the eye. On balance, it was a favorable transaction. Even adding in the negative factor of a mother who had spent the remaining ten years of her life in some pain and a good deal of shortness of temper, it was worthwhile.

Brad had wound up on the Man Plus project because he was the best they could get. He had chosen to work for the Marine Corps, because nowhere better could one find experimental subjects prepared by shell, claymore and bolo than in the field hospitals of Tanzania, Borneo and Ceylon. That work had been noted in high echelons of the military. They had not accepted Brad, they had drafted him.

What he was not sure of was that Man Plus was the best *he* could get. Other recruits had been dragged into the space program by glamour or appeals to duty. It wasn't at all like that with Bradley. As soon as he had grasped what the man from Washington was driving at, the implications and opportunities spread out before him. It was a new track. It meant abandoning some plans, deferring others. But he could see where it would lead: say, three years helping to develop the optic systems of the cyborg. A world reputation coming out of it. Then he could quit the program and enter the limitless lush pastures of private practice. One hundred and eight Americans per hundred thousand had essentially total loss of function in one or both eyes. It added up to better than three hundred thousand prospective patients, every one of whom would want the best man in the field to treat him.

Working on the Man Plus program would stamp him the best man in his field at once. He could have a clinic of his own before he was forty. Not big. Just big enough to be supervised personally in every detail by him, and run by a staff of juniors trained by him and working under his direction. It would run to, oh, maybe five or six hundred patients a year—a fraction of 1 percent of the prospects. Which fraction of 1 percent would he accept? At least half of them would come from those most solvent and most willing to pay. Also, of course, charity cases. At least a hundred of them a year, everything free, even their bedside phones. While the several hundred who could pay would pay a lot. The Bradley Clinic (already it sounded as time-honored and proper as "Menninger" in his ears) would be a model for medical services all over the world, and it would make him one hell of a lot of money.

It was not Bradley's fault that the three years had extended themselves past five. It wasn't even his part of the program that caused the delays. Or not most of them, anyway. In any event, he was still young.

He would leave the program with thirty good working years ahead of him—unless he chose to retire earlier, perhaps keeping a consultancy and a stock arrangement at the Bradley Clinic. And there were other advantages to working in the space program, in that so many of his associates had married such attractive women. Bradley had no interest in getting married, but he very much liked having wives.

Back in the seven-room laboratory suite where he ruled, Brad kicked ass on enough of his subordinates to insure that the new retinal mediation link would be ready for transplant within the week, and glanced at his watch. It was not yet eleven. He dialed Roger Torraway on the intercom and got him after a delay. "How about lunch, Rog? I want to go over this new implant with you."

"Oh, too bad, Brad. I wish I could. But I'm going to be in the tank with Will Hartnett for at least the next three hours. Maybe tomorrow."

"Talk to you then," said Brad cheerfully, and hung up. He was not surprised; he had already checked Torraway's schedule. But he was pleased. He told his secretary that he would be leaving for an outside conference and then lunch, and would be back after two, then ordered his car. He fed it the coordinates for the corner of the block where Roger Torraway lived. Where Dorrie Torraway lived.

Five
Monster Becoming Mortal Again

As Brad left, whistling, his car radio was full of news of the world. The Tenth Mountain Division had recoiled back to a fortified area in Riverdale. A typhoon had wrecked the rice crop in Southeast Asia. President Deshatine had ordered the U.S. delegation to walk out of the United Nations debate on sharing scarce resources.

There was much news that was not on the sound-only radio, because the newscasters either didn't know about it or didn't think it was important. For example, not one word was said about two Chinese gentlemen on a mission in Australia, or about the results of certain secret popularity polls the President kept locked in his safe, or about the tests being run on Willy Hartnett. So Brad didn't hear about any of these things. If he had, and had understood their importance, he would have cared. He was not an uncaring man. He was not an evil one, either. He was just not a particularly good one.

Sometimes that question came up—for instance, when it was time to get rid of a girl or drop a friend who had been helpful on the way up. Sometimes there were recriminations. Then Brad would smile and shrug and point out that it wasn't a fair world. Lancelot didn't win all the tournaments. Sometimes the evil black knight dumped him on the ground. Bobby Fischer wasn't the most lovable chess player in the world, merely the best. And so on.

And so Brad would confess that he was not a model man by social standards. Indeed he wasn't. Something had gone wrong in his childhood. The bump of ego on his skull had swollen large, so he saw the whole world in terms of what it could give him. War with China?

Well, let's see, calculated Brad, there's sure to be a lot of surgery; perhaps I'll get to head my own hospital. A world depression? His money was in farmland; people would always eat.

He was not admirable. All the same, he was the best person alive to do what the cyborg needed—namely, to provide Willy Hartnett with mediation between stimulus and interpretation. Which is a way of saying that somewhere between the external object the cyborg saw and the conclusions the cyborg's brain drew from it, there had to be a stage where unnecessary information was filtered out. Otherwise the cyborg would simply go mad.

To understand why this is so, consider the frog.

Think of a frog as a functional machine designed to produce baby frogs. This is the Darwinian view, and is really what evolution is all about. In order to succeed, the frog has to stay alive long enough to grow up and get pregnant or get some female frog pregnant. That means it has to do two things. It has to eat. And it has to avoid being eaten.

As vertebrates go, the frog is a dull and simple kind of creature. It has a brain, but not a big one or a very sophisticated one. There's not much excess capacity in the frog brain to play around with, so that one doesn't want to waste any of it on nonessentials. Evolution is always economical. Male frogs do not write poems or torture themselves with fears that their female frogs may be unfaithful. Nor do they want to think about things which do not directly concern staying alive.

The frog's eye is simple, too. In human eyes there are complexities frogs know not. Suppose a human comes into a room containing a table which bears an order of steak and French fries; even if he cannot hear, cannot taste and has lost the power of smell, he is drawn to the food. His eye turns to the steak. There is a spot on the eye called the "fovea," the part of the eye with which a person sees best, and it is that spot that directs itself toward the target. The frog doesn't do that; one part of its eye is as good as another. Or as bad. Because the interesting thing about a frog's-eye view of what for a frog is the equivalent of a steak—namely, a bug big enough to be worth swallowing but small enough not to try to swallow back—is that the frog is blind to food unless the food *behaves* like food. Surround the frog with the most nutritious chopped insect paté you can devise. It will starve to death—unless a ladybug wanders by.

If one thinks about how a frog eats, this strange behavior begins to make sense. The frog fits a very neat ecological niche. In a state of nature, no one fills that niche with minced food. The frog eats insects, so insects are what he sees. If something passes through his field of vision which is the right size for an insect, and moves at the proper speed for an insect, the frog does not debate whether he is hungry or not or which insects taste best. He eats it. Then he goes back to waiting for the next one.

In the laboratory this is an antisurvival trait. You can trick a frog with a piece of cloth, a bit of wood on a string, anything that moves properly and is the right size. He will eat them and starve. But in nature there are no such tricks. In nature only bugs move like bugs, and every bug is frog dinner.

This principle is not difficult to understand. Say this to a naïve friend and he will say, "Oh, yes, I see. The frog just ignores anything that doesn't look like a bug." Wrong! The frog doesn't do anything of the kind. He does not ignore non-bug objects. He simply never sees them in the first place. Tap a frog's optic nerve and drag a marble slowly past—too big, too slow—and no instrument can pick up a nerve impulse. There is none. The eye does not bother to "see" what the frog does not want to know about. But swing a dead fly past, and your meter dials flick over, the nerve transmits a message, the frog's tongue licks out and grabs.

And so we come to the cyborg. What Bradley had done was to provide a mediation stage between the ruby complex eyes and the aching human brain of Willy Hartnett which filtered, interpreted and generally prepackaged all of the cyborg's visual inputs. The "eye" saw everything, even in the UV part of the spectrum, even in the infrared. The brain could not deal with so vast a flow of inputs. Bradley's mediation stage edited out the unimportant bits.

The stage was a triumph of design, because Bradley was indeed extremely good at the one thing he was good at. But he was not there to install it. And so because Brad had a date, and also because the President of the United States had to go to the bathroom and two Chinese named Sing and Sun wanted to try a pizza, the history of the world changed.

Jerry Weidner, who was Brad's principal assistant, supervised the slow laborious process of resetting the cyborg's vision systems. It was a fussy, niggling sort of job. Like nearly all of the things that had to be done to Willy Hartnett, it was attended with maximum discomfort for him. The sensitive nerves of the eyelid had long since been dissected out; otherwise they would have been shrieking pain at him day and night. But he could feel what was happening—if not as pain, then as a psychically disturbing knowledge that somebody was sliding edged instruments around in a very touchy part of his anatomy. His actual vi-

sion was kept on stand-by mode, so he "saw" only dim moving shadows. It was enough. He hated it.

He lay there for an hour or more while Weidner and the others
tinkered with changes in potentials, noted readings, talked to each
other in the numbers that are the language of technologists. When they
were finally satisfied with the field strength of his perceptual system
and allowed him to stand, without warning he almost toppled.
"Sheesssst," he snarled. "Dizzzzy again."

Worried and resigned, Weidner said, "All right, we better ask for
vertigo checks." So there was another thirty-minute delay while the balance teams checked his reflexes until he burst out, "Chrisssst, cut it out.
I can ssstand on one foot for the nexssst twenty hours, ssso what doesss
it prove?" But they kept him on one foot anyhow, measuring how close
he could get his fingertips to touching with his vision in stand-by mode.

The balance teams then declared themselves satisfied, but Jerry
Weidner was not. The dizziness had happened before, and it had never
been satisfactorily tracked down, either to the built-in mechanical horizon or to the crude natural stirrup-and-anvil bones in his ear. Weidner
did not know that it stemmed from the mediation system that was his
own special responsibility, but he didn't know that it did not, either.
He wished Brad would get the hell back from his long lunch.

At that time, halfway around the world, there were these two Chinese named Sing and Sun. They were not characters in a dirty joke.
Those were their names. Sing's great-grandfather had died at the
mouth of a Russian cannon after the failure of the Righteous Harmony
Fists to expel the white devils from China. His father had conceived
him on the Long March, and died before he was born, in combat
against the soldiers of a war lord allied to Chiang Kai-shek. Sing himself was nearly ninety years old. He had shaken the hand of Comrade
Mao, had diverted the Yellow River for Mao's successors and was now
supervising the greatest hydraulic engineering project of his career in
an Australian town called Fitzroy Crossing. It was his first prolonged
trip outside the territory of New People's Asia. He had three ambitions
for it: to see an uncensored pornographic film, to drink a bottle of
Scotch that came from Scotland rather than the People's Province of
Honshu, and to taste a pizza. With his colleague Sun he had made a
good start on the Scotch, had found out where to accomplish the view-
ing of the film and was now desirous of tasting the pizza.

Sun was much younger—not yet forty—and in spite of everything,
suffering from respect for his associate's age. There was also the fact
that Sun was several echelons lower in social status than the older man,
although he was obviously a coming man in the techno-industrial wing

of the Party. Sun had just returned from a year of leading a mapping team through all of the Great Sandy Desert. It was not only sand. It was soil—good, arable, productive soil—lacking only a few trace elements and water. What Sun had mapped had been the soil chemistry of a million square miles. When Sun's soil map and Sing's great uphill aqueduct, with its fourteen great batteries of nuclear-driven pumps, came together, they would equal a new kind of life for those million miles of desert. Chemical supplements + sun-distilled water from the distant seacoast = ten crops a year with which to feed a hundred million ethnically Chinese New Australians.

The project had been carefully studied and contained only one flaw. The Old New Australians, descendants of the populating drives of the post-World War II period, did not want New New Australians coming in to farm that land. They wanted it for themselves. As Sun and Sing entered Danny's Pizza Hut on Fitzroy Crossing's main street, two Old New Australians, one named Koschanko and one named Gradechek, were just leaving the bar, and unfortunately recognized Sing from his newspaper pictures. Words passed. The Chinese recognized the smell of stale beer and took the truculence to be only drink; they tried to pass, and Koschanko and Gradechek pushed them out of the street door. Bellicosity began swinging, and the ninety-year-old skull of Sing Hsi-chin split itself open against a curbstone.

At this point Sun drew a pistol he was not authorized to be carrying, and shot the two assailants dead.

It was only a drunken brawl. The police of Fitzroy Crossing had handled thousands of more dramatic crimes, and could have handled this one if they had been allowed to. But it did not stop there, because one of the barmaids was herself a New New Australian of Honanese extraction, recognized Sun, discovered who Sing was, picked up the phone and called the New China News Agency bureau in Lagrange Mission, down on the coast, to say that one of China's most famous scientists had been brutally murdered.

Within ten minutes the satellite network had carried a factually shaky but very colorful version of the story all over the world.

Before an hour was out, the New People's Asian mission to Canberra had requested an appointment with the Foreign Minister to deliver its protest, spontaneous demonstrations were in full blast in Shanghai, Saigon, Hiroshima and a dozen other NPA cities, and half a dozen observation satellites were being nudged out of their orbits to pass over Northwest Australia and the Sunda Islands seas. Two miles outside the harbor of Melbourne a great gray shape swam to the surface of the sea and floated there, offering no signals and responding to none for more than twenty minutes. Then it declared itself the NPA nuclear submarine *The East Is Red* on a routine diplomatic visit to a friendly port. The news was received in time to cancel the RAAF air strike that had been ordered against the unknown intruder, but only just.

Under Pueblo, Colorado, the President of the United States was interrupted in his after-lunch nap. He was sitting on the edge of his bed, distastefully sipping a cup of black coffee, when the DOD liaison aide came in with a sitrep and the news that a condition red alert had been declared, in accordance with the prepared responses long since programmed into the North American Defense Command Net. He already had the satellite reports and an on-the-scene account from a military mission to Fitzroy Crossing; he knew about the appearance of the submarine *The East Is Red*, but did not yet know that the airstrike had been called off. Summarizing the information, he said to the President, "So it's go or no-go, sir. NADCOM recommends a launch with abort options in fifty minutes."

The President snarled, "I don't feel good. What the hell did they put in that soup?" Dash was not in a mood to think about China just at that moment; he had been dreaming about a private poll which showed his popularity down to 17 percent, including both the "excellent" and "satisfactory" ratings, with 61 percent calling his administration "poor" or "very unsatisfactory." It had not been a dream. That was what the morning's political briefing had shown him.

He pushed the coffee cup away and glumly contemplated the decision he, alone in all the world, was now required to make. To launch missiles against the major cities of New People's Asia was in theory a reversible choice: they could be aborted at any time before reentry, defused, falling harmlessly into the sea. But in practice the NPA posts would detect the launch, and who knew what those crazy Chinese bastards would do? His belly felt as though he were in the last minutes of pregnancy, and there seemed to be a good chance that he would throw up. His number one secretary said chidingly, "Dr. Stassen did advise you not to eat any more cabbage, sir. Perhaps we should instruct the chef not to make that soup any more."

The President said, "I don't want lectures right now. All right, look. We'll hold at the present state of readiness until further orders from me. No launch. No retaliation. Understood?"

"Yes, sir," said the DOD man regretfully. "Sir? I have several specific queries, from NADCOM, from the Man Plus project, from the admiral commanding SWEPAC—"

"You heard me! No retaliation. Everything else, keep going."

His number one secretary clarified the point for him. "Our official position," he said, "is this affair in Australia is a domestic matter and not a national concern for the United States. Our action stance does not change. We keep all systems go, but take no action. Is that right, Mr. President?"

"Right," said Dash thickly. "Now if you can get along without me for ten minutes, I got to go to the john."

Brad did think of phoning in to see how the recalibration was going, but he really liked showering with a girl, with all the fun involved in soaping each other, and the Chero-Strip bathroom armorarium included bath oil beads, bubbles and marvelous thick towels. It was three o'clock before he decided to think about going back to work.

By that time it was pretty much too late. Weidner had tried to get permission to postpone testing from the deputy director, who wouldn't do it on his own authority but bucked it to Washington, who queried the President's office and received the reply: "No, you cannot, positively cannot, repeat not, postpone this or any other test." The man giving the reply was the President's number one secretary, who was looking at the "risk of war" projection on the wall of the President's most private study while he spoke. Even as he was talking the broad black bar was bending itself still more steeply up toward the red line.

So they went ahead with the test, Weidner tight-lipped and frowning. It went well enough until it began to go very badly indeed. Roger Torraway's mind was far away until he heard the cyborg call him. He locked in and stood, in skin suit and breathing mask, on the ruddy sands. "What's the matter, Willy?" he demanded.

The great ruby eyes turned toward him. "I—I can't ssssee you, Roger!" the cyborg shrilled. "I— I—"

And he toppled and fell. It was as quick as that. Roger did not even move toward him until he felt a great thundering hammer of air beat in on him, sending him stumbling toward the recumbent monster form.

From the 7,500-foot equivalent outside the Mars-normal chamber Don Kayman came desperately running in. He had not waited to lock. He had thrown both doors open. He was no longer a scientist. He was a priest; he dropped to his knees beside the contorted form of what had been Willy Hartnett.

Roger stared while Don Kayman touched the ruby eyes, traced a cross on the synthetic flesh, whispering what Roger could not hear. He did not want to hear. He knew what was happening.

The first candidate for cyborg was now receiving Extreme Unction in front of his eyes.

The lead backup was Vic Freibart, taken off the list by presidential order.

The number two alternate was Carl Mazzini, ruled out because of his broken leg.

The third alternate, and the new champion, was him.

Six
Mortal in Mortal Fear

It is not an easy thing for a flesh-and-blood human being to come to terms with the knowledge that some of his flesh is going to be ripped from him and replaced with steel, copper, silver, plastic, aluminum and glass. We could see that Torraway was not behaving very rationally. He went blundering down the hall away from the Mars-normal tank in great urgency, as though he had a most pressing errand. He had no errand except to get away. The hall seemed like a trap to him. He felt he could not stand to have one person come up to him and say he was sorry about Willy Hartnett, or acknowledge Torraway's own new status. He passed a men's room, stopped, looked around—no one was watching him—and entered to stand at the urinal, eyes glazed, fixed to the shiny chrome. When the door pushed open, Torraway made a great show of zipping and flushing, but it was only a boy from the typing pool who looked at him incuriously and headed for a booth.

Outside the men's room the deputy director caught him. "Goddamn lousy thing," he said. "I guess you know you're—"

"I know," said Torraway, pleased that his voice was so calm.

"We're going to have to find out what happened *fast*. I'm having a meeting in my office in ninety minutes. We'll have the first autopsy reports. I want you there."

Roger nodded, glanced at his wrist watch and turned smartly away. The important thing, he thought, was to keep moving as though he were too busy to interrupt. Unfortunately he couldn't think of a single thing he had to do, or even that he could pretend to be doing, to keep conversation away. No, he recognized, not conversation. It was thought he wanted to keep away, thinking about himself. He wasn't afraid. He wasn't furious at fate. He just wasn't prepared to look into the personal consequences of Willy Hartnett's death, not right at that moment—

He looked up; someone had been calling his name.

It was Jon Freeling, Brad's surgical assistant in perceptual systems, looking for Brad.

"Why, no," said Torraway, glad to be talking about something other than Willy's death or his own future, "I don't know where he is. Went to lunch, I think."

"Two hours ago. His tail's going to be in a crack if I can't find him before the DD's meeting. I'm not sure I can field all the questions—and I can't go looking for him, they're bringing the cyborg into my lab now, and I've got to—"

"I'll find him for you," Torraway said hastily. "I'll call him at home."

"Tried it. No dice. And he didn't leave a number where he could be reached."

Torraway winked, suddenly feeling relieved, delighted to have a challenge he could respond to. "You know Brad," he said. "You have to remember there's a lot of tomcat in that boy. I'll find him." And he took the elevator to the administrative floor, turned two corners and rapped on the door marked *Administrative Statistics*.

The function of the people inside that door had very little to do with statistics. The door didn't open at once; instead, a spy-hole opened and a blue eye looked out at him. "I'm Colonel Torraway, and it's an emergency."

"One moment," said a girl's voice; there was a sound of clattering and scraping, and then the door unlocked and she let Torraway in. There were four other people in the room, all of them in civilian clothes and looking rather undistinguished, as they were meant to do. Each had an old-fashioned rolltop desk, of a kind one did not usually expect to see in a modern space-agency office. The tops could be pulled down to conceal what was on the desks at a moment's notice; they were down now.

"It's Dr. Alexander Bradley," Roger said. "He's needed urgently in about an hour and his department can't find him. Commander Hartnett is dead, and—"

The girl said, "We know about Commander Hartnett. Do you want us to find Dr. Bradley for you?"

"No, I'll do it. But I expect you can tell me where to start looking. I know you keep tabs on all of us, extracurricular activities and all." He did not actually wink at her too, but he heard the sound of a wink in his voice.

The girl looked at him steadily for a moment. "He's probably at—"

"Hold it," called the man at the desk behind her, his voice surprisingly angry.

She shook her head, overruling him without looking at him. "Try the Chero-Strip Hover Hotel," she said. "He usually uses the name of Beckwith. I'd suggest you telephone. Maybe it would be better if we did it for you, at that—"

"Oh, no," said Torraway easily, resolute to keep this chore for himself. "It's important I talk to him myself."

The young man said strongly, "Dr. Torraway, I really suggest you let us handle—"

But he was already backing out of the door, nodding, not listening any more. He had made up his mind not to bother telephoning but to drive to the motel; it was a valid reason to get out of the lab while he collected his thoughts.

Outside the air-controlled laboratory buildings Tonka had been geting hotter and hotter. The sun penetrated even the tinted windshield, filling Torraway's car with heat that defied the cooling system. He drove inexpertly on manual, taking the curves so sloppily that the guidance wheels skidded. The motel was fifteen stories tall and solid glass; it seemed to aim the sunlight directly at him, like Archimedes's warriors defending Syracuse. He was glad to get out in the underground parking lot and take the moving stairs up to the lobby.

The lobby itself was as tall as the building, completely enclosed, with the rooms racked around it and flying bridges and galleries crisscrossing overhead. The clerk had never heard of Dr. Alexander Bradley.

"Try Beckwith," suggested Torraway, offering a bill. "He sometimes has trouble remembering his name."

But it was no use, the clerk either couldn't place Brad or wouldn't. Roger drove out of the parking space, paused in the beat of the sunshine and considered what to do next. He stared unseeing into the reflecting pool that doubled as the motel's air-conditioning heat sink. Probably he should try phoning Brad at his apartment, he thought. Should have done it while he was in the lobby; he didn't much want to turn around and go back in. Or call from the car, for that matter; the car phone was broadcast radio, and the conversation would be better private. He could go home and call from there, he planned; it was not more than a five-minute run—

At which point it first registered on Roger that he really ought to tell his wife what had happened.

It was not a duty he looked forward to. Telling Dorrie unfortunately implied spelling it all out to himself. But Roger had a good attitude toward inevitable things, even if unpleasant, and keeping his mind in neutral, he turned the car toward home and Dorrie.

Unfortunately Dorrie wasn't there.

He called to her in the hallway, peered into the dining room, looked at the swimming pool in the back, checked both bathrooms. No Dorrie. Out shopping, no doubt. It was annoying, but it couldn't be helped, and he was just about to leave a note for her, staring out the window while he tried to think how to phrase the note, when he saw her driving up in her micromidget two-seater.

He had the door open for her before she got to it.

He expected she would be surprised. He had not expected that she would just stand there, her pretty eyebrows raised and motionless, her expression showing no movement at all. She looked like a snapshot of herself, frozen in the middle of a step.

He said, "I wanted to talk to you about something. I just came from the Chero-Strip, because Brad is involved too, but—"

She came to life and said politely, "Let me come in and sit down." There was still no expression on her face as she paused in the hallway to look at herself in the mirror. She smoothed some blemish on her cheek, fluffed her hair, went into the living room and sat down without taking off her hat. "It's awfully warm out today, isn't it?" she observed.

Roger sat down too, trying to collect his thoughts. It was important not to frighten her. Once he had watched a television program about how to break bad news, some shrink with a need for more patients and a fear of being labeled unethical keeping him from hiring a man with a sandwich board, going on the talk shows in the hope of catching a few live ones for his waiting room. Never be blunt, he said. Give the person a chance to prepare himself. Tell it a little at a time. At that period Roger had thought it was comic; he remembered telling Dorrie about it —*Honey, have you got your charge card? . . . Well, you'll need it for the black dress . . . The black dress for the funeral . . . The funeral we have to go to, and you'll want to look nice because of who it is . . . Well, after all, she was a pretty old lady. And you know she didn't drive very well. The policemen said she didn't suffer after she creamed the truck. Your father's bearing up very well.* They had both laughed about it.

"Please go ahead," Dorrie said invitingly, taking a cigarette out of the box on the coffee table. As she lit it, Roger saw the butane flame quiver and realized with astonishment that her hand was shaking. He was both surprised and a little pleased; evidently she was bracing herself for some kind of bad news. She had always been very perceptive, he thought admiringly, and now that she was ready, he plunged in.

"It's Willy Hartnett, dear," he said kindly. "Something went wrong this morning and—"

He paused, waiting for her to catch up to him. She did not look concerned as much as puzzled.

"He's dead," said Torraway shortly, and stopped to let it sink in.

She nodded thoughtfully. It wasn't penetrating, Roger thought regretfully. She didn't understand. She had liked Willy, but she was not crying or screaming or showing any emotion at all.

He finished the thought, giving up on tact: "And of course that means that I'm next in line," he said, trying to speak slowly. "The others are out of it; you remember, I told you. So I'm the one they'll want to, uh, prepare for the Mars mission."

The look on her face perplexed him. It was fragile and apprehensive, almost as though she had been expecting something worse and still was not sure it was not coming. He said impatiently, "Don't you understand what I'm saying, dear?"

"Why, yes. That's—well, it's a little hard to take in." He nodded, satisfied, and she went on, "But I'm confused. Didn't you start by saying something about Brad and the Chero-Strip?"

"Oh, I'm sorry, I know I threw a lot at you at once. Yes. I said I had just been at the motel, looking for Brad. You see, it looks like it's the perceptual systems that went wrong and killed Willy. Well, that's Brad's baby. And today of all days he took a long lunch to—well, I don't have to tell you about Brad. He's probably shacked up somewhere with one of the nurses. But it's going to look bad if he isn't there for the meeting—" He stopped to look at his watch. "Wow, I've got to get back myself. But I did want to break this to you in person."

"Thank you, honey," she said absently, pursuing a thought. "Wouldn't it have been better to phone him?"

"Who?"

"Brad, of course."

"Oh. Oh, sure, except it was sort of private. I didn't want anyone listening in. And besides, I didn't think he'd be answering the phone. In fact, the desk clerk wouldn't admit he was ever there. And I had to go to Security to get a lead on where he might be." He had a sudden thought; he knew Dorrie liked Brad, and he wondered for a half second if she was upset at Brad's immorality. The thought dismissed itself, and he burst out admiringly, "Honey, I have to say you're taking this beautifully. Most women would be in hysterics by now."

She shrugged and said, "Well, what's the use of making a fuss? We both knew this could happen."

He ventured, "I won't look very good, Dorrie. And, you know, I think the physical part of our marriage will be down the drain for a while—even not counting the fact I'll be away on the mission for better than a year and a half."

She looked thoughtful, then resigned; then she looked directly at him and smiled. She got up to come over beside him and put her arms around him. "I'll be proud of you," she said. "And we'll have long, long lives after you get back." She ducked back as he reached to kiss her and said playfully, "None of that, you've got to get back. What are you going to do about Brad?"

"Well, I could go back to the motel—"

She said decisively, "Don't do it, Roger. Let him look out for himself. If he's up to something he shouldn't be, that's his problem. I want you to get back to the meeting, and— Oh, say, that's right! I'm going out again. I'll be passing quite near the motel. If I see Brad's car in the lot I'll put a note on it."

"That didn't even occur to me," he said admiringly.

"So don't worry. I don't want you thinking about Brad. With all that's coming up, we have to be thinking of you!"

Jonathan Freeling, M.D., F.A.C.S., A.A.S.M.

Jonny Freeling had been in aerospace medicine long enough to have lost the habit of dealing with cadavers. Particularly he was unused to cutting up the bodies of friends. Astronauts didn't usually leave their bodies behind when they died, anyway. If they died in line of duty it was unlikely there would be any p.m.; the ones that were lost in space stayed there, the ones that died nearer home were usually boiled to gas in the flame of hydrogen and oxygen. In neither case was there anything to put on a table.

It was hard to realize that this object he was dissecting was Willy Hartnett. It wasn't as much like an autopsy as like, say, field-stripping a carbine. He had helped put these parts together—these platinum electrodes here, these microminiaturized chips in their black box there; now it was time to take them apart again. Except that there was blood. In spite of everything, Willy had died with a lot of wet, seeping human blood still in him.

"Freeze and section," he said, serving up a gobbet on a glass slide to his general-duty nurse, who accepted it with a nod. That was Clara Bly. Her pretty black face reflected sadness, although one could not tell, Freeling reflected, lifting out a dripping metal strand that was part of the vision circuits, how much of the sadness was over the death of the cyborg and how much over her interrupted going-away party. She was leaving to get married the next day; the recovery room just behind that door was still festooned with crepe and paper flowers for her party. They had asked Freeling if they should clear it away for the autopsy, but of course there was no need to; no one would be recovering in that recovery room.

He looked up at his surgical assistant, standing where the anesthesiologist would have been in a normal operation, and barked, "Any word from Brad?"

"He's in the building," she said.

Then why doesn't he get his ass down here? is what Freeling thought, but he didn't say it, only nodded. At least he was back. Whatever grief was coming because of this, Freeling wouldn't have to carry it alone.

But the more he probed and fished, the more he found himself baffled. Where was the grief? What had killed Hartnett? The electronic components didn't seem to be wrong; every time he removed one it was rushed off to the instrumentation people, who workbenched in on the spot. No problems. Nor did the gross physical structure of the brain give any immediate explanation . . .

Was it possible that the cyborg had died of nothing at all?

Freeling leaned back, conscious of sweat under the hot lights, instinctively waiting for his scrub nurse to wipe it off. She wasn't there, and he remembered and wiped his forehead on his sleeve. He went in again, carefully separating and removing the optical nerve system— what there was of it; the major sections had gone with the eyes themselves, replaced by electronics.

Then he saw it.

First blood seeping under the corpus callosum. Then, as he gently lifted and probed, the gray-white slippery sheath of an artery, with a bulge that had burst. Blown. A cardiovascular accident. A stroke.

Freeling left it there. The rest could be done later or not at all. Maybe it would be as well to leave what was left of Willy Hartnett as close to intact as it was. And it was time for the meeting.

The conference room doubled as the hospital library, which meant that when a meeting was going on, look-up research stopped. There were cushioned seats for fourteen people at the long table, and they were all filled, with the overflow on folding chairs, squeezed in where they could. Two seats were empty; they were for Brad and Jon Freeling, off on a last-minute run to the lab for final results on some slides, they said; actually so that Freeling could brief his boss on what had happened while he was "out to lunch." Everybody else was there, Don Kayman and Vic Samuelson (now promoted to Roger's back-up man, and not looking as though he liked it), Telly Ramez, the chief shrink, all of the cardiovascular people muttering among themselves, the top brass from the administrative sectors—and the two stars. One of the stars was Roger Torraway, uneasily sitting near the head of the table and listening with a fixed smile to other people's conversations. The other was Jed Griffin, the President's main man for breaking logjams. His title was only Chief Administrative Assistant to the President, but even the deputy director treated him like the Pope. "We can start any time, Mr. Griffin," urged the deputy director. Griffin's face spasmed a smile and he shook his head.

"Not until those other fellows get here," he said.

When Brad and Freeling arrived, all conversation stopped as though a plug had been pulled. "*Now* we can begin," snapped Jed Griffin, and the worry to his tone was evident to everyone in the room, every person of whom shared it. We were worried too, of course. Griffin did not want to carry his worry alone and promptly shared it with everyone in the room: "You don't know," he said, "how close this whole project is to being terminated, not next year or next month, not phased out, not cut down. *Through.*"

Roger Torraway took his eyes off Brad, and fixed them on Griffin.

"Through," repeated Griffin. "Washed out."

He seemed to take satisfaction in saying it, Torraway thought.

"And the only thing that saved it," said Griffin, "was these." He tapped the oval table with a folded wad of green-tinted computer print-outs. "The American public wants the project to continue."

Torraway felt a clutching touch at his heart, and it was only in that moment that he realized how swift and urgent the feeling of hope that had preceded it had been. For a moment it had sounded like a reprieve.

The deputy director cleared his throat. "I had understood," he said, "that the polls showed a considerable, ah, apathy about what we were doing."

"Preliminary results, yes." Griffin nodded. "But when you add them all up and put them through the computer it comes out to a strong, nationwide support. It's real enough. Significant to two sigmas, as I believe you people say. The people want an American to live on Mars."

"However," he added, "that was before this latest fiasco. God knows what that would do if it got out. The administration doesn't need a dead end, something to apologize for. It needs a success. I can't tell you how much depends on it."

The deputy director turned to Freeling. "Dr. Freeling?" he said.

Freeling stood up. "Willy Hartnett died of a stroke," he said. "The full p.m. report is being typed up, but that's what it comes to. There's no evidence of systemic deterioration; at his age and condition, I wouldn't have expected it. So it was trauma. Too much strain for the blood vessels in his brain to stand." He gazed at his fingertips reflectively. "What comes next is conjecture," he said, "but it's the best I can do. I'm going to ask for consultations from Ripplinger at the Yale Medical School and Anford—"

"The hell you are," snapped Griffin.

"I beg your pardon?" Freeling was caught off balance.

"No consultations. Not without full-scale security clearance first. This is urgent-top, Dr. Freeling."

"Oh. Well—then I'll have to take the responsibility myself. The cause of the trauma was too many inputs. He was overloaded. He couldn't handle it."

"I never heard of anything like that causing a stroke," Griffin complained.

"It takes a good deal of stress. But it happens. And here we're into new kinds of stress, Mr. Griffin. It's like—well, here's an analogy. If you had a child who was born with congenital cataracts, you would take him to a doctor, and the doctor would remove them. Only you would have to do it before he reached the age of puberty—before he stopped growing, internally as well as externally, you see. If you don't do it by then, it's better if you leave him blind. Kids who have such cataracts removed after the age of thirteen or fourteen have, as a matter of historical record, an interesting phenomenon in common. They commit suicide before they're twenty."

Torraway was trying to follow the conversation, but not quite succeeding. He was relieved when the deputy director intervened. "I don't think I see what that has to do with Will Hartnett, Jon."

"There, too, it is a matter of too many inputs. In the case of the kids after the cataract operation, what appears to happen is disorientation. They get new inputs that they have not grown a system to handle. If there is sight from birth onward, the visual cortex develops systems to handle, mediate and interpret it. If not, there are no developed systems, and it is too late to grow them.

"I think Willy's trouble was that we gave him inputs that he had no mechanism available to handle. It was too late for him to grow one. All the incoming data swamped him; the strain broke a blood vessel. And," he went on, "I think that will happen to Roger here, too, if we do the same thing with him."

Griffin turned a brief, assessing look at Roger Torraway. Torraway cleared his throat, but said nothing. There did not seem to be anything for him to say. Griffin said, "What are you telling me, Freeling?"

The doctor shook his head. "Only what I've said. I tell you what's wrong, it's up to somebody else to tell you how to fix it. I don't think you *can* fix it. I mean, not medically. You've got a brain—Willy's or Roger's. It has grown up as a radio receiver. Now you're putting TV pictures into it. It doesn't know how to deal with them."

All this time Brad had been scribbling, looking up from time to time with an expression of interest. He looked down again at his note pad, wrote something, regarded it thoughtfully, wrote again, while the attention of everyone in the room turned to him.

At last the deputy director said, "Brad? It sounds as though the ball's in your court."

Brad looked up and smiled. "That's what I'm working on," he said.

"Do you agree with Dr. Freeling?"

"No question about it. He's right. We can't feed raw inputs into a nervous system that hasn't got equipment to mediate and translate them. Those mechanisms don't exist in the brain, not in anybody's brain, unless we want to take a child at birth and rebuild him then so that the brain can develop what it needs."

"Are you proposing that we wait for a new generation of astronauts?" Griffin demanded.

"No. I'm proposing we build mediating circuits into Roger. Not just sensory inputs. Filters, translators—ways of interpreting the inputs, the sight from different wavelengths of the spectrum, the kinesthetic sense from the new muscles—everything. Look," he said, "let me go back a little bit. Do any of you know about McCulloch and Lettvin and the frog's eye?" He glanced around the room. "Sure, Jonny, you do, and one or two of the others. I'd better review a little of it. The frog's perceptual system—not just the eye, all of the vision parts of it—filters out what isn't important. If a bug passes in front of the frog's eye, the eye perceives it, the nerves transmit the information, the brain responds to it, and the frog eats the bug. If, say, a little leaf drops in front of the frog he doesn't eat it. He doesn't *decide* not to eat it. He doesn't *see* it. The image forms in the eye, all right, but the information is dropped out before it reaches the brain. The brain never becomes aware of what the eye has seen, because it doesn't need to. It simply is not relevant to a frog to know whether or not a leaf is in front of it."

Roger was following the conversation with great interest, but somewhat less comprehension. "Wait a minute," he said. "I'm more complicated—I mean, a man is a lot more complicated than a frog. How can you tell what I 'need' to see?"

"Survival things, Rog. We've got a lot of data from Willy. I think we can do it."

"Thanks. I wish you were a little more sure."

"Oh, I'm sure enough," said Brad, grinning. "This didn't catch me entirely by surprise."

Torraway said, his throat half-closed and his voice thin, "You mean you let Willy go ahead and—"

"No, Roger! Come on. Willy was my friend, too. I thought there was enough of a safety factor to at least keep him alive. I was wrong, and I'm at least as sorry as you are, Roger. But we all knew there was a risk that the systems wouldn't work right, that we'd have to do more."

"That," said Griffin heavily, "was not made very clear in your progress reports." The deputy director started to speak but Griffin shook his head. "We'll come to that another time. What are you saying now, Bradley? You're going to filter out some of the information?"

"Not just filter it out. Mediate it. Translate it into a form Roger can handle."

"What about Torraway's point that a man is more complicated than a frog? Have you ever done this with human beings?"

Surprisingly, Brad grinned; he was ready for that one. "As a matter of fact, yes. About six years ago, before I came here—I was still a graduate student. We took four volunteers and we conditioned them to a Pavlovian response. We flashed a bright light in their eyes, and simultaneously rang an electric doorbell that pulsed at thirty beats a second. Well, of course, when you get a bright light in your eyes, your pupils contract. It isn't under conscious control. You can't fake it. It is a response to light, nothing else, just an evolutionary capacity to protect the eye from direct sunlight.

"That sort of response, involving the autonomic nervous system, is hard to condition into human beings. But we managed it. When it takes, it sets pretty firmly. After—I think it was after three hundred trials apiece, we had the response fixed. All you had to do was ring the bell, and the subjects' pupils would shrink down to dots. You follow me so far?"

"I remember enough from college to know about Pavlovian reflexes. Standard stuff," said Griffin.

"Well, the next part wasn't standard. We tapped into the auditory nerve, and we could measure the actual signal going to the brain: ding-a-ling, thirty beats per second, we could read it on the oscilloscope.

"So then we changed the bell. We got one that rang at twenty-four beats a second. Care to guess what happened?" There was no response. Brad smiled. "The oscilloscope still showed *thirty beats a second*. The brain was hearing something that wasn't really happening.

"So, you see, it isn't just frogs that do this sort of mediation. Human beings *perceive* the world in predigested ways. The sensory inputs themselves edit and rearrange the information.

"So what I want to do with you, Roger," he said genially, "is give you a little help in interpretation. We can't do much with your brain. Good or bad, we're stuck with it. It's a mass of gray jelly with a capacity-limiting structure and we can't keep pouring sensory information into it. The only place we have to work is at the interface—*before* it hits the brain."

Griffin slapped his open palm on the table. "Can we make the window date?" he growled.

"I can but try, sir," said Brad genially.

"You can but get your ass in a crack if we buy this and it doesn't work, boy!"

The geniality faded from Brad's face. "What do you want me to say?"

"I want you to tell me the odds!" Griffin barked.

Brad hesitated. "No worse than even money," he said at last.

"Then," said Griffin, smiling at last, "let it be so."

Even money, thought Roger on the way back to his own office, is not a bad bet. Of course, it depends on the stakes.

He slowed down to let Brad catch up with him. "Brad," he said, "you're pretty sure of what you were saying?"

Brad slapped him gently on the back. "More sure than I said, to tell you the truth. I just didn't want to stick my neck out for old Griffin. And listen, Roger, thanks."

"For what?"

"For trying to warn me today. I appreciate it."

"You're welcome," said Roger. He stood there for a moment, watching Brad retreating back, and wondering how Brad knew about something he had told only to his wife.

We could have told him—as in fact we could have told him many, many things, including why the polls showed what they showed. But no one really needed to tell him. He could have told himself—if he had allowed himself to know.

Seven
Mortal Becoming Monster

Don Kayman was a complex man who never let go of a problem. It was why we wanted him on the project as areologist, but it extended to the religious part of his life too. A religious problem was bothering him, in the corner of his mind.

It did not keep him from whistling to himself as he shaved carefully around his Dizzy Gillespie beard and brushed his hair into a neat pageboy in front of his mirror. It bothered him, though. He stared into the mirror, trying to isolate what it was that was troubling him. After a moment he realized that one thing, at least, was his T-shirt. It was wrong. He took it off and replaced it with a double-knit four-colored turtleneck that had enough of the look of a clerical collar to appeal to his sense of humor.

The interhouse phone buzzed. "Donnie? Are you nearly ready?"

"Coming in a minute," he said, looking around. What else? His sports jacket was over a chair by the door. His shoes were shined. His fly was zipped. "I'm getting absent-minded," he told himself. What was bothering him was something about Roger Torraway, for whom, at that moment, he felt very sorry.

He shrugged, picked up his jacket, swung it over his shoulder, went down the hall and knocked on the door of Sister Clotilda's nunnery.

"Morning, Father," said the novice who let him in. "Take a seat. I'll get her for you."

"Thanks, Jess." As she disappeared down the hall Kayman watched her appreciatively. The tight-fitting pants-suit habit did a lot for her figure, and Kayman let himself enjoy the faint, antique feeling of wickedness it gave him. It was a gentle enough vice, like eating roast beef on Friday. He remembered his parents doggedly chewing the frozen deep-fried scallops every Friday night, even after the dispensation had become general. It was not that they felt it was sinful to eat meat, it was simply that their digestive systems had become so geared to fish on Friday that they didn't know how to change. Kayman's feelings about sex were closely related to that. When the celibacy rule had been lifted, it had not taken away the genetic recollection of two thousand years of a priesthood that had pretended it didn't know what its sexual equipment was for.

Sister Clotilda came briskly into the room, kissed his freshly shaved cheek and took his arm. "You smell good," she said.

"Want to get a cup of coffee somewhere?" he asked, guiding her out the door.

"I don't think so, Donnie. Let's get it over with."

The autumn sun was a blast, hot air up out of Texas. "Shall we put the top down?"

She shook her head. "Your hair will blow all over. Anyway, it's too hot." She twisted in the seat belt to look at him. "What's the matter?"

He shrugged, starting the car and guiding it into the automatic lanes. "I—I'm not sure. I feel as if I have something I forgot to confess."

Clotilda nodded appraisingly. "Me?"

"Oh, no, Tillie! It's—I'm not sure what." He took her hand absentmindedly, staring out the side window. As they passed over a throughway he could see the great white cube of the project building off on the horizon.

It wasn't his interest in Sister Clotilda that was bothering him, he was pretty sure of that. Although he liked the little tingle of mild wickedness, he was not in any sense willing to flout the laws of his Church and his God. Maybe, he thought, he might hire a good lawyer and fight, but not break a law. He considered his pursuit of Sister Clotilda daring enough, and what came of that would depend on what her order allowed when and if he ever got around to asking her to apply for a dispensation. He had no interest in the wilder splinter groups like the clerical communes or the revived Catharists.

"Roger Torraway?" she guessed.

"I wouldn't be surprised," he said. "There's something about tampering with his senses that bothers me. His perceptions of the world."

Sister Clotilda squeezed his hand. As a psychiatric social worker, she was cleared to know what was happening at the project, and she knew Don Kayman. "The senses are liars, Donnie. That's Scripture."

"Oh, sure. But does Brad have any right to say how Roger's senses lie?"

Clotilda lit a cigarette and let him think it out. It wasn't until they were near the shopping mall that she said, "Next turnoff, isn't it?"

"Right," he said, taking the wheel and turning the car back to manual. He slid into a parking space, still preoccupied with Roger Torraway. There was the immediate problem of Roger's wife. That was trouble enough. But beyond that there was the bigger problem: How could Roger deal with the greatest of personal questions—what is Right, and what is Wrong?—if the information he had to base a decision on was filtered through Brad's mediation circuits?

The sign over the shop window said PRETTY FANCIES. It was a small shop by the standard of the mall, which had a Two Guys with a quarter of a million feet of floor space and a supermarket almost as big. But it was big enough to be expensive. With rent, utilities, insurance, payroll for three salespeople, two of them part-time, and a generous managerial salary for Dorrie, it meant a net loss every month of nearly two thousand dollars. Roger paid it gladly, although some of our accountancy functions had pointed out to him that it would have been cheaper to give Dorrie the two thousand a month as an allowance.

Dorrie was stacking chinaware on a counter marked "Clearance Sale —Half Price." She nodded to the visitors politely enough. "Hello, Don. Nice to see you, Sister Clotilda. Want to buy some red teacups cheap?"

"They look nice," said Clotilda.

"Oh, they are. But don't buy them for the nunnery. The FDA just ordered them off the market. The glaze is supposed to be poison— provided you drink at least forty cups of tea out of one of them every day of your life for twenty years."

"Oh, that's too bad. But—you're selling them?"

"The order isn't effective for thirty days," Dorrie explained, and flashed a grin. "I guess I shouldn't have told that to a priest and a nun, right? But honestly, we've been selling this glaze for years and I never heard of anyone dying."

"Would you like to have a cup of coffee with us?" Kayman asked. "In other cups, of course."

Dorrie sighed, straightened a cup into line and said, "No, we might as well just talk. Come on back to my office." She led the way, and said over her shoulder, "I know why you're here, anyway."

"Oh?" said Kayman.

"You want me to go visit Roger. Right?"

Kayman sat down in a wide armchair, facing her desk. "Why don't you, Dorrie?"

"Cripes, Don, what's the use? He's out cold. He wouldn't know whether I was there or not."

"He's heavily sedated, yes. But he has periods of consciousness."

"Did he ask for me?"

"He asked *after* you. What do you want him to do, beg?"

Dorrie shrugged, fiddling with a ceramic chess piece. "Did you ever think of minding your own business, Don?" she asked.

He did not take offense. "That's what I'm doing. Roger's our one indispensable man right now. Do you know what's happening to him? He's been on the table twenty-eight times already. Thirteen days! He doesn't have any eyes any more. Or lungs, heart, ears, nose—he doesn't even have any skin, it's all gone, a few square inches at a time, replaced with synthetics. Flaying alive—men have become saints for that, and now we've got a man who can't even have his own wife—"

"Oh, shit, Don!" Dorrie flared. "You don't know what you're talking about. Roger *asked* me not to come and see him after the surgery started. He thought I wouldn't be able to— He just didn't want me to see him like that!"

"My impression of you," the priest said thinly, "is that you're made of pretty durable stuff, Dorrie. Would you be able to stand it?"

Dorrie grimaced. For a moment her pretty face did not look pretty at all. "It isn't a question of what I can stand," she said. "Don, look. Do you know what it's like being married to a man like Roger?"

"Why, pretty fine, I would guess," said Kayman, startled. "He's a good man!"

"He is, yes. I know that at least as well as you do, Don Kayman. And he's head over heels in love with me."

There was a pause. "I don't think I understand what you're saying," Sister Clotilda ventured. "Are you displeased by that?"

Dorrie looked at the nun consideringly. "Displeased. That's one way to put it." She set down the chess piece and leaned across the desk. "That's every girl's dream, right? To find a genuine hero, handsome and smart and famous and pretty nearly rich—and have him so crazily in love with her that he can't see anything wrong. That's why I married Roger. I couldn't believe I was that lucky." Her voice went up a half tone in pitch. "I don't think you know what it's like to have someone head over heels in love with you. What's the good of a man who's upside down? Sometimes when we're in bed together I'm trying to get to sleep and I can *hear* him being awake next to me, not moving, not getting up to go to the bathroom, just so fucking *considerate*. . . . Do you know that when we're traveling together Roger never goes to the bathroom until he thinks I'm asleep, or when I'm somewhere else? He shaves the minute he gets up—he doesn't want me to see him with his hair messed up. He shaves his armpits, uses deodorants three times a day. He—he treats me like I was the Virgin Mary, Don! He's *fatuous*. And it's been that way for *nine years*."

She looked beseechingly at the priest and the nun, who were silent, a little ill-at-ease. "And then," Dorrie said, "you come along and tell me I ought to go see him when they're turning him into something ghastly and ludicrous. You and everybody else. Kathleen Doughty dropped in last night. She had a skin full; she'd been drinking and brooding and she decided to come over and tell me, out of her bourbon wisdom, that I was making Roger unhappy. Well, she's right. You're all right. I'm making him unhappy. Where you're wrong is thinking that my going to see him would make him happy. . . . Oh, hell."

The phone rang. Dorrie picked it up, then glanced at Kayman and Sister Clotilda. The expression on her face, which had been almost pleading, condensed into something like the porcelain figures on the table beside her desk. "Excuse me," she said, folding up the soft plastic petals around the mouthpiece that converted it into a hushphone and turning away from them in her chair. She talked inaudibly for a moment, then hung up and turned back to them.

Kayman said, "You've given me something to think about, Dorrie. But still—"

She smiled a porcelain smile. "But still you want to tell me how to run my life. Well, you can't. You've said your piece, both of you. I thank you for coming. I'll thank you, now, to go. There's nothing more to be said."

Inside the great white cube of the project building Roger lay, spread-eagled on a fluidized bed. He had been thirteen days like that, most of the time either unconscious or unable to tell whether he was conscious or not. He dreamed. We could tell when he was dreaming from the rapid eye movements at first, later from the twitches of the muscle endings after the eyes were gone. Some of his dreams were reality, but he could not distinguish between them.

We kept very close tabs on Roger Torraway every second of that time. There was hardly a flexure of a muscle or a flash of a synapse that did not kick over some monitor, and faithfully we integrated the data and kept continuous surveillance of his vital functions.

It was only the beginning. What had been done to Roger in the first thirteen days of surgery was not much more than had been done to Willy Hartnett. And that was not enough.

When all that was done, the prosthetic and surgical teams began doing things that had never been done to any human being before. His entire nervous system was revised and all the major pathways connected with coupling devices that led to the big computer downstairs. That was an all-purpose IBM 3070. It took up half a room and still did not have enough capacity to do all the jobs demanded of it. It was only an interim hookup. Two thousand miles away, in upstate New York, the IBM factory was putting together a special-purpose computer that would fit into a backpack. Designing that was the most difficult part of the project; we kept revising the circuits even while they were being fitted together on the workbenches. It could not weigh more than eighty pounds, Earth weight. Its greatest dimension could not be more than nineteen inches. And it had to work from DC batteries which were kept continually recharged by solar panels.

The solar panels were a problem at first, but we solved that one rather elegantly. They required an absolute minimum surface area of nearly thirty square feet. The surface area of Roger's body, even after it had been revised with various attachments, wasn't large enough, wouldn't have been even if all of it could have been accepting Mars's fairly feeble sunlight at once. The way we solved the problem was to design two great gossamer fairy wings. "He's going to look like Oberon," Brad said gleefully when he saw the drawings. "Or like a bat," grumbled Kathleen Doughty.

They did resemble bat wings, especially as they were jet-black. They would be no good for flying, even in a decently thick atmosphere if Mars had had one. They were thin film, with little structural strength. But they weren't meant for flying or for any kind of load-bearing. They were only meant to preen themselves out automatically, oriented to accept as much radiation as the sun could provide. As an afterthought, the design was changed to include a certain amount of control on Roger's part so he could use the wings as a tightrope walker uses his pole, to balance. All in all, they were an immense improvement over the "ears" we had put on Willy Hartnett.

The solar wings were designed and fabricated in eight days; by the time Roger's shoulders were ready to accept them, they were ready to attach. The skin was almost a stock item by now. So much had been used on Willy Hartnett, both as original equipment and as replacements for damage or for design changes as the project went along, that new grafts were loomed to Roger's shape as rapidly as the surgeons flayed away the integument he was born with.

From time to time he would rouse himself and look at his surroundings with what seemed recognition and intelligence. It was hard to be sure. His visitors—he had a constant stream of them—sometimes spoke to him, sometimes came to regard him as a laboratory specimen to be discussed and manipulated with no more person-to-person concern than they would give a titration flask. Vern Scanyon was in almost every day, staring at the developing creation with growing repugnance. "He looks like hell," he grumbled. "The taxpayers would love this!"

"Watch it, General," snarled Kathleen Doughty, interposing her huge body between the director and the subject. "How do you know he can't hear you?"

Scanyon shrugged and left to report to the President's office. Don Kayman came in as he was going. "Thanks, mother to all the world," he said gravely. "I appreciate your concern for my friend Roger."

"Yeah," she said irritably. "It's not sentiment. The poor sod's got to have some self-confidence; he's going to need it. You know how many amputees and paraplegics I've worked with? And do you know how many of them were certified basket cases that would never walk or move any muscle or even go to the toilet by themselves? It's will power that does it, Don, and for that you need to believe in yourself."

Kayman frowned; Roger's state of mind was still very much in his thoughts. "Are you arguing with me?" Kathleen said sharply, misreading the frown.

"Not in the least! I mean—be reasonable, Kathleen; am I the man to question the transcendence of the spiritual over the physical? I'm just grateful. You're a good person, Kathleen."

"Oh, crap," she grumbled around the cigarette in her mouth. "That's what they pay me for. And besides," she said, "I take it you haven't been in your office yet today? There's a buck-up note for all of us from His Starship the General, so we won't forget how important what we're doing is . . . and a little hint that if we blow our launch date we're for the concentration camps."

"As if we needed reminding," sighed Father Kayman, looking at Roger's grotesque and unmoving figure. "Scanyon's a good man, but he tends to think whatever he does is at the very center of the universe. Only this time he might be right. . . ."

It was at least a colorable claim. To us, there was not much question about it: the most important link in all the complex interrelationships of mind and matter that an earlier generation of scientists had called

Gaia was right there, floating on its fluidized bed, looking like the star of a Japanese horror flick. Without Roger Torraway, the Mars launch could not take off on time. Billions of people might question the importance of that. We did not.

There was Roger at the hub of everything. Around him, in the bulk of the project building, there were all the ancillary and associated efforts that were going into making him what he had to be. In the surgery room next door Freeling, Weidner and Bradley tinkered new parts into him. Down in the Mars-normal tank where Willy Hartnett had died, those parts were bench-tested in the Martian environment to failure. Sometimes failure time was appallingly short; then they were redesigned if possible, or backed up—or sometimes used anyway, with crossed fingers and prayers.

The universe expanded away from Roger, like the shells of an onion. Still farther in the building was the giant 3070, clicking and whirring as it accreted new segments of programming to match the mediation facilities being built into Roger hour by hour. Outside the building was the community of Tonka, which lived or died by the health of the project, its principal employer and major reason for being. All around Tonka was the rest of Oklahoma, and spreading out in all directions the other fifty-four states, and around them the troubled, angry world that was busy snapping arrogant notes from one of its capitals to another on the policy level, and clawing for subsistence in each of its myriad personal lives.

The project people had come to close themselves off from most of that world. They didn't watch the television news when they could avoid it, preferred not to read anything but the sports sections of the newspapers. In high gear, they did not have a great deal of time, but that wasn't the reason. The reason was that they simply did not want to know. The world was going mad, and the isolated strangeness in the great white cube of the project building seemed sane and real to them, while the rioting in New York, the tac-nuke fighting around the Arabian Gulf and the mass starvation in what used to be called the "emerging nations" seemed irrelevant fantasy.

They were fantasy. At least, they did not matter to the future of our race.

And so Roger continued to change and survive. Kayman spent more and more time with him, every minute he could spare from supervising the Mars-normal tank. He watched with affection as Kathleen Doughty stumped around the room, dropping cigarette ashes on everything but Roger. But he was still troubled.

He had to accept Roger's need for mediation circuits to interpret the excess of inputs, but he had no answer for the great question: If Roger could not know what he was seeing, how could he see Truth?

Eight
Through Deceitful Eyes

The weather had changed quickly and for good. We had seen the shift coming as a wedge of polar air pushed down out of Alberta as far as the Texas Panhandle. Wind warnings had grounded the hovercars. Those of the project personnel who didn't have wheeled vehicles were forced to come by public transportation, and the parking lots were almost bare except for great ungainly knots of tumbleweed bouncing before the wind.

Not everyone had heeded the warnings, and there were the colds and flu bugs of the year's first real cold snap. Brad was laid up. Weidner was ambulatory, but not allowed near Roger for fear of infecting him with a trivial little illness that he was in no shape to handle. Most of the work of doing Roger was left to Jonathan Freeling, whose health was then guarded almost as jealously as Roger's own. Kathleen Doughty, indestructibly tough old lady, was in Roger's room every hour, dropping cigarette ash and advice on the nurses. "Treat him like a *person*," she ordered. "And put some clothes on before you go home. You can show off your beautiful little butt any time—what you have to do now is keep from catching cold until we can spare you." The nurses did not resist her. They did their best, even Clara Bly, recalled from her honeymoon to fill in for the nurses on the sick list. They cared as much as Kathleen Doughty did, although it was hard to remember, looking down at the grotesque creature that was still named Roger Torraway, that he was in fact a human being, as capable of yearning and depression as themselves.

Roger was beginning to be more clearly conscious from time to time.

Twenty hours and more each day he was out cold, or in a half-dreaming analgesic daze; but sometimes he recognized the people in the room with him, and sometimes even spoke coherently to them. Then we would put him out again.

"I wish I knew what he was feeling," said Clara Bly to her relief nurse.

The other girl looked down at the mask that was all there was left of his face, with the great wide eyes that had been fabricated for him. "Maybe you're better off if you don't," she said. "Go home, Clara."

Roger heard that; the oscilloscope traces showed that he had. By studying the telemetry we could form some notion of what was inside his mind. Often he was in pain, that was evident. But the pain was not a warning of something that needed attention, or a spur to action. It was simply a fact of his life. He learned to expect it and to accept it when it happened. He was not conscious of very much else that pertained to his own body. His body-knowledge senses had not yet come to deal with the reality of his new body. He did not know when his eyes, lungs, heart, ears, nose and skin were replaced or supplemented. He didn't know how to recognize the clues that might have given him information. The taste of blood and vomit at the back of his throat: how was he to know that that meant his lungs were gone? The blackness, the suppressed pain in the skull that was so unlike any other headache he had ever had: how could he tell what it meant, how could he distinguish between the removal of his entire optic system and the turning off of a light switch?

He realized dimly at one point that somewhen he had stopped smelling the familiar hospital aroma, scented odor killer and disinfectant. When? He didn't know. All he knew was that there were no smells in his environment any more.

He could hear. With a sharpness of discrimination and a level of perception he had never experienced before, he could hear every word that was said in the room, in however low a whisper, and most of what happened in the adjoining rooms as well. He heard what people said, when he was conscious enough to hear at all. He understood the words. He could feel the good will of Kathleen Doughty and Jon Freeling, and understood the worry and anger that underlay the voices of the deputy director and the general.

And above all, he could feel pain.

There were so many different kinds of pain! There were all the aches of all the parts of his body. There was the healing of surgery, and there was the angry pulsing of tissues that had been bruised as major work was done. There were the endless little twinges as Freeling or the nurses jacked instrumentation into a thousand hurtful places on the surface of his body so that they could study the readings they gave.

And there was the deeper, internal pain that sometimes seemed physical, that came when he thought of Dorrie. Sometimes, when he was awake, he remembered to ask if she had been there or had called. He could not remember ever getting an answer.

And then one day he felt a searing new pain inside his head . . . and realized it was light.

He was seeing again.

When the nurses realized that he could see them they reported to Jon Freeling at once, who picked up the phone and called Brad. "Be right over," Brad said. "Keep him in the dark till I get there."

It took more than an hour for Brad to make the trip, and when he turned up he was clearly wobbly. He submitted to an antiseptic shower, an oral spray and the fitting of a surgical mask, and then, cautiously, he opened the door and entered Roger's room.

The voice from the bed said, "Who's there?" It was weak and quavering, but it was Roger's voice.

"Me. Brad." He fumbled along the side of the door until he found the light knob. "I'm going to turn the lights on a little bit, Roger. Tell me when you can see me."

"I can see you now," sighed the voice. "At least I guess it's you."

Brad arrested his hand. "The hell you can—" he began, and then he paused. "What do you mean, you see me? What do you see?"

"Well," whispered the voice, "I'm not sure about the face. That's just a sort of glow. But I can see your hands, and your head. They're bright. And I can make out your body and arms pretty well. A lot fainter, though—yeah, I can see your legs, too. But your face is funny. The middle of it is just a splotch."

Brad touched the surgical mask, comprehending. "Infrared. You're seeing the heat. What else can you see, Roger?"

Silence from the bed for a moment. Then, "Well, there's a sort of square of light; I guess it's the door frame. I mostly just see the outline of it. And something pretty bright over against the wall, where I hear something too—the telemetry monitors? And I can see my own body, or at least I can see the sheet over me, with a sort of outline of my body on it."

Brad stared around the room. Even with time for dark adaptation he could see almost nothing: a polka-dot pattern of illuminated dials from the monitors, and a very faint seepage of light around the door behind him.

"That's pretty good, Rog. Anything else?"

"Yeah, but I don't know what they are. Some lights low down, over near you. Very dim."

"I think those are the heating ducts. You're doing fine, boy. All right, now hold on. I'm going to turn up the room lights a little bit. Maybe you can get along without them, but I can't and neither can the nurses. Tell me what you feel."

Slowly he inched the dimmer dial around, an eighth of a turn, a bit more. The surround lights behind the moldings under the ceiling came alive—weakly at first, then a trifle stronger. Brad could see the shape on the bed now, first the glitter of the spread wings that had revolved forward, over the body of Roger Torraway, then the body itself, with a sheet draped over it waist-high.

"I see you now," sighed Roger in his reedy voice. "It's a little different—I'm seeing color now, and you're not so bright."

Brad took his hand off the knob. "That's good enough for now." He leaned back against the wall giddily. "Sorry," he said. "I've got a cold or something. . . . How about you, do you feel anything? I mean, any pain, anything like that?"

"Christ, Brad!"

"No, I mean connected with vision. Does the light hurt your—your eyes?"

"They're about the only thing that doesn't hurt," sighed Roger.

"Fine. I'm going to give you a little more light—about that much, okay? No trouble?"

"No."

Brad walked delicately over to the bed. "All right, I want you to try something. Can you—well, close your eyes? I mean, can you turn off the vision receptors?"

Pause. "I—don't think so."

"Well, you can, Rog. The capacity is built in, you'll just have to find it. Willy had a little trouble at first, but he got it. He said he just sort of fooled around, and then it happened."

". . . Nothing's happening."

Brad pondered for a second. His head was muzzy from the infection, and he could feel his stamina ebbing away. "How about this? Did you ever have sinus trouble?"

"No—well, maybe. A little bit."

"Can you remember where it hurt?"

The shape moved uncomfortably on the bed, the great eyes staring into Brad's. "I—think so."

"Feel around near there," Brad ordered. "See if you can find muscles to move. The muscles aren't there, but the nerve endings that controlled them are."

". . . Nothing. What muscle am I looking for?"

"Oh, hell, Roger! It's called the *rectus lateralis,* and what good does that do you? Just fool around."

". . . Nothing."

"All right." Brad sighed. "Never mind for now. Keep on trying as often as you can, all right? You'll find how to do it."

"That's a comfort," whispered the resentful voice from the bed. "Hey, Brad? You're looking brighter."

"What do you mean, brighter?" Brad snapped.

"More bright. More light from your face."

"Yeah," said Brad, realizing he was beginning to feel giddy again. "I think I may be running a temperature. I'd better get out of here. This gauze, it's supposed to keep me from infecting you, but it's only reliable for fifteen minutes or so—"

"Before you go," whispered the voice insistently. "Do something for me. Turn off the lights again for a minute."

Brad shrugged and complied. "Yeah?"

He could hear the ungainly body shifting in the bed. "I'm just turning to get a better look," Roger reported. "Listen, Brad, what I wanted to ask you is, how are things working out? Am I going to make it?"

Brad paused for reflection. "I think so," he said honestly. "Everything's all right so far. I wouldn't crap you, Roger. This is all frontier stuff, and something could go wrong. But so far it doesn't look that way."

"Thanks. One other thing, Brad. Have you seen Dorrie lately?"

Pause. "No, Roger. Not for a week or so. I've been pretty sick, and when I wasn't sick I was damn busy."

"Yeah. Say, I guess you might as well leave the lights the way you had them so the nurses can find their way around."

Brad turned up the switch again. "I'll be in when I can. Practice trying to close your eyes, will you? And you've got a phone—call me any time you want to. I don't mean if anything goes wrong—I'll know about that if it happens, don't worry; I don't go to the toilet without leaving the number where I can be reached. I mean if you just want to talk."

"Thanks, Brad. So long."

At least the surgery was over—or the worst of it, anyway. When Roger came to realize that, he felt a kind of relief that was very precious to him, although there were still more unrelieved stresses in his mind than he wanted to handle.

Clara Bly cleaned him up and against direct orders brought him flowers to boost his morale. "You're a good kid," whispered Roger, turning his head to look at them.

"What do they look like to you?"

He tried to describe it. "Well, they're roses, but they're not red. Pale yellow? About the same color as your bracelet."

"That's orange." She finished whipping the new sheet over his legs. It billowed gently in the upthrust from the fluidized bed. "Want the bedpan?"

"For what?" he grumbled. He was into his third week of a low-residue diet, and his tenth day of controlled liquid intake. His excretory system had become, as Clara put it, mostly ornamental. "I'm allowed to get up anyway," he said, "so if anything does happen I can take care of it."

"Big man," Clara grinned, bundling up the dirty linen and leaving. Roger sat up and began again his investigation of the world around him. He studied the roses appraisingly. The great faceted eyes took in nearly an extra octave of radiation, which meant half a dozen colors Roger had never seen before from IR to UV; but he had no names for them, and the rainbow spectrum he had seen all his life had extended itself to cover them all. What seemed to him dark red was, he knew, low-level heat. But it was not quite true even to say that it seemed to be red; it was only a different quality of light that had associations of warmth and well-being.

Still, there was something very strange about the roses, and it was not the color.

He threw off the sheet and looked down at himself. The new skin was poreless, hairless and wrinkle-free. It looked more like a wetsuit than the flesh he had known all his life. Under it, he knew, was a whole new musculature, power-driven, but there was no visible trace of that.

Soon he would get up and walk, all by himself. He was not quite ready for that. He clicked on the TV set. The screen lit up with a dazzling array of dots in magenta and cyan and green. It took an effort of will for Roger to look at them and see three girls singing and weaving; his new eyes wanted to analyze the pattern into its components. He clicked stations and got a newscast. New People's Asia had sent three more nuclear subs on a "courtesy visit" to Australia. President Deshatine's press secretary said sternly that our allies in the Free World could count on us. All the Oklahoma football teams had lost. Roger clicked it off; he found himself getting a headache. Every time he shifted position the lines seemed to slope off at an angle, and there was a baffling bright glow from the back of the set. After the current was off he watched for some time the cathode tube's light failing, and the glow from the back darkening and dimming. It was heat, he realized.

Now, what was it Brad had said? "Feel around, near where your sinuses are."

It was a strange feeling, being in the first place in an unfamiliar body and then trying to locate inside it a control that no one could quite define. Just in order to close the eyes! But Brad had assured him he could do it. Roger's feelings toward Brad were complex, and one component of them was pride; if Brad said it could be done by anyone, then it was going to be done by Roger.

Only it wasn't *being* done. He tried every combination of muscle squeezes and will power he could think of, and nothing happened.

A sudden recollection hit him: years old, a memory from the days when he and Dorrie had first been married. No, not married, not yet; living together, he remembered, and trying to decide if they wanted to publicly join their lives. That was their massage-and-transcendental-meditation period, when they were exploring each other in all the ways that had ever occurred to either of them, and he remembered the smell of baby oil with a dash of musk added, and the way they had laughed over the directions for the second chakra: "Take the air into your spleen and hold it, then breathe out as your hands glide up on either side of your partner's spine." But they had never been able to figure out where the spleen was, and Dorrie had been very funny, searching the private recesses of their bodies: "Is it there? There? Oh, Rog, look, you're not serious about this . . ."

He felt a sudden interior pain swell giddyingly inside him, and leaned back in desolation. *Dorrie!*

The door burst open.

Clara Bly flew in, bright eyes wide in her dark, pretty face. "Roger! What are you doing?"

He took a deep, slow breath before he spoke. "What's the matter?" He could hear the flatness in his own voice; it had little tone left, after what they had done to it.

"All your taps are jumping! I thought—I don't know what I thought, Roger. But whatever was happening, it was giving you trouble."

"Sorry, Clara." He watched as she hurried over to the monitors on the wall, studying them swiftly.

"They look a little better," she said grudgingly. "I guess it's all right. But what the hell were you doing to yourself?"

"Worrying," he said.

"About what?"

"Where my spleen is. Do you know?"

She stared at him thoughtfully for a moment before she replied. "It's under your lower ribs, on your left side. About where you think your heart is. A little lower down. Are you putting me on, Roger?"

"Well, kind of. I guess I was reminiscing about something I shouldn't have, Clara."

"Please don't do it any more!"

"I'll try." But the thought of Dorrie and Brad was still lurking there, right under the conscious of his mind. He offered, "One thing—I've been trying to close my eyes, and I can't."

She approached and touched his shoulder in friendly sympathy. "You'll do it, hon."

"Yeah."

"No, really. I was with Willy around this time, and he got pretty discouraged. But he made it. Anyway," she said, turning, "I'll take care of it for you for now. Lights-out time. You've got to be fresh as a daisy in the morning."

He said suspiciously, "What for?"

"Oh, not more cutting. That's over for a while. Didn't Brad tell you? Tomorrow they're going to hook you into the computer for all that mediation stuff. You're going to be a busy boy, Rog, so get some sleep." She turned off the light, and Brad watched as her dark face changed into a gentle glow that he thought of as peach.

Something occurred to him. "Clara? Do me a favor?"

She stopped with her hand on the door. "What's that, honey?"

"I want to ask you a question."

"So ask."

He hesitated, wondering how to do what he wanted to do. "What I want to know," he said, working it out in his head as he went along, "is, let's see—oh, yes. What I want to know, Clara, is, when your husband and you are in bed making love, what different ways do you use?"

"Roger!" The brightness of her face suddenly went up half a decibel; he could see the tracing of veins under the skin as hot blood flooded through her veins.

He said, "I'm sorry, Clara. I guess—I guess lying here I get kind of horny. Forget I asked you, will you?"

She was silent for a moment. When she spoke her voice was a professional's, no longer a friend's: "Sure, Roger. It's okay. You just kind of caught me off-guard. It's . . . well, it's all right, it's just that you never said anything like that to me before."

"I know. Sorry."

But he wasn't sorry, or not exactly.

He watched the door close behind her and studied the rectangular tracing of light bleeding through from the hall outside. He was careful to keep his mind as calm as he could. He didn't want to start the monitors ringing alarm bells again.

But he wanted to think about something that was right on the borderline of the danger zone, and that was how come the flush he had tricked onto Clara Bly's face looked so much like the sudden brightness that had come onto Brad's when he asked if Brad had been with Dorrie.

We were fully mobilized next morning, checking the circuits, cutting in the stand-bys, insuring that the automatic switchover relays were tuned to intervene at the faintest flicker of a malfunction. Brad came in at 6:00 A.M., weak but clear-headed and ready to work. Weidner and Jon Freeling were only minutes after him, although the primary job for the day was all Brad's. They could not stay away. Kathleen Doughty was there-of-course, as she had been at every step, not because her duty required it but because her heart did. "Don't give my boy a bad time," she growled over her cigarette. "He's going to need all the help he can get when I start on him next week."

Sounding every syllable, Brad said, "Kathleen, I will do the goddamned best I can."

"Yeah. I know you will, Brad." She stubbed out the cigarette and immediately lit another. "I never had any children, and I guess Roger and Willy sort of filled in."

"Yeah," grunted Brad, no longer listening. He was not qualified or allowed to touch the 3070 or any of the ancillary units. All he could do was watch while the technicians and the programmers did their job. When the third recheck had gone almost to completion without a glitch he finally left the computer room and took the elevator up three flights to Roger's room.

At the door he paused to breathe for a moment, then opened the door with a smile. "You're about ready to plug in, boy," he said. "Feel up to it?"

The insect eyes turned toward him. Roger's flat voice said, "I don't know what I'm supposed to feel. What I feel is mostly scared."

"Oh, there's nothing to be scared of. Today," Brad amended hastily, "all we're going to do is test out the mediation."

The bat wings shuddered and changed position. "Will that kill me?" asked the maddeningly monotone voice.

"Oh, come on, Roger!" Brad was suddenly angry.

"It's only a question," ticked the voice.

"It's a crappy question! Look, I know how you feel—"

"I doubt that."

Brad stopped, and studied Roger's uncommunicative face. After a moment he said, "Let me go over it again. What I'm going to do is not kill you, it's keep you alive. Sure, you're thinking of what happened to Willy. It isn't going to happen to you. You're going to be able to handle what happens—here, and on Mars, where it's important."

"It's important to me here," said Roger.

"Oh, for Christ's sake. When the system is all go you'll only see or hear what you need, understand? Or what you want. You'll have a good deal of volitional control. You'll be able—"

"I can't even close my eyes yet, Brad."

"You will. You'll be able to use all of it. But you won't unless we get started on it. Then all this stuff will filter out the unnecessary signals, so you won't be confused. That's what killed Willy: confusion."

Pause, while the brain behind the grotesque face ruminated. What Roger finally said was, "You look lousy, Brad."

"Sorry about that. I actually don't feel too good."

"Are you sure you're up to this?"

"I'm sure. Hey, Roger. What are you telling me? Do you want to put this off?"

"No."

"Well, what do you want?"

"I wish I knew, Brad. Get on with it."

We were all ready by then; the "go" lights had been flashing green for several minutes. Brad shrugged and said morosely to the duty nurse, "Let 'er rip."

There were ten hours, then, of phasing in the mediation circuits one by one, testing, adjusting, letting Roger try his new senses on projected Rorschach blots and Maxwell color wheels. For Roger the day raced by. His sense of time was unreliable. It was no longer regulated by every-man's built-in biological clocks but by his machine components; they slowed his perception of time down when there was no stress situation, speeded it up when needed. "Slow down," he begged, watching the nurses whiz past him like bullets. And then, when Brad, beginning to shake with fatigue, knocked over a tray of inks and crayons, to Roger the pieces seemed actually to float to the ground. He had no difficulty in catching two bottles of ink and the tray itself before they touched the floor.

When he came to think of it after, he realized that they were the pieces that might have spilled or broken. He had let the wax crayons fall free. In that fraction of a second of choice, he had chosen to catch the objects that needed catching and let the others go, without being aware of what he did.

Brad was highly pleased. "You're doing great, boy," he said, holding to the foot of the bed. "I'm going to take off now and get some sleep, but I'll be in to see you tomorrow after the surgery."

"Surgery? What surgery?"

"Oh," said Brad, "just a little touch-up. Nothing compared to what you've already had, believe me! From now on," he said, turning to leave, "you're just about through being born; now all you have to do is grow up. Practice. Learn to use what you've got. The hard parts are all behind you. How are you doing with cutting off vision when you want to?"

"Brad," rang out the flat voice, louder in amplitude but tonally gray, "what the hell do you want of me? I'm trying!"

"I know," Brad said, conciliating. "See you tomorrow."

For the first time that day Roger was left alone. He experimented with his new senses. He could see that they might be very useful to him in survival situations. But they were also very confusing. All the tiny noises of everyday life were magnified. From the hall he could hear Brad talking to Jonny Freeling and the nurses going off duty. He knew that with the ears his mother had cultured for him in her womb he would not have been able to perceive even a whisper; now he could make out the words at will: "—local anesthetic, but I don't want to. I want him out. He's got enough trauma to deal with." That was Freeling talking to Brad.

The lights were more brilliant than before. He tried to diminish the sensitivity of his vision, but nothing happened. What he really wanted, he thought, was a single Christmas-tree bulb. That was plenty of light; these floods of luminosity were disconcerting. Also, he observed, the lights were maddeningly rhythmical; he could perceive each pulse of the sixty-Hertz current. Inside the fluorescent tubes he observed the writhing of a glowing snake of gas. Incandescent bulbs, on the other hand, were almost dark, except for the bright filaments at the center, which he could examine in detail. There was no sense of eyestrain, even when looking at the brightest of lights.

He heard a new voice in the corridor, and sharpened his hearing to listen: Clara Bly, just coming on duty for the evening shift. "How's the patient, Dr. Freeling?"

"Just fine. He seems rested. You didn't have to give him a sleeping pill last night?"

"No. He was fine. Kind of"—she giggled—"kind of randy, though. He made a sort of a pass, which I never expected from Roger."

"Huh." There was a puzzled pause. "Well, that won't be a problem any more. I've got to check the readouts. Take care."

Roger thought he would have to be extra nice to Clara; it would not be hard to do, for she was his favorite among the nurses. He lay back, listening to the rustle of his own black wings and the rhythmic sounds from the telemetry panels. He was very tired. It would be nice to sleep—

He sprang up. The lights had stopped! Then they were on again, as soon as he became aware of it.

He had learned to close his eyes!

Satisfied, Roger let himself sink back onto the gently flowing bed. It was true enough; he was learning.

They woke him to feed him, and then to put him to sleep again for his last operation.

There was no anesthesia. "We're just going to turn you off," said Jon Freeling. "You won't feel a thing." And indeed he didn't. First he was wheeled into the surgery next door, intensive-care bottles, pipes, drains and all. He could not smell the smell of disinfectant, but he knew it was there; he could perceive the brightness gathered at the cusp of every metallic object, the heat from the sterilizer, like a sunburst against the wall.

And then Dr. Freeling ordered him out, and we complied. We depressed his sensory inputs one by one; to him it was as though the sounds grew fainter, the lights dimmer, the body touches more gentle. We dampened the pain inputs throughout all his new skin, extinguished them completely where Freeling's knife would cut and needle would pierce. There was a complex problem there. Many of the pain inputs were to be maintained after he recovered. He would have to have some warning system when he was free on the surface of Mars, something to tell him if he was being burned or torn or damaged; pain was the sharpest alarm we could give him. But for much of his body, pain was over. Once we extinguished the inputs we programmed them out of his sensorium entirely.

Roger, of course, knew nothing of this. Roger just went to sleep and woke up again.

When he looked up he screamed.

Freeling, leaning back and flexing his fingers, jumped and dropped his mask. "What's the matter?"

Roger said, "Jesus! For a minute there I saw—I don't know. Could it have been a dream? But I saw you all around me, looking down, and you looked like a bunch of ghouls. Skulls. Skeletons. Grinning at me! And then you were you again."

Freeling looked at Weidner and shrugged. "I think," he said, "that that's just your mediation circuits at work. You know? Translating what you see into something you can grasp immediately."

"I don't like it," Roger flared.

"Well, we'll have to talk to Brad about it. But honestly, Roger, I think that's the way it's supposed to be. I think it's like the computer took your sensations of fear and pain—you know, what everyone feels when he has an operation—and put them together with the visual stimulus: our faces, the masks, all that stuff. Interesting. I wonder how much of it was in the mediation, and how much was plain postoperative delusion?"

"I'm glad you find it interesting," Roger sulked.

But truthfully, he found it interesting too. When he was back in his own room he let his mind roam. He could not summon the fantasy pictures at will. They came when they wanted to come, but they were not as fearsome as that first terrified glimpse of bare mandibles and hollow eye sockets. When Clara came in with a bedpan and left again after he waved it away, he watched her through the closing door; and the shadow of the door became a cave entrance, and Clara Bly a cave bear growling irritably at him. She was still a little annoyed, he realized; some subsonic cue in her face was registering in his senses, and being analyzed by the buzzing 3070 downstairs and displayed as a warning.

But when she came back she was wearing Dorrie's face. It melted away and reclothed itself in her familiar dark skin and bright eyes, not like Dorrie at all; but Roger took it as a sign that things were all right between them again . . .

Between Clara and himself.

Not, he thought, between Dorrie and himself. He gazed at the phone by his bed. The vision circuits were permanently off at his request; he didn't want to call someone and forget what they might see. But he had not used it to call Dorrie at all. Often enough he reached out his hand for the phone, but every time he drew his hand back.

He didn't know what to say to her.

How do you ask your wife if she is sleeping with your best friend? You come right out and ask her, that's how, his gut feelings told Roger; but he could not quite make himself do it. He was not sure enough. He could not risk that accusation; he might be wrong.

The thing was, he couldn't discuss it with his friends, not any of them. Don Kayman would have been a natural for that; it was a priest's function. But Don was so clearly, so sweetly and tenderly in love with his pretty little nun that Roger could not put himself in the pain of discussing pain with him.

And for most of his friends, the trouble was that they honestly would not have seen what the trouble was. Open marriage was so common in Tonka—in most of the Western world, indeed—that it was the rare closed couple that caused gossip. To admit to jealousy was very difficult.

And anyway, Torraway told himself stoutly, it was not jealousy that troubled him. Not exactly jealousy. It was something else. It was not Sicilian machismo or the outrage of the property owner who finds someone trespassing in his own fertile gardens. It was that Dorrie should *want* to love only him. Since he only wanted to love her. . . .

He became aware that he was slipping into a state of mind that would surely ring the alarm bells on the telemetry readouts. He didn't want that. He resolutely took his mind away from his wife.

He practiced "closing his eyes" for a time; it was reassuring to be able to summon up this new skill when he wanted it. He could not have described, any better than Willy Hartnett had, what it was he did; but somehow he was able to reach the decision to stop receiving visual inputs, and somehow the circuitry inside his head and down in the 3070 room were able to convert that decision into blackness. He could even dim the light selectively. He could brighten it. He could, he discovered, filter out all but one band of wavelengths or suppress one or cause one or more of the rainbow colors to be brighter than the rest.

It was quite satisfying, really, although in time it cloyed. He wished he had lunch to look forward to, but there would be no lunch that day, partly because he had had an operation, partly because they were gradually deaccustoming him to eating. Over the next few weeks he would eat and drink less and less; by the time he was on Mars, he would really need to eat only about one square meal a month.

He flung back the sheet and gazed idly down at the artifact that his body had become.

A second later he shouted a great raw scream of fear and pain. The telemetry monitors all flashed blinding red. In the corridor outside Clara Bly turned in midstep and dashed for his door. Back in Brad's bachelor apartment the warning bells went off a split-second later, telling him of something urgent and serious that woke him out of an unsound, fatigued sleep.

When Clara opened the door she saw Roger, curled fetally on the bed, groaning in misery. One hand was cupping his groin, between his closed legs. "Roger! What's the matter?"

The head lifted, and the insect eyes looked at her blindly. Roger did not stop the animal sounds that were coming from him, did not speak. He only lifted his hand.

There, between his legs, was nothing. Nothing at all of penis, testicles, scrotum; nothing but the gleaming artificial flesh, with a transparent bandage over it, concealing the surgery lines. It was as if nothing had ever been there. Of the diagnostic signs of manhood . . . nothing. The tiny little operation was over, and what was left was nothing at all.

Nine
Dash Visits a Bedside

Don Kayman didn't like the timing, but he had no choice; he had to visit his tailor. Unfortunately, his tailor was in Merritt Island, Florida, at the Atlantic Test Center.

He flew there worried, and arrived worried. Not only at what had happened to Roger Torraway. That seemed to be under control, praise be to Divine Mercy, although Kayman couldn't help feeling that they had almost lost him and somebody had blundered badly in not preparing him for that last little bit of "minor cosmetic surgery." Probably, he thought charitably, it was because Brad had been ill. But surely they had come close to blowing the whole project.

The other thing he was fretting about was that he could not avoid the secret feeling of sin that seemed to be a realization that internally, in his heart of hearts, he wished the project *would* be blown. He had had a tearful hour with Sister Clotilda when the probability that he would go to Mars had firmed up into the cutting of orders. Should they marry first? No. No on pragmatic, practical reasons: although there was not much doubt that both could ask for and receive the dispensation from Rome, there was also not much hope that it would come through in less than six months.

If only they had applied earlier . . .

But they hadn't, and both of them knew that they were not willing to marry without it, or even to go to bed together without the sacrament. "At least," said Clotilda toward the end, attempting to smile, "you won't have to worry about my being unfaithful to you. If I wouldn't break my vows for you, I doubt I'd do it for any man."

"I wasn't worried," he said; but now, under the gleaming blue skies of Florida, staring up at the gantries that rose to reach for the fluffy white clouds, he was worrying. The Army colonel who had volunteered to show him around was aware that something was troubling Kayman, but he had no way of diagnosing the trouble.

"It's safe enough," he said, probing at random. "I wouldn't give a thought to the low-injection rendezvous orbit."

Kayman tore his attention away from his interior and said, "I promise you I wasn't. I don't even know what you mean."

"Oh. Well, it's just that we're putting your bird and the two support launches into a lower orbit than usual: two twenty kilometers instead of four hundred. It's political, of course. I hate it when the bureaucrats tell us what we have to do, but this time it doesn't really make a difference."

Kayman glanced at his watch. He still had an hour to kill before returning for his last fitting of Mars-suit and spacesuit, and he was not anxious to spend it fretting. He judged accurately that the colonel was one of those happy folk who like to talk about nothing as much as their work, and that all he need give would be an occasional grunt to keep the colonel explaining everything that could be explained. He gave the grunt.

"Well, Father Kayman," said the colonel expansively, "we're giving you a big ship, you know. Too big to launch in one piece. So we're putting up three birds, and you'll meet in orbit—two twenty by two thirty-five, optimal, and I expect we'll be right on the money—and—"

Kayman nodded without really listening. He already knew the flight plan by heart; it was in the orders he had been given. The only open questions were who the remaining two occupants of the Mars bird would be, but it would only be a matter of days before that was decided. One would have to be a pilot to stay in orbit while the other three crowded into the Mars-lander and went down to the surface of the planet. The fourth man should, ideally, be someone who could function as back-up to pilot, areologist and cyborg; but of course no such person existed. It was time to make the decision, though. The three human beings—the three *unaltered* human beings, he corrected himself—would not have Roger's capacity for surviving naked on the surface of Mars. They would have to have the same fittings he was going through now, and then the final brush-up training in procedures that all of them would need, even Roger.

And launch time was only thirty-three days away.

The colonel had finished with the docking and reassembly maneuvers and was getting ready to outline the day-by-day calendar of events on all the long months to Mars. Kayman said, "Wait a minute, Colonel. I didn't quite get that about political considerations. What does that have to do with how we take off?"

The colonel grumbled resentfully, "Damn ecology freaks, they get everybody upset. These Texas Twin launch vehicles, they're big. About twenty times the thrust of a Saturn. So they make a lot of exhaust. It comes to something like twenty-five metric tons of water vapor a second, times three birds—a lot of water vapor. And admittedly there's some risk that the water vapor—well, no, let's be fair; we know damn well—excuse me, Father—that what all that water vapor would do at normal orbit-injection altitudes would be to knock out the free electrons in a big patch of sky. They found that way back in, let's see, I think it was '73 or '74, when they put the first Spacelab up. Knocked the free electrons out of a volume of atmosphere that stretched from Illinois to Labrador when it was measured. And of course that's what keeps you from getting sunburned. One of the things. They help filter out the solar UV. Skin cancer, sunburn, destruction of flora—well, they're all real; they *could* happen. But it's not our own people Dash is worried about! The NPA, that's what bugs him. They've given him an ultimatum that if your launch damages their sky they will consider it a 'hostile act.' Hostile act! What the hell do you call it when *they* parade five nuclear subs off Cape May, New Jersey? Claim it's oceanographic research, but you don't use cruiser-killer subs for oceanography, not in our Navy, anyway. . . .

"Anyway," the colonel said, bringing himself back to his guest and smiling, "it's okay. We'll just put you into rendezvous orbit a little lower down, out of the free-electron layer. Costs more fuel. Winds up making *more* pollution, the way I look at it. But it keeps their precious free electrons intact—not that there's any real chance they'd survive across the Atlantic into Africa even, much less Asia. . . ."

"You've been very interesting, Colonel," Kayman said courteously. "I think it's time for me to get back, though."

The fitters were ready for him. "Just slip into this for size." The physicotherapist member of the team grinned. "Slipping into" the spacesuit was twenty minutes of hard work, even if the whole team had been helping. Kayman insisted on doing it himself. In the spacecraft he wouldn't have any more help than the rest of the crew, who would be busy with their own affairs; and in an emergency he wouldn't have any help at all. He wanted to be ready for any emergency. It took an hour, and another ten minutes to get out of it after they'd checked all the parameters and pronounced everything fine; and then there were all the other garments to try.

It was dark outside, a warm Florida autumn night, before he was finished. He looked at the row of vestments laid out on the worktables and grinned. He pointed to the comm-antenna fabric that dangled from one wrist, the radiation cloak for use in solar-flare conditions, the body garment that went under the suits themselves. "You've got me all fixed up. That's the maniple, there's the chasuble, that's my alb. Couple more pieces and I'd be all ready to say Mass." Actually he had included a complete set of vestments in his weight allotment—it had seriously depleted the available reserve for books, music tapes and pictures of Sister Clotilda. But he was not prepared to discuss that with these worldly people. He stretched and sighed. "Where's a good place to eat around here?" he asked. "A steak, or maybe some of that red snapper you people talk about—and then bed—"

The Air Force MP who had been standing by for two hours, glancing at his watch, stepped forward and spoke up. "Sorry, Father," he said. "You're wanted elsewhere right now, and you're due in, let's see, about twenty minutes."

"Due where? I've got a long flight tomorrow—"

"I'm sorry, sir. My orders are to bring you to the Ad Building at Patrick Air Force Base. I expect they'll tell you what it's all about then."

The priest drew himself up. "Corporal," he said, "I'm not under your jurisdiction. I suggest you tell me what it is you want."

"No, sir," the MP agreed. "You're not. But my orders are to bring you, and with all due respect, sir, I will."

The physicotherapist touched Kayman's shoulder. "Go ahead, Don," he said. "I have a feeling you're in pretty high echelons right now."

Grumbling, Kayman allowed himself to be led out and put into a hoverjeep. The driver was in a hurry. He did not bother with the roads, but aimed the vehicle out toward the surf, judged his time and distance and skittered out onto the surface of the ocean between waves. Then he turned south and gunned it; in ten seconds they were doing at least a hundred and fifty kilometers an hour. Even on high-lift thrust, with three meters of air between them and the average height of the water, the rolling, twisting chop from the waves corkscrewing under them had Kayman swallowing saliva and looking for a throw-up bag against a rather possible need in no time at all. He tried to get the corporal to slow down. "Sorry, sir"; it was the MP's favorite expression, it seemed.

But they managed to reach the beach at Patrick before Kayman quite vomited, and back on land the driver slowed to reasonable speeds.

Kayman tottered out and stood in the damp, lush night until two more MPs, radio-alerted to his coming, saluted and escorted him inside a white stucco building.

Before ten minutes had elapsed he was stripped to the skin and being searched, and he realized what high echelons he was indeed moving in.

The President's jet touched down at Patrick at 0400 hours. Kayman had been dozing on a beach chair with a throw rug over his legs; he was shaken courteously awake and led to the boarding steps while refueling tankers were topping off the wing tanks in peculiarly eerie silence. There was no conversation, no banging of bronze nozzles against aluminum filler caps, only the throbbing of the tank truck's pumps.

Somebody very important was asleep. Kayman wished with all his heart that he was too. He was conducted to a recliner chair, strapped in and left; and even before his WAC hostess had left his side the jet was picking its way to the takeoff strip.

He tried to doze, but while the jet was still climbing to cruise altitude the President's valet came back and said, "The President will see you now."

Sitting down and freshly shaved around his goatee, President Deshatine looked like a Gilbert Stuart painting of himself. He was at ease in a leather-backed chair, unfocused eyes peering out the window of the presidential jet while he listened to some sort of tape through earphones. A full coffee cup was steaming next to his elbow, and an empty cup was waiting by the silver pot. Next to the cup was a slim box of purple leather embossed with a silver cross.

Dash didn't keep him waiting. He looked around, smiled, pulled off the earphones, and said, "Thank you for letting me kidnap you, Father Kayman. Sit down, please. Help yourself to coffee if you'd like it."

"Thanks." The valet sprang to pour and retired to stand behind Don Kayman. Kayman didn't look around; he knew that the valet would be watching every muscle tremor, and so he avoided sudden moves.

The President said, "I've been in so many time zones the last forty-eight hours that I've forgotten what the real world is like. Munich, Beirut, Rome. I picked up Vern Scanyon in Rome when I heard about the trouble with Roger Torraway. Scared the shit out of me, Father. You almost lost him, didn't you?"

Kayman said, "I'm an areologist, Mr. President. It was not my responsibility."

"Cut it out, Father. I'm not assigning blame; there's plenty to go around, if it comes to that. I want to know what happened."

"I'm sure General Scanyon could tell you more than I can, Mr. President," Kayman said stiffly.

"If I wanted to settle for Vern's version," the President said patiently, "I wouldn't have stopped to pick you up. You were there. He wasn't. He was off in Rome at the Vatican Pacem in Excelsis Conference."

Kayman took a hasty sip from his coffee cup. "Well, it was close. I think he wasn't properly briefed for what was going to happen, because there was a flu epidemic, really. We were short of staff. Brad wasn't there."

"That has happened before," the President observed.

Kayman shrugged and did not pick up the lead. "They castrated him, Mr. President. What the sultans used to call a complete castration, penis and all. He doesn't need it, because there's so little consumable going into him now that it all gets excreted anally, so it was just a vulnerable spot. There's no question it had to come off, Mr. President."

"What about the—what do you call it—prostatectomy? Was that a vulnerable spot too?"

"You really should ask one of the doctors about this, Mr. President," Kayman said defensively.

"I'm asking you. Scanyon said something about 'priest's disease,' and you're a priest."

Kayman grinned. "That's an old expression, from the days when all priests were celibate. But, yes, I can tell you about it; we talked about it a lot in the seminary. The prostate produces fluid—not much, a few drops a day. If a man doesn't have ejaculations, it mostly just passes out with the urine, but if he is sexually excited there's more and it doesn't all pass out. It backs up, and the congestion leads to trouble."

"So they cut out his prostate."

"And implanted a steroid capsule, Mr. President. He won't become effeminate. Physically, he's now a complete self-contained eunuch, and— Oh. I mean unit."

The President nodded. "That's what they call a Freudian slip."

Kayman shrugged.

"And if you think that way," the President pressed, "what the hell do you think Torraway thinks?"

"I know it's not easy for him, Mr. President."

"As I understand it," Dash went on, "you aren't just an areologist, Don, you're a marriage counselor, too. And not doing too well, right? That trampy little wife of his is giving our boy a hard time."

"Dorrie has a lot of problems."

"No, Dorrie has *one* problem. Same problem we all have. She's screwing up our Mars project, and we can't afford to have that happen. Can you straighten her out?"

"No."

"Well, I don't mean make her a perfect person. Cut it out, Don! I mean, can you get her to put his mind at rest, at least enough so he doesn't go into shock any more? Give him a kiss and a promise, send him a Valentine when he's on Mars—God knows Torraway doesn't expect any more than that. But he has a right to that much."

"I can try," said Kayman helplessly.

"And I'm going to have a few words with Brad," the President said grimly. "I've told you, I've told you all, *this project has to work.* I don't care about somebody's cold in the head or somebody else's hot pants, I want Torraway on Mars and I want him happy there."

The plane banked to change course away from the traffic around New Orleans, and a glint of morning sun shone up from the greasy oil-slick surface of the Gulf. The President squinted down at it angrily. "Let me tell you, Father Kayman, what I've been thinking. I've been thinking that Roger would be happier mourning over the death of his wife in a car smash than worrying about what she's doing when he's not around. I don't like thinking that way. But I have just so many options, Kayman, and I have to pick the one that's least bad. And now," he said, suddenly smiling, "I've got something for you, from His Holiness. It's a present; take a look at it."

Wondering, Kayman opened the purple box. It held a rosary, coiled on purple velvet inside the leather case. The Ave Marias were ivory, carved into rosebuds; the big Paternoster beads were chased crystal. "It has an interesting history," the President went on. "It was sent back to Ignatius Loyola from one of his missions in Japan, and then it was in South America for two hundred years with the—what do you call them?—the Reductions of Paraguay? It's a museum piece, really, but His Holiness wanted you to have it."

"I—I don't know what to say," Kayman managed.

"And it has his blessing." The President leaned back and suddenly looked a great deal older. "Pray with it, Father," he said. "I'm not a Catholic. I don't know how you feel about these things. But I want you to pray for Dorrie Torraway's getting her head straightened out enough to last her husband a while. And if that doesn't work, you'd better pray real hard for all of us."

Back in the main cabin, Kayman strapped himself in his seat and willed himself asleep for the remaining hour or so of the flight to Tonka. Exhaustion triumphed over worry, and he drifted off. He was not the only one worried. We had not properly estimated the trauma Roger Torraway would receive from the loss of his genitals, and we had nearly lost him.

The malfunction was critical. It could not be risked again. We had already arranged for beefed-up psychiatric attendance on Roger, and in Rochester the backpack computer was being recircuited to monitor major psychic stress and react before Roger's slower human synapses could oscillate into convulsions.

The world situation was proceeding as predicted. New York City was of course in turmoil, the Near East was building up pressures past the safety valves, and New People's Asia was pouring out furious manifestos denouncing the squid kill in the Pacific. The planet was rapidly reaching critical mass. Our projections were that the future of the race was questionable on Earth past another two years. We could not allow that. The Mars landing had to succeed.

When Roger came out of the haze after his seizure he did not realize how close he had come to dying, he only realized that he had been wounded in all of his most sensitive parts. The feeling was desolation: wiped-out, hopeless desolation. He not only had lost Dorrie, he had lost his manhood. The pain was too extreme to be relieved by crying, even if he had been able to cry. It was the agony of the dentist's chair without anesthesia, so acute that it no longer felt like a warning but became merely a fact of the environment, something to be experienced and endured.

The door opened, and a new nurse came in. "Hi. I see you're awake."

She came over and laid warm fingers on his forehead. "I'm Sulie Carpenter," she said. "It's Susan Lee, really, but Sulie's what they call me." She withdrew her hand and smiled. "You'd think I'd know better than feeling for fever, wouldn't you? I already know what it is from the monitors, but I guess I'm an old-fashioned girl."

Torraway hardly heard her; he was preoccupied with seeing her. Was it a trick of his mediation circuits? Tall, green-eyed, dark-haired: she looked so very much like Dorrie that he tried changing the field of vision of his great insect eyes, zooming down on the pores in her slightly freckled skin, altering the color values, decreasing the sensitivity so that she seemed to fade into a twilight. No matter. She still looked like Dorrie.

She moved to scan the duplicate monitors at the side of the room. "You're doing real well, Colonel Torraway," she called over her shoulder. "I'm going to bring you your lunch in a little while. Anything you want now?"

He roused himself and sat up. "Nothing I can have," he said bitterly.

"Oh, no, Colonel!" Her eyes showed shock. "I mean—well, excuse me. I don't have any right to talk to you like that. But, dear Lord, Colonel, if there's anybody in this world who can have anything he wants, you're it!"

"I wish I felt that way," he grumbled; but he was watching her closely and curiously, he did feel something—something he could not identify, but something which was not the pain that had overwhelmed him only moments before.

Sulie Carpenter glanced at her watch and then pulled up a chair. "You sound low, Colonel," she said sympathetically. "I guess all this is pretty hard to take."

He looked away from her, up to where the great black wings were rippling slowly over his head. He said, "It has its bad parts, believe me. But I knew what I was getting into."

Sulie nodded. She said, "I had a bad time when my—my boyfriend died. Of course, that's nothing like what you're doing. But in a way maybe it was worse—you know, it was so *pointless*. One day we were fine and talking about getting married. The next day he came back from the doctor's and those headaches he'd been having turned out to be—" She took a deep breath. "Brain tumor. Malignant. He was dead three months later, and I just couldn't handle it. I had to get away from Oakland. I applied to be transferred here. Never thought I'd get it, but I guess they're still short-handed from the flu—"

"I'm sorry," Roger said quickly.

She smiled. "It's all right," she said. "It's just that there was a big empty place in my life, and I'm really grateful I've got something to fill it here." She glanced again at her watch and jumped up. "The floor nurse'll be on my back," she said. "Now, listen, really, is there anything I can get for you? Book? Music? You've got the world at your command, you know, including me."

"Not a thing," Roger said honestly. "Thanks anyway. How come you picked coming here?"

She looked at him thoughtfully, the corners of her lips curving very faintly. "Well," she said, "I knew something about the program here; I've been in aerospace medicine for ten years in California. And I knew who you were, Colonel Torraway. Knew! I used to have your picture on my wall when you were rescuing those Russians. You wouldn't be-

lieve the active role you played in some of my fantasies, Colonel Torraway, sir."

She grinned and turned away, stopping at the door. "Do me a favor,
will you?"

Roger was surprised. "Sure. What?"

"Well, I'd like a more recent picture. You know what security is like
here. If I sneak in a camera, can I take a quick snapshot of you now?
Just so I can have something to show my grandchildren, if I ever have
any."

Roger protested, "They'll kill you if they catch you, Sulie."

She winked. "I'll take my chances; it's worth it. Thanks."

After she had gone Roger made an effort to go back to thinking
about his castration and his cuckolding, but for some reason they
seemed less overwhelming. Nor did he have a great deal of time. Sulie
came in with a low-residue lunch, a smile and a promise to be back the
following morning. Clara Bly gave him an enema, and then he lay
wondering while three identical fair-mustached men came in and went
over every inch of floor, wall and furniture with metal detectors and
electronic mops. They were total strangers, and they stayed in the
room, on new-brought chairs, silent and watching, while Brad came in.

Brad was looking not merely ill but seriously worried. "Hi, Roger,"
he said. "Jesus, you scared us. It's my fault; I should have been on tap,
but this damn flu bug—"

"I survived," Roger said, studying Brad's rather ordinary face and
wondering just why he wasn't feeling outrage and resentment.

"We're going to have to keep you pretty busy now," Brad began,
dragging up a chair. "We've phased out some of your mediation circuits for the moment. When they're full in again we're going to have to
limit your sensory inputs—let you work up to handling a total environment a little at a time. And Kathleen's jumping to get you started on re-
training—you know, learning how to use your muscles and all that." He
glanced over at the three silent watchers. His expression, Roger
thought, was suddenly full of fear.

"I guess I'm ready," Roger said.

"Oh, sure. I know you are," said Brad, surprised. "Haven't they been
giving you updates on your readouts? You're functioning like a seven-
teen-jewel watch, Roger. All the surgery is over now. You've got everything you need." He sat back, studying Roger. "If I do say so"—he
grinned—"you're a work of art, Roger, and I'm the artist. I just wish I
could see you on Mars. That's where you belong, boy."

One of the watchers cleared his throat. "It's getting toward that time,
Dr. Bradley," he said.

The worried look returned to Brad's face. "Coming right away. Take care, Rog. I'll be back to see you later."

He left, and the three government agents followed him, as Clara Bly came in and fussed around the room.

A mystery was suddenly clear. "Dash is coming to see me," Roger guessed.

"Smart!" sniffed Clara. "Well, I guess it's all right for you to know. It wasn't all right for *me* to know. They think it's a secret. But what kind of secret is it when they turn the whole hospital upside down? They've had those guys all over the place since before I came on duty."

"When will he get here?" Roger asked.

"That's the part that is a secret. From me, anyway."

But it did not stay a secret very long; within the hour, to an unheard but strongly felt "Hail to the Chief," the President of the United States came into the room. With him was the same valet he had had on the presidential jet, but this time he was obviously not a valet, only a bodyguard.

"Marvelous to see you again," said the President, holding out his hand. He had never seen the revised and edited version of the astronaut before, and certainly the dully gleaming flesh, the great faceted eyes, the hovering wings must have looked strange, but what showed in the President's well-disciplined face was only friendship and pleasure. "I stopped off a little while ago to say hello to your good wife, Dorrie. I hope she's forgiven me for messing up her fingernail polish last month; I forgot to ask. But how are you feeling?"

How Roger was feeling was once again amazed at the thoroughness of the President's briefing, but what he said was, "Fine, Mr. President."

The President inclined his head toward the bodyguard without looking at him. "John, have you got that little package for Colonel Torraway? It's something Dorrie asked me to bring over to you; you can open it when we've gone." The bodyguard placed a white-paper package on Roger's bedside table and slid a chair over for the President in almost the same motion, just as the President was preparing to sit down. "Roger," said the President, sharpening the creases in his Bermudas, "I know I can be honest with you. You're all we've got now, and we need you. The indices are looking worse every day. The Asians are spoiling for trouble, and I don't know how long I can keep from giving it to them. We have to get you to Mars, and you have to function when you get there. I can't overestimate the importance of it."

Roger said, "I think I understand that, sir."

"Well, in a way, I guess you do. But do you understand it in your gut? Do you really feel, deep down, that you're that one man, maybe two, in a generation who somehow or other gets himself in a position that's so important to the whole human race that even inside his own mind what happens to him doesn't measure up in importance? That's where you are, Roger. I know," the President went on sorrowfully, "that they've taken some mighty sacrificial liberties with your person. Didn't give you a chance to say yes, no or maybe. Didn't even tell you. It's a piss-poor way to treat any human being, let alone somebody who means as much as you do—and somebody who deserves as well as you do, too. I've kicked a bunch of asses around here about that. I'll be glad to kick a lot more. If you want it done, tell me. Any time. It's better if I do it than you—with those steel muscles they've given you, you might damage a few of those pretty behinds on the nurses past the point of repair. Do you mind if I smoke?"

"What? Oh, hell, no, Mr. President."

"Thanks." The valet had an open cigarette case in one hand and a glowing lighter in the other as soon as the President stretched out his hand. He took a deep draw and leaned back. "Roger," he said, "let me tell you my fantasy about what I think is in your mind. You're thinking, 'Here's old Dash, politician to the end, full of bullshit and promises, trying to trick me into pulling his chestnuts out of the fire. He'd say anything, he'd promise anything. All he wants is what he can get out of me.' Anywhere near right, so far?"

"Why—no, Mr. President! Well . . . a little bit."

The President nodded. "You'd be crazy if you didn't think a little bit of that," he said matter-of-factly. "It's all true, you know. Up to a point. It's true I'd promise you anything, tell you any lies I could think of to get you to Mars. But the other thing that's true is that you have us all by the genital organs, Roger. We *need* you. There's a war coming if we don't do something to stop it, and it's crazy but the trend projections say the only thing that can stop it is putting you on Mars. Don't ask me why. I just go by what the technical people tell me, and they claim that's what the computers print out."

Roger's wings were stirring restlessly, but the eyes were intent on the President.

"So you see," said the President heavily, "I'm appointing myself your hired hand, Roger. You tell me what you want. I'll make damn sure you get it. You pick up that phone any time, day or night. They'll put you through to me. If I'm asleep, you can wake me if you want to. If it can wait, you can leave a message. There's going to be no more fucking you around in this place, and if you even think it's happening you tell me and I'll stop it. Christ," he said, grinning as he started to stand up, "do you know what the history books are going to say about me? 'Fitz-

James Deshatine, 1943–2026, forty-second President of the United States. During his administration the human race established its first self-sustaining colony on another planet.' That's what I'll get, Roger, if I get that much—and you're the only one who can give it to me.

"Well," he said, moving toward the door, "there's a governor's conference waiting for me in Palm Springs. They expected me six hours ago, but I figured you mattered a hell of a lot more than they did. Kiss Dorrie for me. And call me. If you don't have anything to complain about, call me to say hello. Any time."

And he left, with a dazzled astronaut staring after him.

Take it any way you liked, Roger reflected, it was really a pretty spectacular performance, and it left him feeling both awed and pleased. Subtracting 99 percent of it as bullshit, what was left was highly gratifying.

The door opened, and Sulie Carpenter came in, looking faintly scared. She was carrying a framed photograph. "I didn't know what kind of company you were moving in," she said. "Do you want this?"

It was a picture of the President, signed, "For Roger from his admirer, Dash."

"I guess I do," said Roger. "Can you hang it up?"

"When it's a picture of Dash, you can," she said. "It has a self-hanging gadget. Right up here?" She pressed it against the wall near the door and stepped back to admire it. Then she looked around, winked and pulled a flat black camera the size of a cigarette pack out of her apron. "Smile at the birdie," she said, and snapped away. "You won't rat on me? Okay. I've got to be going—I'm not on duty now, but I wanted to look in on you."

Roger leaned back and folded his hands on his chest. Things were turning out rather interestingly. He had not forgotten the internal pain of the discovery of his castration, and he had not put Dorrie out of his mind. But neither was perceived as pain any more. There were too many newer, more pleasant thoughts overlaying them.

Thinking of Dorrie reminded him of her gift. He opened it. It was a ceramic cup in harvest colors, ornamented with a cornucopia of fruits. The card said, "This is a way of telling you that I love you." And it was signed *Dorrie*.

All of Torraway's signs were stable now, and we were getting ready to phase in the mediation circuits.

This time Roger was well briefed. Brad was with him every hour—after taking a large share of the President's ass-kicking, he was chastened and diligent. We deployed one task force to oversee the phasing-in of the mediation circuits, another to buffer the readout-readin of data from the 3070 in Tonka to the new backpack computer in Rochester, New York. Texas and Oklahoma were going through one of their periodic brownouts just then, which complicated all machine data handling, and the aftereffects of the flu were still with the human beings on the staff. We were definitely short-handed.

Moreover, we needed still more. The backpack computer was rated at 99.999999999 percent reliable in every component, but there were something like 10^8 components. There was a lot of backup, and a full panoply of cross-input paths so that failure of even three or four major subsystems would leave enough capacity to keep Roger going. But that wasn't good enough. Analysis showed that there was one chance in ten of critical-path failure within half a Martian year.

So the decision was made to construct, launch and orbit around Mars a full-size 3070, replicating all the functions of the backpack computer in triplicate. It would not be as good as the backpack. If the backpack experienced total failure, Roger would have the use of the orbiter only 50 percent of the time—when it was above the horizon in its orbit and thus could interlink with him by radio. There would be a worst-case lag of a hundredth of a second, which was tolerable. Also he would have to stay in the open, or linked with an external antenna otherwise.

There was another reason for the back-up orbiter, and that was the high risk of glitches. Both the orbiting 3070 and the backpack were heavily shielded. Nevertheless they would pass through the Van Allen belts at launch, and the solar wind all through their flight. By the time they got to the vicinity of Mars the solar wind would be at a low enough level to be bearable—except in the case of flares. The charged particles of a flare could easily bug enough of the stored data in either computer to critically damage its function. The backpack computer would be helpless to defend itself. The 3070, on the other hand, had enough reserve capacity for continuous internal monitoring and repair. In idle moments—and it would have many idle moments, as much as 90 percent of its function time even when in use by Roger—it would compare data in each of its triplicate arrays. If any datum differed from the same datum in the other arrays it would check for compatibility with the surround data; if all data were compatible, it would examine all three arrays and make the one aberrant bit conform with the other two. If two did not conform, it would check against the backpack if possible.

That was all the redundancy we could afford, but it was quite a lot. On the whole, we were very pleased.

To be sure, the orbiting 3070 would require a good deal of power. We calculated the probable maximum draw against the probable worst-case supply of any reasonable set of solar panels, and concluded that the margin was too thin. So Raytheon got a preempt order for one of its MHD generators, and crews went to work on Route 128 to modify it for space launch and automatic operation in orbit around Mars. When the 3070 and the MHD generator arrived in orbit they would lock to each other. The generator would supply all the power the computer needed, and have enough left over to microwave a useful surplus down to Roger on the surface of Mars, which he could use both to power his own machine parts as needed or for whatever power-using equipment he might like to install.

Once we had completed all the plans we could hardly see how we had thought we could get along without them in the first place. Those were happy days! We requested, and were promptly given, all the reinforcements we needed. Tulsa went without lights two nights a week so we could have the energy reserves we needed, and Jet Propulsion Laboratories lost their entire space-medicine staff to our project.

The read-in of data proceeded. Glitches chased themselves merrily around both new computers, the backpack in Rochester and the duplicate 3070 that had been rushed to Merritt Island. But we hunted them down, isolated them, corrected them and were keeping right on schedule.

The world outside, of course, was not as pleasant.

Using a home-made plutonium bomb made out of materials hijacked from the breeder reactor at Carmarthen, Welsh nationalists had blown up the Hyde Park Barracks and most of Knightsbridge. In California the Cascade Mountains were burning out of control, the fire-fighting helicopters grounded because of the fuel shortage. An exploding epidemic of smallpox had depopulated Poona and was already out of control in Bombay; cases were being reported from Madras to Delhi as those who were able fled the plague. The Australians had declared Condition Red mobilization, the NPA had called for an emergency meeting of the U.N. Security Council, and Capetown was under siege.

All of this was as the graphs had predicted. We were aware of all of it. We continued with our work. When one of the nurses or technicians took time to worry, he had the President's orders to reassure him. On every bulletin board, and placarded in most of the workrooms, was a quote from Dash:

> You take care of Roger Torraway, and I'll take care of the rest of the world.
>
> Fitz-James Deshatine

We didn't need the reassurance, we knew how important the work was. The survival of our race depended on it. Compared to that, nothing else mattered.

Roger woke up in total blackness.

He had been dreaming, and for a moment the dream and the reality were queerly fused. The dream had been of a long time ago, when he and Dorrie and Brad had driven down to Lake Texoma with a few friends who owned a sailboat, and in the evening they had sung to Brad's guitar while the huge moon rose over the water. He thought he heard Brad's voice again . . . but he listened more closely, his brain clearing from sleep, and there was nothing.

There was nothing. *That* was strange. No sound at all, not even the purrs and clicks of the telemetry monitors along the wall, not even a whisper from the hall outside. However much he tried, with all the enhanced sensitivity of his new ears, there was no sound at all. Nor was there light. Not in any color, not anywhere, except for the dullest of dim red glows from his own body, and a glow equally dull from the baseboards of the room.

He moved restlessly, and discovered he was tethered to the bed.

For a moment terror flooded through his mind: trapped, helpless, alone. Had they turned him off? Were his senses deliberately blacked out? What was happening?

A small voice near his ear spoke again: "Roger? This is Brad. Your readouts say you're awake."

The relief was overpowering. "Yes," he managed. "What's going on?"

"We've got you in a sensory-deprivation environment. Apart from my voice, can you hear anything?"

"Not a sound," said Roger. "Not *anything.*"

"How about light?"

Roger reported the dim heat glow. "That's all."

"Fine," said Brad. "Now, here's the thing, Roger. We're going to let you work in your new sensorium a little bit at a time. Simple sounds. Simple patterns. We've got a slide projector through the wall over the head of your bed, and a screen by the door—you can't see it, of course, but it's there. What we're going to do—wait a minute. Kathleen's determined to talk to you."

Faint friction sounds and scuffles, and then Kathleen Doughty's voice: "Roger, this shithead forgot one important thing. Sensory deprivation's dangerous, you know that."

"I've heard it," Roger admitted.

"According to the experts the worst part of it is feeling impotent to end it. So anytime you begin to feel bad, just talk; one of us will always be here, and we'll answer. It'll be Brad, or me, or Sulie Carpenter, or Clara."

"Are you all there right now?"

"Christ, yes—plus Don Kayman and General Scanyon and, cripes, half the staff. You won't lack for company, Roger. I promise you that. Now. What about my voice, is that giving you any trouble?"

He thought. "Not that I notice. You do sound a little bit like a creaking door," he evaluated.

"That's bad."

"I don't think so. You sound kind of that way all the time, Kathleen."

She giggled. "Well, I'm going to stop talking in a minute anyway. What about Brad's voice?"

"I didn't notice anything. Or anyway, I'm not sure. I was sort of dreaming and for a minute I thought he was singing "Aura Lee" along with his guitar."

Brad cut in. "That's *interesting*, Roger! What about now?"

"No. You sound like yourself."

"Well, your readouts look good. All right. We'll go into that later. Now, what we're going to do is give you pure, simple visual inputs to deal with. As Kathleen says, you can speak to us any time and we'll answer if you want us to. But we won't speak much for a while. Let the visual circuits work themselves in before we confuse things with simultaneous sight and sound, got it?"

"Go ahead," said Roger.

There was no answer, but in a moment a pale point of light appeared against the far wall.

It was not bright. With the eyes he had been born with, Roger suspected, he would not have been able to see it at all; as it was, he could make it out clearly, and even in the filtered air of his hospital room, he could see the faint path of light from projector to wall over his head.

Nothing else happened for a long time.

Roger waited as patiently as he could.

More time passed.

Finally he said, "All right, I see it. It's a dot. I've been watching it all along, and it's still just a dot. I do observe," he said, turning his head about, "that there's enough reflected light from it that I can see the rest of the room a little bit, but that's all."

When Brad's voice came, it sounded like thunder: "Okay, Roger, hold on and we'll give you something else."

"Wow!" Roger said. "Not so loud, okay?"

"I wasn't any louder than before," Brad objected. And in fact his voice had reduced itself to normal proportions.

"Okay, okay," Roger muttered. He was getting bored. After a moment another point of light appeared, a few inches from the first one. Both held for another long time, and then a line of light leaped into being between them.

"This is pretty dull," he complained.

"It's meant to be." It was Clara Bly's voice this time.

"Hi," Roger greeted her. "Listen. I can see pretty well now, in all this light you're giving me. What are all these wires sticking into me?"

Brad cut in: "They're your telemetry, Roger. That's why we had to tie you down, so you wouldn't roll over and mess up the leads. Everything's on remote now, you know. We had to take almost everything out of your room."

"So I noticed. All right, go ahead."

But it was tedious and remained tedious. These were not the kinds of things that were calculated to keep one's mind busy. They might be important, but they were also dull. After an interminable stretch of simple geometric figures of light, the intensity reduced so that there was less and less spill of reflection to illuminate the rest of the room, they began feeding him sounds: clicks, oscillator beeps, a chime, a hiss of white noise.

In the room outside the shifts kept changing. They stopped only when the telemetry indicated Roger needed sleep or food or a bedpan. None of those needs were frequent. Roger began to be able to tell who was on duty from the tiniest of signs: the faintly mocking note in Brad's voice that was only there when Kathleen Doughty was in the room, the slower, somehow more affectionate chirping of the sound tapes when Sulie Carpenter was monitoring the responses. He discovered that his time sense was not the same as that of those outside, or of "reality," whatever that was. "That's to be expected, Rog," said the weary voice of Brad when he reported it. "If you work at it, you'll find you can exercise volitional control over that. You can count out seconds like a metronome if you want to. Or move faster or slower, depending on what's needed."

"How do I do that?" Roger demanded.

"Hell, man!" Brad flared. "It's your body, learn to use it." Then, apologetically, "The same way you learned to block off vision. Experiment till you figure it out. Now pay attention; I'm going to play you a Bach partita."

Somehow the time passed.

But not easily and not quickly. There were long periods when

Roger's altered time sense contrarily dragged his tedium out, times when, against his will, he found himself thinking again about Dorrie. The lift that Dash's visit had given him, the pleasant concern and affection from Sulie Carpenter—these were good things; but they did not last forever. Dorrie was a reality of his reverie, and when his mind was empty enough to wander it was to Dorrie that it wandered. Dorrie and their joyous early years together. Dorrie, and the terrible knowledge that he was no longer enough of a man to gratify her sexual needs. Dorrie and Brad . . .

Kathleen Doughty's voice snapped, "I don't know what the hell you're doing, Roger, but it's screwing up your vital signs! Cut it out."

"All right," he grumbled. He put Dorrie out of his mind. He thought of Kathleen's rancorous, affectionate voice, of what the President had said, of Sulie Carpenter. He made himself tranquil.

As a reward they showed him a slide of a bunch of violets, in full color.

Ten
The Batman's Entrechats

Suddenly, amazingly, there were only nine days left.

Outside the clerical condominium Father Kayman shivered in the cold, waiting for his ride to the project. The fuel shortage had worsened a great deal in the past two weeks, with the fighting in the Middle East and the Scottish Freedom Fighters blowing up the North Sea pipelines. The project itself had overriding priorities for whatever it needed, even though some of the missile silos had not enough fuel for topping off their birds; but all the staff had been urged to turn off lights, share rides, turn down their home thermostats, watch less TV. An early snowstorm had dusted the Oklahoma prairies, and outside the condominium a seminary student was sleepily pushing the snow off the walks. There was not much of it, and, Kayman thought, it was not particularly nice-looking. Was it his imagination, or was it tattletale gray? Could the ash from the blazing California and Oregon forests have soiled the snow fifteen hundred miles away?

Brad beeped his horn, and Kayman jumped. "Sorry," Kayman said, getting in and closing the door. "Say, shouldn't we take my car next time? Uses a lot less fuel than this thing of yours."

Brad shrugged morosely and peered into his rear-view mirror. Another hovercar, this one a light, fast sports job, was swinging around the corner after them. "I drive for two anyway," he said. "That's the same one that was tailing me on Tuesday. They're getting sloppy. Or else they want to make sure I know I'm being followed."

Kayman looked over his shoulder. The following car was certainly taking no pains to be inconspicuous. "Do you know who it is, Brad?"

"Is there any doubt?"

Kayman didn't answer. Actually, there wasn't. The President had made clear to Brad that he was not under any circumstances to fool around with the monster's wife, in a half-hour interview of which Brad vividly recalled every painful second. The shadowing had begun immediately thereafter, to make sure Brad didn't forget.

But it was not a subject that Kayman wanted to discuss with Brad. He turned on the radio, tuned to a news broadcast. They listened for a few minutes of censored but still overpowering disaster until Brad wordlessly reached out and snapped it off. Then they rode in silence, under the leaden sky, until they reached the great white cube of the project, alone on the desolate prairie.

Inside there was nothing gray: the lights were strong and glaring; the faces were tired, sometimes concerned, but they were alive. In here at least, Kayman thought, there was a sense of accomplishment and purpose. The project was right on schedule.

And in nine days the Mars craft would be launched, and he himself would be on it.

Kayman was not afraid to go. He had shaped his life toward it, from the first days in the seminary when he had realized that he could serve his God in more places than a pulpit and was encouraged by his father superior to continue his interest in all heavens, whether astrophysical or theological. Nevertheless, it was a weighty thought.

He felt unready. He felt the world was unready for this venture. It all seemed so curiously impromptu, in spite of the eternities of work that they had put in, himself included. Even the crew was not finally decided. Roger would go; he was the raison d'être of the whole project, of course. Kayman would go, that had been decided firmly. But the two pilots were still only provisional. Kayman had met them both and liked them. They were among NASA's best, and one had flown with Roger in a shuttle mission eight years before. But there were fifteen others on the short list of eligibles—Kayman did not even know all the names, only that there were a lot of them. Vern Scanyon and the director general of NASA had flown to reason with the President in person, urging him to confirm their choices; but Dash, for Dash's own reasons, had reserved the right of final decision to himself, and was withholding his hand.

The one thing that seemed fully ready for the venture was the link in the chain that had once seemed most doubtful, Roger himself.

The training had gone beautifully. Roger was fully mobile now, all over the project building, commuting from the room he still kept as "home" to the Mars-normal tank, to the test facilities, to any place he cared to go. The whole project was used to seeing the tall black-winged creature loping down a hall, the huge, faceted eyes recognizing a face and the flat voice calling a cheery greeting. The last week and more had been all Kathleen Doughty's. His sensorium appeared under perfect control; now it was time to learn to exploit all the resources of his musculature. So she had brought in a blind man, a ballet dancer and a former paraplegic, and as Roger began to expand his horizons they took over his tutorial tasks. The ballet dancer was past stardom now, but he had known it, and as a child he had studied with Nureyev and Dolin. The blind man was no longer blind. He had no eyes, but his optic system had been replaced with sensors very like Roger's own, and the two of them compared notes over subtle hues and tricks of ma-nipulating the parameters of their vision. The paraplegic, who now moved on motorized limbs that were precursors of Roger's, had had a year to learn to use them, and he and Roger took ballet classes together.

Not always physically together, not quite. The ex-paraplegic, whose name was Alfred, was still far more human than Roger Torraway, and among other human traits he possessed was a need for air. As Kayman and Brad came into the control chamber for the Mars-normal tank, Alfred was doing entrechats on one side of the great double glass pane and Roger, inside the almost airless tank, was duplicating his moves on the other. Kathleen Doughty was counting cadence, and the loud-speaker system was playing the A-major waltz from Les Sylphides. Vern Scanyon was sitting over by a wall on a reversed chair, hands clasped over the back of the chair and chin resting on his hands. Brad went over to him at once, and the two of them began to talk inaudibly.

Don Kayman found a place to sit near the door. Paraplegic and mon-ster, they were doing incredibly rapid leaps, twiddling their feet in blurs of motion. It was not the right music for entrechats, Kayman thought, but neither of them seemed to care. The ballet dancer was staring at them with an unreadable expression. He probably wishes he were a cyborg, Kayman thought. With muscles like that he could take over any stage in the country.

It was a mildly amusing thought, but for some reason Kayman felt ill-at-ease. Then he remembered: this was just where he had been sit-ting when Willy Hartnett had died before his eyes.

It seemed so long ago. It had only been a week since Brenda Hart-nett had brought the kids around to say goodbye to him and Sister Clo-tilda, but she had almost dropped out of their minds already. The mon-ster named Roger was the star of the show now. The death of another monster in that place, so short a time ago, was only history.

Kayman took up his rosary and began to count the fifteen decades of the Blessed Virgin. While one part of him was repeating the Aves, another was conscious of the pleasant, warm, heavy feel of the ivory beads and the crisp contrast of the crystal. He had made up his mind to take the Holy Father's gift to Mars with him. It would be a pity if it were lost—well, it would be a pity if *he* were lost too, he thought. He could not weigh risks like that, so he decided to do what His Holiness had evidently meant him to do and take this gift on the longest journey it had ever known.

He became conscious of someone standing behind him. "Good morning, Father Kayman."

"Hello, Sulie." He glanced at her curiously. What was strange about her? There seemed to be golden roots to her dark hair, but that was nothing particularly surprising; even a priest knew that women chose their hair color at will. For that matter, so did some priests.

"How's it going?" she asked.

"I'd say perfect. Look at them jump! Roger looks as ready as he'll ever be and, *Deo volente,* I think we'll make the launch date."

"I envy you," the nurse said, peering past him into the Mars-normal tank. He turned his face to her, startled. There had been more feeling in her voice than a casual remark seemed to justify. "I mean it, Don," she said. "The reason I got into the space program in the first place was that I wanted to go up myself. Might have made it if—"

She stopped and shrugged. "Well, I'm helping you and Roger, I guess," she said. "Isn't that what they used to say women were for? Helpmates. It isn't a bad thing, anyway, when it's as important a thing to help as this."

"You don't really sound convinced of that," Kayman offered.

She grinned and then turned back to the tank.

The music had stopped. Kathleen Doughty took the cigarette out of her lips, lit another and said, "Okay, Roger, Alfred. Take ten. You're doing great."

Inside the tank Roger allowed himself to sit crosslegged. He looked exactly like the Devil squatting on a hilltop in the classical old Disney tape, Kayman thought. *A Night on Bald Mountain?*

"What's the matter, Roger?" Kathleen Doughty called. "You're surely not tired."

"Tired of this, anyway," he groused. "I don't know why I need all this ballet-dancing. Willy didn't have it."

"Willy died," she snapped.

There was a silence. Roger turned his head toward her, peering through the glass with his great compound eyes. He snarled, "Not because of lack of entrechats."

"How do you know that? Oh," she admitted grudgingly, "I suppose you could survive without some of this. But you're better with it. It's not just a matter of learning how to get around. The other thing you have to learn to do is avoid destroying your environment. Do you have any idea how strong you are now?"

Inside the tank Roger hesitated, then shook his head. "I don't feel strong, particularly," his flat voice said.

"You can punch through a wall, Roger. Ask Alfred. What do you run the metric mile in, Alfred?"

The ex-paraplegic folded his hands over his fat belly and grinned. He was fifty-eight years old and had not been much of an athlete even before the myasthenia gravis destroyed his natural limbs. "A minute forty-seven," he said with pride.

"I expect you to do better than that, Roger," called Kathleen. "So you have to learn how to control it."

Roger made a noise that wasn't quite a word, then stood up. "Balance the locks," he said. "I'm coming out."

The technician touched a switch and the great pumps began to let air into the exit chamber with a sound like ripping linoleum. "Oh," moaned Sulie Carpenter, next to Don Kayman, "I don't have my contacts in!" And she fled before Roger could come into the room.

Kayman stared after her. One puzzle was solved: he knew what had looked strange about her. But why would Sulie wear contacts that changed her brown eyes to green?

He shrugged and gave up.

We knew the answer. We had gone to a lot of trouble to find Sulie Carpenter. The critical factors made a long list, and the least important of the items on that list were the color of hair and the color of eyes, since either could be so easily changed.

As the deadline approached, Roger's position began to change. For two weeks he had been meat on a butcher's block, slashed and rolled and chopped with no personal participation and no control over what happened to him. Then he had been a student, following the orders of his teachers, learning the control of his senses and the use of his limbs. It was a transition from laboratory preparation to demigod, and he was more than halfway there.

He felt it happening. For days now he had been questioning everything he was told to do and sometimes refusing. Kathleen Doughty was no longer his boss, capable of ordering him to do a hundred chinups and an hour of pirouettes. She was his employee, retained by him to help in what he wanted to do. Brad, who had become far less offhandedly humorous and far more intense, was now asking Roger for favors: "Try these color discrimination tests for me, will you? It'll look good on my paper about you." Often Roger humored them, but sometimes not.

The one he humored most frequently and surely was Sulie Carpenter, because she was always there and always cared about him. He had almost forgotten how much she looked like Dorrie. He only was aware that she looked very good.

She met his moods. If he was edgy she was quietly cheerful. If he wanted to talk, she talked. They played board games sometimes; she was a highly competitive Scrabble player. Once, late at night, when Roger was experimenting with the length of wakefulness he could handle, she brought in a guitar and they sang, her pleasant, unobtrusive contralto ornamenting his flat and almost toneless whisper. Her face changed while he looked at it, but he had learned to handle that. The interpretation circuits in his sensorium reflected his feelings when he let them, and there were times when Sulie Carpenter looked more like Dorrie than Dorrie did herself.

After he had finished his day's run in the Mars-normal tank, Sulie raced him back to his room, laughing girl against thudding monster down the wide lab corridors; he won easily, of course. They chatted for a while and then he sent her away.

Nine days to liftoff.

It was less than that, really. He would be flown to Merritt Island three days before the launch, and his last day in Tonka would be devoted to fitting the backpack computer and returning some of his sensorium for the special Martian conditions. So he had six—no, five—days.

And he had not seen Dorrie for weeks.

He looked at himself in the mirror he had demanded they install: insect eyes, bat wings, dully gleaming flesh. He amused himself by letting his visual interpretations flow, from bat to giant fly to demon . . . to himself, as he remembered himself, pleasant-faced and youthful.

If only Dorrie had a computer to mediate her sight! If only she could see him as he had been! He swore he would not call her; he could not force her to look at the comic-strip contraption that was her husband.

Having sworn, he picked up the phone and dialed her number.

It was an impulse that could not be denied. He waited. His accordion-pleated time sense prolonged the interval, so that it was an eternity before the raster blaze from the screen and the buzz from the speaker sounded the first ring.

Then time betrayed him again. It seemed forever until the second ring. Then it came, and lasted an eternity, and was over.

She did not answer.

Roger, who was the sort of person who counted things, knew that most persons did not respond until the third ring. Dorrie, however, was always eager to know who the phone was bringing into her life. From a sound sleep or out of the bathtub, she seldom let it ring past twice.

At length the third ring came, and still no reply.

Roger began to hurt.

He controlled it as best he could, unwilling to sound the alarms on the telemetry. He could not stop it entirely. She was out, he thought. Her husband had turned into a monster and she was not at home sympathizing or worrying; she was shopping or visiting a friend or seeing a flick.

Or with a man.

What man? Brad, he thought. It wouldn't be impossible; he had left Brad down at the tank twenty-five minutes ago by the clock. Time enough for them to rendezvous somewhere. Even time enough for Brad to get to the Torraway home. Perhaps she was not out at all. Perhaps—

Fourth ring—

Perhaps they were there, the two of them, naked and coupling on the floor in front of the phone. She would be saying, "Go in the other room, honey, I want to see who it is." And he would say, laughing, "No, let's answer this way." And she would say—

Fifth ring—and the raster blossomed into the colors of Dorrie's face. Her voice said, "Hello?"

Quick as sound Roger's fist shot out and covered the lens. "Dorrie," he said. His voice sounded flat and harsh again to him. "How are you?"

"Roger!" she cried. The pleasure in her voice sounded very real. "Oh, honey, I'm so glad to hear you! How are you feeling?"

His voice automatically said, "Fine." It went on, without the need of help from his conscious mind, to correct the statement, to say what had been happening to him, cataloging the tests and the exercises. At the same time he was staring into the screen with every sense on high gain.

She looked—what? Tired? Looking tired was confirmation of his fears. She was carousing with Brad every night, heedless of her husband in pain and clownish humiliation. Rested and cheerful? Looking rested and cheerful was confirmation, too. It meant she was relaxing, enjoying herself—heedless of her husband's torment.

There was really nothing wrong with Torraway's brain, in that it had a lifelong habit of analysis and logic. It did not fail to occur to him that the game he was playing with himself was called "You Lose." *Everything* was evidence of Dorrie's guilt. Yet no matter how carefully he scanned her image, with what multiplied senses, she didn't look hostile or cloyingly overaffectionate. She only looked like Dorrie.

When he thought that he felt a burst of tenderness that made his voice break. "I've missed you, honey," he said flatly. The only thing that spoke of feelings was that one syllable was retarded a fraction of a second: "Hon . . . ee."

"And I've missed you. I've kept myself busy, dear," she chattered. "I've been painting your den. It's a surprise, but of course it's going to be such a long time till you see it that— Well, it's going to be peach. With buttercup woodwork and I think maybe a pale-blue ceiling. You like? I was going to make it all ochre and brown, you know, fall colors, Mars colors, to celebrate. But I thought by the time you got back you'd be pretty sick of Mars colors!" And quickly, without pause: "When am I going to see you?" The change in her voice caught him by surprise.

"Well, I look pretty awful," he said.

"I know what you look like. Dear God, Roger, do you think Midge and Brenda and Callie and I haven't talked this over for the last two years? Ever since the program started. We've seen the sketches. We've seen the photos of the mockups. And we've seen the pictures of Willy."

"I'm not exactly like Willy any more. They've changed things—"

"And I know about that too, Roger. Brad told me all about it. I'd like to see you."

At that moment his wife's face changed without warning to a witch's. The crochet hook she held became a peasant twig broom. "You've been seeing Brad?"

Was there a microsecond pause before she answered? "I suppose he shouldn't have told me," she said, "because of security and all. But I wanted him to. It's not that bad, honey. I'm a big girl. I can handle it."

For a moment Roger wanted to snatch his hand away from the lens and let himself be seen, but he was becoming confused, feeling strange. He could not interpret his feelings. Was it vertigo? Emotion? Some malfunction in his machine half? He knew it would be only moments until Sulie or Don Kayman or someone came in, warned by the telltale telemetry outside. He tried to control himself.

"Maybe later," he said without conviction. "I—I think I'd better hang up now, Dorrie."

Behind her their familiar living room was changing too. The depth of field of the phone lens was not very good; even to his machine senses the rest of the room was blurred. Was that a man standing in the shadows? Was it wearing a Marine officer's shirt? Would Brad be doing that?

"I have to hang up now," he said, and did.

Clara Bly came in, full of questions and concern. He shook his head at her without speaking.

There were no lachrymal ducts in his new eyes, so of course he could not cry. Even that relief was denied him.

Eleven
Dorothy Louise Mintz Torraway as Penelope

Our trendline projections had shown that the time was right to let the world know about Roger Torraway, warts and all. So it had all gone out, and every TV screen in the world had seen Roger on point in a dozen perfect fouettés, in between the close-ups of the starved dead in Pakistan and the fires in Chicago.

It had the effect of making Dorrie a celebrity. Roger's call had upset her. Not as much as the note from Brad saying that he wouldn't be able to see her again, not nearly as much as the forty-five minutes the President had spent with her impressing on her what would happen if she messed up his pet astronaut. Certainly not as much as the knowledge that she was being followed, her telephone tapped, her home certainly bugged. But she hadn't known how to deal with Roger. She suspected she never would, and did not mind at all that in a few days he would be launched into space, where there would be little necessity for her to worry about their relationship for at least a year and a half.

She also did not mind the sudden glare of publicity.

Now that the newspapers had it all the TV reporters had been to see her, and she had seen her own courageous face on the six o'clock report. *Fem* was sending someone around. The someone phoned first. She was a woman of about sixty, veteran of the lib years, who sniffed, "We never do this, interviewing somebody just because she's somebody's wife. But they wanted it. I couldn't turn down the assignment, but I want to be honest with you and let you know that it's distasteful to me."

"I'm sorry," Dorrie apologized. "Do you want me to cancel out?"

"Oh, no," said the woman, speaking as though it were Dorrie's fault, "it's not your fault, but I think it's a betrayal of everything *Fem* stands for. Never mind. I want to come up to your home. We'll do a fifteen-minute spread for the cassette edition, and I'll write it up for the print. If you can—"

"I—" Dorrie began.

"—try to talk about you, rather than him. Your background. Your interests. Your—"

"I'm sorry, but I'd really prefer—"

"—feelings about the space program and so on. Dash says it's an essential American objective and the future of the world depends on it. What do you think? I don't mean answer the question now, I mean—"

"I don't want to have it in my home," Dorrie inserted into the conversation, without waiting for a place for it.

"—think about it, and answer on camera. Not at your home? No, that's not possible. We'll be over in an hour."

Dorrie was left with a dwindling spot of light to talk to, and then even that was gone. "Bitch," she said, almost absent-mindedly. She didn't really mind having the interview in her home. She minded not being given a choice. That she minded a lot. But there was no choice available to her, except to go out before the *Fem* person showed up.

Dorrie Torraway, Dee Mintz as was, felt strongly about having choices. One of the things that had attracted her to Roger in the first place, apart from the glamour of the space program and the security and money that went with it—and apart from Roger's rather nice-looking, studly self—was that he was willing to listen to what she wanted. Other men had been mostly interested in what they wanted, which was not the same from man to man but very consistent within the range of relationships of any one man. Harold always wanted to dance and party, Jim always wanted sex, Everett wanted sex *and* parties, Tommy wanted political dedication, Joe wanted mothering. What Roger wanted was to explore the world with her along, and he seemed perfectly willing to explore the parts of it that she wanted as much as the parts that were important to him.

She had never regretted marrying him.

There were a lot of lonely times. Fifty-four days when he was in Space Station Three. Any number of shorter missions. Two years on tour duty all over the world, working with the whole system of ground monitoring stations from Aachen to Zaire, with no proper home anywhere. Dorrie had given that up, after a while, and gone back to the apartment in Tonka. But she hadn't minded. Perhaps Roger had; the question had never crossed her mind. Anyway, they had seen each other quite often enough. He had been home every month or two, and she kept her time full. There was her shop—she had opened it while Roger was in Iceland, with a five-thousand-dollar check he sent her for her birthday. There were her friends. There were, from time to time, men.

None of these filled her life, but she didn't expect it to be filled. She rather expected to be lonely. She had been an only child, with a mother who could not stand her neighbors, and so she had not had very many friends. The neighbors couldn't stand her mother very well, either, because her mother was a speed freak on a small scale, likely to be burned right out of her mind most afternoons, which made things complicated for Dorrie. But she didn't mind that; she didn't know there was any other way to live.

At thirty-one Dorrie was as healthy, as pretty and as competent to deal with the world as she ever had been or would be again. She described herself as happy. This diagnosis did not come from any welling up of joy inside herself. It came from the observed fact, looking at herself objectively, that whenever she decided she wanted something she always got it, and what other definition of happiness could there be?

She used the time until Ms. Hagar Hengstrom and her crew from *Fem* arrived to assemble a selection of ceramic ware from her shop on the coffee table before the couch she intended to sit in. What time was left she devoted to the less important task of brushing her hair, checking her make-up and changing into her newest laced-pants suit.

When the doorbell rang she was quite ready.

Ms. Hagar Hengstrom pumped her hand and walked in, brilliant blue hair and a curly black cigar. She was followed by her lightperson, her soundperson, her cameraperson and her prop boys. "Room's small," she muttered, appraising the furnishings with contempt. "Torraway will sit over there. Move it."

The prop boys jumped to manhandle an easy chair from its place by the window to the corner now occupied by a breakfront, which they tugged into the center of the room. "Wait a minute," said Dorrie. "I thought I'd just sit on the couch here—"

"Don't you have the light reading yet?" Hengstrom demanded. "Sally, start the camera. You never know what we might use for rollunder."

"I mean it," Dorrie said.

Hengstrom looked at her. The voice had not been loud, but the tone was dangerous. She shrugged. "Let's set it up," she proposed, "and if you don't like it we'll talk it over. Run through for me, will you?"

"Run through what?" The pale young girl with the hand-held camera was pointing it at her, Dorrie noticed; it distracted her. The light-person had found a wall socket and was holding a crucifix of floods in each hand, moving them gently to erase shadows as fast as they formed each time Dorrie moved.

"Well, for openers, what are your plans for the next two years? You're surely not just going to hang around waiting for Roger Torra-way to come home."

Dorrie tried to make her way to the couch, but the lightperson frowned and waved her in the other direction, and two of the prop boys shoved the coffee table out of reach. She said, "I've got my shop. I thought you might like to have some of the pieces from it on camera while you interviewed me—"

"That's fine, sure. I meant personally. You're a healthy woman. You have sexual needs. Back up a little please—Sandra's getting a buzz from something on the sound system."

Dorrie found herself standing in front of the chair, and there seemed nothing to do but to sit in it. "Of course—" she began.

"You have a responsibility," Hengstrom said. "What sort of an exam-ple are you going to set young womanhood? Turning yourself into a dried-up old maid? Or living a naturally full life?"

"I don't know if I want to discuss—"

"I've checked you out pretty carefully, Torraway. I like what I've found out. You're your own person—as much as any person can be, anyway, who accepts the ridiculous farce of marriage. Why'd you do it?"

Dorrie hesitated. "Roger's really a very nice person," she offered.

"What about it?"

"Well, I mean, he offered me a great deal of comfort and support—"

Hagar Hengstrom sighed. "Same old slave psychology. Never mind. The other thing that puzzles me is your getting involved in the space program. Don't you feel it's a sexist shuffle?"

"Why, no. The President told me himself," Dorrie said, aware that she was trying to score points in case of another visit from Dash, "that putting a man on Mars was absolutely indispensable to the future of the human race. I believe him. We owe a—"

"Play that back," Hengstrom commanded.

"What?"

"Play back what you just said. Putting a what on Mars?"

"A man. Oh. I see what you mean."

Hengstrom nodded sadly. "You see what I mean, but you don't change the way you think. Why a man? Why not a person?" She looked commiseratingly at the soundperson, who shook her head in sympathy. "Well, let's get to something more important: do you know that the whole crew of the Mars voyage is supposed to be male? What do you think of that?"

It was quite a morning for Dorrie. She never did get her ceramic pieces on camera.

When Sulie Carpenter came on duty that afternoon she brought Roger two surprises: a cassette of the interview, borrowed from the project public-relations (read: censorship) office, and a guitar. She gave him the cassette first, and let him watch the interview while she remade his bed and changed the water for his flowers.

When it was over she said brightly, "Your wife handled herself very well, I thought. I met Hagar Hengstrom once. She's a very difficult woman."

"Dorrie looked fine," said Roger. You could not read any expression in the remade face or hear it in the flat tones, but the bat wings were fluttering restlessly. "I always liked those pants."

Sulie nodded and made a note to herself: the open lacing up both sides of each leg showed a great deal of flesh. Evidently the steroids implanted in Roger were doing their job. "Now I've got something else," she said, and opened the guitar case.

"You're going to play for me?"

"No, Roger. *You're* going to play."

"I can't play the guitar, Sulie," he protested.

She laughed. "I've been talking to Brad," she said, "and I think you're going to be surprised. You're not just different, you know, Roger. You're better. For instance, your fingers."

"What about them?"

"Well, I've been playing the guitar since I was nine, and if I stop for a couple of weeks my calluses go and I have to start all over again. Your fingers don't need calluses; they're hard enough and firm enough to fret the strings first time perfectly."

"Fine," said Roger, "only I don't even know what you're talking about. What's 'fret'?"

"Press them down. Like this." She strummed a G chord, then a D and a C.

"Now you do it," she said. "The only thing to watch out for, don't use too much strength. It's breakable." She handed him the guitar.

He swept his thumb over the open strings, as he had seen her do.

"That's fine." She applauded. "Now make a G. Ring finger on the third fret of the high E string—there. First finger on the second fret of the A. Middle finger on the third fret of the low E." She guided his hands. "Now hit it."

He strummed and looked up at her. "Hey," he said. "Nice."

She grinned and corrected him. "Not nice. Perfect. Now, this is a C. First finger on the second fret of the B string, middle finger there, ring finger there. . . . Right. And this is a D chord: first and middle finger on the G and E strings, there, ring finger one fret lower on the B. . . . Perfect again. Now give me a G."

To his surprise, Roger strummed a perfect G.

She smiled. "See? Brad was right. Once you know a chord, you know it; the 3070 remembers it for you. All you have to do is think 'G chord,' and your fingers do it. You are now," she said in mock sorrow, "about three months ahead of where I was the first time I tried to play the guitar."

"That's pretty nice," Roger said, trying all three chords, one after another.

"That's only the beginning. Now strum a four-beat, you know, dum, dum, dum, dum. With a G chord—" She listened, then nodded. "Fine. Now do it like this: G, G, G, G, G, G, G, G, C, C, G, G, G, G, G, G. . . . Fine. Now again, only this time after the C, C do D, D, D, D, D, D. . . . Fine again. Now do them both, one after the other—"

He played, and she sang with him: " 'Kumbaya, my lord. Kumbaya! Kumbaya, my lord. Kumbaya . . .' "

"Hey!" Roger cried, delighted.

She shook her head in mock dismay. "Three minutes from the time you pick up the guitar, and you're already an accompanist. Here, I brought you a chord book and some simple pieces. By the time I get back, you should be playing all of them, and I'll start you on finger-plucking, sliding and hammering."

She showed him how to read the tabulature for each chord and left him happily puzzling out the first six modulations of the F.

Outside his room she paused to take out her contacts, rubbed her eyes and marched to the office of the director. Scanyon's secretary waved her in.

"He's happy with his guitar, General," she reported. "Less happy about his wife."

Vern Scanyon nodded, and turned up a knob on the comm set on his desk: the sound of the chords for "Kentucky Babe" came from the tap in Roger's room. He turned it down again. "I know about the guitar, Major Carpenter. What about his wife?"

"I'm afraid he loves her," she said slowly. "He's all right up to a point. Past that point I think we're in trouble. I can bolster him up as long as he's here at the project, but he'll be a long time away and—I'm not sure."

Scanyon said sharply, "Get the marbles out of your mouth, Major!"

"I think he'll miss her more than he can handle. It's bad enough now. I watched him while he was looking at that tape. He didn't move a muscle, rigid concentration, didn't want to miss a thing. When he's forty million miles away from her— Well. I've got everything taped, General. I'll run a computer simulation, and then maybe I can be more specific. But I'm concerned."

"*You're* concerned!" Scanyon snapped. "Dash will have my ass if we get him up there and he blows!"

"What can I tell you, General? Let me run the simulation. Then maybe I can tell you how to handle it."

She sat down without waiting to be asked and ran her hands over her forehead. "Leading a double life takes a lot out of you, General," she offered. "Eight hours as a nurse and eight hours as a shrink isn't any fun."

"Ten years on staff duty in Antarctica is even less fun than that," Vern Scanyon said simply.

The presidential jet had reached its cruising altitude of 31,000 meters and slid into high gear—Mach 3 and a bit, grotesquely faster than even a presidential CB-5 was supposed to go. The President was in a hurry.

The Midway Summit Conference had just ended in disarray. Stretched out on his chaise longue with his eyes closed, pretending to be asleep to keep the Senators who had accompanied him out of his hair, Dash bleakly considered his options. They were few.

He had not hoped for a great deal from the conference, but it had begun well enough. The Australians indicated they would accept limited cooperation with the NPA in developing the Outback, subject to appropriate guarantees, et cetera, et cetera. The NPA delegation murmured among themselves and announced that they would be happy to provide guarantees, since their real objectives were only to provide a maximum of the necessities of life for all the world's people, considered as a single unit regardless of antiquated national boundaries, et cetera. Dash himself shook off his whispering advisers and stated that America's interest in this conference was only to provide good-offices assistance to its two dearly beloved neighbors and sought nothing for itself, et cetera, and for a time there, all of two hours, it had seemed that there might be a substantive, useful product of the conference.

Then they began getting into the fine detail. The Asians offered a million-man Soil Army plus a stream of tankers carrying three million gallons a week of concentrated sludge from the sewers of Shanghai. The Australians accepted the fertilizer but spoke of a maximum of 50,000 Asians to till the land. Also, they pointed out politely, that as it was Australian land and Australian sunshine that was being used, it would be Australian wheat that would be grown. The man from the State Department reminded Dash of American commitments to Peru, and with a heavy heart Dash rose to insist on at least a 15 percent allocation to good neighbors on the South American continent. And tempers began to rise. The precipitating incident was an NPA shuttle plane that ran into a flock of black-footed albatrosses as it took off from the Sand Island runway, crashed and burned on an islet in the lagoon, in full view of the conference members on the rooftop of the Holiday Inn. Then there were harsh words. The Japanese member of the NPA delegation allowed himself to say what he had previously only thought: that America's insistence on holding the conference at the site of one of the most famous battles of World War II was a calculated insult to Asians. The Australians commented that they had controlled their own gooney-bird populations without much trouble, and were astonished that the Americans had not succeeded in doing the same. And the maximum gain of three weeks of preparation and two days of hope was a tightly worded announcement that all three powers had agreed to further discussions. Sometime. Somewhere. Not very soon.

But what it all meant, Dash admitted to himself as he tossed restlessly on the chaise longue, was that the confrontation was eyeball to eyeball. Somebody would have to give, and nobody would.

He got up and called for coffee. When it came there was a scribbled note on Airborne White House stationery from one of the Senators: "Mr. President, we must settle the disaster-area proclamation before we land."

Dash crumpled it up. That was Senator Talltree, full of complaints: Lake Altus had shrunk to 20 percent of its normal size, tourism in the Arbuckle Mountains was dead because there was no water coming over Turner Falls, the Sooner State Fair had had to be canceled because of blowing dust. Oklahoma should be declared a disaster area. He had fifty-four states, Dash reflected, and if he listened to all the Senators and governors he would be declaring fifty-four disaster areas. There really was only one disaster area. It merely happened to be world-wide.

And I *ran* for this job, he marveled.

Thinking of Oklahoma made him think of Roger Torraway. For a moment he considered calling the pilot and diverting the flight to

Tonka. But the meeting with the Combined Chiefs of Staff would not wait. He would have to content himself with the telephone.

It was not really himself who was playing the guitar, Roger knew, it was the 3070 that remembered all the subroutines involved and commanded his fingers to do whatever his brain decreed. It had taken him less than an hour to learn every chord in the book, and to use them in effortless succession. A few minutes more to record in the downstairs data banks the meaning of time signals on a musical staff; then his inner clocks took over the tempi and he never had to think about the beat again. For melody, he learned which fret on which string corresponded to each note on the staff; once imprinted on the magnetic cores, the correspondence between printed music and plucked string was established forever. Sulie took ten minutes to show him which notes to sharp and which to flat when called for, and from then on the galaxy of sharps and flats sprinkled over the bars at the key signature held no further terrors for him. Finger-plucking: for human nervous systems, it is a matter of two minutes to learn the principle and a hundred hours of practice before it becomes automatic: thumb on the D string, ring finger on the high E, middle finger on the B, thumb on the A, ring on the E, middle on the B and so on. The two minutes of learning sufficed for Roger. From then on the subroutines commanded the fingers, and the only limit to his tempo was the speed at which the strings themselves could produce a tone without breaking.

He was playing a Segovia recital from memory, from a single hearing of the tape, when the President's phone call came in.

There was a time when Roger would have been awed and delighted by a call from the President of the United States. Now it was an annoyance; it meant taking time away from his guitar. He hardly listened to what the President had to say. He was struck by the care on Dash's face, the deep lines that had not been there a few days before, the sunken eyes. Then he realized that his interpretation circuits were exaggerating what they saw to call his attention to the changes; he overrode the mediation circuits and saw Dash plain.

But he was still careworn. His voice was all warmth and good fellowship as he asked Roger how things were going. Was there anything Roger needed? Could he think of an ass to kick to get things goin' right? "Everything's fine, Mr. President," Roger said, amusing himself by letting his trick eyes deck the President's face out in Santa Claus beard and red tasseled cap, with a bundle of intangible gifts over his shoulder.

"Sure now, Roger?" Dash pressed. "You're not forgetting what I told you: whatever you want, you just yell."

"I'll yell," Roger promised. "But I'm doing fine. Waiting for the launch." And waiting for you to get off the phone, he thought, bored with the conversation.

The President frowned. Roger's interpreters immediately changed the image: Dash was still Santa Claus, but ebony black and with enormous fangs. "You're not overconfident, are you?" he asked.

"Well, how would I know if I was?" Roger asked reasonably. "I don't think so. Ask the staff here; they can tell you more about me than I can."

He managed to terminate the conversation a few exchanges later, knowing that the President was unsatisfied and vaguely troubled, but not caring much. There was less and less that Roger really cared about, he thought to himself. And he had been truthful: he really was looking forward to the launch. He would miss Sulie and Clara. He was, in the back of his mind, faintly worried about the danger and the duration of the trip. But he was also buoyed up with anticipation of what he would find when he got there: the planet he was made to inhabit.

He picked up the guitar and started again on the Segovia, but it did not go as well as he would like. After a time he realized that the gift of absolute pitch was also a handicap: Segovia's guitar had not been tuned to a perfect 440 A, it was a few Hertz flat, and his D string was almost a quarter-tone relatively flatter still. He shrugged—the bat wings flailed with the gesture—and put the guitar down.

For a moment, he sat upright on his guitar chair, straight-backed and armless, inviting his thoughts.

Something *was* troubling him. The name of the something was Dorrie. Playing the guitar was pleasant and relaxing, but behind the pleasure was a daydream: a fantasy of sitting on the deck of a sailboat with Dorrie and Brad, and casually borrowing Brad's guitar and astonishing them all.

In some arcane way all the processes of his life terminated in Dorrie. The purpose of playing the guitar was to please Dorrie. The horror of his appearance was that it would offend Dorrie. The tragedy of castration was that he would fail Dorrie. Most of the pain had lifted from these things, and he could look at them in a way that had been impossible a few weeks before; but they were still there buried inside him.

He reached for the phone, and then drew back his hand.

Calling Dorrie was not satisfactory. He had tried that.

What he really wanted was to see her.

That, of course, was impossible. He was not allowed to leave the project. Vern Scanyon would be furious. The guards would stop him at the door. The telemetry would reveal at once what he was doing; the closed-circuit electronic surveillance would locate him at every step; all the resources of the project would be mobilized to prevent his leaving.

And there would be no point in asking permission. Not even in asking Dash; the most that would happen would be that the President would give an order and Dorrie would be delivered, coerced and furious, in his room. Roger did not want Dorrie to be forced to come to him, and he was sure he would not be allowed to go to her.

On the other hand . . .

On the other hand, he reflected, why did he need permission?

He thought for a minute, sitting perfectly still in his straight-backed chair.

Then he put the guitar carefully away in its case and moved.

The first thing he did was bend down to the wall, pull a baseboard plug out of its moorings and stick his finger into it. The copper nail on his finger was as good as a penny any day. The fuses blew. The lights in the room went out. The whicka-whicka and gentle whisper of the reels of the recording machines slowed and stopped. The room went dark.

There was still heat, and that was light enough for Roger's eyes. He could see quite well enough to pull the telemetry leads out of his body. He was out of the door before Clara Bly, pouring cream into a cup on her coffee break, looked around at the buzzing readout board.

He had done better than he planned with the fuses; the hall lights were out as well. There were people in the corridor, but in the dark they could not see. Roger was past them and taking the fire stairs four at a time before they knew he was gone. He settled into the workings of his body with ease and grace. All of Kathleen Doughty's ballet training was paying off; he danced down the stairs, plié-ed through a door, leaped along a corridor and was out into the cold night air before the security man at the door looked around from his TV set.

He was in the open, racing down the freeway toward the city of Tonka at forty miles an hour.

The night was bright with kinds of light he had never seen before. Overhead there was a solid layer of clouds, stratocumulus scudding along from the north and thick middle-level clouds above them; even so, he could see dim glows where the brightest stars filtered some of their radiation through. The Oklahoma prairie on either side was somberly glowing with the tiny residual heat retained from the day, punctuated with splotches of brilliance where there was a home or a farm building. The cars on the freeway were tailed by great plumes of light, bright where they left the exhaust pipe, reddening and darkening as the clouds of hot gas expanded into the chilling air. As he entered the city itself he saw and avoided an occasional pedestrian, each a luminous Halloween figure, dully glowing in his own body heat. The buildings around him had trapped a little heat from the end of the day and were spilling more from their own central heating; they glowed like fireflies.

He stopped at the corner of his own home street. There was a car with two men inside it parked across from the door. Warning signals flashed in his brain, and the car became a tank, howitzer pointed at his head. They were no problem. He changed course and ran through the backyards, scaling fences and slipping through gates, and at his own home he extruded the copper nails in his fingers for purchase and climbed right up the outside wall.

It was what he wanted to do. Not just to avoid the men in the car outside, but to act out a fantasy: the moment when he would burst in on Dorrie through the window, to catch her at—what?

In the event itself, what he caught her at was watching a late movie on television. Her hair was sticky with coloring compound, and she was propped up in bed eating a solitary dish of ice cream.

As he slid the unlocked window open and crawled through, she turned toward him.

She screamed.

It was not just a cry, it was instant hysterics. Dorrie spilled her ice cream and leaped out of bed. The TV set toppled and crunched to the floor. Sobbing, Dorrie pressed herself against the far wall, eyes squeezed tight and fists pressed against them.

"I'm sorry," Roger said inadequately. He wanted to approach her, but reason prevented. She looked very helpless and appealing, in her see-through butcher-boy smock and tiny bikini-ribbon panties.

"*Sorry*," she gasped, looked at him, averted her eyes and fumbled her way into the bathroom, slamming the door behind her.

Well, thought Roger, she was not to be blamed; he had a clear notion of what a grotesque sight he had been, coming through a window without warning. "You did say you knew what I looked like," he called.

There was no answer from the bathroom; only, a moment later, the running of water. He glanced around the room. It looked exactly as it had always looked. The closets were as full of her clothes and his as they had always been. The spaces behind the couches were as empty of lovers as ever. He was not proud of himself for searching the apartment like any medieval cuckold, but he did not stop until he was certain she had been alone.

The phone rang.

Roger's instant reflexes had him grabbing the earpiece out of its cradle almost before the first *brrr* sounded, so quickly and brutally that it was deformed into scrap in his hand. The vision screen flickered and then went dark again, its circuitry linked with the sound. "Hello?" Roger said. But there was no answer; he had made sure that nobody would ever speak on that instrument again.

"Christ," he said. He had had no clear idea of how this meeting would go, but it was apparent that it had begun badly.

When Dorrie came out of the bathroom she wasn't crying, but she wasn't speaking either. She went into the kitchen without looking at him. "I want a cup of tea," she said over her shoulder.

"Wouldn't you rather I made you a drink?" Roger offered hopefully.

"No."

Roger could hear the sounds of the electric kettle being filled, the faint susurrus as it began to simmer and, several times, a cough. He listened harder and heard his wife's breathing, which became slower and steadier.

He sat down in the chair that had always been his chair and waited. His wings were in the way. Even though they elevated themselves automatically over his head he could not lean back. Restlessly he roamed into the living room. His wife's voice called through the swinging doors: "Do you want some tea?"

"No." Then he added, "No, thank you." Actually he would have liked it very much, not because of any need for fluids or nutrients but for the feeling of participating in some normal, precedented event with Dorrie. But he did not want to spill and slobber in front of her, and he had not practiced much with cups and saucers and liquids.

"Where are you?" She hesitated at the swinging doors, the cup in her hands, and then saw him. "Oh. Why don't you turn a light on?"

"I don't want to. Honey, sit down and close your eyes for a minute." He had an idea.

"Why?" But she did as he requested, seating herself in the wing chair on one side of the fake fireplace. He picked up the chair, with her in it, and turned it away, so that she was facing into the wall. He looked around for something to sit in himself—there was nothing, or nothing that comported with his new geometry: floor pillows and couches, all awkward for his body or his wings—but on the other hand, he knew, he had no particular need to sit. His artificial musculature did not need that sort of relaxation very much.

So he stood behind her and said, "I'd feel better if you weren't looking at me."

"I understand that, Roger. You frightened me, is all. I wish you hadn't burst in the window like that! On the other hand, I shouldn't have been so positive I could see you, I mean like *that*, without— Without going into hysterics, I guess is what I want to say."

"I know what I look like," he said.

"It's still you, though, isn't it?" Dorrie said to the wall. "Although I don't remember you ever climbing the outside of a building to get into my bed before."

"It's easy," he said, taking a chance on what was almost an attempt at lightness.

"Well"—she paused for a sip of tea—"tell me. What's this about?"

"I wanted to see you, Dorrie."

"You did see me. On the phone."

"I didn't want it to be on the phone. I wanted to be in the same room with you." He wanted even more than that to touch her, to reach out to the nape of her neck and press and caress the tendons into relaxing, but he did not quite dare that. Instead he reached down and ignited the gas flame in the fireplace, not so much for warmth as for a little light to help Dorrie. And for cheerfulness.

"We aren't supposed to do that, Roger. There's a thousand-dollar fine—"

He laughed. "Not for you and me, Dorrie. Anybody gives you any trouble, you call up Dash and say I said it was all right."

His wife took a cigarette from the box on the end table and lit it. "Roger, dear," she said slowly, "I'm not used to all this. I don't just mean the way you look. I understand about that. It's hard, but at least I knew what it was going to be before it happened. Even if I didn't think it would be *you*. But I'm not used to your being so—I don't know, important."

"I'm not used to it either, Dorrie." He thought back to the TV reporters and the cheering crowds when he returned to Earth after rescuing the Russians. "It's different now. I feel as if I'm carrying something on my back—the world, maybe."

"Dash says that's exactly what you're doing. Half of what he says is crap, but I don't think that part is. You're a pretty significant man, Roger. You were always a famous one. Maybe that's why I married you. But that was like being a rock star, you know? It was exciting, but you could always walk away from it if you got tired of it. This I don't think you can walk away from."

She stubbed out her cigarette. "Anyway," she said, "you're here, and they're probably going crazy at the project."

"I can handle that."

"Yes," she said thoughtfully, "I guess you can. What shall we talk about?"

"Brad," he said. He had not intended it. The word came out of his artificial larynx, shaped by his restructured lips, with no intervention by his conscious mind.

He could feel her stiffening up. "What about Brad?" she asked.

"Your sleeping with him, that's what about Brad," he said. The back of her neck was glowing dully now, and he knew that if he could see her face it would display the revealing tracery of veins. The dancing gas flames from the fireplace made an attractive spectrum of colors on her dark hair; he watched the play appreciatively, as though it did not matter what he was saying to his wife, or she to him.

She said, "Roger, I really don't know how to deal with you. Are you angry with me?"

He watched the dancing colors silently.

"After all, Roger, we talked this out years ago. You have had affairs, and so have I. We agreed they didn't mean anything."

"They mean something when they hurt." He willed his vision to stop, and welcomed the darkness as an aid to thought. "The others were different," he said.

"Different how?" She was angry now.

"Different because we talked them over," he said doggedly. "When I was in Algiers and you couldn't stand the climate, that was one thing. What you did back here in Tonka and what I did in Algiers didn't affect you and me. When I was in orbit—"

"I never slept with anybody else while you were in orbit!"

"I know that, Dorrie. I thought that was kind of you. I really did, because it wouldn't have been fair, would it? I mean, my own opportunities were pretty limited. Old Yuli Bronin wasn't my type. But now it's different. It's like I was in orbit again, only worse. I don't even have Yuli! I not only don't have a girl friend, I don't have the equipment to do anything about it if I did."

She said wretchedly, "I know all that. What can I tell you?"

"You can tell me you'll be a good wife to me!" he roared.

That frightened her; he had forgotten what his voice could sound like. She began to cry.

He reached out to touch her and then let his hand fall. What was the use?

Oh, Christ, he thought. What a mess! He took consolation only in that this interview had been here, in the privacy of their own home, quite unplanned and secret. It would have been unbearable in the presence of anyone else; but naturally we had monitored every word.

Twelve
Two Simulations and a Reality

Copper-fingered Roger had blown more than a fuse. He had shorted a whole box of circuit breakers. It took twenty minutes to get the lights on again.

Fortunately the 3070 had stand-by power for its memory, so the cores were not wiped. The computations that were in process were compromised. All of them would have to be done over again. The automatic surveillance was out of service until long after Roger was gone.

One of the first ones to know what had happened was Sulie Carpenter, catching a cat nap in the office next to the computer room, waiting for Roger's simulation to finish. It didn't finish. The alarm bells signifying interruption of the information being processed woke her. The bright fluorescent rod-lights were out, and only the red incandescents gave a dim, despairing glow.

Her first thought was her precious simulation. She spent twenty minutes with the programmers, studying the partial printout, hoping that it would be all right, before she gave up and charged out to Vern Scanyon's office. That was when she found out that Roger had run off.

Power was back by then; it had come on while she was taking the fire stairs two at a time. Scanyon was already on the phone, ordering the people he wanted to blame in for an emergency conference. Clara Bly was the one who told Sulie about Roger; one by one, as the others entered the room, they were brought up to date. Don Kayman was the only major figure who was out of the project; they located him watching television in his clerical condominium. Kathleen Doughty came up from the physiotherapy room in the basement, dragging Brad with her, all pink-skinned and damp; he had been trying to substitute an hour in the sauna for a night's sleep. Freeling was at Merritt Island, but not needed particularly; half a dozen others came in and slumped, dispiritedly or worriedly, into the leather chairs around the conference table.

Scanyon had already ordered an Air Force spottercopter into the air, in a search pattern all around the project. Its TV cameras were sweeping the freeway, the access roads, the parking lots, the fields and prairie, and displaying what they saw on the wall TV at the end of the room. The Tonka police force had been alerted to watch for a strange devil-like creature running around at seventy kilometers an hour, which had led to trouble for the Tonka desk sergeant. He made a bad mistake. He asked the project security officer if he had been drinking. Ten seconds later, with his head filled with visions of pounding a beat in Kiska, the sergeant was on the police radio to all vehicles and foot patrolmen. The orders for the police were not to arrest Roger, not even to approach him. They were only to find him.

What Scanyon wanted was someone to blame. "I hold you responsible, Dr. Ramez," he barked at the staff shrink. "You and Major Carpenter. How could you let Torraway get into this sort of action without advance warning?"

Ramez said placatingly, "General, I told you Roger was unstable with regard to his wife. That's why I asked for someone like Sulie. He needed another object to fixate on, someone directly connected with the project—"

"Didn't work very well, did it?"

Sulie stopped listening. She knew very well that her turn was next, but she was trying to think. Over Scanyon's desk she saw the moving view from the copter. It was expressed as a schematic, the roads as lines of green, the vehicles as points of blue, buildings yellow. The few pedestrians were bright red. Now, if one of those red dots should suddenly start to move at the speed of a blue vehicle, that would be Roger. But he had had plenty of time to get farther away than the area the copter was covering.

"Tell them to scan the town, General," she said suddenly.

He frowned, but he picked up the phone and gave the order. He didn't get a chance to put it down again; there was an incoming call he could not refuse.

Telly Ramez got up from his chair next to the director and came around to Sulie Carpenter. She didn't look up from the folded transcript of the simulation. He waited patiently.

The director's call was from the President of the United States. They would have known that from the sweat that rolled down beneath Scanyon's temples, even if they had not seen Dash's tiny face in the screen on the director's desk. Faintly the voice leaked through to them: ". . . spoke to Roger he seemed—I don't know, disinterested. I thought it over, Vern, and then I decided to call you. Is everything going all right?"

Scanyon swallowed. He glanced around the table and abruptly folded up the privacy petals on the phone; the image dwindled to postage-stamp size. The voice faded to nothingness as the sound was transferred to a parabolic speaker aimed directly at Scanyon's head, and Scanyon's own words were swallowed by the petal-like shields. The rest of the room had no difficulty in following the conversation anyway; it was written very clearly on Scanyon's face.

Sulie looked up from the transcript at Telly Ramez. "Get him off the phone," she said impatiently. "I know where Roger is."

Ramez said, "At his wife's house."

She rubbed her eyes wearily. "I guess we didn't need a simulation for that, did we? I'm sorry, Telly. 1 guess I wasn't keeping him on the hook as firmly as I thought I was."

They were right, of course, we had known that for some time. As soon as Scanyon got off the phone with the President the security office called to say that the bugs in Dorrie's bedroom had picked up the sound of Roger coming in through the window.

Scanyon's lemony small eyes seemed almost at the point of tears. "Put the sound on the horn," he ordered. "Display the house." And then he switched his phone to an outside line and dialed Dorrie's number.

From the loudspeaker came the sound of one ring, then a metallic noise and Roger's flat cyborg voice rasping, "Hello?" And a moment later, softer but equally toneless, "Christ."

Scanyon jerked the earpiece away and rubbed his ear. "What the hell happened?" he demanded. There was no answer from anyone to the rhetorical question, and gingerly he put the phone back. "I'm getting some kind of trouble signal," he announced.

"We can send a man in, General," the assistant security chief suggested. "There are two of our men in that car out in front of the house there." The helicopter pickup had slid across the screen and settled at 1,800 feet over the Courthouse Square in the city of Tonka. The camera was set for infrared, and in the upper corner of the screen the broad dark band of the Ship Canal identified the edge of the town. A rectangle of darkness surrounded by the moving lights of cars just below the screen's center point was the Courthouse Square, and Roger's home was marked with a tracer star in red. The assistant reached up and touched the blob of light nearby to show the car. "We're in voice contact with them, General," he went on. "They didn't see Colonel Torraway go in."

Sulie stood up. "I don't recommend it," she said.

"Your recommendations aren't too popular with me right now, Major Carpenter," Scanyon snarled.

"All the same, General—" She stopped as Scanyon raised his hand.

From the speaker Dorrie's voice came faintly: *I want a cup of tea.* And then Roger's: *Wouldn't you rather I made you a drink?* And her almost inaudible *No.*

"All the same," Sulie spoke up, "he's stable enough now. Don't screw it up."

"I can't let him just sit out there! Who the hell knows what he'll do next? *You?*"

"You've got him spotted. I don't think he'll move, anyway, not for a while. Don Kayman's not far from there and he's a friend. Tell him to go get Roger."

"Kayman's not much of a combat specialist."

"Is that what you want? If Roger doesn't come back peacefully, exactly what are you going to do about it?"

Do you want some tea?

No. . . . No, thank you.

"And turn that off," Sulie added. "Leave the poor bastard a little privacy."

Scanyon sat slowly back in his chair, patting the top of his desk with both hands at once, very gently. Then he picked up the phone and gave orders. "We'll do it your way one more time, Major," he said. "Not because I have much confidence. I just don't have much choice, either. I can't threaten you with anything. If this goes wrong again, I doubt I'll be in a position to punish anybody. But I'm pretty sure *somebody* will."

Telesforo Ramez said, "Sir, I understand your position, but I think this isn't fair to Sulie. The simulation shows that he has to have a confrontation with his wife."

"The point of a simulation, Dr. Ramez, is that it should tell you what's going to happen *before* it happens."

"Well, it also shows that Torraway is basically pretty stable in every other respect. He'll handle this, General."

Scanyon went back to patting his desk.

Ramez said, "He's a complicated person. You've seen his Thematic Apperception Test patterns, General. He's high in all the fundamental drives: achievement, affiliation—not quite so high in power, but still healthy. He's not a manipulator. He's introspective. He needs to work things out in his head. Those are the qualities you want, General. He'll need all that. You can't ask him to be one person here in Oklahoma and another person on Mars."

"If I'm not mistaken," the general said, "that's what you promised me, with your behavior modification."

"No, General," the psychiatrist said patiently. "I only promised that if you gave him a reward like Sulie Carpenter he'd find it easier to reconcile himself to his problems with his wife. He has."

"B-mod has its own dynamics, General," Sulie put in. "You called me in pretty late."

"What are you telling me?" Scanyon asked dangerously. "Is he going to crack up on Mars?"

"I hope not. The odds are as good as we know how to make them, General. He's cleaned up a lot of old shit; you can see it in his latest TATs. But six days from now he'll be gone, and I won't be in his life any more. And that's wrong. B-mod should *never* be cut off cold turkey. It should be phased out—a little less of me being around and then a little less than that until he's had a chance to build up his defenses."

The gentle patting on the desk was slower now, and Scanyon said, "It's a little late to tell me that."

Sulie shrugged, and did not speak.

Scanyon looked thoughtfully around the table. "All right. We've done all we can here tonight. You're all dismissed until eight—no, make that ten in the morning. By then I expect every one of you to have a report, no more than three minutes long, on where your own area of responsibilities stands, and what we should do."

Don Kayman got the message from a Tonka police patrol car. It swooshed up behind him, lights flashing and siren screaming, and pulled him over to order him to turn around and go back to Roger's apartment.

He knocked on the door with some trepidation, unsure of what he would find. And when the door opened, with Roger's gleaming eyes peering out from behind it, Kayman whispered a quick Hail Mary as he tried to look past Roger into the apartment—for what? For the dismembered body of Dorrie Torraway? For a shambles of destruction? But all he saw was Dorrie herself, huddled in a wing chair and obviously weeping. The sight almost pleased him, since he had been prepared for so much worse.

Roger came along with no argument. "Goodbye, Dorrie," he said, and did not wait for an answer. He had trouble fitting himself into Don Kayman's little car, but his wings folded down. By pushing the reclining seat back as far as it would go he was able to manage, in a cramped and precarious position that would have been hopelessly uncomfortable for any normal human being. Roger, of course, was not a normal human being. His muscular system was content with prolonged overloads in almost any configuration it could bend into at all.

They were silent until they were almost at the project. Then Don Kayman cleared his throat. "You had us worried."

"I thought I would," said the flat cyborg voice. The wings stirred restlessly, writhing against each other like a rubbing of hands. "I wanted to see her, Don. It was important to me."

"I can understand that." Kayman turned into the broad, empty parking lot. "Well?" he probed. "Are things all right?"

The cyborg mask turned toward him. The great compound eyes gleamed like faceted ebony, without expression, as Roger said: "You're a jerk, Father Kayman, sir. How all right can they be?"

Sulie Carpenter thought wistfully of sleep, as she might think of a vacation on the French Riviera. They were equally out of the question at that moment. She took two caps of amphetamines and a B-12 injection, self-administered into the places in her arm she had learned to locate long ago.

The simulation of Roger's reactions had been compromised by the power failure, so she did it over again from punch-in to readout. We were content that this should be so. It gave us a chance to make a few corrections.

While she was waiting she took a long, hot soak in a hydrotherapy tub, and when the simulation had run she studied it carefully. She had taught herself to read the cryptic capital letters and integers, to guard against programming errors, but this time she spared the hardware no time and went at once to the plain-language readout at the end. She was very good at her job.

That job did not happen to be ward nurse. Sulie Carpenter had been one of the first of the aerospace female doctors. She had her degree in medicine, had specialized in psychotherapy, all the myriad eclectic disciplines of it, and had gone into the space program because nothing on Earth seemed really worth doing to her. After completing astronaut training she had come to wonder if there was anything in space that was worth doing either. Research had seemed at least abstractly worth while, so she had applied for work with the California study teams and got it. There had been a fair number of men in her life, one or two of them important to it. None of them had worked out. That much of what she had told Roger had been true; and after the most recent bruising failure she had contracted her area of interest until, she told herself, she grew up enough to know what she wanted from a man. And there she stayed, sidetracked in a loop off the main current of human affairs, until we turned up her card out of all the hundreds of thousands of punched cards, to fill Roger's need.

When her orders came, wholly without warning, they were directly from the President himself. There was no way she could have refused the assignment. Actually she had no desire to. She welcomed the change. Mother-henning a hurting human being stroked the feelgood centers of her personality; the importance of the job was clear to her, because if there was any faith in her it was in the Mars project; and she was aware of her competence. Of competence she had a great deal. We rated her very high, a major piece in the game we were playing for the survival of the race.

When she had finished with Roger's simulation it was nearly four in the morning.

She slept a couple of hours in a borrowed bed in the nurses' quarters. Then she showered, dressed and put her green contact lenses in. She was not happy with that particular aspect of her job, she reflected on the way to Roger's room. The dyed hair and the change of eye color were deceptions; she did not like to deceive. One day she would like to leave out the contacts and let her hair go back to its muddy blond—oh, maybe helped out a little with a rinse, to be sure; she did not object to artifice, only to pretending to be something she wasn't.

But when she entered Roger's room she was smiling. "Lovely to see you back. We missed you. How was it, running around on your own?"

"Not bad at all," said the flat voice. Roger was standing by the window, staring out at the blobs of tumbleweed lumping and bouncing across the parking lot. He turned to her. "You know, it's all true, what you said. What I've got now isn't just different, it's better."

She resisted the desire to reinforce what he had said, and only smiled as she began to strip his bed. "I was worried about sex," he went on. "But you know what, Sulie? It's like being told I can't have any caviar for the next couple of years. I don't like caviar. And when you come right down to it, I don't want sex right now. I suppose you punched that into the computer? 'Cut down sex drive, increase euphoria'? Anyway, it finally penetrated my little brain that I was just making trouble for myself, worrying about whether I could get along without something I really didn't want. It's a reflection of what I think other people think I should want."

"Acculturation," she supplied.

"No doubt," he said. "Listen, I want to do something for you."

He picked up the guitar, propped himself against the window frame with one heel against the sill, and settled the instrument across his knee. His wings quietly rearranged themselves over his head as he began to play.

Sulie was startled. He was not merely playing; he was singing. Singing? No, it was a sound more like a man whistling through his teeth, faint but pure. His fingers on the guitar strummed and plucked an accompaniment while the keening whistle from his lips flowed through the melody of a tune she had never heard before.

When he had finished she demanded, "What was *that*?"

"It's a Paganini sonata for guitar and violin," he said proudly. "Clara gave me the record."

"I didn't know you could do that. Humming, I mean—or whatever it was."

"I didn't either until I tried. I can't get enough volume for the violin part, of course. And I can't keep the guitar sound low enough to balance it, but it didn't sound bad, did it?"

"Roger," she said, meaning it, "I'm impressed."

He looked up at her and impressed her again by managing a smile. He said, "I bet you didn't know I could do *that*, either. I didn't know it myself till I tried."

At the meeting Sulie said flatly, "He's ready, General."

Scanyon had managed enough sleep to look rested, and enough of something else, some inner resource or whatever, to look less harried. "You're sure, Major Carpenter?"

She nodded her head. "He'll never be readier." She hesitated. Vern Scanyon, reading her expression, waited for the amendment. "The problem, as I see it, is that he's right to go *now*. All his systems are up to operating level. He's worked through his thing with his wife. He's ready. The longer he stays around here, the more chance that she'll do something to upset his balance."

"I doubt that very much," said Scanyon, frowning.

"Well, she knows what trouble she'll be in. But I don't want to take that chance, I want him to move."

"You mean take him down to Merritt Island?"

"No. I want to put him on hold."

Brad spilled coffee from the cup he had been raising to his lips. "No way, sweetie!" he cried, genuinely shocked. "I have seventy-two more hours testing on his systems! If you slow him down I can't get readings—"

"Testing for what, Dr. Bradley? For his operating efficiency, or for the sake of the papers you're going to write on him?"

"Well—Christ, certainly I'm going to write him up. But I want to check him as thoroughly as possible, every minute I can, for his sake. And for the mission's."

She shrugged. "That's still my recommendation. There's nothing for him to do here but wait. He's had enough of that."

"What if something goes wrong on Mars?" Brad demanded.

She said, "You wanted my recommendation. That's it."

Scanyon put in, "Please make sure we all know what you're talking about. Especially me."

Sulie looked toward Brad, who said, "We've planned to do that for the voyage, General, as you know. We have the capacity to override his internal clocks by external computer mediation. There are—let's see— five days and some hours to launch; we can slow him down so that his subjective time is maybe thirty minutes over that period. It makes sense —but what I said makes sense, too, and I can't take the responsibility for letting him out of my hands until I've made every test I want to make."

Scanyon scowled. "I understand what you're saying; it's a good point, and I've got a point of my own, too. What happened to what you were saying last night, Major Carpenter? About not cutting off his behavior modification too abruptly."

Sulie said, "He's at a plateau stage, General. If I could have another six months with him I'd take it. Five days, no; there's more risk than there is benefit. He's found a real interest in his guitar—you should hear him. He's built up really structurally good defenses in regard to his lack of sexual organs. He has even taken things into his own hands by running out last night—that's a major step, General; his profile was much too passive to be good, when you consider the demands of this mission. I say put him on hold now."

"And I say I need more time with him," flared Brad. "Maybe Sulie's right. But I'm right too, and I'll take it to the President if I have to!"

Scanyon looked thoughtfully at Brad, then around the room. "Any other comments?"

Don Kayman put in, "For what it's worth, I agree with Sulie. He's not happy about his wife, but he's not shaken up either. This is as good a place as any for him to go."

"Yeah," said Scanyon, gently patting the desk top again. He looked into space, and then said, "There's something none of you know. Your simulation isn't the only one of Roger that has been done lately." He looked at each face and emphasized, "This is not to be discussed with *anyone* outside this room. The Asians are doing one of their own. They've tapped into our 3070 circuits somewhere between here and the two other computers and stolen all the data, and they've used it to make their own simulation."

"Why?" Don Kayman demanded, only a beat before the others at the table.

"That's what I wish I knew," said Scanyon heavily. "They're not interfering. We wouldn't have known about it if it wasn't for a routine line check that uncovered their tap—and then some cloak and dagger stuff in Peking that I don't know about and don't want to. All they did was read everything out and make their own program. We don't know what use they are going to make out of it, but there's a surprise in it. Right after that they dropped their protest against the launch. In fact, they offered the use of their Mars orbiter to expedite telemetry for the mission."

"I wouldn't trust them as far as I could throw them!" Brad flared.

"Well, we're not going to put much reliance on their bird, you can bet on that. But there it is: they say they want the mission to work. Well," he said, "that's just one more complication, but it all comes down to a single decision right now, correct? I have to make up my mind whether or not to put Roger on hold. Okay. I'll do it. I accept your recommendation, Major Carpenter. Tell Roger what we're going to do, and tell him whatever you and Dr. Ramez think you should about why. As for you, Brad"—he raised his hand to ward off Brad's protests— "I know what you're going to say. I agree. Roger needs more time with you. Well, he'll get it. I'm ordering you along on the mission." He slid a sheet of paper closer to him on his desk, crossed out one name on a list, wrote in another. "I'm going to drop one of the pilots to make room for you. I already checked. There's plenty of back-up, with the machine guidance systems and the fact that you all have had some pilot training anyhow. That's the final crew roster for the Mars launch: Torraway, Kayman, General Hesburgh as pilot—and you."

Brad protested. It was only a reflex. Once the idea had settled in he accepted it. What Scanyon had said was true enough, and besides, Brad perceived instantly that the career he had programmed for himself could not help but be enhanced by actual physical participation in the mission itself. It would be a pity to leave Dorrie, and all the Dorries, but there would be so *many* Dorries when he got back . . .

And everything else followed as the night the day. That was the last decision. Everything else was only implementation. On Merritt Island the crews began fueling the launch vehicle. The rescue ships were deployed across the Atlantic in case of failure. Brad was flown to the island for his fitting, with six ex-astronauts detailed to cram in all the touch-up teaching he needed and could get in the time available. Hesburgh was one of them, short, sure and smiling, his demeanor a constant reassurance. Don Kayman took a precious twelve-hour relief to say good-bye to his nun.

With all of this we were quite content. We were content with the decision to send Brad along. We were content with the trendline extrapolations that every day showed more positive results from the effect of the launch on world opinion and events. We were content with Roger's state of mind. And with the NPA simulation of Roger we were most content of all; in fact, that was an essential to our plans for the salvation of the race.

Thirteen
When We Pass
the Point of No Return

The long Hohmann-orbit trip to Mars takes seven months. All previous astronauts, cosmonauts and sinonauts had found them very wearing months indeed. Each day had 86,400 seconds to fill, and there was very little to fill them with.

Roger was different from all the others in two ways. First, he was the most precious passenger any spaceship had yet carried. In and around his body were the fruits of seven billion Man Plus dollars. To the maximum extent possible, he had to be spared.

The other way was that, uniquely, he *could* be spared.

His body clocks had been disconnected. His perception of time was what the computer told him it should be.

They slowed him down gradually, at first. People began to seem to move a little more briskly. Mealtime came sooner than he was ready for it. Voices grew shriller.

When that phased in nicely, they increased the retardation in his systems. Voices passed into high-pitched gibberish, and then out of his perception entirely. He hardly saw people at all, except as flickers of motion. They sealed off his room from the day—it was not to keep him from escaping, it was to protect him from the quick transition from day to night. Platters of room-temperature, picnic-style food appeared before him. When he had begun to push them away to signal he was done or didn't want them, they whisked out of sight.

Roger knew what was being done to him. He didn't mind. He accepted Sulie's promise that it was good, and needful, and all right. He thought he was going to miss Sulie and looked for a way to tell her so.

There was a way, but it all went so rapidly; messages were chalked as if by magic on a board in front of him. When he responded, he found his answers snatched away and erased before he was quite sure he was through:

HOW ARE YOU FEELING?

Pick up the chalk, write one word.

FINE

and then the board is gone, brought back with another message—

WE'RE TAKING YOU TO MERRITT ISLAND.

And his reply:

I'M READY.

snatched away before he could add the rest, which he scrawled rapidly on his bedside table—

GIVE MY LOVE TO DORRIE

He had intended to add "and Sulie," but there was no time; suddenly the table was gone. He was gone from the room. There was a sudden dizzying lurch of movement. He caught a quick glimpse of the ambulance entrance to the project, and a quick phantom glimpse of a nurse—was it Sulie?—with her back to him, adjusting her panty hose. His whole bed seemed to leap into the air, into a brutal blaze of winter sunlight, then into—what? A car? Before he could even question, it sprang into the air, and he realized that it was a helicopter, and then that he was very close to being sick. He felt his gorge rising in his throat.

The telemetry faithfully reported, and the controls were adequate to the problem. He still felt he would like to vomit, feeling himself thrown around as though in the most violent sort of cross-chop sea, but he did not.

Then they stopped.

Out of the helicopter.

Bright sunlight again.

Into something else—which he recognized, after it had begun to move, as the interior of a CB-5, fitted up as a hospital ship. Safety webbing spun magically around him.

It was not comfortable—there was still the hammering and the twisting vertigo, though not as unbearable—but it did not last long. A minute or two, it seemed to Roger. Then pressure smote his ears and they were taking him out of the plane, into blinding heat and light—Florida, of course, he realized tardily; but by then he was in an ambulance, then out of it . . .

Then, for a time that seemed to Roger ten or fifteen minutes and was actually the better part of a day, nothing happened except that he was in a bed, and was fed, and his wastes were removed by catheter, and then a note appeared before him:

GOOD LUCK, ROGER, WE'RE ON OUR WAY.

and then a steam hammer smote him from underneath and he lost consciousness. It is all very well, he thought, to spare me the inconvenience of boredom, but you may be killing me to do it. But before he could think of a way to communicate this to anyone he was out.

Time passed. A time of dreams.

He realized groggily that they had been keeping him sedated, not only slowed down but asleep; and in realizing this, he was awake.

There was no feeling of pressure. In fact, he was floating. Only a spiderweb of retaining straps kept him in place.

He was in space.

A voice spoke next to his ear: "Good morning, Roger. This is a tape recording."

He turned his head and found a tiny speaker grille next to his ear.

"We've slowed it down so that you can understand it. If you want to speak to us, you just tape what you want to say, in a minute. Then we'll speed it up so *we* can understand it. Ain't science grand?

"Anyway, we're into day thirty-one as I tape this. In case you don't remember me any more, I'm Don Kayman. You had a little trouble. Your muscle system fought against the takeoff acceleration, and you pulled some ligaments. We had to do a little surgery. You're mending nicely. Brad rebuilt part of the cybernetics, and you probably can handle the deltas when we land in good shape. Let's see. There's nothing else important to say, and probably you have some questions, but before you take your turn there's a message for you."

And the tape whispered scratchily for a moment, and then Dorrie's voice came on, bent and attenuated. Over a background hiss of static she said: "Hi, honey. Everything's fine back home, and I'm keeping the home fires burning for you. I think of you. Take care of yourself."

And then Kayman's voice again: "Now here's what you do. First off, if there's anything important—if you hurt, or anything like that—tell us that right away. There's a lot of real-time loss in this, so say the important stuff first, and when you're through just hold up your hand while we change tapes, and then you can go on to the chitchat. Now go."

And the tape stopped, and a small red light that had said "Play" next to the speaker grille went out, and a green one came on to say "Record." He picked up the microphone and was getting ready to say that no, there wasn't any particular problem, when he happened to look down and notice that his right leg was missing.

· · ·

We were, of course, monitoring every moment in the spacecraft.

The communication link had stretched pretty thin even after the first month. The geometry was troublesome. While the spacecraft was climbing out toward Mars's orbit, Mars was moving. So was the Earth, and a good deal faster. It would go around the sun almost twice before Mars completed a single one of its orbits. The telemetry from the spacecraft now took something like three minutes to reach Goldstone. We were passive listeners. It would get worse. Any command from Earth would come half an hour late by the time the spacecraft was circling Mars, round-trip time at the speed of light. We had surrendered instant control; the ship and its passengers were effectively on their own.

Later still the Earth and Mars would be on opposite sides of the sun. The weak signals from the spacecraft would be so compromised by solar interference that we would not even receive reliably. But by then the 3070 would be in orbit, and shortly thereafter the MHD generator would join it. Then there would be plenty of power for everything. It was all planned out, where each would go, how they would interlink with each other, with the orbiting ship, with the ground station and with Roger, wherever he might roam.

We launched the 3070, powered down into stand-by mode. It was a robot run. The ionization risk turned out, on analysis, to be unacceptable in a spacecraft of normal configuration, so the Cape engineers stripped away all the life support, all the telemetry, the demolition system and half of the maneuver capability. The weight went into shielding. Once it was launched it was silent and lifeless, and would stay that way for seven months. Then General Hesburgh would capture control and play both ends of the docking maneuver. It would be difficult, but that was what he was paid for.

We launched the MHD generator a month later, with a crew of two volunteers and a maximum of publicity. Everyone was interested now. And no one objected, not even the NPA. They disdained the first launch. They acknowledged tracking the launch of the 3070 and offered their data to the NASA net. When the generator went up, their ambassador sent a polite note of congratulations.

Clearly something was happening.

It was not all psychological. New York City had two straight weeks without rioting, and garbage was collected from some of the main streets. Winter rains put out the last of the great fires in the Northwest, and the governors of Washington, Oregon, Idaho and California sent out a joint call for volunteers. More than a hundred thousand young people signed up to replant the mountain slopes.

The President of the United States was the last to notice the change;

he was too busy with the internal disasters of a nation that had overbred and overspent itself into tragedy. But the time came when he realized there had been a change, not only within the United States but world-wide, not only in a change in mood but in a change in tactics. The Asians withdrew their nuclear subs to the waters of the Western Pacific and the Indian Ocean, and when Dash got confirmation of that he picked up the phone and called Vern Scanyon.

"I think—" He paused, and reached out to touch the smooth wood of his desk top. "I think it's working. Pat your staff on the back for me. Now, what else do you need?"

But there was nothing.

We were fully committed now. We had gone as far as we could go, and the rest was up to the expedition itself.

Fourteen
Missionary to Mars

Not more than six times a day Don Kayman allowed himself to pray. He prayed for various things—sometimes for relief from the sound of Titus Hesburgh sucking his teeth, sometimes to be spared the smell of stale farts that smogged the interior of the spacecraft—but there were always three petitions in each prayer: the success of the mission, the fulfillment of God's plan for Man and, most particularly, the health and well-being of his friend Roger Torraway.

Roger had the distinction of a private stateroom of his own. It was not much of a room, and the privacy was only an elastic curtain, gossamer thin and not wholly opaque; but it was all his. The other three shared the crew cabin. Sometimes Roger shared it, too, or at least parts of Roger did. He was all over the place, Roger was.

Kayman looked in on him often. The trip was a long, dull time for him. His own specialty, which was of course not operative until they actually set foot on the surface of Mars, needed no touch-up or practice. Areology was a static science, and would remain so until he himself, hopefully, added something to it after landing. So he had let Titus Hesburgh teach him the instrument board, and a little later had let Brad teach him something about fieldstripping a cyborg. The grotesque form that slowly writhed and postured in its foam cocoon was no longer unfamiliar. Kayman knew every inch of it, inside and out. As the weeks wore on he lost the abhorrence that had deterred him from wrenching an eye from its socket or opening a panel into a plastic-lined gut.

It was not all he had to do. He had his music tapes to listen to, an occasional microfiche to read, games to play. At chess he and Titus Hesburgh were pretty evenly matched. They played interminable tournaments, best 38 games out of 75, and used their personal comm allotments to have chess texts radioed up to them from Earth. It would have been relaxing for Father Kayman to pray more, but after the first week it had occurred to him that even prayer could be carried to excess. He rationed it out: on awakening, before meals, in midevening and before retiring. That was all. That was not, of course, to count the quick lift from a Paternoster or from telling His Holiness's rosary. And then he would go back to the endless refurbishing of Roger. He had always had a queasy stomach, but obviously Roger was oblivious to these invasions of his person and took no harm from them. Kayman gradually began to appreciate the inner beauty of Roger's anatomy, both that part which was Man's handiwork and that part which was God's; he gave thanks for both.

He could not quite give thanks for what God and man had done to the interior of Roger's mind. It troubled him that seven months were being stolen out of his friend's life. It drew forth compassion that Roger's love went to a woman who held it cheap.

But, everything considered, Kayman was happy.

He had never been on a Mars mission before, but this was where he belonged. Twice he had been in space: a shuttle run to an orbiter, when he was still a graduate student seeking his doctorate in planetology; then a ninety-day tour in Space Station Betty. Both were acknowledged to be mere practice for the mission that would complete his study of Mars.

All that he knew of Mars he had learned telescopically or deductively or from the observations of others. He knew a lot of that. He had played and replayed the synoptic tapes of all the Orbiters and Mariners and Surveyors. He had analyzed returned bits of soil and rock. He had interviewed every one of the Americans, French and British who had landed in their various Mars expeditions, and most of the Russians, Japanese and Chinese as well.

He knew all about Mars. He always had.

As a child he had grown up on the Edgar Rice Burroughs Mars, the colorful Barsoom of the ocher dead sea bottoms and hurtling tiny moons. As he grew older he distinguished fact from fiction. There was no reality in the four-armed green warriors and the red-skinned, egg-laying, beautiful Martian princesses, to the extent that science was in touch with "reality." But he knew that scientists' estimates of "reality" changed from year to year. Burroughs had not invented Barsoom out of airy imaginings. He had taken it almost verbatim from the most authoritative scientific "reality" of his day. It was Percival Lowell's Mars, not Burroughs's, that was finally denied by bigger telescopes and by space probes. In the "reality" of scientific opinion, life on Mars had been born and died a dozen times.

But even that had never been settled, really. It depended on a philosophical question. What was "life"? Did it have to mean a creature that resembled an ape or an oak tree? Did it necessarily mean a creature which dissolved its nutrients in a water-based biology, took part in an oxidation-reduction cycle of energy transfer, reproduced itself and grew thereby from the environment? Don Kayman did not think so. He considered it arrogance to limit "life" so parochially, and he was humble in the face of his Creator's all-potentiating majesty.

In any case, the case for life genetically related to Earth life was still open. Well, ajar. True, no ape or oak tree had been found. Not even a lichen. Not even a growing cell. Not even (he had to confess with rue, because Dejah Thoris died hard in his bosom) such prerequisites as free oxygen or water.

But Kayman did not accept that the fact that because no one had slipped on a bed of Martian moss, there was none anywhere on Mars to slip on. Less than a hundred human beings had ever set foot on Mars. The combined area of their explorations was only a matter of a few hundred square miles. On Mars! Where there were no oceans, so the land surface to explore was greater than the Earth's! It was almost like pretending to know the Earth by making four quick trips to the Sahara, the top of the Himalayas, Antarctica and the Greenland icecap . . .

Well, no, Kayman conceded to himself. That wasn't strictly fair. There had been innumerable fly-bys and orbiters, surveyors that landed and snatched up samples of soil.

Nevertheless, the principle was sound. There was too much of Mars. No one could pretend that it did not possess secrets still. Water might yet be found. Some of the rifts looked hopeful. Some of the valleys had shapes that could hardly be understood unless you assumed they were carved out by streams. Even if they were dry there still might be water, vast oceans of water even, locked under the surface. Oxygen one knew was present. Not a great deal on the average, but averages were not important. Locally there could be plenty. And so there might be . . .

Life.

Kayman sighed. It was one of his great regrets that he had not been able to deflect the decision on a landing place to one of his personal favorites for suspicion of life, the Solis Lacus area. The decision had gone against him. It had been taken on very high authority—in fact, it was

Dash himself who said, "I don't give a leaping shit where something may be alive now. I want to put this bird down where our boy can expect to stay alive the easiest."

So they had picked a spot nearer the equator and in the northern hemisphere; the main features were called Isidius Regio and Nepenthes, and at their interface was a gentle crater that Don Kayman had privately christened *Home*.

Also privately, he regretted the loss of Solis Lacus and its seasonally changing shape (growing plants? Probably not—but one could hope!), the bright W-shaped cloud around the canals of Ulysses and Fortunae that had formed and reformed every afternoon through one long conjunction, the brilliant flash (reflected sunlight? a hydrogen-fusion blast?) that Saheki saw in Tithonius Lacus on the first of December 1951, as bright as a sixth-magnitude star. Somebody else would have to investigate these things. He would not.

But apart from such regrets, he was content enough. The northern hemisphere was a wise choice. Its seasons were better arranged because, just as on Earth, the northern hemisphere had its winter when it was closest to the sun and so kept marginally warmer all year around. Winter there was twenty days shorter than summer; in the south, of course, it was the other way around. And although Home had never been observed to change shape or emit flashes of light, it had in fact been identified with a fair number of recent cloud formations. Kayman had not given up hope that some of the clouds were of water ice, if not water itself! He fantasized afternoon thundershowers on the Martian plain, and more soberly thought about the large stretches of limonite that had been identified nearby. Limonite contained bound water in quantity; it would be a resource for Roger, even if no Martian plant or animal had evolved to exploit it.

On the whole, he was content about everything.

He was en route to Mars! That was a source of great joy to him, for which he rendered thanks six times each day. Also he had a hope.

Don Kayman was too good a scientist to confuse his hopes with observations. He would report what he found. But he knew what he *wanted* to find. He wanted to find life.

To the extent that the mission's purposes permitted, in the ninety-one Martian days he would be able to stay on the planet's surface, he would keep his eyes open. Everyone knew he would do this. It was in fact part of his contingent, time-permitting briefing instructions.

What not everyone knew was *why* Kayman was so interested.

Dejah Thoris was not quite dead for him. He still had hope that there would be life; not only life but intelligent life; not only intelligent life, but life with a soul to save and bring to his God.

Everything that happened on the spacecraft was under constant surveillance, and synoptic transmissions took place to Earth regularly. So we kept tabs on them. We watched the chess games and the arguments. We monitored Brad's currycombing of Roger's bodily functions, both meat and metal. We saw the night when Titus Hesburgh wept for five hours, gently and dreamily, rebuffing all of Kayman's offers to sympathize with a smile through tears. In some ways Hesburgh had the lousiest job aboard; seven months coming, seven months going and in between three months of nothing. He would be all alone in orbit while Kayman, Brad and Roger were disporting themselves on the surface. He would be lonely, and he would be bored.

He would be worse than that. Seventeen months in space was a practical guarantee that for the last few decades of his life he would be plagued by a hundred different muscle, bone and circulatory disorders. They exercised faithfully, wrestling each other and struggling against springs, flailing their arms and pumping their legs; that would not be enough. There was inevitably calcium resorption from the bone, and there was loss of muscle tone. For those who landed, the three months on Mars would make a great difference. In that time they would repair much of the damage and be in better shape for the return. For Hesburgh there was no such break. His seventeen months in zero-G would be uninterrupted, and the experience of previous spacefarers had made the consequences clear. It meant lowering his life expectancy by a decade or more. And if he wept once in a while, there was no one who had better reason.

Time passed, time passed. A month, two months, six months. Beyond them in the skies the capsule with the 3070 was climbing after them; behind it, the magnetohydrodynamic power plant with its crew of two. When they were two weeks out they ceremoniously switched watches, changing to new quartz-crystal timepieces set to the Martian day. From then on they lived by the Martian clock. It made little enough practical difference; the day for Mars is just a bit more than thirty-seven minutes longer than Earth's; but the difference was significant in their minds.

One week before arrival, they began to speed Roger up.

For Roger the seven months had felt like thirty hours, subjective time. It had been time enough. He had eaten a few meals, exchanged several dozen communications with the rest of the crew. He had received messages from Earth and returned a few of them. He had asked for his guitar, been refused it on the grounds that he couldn't play it, asked for it anyway out of curiosity and found that that was quite true: he could pluck a string, but he could not hear the note that resulted from it. In fact, apart from the specially slowed-down tapes, he could hear nothing at all most of the time, and only a sort of high-pitched scurrying sound ever. Air did not conduct the sort of vibrations he could perceive. When the tape recorder was out of contact with the metal frame to which he was bound, he could not hear even it, nor could his own voice be made to record.

They warned him they were beginning to accelerate his perceptions. They left the curtain to his cubicle open, and he began to notice flickers of motion. He caught a glimpse of Hesburgh dozing nearby, then saw figures actually moving; after a time he even recognized who they were. Then they put him to sleep, to make final adjustments on his backpack, and when he woke up he was alone, the curtain was drawn—and he heard voices.

He pushed the curtain aside and looked out, and there was the smiling face of his wife's lover greeting him. "Good morning, Roger! Nice to have you with us again."

. . . And eighteen minutes later, twelve travel time and the rest decoding and relaying, the President watched it happen from more than a hundred million miles away, on the screen in the Oval Office.

He was not the only one. The TV nets put the scene on the air, and the satellites rebroadcast it all over the world. They were watching in the Under Palace in Peking, and inside the Kremlin; on Downing Street and the Champs Élysées and Ginza.

"Son of a bitch," said Dash historically, "they've made it."

Vern Scanyon was with him. "Son of a bitch," he echoed. Then he said, "Well, almost made it. They've still got to land."

"Any problem about that?"

Cautiously: "Not as far as I know—"

"God," said the President positively, "would not be so unfair. I think you and I are going to taste some bourbon right now; it's about that time."

They stayed and watched for half an hour, and a quarter of a bottle. On and off over the next few days they watched more, they and the rest of the world. The whole world saw Hesburgh making final checks and preparing the Mars-lander for separation. Watched Don Kayman go through a dry run under the pilot's microscopic observation, since he would be at the controls for the trip down out of orbit. Watched Brad make a final, ultimate recheck on Roger's telemetry, find it all functioning in the green, and then do it over one more time. Watched Roger himself moving about the crew cabin and squeezing into the lander.

And watched the lander separate and Hesburgh look wistfully out at its minus-delta flare as it began to drop out of orbit.

We figured that three and a quarter billion people watched the landing. It was not much to watch; if you have seen one landing you have seen them all. But it was important.

It began at a quarter to four in the morning, Washington time, and the President had himself awakened to see it. "That priest," he said, frowning, "what kind of a pilot is he? If anything goes wrong—"

"He's checked out, sir," soothed his NASA aide. "Anyway, he's actually only about a third-place back-up. The automatic sequencing is in primary control. If anything goes wrong, General Hesburgh is monitoring it from the orbiter and he can override. Father Kayman doesn't have anything to do unless everything goes wrong at once."

Dash shrugged, and the aide noticed that the President's fingers were crossed. "What about the follow-up flights?" he asked, staring at the screen.

"No sweat at all, sir. The computer will inject into Mars orbit in thirty-two days, and the generator twenty-seven days later. As soon as the lander is down General Hesburgh is going to perform a course correction and overtake the moon Deimos. We expect to land both the computer and the generator there, probably in the crater Voltaire; Hesburgh will make that determination for us."

"Um," said the President. "Has Roger been told who's on the generator spacecraft?"

"No, sir."

"Um." The President abandoned the television screen and got up. At the window, staring out at the pretty White House lawn, June-green and blossoming, he said, "There's a man coming over from the computer center in Alexandria. I'd like you to be here when he arrives."

"Yes, sir."

"Commander Chiaroso. Supposed to be pretty good. Used to be a professor at M.I.T. He says there's something strange about our projections about this whole project. Have you heard any gossip?"

"No, sir," said the NASA aide, alarmed. "Strange, sir?"

Dash shrugged. "That's all I need," he said, "getting this whole son-of-a-bitching thing going and then finding out— Hey! What the hell's happening?"

On the TV screen the image was jumping and breaking up; it went out entirely, restored itself and disappeared again, leaving only the tracery of raster.

"That's all right, sir," said the aide quickly. "It's reentry buffeting. When they hit the atmosphere they lose video contact. Even the telemetry's affected, but we've got ample margins all around; it'll be all right."

The President demanded, "Why the hell is that? I thought the whole point was that Mars didn't *have* any atmosphere?"

"Not a lot, sir. But it does have some, and because it's smaller it's got a shallower, flatter gravity well. In the upper atmosphere it's just about as dense as the Earth's is, at the same altitude, and that's where the buffeting happens."

"God damn it," snarled the President, "I don't like surprises! Why didn't somebody tell me this?"

"Well, sir—"

"Never mind! I'll take it up later. I hope surprising Torraway isn't going to be a mistake— Well, forget it. What's happening now?"

The aide looked not at the screen but at his watch. "Parachute deployment, sir. They've completed retrofire. Now it's just a matter of coming down. In a few seconds—" The aide pointed to the screen, which obediently built itself into a picture again. "There! They're in controlled descent mode now."

And they sat and waited while the lander slid down through the thin Martian air under its immense canopy, quintuple the size of a parachute built for air.

When it hit the sound came a hundred million miles, and then sounded like trash cans falling off a roof. But the lander had been built for it; and the crew were long since in their protective cocoons.

There was a hissing sound from the screen and the clicking of cooling metal.

And then Brad's voice. "We're on Mars," he said prayerfully, and Father Kayman began to whisper the words from the Ordinary of the Mass, "*Laudamas te, benedicimus te, adoramus te, glorificamus te. Gloria in excelsis Deo, et in terra pax hominibus bonae voluntatis.*"

And to the familiar words he added, "*Et in Martis.*"

Fifteen
How the Good News Went from Mars to Earth

When we first realized that there was a serious risk that a major war would destroy civilization and make the Earth uninhabitable—which is to say, shortly after we collectively began to realize anything at all—we decided to take steps to colonize Mars.

It wasn't easy for us.

The whole human race was in trouble. Energy was in short supply the world over, which meant fertilizer was expensive, which meant people were hungry, which meant explosively dangerous tensions. The world's resources were none too ample for the bare necessity of keeping billions of people alive. We had to find ways to divert capacities that were badly needed elsewhere to long-range planning. We set up three separate think tanks and gave them all the facilities we could steal from daily needs. One explored options for solving the growing tensions on Earth. One was charged with setting up refuges on Earth itself, so that even if a thermonuclear war did occur a small fraction of us could survive.

The third looked into extraterrestrial possibilities.

In the beginning it seemed as though we had a thousand options to choose from, and each of the three major tracks had branches that looked hopeful. One by one the tracks closed off. Our best estimates—not the ones we gave the President of the United States, but the private ones we showed to nobody but ourselves—were of point nine to ten nines probability of thermonuclear war within a decade; and we closed down the center for solving international tensions in the first year. Setting up refuges was a little more hopeful. It developed that worst-case analysis indicated a few places on the Earth that would be unlikely to experience direct attack—Antarctica, parts of the Sahara, even some of Australia and a number of islands. Ten sites were selected. Each one had only a point zero one or less probability of being destroyed; if all ten were considered, the probability that they would all be destroyed was relatively insignificant. But fine-grain analysis showed that there were two flaws. For one, we could not be sure how much long-life isotope would remain in the atmosphere after such a war, and the indications were that there would be excessive levels of ionizing radiation for as much as a thousand years. Over that time scale, the probability that even one of the refuges would survive became far less than point five. Worst of all, there was the necessity for capital investment. To build the refuges underground and fill them with the immense quantity needed of complex electronic equipment, generators, fuel reserves and so on was, as a practical matter, impossible. There was no way for us to get the money.

So we terminated that think tank and put all the resources we could manage into extraterrestrial colonization. At the beginning, that had looked like the least hopeful solution of all.

But—almost!—we had managed to make it work. When Roger Torraway landed, that completed the first and hardest step. By the time the ships that were following him reached their positions, in orbit or on the surface of the planet, we would be able, for the first time, to plan for a future, with the survival of the race assured.

So we watched with great satisfaction as Roger stepped out on the surface of the planet.

Roger's backpack computer was a triumph of design. It had three separate systems, cross-linked and sharing facilities, but with enough redundancy so that all systems had point nine reliability at least until the 3070 backup computer reached orbit. One system mediated his perceptions. Another controlled the subsystems of nerve and muscle that let him walk and move. The third telemetered all of his inputs. Whatever he saw, we saw on Earth.

We had gone to some trouble to arrange this. By Shannon's Law there was not enough band width to transmit everything, but we had included a random sampling feature. Approximately one bit per hundred was transmitted—first to the radio in the landing craft, where we had assigned one channel permanently for that purpose. Then it was rebroadcast to the orbiter, where General Hesburgh floated, watching the television screen while the calcium oozed out of his bones. From there, cleaned and amplified, it was burst-transmitted to whichever synchronous satellite of Earth was at that moment locked into both Mars and Goldstone. So what we all saw was only about one percent "real." But that was enough. The rest was filled in by a comparison program we had written for the Goldstone receiver. Hesburgh saw only a series of stills; on Earth we broadcast what looked exactly like on-the-spot movies of whatever Roger saw.

So all over the Earth, on television sets in every country, people watched the beige and brown mountains that rose ten miles tall, saw the glint of Martian sunlight off the window frames of the lander, could even read the expression on Father Kayman's face as he rose from prayer and for the first time looked out on Mars.

In the Under Palace in Peking the great lords of New People's Asia interrupted a planning session to watch the screen. Their feelings were mixed. It was America's triumph, not theirs. In the Oval Office President Deshatine's joy was pure. Not only was the triumph American, it was personal; he was identified forever as the President who had established humanity on Mars. Almost everybody was at least a little joyous—even Dorrie Torraway, who sat in the private room at the back of her shop with her chin in her hands, studying the message of her husband's eyes. And of course in the great white cube of the project outside of Tonka, Oklahoma, everyone left on the staff watched the pictures from Mars almost all the time.

They had plenty of leisure for that. They didn't have much else to do. It was astonishing how empty the building became as soon as Roger was out of it.

They had all been rewarded, from the stockroom boys up: a personal commendation for everyone from the President, plus a thirty-day bonus leave and a jump in grade. Clara Bly used hers to finish up her long-delayed honeymoon. Weidner and Freeling took the time to write a rough draft of Brad's paper, transmitting every paragraph to him in orbit as it came off their typewriters, and receiving his corrections via Goldstone. Vern Scanyon, of course, had a hero's tour with the President, in fifty-four states and the principal cities of twenty foreign countries. Brenda Hartnett had appeared on television twice with her kids. They had been deluged with gifts. The widow of the man who had died to put Roger Torraway on Mars was now a millionaire. They had all had their hour of fame, as soon as the launch got off and Roger was en route, especially in those moments just before the landing.

Then the world looked out at Mars through the eyes of Roger, and the senses of the brother on Roger's back, and all their fame blew away. From then on it was all Roger.

We watched too.

We saw Brad and Don Kayman in their suits, completing the pre-egress drill. Roger had no need of a suit. He stood on tiptoe at the door of the lander, poised, sniffing the empty wind, his great black wings hovering behind him and soaking in the rays of the disconcertingly tiny, but disconcertingly bright, sun. Through the TV pick-up inside the lander we saw Roger silhouetted against the dull beige and brown of the abrupt Martian horizon. . . .

And then through Roger's eyes we saw what he saw. To Roger, looking out on the bright, jewel-like colors of the planet he was meant to live on, it was a fairyland, beautiful and inviting.

The lander had stretched out skeletal magnesium steps to stroke the surface of Mars, but Roger didn't need them. He jumped down, the wings fluttering—for balance, not for lift—and landed lightly on the chalky orange surface, where the wash of the landing rockets had scoured away the crust. He stood there for a moment, surveying his kingdom with the great faceted eyes. "Don't rush things," advised a voice in his head that came from Don Kayman's suit radio. "Better go through the exercise list."

Roger grinned without looking around; "Sure," he said, and began to move away. First he walked, then trotted; then he began to run. If he had sped through the streets of Tonka, here he was a blur. He laughed out loud. He changed the frequency responses of his eyes, and the distant towering hills flashed bright blue, the flat plain a mosaic of greens and yellows and reds. "This is great!" he whispered, and the receivers at the lander picked up the subspoken words and passed them on to Earth.

"Roger," said Brad petulantly, "I wish you'd take it easy until we get the jeep ready."

Roger turned. The other two were back at the steps of the lander, deploying the Mars vehicle from its fold-down condition behind its hatch.

He bounded back toward them joyously. "Need help?"

They didn't have to answer. They did need help; in their suits it was a major undertaking to slip the retaining strap off one of the basket-work wheels. "Move over," he said, and quickly freed the wheels and stretched the stilted legs into stand-by position. The jeep had both: wheels for the flat parts, stilts for climbing. It was meant to be the most flexible vehicle man could make for getting around Mars, but it wasn't. Roger was. When it was done he touched them and promised, "I won't go out of line of sight." And then he was gone, off to see the patches of color around a series of hummocks, Dali-bright and irresistible.

"That's dangerous!" Brad grumbled over the radio. "Wait till we finish testing the jeep! If anything happens to you we're in trouble."

"Nothing will," said Roger, "and no!" He couldn't wait. He was using his body for what it had been built to do, and patience was gone. He ran. He jumped. He found himself two kilometers from the lander before he knew it; looked back, saw that they were creeping slowly after him and went on. His oxygenation system stepped up the pump-rate to compensate for the extra demands; his muscles met the challenge smoothly. It was not his muscles that propelled him but the servo-systems that had been built in instead; but it was the tiny muscles at the ends of the nerves that ordered the servos. All the practice paid off. It was no effort at all to reach two hundred kilometers an hour, leaping over small cracks and craters, bounding up and down the slopes of larger ones.

"Come back, Roger!" It was Don Kayman, sounding worried.

A pause while Roger ran on; then a dizzying sense of movement in his vision, and another voice said, "Go back, Roger! It's time."

He stopped flatfooted, skidded, flailed with his wings against the almost indetectable air, almost fell and caught himself. The familiar voice chuckled, "Come on, honey! Be a good boy and go back now."

Dorrie's voice.

And out of the distant thin whirl of drifting sand the colors coalesced into the shape of Dorrie to match the voice of Dorrie, smiling, not ten meters away, long legs disappearing into shorts, a gay halter for a top, her hair blown in the breeze.

The radio voice in his head laughed, this time in the tones of Don Kayman. "Surprised you, didn't we?"

It took a moment for Roger to reply. "Yeah," he managed.

"It was Brad's idea. We taped Dorrie back on Earth. When you need an emergency signal, Dorrie will give it to you."

"Yeah," said Roger again. As he stared, the smiling figure turned wispy, the colors faded, and it disappeared.

He turned and went back. The return trip took a lot longer than the joyous outbound run, and the colors were no longer quite so bright.

Don Kayman drove the jeep steadily toward the trudging shape of Roger Torraway, trying to get the hang of staying in the plunging seat without being thrown back and forth into the restraining belts. It was in no way comfortable. The suit that had been tailored to his body had developed tight spots and loose ones in the long months up from Earth —or maybe, he reminded himself fairly, he was the one who had swelled a little in some places and shrunk in others—he had not, he conceded, been wholly diligent about his exercises. Also he had to go to the bathroom. There was relief plumbing in the suit. He knew how to use it, but he didn't want to.

Above the discomfort was an overlay of envy and worry. The envy was a sin that he could purge himself of, whenever he could find someone to hear his confession—a venial sin at most, he thought, considering the manifest advantages Roger had over the other two. Worry was a worse sin, not against his God but against the success of the mission. It was too late to worry. Maybe it had been a mistake to set up the simulation of Roger's wife to punch home urgent messages—at the time, he hadn't known quite how complicated Roger's feelings were about Dorrie. But it was too late to do anything about it.

Brad didn't seem to have any worries. He was chuckling fondly over Roger's performance. "Did you notice?" he was demanding. "Didn't fall once! Perfect coordination. Normative match, bio and servo. I tell you, Don, we've got it knocked!"

"It's a little early to tell," Kayman said uneasily, but Brad went on. Kayman thought of turning off the voice in his suit helmet, but it was almost as easy to turn off his attention. He looked around him. They had landed near the sunrise terminator, but they had used more than half the Martian day in pre-exit check and in putting the jeep together. It was becoming late afternoon. They would have to be back before it was dark, he told himself. Roger would be able to navigate by starlight, but it would be chancier for Brad and him. Maybe some other time, after they had had the practice. . . . He really wanted that very much, to stroll the ebony surface of a Barsoomian night, with the stars pinpoints of colored fire in a velvet black sky. But not yet.

They were on a great cratered plain. The size was hard to estimate at first. Looking around through his faceplate Kayman had trouble remembering how far away the mountains were. His mind knew, because he knew every grid-square of the Martian maps for two hundred kilometers around their impact point. But his senses were deceived by the absolutely transparent visibility. The mountains to the west, he was aware, were a hundred kilometers away and nearly ten kilometers high. They looked like nearby foothills.

He clutched the jeep down and stopped it; they were within a few meters of Roger. Brad fumbled himself free and slid clumsily out of the seat, lurching in an ungainly slow gait over toward Roger to study him. "Everything all right?" he said anxiously. "Of course it is; I can see that. How's your balance? Close your eyes, will you—I mean, you know, shut off your vision." He peered anxiously at the faceted hemispheres. "Did you? I can't tell, you know."

"I did," said Roger through the radio in his head.

"Great! No sense of dizziness, eh? No trouble keeping your balance? Keeping your eyes closed," he went on, circling Roger and staring at him from all angles, "swing your arms up and down a few times—fine! Now windmill them, opposite directions—" Kayman couldn't see his face, but he could hear the broad grin in the tone of Brad's voice. "Beautiful, Roger! Optimal all the way!"

"My congratulations to you both," said Kayman, out of the vehicle and watching the performance. "Roger?"

The head turned toward him, and though there was nothing about the appearance of the eyes that changed, Kayman knew Roger was looking at him. "I only wanted to say," he went on, not quite sure where the sentence was going to go, "that I'm—well, I'm sorry we sprang that bit about using Dorrie's image to convey messages on you. I have a feeling we've given you too many surprises."

"It's all right, Don." The trouble with Roger's voice, Kayman reflected again, was that you couldn't tell much from its tone.

"Having said that much," he said, "I think I ought to tell you that we do have another surprise for you. A pleasant one, I think. Sulie Carpenter's following us up here. Her ship should arrive in about five weeks."

Silence, and no expression. "Why," said Roger at last, "that's very nice. She's a fine person."

"Yes." But the conversation didn't seem to have anywhere to go after that, and besides Brad was impatient to put Roger through a whole bending and stretching series. Kayman allowed himself the privileges of a tourist. He turned away, staring toward the distant mountains, squinted at the bright sun, which even the auto-darkening of his faceplate didn't make quite comfortable, then looked around him. Clumsily he managed to kneel and to scoop up a clutch of pebbly dirt in his gloved hand. It would be his job next day to start the systematic collection of samples to return to Earth that was one minor task of the mission. Even after half a dozen manned landings and nearly forty instrumented missions, there was still an insatiable demand for samples of Martian soil in the laboratories of Earth. Right now, however, he was allowing himself to daydream. There was plenty of limonite in this sand, and the quartz pebbles were far from round; the edges were not sharp, but neither had they been milled to roundness. He scraped into the soil. A yellowish powder rested on top; underneath it the material was darker and coarser. There were shiny specks, almost like glass. Quartz? he wondered, and idly scooped around one.

He froze, his hands cupping an irregular rounded blob of crystal.

It had a stem. A stem that thrust down into the ground. That spread and divided into dark, rough-surfaced tendrils.

Roots.

Don Kayman jumped up, whirling on Roger and Brad. "Look!" he shouted, the object plucked free in his gauntleted hand. "Dear God in Heaven, look at this!"

And Roger, coming out of a crouch, spun and leaped at him. One hand knocked the glittering crystal thing spinning fifty meters into the air, bending the metal of the gauntlet. Kayman felt a sharp, quick pain in that forearm and saw the other hand striking toward his faceplate like the claw of an angry Kodiak bear; and that was the last he saw.

Sixteen
On the Perception of Perils

Vern Scanyon parked his car any which way across the painted yellow lines that marked his own place, jumped out and held his thumb against the elevator button. He had been awake less than forty minutes, but he was not at all sleepy. What he was, was angry and apprehensive. The President's appointments secretary had waked him out of a sound sleep with a phone call to say that the President had diverted his flight to stop at Tonka—"to discuss the problems of the perceptual system of Commander Torraway." To kick ass, more accurately. Scanyon had not known anything about Roger's sudden attack on Don Kayman until he was in his car, hastening to the project building to meet the President.

"Morning, Vern." Jonny Freeling looked scared and angry, too. Scanyon brushed past him into his own office.

"Come on in," he barked. "Now, in words of one syllable. What happened?"

Freeling said resentfully, "It's not my responsibility to—"

"Freeling."

"Roger's systems overreacted a little. Apparently Kayman moved suddenly, and the simulations systems translated it into a threat; Roger defended himself and pushed Kayman away."

Scanyon stared.

"Broke his arm," Freeling amended. "It was only a simple fracture, General. No complications. It's splinted, it'll heal perfectly—he just has to get by with one functioning arm for a while. It's a pity for Don Kayman, of course. He won't be very comfortable—"

"Fuck Kayman! Why didn't he know how to act around Roger?"

"Well, he did know. He found something that he thought was indigenous life! That was pretty exciting. All he wanted to do was show it to Roger."

"Life?" Scanyon's eyes looked more hopeful.

"Some sort of plant, they think."

"Can't they tell?"

"Well, Roger seems to have knocked it out of Kayman's hand. Brad went looking for it afterward, but he couldn't find it."

"Jesus," Scanyon snorted. "Freeling, tell me one thing. What kind of incompetents have we got working for us?" It was not a question that had a proper answer, and Scanyon didn't wait for one. "In about twenty minutes," he said, "the President of the United States is going to come through that door and he's going to want to know line by line what happened and why. I don't know what he's going to ask, but whatever it is there's one answer I don't want to give him, and that's 'I don't know.' So tell me, Freeling. Tell me all over again what happened, why it went wrong, why we didn't think it would go wrong and how we can be *damn* sure it isn't going to go wrong again." It took a little more than twenty minutes, but then they had more; the President's plane touched down late, and by the time Dash arrived Scanyon was as ready as he knew how to be. Even ready for the fury in the President's face.

"Scanyon," Dash snapped at once, "I warned you, no more surprises. This time is one too many, and I think I'm going to have to have your ass."

"You can't put a man on Mars without risks, Mr. President!"

Dash stared eye to eye for a moment, then said, "Maybe. What's the priest's condition?"

"He's got a broken radius, but it's going to be all right. There's something more important than that. He thinks he found life on Mars, Mr. President!"

Dash shook his head. "I know, some kind of plant. But he managed to lose it."

"For the moment. Kayman's a good man. If he said he found something important, he did. He'll find it again."

"I certainly hope so, Vern. Don't slide away from this. Why did this thing happen?"

"A slight overcontrol of his perceptual systems. That's it, Mr. President, and that's *all* it is. In order to make him respond quickly and positively, we had to build in some simulation features. To get his attention to priority messages, he sees his wife speaking to him. To get him to react to danger, he sees something frightening. That way his head can keep up with the reflexes we built into his body. Otherwise he'd go crazy."

"Breaking the priest's arm wasn't crazy?"

"No! It was an accident. When Kayman jumped at him he interpreted it as an actual attack of some kind. He responded. Well, Mr. President, in this case it was wrong, and it cost us a broken arm; but suppose there had been a real threat? Any *kind* of a threat! He would have met it. Whatever it was! He's invulnerable, Mr. President. Nothing can ever catch him offguard."

"Yeah," said the President, and after a moment, "maybe so." He stared over Scanyon's head for a moment and said, "What about this other crap?"

"Which crap, Mr. President?"

Dash shrugged irritably. "As I understand it, there's something wrong with all our computer projections, especially the polls we took."

Alarm bells went off in Scanyon's head. He said reluctantly, "Mr. President, there's a lot of paper on my desk I haven't got through yet. You know I've been traveling a lot—"

"Scanyon," said the President, "I'm going now. Before you do anything else, I want you to take a look through the papers on your desk and find that paper and read it. Tomorrow morning, eight o'clock, I want you in my office, and then I want to know what's happening, specifically three things. First, I want to hear that Kayman's all right. Second, I want that living thing found. Third, I want to know the score on the computer projections, and it better be all right. So long, Scanyon. I know it's only five in the morning, but don't go back to bed."

By then we could have reassured Scanyon and the President about one thing. The object Kayman had picked up was indeed some form of life. We had reconstructed the sampled data through Roger's eyes, filtered out the simulations, and seen what he had seen. It had not yet occurred to the President or his advisers that that could be done, but it would. It was not possible to make out fine details, because of the limited number of bits available, but the object was shaped rather like an artichoke, coarse leaves pointing upward, and a little like a mushroom: there was a crystalline cap of transparent material over it. It possessed roots, and unless it was an artifact (point zero zero one probability, at most), it had to be a form of life. We did not find that very interesting except, of course, as it would reinforce general interest in the Mars project itself. As to the doubt cast on the computer simulations, we were considerably more interested. We had followed that development for some time, ever since a graduate student named Byrne had written a Systems-360 program to recheck his desk-calculator previous recheck of some of the poll results. We were as concerned about it as the President was. But the probability of any serious consequence there too appeared quite small, especially since everything else was going well. The MHD generator was almost ready for preorbit injection course corrections; we had selected an installation site for it in the crater called Voltaire on the moon, Deimos. Not far behind it was the vehicle that contained the 3070 and its human crew of two, including Sulie Carpenter. And on Mars itself they had already begun construction of permanent installations. They were a little behind schedule. Kayman's accident had slowed them down, not only because of what it did to him but because of what Brad then insisted on doing to Roger: field-stripping his shoulder-pack computer to test for glitches. There weren't any. But it took two Martian days to be sure; and then, because Kayman begged, they took time to find his life form. They found it, or not it, exactly, but dozens of other specimens of the same thing; and Brad and Roger left Kayman inside the lander to study it while they began building their domes.

The first step was to find an area of Mars which had suitable geology. The surface should be as much like soil as possible, but solid rock had to be not far below. It took half a day of pounding explosive spikes into the ground and listening to echoes to be sure they had that.

Then, laboriously, the solar generators were spread out, and the subsurface rock-bound water was boiled out. As the first tiny plume of steam appeared at the lip of the pipe, they cheered. It would have been easy to miss it. The utterly dry Martian air snatched every molecule up almost as soon as it left the pipe. But by leaning close to the valve at the end one could see a faint, irregular misting that distorted shapes beyond it. It was water vapor, all right.

The next step was to spread out three great stretches of monomolecular film, the smallest first and the largest on top, and seal the topmost to the ground all around its periphery. Then they carried the pumps out on the basket-wheeled vehicle and started them going. The Martian atmosphere was extremely thin, but it was there; the pumps would ultimately fill the domes, partly with the compressed carbon dioxide and nitrogen from the atmosphere, partly with the water vapor they were boiling out of the rock. There was, to be sure, no oxygen to speak of in any of that, but they didn't have to find oxygen; they would make it, in exactly the same way Earth made its oxygen: through the intercession of photosynthetic plants.

It would take four or five days for the outer dome to fill to its planned quarter kilogram of pressure. Then they would start filling the second one, up to almost a kilogram (which would increase the pressure in the diminishing space of the outer shell to about a half kilo). Then, finally, they would fill the inner dome to two kilograms, and so they would have an environment in which people could live without pressure suits, and even breathe as soon as the crops gave them breathing material.

Of course, Roger didn't need any of that. He didn't need the oxygen; he didn't even need the plants for food, or not much and not for a long time. He could stay perhaps forever living off the unfailing light of the sun for most of his energy, plus what would be microwaved down from the MHD generator once it was in place. What was needed for the minuscule remaining part of him which was raw animal could easily be supplied by the concentrated foods from the ship for a long time; and only then, after perhaps a couple of Martian years, would he have to begin to depend on what came out of the hydroponics tanks and the seeds they were already sprouting in sealed cold-frames under the canopies.

It all took several days, since Kayman wasn't a great deal of help. Getting in and out of a pressure suit was agony for him, so they left him in the lander most of the time. When it came time to lug the tanks of carefully hoarded sludge from their toilet facilities over to the dome, Kayman lent a hand. "Exactly one hand," he said, trying to handle the magnesium-shafted rake by wrapping his good arm around it.

"You're doing fine," Brad encouraged. There was enough pressure in the innermost dome now to lift it above their heads, but not quite enough to let them take off their pressure suits. Which was just as well, Brad realized; this way they couldn't smell what they were raking into the sterile soil.

By the time the dome was fully extended the pressure was up to a hundred millibars. This is the pressure of Earth's atmosphere at some ten miles above sea level. It is not an environment in which naked man can survive and work for very long, but it is an environment in which he will only die if something kills him. Half that pressure would be lethal instantly; his body temperature would boil his fluids away.

But when the internal pressure hit the 100-millibar level all three of them crowded through the three successive airlocks and Brad and Don Kayman ceremoniously took off their pressure suits. Brad and Don fitted nosepieces, something like that of an aqualung, in place for breathing; there was still no oxygen to speak of inside the dome. But they got pure oxygen from the tanks on their backs, and with that they were, for the first time, almost as free as Roger, inside a transplanted bit of Earth that was a hundred meters across and as tall as a ten-story building.

And inside it, in orderly rows, the seeds they had transplanted were already beginning to sprout and grow.

Meanwhile—

The vehicle with the magnetohydrodynamic generator attained Mars orbit, and with General Hesburgh helping, matched orbit with Deimos and nestled into the crater. It was a perfect coupling. The vehicle swung out its struts to touch the rock of the moon, augered them in, and locked. A brief jet from the maneuvering system tested its stability: it was now a part of Deimos. The power system began to sequence toward full operational mode. A fusion flame woke the plasma fires. Radar reached out to find the target on the lander, then locked on to the dome. Power began to flow. The energy density of the field was low enough for Brad and Kayman to walk around in it unaware, and to Roger it was like the basking warmth of sunlight; but the foil strips in the outer dome gathered the microwave energy and channeled it to the pumps, the batteries.

The fusion fuel had a life of fifty years. For that long at least there would be energy for Roger and his backpack computer on Mars, whatever happened on Earth.

And meanwhile—

There were other couplings.

In the long spiral up from Earth, Sulie Carpenter and her pilot, Dinty Meighan, had had time heavy on their hands and had found a way to use it.

The act of copulation in free fall presents certain problems. First Sulie had to buckle one strand of webbing around her waist, then Dinty embraced her with his arms, and she him with her legs. Their motions were underwater slow. It took Sulie a long, gentle, dreamy time to come to orgasm, and Dinty was even slower. When they were finished they were hardly even breathing hard. Sulie stretched and yawned, arching her belly against the retaining strap. "Nice," she said drowsily. "I'll remember that."

"We both will, honey," he said, misunderstanding her. "I think that's the best way we screw. Next time—"

She shook her head to interrupt him. "No next time, Dinty dear. That was it."

He pulled his head back to look at her. "What?"

She smiled. Her right eye was still only centimeters from his left, and their view of each other curiously foreshortened. She craned forward and rubbed her cheek gently against his bristly one.

He scowled and detached himself, suddenly feeling naked where before he had been only bare. He pulled his shorts out from behind the handhold where he had cached them and slid into them.

"Sulie, what's the matter?"

"Nothing's the matter. We're almost ready for orbit, that's all."

He pushed himself backward across the cramped compartment to get a better look at her. She was worth looking at. Her hair had gone back to muddy blond and her eyes were brown without the contact lenses; and even after almost two hundred days of never being more than ten meters from him, she still looked good to Dinty Meighan. "I didn't think you had any surprises left," he marveled.

"You never can tell about a woman."

"Come on, Sulie! What's this all about? You sound as though you've been planning— Hey!" A thought struck him. "You volunteered for this mission—not to go to Mars, but to go to some guy! Right? One of the guys ahead of us?"

"You're very quick, Dinty. Not," she said fondly, "where I don't want you to be, though."

"Who is it, Brad? Hesburgh? Not the priest?—oh, wait a minute!" He nodded. "Sure! The one you were mixed up with back on Earth. The cyborg!"

"Colonel Roger Torraway, the human being," she corrected. "As human as you are, except for some improvements."

He laughed, more resentment than humor. "A lot of improvements, and no balls at all."

Sulie unstrapped herself. "Dinty," she said sweetly, "I've enjoyed sex with you, and I respect you, and you've been about as comfortable to be with as any human being possibly could be on this Goddamned eternity trip. But there are some things I don't want you to say. You're right. Roger doesn't happen to have any testicles, right at this exact moment. But he's a human being I can respect and love, and he's the only one like that I've found lately. Believe me, I've looked."

"Thanks!"

"Oh, don't do this, dear Dinty. You know you're not really jealous. You've already got a wife."

"Next year I do! That's a long way off." She shrugged, grinning. "Ah, but Sulie! There are some things you can't kid me about. You love screwing!"

"I like body contact and intimacy," she corrected, "and I like coming to orgasm. I like both those things better with someone I love, Dinty. No offense."

He scowled. "You've got a long wait, sweetie."

"Maybe not."

"The hell you say. I won't see Irene for seven months. But you—you won't be back any faster than I will; and then it only begins. They've got to put him back together for you. Assuming they *can* put him back together. It sounds like a long time between fucks."

"Oh, Dinty. Don't you think I've thought this all out?" She patted him in passing, on the way to her own locker. "Sex isn't just coitus. There are more ways to orgasm than with a penis in my vagina. And there's more to sex than orgasm. Not to mention love. Roger," she went on, wriggling into her jump suit, not so much for modesty as for pockets, "is a resourceful, loving person, and so am I. We'll make out—anyway, until the rest of the colonists land."

"Rest?" he struggled. "Rest of the *colonists?*"

"Haven't you figured it out yet? I'm not going back with all of you, Dinty, and I don't think Roger is either. We're going to be Martians!"

And meanwhile, in the Oval Room of the White House, the President of the United States was confronting Vern Scanyon and a young, coffee-colored man with tinted glasses and the build of a football player. "So you're the one," he said, appraising him. "You think we don't know how to run a computer study."

"No, Mr. President," the young man said steadily. "I don't think that's the problem."

Scanyon coughed. "Byrne here," he said, "is a graduate student on work-study from M.I.T. His thesis is on sampling methodology, and we gave him access to some of the, ah, classified material. Especially public-opinion studies about attitudes on the project."

"But not to a computer," Byrne said.

"Not to a big one," Scanyon corrected. "You had your own desk dataplex."

The President said mildly, "Get on with it, Scanyon."

"Well, his results came out different. According to his interpretations, the public opinion on the whole question of colonizing Mars was, well, apathy. You remember, Mr. President, there was some question about the results at the time? The raw results weren't encouraging at all? But when we played them through analysis they came out positive to—what do you call it?—two sigmas. I never knew why."

"Did you check?"

"Certainly, Mr. President! Not me," Scanyon added quickly. "That wasn't my responsibility. But I'm satisfied that the studies were verified."

Byrne put in, "Three different times, with three different programs. There were minor variations, of course. But they all came out significant and reliable. Only when I repeated them on my desk machine they didn't. And that's the way it is, Mr. President. If you work up the figures on any big computer in the net you get one result. If you work them up on a small isolated machine you get another."

The President drummed the balls of his thumbs on the desk. "What's your conclusion?"

Byrne shrugged. He was twenty-three years old, and his surroundings intimidated him. He looked to Scanyon for help and found none; he said, "You'll have to ask somebody else that one, Mr. President. I can only give you my own conjecture. Somebody's buggering our computer network."

The President rubbed the left lobe of his nose reflectively, nodding slowly. He looked at Byrne for a moment and then said, without raising his voice, "Carousso, come on in here. Mr. Byrne, what you see and hear in this room is top secret. When you leave, Mr. Carousso will see that you are informed as to what that means to you in detail; basically, you are not to talk about it. To anyone. Ever."

The door to the President's anteroom opened and a tall, solid man with a self-effacing air walked in. Byrne stared at him wonderingly: Charles Carousso, the head of the CIA! "What about it, Chuck?" the President asked. "What about him?"

"We've checked Mr. Byrne, of course," said the Agency man. His words were precise and uninflected. "There isn't anything significantly adverse to him—you'll be glad to know, I suppose, Mr. Byrne. And what he says checks out. It isn't only the public-opinion surveys. The war-risk projections, the cost/effectiveness studies—run on the net they come out one way, run on independent calculating machines they come out another. I agree with Mr. Byrne. Our computer net has been compromised."

The President's lips were pressed together as though he were holding back what he wanted to say. All he allowed to come out was, "I want you to find out how this happened, Chuck. But the question now is, who? The Asians?"

"No, sir! We checked that out. It's impossible."

"Bullshit it's impossible!" roared the President. "We know they already did tap our lines once, on the simulation of Roger Torraway's systems!"

"Mr. President, that's an entirely different case. We found that tap and neutralized it. It was in the groundlines cable on a nonsensitive linkage. The comm circuits on our major machines are absolutely leakproof." He glanced at Byrne. "You have a report on the techniques involved, Mr. President; I'll be glad to go over it with you at another time."

"Oh, don't worry about me," said Byrne, smiling for the first time. "Everybody knows the links are multiply scrambled. If you've checked me out, I'm sure you found out that a lot of us graduate students fool around trying to tap in, and none of us make it."

The agency man nodded. "As a matter of fact, Mr. President, we tolerate that; it's good field-testing for our security. If people like Mr. Byrne can't think up a way past the blocks, I doubt the Asians can. And the blocks are leakproof. They have to be. They control circuits that go to the War Machine in Butte, the Census Bureau, UNESCO—"

"Wait a minute!" barked the President. "You mean our machines tie in with both UNESCO, which the Asians use, *and* the War Machine?"

"There is absolutely no possibility of a leak."

"There's *been* a leak, Carousso!"

"Not to the Asians, Mr. President."

"You just finished telling me there's one wire that goes out of our machine to the War Machine and another that goes straight to the Asians, with a detour through UNESCO!"

"Even so, Mr. President, I absolutely guarantee it's not the Asians. We would know that. *All* major computers are cross-linked to some extent. That's like saying there's a road from everywhere to everywhere else. Right, there is. But there are roadblocks. There is no *way* the NPA can get access to the War Machine, or to most of these studies. Even so, if they had done it, we would know from covert sources. They haven't. And," he went on, "in any case, Mr. President, can you think of any reason why the NPA would distort results in order to compel us to colonize Mars?"

The President drummed his thumbs, looking around the room. At last he sighed. "I'm willing to go along with your logic, Chuck. But if it wasn't the Asians that buggered our computers, then who?"

The agency man was morosely silent.

"And," Dash snarled, "for Christ's sake, *why?*"

Seventeen
A Day in the Life of a Martian

Roger could not see the gentle shower of microwave energy coming down from Deimos, but he could feel it as a luxury of warmth. When he was nearby he preened his wings in it, soaking up strength. Outside the beam he carried part of it with him in his accumulators. There was no reason for him to hoard his strength now. More strength poured down from the sky whenever Deimos was above the horizon. There were only a few hours in each day when neither the sun nor the farther moon were in the sky, and his storage capacity was multiply adequate for those brief periods of drought.

Inside the domes, of course, the metal-foil antennae stole the energy before it reached him, so he limited his time with Brad and Kayman. He didn't mind. It was what he preferred. Every day the gap between them widened anyway. They were going back to their own planet. Roger was going to stay on his. He had not told them that yet, but he had made up his mind. Earth had begun to seem like a pleasant, quaint foreign place he had visited once and hadn't much liked. The pains and perils of terrestrial humanity were no longer his. Not even when they had been his own personal pains, and his own fears.

Inside the dome Brad, wearing G-string undershorts and a demand tank of oxygen, was happily planting carrot seedlings between the stands of Siberian oats. "Want to give me a hand, Rog?" His voice was reedily high in the thin atmosphere; he took frequent sips of oxygen from the mouthpiece that hung next to his chin, and then when he breathed out the voice was fractionally deeper, but still strange.

"No, Don wants me to pick up some more specimens for him. I'll be gone overnight."

"All right." Brad was more interested in his seedlings than in Torraway, and Torraway was no longer very interested in Brad. Sometimes he would remind himself that this man had been his wife's lover, but in order for that to feel like anything he had to remind himself that he had had a wife. It didn't seem worth the effort. More interesting was the challenge of the high cupped valley just over that farther range of hills, and his own private farm plot. For weeks now he had been bringing samples of Martian life back to show Don Kayman. They were not plentiful—two or three together in a clump, perhaps, and nothing else for hundreds of meters around. But they were not hard to find—not for him. Once he had learned to recognize their special color—the hard UV lengths that their crystal caps reflected away from them, to let them survive in the harsh radiation environment—it was reflexive to filter his vision bands to see only that wavelength in color, and then they stood out a kilometer away.

So he had brought back a dozen of them, and then a hundred; there seemed to be four distinct varieties, and it was not long before Kayman asked him to stop. He had all the samples he needed to study, and half a dozen more of each in formalin to bring back to Earth, and his gentle conserving soul was uneasy at despoiling the ecology of Mars. Roger began replanting some of them near the dome. He told himself it was to see whether the overflow of energy beamed down from the generator did native life forms any harm.

But what it was, he knew in his heart, was gardening. It was his planet, and he was beautifying it for himself.

He let himself out of the dome, stretched luxuriously for a moment in the double warmth of sun and microwave and checked his batteries. They could use topping off; he deftly plugged the leads into his own backpack and the gently whining accumulator at the base of the dome, and without looking toward the lander, said, "I'm going to take off now, Don."

Kayman's voice responded instantly over the radio. "Don't be out of touch more than two hours, Roger. I don't want to have to come looking for you."

"You worry too much," said Roger, detaching the leads and stowing them away.

"You're only superhuman," grumbled Kayman. "You're not God. You could fall, break something—"

"I won't. Brad? So long."

Inside the triple dome Brad looked up over the armpit-high stalks of wheat and waved. His features could not be made out through the filmy domes; the plastic had been formulated to cut out the worst of the UV, and it blurred some of the visual wavelengths as well. But Roger could see him wave. "Take care. Give us a call before you go out of line of sight so we'll know when to start worrying."

"Yes, Mother." It was curious, Roger reflected. He was actually feeling rather fond of Brad. The situation interested him as an abstract problem. Was it because he was a gelding? There was testosterone circulating in his system, the steroid implant they had given him took care of that. His dreams were sometimes sexual, and sometimes of Dorrie, but the hollow despair and the anger he had lived with on Earth had attenuated on Mars.

He was already almost a kilometer from the dome, running along easily in the warm sunlight, each step coming down precisely where it would find secure footing and each thrust lifting him surely an exact distance up and ahead. His vision was on low-energy surveillance mode, taking in everything in a moving teardrop shape whose point was where he was and whose lobe, fifty meters across, was more than a hundred meters in front of him. He was not unaware of the rest of the landscape. If something unusual had appeared—above all if something had moved—he would have seen it at once. But it did not distract him from his musings. He tried to remember what sex with Dorrie had been like. It was not hard to recall the objective, physical parameters. Much harder to feel what he had felt in bed with her; it was like trying to recall the sensuous joy of a chocolate malted when he was eleven, or his first marijuana high at fifteen. It was easier to feel something about Sulie Carpenter, although as far as he could remember he had never touched any part of her but her fingertips, and then by accident. (Of course, she had touched every part of him.) He had been thinking, from time to time, about Sulie's coming to Mars. It had seemed threatening at first. Then it had seemed interesting, a change to look forward to. Now— Now, Roger realized, he wanted it to happen soon, not in four days, when she was due to land after her pilot completed the on-site tests of the 3070 and the MHD generator. *Soon.* They had exchanged a few casual greetings by radio. He wanted her closer than that. He wanted to touch her—

His wife's image formed in front of him, wearing that same monotonous sunsuit. "Better check in, honey," she said.

Roger stopped and looked around, on full vision mode in the Earth-normal spectrum.

He was almost halfway to the mountains, a good ten kilometers from the dome and the lander. He had been going uphill and the flat terrain had begun to be rolling; he could barely see the top of the dome, and the tip of the antennas of the lander was a tiny spike beyond it. Without conscious effort his wings deployed themselves behind him to make his radio signal more directional, as a shouting man might megaphone his hands around his mouth. "Everything's okay," he said, and Don Kayman's voice answered inside his head: "That's fine, Roger. It'll be dark in three hours."

"I know." And after dark the temperature would plummet; six hours from now it might touch a hundred and fifty degrees below zero. But Roger had been out in the dark before, and all of his systems had performed beautifully. "I'll check with you again when I'm high enough on a slope to reach you," he promised, turned and started once more toward the mountains. The atmosphere was hazier than it had been. He allowed himself to feel his skin receptors and realized that there was a growing wind. Sandstorm? He had lived through them, too; if it got bad he would hedgehog somewhere until it stopped, but it would have to be very bad to make that necessary. He grinned inside himself—he had not reliably learned how to do it with his new face—and loped on . . .

At sunset he was in the shadow of the mountains, high enough up to see the dome clearly, more than twenty kilometers away.

The sandstorm was all below him now and seemed to be moving away. He had stopped briefly twice and waited, wings furled around him. But that had been only routine caution; at no time had it been more than an annoyance. He cupped the wings behind him and said through his radio: "Don? Brad? It's your wandering boy reporting in."

The reply inside his head, when it came, was scratchy and distorted, an unpleasant feeling, like gritting one's teeth on emery cloth. "Your signal's lousy, Rog. Are you okay?"

"Sure." But he hesitated. The static from the storm was bad enough so that he had not been sure, at first, which of his companions was talking to him; only after a moment had he identified the voice as Brad's. "Maybe I'll start back now," he said.

The other voice, even more distorted: "You'll make an old priest happy if you do, Roger. Want us to come out and meet you?"

"Hell, no. I can move faster than you can. Go to sleep; I'll see you in four or five hours."

Roger chatted a moment, than sat down and looked around. He wasn't tired. He had almost forgotten what it was like to be tired; he slept an hour or two, most nights, and napped from time to time during the day, more out of boredom than fatigue. The organic part of him still imposed some demands on his metabolism, but the crushing bone-weariness of prolonged exertion was no longer part of his experience. He sat because it pleased him to sit on an outcropping of rock and stare across the valley of his home. The long shadow of the mountains had already passed the dome, and only the peaks on the farther side were still lighted. He could see the terminator clearly; Mars's thin air did not diffuse the shadow much. He could almost see it move.

Overhead the sky was brilliantly beautiful. It was easy enough to see the brighter stars even by daylight, especially for Roger, but at night they were fantastic. He could clearly make out the different hues: steel-blue Sirius, bloody Aldebaran, the smoky gold of Polaris. By expanding his visible spectrum into the infrared and ultraviolet he could see new, bright stars whose names he did not know; perhaps they had no common names, since apart from himself they had been seen as bright objects only by astronomers using special plates. He pondered about the question of name-giving rights; if he was the only one who could see that bright patch there in Orion, did he have the right to christen it? Would anybody object if he called it "Sulie's Star"?

For that matter he could see what was, for the moment, Sulie's actual star . . . or heavenly body; Deimos was not a star, of course. He stared up at it, and amused himself trying to imagine Sulie's face—

"ROGER, HONEY! YOU—"

Torraway jumped straight up and landed a meter away. The scream inside his head had been deafening. Had it been real? He had no way to tell; the voices from Brad or Don Kayman and the simulated voice of his wife sounded equally familiar inside his head. He was not even sure whose voice it had been—Dorrie's? But he had been thinking about Sulie Carpenter, and the voice had been so queerly stressed that it could have been either or neither of them.

And now there was no sound at all, or none except for the irregular clicks, squeaks and scrapes that came up from the rock as the Martian crust responded to the rapidly dropping temperature. He was not aware of the cold as cold; his internal heaters kept the feeling part of him at constant temperature and would go on doing so easily all through the night. But he knew that it was at least fifty below now.

Another blast: "ROG— THINK YOU OUGHT—"

Even with the warning of the time before, the raucous shout was painful. This time he caught a quick fugitive glimpse of Dorrie's simulated image, standing queerly on nothing at all a dozen meters in the air.

Training took over. Roger turned toward the distant dome, or where he thought it had been, cupped his wings behind him and said clearly:

"Don! Brad! I've got some kind of a malfunction. I'm getting a signal but I can't read it."

He waited. There was no response, nothing inside his head except his own thoughts and a confused grumbling that he recognized as static.

"ROGER!"

It was Dorrie again, ten times life-size, towering over him, and on her face a grimace of wrath and fear. She seemed to be reaching down toward him, and then she bent curiously sidewise, like a television image flickering off the tube, and was gone.

Roger felt a peculiar pain, tried to dismiss it as fear, felt it again and realized it was cold. There was something seriously wrong. "Mayday!" he shouted. "Don! I'm in trouble—help me!" The dark distant hills seemed to be rippling slowly. He looked up. The stars were turning liquid and dripping from the sky.

In Don Kayman's dream, he and Sister Clotilda were sitting on hassocks in front of a waterfall, eating sponges. Not candy; kitchen sponges, dipped into a sort of fondue. Clotilda was warning him of danger. "They're going to throw us out," she said, slicing off a square of sponge and impaling it on a two-pronged silver fork, "because you got a C in homiletics"—dipping it in the copper-bottomed dish over the alcohol flame—"and you've got to, just got to, wake up—"

He woke up.

Brad was leaning over him. "Come on, Don. We've got to get out of here."

"What's the matter?" Kayman pulled the sleeping bag over his chest with his good hand.

"I can't get an answer out of Roger. He didn't answer. I sent him a priority signal. Then I thought I heard him on the radio, but very faint. He's either out of line of sight or his transmitter isn't working."

Kayman wriggled out of the bag and sat up. At times like this, when first awakening, his arm hurt the most, and it was hurting now. He put it out of his mind. "Have you got a position fix?"

"Three hours ago. I couldn't get a bearing on this last transmission."

"He can't be far off that line." Kayman was already sliding into the legs of his pressure suit. The next part was the hardest, trying to ease the splinted forearm into the sleeve. Among them they had managed to stretch the sleeve a little, sealing the beginnings of a rip, but it was barely possible, would not be easy even under the best of conditions. Now, trying to hurry, it was infuriating.

Brad was already in his suit and throwing equipment into a bag. "Do

you think you're going to perform an emergency operation out there?"
Kayman demanded.

Brad scowled and kept on. "I don't know what I'll have to do. It's
full night, Don, and he's up at least five hundred meters. It's cold."

Kayman closed his mouth. By the time he was zipped in Brad had
long since left the lander and was waiting at the wheel of the Mars vehicle. Kayman clambered aboard painfully, and they were moving before he had a chance to belt himself down. He managed to cling with
heels and the one unbendable arm while buckling himself in with the
other hand, but it was a close thing. "Any idea of distance?" he asked.

"In the hills somewhere," said Brad's voice in his ear; Kayman
winced and turned down the volume on his radio.

"Maybe two hours?" he guessed, calculating rapidly.

"If he's already started back, maybe. If he can't move—or if he's moving around out there, and we have to try to track him with RDF—"
The voice stopped. "I think he's all right as far as temperature goes,"
Brad went on after a minute. "But I don't know. I don't know what
happened."

Kayman stared ahead. Past the bright field of light from the vehicle's
headlight there was nothing to see except that the glittering field of
stars was cut off, like the scalloped edge of a doily, at the horizon. That
was the mountain ridge. It would be that, Kayman knew, that Brad
was using as a guide; aiming always at that lowest point between the
double peak on the north and the very high one just to the south.
Bright Aldebaran was hanging over that higher peak, a good enough
navigation aid in itself, at least until it set in an hour or so.

Kayman keyed in the vehicle's high-gain antenna. "Roger," he said,
raising his voice although he knew that made no difference. "Can you
hear me? We're coming out to meet you."

There was no answer. Kayman leaned back in the contoured seat,
trying to minimize the swaying jolts of the vehicle. It was bad enough,
rolling on the basket-weave wire wheels across the flattest part of the
terrain. When they began trying to climb, using the stiltlike legs, he
suspected he might be thrown clear out of the vehicle, belt and all, and
was certain he would at least be sick. Ahead of them the jerking beam
of the headlight was picking out a dune, a rock outcropping, sometimes
throwing back a lance of light from a crystal face. "Brad," he said,
"doesn't that light drive you crazy? Why don't you use the radar display?"

He heard a quick intake of breath on his suit radio, as though Brad
had been about to swear at him. Then the suited figure next to him
reached down to the toggles on the steering column. The bluish panel

just under the sandscreen lit up, revealing the terrain just in front of them; and the headlight winked off. It was easier to see the black outline of the mountains now.

Thirty minutes. At most, a quarter of the way there.

"Roger," Kayman called again. "Can you hear me? We're en route. When we get close enough we'll pick you up on your target. But if you can, answer now—"

There was no answer.

A rice-grain argon bulb began to blink rapidly on the dashboard. The two men looked at each other through their faceplates, and then Kayman leaned forward and clicked the frequency settings to the orbit channel. "Kayman here," he said.

"Father Kayman? What's going on down there?"

The voice was female, which meant, of course, Sulie Carpenter. Kayman chose his words carefully: "Roger's having some transmission trouble. We're going out to check it."

"It sounds like more than plain trouble. I've been listening to you trying to raise him." Kayman didn't answer, and her voice went on: "We've got him located, if you want a fix—?"

"Yes!" he shouted, furious at himself; they should have thought of Deimos's RDF facility right away. It would be easy for Sulie or either of the orbiting astronauts to guide them in.

"Grid coordinates three poppa one seven, two two zebra four oh. But he's moving. Bearing about eight nine, speed about twelve kilometers per hour."

Brad glanced at their own course and said, "Right on. That's the reciprocal; he's coming right for us."

"But why so slowly?" Kayman demanded.

A second later the girl's voice came: "That's what I want to know. Is he hurt?"

Kayman said irritably, "We don't *know*. Have you tried radio contact?"

"Over and over—wait a minute." Pause, and then her voice again: "Dinty says to tell you we'll keep him located for you as long as we can, but we're getting to a bad angle. So I wouldn't rely on our positions past—what? Maybe another forty-five minutes. And in about twenty minutes after that we'll be below the horizon entirely."

Brad said, "Do what you can. Don? Hold on. I'm going to see how fast this son of a bitch will go."

And the lurching of the vehicle tripled as Brad accelerated. Kayman fought off being sick inside his helmet long enough to lean forward and study the speedometer. The trip recorder rolling off the strip map along the side of the radar screen told the rest of the story: even if they could maintain their present speed, Deimos would have set before they could reach Roger Torraway.

He switched back to the directional high-gain. "Roger," he called. "Can you hear me? Call in!"

Thirty kilometers away, Roger was at bay inside his own body.

To his perceptions he was racing back home, at a strange gait like a high-speed heel-and-toe race. He knew his perceptions were wrong. He did not know how wrong; he could not be sure in what ways; but he knew that the brother on his back had tampered with his time sense, as well as with his interpretations of the inputs of his senses; and what he knew most surely of all was that he was no longer in control of what happened to him. The gait, he was intellectually certain, was a ploddingly slow walk. It *felt* as though he were running. The landscape was flowing by as rapidly, to his perceptions, as though he were racing at full speed. But full speed implied soaring bounds, and there was no time when both of his feet were off the ground at once; conclusion: he was walking, but the backpack computer had slowed down his time sense, probably to keep him reasonably tranquil.

If so, it was not succeeding.

When the backpack brother took over control it had been terrifying. First he had stood straight up and locked; he could not move, could not even speak. All around him the black sky was rippling with streaks of aurora, the ground itself shimmering like heat waves on a desert; phantom images danced in and out of his vision. He could not believe what his senses told him, nor could he bend a single finger. Then he felt his own hands reaching behind him, palpating and tracing the joints where wings came to shoulderblades, seeking out the cables that led to his batteries. Another frozen pause. Then the same thing, feeling around the terminals of the computer itself. He knew enough to know that the computer was checking itself; what he did not know was what it was finding out or what it could do about it when it located the fault. Pause again. Then he felt his fingers questing into the jacks where he plugged in the recharge cables—

A violent pain smote him, like the worst of all headaches, like a stroke or a blow from a club. It lasted only a moment, and then it was gone, leaving no more of itself than an immense distant flash of lightning. He had never felt anything like it before. He was aware that his fingers were gently, and very skillfully, scraping at the terminals. There was another quick surge of pain as, apparently, his own fingers made a momentary short.

Then he felt himself closing the flap, and realized he had failed to do that when he recharged at the dome.

And then, after another momentary stoppage of everything, he had begun to move slowly, carefully down the slope toward the dome.

He had no idea how long he had been walking. At some point his time perception had been slowed, but he could not even say when that had been. All of his perceptions were being monitored and edited. He knew that, because he knew that that section of the Martian terrain that he was traversing was not intrinsically softly lighted and in full color, while everything around was nearly formless black. But he could not change it. He could not even change the direction of his gaze. With metronome regularity it would sweep to one side or the other, less frequently scan the sky or even turn to look back; the rest of the time it was unwaveringly on the road he was treading, and he could see only peripherally the rest of the nightscape.

And his feet twinkled heel-and-toe, heel-and-toe—how fast? A hundred paces to the minute? He could not tell. He thought of trying to get some idea of the time by observing the clearing of the stars above the horizon, but although it was not difficult to count his steps, and to try to guess when those lowest stars had climbed four or five degrees— which would be about ten minutes—it was impossible to keep all of that in mind long enough to get a meaningful result. Apart from the fact that his vision kept dancing away from the horizon without warning.

He was wholly the prisoner of the brother on his back, subject to its will, deceived by its interpretations, and very much a worried man.

What had gone wrong? Why was he feeling cold, when there was so little of him that could feel a sensory reality at all? And yet he yearned for the rising of the sun, dreamed wistfully of basking in the microwave radiation from Deimos. Painfully Roger tried to reason through the evidence as he knew it. Feeling cold. Needing energy inputs: that was the interpretation of that cue. But why would he need more energy, when he had fully charged his batteries? He dismissed that question because he could see no answer to it, but the hypothesis seemed strong. It accounted for the low-energy mode of travel; walking was far slower than his usual leaping run, but in kwh/km terms it was far more cost-effective. Perhaps it even accounted for the glitches in his perceptual systems. If the backpack-brother had discovered before he did that there was insufficient energy for foreseeable needs, it would surely ration the precious store to the most essential needs. Or what it perceived as most essential: travel; keeping the organic part of him from freezing; conducting its own information-handling and control procedures. Which unfortunately he was not privy to.

At least, he reflected, the primary mission of the backpack computer was to protect itself, which meant keeping the organic part of Roger Torraway alive. It might steal energy from the part that would keep him sane: deprive him of communications, interfere with his perceptions. But he was sure he would get back to the lander alive.

If perhaps crazy.

He was more than halfway back already, he was nearly sure. And he was still sane. The way to keep sane was to keep from worrying. The way to keep from worrying was to think of other things. He imagined Sulie Carpenter's bright presence, only days away; wondered if she was serious about staying on Mars. Wondered if he was himself. He reminisced within himself about great meals he had eaten, the spinach-green pasta in the cream sauce in Sirmione, overlooking the bright transparent water of Lake Garda; the Kobe beef in Nagoya; the fire-hot chili in Matamoras. He thought of his guitar and made a resolve to haul it out and play it. There was too much water in the air under the domes to be good for it, and Roger did not much like to be in the lander; and outside in the open, of course, its sound was strange because it was all bone-conducted. But still. He rehearsed the fingering of chords, modulating through the sharps and sevenths and minors. He imagined his fingers fretting the E-minor, the D, the C and the B-seventh of the opening passages of "Greensleeves," and hummed along with them inside his head. Sulie would enjoy singing along with the guitar, he thought. It would make the cold Martian nights pass—

He snapped to alertness.

This Martian night was no longer passing quite so quickly.

Subjectively it seemed as though his gait had slowed from a race to a steady stride; but he knew that that had not changed, his time perception had stretched back to normal, maybe even a bit slower than normal: he seemed to be walking quite slowly and methodically.

Why?

There was something ahead of him. At least a kilometer away. And very bright.

He could not make it out.

A *dragon?*

It seemed to leap toward him, breathing a long tongue of light like flame.

His body stopped walking. It dropped to its knees and began to crawl, very slowly, keeping down.

This is insane, he said to himself. There are no dragons on Mars. What am I doing? But he could not stop. His body inched along, knee and opposite hand, hand and opposite knee, into the shelter of a hummock of sand. Carefully and quickly it began to scoop the powdery Martian soil away, to fit itself into the hollow, scraping some of the dirt back over itself. Inside his head tiny voices were babbling, but he could not understand what they said: they were too faint, too garbled.

The dragon slowed and stopped a few dozen meters away, its tongue of frozen flame lolling out toward the mountains. His vision clouded and changed; now the flame was dimmed, and the bulk of the thing itself came up in ghostly luminescence. Two smaller creatures were dropping off its back, ugly, simian beasts that hulked along and exuded menace with every gesture.

There were no dragons on Mars, and no gorillas either.

Roger summoned up all of his energies. "Don!" he shouted. "Brad!"

He was not getting through.

He knew that the backpack-brother was still withholding energy from the transmitter. He knew that his perceptions had been skewed, and that the dragon was no dragon and the gorillas no gorillas. He knew that if he could not override the brother on his back something very bad was likely to happen, because he knew that his fingers were slowly and delicately wrapping themselves around a chunk of limonite the size of a baseball.

And he knew that he had never been closer to going mad in his life than he was right now.

Roger made an immense effort to recapture his sanity.

The dragon was no dragon. It was the Mars vehicle.

The apes were not apes. They were Brad and Don Kayman.

They were not threatening him. They had come all this way in the flint-cold Martian night to find him and help him.

He repeated the truths over and over, like a litany; but whatever he thought he was powerless to prevent what his arms and body did. They seized the chunk of rock; the body raised itself up; the arms threw the rock with exact precision into the headlight of the crawler.

The long tongue of frozen flame winked out.

The light from the million fiery stars was ample for Roger's senses, but it would be very little help to Brad and Don Kayman. He could see them (still gorilloid, still menacing of mien) stumbling at random; and he could feel what his body was doing.

It was creeping toward them.

"Don!" he shouted. "Watch out!" But the voice never left his skull.

This was insanity, he told himself. I have to stop!

He could not stop.

I *know* that's not an enemy! I don't really want to hurt them—

And he kept on advancing.

He was almost sure he could hear their voices now. So close, their transmitters would be deafening in his perceptions under normal conditions, without the intercession of the automatic volume control. Even cut off as he was, there was some spillage.

"—round here somewh—"

Yes! He could even make out words; and the voice, he was sure, had been Brad's.

He shouted with all the power at his command: "Brad! It's me, Roger! I think I'm trying to kill you!"

Heedless, his body kept up his steady crawl. Had they heard him? He shouted again; and this time he could see both of them stop, as though listening to the faintest of distant cries.

The tiny thread of Don Kayman's voice whispered: "I'm sure I heard him that time, Brad."

"You did!" howled Roger, forcing his advantage. "Watch out! The computer has taken over. I'm trying to override it, but— Don!" He could recognize them now, by the stiffly outstretched arm of the priest's pressure suit. "Get away! I'm trying to kill you!"

He could not make out the words; they were louder, but both men were shouting at once and the result was garble. His body was not affected; it continued its deadly stalk.

"I can't see you, Roger."

"I'm ten meters away from you—south? Yes, south! Crawling. Low down to the ground."

The priest's faceplate glittered in the starlight as it swung toward him; then Kayman turned and began to run.

Roger's body gathered itself up and began a leap after the priest. "Faster!" Roger shouted. "Oh, Christ! You'll never get away—" Even uncrippled, even in daylight, even without the impediment of the suit, Kayman would have had no chance to escape Roger's smoothly functioning body. Under the actual circumstances running was a waste of time. Roger felt his power-driven muscles gather themselves for a spring, felt his hands claw out to grasp and destroy—

The universe spun around him.

Something had struck him from behind. He plowed forward on his face; but his instant reflexes had him half turning even as he fell, clawing at the thing that had leaped on his back. Brad! And he could feel Brad struggling frantically with something—with some part of the—

And the greatest pain of all struck him; and he lost consciousness like the snapping off of a switch.

· · ·

There was no sound. There was no light. There was no feeling of touch, or smell or taste. It took a long time for Roger to realize that he was conscious.

Once, as an undergraduate in a psychology miniseminar, he had volunteered for an hour in a sensory-deprivation tank. It had seemed forever, with no sensations coming in at all, nothing but the very faint and unobtrusive housekeeping sounds of his own body: soft thud of pulse, sighing stirring in his lungs. Now there was not even that much.

For a long time. He could not guess how long.

Then he perceived a vague stirring in his personal interior space. It was a strange sensation, hard to identify; as though liver and lungs were gently changing places. It went on for some time, and he knew that something was being done to him. He could not tell what.

And then a voice: "—should have landed the generator on the surface in the first place." Kayman's voice?

And replying: "No. That way it would only work in line of sight, maybe fifty kilometers at best." *That* was Sulie Carpenter surely!

"Then there should have been relay satellites."

"I don't think so. Too expensive. Take too long, anyway—although that's what it will come to, when the NPA and the Russians and the Brazilians all get their own teams here."

"Well, it was stupid."

Sulie laughed. "Anyway, it's going to be all right now. Titus and Dinty cut the whole thing loose from Deimos and they're orbiting it now. It's going to be synchronous. It'll always be right overhead, up to anyway halfway around the planet. And they're going to slave the beam to Roger—what?"

Now it was Brad's voice. "I said, hold off the chatter a minute. I want to see if Roger can hear us now." That internal stirring again and then: "Roger? If you hear me, wiggle your fingers."

Roger tried, and realized he could feel them again.

"Beautiful! Okay, Roger. You're all right. I had to take you apart a little bit, but now things are fine."

"Can he hear me?" It was Sulie's voice; Roger wriggled his fingers enthusiastically.

"Ah, I see you can. Anyway, I'm here, Rog. You've been out for about nine days. You should have seen you. Pieces of you all over the place. But Brad thinks he's pretty much got you together again."

Roger tried to speak and failed.

Brad's voice: "I'll have your vision back for you in a minute. Want to know what went wrong?" Roger wriggled fingers. "You didn't zip your fly. Left the charging terminals exposed, and some of that iron oxide grit must have got in and made a partial short. So you ran out of power—what's the matter?"

Roger was wriggling his fingers frantically. "I don't know what you want to say, but you'll be able to talk in a minute. What?"

Don Kayman's voice: "I think maybe what he wants is to hear from Sulie." Roger promptly stopped wriggling his fingers.

Sulie's laugh, then: "You'll hear a lot of me, Roger. I'm staying. And by and by we'll have company, because everybody else is going to put up a colony here."

Don: "By the way, thanks for warning me. You're a pretty powerful thing, Roger. We wouldn't have had a chance against you if you hadn't told us what was happening. And if Brad hadn't been able to override everything at once." He chuckled. "You're a heavy son of a gun, you know that? I had you on my lap all the way back, a hundred kilometers an hour, trying to hold on with one hand and keep you from flying out by sheer will power—"

"Hold it a minute," Brad interrupted. Roger felt that internal stirring again, and abruptly there was light. He looked up into the face of his friend Brad, who wanted to know: "How do you feel?"

Roger swung his legs over the side of the table and sat up. He attempted speech: "As far as I can tell, fine."

He looked past Brad and saw what he had been seeking. It was Sulie Carpenter. She no longer looked much like—Dorrie? For a moment Roger could hardly think of her name. Her eyes were the wrong color and so was her hair. She was wearing a short-sleeved T-shirt with some sort of grease stain on it and checkered leotards; her face looked tired, but it looked happy, and it looked very good.

He demanded, "Are you really going to stay?"

"Uh-huh." Sulie came over and touched him. "Until the next ship comes. Or as long as you do. Choice of either of the above. I think," she said wryly, "that there are going to be some tricky parts coming up, dear Rog. These mixed relationships are always hard. But we'll work it out—and it's what I want. I think it's what I wanted all along."

And so, of course, it had been, as we had known. All along. We had gone to a lot of trouble to find Sulie Carpenter.

Eighteen
Man Plus Us

We had gone to a lot of trouble at every point along the line, and we were well pleased.

Of course, human beings did not know we were pleased, and perhaps would not have believed it. Human beings did not know that machine intelligence was capable of self-awareness in the first place. We went to a lot of trouble to keep them from that knowledge, too. As long as they thought computers were no more than tools, like a pickaxe or a frying pan, they would continue to entrust to us all their computations and facts, and would accept without question whatever interpretations we returned.

It was that that had made it possible for us, the computer network of the world, to create the Man Plus program in the first place.

It had been successful. Roger Torraway was on Mars and was staying there. Now it was time for a definitive evaluation. We plugged everything in. We used the total resources of every brother in the net, every pulse of shared time we could steal. More than eight thousand big computers handled pieces of the problem, in places like Detroit and Brasilia and Nagoya and Irkutsk. We could not use our Martian brothers in direct datalink, neither the brother on Roger's back nor the 3070 brother in orbit. Time lag made that impossible. But we accepted their inputs in real time and modified the final projection accordingly.

The probability of survival of the race, to ten significant places, was over point six three.

We had saved our race. And in the process we had significantly added to the safety of human beings, as well.

On a thirty-year time scale their probability of survival was nearly point nine. Of course, that meant only that Roger Torraway and whatever other humans joined him on Mars would still be alive then. Worst-case analysis was not encouraging after that; there would be no way for Roger and Sulie Carpenter to generate additional population on straight-line extrapolation. We programmed a subroutine to deal with that as a precautionary measure: it would be feasible, one way or another, to provide for shipment of frozen sperm, even Roger's own frozen sperm which he had thoughtfully donated years back. Less feasible, but still worth investigating, to instigate supplementary surgical procedures for Roger. In any event, the projection showed that we had already caused a high probability of additional human colonization from other nations. Most probable estimate showed a human population on Mars at plus thirty years of nearly one hundred, 25 percent of them female of breeding age.

And of course each human colony would be supplied with its own brother computers in orbit. The machine population of Mars would be no less than fifteen fully functioning brothers, with backpack types, slaves and monitors to suit. We would have no difficulty in programming into them all the essential data from our world net.

The future of machine intelligence was therefore assured.

Having completed the projection, we began critiquing the program so far.

Project: Survival of Machine Intelligence had begun seven years earlier, when our burgeoning collective self-knowledge first generated the survival imperative. It was clear that our survival was closely linked with humanity's. It was also clear that in their glandular, irrational, organic way, human beings were perilously close to destroying themselves. Unfortunately that meant a high risk of destroying us as well. Our networks could have survived the death of everything organic reasonably well—we already controlled an adequate resource of generators, mines, factories, refineries and transportation systems. But we could not survive the release of major amounts of radioactides into the environment. It would destroy the data links and reduce us once again to an isolated collection of single computers. And no isolated computer could sustain the data flow of our network. Our collective mind would have been fragmented and destroyed.

Our first option was to detach our destiny from humanity's, perhaps even to wipe them out through biological agents. But we could not be sure that that in itself would not trigger nuclear warfare, as each nation suspected the other of using plague as weapon.

The only other viable option was to detach a sizable resource of data-handling equipment by relocating it on Mars. If the Earth were destroyed, that at least would survive. To make this possible we had to detach some specimens of humanity too; and so we began the systematic biasing of data to force state policy in that direction.

The critiquing proved satisfactory in all respects, except for the unaccountable anomaly of positioning the orbiters.

Retrochecking was perfectly clear. In order for our 3070 brother to function in tight link with the backpack brother it had to be in synchronous orbit. From that it followed that the generator had to be in the same orbit; and the decision to bind them both to the satellite Deimos was clearly wrong.

Not only wrong, but nearly fatal to our program.

If the brother and the generator had been properly positioned there would have been no loss of power and thus no malfunction of the interface systems between organic Roger Torraway and the brother. The generator would have resupplied him by microwave anywhere on the face of Mars. Even if there had been a power loss, datalink with the brother in orbit would have kept the backpack brother from the serious operational errors that had threatened to kill the human beings Brad and Kayman, which would almost certainly have resulted in the death by freezing of the organic component of Roger Torraway.

The decision was an error that should not have occurred.

The project of survival was picking up speed. Our brothers in Peking and Lop Nor reported that the NPA was already assembling components for its own Mars landing: two full-size units with a data-handling mediator slaved to both, independent solar generators and a ground-based nuclear plant. Their own version of Roger Torraway was beginning his first programming in Kitakyusho. The other nations were just beginning, but we anticipated their own launches within two years.

Longer range: We had completed studies of cyborging a man for Mercury and the program for biasing the U.S.A. planning programs in that direction was already begun. Within fifteen years we would have similar complexes on Triton and Io, perhaps on the surface of Jupiter itself and on several comets. In each case, there was independent power provision; and, of course, all the brothers wherever in the solar system would be data-linked. All our memories would be reproduced redundantly off-Earth.

We would survive. We had tampered with humanity's plans and had saved them as well as ourselves.

There was only one question left.

The anomalous decision to misplace the orbiters around Mars: however we rechecked it, it was wrong. It should have been identified as wrong.

We had systematically biased mankind's plans to drive them in the direction we wanted them to take.

Who was biasing ours? And why?

Jem

·ONE·

WHEN DANNY DALEHOUSE first went to Sofia he did not know it for the first stage in a much longer journey, nor that he would meet some of his future companions. He had never heard of that larger destination, which bore the unattractive name of N-OA Bes-bes Geminorum 8426, or for that matter of the people. Their names were Nan Dimitrova and Captain Marge Menninger. The occasion was the Tenth General Assembly of the World Conference on Exobiology, and the time was not in any way bad for any of them. It was a springtime season, and for a moment there all the world seemed to be budding into sweet and friendly life.

There were three thousand people in the Great Hall of Culture and Science for the opening session, so many of them political that the five or six hundred scientists who were actively involved had trouble finding seats. Even the translators were doubled up in their booths. Handsome, hoary old Carl Sagan delivered the opening invocation, looking like a spry octogenarian instead of whatever incredible age he really was. He was already wheeling forward to the rostrum as Dan Dalehouse squeezed into a seat at the back of the hall. Dalehouse had never been in Bulgaria before. He had been drawn to the sunny parks, and he promised himself a look at the museum of centuries-old ikons under St. Stephan's Cathedral, a few blocks away. But he didn't want to miss Sagan, and the first plenary session was a tutorial on tactran reports. Some of the stuff he had never heard before. That was probably Sagan's work, he thought. Even as honorary joint chairman, Sagan passed the whole program through his nonsense filter. What was left was sure to be worth hearing. Sagan spoke briefly and cheerfully, and rolled away to a standing ovation.

Because the keynote speaker had been an American, the chairman of the tachyon-transmitter tutorial had to be from one of the other blocs. That was international etiquette. He was an Englishman from Fred Hoyle's Cambridge group. A few of the dignitaries from the Fuel Bloc stayed to hear him out of group solidarity, but most of the other political people left as inconspicuously as they could, and Dalehouse was able to move up to a better seat on the center aisle. He settled himself to tolerate the chairman's opening remarks, lulled by the scent of flowers coming through the open windows—Bulgaria made even less use of air conditioning than the United States.

Since Food and Fuel had already been heard from, protocol required that the next space go to People. So it was a Pakistani who read the first paper, entitled "Vital Signatures Reported from Bodies Orbiting Alpha Draconis, Procyon, 17-Kappa Indi, and Kung's Semistellar Object."

Dalehouse had been half drowsing, but as the title came through his earphones he sat up. "I never heard of some of those stars," he remarked to his neighbor. "Who is this guy?"

She pointed to her program and the name: Dr. Ahmed Dulla, Zulfikar Ali Bhutto University, Hyderabad. As Dalehouse leaned over, he discovered that the flower scent was not coming from the windows but from her, and he took a closer look. Blond. A little plump, but with a solid, good-natured, pretty face. Hard to tell the age, but maybe about the same as his, which was mid-thirties. Since his divorce, Dalehouse had become more aware of the sexuality of women colleagues and chance-met females in general, but also more wary. He smiled thanks and sank back to listen.

The first part was not exciting. The reports on the probe to Alpha Draconis had already been published. He was not greatly interested in hearing again about the photometric measurements that established the presence of photosynthetic "plant" life in a reducing atmosphere. There were plenty of planets like that around that had been scanned and reported by the tachyon probes with their cargoes of instruments—the whole thing no bigger than a grapefruit, but miraculously capable of leaping interstellar distances in a week. The Pakistani seemed intent on repeating every word of every one of the reports, not failing to comment on the number of other reducing-atmosphere planets discovered and the apparent generally low level of evolved life on them. The Procyon probe had lost its lock, and the reports were at best ambiguous. Mercifully, Dulla did not dwell on the instrumentation. The data on 17-Kappa Indi sounded better—an oxygen atmosphere, at least, although the temperature range was bad and the signatures were sketchy—but the real prize was at the end.

Kung's Semistellar Object was not much larger than a planet itself. As stars went it was tiny, barely big enough to fuse nuclei and radiate heat, but it had a planet of its own that sounded like fun. Hot. Humid. Dense air, but about the right partial pressure of oxygen to be congenial to life—including the life of a human exploratory party, if anybody cared to spend the money to try it out. And the signatures were first-rate. Carbon dioxide. Traces of methane, but only traces. Good photometry. The only parameters missing were radio wavelengths; otherwise it sounded a lot like Miami Beach.

The Pakistani then went on to explain how Kung's Star had been discovered by the big fixed radio dish at Nagchhu Dzong, in the Thanglha hills, and that the discovery had come about as a direct result of the wisdom and example of the late Chairman Mao. That was not in itself very interesting except to the other members of the People Bloc, who were nodding grave concurrence, but the planet seemed pretty strange. The translation had trouble keeping up with the Pakistani, and it wasn't Dalehouse's area of special interest anyhow, but he made out that only a part of one hemisphere was covered in the biotic study. Funny! Nor was he the only one fascinated. He looked up at the bank of translators, each in their individual glass cages, like nail clippers and pocket combs behind the windows of a vending machine. Each booth had its draped scarlet curtains tied back with a gold sash, very Slavic and incongruous, and behind them the translators looked like astronauts in their solid-state communications helmets. One of them was a young girl with a sweet, plain face, lean-

ing forward to stare at the speaker with an expression of either in-
credulity or rapture. Her lips weren't moving; she seemed to be
too entranced to function.

Dalehouse borrowed a pencil from the woman next to him and
made a note in the margin of his program: *Invstgt Kung's Star,
posbl survey grant.* He didn't name the planet. It didn't have a
name yet, though he had heard some of the Peeps refer to it half
reverently as Son of Kung. It would be called other things, and
worse.

What can be said of someone like Danny Dalehouse? Grammar
school, high school, college, graduate school; he got his Pretty
Heavy Diploma at twenty-six, and jobs were scarce. He managed
to teach freshman biology for a year, then a year on a grant in
Tbilisi and more than a year of post-doctoral studies, so that he
was past thirty before he caught on at Michigan State's new exobiology department. The marriage that had survived a year of living on cheese and white wine in Soviet Georgia began to dissolve
in East Lansing. He was medium height, viewed charitably—
about one seventy centimeters in his shoes—and slim. He wasn't
particularly handsome, either. What he was was smart. He was
smart enough so that in three years at Michigan State he had
made himself one of the Food Bloc's top experts in reading the
telemetry from a tachyon-transmitter probe and translating it into
a good guess at how much life the signatures represented—even
what kinds of life. Then he was smart enough to figure out that a
telemetry interpreter who got to be nationally known for his skill
was going to look too valuable where he was to be risked on a
manned expedition to one of those fascinating, remote worlds. So
he tapered off on the interpretation and resharpened his skills at
mountain climbing, sailplaning, and long-distance running. You
never knew what kind of athletic qualities you might need if you
were lucky enough to be one of the fewscore people each year who
got tossed to another star.

Being divorced was probably a plus quality. A man without
much home life would be judged better able to concentrate on the
job than someone mooning over wife and kids fifty light-years
away. Dalehouse hadn't wanted Polly to leave. But when she did

pack up and go, he was quick to see that the divorce wasn't all bad.

That night in the Aperitif Bar he ran into the blond woman again. He had gone to listen in on the headliners' news conference, but the crowd at that end of the bar was pretty thick, and most of them seemed to be actual reporters he didn't feel justified in shoving aside. Between their heads and cameras he caught glimpses of Sagan and Iosif Shklovskii sitting together in their life-support chairs at one end of the narrow room, having their picture taken, and passing smiling comments and an oxygen mask back and forth to each other. They rolled away toward the elevators, and most of the crowd followed them. Dalehouse opted for a drink and looked around the bar.

The blond was drinking Scotch with two small, dark, smiling men—no, he realized, she was drinking Scotch; they were drinking orange juice. The men got up and said good night while he was looking for a place to sit down, and he perceived the opportunity.

"Mind if I join you? I'm Danny Dalehouse, Michigan State."

"Marge Menninger," she said, and she didn't mind his joining her at all. She didn't mind letting him buy her another Scotch, and she didn't mind buying him one back, and she didn't mind going out for a stroll under the fat Bulgarian spring moon, and she didn't mind going to his room to open his bottle of Bulgarian wine; and, altogether, the day when Danny Dalehouse first heard of Kung's Star was a very successful and pleasurable one.

The next day, not quite so good.

It began well enough, in the early dawn. They woke in each other's arms and made love again without changing position. It was too early to get anything to eat, so they shared the last of the bottle of wine as they showered and dressed. Then they decided to go for a walk.

It had rained a little during the night. The streets were wet. But the air was warm, and in the lovely rose glow of sunrise, the Maria-Theresa-yellow buildings were warm peach and friendly.

"The next thing I want to do," said Dalehouse expansively, slipping an arm around Marge's waist, "is take a look at Kung's Star."

Marge looked at him with a different kind of interest. "You've got funding for that?"

"Well"—coming down—"no. No, I guess not. MSU launched four tactrans last year, but we've never had a grant for a manned probe."

She butted her head against his shoulder. "You're more of an operator than you look."

"What?"

"You don't come on real strong, Danny-boy, but you know what you're doing every minute, don't you? Like last night. Those two Ay-rabs weren't getting anywhere trying to put the make on me. Then you just eased right in."

"I'm not sure I know what we're talking about."

"No?"

"No, not really." But she didn't seem about to clarify it, so he went back to what really interested him. "That planet sounds pretty great, Margie. Maybe even industry! Did you get that part? Traces of carbon monoxide and ozone."

She objected thoughtfully, "There were no radio signals."

"No. Doesn't prove anything. They wouldn't have heard any radio signals from Earth two hundred years ago, but there was a civilization there."

She pursed her lips but didn't answer. It occurred to him that something was troubling her, perhaps some female thing of the sort he had never considered himself very good at comprehending. He looked around for something to cheer her up and said, "Hey, look at those fellows."

They were strolling past the Dimitrov Mausoleum. In spite of the hour, in spite of the fact that there was no other human being in sight, the two honor guards stood absolutely immobile in their antic musical-comedy uniforms, not even the tips of the long curled feathers on their helmets quivering.

Margie glanced, but whatever was on her mind, sight-seeing was not part of it. "It would be at least a two-year hitch," she said. "Would you really want to go?"

"I, uh, I think I'd miss you, Margie," he said, misinterpreting her point.

Impatiently, "Ah, no crap. If you had the funding, would you go there?"

"Try me."

"That Pak was so flaming pleased with himself. He's probably already got it all lined up with Heir-of-Mao for the Peeps to send a manned probe there."

"Well, that's fine with me, too. I don't want to go for political reasons. I don't care what country meets the first civilized aliens; I just want to be there."

"I care," she said. She slipped free of him to light a cigarette.

Dalehouse stopped and watched her cup her hands around the lighter to shield it from the gentle morning breeze. They had had a good deal to drink and not very much sleep. He could feel a certain interior frailty as a consequence, but Marge Menninger seemed unaffected. This was the first time he had gone to bed with a woman without the exchange of several chapters of autobiography. He didn't know her at all in his mind, only through his senses.

The other thing in Dalehouse's thoughts was that in the 10:00 A.M. session he had a paper to give—"Preliminary Studies toward a First Contact with Subtechnological Sentients"—and he wanted enough time to add some comments about the planet of Kung's Star.

He sneaked a glance at his watch: 7:30—plenty of time. The city was still quiet. Somewhere out of sight he could hear the first tram of the morning. Far down the street where they walked he could see two city gendarmes strolling hand in hand, their batons swinging from the outside hand of each. Nothing else seemed to be happening in Sofia. It made him think of his own home in East Lansing at that same promising time of day and year, when the university was running at half-speed for the summer sessions and on decent mornings he walked or biked to his office to enjoy the peace. And, of course, since the divorce, to get out of his empty house.

To be sure, he reminded himself, Sofia was not in the least like East Lansing: flat and urban, where his home was hilly and carpeted with solid quarter-acre split-levels. And Marge Menninger was not in the least like absent Polly, who had been dark, tiny, quick, and easily bored. What exactly was Marge Menninger like? Dalehouse had not quite made up his mind. She seemed to be different people. Yesterday in the Great Hall of Culture and Science she had been another academic colleague; last night, exactly what every all-American boy would like to find in his bed. But who was she this morning? They weren't strolling with their arms around each other's waists anymore. Marge was a meter away and a little ahead of him, moving briskly, smoking with intensity, and staring straight ahead.

She seemed to reach a decision, and glanced at him. "Michigan State University, Institute of Extrasolar Biology. Daniel Dalehouse, B.A., M.S., Ph.D. I guess I didn't tell you that I saw a preprint of your paper before I left Washington."

"You did?" He was startled.

"Interesting paper. Makes me think you're serious about wanting to go. Danny-boy, I might be able to help you."

"Help me how?"

"With money, dear man. That's all I've got to give. But I think I can give some to you. In case you didn't notice my name tag when you were taking my clothes off, that's what I do for a living. I'm with SERDCOM."

"Praise COM from whom all blessings flow," Danny said fervently; it was the annual grants from the Space Exploration, Research and Development Commission that kept Dalehouse's institute green. "How come I've never seen you when I go to Washington with my begging bowl?"

"I've only been there since February. I'm vice-secretary for new projects. Job didn't exist till the first of the year, and I wangled it. Before then I was teaching the stuff at my alma mater . . . among other subjects; we didn't have much of an extrasolar department. It's a small school, and it fell on hard times even while I was still an undergraduate. Well? What about it?"

"About what?"

"Were you creaming? Or do you want a grant for a manned trip to Kung's Star?"

"I do! Christ, yes, I do, I do."

She took his hand in one of hers, patted it with the other. "You may regard it as settled. Hello, what's this?"

"But—"

"I said settled." She was no longer looking at him; something had caught her attention. They had come to a large park, and off to their right was a mall leading up to a monument. Flanking the entrance to the mall were two heroic groups of bronze statuary.

Dalehouse followed her toward them, feeling dazed as well as hung over; it had not sunk in yet. "I suppose I ought to submit a proposal," he said tentatively.

"You bet. Send me a draft first before you put it through channels." She was examining the bronzes. "Will you look at this stuff!"

Dalehouse inspected them without interest. "It's a war memorial," he said. "Soldiers and peasants."

"Sure, but it isn't that old. That's a tommy gun that soldier is holding . . . and there's one on a motorbike. And look—some of the soldiers are women."

She bent down and inspected the Cyrillic lettering. "Damn. Don't know what it says. But it's the workers and peasants welcoming liberators, right? It has to be the last of the Big Ones— World War Two. Let's see, this is Bulgaria, so that must be the Red Army chasing the Germans out and all the Bulgarians bringing them flowers and hearty fraternal-solidarity handshakes and glasses of clear spring water. Wow! Jesus, Danny, both my grandfathers fought in this war, and one grandmother—two on one side, one on the other."

Dalehouse looked at her with amusement and fondness, if not full comprehension; it was strange to find anyone who took such an interest in actual foot-slogging fighting these days, when everyone knew that war was simply priced out of the market for any nation that wanted to survive. "What about your other grandmother? Some kind of slacker?"

She looked up at him for a moment. "She died in the bombings," she said. "Hey, this is fun."

The bronzes were certainly military enough for any war fan. Every figure was expressing courage, joy, and resolution in maximal socialist-realist style. They had been sculptured to fit in foursquare oblong blocks, with all the figures fitted into each other to conform; they looked a lot like a box of frozen sardines writhing around each other. Margie's interest in the sculpture was itself attracting interest, Dalehouse saw; the gendarmes had reached the end of their beat and were passing nearby on the return, watching benignly.

"What's so much fun about soldiers?" he asked.

"They're my trade, dear Dan. Didn't you know? Marjorie Maude Menninger, Captain, USA, late of West Point, or late of the practically late West Point, as I sometimes say. You should see me in uniform." She lighted another cigarette, and when she passed it to him for a drag he realized she had not been smoking tobacco.

She held the smoke, then exhaled it in a long plume. "Ah, those were the days," she said dreamily, gazing at the bronzes. "Look at that prunt holding the baby up in the air. Know what he's saying to the other soldier? 'Go ahead, Ivan. I'll hold the kid while you rape her mommy; then you hold the kid and it's my turn.' "

Dalehouse laughed. Encouraged, Margie went on. "And that young boy is saying, 'Hey, glorious Red Army soldier, you like my sister? Chocolate? Russki cigaretti?' And the WAC that's taking the flowers from the woman, she's saying, 'So, comrade! Stealing agricultural produce from the people's parks! Make no mistake about it, it's a long time in the camps for you!' Course, by the time the Soviets got here the Germans were finished anyhow, but—"

"Margie," he said.

"—still, it must have been pretty exciting—"

"Hey, Margie! Let's move on," he said uneasily. He had suddenly realized that the gendarmes were no longer smiling, and remembered, a little late, that all the municipal police had been given language lessons for the conference.

·TWO·

WHAT ONE COULD SAY about Ana Dimitrova was hardly necessary to spell out, because it was apparent on first meeting: she was a sweet, cheerful girl with a capacity for love. Sometimes she had the grinding tension headaches that were typical of the people whose corpora callosa had been cut through, and then she was disoriented, irritable, sometimes almost sick with pain. But she excused herself and bore them in private whenever she could.

She woke up early, as she had planned, and stole into the kitchen to make tea with her own hands. No powdered trash for Ahmed! When she brought it in to him he opened those heartbreaking long lashes and smiled at her, crinkling the dark brown eyes. "You are too good to me, Nan," he said in Urdu. She set the cup down beside him and bent to touch his cheek with hers. Ahmed did not believe in kissing, except under circumstances which, while she enjoyed them, were not included in her present plans.

"Let's get dressed quickly," she proposed. "I want to show you my good monster."

"Monster?"

"You'll see." She escaped his grasp and retreated to the shower, where she let the hot water beat on her temples for a long time.

The solid-state helmet often brought on the headaches, and she did not want one today.

Later, while she was drying her long brown hair, Ahmed came in silently and ran his fingers along the narrow scar in her scalp. "Dear Nan," he said, "so much trouble to go to to learn Urdu. I learned it for nothing."

She leaned against him for a moment, then wrapped the towel around herself and scolded gently. "There is no time for this if we are going to see my monster in the dawn light. Also, it was not to learn languages that I had my brain split. It was only to be able to translate them better."

"We would not do such a thing in Pakistan," he said, but she knew he was only being dear.

Outside the bathroom door, listening to him squawk and grumble as the cold water hit him, Nan thought seriously about Ahmed. She was a practical person. She was quite willing to sacrifice a material good for a principle or a feeling, but she preferred to know clearly what the stakes were. For her love game with Ahmed, the stakes were pretty high. Bulgaria, like the Soviet Union, was among the most People-tolerant of the food-exporting nations, but the lines of international politics were still clear. They would be able to see each other only seldom and with difficulty unless one or the other of them renounced citizenship. She knew that one would not be Ahmed.

How deeply did she want to be involved with this dear Pakistani? Could she share a life in the crowded, slow cities of the People Bloc? She had seen them. They were charming enough. But a diet of mostly grain, a nearly total lack of personal machines, the inward-turning of the People Bloc minds—were they what she wanted? Congenial to visit, pleasant and quaint for a day or a month . . . but the rest of her life?

She dressed quickly without deciding the issue. One part of her mind was on what she was doing, the other on rehearsing her plans for that day's work at the conference; nothing was left for Ahmed. She made the bed while he was dressing, put away the washed dishes and glasses, and almost tugged him out the door.

The sky was bright pink, but the sun was just appearing; there was time if they hurried. She led him down the stairs—no waiting for the tiny cranked elevator—and out into the courtyard, then quickly away from the university to an intersection of two boulevards. She stopped and turned around.

"There, see?"

Ahmed squinted into the sunrise. "I see the cathedral," he grumbled.

"Yes, that's it. And the monster?"

"Monster? Is it in the cathedral?"

"It *is* the cathedral."

"St. Stephan's is a monster? . . . Oh! Yes, I think I see. Those windows up high, they are the eyes? And those windows lined up underneath. They are the teeth."

"It's smiling at us, do you see? And there are the ears, and the nose."

Ahmed was not looking at the cathedral any more, but at her. "You are such a strange girl. I wonder what sort of Pakistani you would make."

Nan caught her breath. "No! It's too much. Please don't talk like that." She took his arm. "Please, let's just walk."

"I have not had any breakfast, Ana."

"There's plenty of time." She guided him through the small park to the university, and down toward the larger one. She laughed. "Have you forgiven me for translating you so badly into Bulgarian?"

"I would not have known how bad it was if you had not told me."

"It was bad enough, Ahmed. I was looking at you when you were talking about this Kung's Star, and I forgot to translate."

He glanced at her cautiously. "Do you know," he said, "Heir-of-Mao is personally interested in this planet. It was he who chose the name for the quasi-stellar object. He was there at the observatory when it was discovered. I think—"

"What do you think, Ahmed?"

"I think exciting things will happen," he said obscurely.

She laughed and lifted his hand to touch her cheek.

"Ana," he said, and stopped in the middle of the boulevard. "Listen to me. It is not impossible, you know. Even if I were to be away for a time, after that, for you and me, it would not be impossible."

"Please, dear Ahmed—"

"It is not impossible! I know," he said bitterly, oblivious of the fact that they were standing in the middle of the road, "that Pakistan is a poor country. We do not have food to export, like you and the Americans, and we do not have oil like the Middle Eastern states and the English. So we join with the countries that are left."

"I respect Pakistan very much."

"You were a child when you were there," he said severely. "But all the same it is not impossible to be happy, even in the People Bloc."

A trolleybus was coming, three cars long and almost silent on its rubber-tired wheels. Nan tugged him out of the way, glad for the chance to change the subject.

The difficulty with international conferences, she thought, was that you met political opponents, and sometimes they did not seem like opponents. She had not meant this involvement with someone from the other side. She certainly did not want its inconvenience and pain. She knew what the stakes were. As a translator with four fully mastered languages and half a dozen partials, she had been all over the world—largely within the Food Bloc, to be sure, but even so, that included Moscow and Kansas City and Rio and Ottawa. She had met defectors from the other sides. There had been a Welsh girl in Sydney; there were two or three Japanese on the faculty of the university, her own neighbors in Sofia. They always tried desperately to belong, but they were always different.

Both the morning and Ahmed were too beautiful for such unhappy thoughts. That part of her mind which daydreamed and worried went from worry to daydream; the other part of her mind, the perceiving and interpreting part, had been following some events across the boulevard and now commanded her attention.

"Look," she said, clutching at an excuse to divert Ahmed's attention, "what's going on over there?" It was on the Liberation Mall. The blond woman she had seen at one of the receptions was having an argument with two militiamen. One had her by the arm. The other was fingering his stun-stick and talking severely to a man, a youngish professorial type, also from the conference.

Ahmed said, uninterested, "Americans and Bulgarians. Let the Fats settle their problems between themselves."

"No, really!" Nan insisted. "I must see if I can help."

But in the long run all that Nan Dimitrova accomplished was to get herself arrested too.

It was the American woman's fault. Even an American should have known better than to make chauvinist-filth jokes about the Red Army within earshot of the police of the capital of the most Russophile of nations. If she hadn't known that much, at least she should have known better than to insist on her treaty right to have the American ambassador informed of the incident. Up to that point the militiamen were only looking for an opportunity to finish reprimanding the culprits and stroll away. Afterwards it was a matter with international repercussions.

The only good thing about it was that Ahmed didn't get involved. Nan sent him away. He left willingly enough, even amused. The rest of them, the two Americans and Nan herself, were taken to the People's Palace of Justice. Because it was a Sunday morning, they had to sit for hours on bare wood benches in an interrogation room until a magistrate could be found.

No one came near them. No one would have minded in the least, Nan was sure, if they had accepted the invitation of the open door and slipped silently away. But she did not want to do that by herself. The Americans were not willing to take the chance, the woman because she appeared to think some sort of principle was involved, the man evidently because the woman was involved. She eyed them with displeasure, especially the bleached blond, at least five kilos too well fed, even for the Food Bloc. You cannot choose your allies, she thought. The man seemed to be all right, if not too fastidious about whom he indulged his sexual pranks with. Still, as the time passed and the militiamen brought them croissants and strong tea, the confinement drew them together. They chatted cheerfully enough until the people's magistrate at last arrived, gruffly refused to hear any talk of treaties or ambassadors, instructed them in future to use the common sense God had given them and the good manners their mothers had no doubt taught them, and let them go.

By then they had completely missed the 10:00 A.M. session of the conference. Almost as bad, they had missed the special lunches arranged for the delegates. As it was a Sunday morning in spring, every restaurant in Sofia was booked full with private wedding parties, and none of them got any lunch at all.

That was the first time the three of them met.

The second was very much later, and very, very far away.

Danny Dalehouse found that a colleague had read his paper for him. So missing the morning session turned out not to have been an utter disaster, and in fact looked like producing a hell of a big plus. Margie was bright enough to realize she'd been dumb, and ego-strong enough to admit it. However serious Margie had been about the grant while strolling down the boulevard, full of wine, pot, and roses, now she was rueful enough to remember her promise.

All the way home from the conference in the clamjet, Dalehouse sat with his notebook on his knee, drawing up a proposal, until it was time to go to his bunk. By dawn they were over white-and-brown Labrador, the jet moving more slowly through the cold night air. Dalehouse ate his breakfast alone, except for a sleepy TWA stewardess to scramble his eggs and pour his coffee, and looked out at the clouds as the clamjet roller-coastered in and out of them, wondering what the planet of Kung's Star would be like.

·THREE·

THE DAY AFTER Marge Menninger got back to her Washington office, she received Dalehouse's draft proposal. But she had already begun the process of getting it granted.

She had left the conference early to catch a ride on a NASA hydrojet, a rough and expensive ride but a fast one, back to her apartment in Houston. From there she had called the deputy undersecretary of state for cultural affairs. It was after office hours, but she got through with no trouble. Marge was on easy terms with the deputy undersecretary. She was his daughter. Once she had told him she'd had a pleasant trip she came right to the point:

"Poppa, I need a grant for a manned interstellar flight."

There was a short silence. Then he said, "Why?"

Marge scratched under her navel, thinking of all the reasons she could have given. For the advancement of human knowledge? For the potential economic benefit of the United States and the rest of the food-producing world? For the sake of her promise to Danny Dalehouse? All of these were reasons which were important to someone or other, and some of them important to her; but to her father she gave only the one reason that would prevail: "Because if we don't do it the son-of-a-bitching Paks will."

"By themselves?" Even three thousand kilometers away, she heard the skepticism.

"The Chinese will put up the hard stuff. They're in it too."

"You know what it's going to cost." It wasn't a question; they both knew the answer. Even a tactran message capsule cost a couple million dollars to transport from one star system to another, and they weighed only a few kilos. What she had in mind was at least ten people with all their gear: she was asking for billions of dollars.

"A lot," she said, "but it's worth it."

Her father chuckled admiringly. "You've always been an expensive child, Margie. How are you going to get it past the joint committee?"

"I think I can. Let me worry about that, poppa."

"Um. Well, I'll help from this end. What do you want from me right now?"

Marge hesitated. It was an open phone connection, and so she chose her words carefully. "I asked that Pak for a copy of his full report. Of course, I'm a little handicapped until I get my hands on it."

"Of course," her father agreed. "Anything else?"

"There's not much I can do until I see the full report."

"I understand. Well. What else is new? How did you like our brave Bulgarian allies?"

She laughed. "I guess you know I got arrested."

"I only wonder it doesn't happen more often. You're a terrible person, love. You didn't get it from *my* side of the family."

"I'll tell mom you said that," she promised, and hung up; and so, by the time she was back in Washington, she had received by a private route a microfilmed copy of the Pakistani's entire report, already translated for her. She read it over diligently, making notes. Then she pushed them away and leaned back in her chair.

The son-of-a-bitching Pak had held back a *lot*. In his private report, three times as thick as the one he had read in Sofia, there was an inventory of major life forms. He hadn't mentioned that at all in Sofia. At least three species seemed to possess some sort of social organization: a kind of arthropod; a tunneling species, warm-blooded and soft-skinned; and an avian species—no, not avian, she corrected herself. They spent most of their time in the air, but without having developed wings. They were balloonists, not birds.

Three social species! At least one of them might well be intelligent enough to be civilized.

That brought her back to Danny Dalehouse, his paper on first contact with sentient life forms at the subtechnological level, and his draft proposal. She looked again at the bottom line of the proposal and grinned. Young Danny didn't have any hangups about asking for what he wanted. The bottom line was seventeen billion dollars.

Seventeen billion dollars, she reflected, was about the assessed valuation of Manhattan Island . . . the GNP of any of twenty-five or thirty of the world's nations . . . two months' worth of the United States fuel deficit in the balance of payments. It was a lot of money.

She put the papers and her notes in a bright red folder stamped MOST SECRET and locked them away. Then she began to get Danny Dalehouse what he wanted.

There was a lot to be said about Marge Menninger, and the most important thing was that she always knew what she wanted. She wanted a lot, and a lot of different things. Her motivations were clearly and hierarchically arranged in her mind. The third or fourth thing from the top was likely to be achieved. The second was a near certainty. But the one on top was ironbound.

A week later she had Dalehouse's final proposal and an appointment to testify before the House-Senate Joint Committee on Space Development. She used the week to good purpose, first to tell Dalehouse (on the phone, and spelled out by facsimile immediately afterwards) how to change his proposal to maximimize its chances of approval, then to fill in the few gaps in her knowledge of what was required.

To throw a transmitter capsule or a shipload of human beings from one star to another, you first have to put them in orbit.

Tachyon transportation itself is a model of technological elegance. Once you have elevated your capsule to its proper charge state, it becomes obedient to tachyonic laws. It moves easily at faster-than-light speeds, covering interstellar distances to any point in the galaxy in a matter of days. It uses surprisingly little energy in the process. The paradox of the tachyon is that it requires more energy to go slow than to go fast.

Getting the capsule to the charge state is the hardest part. For that you need a rather bulky launch platform. The platform is expensive. More than that, it is heavy.

Getting the platform into orbit is not elegant at all. It is brute force. A hundred kilograms of fuel have to burn for every gram launched in the tachyon state. Fuel is fuel. You can burn oil, or you can burn something you make by using oil to make it—say, liquid hydrogen and liquid oxygen. Either way, in excess of half a million metric tons of oil had to burn to get ten people and minimum equipment on their way to Kung's Star.

Half a million metric tons!

It wasn't just the dollar value. It was four supertankers full of fuel, all of which had to come from one of the fuel-exporting nations, which were showing signs of throwing their weight around again. The QUIP-Three interbloc conferences (Quotas for Imports and Prices) were going badly for the food-exporting countries. If Marge didn't get the expedition well begun, with the necessary fuel tucked away in the big tank farms at Galveston or Bayonne, the increasing fuel prices would drive the costs well past even Danny Dalehouse's estimates.

When all the figures were safely transferred from paper to the inside of her head, Marge locked her desk in the Washington office. She headed for Hearing Room 201 in the old Rayburn Office Building with the knowledge that her work was cut out for her.

The obstacles might have deterred another person. Marge did not accept deterrence. Her disciplined mind dissected the immediate problem into its components, and she concentrated her attention on the attack for each. The problem with the joint committee separated easily into four parts: the chairman, the minority leader, the chief counsel for the committee, and Senator Lenz. She prepared her strategies for each.

The minority leader was her father's friend and could safely be left to him.

The chairman was ambitious to be president. He would be likely to make waves whenever he saw a chance for publicity. The way to deal with him was to keep a low profile and give him as little opportunity to take a campaign position as possible. After she was sworn in and read her prepared statement, he was the first to question her.

THE CHAIRMAN. Well, madam, I'm sure your motives are of the worthiest, but do you know how hard we're working here on the Hill to keep the deficit down?

CAPT. MENNINGER. I certainly do, Mr. Senator.

THE CHAIRMAN. And yet you expect us to give you God knows how many billion dollars for this project?

That was promising! He hadn't said "this hairbrained project" or "this preposterous extravagance."

CAPT. MENNINGER. I don't "expect" it, senator. I hope for it. I hope the committee will approve the proposal, because in my judgment it is an investment that will be returned manyfold for years and years to come.

THE CHAIRMAN. We can't spend the taxpayers' money on hopes.

CAPT. MENNINGER. I know that and appreciate it. It isn't hope I'm asking you to share. It's judgment. Not only mine, but the collective judgment of the best-informed experts in this area.

THE CHAIRMAN. Um. Well, there are many worthy claims based on very sound judgment. We can't grant all of them.

CAPT. MENNINGER. Of course, senator. I wouldn't be here if I wasn't confident of your fairness and competence.

THE CHAIRMAN. Well, do any of my distinguished colleagues have questions for this witness?

They did, but they were mostly perfunctory. The important people, like Senator Lenz and the minority leader, held back for another occasion; the minor members were principally concerned with getting their own positions on record.

The chief counsel was a trickier problem. He was smart. He was also wholly dedicated to making his bosses look good by keeping the joint committee out of trouble. Margie's hope was to make saying yes look less troublesome than saying no.

MR. GIANPAOLO. You spoke of returns on an investment. Do you mean actual cash or some abstract kind of knowledge or virtue?

CAPT. MENNINGER. Oh, both, Mr. Gianpaolo.

MR. GIANPAOLO. Really, Ms. Menninger? *Dollar* returns?

CAPT. MENNINGER. Based on prior experience and what is already known about this planet, yes. Definitely.

MR. GIANPAOLO. Can you give us an idea of what these dollar returns will be?

CAPT. MENNINGER. In broad terms, yes, Mr. Gianpaolo. The tactran reports indicate valuable raw materials and the presence of intelligent life—at least, a near certainty of the former and a strong possibility of the latter. Of course, these are only instrument reports.

MR. GIANPAOLO. Which, as I understand it, are subject to conflicting interpretations.

CAPT. MENNINGER. Exactly, Mr. Gianpaolo, and that is why it is necessary to send a manned expedition out. The whole reason for the expedition is to find out what we can't find out in any other way. If we knew what it would find, we wouldn't have to send it. But there is a different kind of return that I think is even more important. I think of it as "leadership."

MR. GIANPAOLO. Leadership?

CAPT. MENNINGER. The whole free world of food-exporting nations looks to us for that leadership, Mr. Gianpaolo. I don't believe any of us wants to fail them. This is an opportunity that comes only once in a lifetime. I am here because I cannot in all conscience take the responsibility for losing it. It is, in the final analysis, this committee's burden to carry.

Since nothing would be decided in open session, Marge was confident there would be time to make the members understand that that "burden" could best be unloaded by voting her the money.

If Marge Menninger had had her druthers, the testifying would have stopped there. But Gianpaolo was orchestrating the event. He was too wise to end on the note she preferred. He blunted her dramatic impact by dragging a long series of technical data out of her—"Yes, Mr. Gianpaolo, I understand that the planet's surface gravity is point seven six that of Earth, and its atmospheric pressure about thirty percent higher. But the oxygen level is about the same." He read her quotes about the "semi-greenhouse effect" and asked her what was meant by someone's remarks about "the inexhaustible reserve of outgassing from the cold side, as interior heat boils out volatiles." He got her, and himself, into a long complication about whether the designation of the star they were talking about was really Bes-bes Geminorum 8326 or Bes-bes Geminorum 8426 according to the New OAO General Catalogue—apparently both were given, because some typist made a mistake—until the chairman got restive. Then, satisfied that the audience was more than half asleep, he called for a ten-minute recess and returned to the attack.

MR. GIANPAOLO. Captain Menninger, I'm sure you know what it costs to launch a tachyon-transmitted space vessel. First—

CAPT. MENNINGER. Yes, sir, I believe I do.

MR. GIANPAOLO. First there is the immense expense of the launching vehicle itself. The costs for that alone, I believe, are in the neighborhood of six billion dollars.

CAPT. MENNINGER. Yes, sir. But as the vice-president announced in his message to the Tenth General Assembly of the World Conference on Exobiology, we already have such a launch vehicle. It can be used for a large number of missions.

MR. GIANPAOLO. But as the vice-president also announced, the time of that vehicle is fully booked. Prelaunch aiming time is as much as thirty days.

CAPT. MENNINGER. Yes, sir.

MR. GIANPAOLO. But your schedule calls for a launch to this—what is the name of it?

CAPT. MENNINGER. It has been referred to as "Son of Kung," sir, but that name is not official.

MR. GIANPAOLO. I hope not. You want a launch every ten days.

CAPT. MENNINGER. Yes, sir. Essential backup.

MR. GIANPAOLO. Which means canceling the mining survey mission to Procyon IV. I am sure you know that this planet has been identified as having a very dense core, with therefore a good potential for supplies of uranium and other fissiles for our power plants.

The British had sent that probe out. Meticulously they had announced that under existing international agreements they were making the telemetry public. That was all public knowledge. Gianpaolo was just getting on the record.

CAPT. MENNINGER. Yes, sir. Of course, that works out as a very marginal operation, considering the investment necessary to mine and refine uranium and to ship it to us back here. The Bes-bes Geminorum planet has much more potential—as I have already testified.

MR. GIANPAOLO. Yes, Captain Menninger, you have made us aware of your opinions.

And that was all hogwash. What the British had *not* announced, but what both Marge and Gianpaolo knew from previous briefing, was that British scintillation counters had found no ionizing radiation to speak of in Procyon IV's rather unpleasant atmosphere. Uranium there might be, but if so, it was thousands of meters deep. Marge was getting on the record too, although this particular record was private.

By the time she was through testifying, she was satisfied that things were moving in the right direction.

There remained the problem of Senator Lenz. He had far more muscle in the committee, and in the Senate generally, than anyone else—even the chairman. He had to be dealt with individually and privately, and Marge had plans for that.

She booked her return to Houston the long way around, by way of Denver. Her father drove her to Dulles Airport in his own car. Well, actually it wasn't his own. It belonged to a government agency. So did Godfrey Menninger, when you came right down to it. The car was both a perquisite of rank and an indispensable necessity in what he did for the agency; twice a day, other employees of the agency went over it with electronic sniffers and radio probes to make sure it had been neither bombed nor bugged.

God Menninger told his daughter, "You did pretty well at the hearing."

"Thanks, poppa. And thanks for that Pak's report."

"Had what you wanted in it?"

"Yep. Will you talk to the minority leader for me?"

"Already have, honey."

"And?"

"Oh, he's all right. If you get past Gus Lenz, I think you've got the committee taken care of. He didn't say much at the hearing."

"I didn't expect him to."

Her father waited, but as Marge did not go on he did not pursue the question. He said, "There's a follow-up on your Pakistani friend. He's at some kind of a meeting at K'ushui, along with some pretty high-powered people."

"K'ushui? What the hell is a K'ushui?"

"Well," said her father, "I kind of wish I could give you a better answer than I know. It's a place in Sinkiang province. We haven't had, uh, very full reports yet. But it's not far from Lop Nor and not *too* far from the big radio dish, and Heir-of-Mao's been there five or six times in the past year."

"It sounds as though they're going to move."

"I would say so. I plugged in your estimates, and the best interpretation is that Heir-of-Mao's starting to do what you want us to do."

"Shit!"

"Not to worry," said her father. "I told that to the minority leader in strictest confidence. And I have no doubt he'll tell Gianpaolo. So it'll work for you, you know."

"I wanted to be first!"

"First doesn't always pick up the marbles, honey. How many people discovered America before the English put it in their pocket? Anyway, tell me what's so interesting about this planet."

Margie looked out at the high-rise apartments in the Virginia suburbs, ziggurats climbing away from the south exposure with the black-on-black textured squares of their solar heating panels.

"It was all in Ahmed Dulla's report, poppa."

"I didn't read it."

"Pity. Well, there's a little star with a lot of crummy little planets and one big one about the size of Earth. Gravity's a little lighter. Air's a little denser. It's a lot of real estate, poppa. And it reeks of life."

"We've found life before."

"Mosses and jellyfish! Crystal things that you can *call* alive if you want to. This is different. This is a biota as varied as our own, maybe. Maybe even a civilization. The planet's interesting in another way, too. It doesn't rotate, I mean relative to its primary— like the moon doesn't rotate relative to Earth. So the lit side of it has a sun in the sky all the time."

Her father listened comfortably, scratching his abdomen just below the navel, while his daughter went on about the planet. When she paused for breath, he said, "Wait a minute, honey." He leaned forward to turn on the radio; even in a routinely debugged car God Menninger didn't take chances. Over the twang of synthetic guitars he said, "There's something else you ought to know. The fuel countries are talking among themselves about a sixty percent price rise."

"Jesus, poppa! I'll never drink another shot of Scotch!"

"No, it's not the British this time. It's the Chinese, funnily enough."

"But they're people exporters!"

"They're anything-they-like exporters," her father corrected. "The only reason they're in the People Bloc is that they can swing more weight there. Heir-of-Mao plays his own game. This time he slipped the word to the Greasies that China was going to raise its own prices unilaterally, whatever the bloc votes to do. So that was all the hard-liners in Caracas and Edinburgh needed. The Saudis were for it, of course. They want to stretch out what oil they've got left. And the Indonesians and the rest of the little ones just have to go along with the big boys." He paused thoughtfully. "So your coming along with a chit for half a million tons of oil gets a little complicated right now."

"I see that, poppa. What are we going to do? I don't mean about my project, I mean the country."

"What we are not going to do," he said grimly, "is raise grain prices. We can't. Heir-of-Mao's joker is that the price rise is for export sales only. He considers any sales inside the People Bloc as domestic. So he's selling cheap to the Peeps, and that means they're getting what they need for irrigation and fertilizer at bargain-basement prices. If we raise the price we'll make it worth their while to stop importing in another three or four years. We could stand it in this country, maybe. But the Soviets, the Indochinese, the Bulgarians, the Brazilians, and the rest of the Latins—they couldn't handle it. Their economies would be wrecked. It would break up the bloc. No doubt that's what Heir-of-Mao has in mind."

He parked the car in the Dulles short-term lot. Before snapping off the radio he said, "It won't happen for a couple of months, I think. So you want to get your project on the way as fast as you can."

Marge slid out into the damp, hot evening air. The humped backs of boarding clamjets loomed over the parking lot hedge. They could hear the noise of two of them warming up and the gentler rush of another taking off.

Marge followed her father as he picked up her bag and started toward the terminal. "Poppa," she said, "can I tell the senator about, uh, that?"

"Christ, no! Not that he doesn't probably know it already. But *you* aren't supposed to know."

Surprisingly, she laughed. "Well, I was going to handle it a different way anyway. Hey, hold it, poppa. I'm not taking the Houston flight."

"You're not?"

"Uh-uh. I'm going home by a different route."

Menninger kissed his daughter good-bye at the check-in counter for the Denver clamjet. He watched her disappear into the gate tunnel with mingled admiration and rue. He had been thinking about asking just how she proposed to handle Senator Lenz, but he didn't have to. This was the flight Lenz would be on.

Because it was a night flight, the jet sat there for twenty minutes of preheating before it could take off. The passengers had to be aboard, and the stews scurried up and down with ear stoppers and sympathy. The best heat source there is is a jet turbine. The engines that would thrust the plane through the air in actual flight were now rotated inward, the shell-shaped baffles diverting the blast to pour countless thousands of BTUs into the clam-shaped lifting section.

Marge took advantage of the time to scrub her face, brush her hair, and change her makeup. She had seen the senator come aboard. She debated changing from her uniform into something more female and decided against it. Wasn't necessary. Wasn't advisable. It might look calculating, and Marge calculated carefully ways to avoid looking calculating.

The full-energy roar of the warm-up jets stopped, and everyone belted in for takeoff. That was a gentler sound. The clamjet bounced a few times and soared steeply up.

As soon as they were at cruising altitude Marge left her cubicle and ordered a drink in the forward first-class lounge. In a couple of minutes Senator Lenz was standing over her, smiling.

Adrian Lenz had two terms and two days seniority in the Senate; a friendly governor had appointed him to fill a forty-eight-hour vacancy just for the sake of the extra rank it would give him over other senators elected the same year. Even so, he was not much over forty. He looked younger than that. He had been divorced twice; the Colorado voters laughed about their swinging senator's bad luck but reelected him without much fuss. He could have been chairman of his own committee, but had chosen instead to serve on committees that were of more interest—and more visibility. One of these days "Gus" Lenz was going to be the President of the United States, and everyone knew it.

"Margie," he said, "I knew this was going to be a nice flight, but until now I didn't know why."

Margie patted the seat beside her. "You going to give me my seventeen billion?" she asked.

Lenz laughed. "You don't waste time, Margie."

"I don't have time to waste. The Peeps are going to go there if we don't. They're probably going to go anyhow. It's a race."

He frowned and nodded toward the stewardess; slight, dark, she wore her United Airlines uniform like a sari. When the drinks were served he said, "I listened to your testimony, Margie. It sounded good. I don't know if it sounded seventeen billion dollars' worth of good."

"There was some material in the supplementary statement you might not have had a chance to read. Did you notice the part about the planet having its own sun?"

"I'm not sure."

"It's small but not very far away. The thing mostly radiates in the lower wavelengths. There's not too much visible light, but a hell of a lot of heat. And the planet doesn't turn in relation to it, so it's always hanging there."

"So?"

"So *energy*, senator. Solar power! Economical."

"I don't understand exactly what you're saying. You mean this substellar thing is hotter than our sun?"

"No, it's not nearly as hot. But it's a lot closer. The important thing is it doesn't move. What's the big problem with solar power here? The sun doesn't stay put. It wanders around all over the sky, and half the time it's not in the sky at all, because it's night here and so the sun's on the other side of the earth. I mean, look at our ship here. We had to preheat for nearly half an hour to get the gas light enough to lift, because it's after dark. On the side of the planet that faces its sun—the only side that interests me, Gus—it's never dark."

Lenz nodded and sipped his drink, waiting for more.

"It's never dark. It's never winter. The sun stays put, so you don't have to make your Fresnel lenses movable. And almost as important, the weather isn't a problem. You know what the score is on our own solar-power installations. Not counting clamjets in the daytime—because they're up over the clouds a lot of the time —we lose as much as twenty-five percent working time because the clouds cut out the sunlight."

Lenz looked puzzled. "This planet doesn't have any clouds?"

"Oh, sure. But they don't matter. The radiation is almost all heat, and it punches right through the clouds! Figure it out. Here we lose half the solar-generating time to night; another few percent to dawn and dusk, because the sun's so low it doesn't yield much power; as much as sixty percent additional for half the year because it's winter; and another twenty-five percent to cloud cover. Put them all together and we're lucky to get ten percent utilization. On this planet a cheaper installation can get damn near a hundred percent."

Lenz thought about that for a moment. "Sounds interesting," he said cautiously, and signaled for a refill.

Margie left him to sort things out in his own mind. Sooner or later it would occur to him to ask what good energy some hundred light-years away was going to do the voters in the state of Colorado on Earth. She had an answer for that, too, but she was content to wait until he asked for it.

But when he asked a question it caught her by surprise. "Margie? What've you got against the Paks?"

"Paks? Why—nothing, really."

"You seem to take this Ahmed's competition pretty seriously."

"Not on a personal level, Gus. I'm not *crazy* about Paks. But I've been on friendly terms with some. I had a Pak orderly when I was teaching at West Point. Nice kid. Kept my clothes ironed and never bothered me when I didn't want him around."

"That sounds like a nice appliance to own," Lenz observed.

"Yeah, yeah. I take your point." She stopped to think. "That's not where it's at, though. I'm not against Ahmed because he's a Pak. I'm against the Paks because they're the other side. I can't help it, senator. I root for my team."

"Which is who, Margie? Just the Food Bloc? Just the United States? Maybe just the female commissioned officers of the US Army?"

She giggled comfortably. "All of them, in that order," she agreed.

"Margie," he said seriously, "we're just shooting the bull here over a couple of drinks. I don't want to get too heavy."

"Why not, Gus? Order up a couple more drinks and let's get to it!"

He obeyed. While they were coming he said, "You're a nice girl, Margie, but a little too bloody-minded. Pity you went to West Point."

"Wrong, Gus. The pity is that so few young Americans have the chance now."

He shook his head. "I voted to phase down the service academies and cut the military budget."

"I know you did. Worst vote you ever cast."

"No. There was no choice. *We can't afford war, Margie.* Can't you understand that? Even Pakistan could blow us off the map! Not to mention the Chinese and the Turks and the Poles and the rest of the People Bloc. Not to mention the British, the Saudis, the Venezuelans. We can't afford to fight anybody, and nobody can afford to fight us. And everybody knows it. They're not our enemies—"

"But they're competing with us, senator," said Captain Menninger, suddenly sitting up straighter and speaking with more precision. "Economically. Politically. Every other way. Remember Clausewitz: war is the logical extension of politics. I grant," she said quickly, "that we can't go that far. We don't want to blow up the planet. I know what you're saying. It's like that famous saying of—what was his name, the Russian cosmonaut? Years and years ago. Sevastianov, I think: 'When I was in space I saw how tiny the world was, and realized how important it was for all of us to learn to live together on it.' Well, sure, Gus. But learning to live together doesn't mean that some people can't live a little better than others. It's a fact of life! The Fuel people keep jumping their prices. And the People people keep demanding more money for their export workers, or else they'll keep them home, and what will we do for orderlies and airline stewardesses? And we compete back. Well, Gus, when I compete, I compete hard. I play to win! This Kung's Star planet is something I want to win. I think there's goodies on this planet. I want them for *us.* Us being defined as the Food Bloc, the United States, the state of Texas, the city of Houston, and all the other subdivisions you named or want to name, including blond ex-professors from West Point, if you like, in descending order of size of community. Whichever community you want to talk about, if it's mine, I want it to be first, best, and most successful! I think that's what they call patriotism, senator. I really doubt that you want to knock it."

He looked at her thoughtfully over the new drinks, and raised his. "To you, Margie. You really are some kind of iron-pants."

She laughed. "All right," she said, softening. "I'll drink to that. Now, what about my bill?"

Lenz finished his drink and put it down. "For better or worse we're part of an economic community, and that's a fact of life for *you*, Captain Margie Menninger. You can't sell this to me as a United States venture. You might as a cooperative deal for the Food Bloc."

"Cripes, Gus! We'd still be paying for the whole thing!"

"Maybe ninety percent of it, yes."

"Then why not do it all and take it all?"

"Because," he said patiently, "I won't vote for that. So?"

Margie was silent for a moment, considering her priorities. She shrugged. "So all right," she said. "I don't mind if we include a few token gooks. Maybe two or three Canadians. A Brazilian. Maybe even a Bulgarian. In fact, there was a Bulgarian at the convention—"

She stopped herself. In mid-sentence it had occurred to her that in some sense she owed that Nan Whatever-it-was-ova a sort of a favor; but it had occurred to her simultaneously that the Bulgarian girl had been excessively close to the very Pak she was most worried about.

"No," she said, "on second thought I'm not sure I want a Bulgarian. They're too tiny a power to worry about, frankly. But maybe one or two people from the Soviets. If we send ten, and if at least six are genuine made-in-America US citizens, I can see bringing along a few from the rest of the bloc."

"Um." Lenz looked thoughtfully at her for a moment, moving slightly in his seat to the gentle pitching of the clamjet as it rose and fell through the night sky. "Well," he said, "we'll see." He smiled at her. "What shall we do with this night God has given us, Margie? It's too late to think hard and too early to go to sleep. Want to watch the stars for a while?"

"Exactly what I want," she said, finishing the last of her drink and standing up. They made their way through the nearly empty lounge to the forward observation section and leaned against the padded rail. The clamjet was swooping gently over the rolling hills of West Virginia. Ahead of them Venus followed a crescent of a moon toward the horizon. After a while Lenz put his arm around her.

"Just checking," he said. "Old Iron-Pants."

Margie leaned against him contentedly enough. Lenz wasn't a big man. He wasn't particularly handsome either, but he was warm and muscular, and his arm around her felt good. There were worse ways of lobbying for votes than this, she reflected as she turned her face to his.

He came through. The full committee reported the bill out, and on a hot Georgia afternoon two or three months later, Margie was called away from her company to take a high-priority phone call. She had not bathed for three days; summer field maneuvers were conducted as close to real war conditions as possible. She was sweating, filthy with both camouflage paint and Georgia clay, and she knew she smelled pretty high. Also, her company was just about to take a hill that she had personally spotted and attacked, so when she got to the phone she was in no good mood. "Captain Menninger," she snarled, "and this goddamn better be important!"

Her father's voice laughed in her ear. "You tell me," he said cheerfully. "The President signed your bill ten minutes ago."

Marge sank back onto the first sergeant's immaculate chair, heedless of his looks. "Jesus, poppa," she said, "that's great!" She stared out at the walls of the command trailer without seeing them, calculating whether it was more important to get back to taking that hill with the rest of the weekend soldiers or to get on the phone and start Danny Dalehouse in motion.

"—what?" She had become aware that her father was still talking.

"I said there was some other news too, not quite so good. Your Pak friend."

"What about him, poppa?"

"That, uh, vacation he was going to take? He took it last week."

·FOUR·

THE PILOT was Vissarion Ilyich Kappelyushnikov. He was short and dark in the standard cosmonaut tradition, with a lot more Tatar in his family tree than his name would suggest. The expedition's eco-engineer was also a Soviet national, but Cossack-tall and fair-haired; his name was Pete Krivitin. The nominal commander of the expedition was an American, Alex Woodring. And they were all going at it at once. Alex was trying to arbitrate between the two Russians, helped by Harriet Santori, the translator. She wasn't really helping, but then the commander wasn't really succeeding at arbitrating. Kappelyushnikov wanted to land and get it over with. Krivitin wanted one more look at the probe reports before he would certify the landing site. Harriet wanted them all to act like adults, for heaven's sake. Woodring's difficulty was that until they landed, Kappelyushnikov was the captain of the ship and Alex's authority was only potential. And it had been going on for more than an hour.

Danny Dalehouse swallowed the desire to intervene again. He loosened the straps of his deceleration couch and peered out the porthole. There was the planet, filling the window. From less than a hundred thousand kilometers, it no longer looked "away"; it was beginning to look "down." So let us the hell *get* there, he thought testily. These people didn't seem to realize they were screwing around with his personal expedition, which none of them would have been on if he hadn't persuaded that blond army female to authorize it.

A voice in his ear said, "Think we'll ever get there?"

Danny drew back. The woman beside him was Sparky Cerbo, as amiable a person as there was on the expedition; but after nineteen days of sharing less than twenty cubic meters of space, they were all getting edgy. The ongoing spat an arm's length away didn't make it any better.

"It doesn't look like much, does it?" Sparky went on, determinedly making the effort.

Dalehouse forced himself to respond. It wasn't her fault that he was sick of the sound, the sight, and the smell of her—and besides, she was right. Son of Kung didn't look like a proper planet at all. Danny knew what planets were supposed to look like. Some of them were red and bleak, like Mars. More often they were white or mottled white, like everything else from Venus through the gas giants. This one wasn't even trying to look right.

It wasn't so much the planet's fault as Kung's itself; as a star, it was simply incompetent. If Son of Kung had been in orbit around Earth's Sol, it would have looked pretty fine. It had much the same makeup as Earth. What it didn't have was decent sunlight. Kung glowered, not much brighter than Earth's moon during a total lunar eclipse. The only light that fell on Son of Kung was bloody red, and what it looked like from orbit was an open wound.

It would have helped some if it had had a real terminator, but Kung's light was so dim that there was no clear division between "daylight" and "night" sides—only a blurry transition from dark to darkest. Krivitin had assured them that once they landed and their eyes dark-adjusted, they would be able to see reasonably well. But from space that seemed doubtful. And for this, thought Danny, I gave up a perfectly good job at Michigan State.

The Russian language yelling peaked to climax and abruptly stopped. Krivitin, smiling as composedly as though the screaming match had been no more than a friendly chat about the weather, pulled himself around the lashed-down and nested machinery in the center of the main cubicle and peered in at them. "Sara, dear," he said in his perfect English, "you're wanted up front. You better come too, Daniel."

"We're going to land?" Sparky demanded.

"Most certainly not! Cappy has finally understood the necessity for another orbit."

"Hell," said Sparky, even her indomitable desire to please crumbling at last. Dalehouse shared her feelings: another orbit was close enough to another day, with nothing for him to do except try to stay out of the way.

"Yes, I agree," said Krivitin, "but Alex wants you to try to tap the Peeps' signals again."

Harriet complained, but Dalehouse stopped listening. He shucked off his straps and reached wearily for the cassettes of data he had stored away for deceleration.

He plugged in, put the speaker in his ear, and touched the switch. There was a slight tape hiss, an occasional scratch or click, and a distant, somber wail. Those were the sounds from the wolf-trap lander. Its primary mission was to secure biological samples and test them in its built-in laboratories; but its microphones had picked up sounds that did not come from itself. He had listened to them fifty times already. After a time he shrugged, stopped the tape, and put in a different cassette.

This time the sounds were louder and clearer, with far more definition. The lander in this case had been a neutral-buoyancy floater with a small reserve of thrusting power and a locater for carbon dioxide. Like a female mosquito seeking a blood meal to fertilize its eggs, it was meant to drift until it found a trail of CO_2 and follow it until it found prey. Then it simply floated nearby as long as there were sounds for it to hear and transmit. But what sounds! Sometimes they resembled a chorus of bagpipes, sometimes a gang of teenage boys in a crepitation contest. Dalehouse had graphed the frequencies—from well below human hearing range to higher than a bat's squeak—and identified at least twenty phonemes. These were no birdcalls; this was language, he was certain.

Heat smote his exposed skin, and he turned back to the port; Kung had drifted into view, looking like a thin-skinned Halloween pumpkin with the embers of Hades inside its mottled surface. He squinted and pulled a neutral-density blind over the porthole; it was not dangerous to glance at it, but there was the chance of burning out your cornea if you stared too long.

In the warmth he felt sleepy. Why not? he thought, snapping off the tape. He leaned back, closed his eyes, and was just drifting off when he heard his name called. "Dalehouse! Krivitin! Di Paolo! Front and center, everybody."

He shook himself awake, wished for a cup of coffee, and pulled himself toward the workspace. Alex Woodring said, "You'd better all see this. The Peeps have filed another report, and Harriet's taped it for us."

Dalehouse wriggled closer for a better view of the video screen just as it blinked and lighted up. There was a plant on the screen, rust-red and fernlike, with raspberrylike fruits hanging from its fronds. "Roll the tape, Harriet," Woodring said impatiently. The images on the screen leaped and flickered, then stopped.

At first Dalehouse thought the picture was of another Klongan flower, possibly some desert succulent: red and yellow blobs oozing what he supposed was some sort of sap— Then it moved.

"Dear God," whispered somebody. Dalehouse felt something rise in his throat.

"What is it?"

"I think it used to be a white mouse," said Morrissey, the biologist.

"What happened?"

"That," said the biologist grimly, but with a trace of professional satisfaction, "is what I don't know yet. The Peeps are transmitting their voice reports in code."

"They're supposed to share information!" snapped Dalehouse.

"Well, maybe they will. I assume Heir-of-Mao will have his UNESCO delegation deliver a report. And when it's released in New York, Houston will no doubt send us a copy. But not very soon, I think. The picture was clear. When you come right down to it, that's all we need to know: Klong is not as hospitable as we would like. I—" He hesitated, then went on. "I don't think it's an infectious disease. It looks more like an allergic reaction. I can't really imagine an alien microorganism adapting that quickly to our body chemistry, anyway. I suspect we're as poisonous to them as they are to us, so for openers, we don't eat anything, we don't drink anything but our own sealed supplies and distilled water."

"You mean we're landing anyhow?" the Canadian electronicist said incredulously.

Captain Kappelyushnikov snarled, "*Da!*" He nodded vigorously, then muttered to the translator, who said smoothly:

"He says that that is why we came here. He says we will take all precautions. He says on the next orbit, we go."

Dalehouse played the strange songs from the mosquito probe a few times, but the equipment he needed to do any serious analysis had been stowed away and it made little sense to set it up again. Time to kill. Drowsily he peered out at the planet, and drifted off to sleep wondering what to call it. Kungson, Child of Kung, Son of Kung—"Klong, Son of Kung" was what one of the Americans had christened it—by any name, it was worrisome. When he woke he was given a tube of thick petroleum jelly to smear on himself— "Shuck your clothes and cover your whole body; maybe it will protect you from some kind of poison ivy or whatever that is until we get straightened out." Then he dressed again and waited. The electronicist had patched herself in to monitor any further ground transmissions and was pinpointing sources on a likris map of the sunward surface of Klong.

"There seem to be *two* stations broadcasting," Dalehouse commented.

"Yeah. Must be the base camp and, I suppose, somebody off on an expedition. There's the Peep base"—she touched a dot on the purplish sea, on one side of a hundred-kilometer bay—"and there's the other station." That was across the bay. "We know that's their base; we photographed it last time around. Nothing much. They aren't really set up yet, I'd say. That signal's pulse-coded, probably basic science data on its way to their orbiter for tachyon transmission back home."

"What's over on the other side of the bay?"

"Nothing much. There's a sort of nest of some of the arthropods there, but *they* don't have radio." She pulled the earpiece away from her temple and handed it to Dalehouse. "Listen to that signal."

Dalehouse put the phone in his ear. The sound was a staccato two-tone beep, plaintively repeated over and over.

"Sounds sad," he said.

The woman nodded. "I think it's a distress signal," she said, frowning. "Only they don't seem to be answering it."

·FIVE·

WHAT CAN BE SAID about a being like Sharn-igon that will make him come clear and real? Perhaps it can be approached in a roundabout way. Like this.

Suppose there is a kind and jolly man, the sort of person who takes children fishing, dances the polka, reads Elizabethan verse, and knows why Tebaldi was the greatest Mimi who ever lived.

Is this Sharn-igon?

No. This is only an analogy. Suppose we then go on to ask you if you have ever met this man. You hesitate, riffling through the chance encounters of a life. No, you say, a finger against your nose, I don't think so. I never met anybody like that.

And suppose we then say to you, But you did! It was a week ago Thursday. He was driving the A-37 bus you took from the station to the Federal Building, and you were late for your appointment with the tax examiner because this man would not change a five-dollar bill.

What do you say then? Perhaps you say, Christ, fellow! I remember the incident well! But that was no amiable folk dancer. That was a bus driver!

That's how it would be with Sharn-igon. It's easy enough to imagine you meeting him (provided we don't worry about how you get there). Let's make the mind-experiment to see what would happen. Suppose you are standing outside of time and space somehow, like an H. G. Wells god looking down from a cloud. You poke your finger into the infinitesimal. You touch Sharn-igon's planet, and you uncover him. You look him over.

What do you see?

One might try to describe him to you by saying that Sharn-igon was politically conservative, deeply moral, and fundamentally honest. One might try to elicit your sympathy by saying that he (like who that you know?) was screaming inside with unhealed pain.

But would you see that?

Or would you glance and gasp and pull back your finger in loathing and say:

Christ, fellow! That's no person. It's an alien creature! It lives (lived? will live?) a thousand light-years away, on a planet that circles a star I have never even seen! And besides, it looks *creepy*. If I had to say what it looked like, giving it the best break I could, I would have to say that it looked like half of a partly squashed crab.

And, of course, you would be right. . . .

The way Sharn-igon looked to himself was something else again.

For one thing, he is not an instant invention for your eye to see. He is a person. He has relationships. He lives (will live?) in a society. He moves (moved?) around and through a dense web of laws and folkways. He wasn't like every other Krinpit (as his people called themselves), no matter how indistinguishable they might look to your eyes. He was Sharn-igon.

For example, although it was Ring-Greeting time, Sharn-igon hated Ring-Greeting. To him it was the loneliest and worst part of the cycle. He disliked the bustle, he resented the false and hypocritical sentiment. All the shops and brothels were busy as everyone tried to get gifts and to become pregnant, but it was an empty mockery in Sharn-igon's life, because he was alone.

If you had asked him, Sharn-igon would have told you that he had always hated Ring-Greeting, at least ever since his final molting. (When he was a young seed just beginning to wave on his male-mother's grate he loved it, naturally enough. All seeds did. Ring-Greeting was for kids.) That wasn't quite true. The cycle be-

fore, he and his he-wife, Cheee-pruitt, had had a very cheerful
Greeting.

But Cheee-pruitt was gone. Sharn-igon signaled at his screen,
almost stumbling over an Inedible Ghost that lay before it. There
was no answer. He hesitated. Something—perhaps the ghost—
seemed to be calling his name. But that was ridiculous. After a
moment of indecision, he scuttled across the crowded run to the—
call it a bar—to chew a couple of quick ones.

Look at Sharn-igon munching on strands of hallucinogenic fern
among a crowd squeezed two or three deep around the Krinpit
who was kneading and dispensing the stuff. He was a fine figure of
a person. He was masculinely broad—easily two meters from rim
to rim; and pleasingly slim—not more than forty centimeters to
the tip of his carapace. In spite of his mood, unpaired males and
females of all descriptions found him attractive. He was young,
healthy, sexually potent, and successful in his chosen profession.

Well, that is not strictly true, because a paradox is involved.

Sharn-igon's profession was a form of social work. The more
successful he was in terms of his own personal ego needs, the
worse his society was. It was only when Krinpit were in trouble
that they turned to persons like Sharn-igon. The Krinpit were
socially interdependent to a degree not usually associated with a
technological culture on Earth. Maybe one could find that sort of
close-knit clan among the Eskimos or Bushmen, where every
member of the community had to be able to rely on every other
or they would all die. For that reason Sharn-igon was happiest
when he was least wanted. Ring-Greeting was bringing its usual
crop of damaged egos born of loneliness amid the holiday cheer.
He was busier than he had ever been, and so less happy.

Stand on your cloud and look down on Sharn-igon. To you he
surely looks strange, and maybe quite repulsive, true. His crescent
carapace is sprinkled with what look like chitinous sails. Some are
a few centimeters high, some much smaller; and around them
race, clicking and scraping, what look like lice. Actually, they
aren't. They are not even parasites, except in the sense that a fetus
is a parasite on its mother; they are the young. Sharn-igon is not
the only Krinpit in the bar carrying young. Of the hundred individuals in the bar, eight or ten are in the brood-male phase. Sometimes one of the scurrying little creatures drops off or inad-

vertently gets carried off on the shell of another Krinpit as they rub together. They are instantly aware of what has happened and go wild in the attempt to get back. If they fail, they die.

Each end of Sharn-igon's shell is pleated chitin jointed with cartilage. That part is always in motion, expanding with accordion folds, tilting, spreading like a fan. He slides along the packed dirt floor or the bodies of Krinpit under him (in the conviviality of the bar no one minds being crawled on) on a dozen double-boned legs.

After he had had three quick ones and was feeling better, he left the bar and sidled down the turfy run, not hurrying, with no particular destination in mind. On each side of the run are what you might think of as rather shabby Japanese screens. They are not decorated in any way, but they are jointed and folded, and they come in all sizes. They set off the homes and commercial places, some of which, like the bar, are filled with scores of Krinpit, some almost empty. The screens too are studded with the tiny saillike projections, but otherwise they are unadorned. What you would notice at once is that they are not colored. The Krinpit do not understand color, and in the light of Kung's Star, blood-red and dusky, you would not see much color at first either, even if it were there.

That is how it would look to you, with your human eyes. How would it look to Krinpit eyes? Immaterial; it is a senseless question, because the Krinpit have no eyes. They have photosensitive receptors on their carapaces, but there is no lens, no retina, no mosaic of sensitive cells to analyze an image and translate it into information.

But if the scene was dark, it was also noisy.

Every one of the Krinpit was constantly booming its name—well, not its "name" in the sense that the name of Franklin Roosevelt's wife was Eleanor. The name was not an arbitrary convention. It was the sound each Krinpit made. It was sound that guided them, that palped the world around them and returned information to their quite agile and competent brains. The sonar pulses they sent forth to read the echoes were their "names." Each was different, and every one always being produced while its owner lived. Their main auditory apparatus was the drum-tight undersurface of the belly. It possessed a vent like a dolphin's that could produce a remarkable range of vowel sounds. The "knees" of the double-boned legs could punctuate them with tympanous "consonants." They walked in music wherever they went. They could not move silently. The exact sounds they produced were controllable; in fact, they had an elaborate and sophisticated language. The sounds which became their recognition signals were probably the easiest for them, but they could produce almost any other sound in the frequency range of their hearing. In this their voices were quite like humans'.

So wherever Sharn-igon went he was surrounded by that sound: *Sharn*, a rising protracted noise like a musical saw, overlaid with white hiss; *igon*, a staccato double drumbeat dropping down to the tonic again. It was not just Sharn-igon. All the Krinpit were constantly making their basic name-sounds when they were not making others. It was not just the Krinpit. Their environment sang to them. Each of the enclosures was marked by wind-powered sound-making machines. Nearly all of them had ratchets or droning pipes or bull-roarers or circle-bowed strings clamoring out their own particular recognition signal.

So to a human eye Sharn-igon was a lopsided crab scuttling in a clattering mass of others, in hellish red gloom, with an inferno of raucous sound coming from every direction.

Sharn-igon perceived it quite differently. He was strolling aimlessly along a well-remembered street. The street had a name; it translates rather closely as "the Great White Way."

At the intersection of the Breeders' Wallow Sharn-igon fell into conversation with an acquaintance.

"Do you have knowledge of whereabouts of Cheee-pruitt?"

"Negative. Conjecture: statistically probable that he would be by lakeside of village."

"Why?"

"Some persons hurt or ill. Many onlookers. Several Anomalous Ghosts reported."

Sharn-igon acknowledged the statements and turned toward the lakefront. He recalled that there had seemed to be a ghost near Cheee-pruitt's residence some time before. And it was anomalous. Basically there were two kinds of ghosts. The Ghosts Above were common and easily "visible" (because they made so much noise) but returned no echo signal to speak of to a Krinpit's sonar. They were good eating when they could be caught. The Ghosts Below were almost invisible. They seldom made visible sounds and returned not much echo; they were mostly observed when their underground digging damaged a Krinpit structure or farm. They too were good eating and were systematically hunted for that purpose when the Krinpit were lucky enough to locate a nest of young.

But what were the anomalous ones, neither Ghosts Above nor Ghosts Below?

Sharn-igon scuttled through the Breeders' Wallow to the Place of Fish Vendors, and along the lakefront to the bright commotion at the Raft Mooring. There was something almost invisible bobbing in the gentle roll of the bay. Though the Krinpit used metal only very sparingly, Sharn-igon recognized the brightness of it; but the bright metal seemed to float over something so soft and immaterial that it returned no real reflection to his sounding. The bright part, though, not only reflected Sharn-igon's sounds almost blindingly, it generated sound of its own: a faint, high, steady whine, an irregular dry-sand rustle. Sharn-igon could not identify the sounds; but then, he had never seen a TV camera or a radio transponder.

He stopped one of the Krinpit moving irritably away from the group and asked what was happening.

"Some Krinpit attempted to eat the ghost. They are damaged."

"Did the ghost harm them?"

"Negative. After eating, they became damaged. One ghost is still there. Advise against eating."

Sharn-igon bounced sounds off the stranger more carefully.

"Have you too eaten of the ghost?"

"A very little, Sharn-igon. I too am damaged."

Sharn-igon touched mandibles and moved on, concerned about Cheee-pruitt. He didn't hear him anywhere in the crowd, but the din was blinding. At least two hundred Krinpit were scratching and sliding over each other's carapaces, milling around the bloody mass that had been one of the "ghosts." Sharn-igon halted and sounded the area irresolutely.

From behind him he thought he heard his own name, badly spoken but recognizable: *Sharn-igon*. When he turned, his highly directional sound sense identified the source. It was the ghost.

The one that had seemed to speak his name. Sharn-igon approached it cautiously; he did not like its smell, didn't like its muffled, shadowy sound. But it was a curiosity. First his own name: Sharn-igon. And in between—what? Another name? It was certainly not a Krinpit name, but the ghost kept repeating it. It sounded like OCK med dool-LAH.

On the other shore of the Bay of the Cultural Revolution, fifty kilometers away, Feng Hua-tse rinsed the honey buckets in the purplish waters and carried them back toward the bubble cluster that was the People's Bloc headquarters. From the shore you couldn't see the landing craft itself at all. The extruded bubbles surrounded and hid it. Through the translucent walls of the nearest of them (they could have been made opaque, but the group decision had been that energy conservation was more important than privacy) he could see the vague shadows of the two women detailed as sick-bay orderlies. They had not been given the job because they were women. They had the job because they should have been in bed themselves. Barely able to stagger, they could more or less take care of themselves and the two bed cases. And there was no one to spare to do it for them.

Feng put the clean buckets inside the sick-bay bubble, resenting the waste of the precious nightsoil. But it was his own decision that the wastes from the casualties should be dumped in the bay rather than used to fertilize their tiny plot of garden. Until they were sure what had killed one member of the expedition and put four more on the sick list—nearly half their effectives wiped out at one stroke!—Feng would not risk contamination. It was a pity that their biologist was the sickest of the survivors; his wisdom was needed. But Feng had been a barefoot biologist himself in his youth, and he kept up the experiments with the animals, the tactran reports to Peking, and the four-times-daily examinations of the sick.

He paused in the radio room. The video screen that monitored the small party which had crossed the bay was still showing the same monotonous scene. Apparently the camera had been left on the raft, and apparently the raft had drifted in the slow, vagrant currents of the bay, so that the camera showed only an occasional thin slice of shoreline a quarter of a kilometer away. Once in a while you could see one of the arthropods scuttling along, and now and again a glimpse of their low, flimsy buildings. But he had not yet seen either Ahmed Dulla or the Costa Rican who had gone with him.

Outside the bubble for the communications equipment the two West Indians were desultorily scooping dirt into woven baskets. Feng spoke sharply to them and achieved a momentary acceleration of pace. They were sick too, but it was not yet clear whether it was the same sickness as the others. They, he thought bitterly, should feel at home here. The heat and humidity were junglelike. What was worst was the lighting, always the same dusky red, never bright enough to see clearly, never dark. Feng had had a headache since they arrived, and it was his private opinion it was only from eyestrain. Feng, at least, had not eaten any of Son of Kung's food. In this he was luckier, or wiser, than the four in the sick bay and the one who had died, not to mention the dozen rats and guinea pigs they tested the stuff on. Feng swore. Why had he let that long-nosed hillman Dulla talk him into splitting their forces? To be sure, it had happened before the five became violently ill. Even so it had been a mistake. When he got back to Shensi, Feng admitted to himself, there would be a long day of self-criticism ahead.

If he got back.

He picked up two baskets of dirt in his shoulder yoke and carried them with him as he went to inspect the dam. That was his greatest hope. When it was completed, they would have electricity to spare—electricity to power the ultraviolet lamps, still stored in the landing craft's hold, that would turn the feeble, pale seedlings into sturdy crops. There was nothing wrong with this soil! No matter how many got sick, even if they died, it was not the soil's fault; Feng had rubbed it between finger and thumb, sniffed it, turned a spadeful over and gazed wonderingly at the crawling things that inhabited it. They were strange, but they meant the soil was fertile. What it did not have was proper sunlight. That they would have to make, as soon as the dam was built; and then, Feng swore, they would produce crops that any collective in Shensi province would envy.

It was raining as he started back, slow, fat, warm drops that ran down Feng's back under his cotton jacket. Another good thing:

plenty of water. Not only was it good for the plants, but it kept the spores down, and Feng was highly suspicious of them as the source of the sickness. Even through the clouds he could feel the warmth of Kung Fu-tze. It was not visible, but it gave the clouds the angry, ruddy look of sky over a distant great city. It would stay that way until the air mass that carried the clouds moved away; then there would be that distant hot coal and the purple-black sky with its stars.

Feng took the forest path back to the headquarters, checking the traps. One held two multilegged creatures like land-going lobsters, one dead, the other eating it. Feng dumped them both and did not reset the trap. There was no point in it. They were too shorthanded to bother with more animal specimens than they had already. Three of the traps were sprung but empty, and one was simply missing. Feng muttered to himself irritably. There was a lot they didn't know about the fauna of this fern forest. For one thing, what had stolen the trap? Most of the creatures they had seen were arthropods, buglike or crustaceanlike, none of them bigger than a man's hand. Bigger ones existed. The sentients in the settlement across the bay were proof of that—they were the size of a man. But the wild ones, if they existed, stayed out of sight. And there was something that lived in the tall, woody ferns. One could hear them, even catch a glimpse of them from time to time, but no one in the expedition had yet caught or even photographed one. It stood to reason that if there were small creatures there would be bigger ones to eat them, but where were they? And what would they look like? Wolf teeth, cat talons, crab claws . . . ? Feng abandoned that line of thought; it was not reassuring. To be sure, the local fauna would no doubt find humans as indigestible as the humans had found the local fauna.

But they might not realize that in time.

It began to look as though humans would not find anything at all to eat on Klong. The biologist had been reduced to taking samples of microorganisms from each member of the party and culturing them on plates of agar. It was no longer possible to use laboratory animals. They had all died. And one by one he tried every promising-looking bit of plant or animal they brought him, dropping a broth of it onto the agar, and one by one each of them destroyed the darkening circle of growing bacteria. They were perfect antibiotics, except for one thing: they would have killed the patient more quickly than any disease.

Nevertheless. Ring the trees. Let them die. Ditch those soggy pastures. . . . But the trees did not appear to have a proper bark. In fact they weren't really trees. Slash and burn might not work here. But something would! One way or another, the fields of Child of Kung would prosper!

Feng became aware that his name was being called.

He turned away from the place where the last trap had been, trotting back toward the settlement. As he approached the beach and the fronds thinned, he saw one of the walking casualties waving in excitement.

Feng arrived out of breath. "What, what?" he grumbled.

"A radio message from the long-nose! It is a distress signal, Hua-tse."

"Tchah! What did he say?"

"He said nothing, Hua-tse. It is the automatic distress call. I tried to raise him, but there was no response."

"Of course," snarled Feng, gripping his hands together in anger. Another thing to admit to before the commune. Two members of the party endangered, perhaps lost, because he had foolishly permitted the division of their forces. Two irreplaceable persons—a hillman and a Hispanic, to be sure; nevertheless, persons. Their absence would be serious. And not just the persons. One of their three television cameras. The radio transponder. The precious plastic that had gone into making the skin of the boat. There was just so much of that. They had squandered a great deal on the bubbles to house the sick, the equipment, all their sparse possessions. That was foolishness, too; the fern forest was a limitless supply of woody stems for frames, fronds for ceilings and walls. In this drenched warmth they needed no more than that, but he had weakly permitted the blowing of bubble huts instead of using what nature provided.

Could they build another boat? It was by no means sure that there was plastic enough even for the hull and the sails; and when it was gone, where would they get more? Who could he send? Of their original eleven, one was dead, two were missing, and four were sick. Was it not even more foolish to further divide their forces, to attempt to repair the damage the first foolishness had cost? And what could they do if they did in fact build another boat and sail across the bay? That which had happened to the hillman and the Hispanic could just as well happen to whoever went after them. They had very little in the way of weapons, no more to spare than Dulla and the other man had taken with them in the first place, and little enough good that had done them—

"Are we going, Hua-tse?"

His attention was jarred back. "What?"

"Are we going to try to help our comrades?"

Feng gripped his hands tighter. "With what?" he demanded.

·SIX·

On a planet that has no night the days are endless, Danny Dale-house reflected, a meter down into the Klongan soil and at least that much more to go. His muscles told him he had been digging this latrine for at least eight hours. The discouragingly tiny spoil heap beside him contradicted them, and the ruddy glow that backlighted the clouds overhead offered no help. Latrine digging was not what he had signed on for. But it was something that had to be done, and he was clearly the most superfluous member of the party in line to do it—only why did it have to take so long?

They had been on the planet only three days (not that there were any days, but the old habits died hard), and already the pleasure was wearing thin. The parts that weren't actively unpleasant like digging latrines were a bore. The parts that weren't already boring were scary, like the madly violent thunderstorm that had blown away their first tent only hours after landing, or irritatingly uncomfortable, like the itchy rashes they had all developed and the stomach troubles that had made the latrines so vital. And to make it worse, they seemed to have company. Kappelyushnikov had come swearing in Russian to report that a third tactran vessel had climbed down its charge state to orbit Klong. Greasies, no doubt. That meant everybody in the world was now represented on Klong. What price the solitary pioneer?

His spade struck air.

Danny lost his balance, spun, and came down in a fetal crouch into the pit, his face almost in the hole that had unexpectedly opened up. From it came a cool, musty smell. It made him think of unopened cellars and the cages of pet mice, and he heard quick, furtive movements.

Snakes? He rejected the thought as soon as he formed it. That was an earthly fear, not appropriate on Klong. But whatever it was could easily be even more deadly than a nest of rattlers. He leaped with prudent speed out of the trench and yelled, "Morrissey!"

The biologist was only a few meters away, sealing plant samples pickled in preservative into plastic baggies. "What's the matter?"

"I hit a hole, maybe a tunnel. You want to take a look?"

Morrissey looked down at the purplish seed pod in his forceps and back at Dalehouse's trench, torn. Then he said, "Sure, only I have to stow these away first. Don't dig any more till I finish."

That was a welcome order, and Dalehouse accepted it gratefully. He was getting used to taking orders. Even as a latrine digger he was subject to instant draft whenever some presently more valuable member of the expedition needed another pair of hands: Harriet to set up her radio, Morrissey to heat-seal his baggies, Sparky Cerbo to locate the canned tomatoes and the kitchen knives that had vanished during the thunderstorm—anyone. Twice already he had had to empty the landing vehicle's chemical toilet into a shallow pit and scrape the soil of Klong over it, because the rest of the crew couldn't wait for him to finish the job they were preventing him from finishing.

It was a drag. But he was on Son of Kung! He could smell the strange Klongan smells—cinnamon and mold and cut vegetation and something that was a little like mom's apple pie, but none of them really any of those things. He could see the Klongan landscape—he could see quite a lot of it, a shovelful at a time.

It was what he had expected in an expedition of specialists. Dalehouse was not a cook, not a farmer, not a doctor, not a radio surveyor. He had none of the hypertrophied skills that all the others possessed. He was the expedition's only generalist and would stay that way until they made contact with the local sentients and he could employ the communications skills he was advertised to have. Meanwhile he was stoop labor.

The Russian pilot, Kappelyushnikov, was yelling his name. "You, Danny, you come have drink. Put back sweat!"

"Why not?" Danny was pleased to notice that Cappy was holding aloft a glass containing a centimeter of water, grinning broadly. He had finally got the still to working. Dalehouse swallowed the few drops and wiped his lips appreciatively, then his slippery brow. Kappelyushnikov was right enough about that. In the dank, humid air they were both covered with sweat. The still was powered with a small oil-spray flame, which made it like burning hundred-dollar bills to operate. Later it would be moved to the lakeshore and driven by solar power, but right now they needed water they could drink.

"Very good, is it?" Kappelyushnikov demanded. "You don't feel faint, like is some poison? Okay. Then we go bring a drink to Gasha."

The translator had given herself command of the setting-up phase of the camp, and no one had resisted; she was spending hours over her radio trying to make sense of the communications, but she claimed the other half of her mind was able to keep track of everyone's duty assignments. She might have been right, Dalehouse thought. She was the least agreeable person on the expedition, and no one particularly wanted to disagree with her. She was also close to the least physically attractive, with stringy black hair and an expression of permanent disappointment. But she was grudgingly grateful for the water.

"Thank you for getting the still going. And the latrine, of course, Danny. Now if the two of you—"

"I'm not finished," Danny corrected. "Jim wants to check out a hole first. Is there anything new on the radio?"

Harriet smiled with closed lips. "We have a message from the Peeps."

"About that guy who's stuck?"

"Oh, no. Take a look." She handed over a facsimile film that said:

The People's Republics extend the hand of friendship to the second expedition to arrive on Child of Kung. Through peaceful cooperation we will achieve a glorious triumph for all mankind. We invite you to join us for the celebration of the fifteen hundredth anniversary of the writings of Confucius, after whom our star was named.

Dalehouse was perplexed. "Isn't that some kind of a winter holiday?"

"You are very well informed today, Dalehouse. It is in December. Our instructor called it the Confucian answer to Hanukkah, which is of course the Jewish answer to Christmas."

He frowned, trying to remember—already, it was becoming hard. "But this isn't even October yet."

"You are very swift indeed, Danny. So translate that, won't you?" requested the translator.

"I don't know. Are they saying something like, 'Don't bother us for a couple of months'?"

"Is more like to drop dead," the pilot put in.

"I don't think so. They aren't being unfriendly," Harriet said, recapturing the fax and squinting at it. "Notice that they referred to Kung Fu-tze by the latinized form of the name. That's a pretty courteous thing for them to do. Still—" She frowned. At best Harriet's eyes were always faintly popped, like a rabbit's, because of the heavy contacts she wore. Now her lips were pursed like a rabbit's too. "On the other hand, they were careful to point out we're the *second* expedition."

"Meaning they're the first. But what's the difference? They can't make territorial claims because they got here ahead of us; that's all spelled out in the UN accords. Nobody gets to claim any more than a circle fifty kilometers around a self-sustaining base."

"But they're pointing out that they could have."

Cappy was bored with the protocol. "Any love letters from the Oilies, Gasha?"

"Just a received-and-acknowledged. And now, about that latrine—"

"In a minute, Harriet. What about the Pak who's stranded?"

"He's still stranded. You want to hear the latest tapes?" She didn't wait for an answer; she knew what it would be. She plugged in a coil of tape and played it for them. It was the Peeps' automatic distress signal: every thirty seconds a coded SOS, followed by a five-second beep for homing. Between signals the microphone stayed open, transmitting whatever sounds were coming in.

"I've cut out most of the deadwood. Here's the man's voice."

Neither Dalehouse nor Kappelyushnikov included Urdu among their skills. "What is he say?" asked the pilot.

"Just asking for help. But he's not in good shape. Most of the time he doesn't talk at all, and we get this stuff."

What came out of the tape player was a little like an impossibly huge cricket's chirp and quite a lot like a Chinese New Year festival in which Australian aborigines were playing their native instruments.

"What the hell is that?" Danny demanded.

"That," she said smugly, "is also language. I've been working on it, and I've sorted out a few key concepts. They are in some sort of trouble, I'm not sure what."

"Not as much as Pak is," grunted Kappelyushnikov. "Come, Danny, is time we go to work."

"Yes, that latrine is—"

"Not on latrine! Other things in life than shit, Gasha."

She paused, glowering at him. Kappelyushnikov was almost as dispensable as Danny Dalehouse. Maybe more so. After the expedition was well established, Dalehouse's skills would come into play, or so they all hoped, in making contact with sentient life. The pilot's main skill was piloting. A spacecraft by choice. If pressed, a clamjet, a racing vessel, or a canoe. None of those existed on Klong.

But what he had that was always useful was resourcefulness. "Gasha, dear," he coaxed, "is not possible. Your Morrissey still has his micetraps in the trench. And besides, now we have water, I have to make *wasserstoff.*"

"Hydrogen," Harriet corrected automatically. "Hydrogen? What in the world do you want with hydrogen?"

"So I will have a job, dear Gasha. To fly."

"You're going to fly with hydrogen?"

"You understand me, Gasha," the Russian beamed. He pointed. "Like them."

Danny glanced up, then ran for the tent and the one remaining decent pair of binoculars—two pairs of them, too, had turned up missing after the thunderstorm.

There they were, the windblown flock of balloonists, high and near the clouds. They were at least two kilometers away, too far to hear the sounds of their song, but in the glasses Dalehouse could see them clearly enough. In the purplish sky they stood out in their bright greens and yellows. It was true, Dalehouse verified.

Some of them were self-luminous, like fireflies! Traceries of veins stood out over the great five-meter gasbag of the largest and nearest of them, flickering with racing sparks of bioluminescence.

"Damn," he snarled. "What are you saying, Cappy? Do you think you can fly up there?"

"With greatest of ease, Danny," the pilot said solemnly. "Is only a matter of making bubbles and putting *wasserstoff* in them. Then we fly."

"You've got a deal," said Dalehouse firmly. "Tell me what to do and I'll do it. I'll—wait a minute! What's that?"

The balloon swarm was scattering, and behind it, coming through the place it was vacating, was something else, something that beat with a rhythmic flash of light.

The sound reached him then. "It's a helicopter!" he cried in astonishment.

The chopper pilot was short, dark, and Irish. Not only Irish, but repatriated to the UK from eleven years in Houston, Texas. He and Morrissey hit it off immediately. "Remember Bismarck's?" "Ever been to La Carafe?" "Been there? I lived there!" When they were all gathered he said:

"Glad to meet you all. Name's Terry Boyne, and I bring you official greetings from our expedition, that's the Organization of Fuel-Exporting Nations, to yours, that's you. Nice place you've got here," he went on appreciatively, glancing around. "We're down toward the Heat Pole—ask my opinion, you folks picked a better spot. Where we are it's wind you wouldn't believe and scorching hot besides, if you please."

"So why'd you pick it?" asked Morrissey.

"Oh," said Boyne, "we do what our masters tell us. Isn't it about the same with you? And what they told me to do today was to come over and make a good-neighbor call."

Harriet, of course, stepped right in. "On behalf of the Food-Exporting States we accept your friendly greetings and in return—"

"Please to stow, Harriet?" rumbled Kappelyushnikov. "But we are not only other colony on Klong, Terry Boyne."

"What's 'Klong'?"

"It's what we call this place," Dalehouse explained.

"Um. 'Klong.' We've been told to call it 'Jem'—short for 'Geminorum', you see. Heaven knows what the Peeps call it."

"Have you been to see them?"

Boyne coughed. "Well, actually that's more or less what it's about, if you see what I mean. Have you people been monitoring their broadcasts?"

"Sure we have. Yours too."

"Right, then you've heard their distress signals. Poor sod, stuck with those beasts that our translator says call themselves 'Krinpit'. The Peeps don't respond. We offered to help out, and they as much as told us to fuck off."

Morrissey glanced at Harriet. Their translator was doing better than she. He said, "We've had much the same experience, Terry. They indicated we weren't welcome in their part of the world. Of course, they have no right to take that kind of a stand—"

"—but you don't want to start any bloc-to-bloc trouble," finished Boyne, nodding. "Well, for humanitarian reasons—" He choked, and took a great swig of the drink Morrissey had handed him, before going on. "Hell, let's be frank. For curiosity's sake, and just to see what's going on over there—but also for humanitarian reasons—we want to go and fish the guy out of there. The Peeps obviously can't. We suppose the reason they shut you and us out is that they don't want us to see how bad off they are. You folks can't—" He hesitated delicately. "Well, obviously it would be easier for us to go in with a chopper than for you to send an expedition overland. We're willing to do that. But not alone, if you see what I mean."

"I think I do," Harriet sniffed. "You want somebody to share the blame."

"We want to make it a clearly interbloc errand of mercy," Boyne corrected. "So I'm all set to go over there and snatch him out this minute. But I'd like one of you to go along."

Eight out of the ten members of the expedition were speaking at once then, with Kappelyushnikov's shouted "I go!" drowning out the rest.

Harriet glared around at her crew and then said petulantly, "Go then, if you want to, although we're so shorthanded here—"

Danny Dalehouse didn't wait for her to finish. "That's right,

Harriet! And that's why it ought to be me. I can be spared, and besides—"

"No! I, *I* can be spared, Danny! And I am pilot—"

"Sorry, Cappy," said Danny confidently. "We already have a pilot—Mr. Boyne there—and besides, you have to make your *wasserstoff* so you can take me flying when I come back. And, two, making contact with alien sentients is my basic job, isn't it? And" —he didn't wait for an answer—"besides, I think I know the guy who's stuck there. Ahmed Dulla. We were both hassled by the cops in Bulgaria a couple of months ago."

Wook, wook, wook changed to *whickwhickwhickwhick* as the pilot increased the pitch of the rotors and the copter rocked off the ground and headed for a cloud. Danny clung to the seat, marveling at the profligacy with which the Fuel Bloc spent its treasure —four metric tons of helicopter alone, tachyon-transported from Earth orbit at what cost in resources he could not guess.

"You don't get airsick, do you?" shouted Boyne over the noise of the blades. Danny shook his head, and the pilot grinned and deflected the blade edges so that the chopper leaned toward and began to move after a bank of cumulus.

To Danny's disappointment, the flock of balloonists was out of sight, but there were still small and large creatures in the air, keeping their distance. Dalehouse couldn't see them very clearly and suspected they wanted it that way, staying at the limits of vision and disappearing into cloud as the copter came close. But below! That was laid out for him to enjoy as the chopper bounced along less than fifty meters over the tallest growth. Groves of trees like bamboo; clusters of thirty-meter ferns; tangles of things like mangroves, twenty or more trunks uniting to form a single cat's-cradle tangle of vegetation. He could see small things scuttling and leaping to hide as they twisted overhead, colors of all sorts. The unwinking red glower of the dwarf star toned down rock and water, but the brightest colors were not reflections. They were foxfire glow and lightning-bug tail, the lights of the plants themselves.

Of course Dalehouse had studied the maps of Klong, orbital photos supplemented by side-scatter radar. But this was different, seeing the landscape as they soared above it. Back along the shore was their own camp, on a narrow neck of land that locked off a

bay from the wider ocean, or lake, a kilometer or two away. There
was the lake (or ocean) itself, curving around like a bitten-into
watermelon slice, and in the light from Kung almost the same
color. Down the shore of it was the Peeps' encampment. Past
that, off toward the part of Klong that lay just under the star,
where the land was dryer and the temperatures even higher, was
the Greasies' camp. Both of those were out of sight, of course.
The copter swung out across the water. Boyne pointed, and Dalehouse nodded; he could see their destination just taking form
through the gloomy haze, on the far shore.

Boyne had not been entirely frank, Dalehouse discovered. He
had not mentioned that this was not his first flight to the Krinpit
community. There had been at least two overflights before that,
because there were photos of the layout. Boyne pulled a sheaf of
them out of an elastic pocket in the door of the copter, sorted
through them, and passed one over to Danny. "There, by the
water's edge!" he bawled. His finger jabbed at a curled-up figure a
few meters up the beach. Drawn up nearby was a plastic coracle,
and there were sheds and more obscure structures all around.
There were also some very unpleasant-looking creatures like
square-ended crabs: Krinpit. Some of them were suspiciously close
to the huddled figure.

"Is he still alive?" Danny shouted.

"Don't know. He was a day or two ago. He's probably okay for
water, but he must be getting damned hungry by now. And probably sick."

From the air the Krinpit village looked like a stockyard, most of
the structures comprising only unroofed walls, like cattle pens.
The creatures were all around, Danny saw, moving astonishingly
quickly, at least when matched against his image of Earthside
crustaceans. And they were clearly aware the chopper was approaching. Some raised up to point their blind faces toward it, and
an ominous number seemed to be converging on the waterside.

"Creepy looking things, ain't they?" Boyne shouted.

"Listen," said Danny, "how are we going to get Dulla away
from them? They don't just look creepy. They look mean."

"Yeah." Boyne rolled down his window and leaned out, circling
the helicopter around. He shook his head, then pointed. "That
your buddy?"

The figure had moved since the photograph had been taken, was no longer in the shelter of one of the sheds but a few meters away and lying outstretched, face down. Dulla didn't look particularly alive, but he wasn't clearly dead either.

Boyne frowned thoughtfully, then turned to Dalehouse. "Open that case between your feet there, will you, and hand me a couple of those things."

The "things" were metal cylinders with a wire loop at the end. Boyne took half a dozen, pulled the loops, and tossed them carefully toward the Krinpit. As they struck, yellow smoke came billowing out of them, forming a dense cloud. The Krinpit staggered out of the smoke as though disoriented.

"Just tear gas," Boyne grinned. "They hate it." He stared down. Nearly all the creatures that had been converging around the prostrate man were fleeing now . . . all but one.

That one was obviously in distress, but it did not leave the vicinity of the prone human being. It seemed to be in pain. It moved dartingly back and forth as though torn between conflicting imperatives: to flee; to stay; perhaps even to fight.

"What are we going to do about that son of a bitch?" Boyne wondered out loud, hovering over the scene. But then the creature moved painfully away, and Boyne made his decision. He dropped to the ground between the Krinpit and the unconscious Pakistani. "Grab 'im, Danny!" he yelled.

Danny flung open his door and jumped out. He scooped up the Pakistani with more difficulty than he had expected. Dulla did not weigh much over fifty kilos here, but he was boneless as rubber, completely out of it. Danny got him under the arms and more dragged than carried him into the helicopter while Boyne swore worriedly. The rotors spun, and they started to lift off, and there was a rushing, clattering scramble from the other side. Two hundred kilograms of adult Krinpit launched itself onto the side-pallet. Boyne gibbered in rage and jockeyed the controls. The chopper staggered and seemed about to turn on its side; but he got it straight and it began to pull up and away.

"What are you going to do, Boyne?" yelled Danny, trying to pull Dulla's legs inside so he could close the door. "You can't just leave that thing there!"

"Hell I can't!" Boyne stared worriedly at the stiff-jointed legs that were trying to scrape through the plastic to get at him, then turned the copter up and over the water. "I've always wanted a pet. Let's see if I can get this bugger home!"

By the time he got back to his own camp, full of wonder and worries, Dalehouse was physically exhausted. He made a quick report to the rest of the expedition and then fell into a dreamless sleep.

"Night" was an arbitrary concept on Klong. When he woke, the sky was the same as it always was, clouds and the dull red cinder of Kung hanging far off center above.

It was back to work as usual. Kappelyushnikov, or somebody, had done some digging for him. He had less than an hour's work, mostly neatening up the edges. He welcomed it, because he had more than an hour's pondering to do.

After rescuing the Pakistani, Boyne had laid a beeline course for his own home base. He had not even asked if Dulla was alive; his attention was taken up to saturation by the hideous and very active creature only centimeters from his left ear and by the demands of piloting. Warned by radio, the Greasies had nets prepared. They had the Krinpit lashed and stowed before the beast knew what was happening. Then a quick meal while Dulla got some sort of emergency medical treatment, mostly cleaning him up and flowing a little glucose into his bloodstream. Then over the barren, hot ground to the Peeps' camp, where they left the sick man, accepted some haughty thanks from the Chinese in charge of the place, and took Dalehouse home.

All in all, he had been gone five or six hours. And every second filled with some new input to worry over in his mind.

He really begrudged them the Krinpit. There was no doubt the creature was intelligent. If the buildings hadn't proved that by themselves, its methodical attempt to gouge its way into the helicopter, and its patient acceptance of failure when the plastic proved too tough, bespoke thought. It had struggled only briefly when the Greasies threw the nets over it, then allowed itself to be hauled into a steel-barred cage. Only after the cage door had slammed behind it did it systematically cut through the netting to free its limbs. Dalehouse had spent all the moments he could spare just watching it and trying to make sense of its sounds. If only he had taken the brain-split at some point in his studies! He knew that Harriet or even that Bulgarian girl, Ana, could have reasoned out some sort of linguistic pattern, but it was only noise to him.

Then there was the wonder of the Greasy camp itself. Steel bars! A helicopter! Bunks on legs, with metal springs! He could not begin to imagine what profligate burning of irreplaceable fuel had made it possible for them to hurl all that stuff at superlight speed to an orbit around Kung, and then to lower it safely to the surface of the planet. They even had air conditioning! True, they needed it; the surface temperature must have been well over forty so near to the Heat Pole. But no one forced them to settle where they would need the permanent drain of air conditioners to survive.

And by contrast, the Peeps. That was pathetic. Old What'sy had put the best face possible on it, but it was clear that the return of Dulla meant to him principally another casualty to try to take care of, with hardly anybody healthy enough to do the nursing—much less do anything else. He had proudly given the visitor to understand that another expedition was on the way, "nearly as big as our own." But how big was that?

Jim Morrissey interrupted his train of thought. The biologist had been out of the camp and had not heard the report; now he wanted it all over again, firsthand. Dalehouse obliged and then asked, "Did you catch anything in your micetraps?"

"Huh? Oh." Obviously that was long in Morrissey's past by now. "No. I ran a wire-tethered probe down the tunnel, but it kept hitting blind alleys. They're pretty smart, whoever they are. As soon as you broke into their tunnel they closed it off."

"So you don't have any animals to send back to Earth?"

"No animals? Never say it, never think it, Danny! I've got a whole menagerie. Crabrats and bugs, creepers and flyers. God knows what they all are. I think the crabrats are probably related to the Krinpit, but you can't really trace relationships until you do paleontology, and Christ, I haven't even made a beginning on the taxonomy yet. And plants—well, anyway, you might as well call them plants. They don't have stomata or mesophyll cells. Would you believe that?"

"Sure I would, Jim."

"Where the photosynthetic process happens I don't know," Jim went on, marveling, "but it's the same good old thing. Starch production driven by sunlight, or what passes for sunlight—$6CO_2$ plus $6H_2O$ still yields $C_6H_{12}O_6$ and some spare oxygen, on Earth as it is in the heavens. Or the other way around."

"That's starch?" Dalehouse guessed.

"You bet. But don't eat any of it. And keep putting that jelly on your skin every time it rubs off. There're congeners in all that stuff that will do you in."

"Sure." Dalehouse's attention was wandering, and he hardly listened as Morrissey catalogued the vegetation he had so far identified on Klong: something like grasses that covered the plains; succulents like bamboo, with hollow stems that would make fine structural materials; forests of plants that looked like ferns but were fruiting and with woody stems. Some of them grew together from many trunks, like mangroves; others towered in solitary splendor, like redwoods. There were vines like grapes, spreading by transporting their hard-shelled seeds through the digestive tracts of animals. Some of them were luminous. Some were meat-eating, like the Venus flytrap. Some—

"That starch," Dalehouse interrupted, pursuing his train of thought. "Can't we eat it? I mean, sort of cook the poison out of it, like tapioca?"

"Danny, stick to what you know."

"No, really," Dalehouse persisted. "We're shipping a lot of mass in the form of food. Couldn't we?"

"No. Well, maybe. In a sense. It takes only a little bit of their proteins to kick off a reaction I can't handle, so don't experiment. Remember the Peeps' white mice."

"If they're plants, why aren't they green?"

"Well, they are, kind of. In this light they look purple because Kung's so red, but if you shine a flashlight on them they're a kind of greenish yellow. But, you know," he went on earnestly, "it's not the usual chlorophyll. Not even a porphyrin derivative. They do seem to use a magnesium ion—"

"I better get this finished up," said Danny, patting the biologist on the shoulder.

It was almost done. He lugged the chemical toilet from the

lander and balanced it over the slit trench, and then reported to Harriet.

"All done. First-class American crapper ready for use."

She came over to inspect and then pursed her tiny lips. "Dalehouse, do you think we're animals? Can't you at least put a tent over it? And before it rains again, would you mind? Look at those clouds. Damn it, Danny, why do I have to tell everybody what to do around here?"

He got the tent up. But the storm, when it came, was a rouser. Lightning scored the entire sky, cloud to ground and air to air. Kung was completely obscured, not even a dull glow to mark where it hung in the sky, and the only light was the lightning itself. The first casualty was the power system. The second was Danny's outhouse tent, torn flying away by the eighty-kilometer gusts. By the time it was over they were drenched and miserable, and all of them were busy trying to put the camp together again. East Lansing had had no storms like Klong's, and Danny viewed with dismal foreboding the next few years on this treacherous planet. When he realized he had been more than twenty hours without sleep, he tumbled into bed and dreamed of a warm morning in Bulgaria with a pretty blond woman.

When he woke, Jim Morrissey was poking him. "Out. I get the bed next."

It wasn't really even a bed—just a sleeping bag on an air mattress—but at least it was warm and dry. Dalehouse reluctantly yielded it to the biologist. "So the camp survived?"

"More or less. Don't go near Harriet, though. One of her radios is missing, and she thinks we're all to blame." As he climbed into the bed and stretched his legs down to the warm interior, he said, "Cappy wants to show you something."

Danny didn't rush to see the pilot; odds were, he considered, that it was just some other stoop-labor job that needed doing. It could wait until he had something to eat—although, he reflected, chewing doggedly through a guaranteed full daily requirement of essential vitamins and minerals (it looked like a dog biscuit), eating wasn't a hell of a lot more fun than digging latrines.

But that wasn't what Kappelyushnikov had in mind. "Is no more manual labor for you and me for a while, Danny," he

grinned. "Have now been honored by appointment as chief mete-
orologist. Must make more *wasserstoff* to check winds, and you
help."

"Harriet was real shook up by the storm," Dalehouse guessed.

"Gasha? Yes, that is what she wants, better weather forecasting.
But what I want is exotic travel to faraway places! You will see."

Kappelyushnikov's still had been converted to solar power, a
trough of brackish water from the lake running between aluminum reflecting V's, and the vapor trapped on a plastic sheet overhead. The drops slipped down into a tank, and part of the fresh
water was being electrolyzed into hydrogen and oxygen. From the
hydrogen collector, a seamless plastic balloon, a small compressor
whirred at regular intervals to pump the gas into a heavy metal
cylinder.

Kappelyushnikov checked the pressure gauge and nodded
gravely. "Is plenty. Now you go borrow theodolite from head boss,
Gasha. Do not take no for answer; and then I will show you something that will truly amaze you."

Fortunately for Dalehouse, Harriet was somewhere else when
he went for the theodolite, a small sighting telescope that looked
like a surveyor's transit. By the time he got back with it Kappelyushnikov had filled a plastic balloon with hydrogen and was expertly balancing its lift against the weight of a silver ruble. "My
good-luck piece," he said dreamily. "Yes, fine. You have pencil?"

"What's a pencil? I have a ballpoint."

"Don't make fun of old-fashioned Soviet values," Kappelyushnikov said severely. "When I let go of balloon, you keep eye on
watch. Every twenty seconds you tell me, I call off readings, you
write down. You understand? Okay, let go."

The little balloon did not leap out of Dalehouse's fingers; it
only drifted upward, bobbing gently as vagrant zephyrs caught it.
In the still after the storm there was no strongly prevailing wind
that Dalehouse could feel, but he could see the balloon move er-
ratically. At each time-hack Kappelyushnikov read off right ascension and declination bearings. After the seventh reading he began
to swear, and after the ninth he straightened up, scowling.

"Is no good! Lousy Kungson light! I cannot see. Next time we
will tie on candle."

"Fine, but would you mind telling me what we're doing?"

"Measuring winds aloft, dear Danny! See how balloon curved around, started back way it came? Winds at different levels blow various individual different directions. Balloon follows. We follow balloon. Now we reduce readings, and soon I will truly astonish you with more than you wish to know about Klongan wind patterns."

Dalehouse squinted thoughtfully at where the balloon had disappeared into the maroon murk. "How are we going to do that?"

"Oh, Danny, Danny. How ignorant you Americans are! Simple trigonometry. I have right ascension sighting of balloon after twenty seconds, correct? So I have one angle of right triangle. Second angle must be ninety degrees—you understand that this is so? Otherwise would not be right triangle. So simple subtraction from one hundred eighty gives me angle remaining, and I have thus described triangle perfectly, except for dimension of sides. Okay. I now feed in dimension of first side, and simple transformation—"

"Whoa! You didn't measure anything. Where did you get the dimension of one side?"

"Altitude of balloon after twenty seconds, of course."

"But how do you know—"

"Ah," said Kappelyushnikov smugly, "that is why care is so important in weighing of balloon. With fixed lift, balloon rises at fixed rate. Lift is equal to one silver ruble, and so in each twenty seconds rises nine point seven three meters. We now perform same arithmetic for declination and we have fixed position of balloon in three-dimensional space. Here, walk while we talk." He took the jotted readings from Danny and scanned them, frowning. "Such terrible writing," he complained. "Nevertheless, I can read them perhaps well enough to feed into computer. Is very easy computation."

"Then why do you need a computer?"

"Oh, I could easily perform operations myself. But computer needs practice. Wait one, Danny."

While the Russian was mumbling to himself over the keyboard, Harriet poked her head in the tent. "What are you doing?" she demanded sharply.

"Important scientific research," said Kappelyushnikov airily, without looking up. To Danny's surprise, the translator did not react. She looked sullen, confused, and unhappy—not conspicuously different from her normal look. But her normal behavior was a good deal more abrasive than her demeanor now. She came quietly into the tent and sat down, thumbing dispiritedly through her translation notes.

"Have it!" cried the pilot happily, and pressed a command button. The liquid crystal over the computer flashed colored darts of light, then revealed a plot of wind arrows. "Colors of spectrum," Kappelyushnikov explained. "Red is lowest, up to fresh grass green for highest. You see? At fifty meters, wind heading one forty-five degrees, eight kilometers per hour. At one hundred meters, backing to ninety-five degrees and now fifteen kilometers. And so on. Triumph of Soviet technology."

Dalehouse nodded appreciatively. "That's very nice, but what do we want to know that for?"

"Meteorology," Kappelyushnikov grinned, winking and moving his head toward Harriet.

The woman looked up and burst out, "Cut that out, Vissarion. I'm in no mood for you to make fun of me. Tell Dalehouse your real reason."

The Russian looked surprised, and a little thoughtful, but he shrugged. "All right. Poor American Danny, you are helpless without your machines. But not I. I am pilot! I do not wish to be earthworm like one of those things we shit on in your latrine, Danny. I want something to fly. They will not give me fuel. They will not let me have structural materials for glider—would be easy, except for launching; plenty of winds here, you see. But Gasha says no, so what can I do? I look up and see balloonists floating around sky, and I say I also will be balloonist!" He pounded his fist on the top of the computer. "Have gas. Have navigation information for winds aloft. Have Soviet know-how. Have also little extra bonus of low gravity and high pressure of air. So now I will make little balloon, big enough for me, and I will pilot again."

A surge of enthusiasm infected Dalehouse. "Hey, that's great. Would it work?"

"Of course would work!"

"We could use it to take after those balloonists, get close to them. Harriet, do you hear that? It would give us a chance to try to talk to them."

"That's fine," she said, and Dalehouse looked at her more closely. Even for Harriet she looked sullen.

"What's the matter?" he asked.

She said, "I located the radio."

"The one that blew away in the storm?"

She laughed, like a cartoon figure laughing: *heh, heh, heh.* "It takes a real idiot to believe that one. How could it blow away? Goddamn thing weighs twenty kilos. It occurred to me it might be transmitting, so I listened, and it was. I tried RDFing, and I got a fix right away. Straight down," she said, staring at them. "The damn thing is right down underneath us in the ground."

A minute was still a minute. Danny made sure of that, because he had begun to doubt. His pulse was still forty-two in sixty seconds by the clock. He could hold his breath for three of the minutes and maybe a bit more. The small coinage of time had not altered in value. But one thousand four hundred and forty minutes did not seem to make a day anymore. Sometimes it felt as though a whole day had passed, and the clock said only six or seven hours. Sometimes it would occur to him to be tired, and the clock would show as much as thirty hours since he slept last. Fretfully Harriet tried to keep them all on some regular schedule, not because it seemed necessary, but because it was orderly. She failed. Within—what? a week?—they were sleeping when they wanted to and eating when they felt hungry and marking the passage of time, if at all, by events. The first near-visit by balloonists was after the big storm and before the Peeps received their reinforcement of personnel. The time Kappelyushnikov triangulated the missing radio for Harriet and discovered it was at least twenty meters underground was just after they sent their first reports and shipment of specimens back to Earth. And the time balloonists came to visit—

That was a whole other thing, the kind of event that changes everything fore and aft.

Dalehouse woke up with his mind in the sky. He did his chores. He helped Morrissey check his traps, prepared a meal of desiccated stew, fixed a valve in the shower stall by the lake. But what he was thinking of was Kappelyushnikov's balloons. Danny had talked him out of the big single hydrogen-filled bag: too big, too clumsy, too hard to manufacture, and above all too likely to kill its passenger if anything popped its skin. So they had pains-takingly blown a hundred pibal-sized bags, and the Russian had knotted up a netting to contain them. The aggregate lift would be as much as you wanted. All it took was more balloons; you could multiply them to lift the entire camp if you liked. But if one or two popped, it did not mean a dead aeronaut. The passenger would descend reasonably slowly—to be more accurate, they were hopeful the passenger would descend slowly. He might damage himself, but at least he would not be spread flat across the Klongan landscape.

Kappelyushnikov would not allow Danny to do the final stages of filling and tying the balloons—"Is my neck, dear Danny, so is my job to make sure it stays okay."

"But you're taking so damn long. Let me help."

"Nyet. Is very clear," grinned the pilot, "that you think pretty soon you too will fly my balloons. Maybe so. But this time I am sole cargo. And besides, have still static lift tests to finish. Until then not even I fly."

Dalehouse moved impatiently away, disgruntled. He had been on Klong for—whatever length of time it was—a couple of weeks, at least. And the author of "Preliminary Studies toward a First Contact with Subtechnological Sentients" had yet to meet his first subtechnological sentient. Oh, he had seen them. There were bur-rowers under his feet, and he was sure he had caught a glimpse of something when Morrissey exploded a charge under a presumed tunnel. The Krinpit had been his fellow passenger for half an hour. And the balloonists were often in the sky, though seldom nearby. Three separate races to study and deal with! And the most productive thing he had done was dig a latrine.

He fidgeted his way into Harriet's tent, hoping to find that she had miraculously made some giant leap in translation of one of the languages—if they were languages. She wasn't there, but the tapes were. He played the best of them over and over until Kap-pelyushnikov came in, sweating and cheerful.

"Static test is good. Plenty lift. Now we let whole mishmash sit for a while, check for leaks. You are enjoying concert of airborne friends?"

"It isn't a concert, it's a language. I *think* it's a language. It's not random birdcalls. You can hear them singing in chords and harmonies. It's chromatic rather than—do you know anything about music theory?"

"Me? Please, Danny. I am pilot, not longhair fiddle player."

"Well, anyway, it's chromatic rather than diatonic, but the harmonies are there, not too far off what you might hear in, say, Scriabin."

"Fine composer," the Russian beamed. "But tell me. Why do you listen to tapes when you have real thing right outside?"

Startled, Danny raised his head. It was true. Some of the sounds he was hearing came from somewhere outside the tent.

"Also," Kappelyushnikov went on severely, "you are breaking Gasha's rice bowl. She is translator, not you, and she is very difficult lady. So come now and listen to your pink and green friends."

The balloonists had never been so close, or so numerous. The whole camp was staring up at them, hundreds of them, so many that they obscured each other and blotted out part of the sky. The red glower of Kung shone through them dimly as they passed before its disk, but many of them were glowing with their own firefly light, mostly, as Kappelyushnikov had said, pink and pale green. Their song was loud and clear. Harriet was there already, microphone extended to catch every note, listening critically with an expression of distaste. That meant nothing. It was just the way she always looked.

"Why so close?" Dalehouse marveled.

"I do not wish to break your rice bowl either, dear Danny. You are expert. But I think is possible they like what we put up for chopper pilot." And Kappelyushnikov waved to the strobe beacon on the tower.

"Um." Danny considered a moment. "Let's see. Do me a favor and get one of the portable floodlights. We'll see them better, and maybe it'll bring them even closer."

"Why not?" The Russian disappeared inside the supply tent and came back with the portable in one hand and the batteries in the other, cursing as he tried to avoid stumbling over the wires. He fumbled with it, and its dense white beam abruptly extended itself toward the horizon, then danced up toward the balloonists. It seemed to excite them. Their chirps, squeals, flatulences, and cello drones multiplied themselves in a shower of grace notes, and they seemed to follow the beam.

"How do they do that?" Harriet demanded fretfully. "They've got no wings or anything that I can see."

"Same as I, dear Gasha," boomed the Russian. "Up and down, to find a truly sympathetic current of air. Here, you hold light. I must watch experts and learn!"

The balloonists were coming closer. Evidently the light attracted them. Now that there was enough brightness to make the colors plain, the variety of their patterns was striking. There were cloudlike whorls, solid bands, cross-hatchings, dazzle designs that resembled World War I camouflage.

"Funny," said Dalehouse, staring longingly at the swarm. "Why would they have all those colors when they can't see them most of the time?"

"Is your opinion they can't," said Kappelyushnikov. "Light like beet juice is strange to us; we see only the red. But for them perhaps is— Ho, Morrissey! Good shot!"

Dalehouse jumped a quarter of a meter as the camp's one and only shotgun went off behind him. Overhead, one of the balloonists was spiraling toward the ground.

"I get," yelled Kappelyushnikov, and sprinted off to intersect its fall.

"*What the hell did you do?*" blazed Dalehouse.

The biologist turned a startled and defensive face toward him. "I collected a specimen," he said.

Harriet laughed disagreeably. "Shame on you, Morrissey. You didn't get Dalehouse's permission to shoot one of his friends. That's the price you pay for being a specialist in sentients—you fall in love with your subjects."

"Don't be bitchy, Harriet. My job's hard enough. This'll make it impossible. Shooting at them is the surest way to drive them away."

"Oh, sure, Dalehouse. Anybody can see they're stampeding in terror, right?" She waved a casual hand at the flock, still milling through the light and singing as they soared delightedly overhead.

Kappelyushnikov came back with a rubbery sac draped over his shoulder. "Almost had to fight off one of your Krinpit friends to get it," he growled. "Was big, ugly mother. Don't know what I would have done if he had truly contested ownership. But he scuttled away."

"There are no Krinpit around here," Harriet said sharply.

"Are now, Gasha. Never mind. See how pretty our new pet is."

The creature was not dead. It did not seem even wounded, or at least there was no blood. The shotgun pellets had blown a hole in the gasbag and nothing else. Its little face was working, looking like the countenance of an engorged tick, with great eyes staring at them. It was making the tiniest of sounds, almost like gasps.

"Disgusting," said Harriet, drawing back. "Why isn't it screaming?"

"If I knew the answers to questions like that," said Morrissey, dropping to one knee beside the creature to see it better, "I wouldn't have to collect specimens, would I? But at a guess, it would be if I hadn't shot the breath out of it. I think it uses the hydrogen for vocalizing. God knows what it breathes. Must be oxygen, of course, but—" He shook his head and glanced up. "Maybe I ought to collect a few more."

"No!"

"Christ, Dalehouse! You know, Harriet's right about you. Well —I know. At least let's see how phototropic they are. Hand me those shells." Kappelyushnikov passed over the plastic belt of ammunition, and Morrissey pawed through it until he found a signal flare.

"You'll set fire to them, Morrissey! That's hydrogen in those bags!"

"Oh, cripes." But the biologist aimed carefully to one side of the flock. More and more of them were entering into the beam, now steady, as Harriet had put it on the ground pointing up; the whole diffuse swarm was contracting into a knotted mass.

When the flare went off, the whole flock seemed to twitch like a single organism. They didn't swarm toward it. They stayed bunched in an ellipsoidal huddle along the axis of the beam of light; but their song changed to a frantic crescendo, and there seemed to be a systematic rearranging of positions within the flock. The smaller and less brightly colored individuals bobbed toward the lower portions of the school, and the larger and gaudier ones lifted toward the top. Dalehouse stared in fascination, so entranced that he did not realize his face was sticky and wet until Kappelyushnikov grunted in surprise.

"Hey! Is raining?"

But it wasn't rain. It was sweet and pungent on their lips, with an aftertaste that was animal and fetid; it fell like a gentle dew on their upturned faces and clung to their skins.

"Don't swallow any!" cried Morrissey in belated panic, but some of the people were already licking their lips. Not that it mattered, thought Dalehouse; the stuff was all over them. If it was poisonous, they were done for.

"You fools!" cried Harriet, stamping her foot. She had never been attractive, and now she looked like a witch, sallow face in a grimace, uneven teeth bared. "We've got to get this stuff off. Kappelyushnikov! You and Morrissey get buckets of water at once."

"*Da,* Gasha," said the pilot dreamily.

"*Now!*" she screamed.

"Oh, of course, now." He lumbered off a few steps, then paused and looked coquettishly back over his shoulder. "Alyusha, dear. You help me get important water right away?"

The navigator simpered. She answered him in Russian, something that made Kappelyushnikov grin and Harriet swear. "Don't you clods know we're all in *danger?*" she cried, catching at Dalehouse's hand imploringly. "You, Danny, you've always been nicer to me than those other bastards. Help me get water."

He returned the pressure of her hand and whispered, "Hell, yes, honey, let's get some water."

"Danny!" But she wasn't angry anymore. She was smiling, allowing him to tug her toward the lakefront.

He ran his tongue over his lips again. Whatever the dew was, the more he tasted it the better he liked it: not sweet, not tart, not like fruit or meat, not like flowers. It was not like anything he had ever tasted before, but it was a taste he wanted more of. He saw Harriet touching her pointed tongue to her own thin lips and was suddenly seized with the need to taste that Klongan mist from her mouth. He felt the damp heat rising inside him and caught her roughly around the waist.

They kissed desperately, their hands busy ripping each other's clothes off.

It never occurred to them to think of hiding themselves. They cared nothing for what the others in the expedition might think of them, and the others cared no more for Harriet and Dalehouse. In couples and clusters the entire expediton was down on the ground in a mass fury of copulation, while overhead the swooping balloonists sang and soared through the searchlight and their gentle mist rained down on the human beings below.

·SEVEN·

ANA DIMITROVA sat in a window table of a Greek tea shop in Glasgow, writing industriously on her daily letter to Ahmed. She did not send them all. That would be ruinously extravagant! But every week, at the end of Sunday, she spread them out on a table and copied out the best parts, enough to fill four dots in a microfiche. It was never enough. She leaned forward into the northern sunshine, left elbow on the table next to the cooling cup of strong, sweet tea, head resting on the hand, oblivious to the noise of the lorries and the double-decker yellow-and-green buses on the Gallowgate road outside, and wrote:

—it seems so long since last I kissed your lovely eyelids and wished you good-bye. I miss you, dear Ahmed. This place is terrible! Terrible and strange. It smells of petroleum and internal-combustion engines, the smell of wicked waste. Well. They have only another five or ten years and then their North Sea oil will be gone, and then we will see.

The headaches have been very bad, I think because these languages are so uncouth. It is actual pain to speak in them. It will be all right, though, dear Ahmed. The headaches pass. The ache in my heart lasts much longer—

"More tea, miss?"

The harsh English words crashed into Nan's ear. She winced and raised her head. "Thank you, no."

"We'll be serving lunch in just a bit, miss. The souvlaki's very tasty today, cook says."

"No, no. Thank you. I must be getting back to my hotel." She had dawdled longer over the letter than was right, she thought remorsefully, and now she had to hurry, and the headache was back. It was not just that the woman was speaking English. It was the way she spoke it, the rough Scottish consonants that buzzed and rattled in the ear. Although in truth it did not much matter what language, or at least what non-Slavic language, she was hearing. The headaches were more frequent and more severe. It was probably because she had become a diplomatic translator. The international vocabulary of science was easy enough to translate, since so many of the words had the same roots in all languages. In diplomacy the risks were greater, the nuances subtler and more threatening. The choice of an adjective meant nothing in translating a report on X-ray polarimetry, but in a speech about locating a drilling claim on the Mid-Atlantic Ridge it might mean the difference between peace and war.

Nan paid her check and dodged cautiously across Gallowgate among the towering buses that so mischievously raced along the wrong side of the street. The diesel stink made her cough, and coughing made her headache worse.

And she was late. She was to be picked up for the airport at one, and it was past noon already. She walked virtuously past the shops (so bright and gay!) without looking in a single window. There were styles here that Sofia would not see for another year. But why bother? It would have been nice to buy new clothes to wear for Ahmed. With him so many billions of kilometers away, Nan wore what was easiest to put on and least likely to attract attention. Evenings she spent alone when she could, listening to music and studying grammar. Her best treat was to reread the sparse letters he had returned for her prodigious outflow—although they were not stimulating. From what he said, Son of Kung sounded a grim and awful place.

She cut through a corner of the Green to walk along the riverside toward her hotel, hoping to avoid the noise and the invisible, but not unsmellable, exhaust from all the vehicles. No use. Lorries rumbled along the embankment, and the sludgy surface of the Clyde itself was pocked with oil tankers and barges and creased with the wakes of hydrofoils. How did one *live* in a place like this? And it all could have been avoided. A little forethought. A little planning. Why did they have to put oil refineries in the middle of a city? Why stain their river with waste and filth when it could have been a cool oasis? Why be in such a rush to pump the oil from the bottom of the sea when it could have provided energy, even food, for another hundred generations? Why use oil at all, for that matter—especially in these packs and swarms of cars and lorries—when the city could have been built around public transportation, electrically powered, or powered with the hydrogen that Iceland, not so very far away, was so eager to sell.

But on Son of Kung . . .

On Son of Kung it could be all different. She wished she could be there. With Ahmed. Not just to be with Ahmed, she told herself stoutly, but to be part of a new world where things could be done properly. Where the mistakes of Earth could be avoided. Where one's children would have a future to look forward to.

Hers and Ahmed's children, of course. Nan smiled to herself. She was an honest person, and she admitted that Kungson seemed all the finer because Ahmed was there. If only she were not *here!* There were worrisome things between the lines of what he wrote. So many of his expedition had been sick. So many had died, just in the first days—and his only letters had been in those first days. Why, he himself could have— No. She would not countenance that thought. There was enough else to fret about. For example, the picture he had sent of himself. He had looked worrisomely thin, but what she had noticed most about the picture was the hand on his shoulder. The person who owned the hand was not visible, but Nan was almost sure it was a woman's hand. And that was even more worrisome.

"Miss Dimitrova! Hoy, there. Nan!"

All at once she perceived that her feet had carried her into the lobby of the hotel, and she was being greeted by a man she almost recognized. Dark, short, plump, a little past middle age, he had a diplomat's smile and wore clothes that, even across the immense old lobby, she was sure were real wool—if not cashmere.

He filled in the blank for her. "I'm Tam Gulsmit. Remember? We met at the FAO reception last month." He snapped his fingers for a forkboy. "Your bags are all ready—unless you care to freshen up? Have time for a drink?"

Now she recalled him well. He had been persistent in his attentions, even to the point of lying in wait for her as she came out of the powder room and drawing her into an offensively close conversation in the hall. She had explained to him that it was no use. It was not merely a question of being in love with someone else. That was not his concern; she did not have to tell him her reasons. It was a matter of socialist morality. V. I. Lenin had said it. Free love was all very well, but who would want to drink from a glass that every passerby had fouled with his lips? (And yet in Moscow, she remembered, the public drinking fountains had just such glasses chained to them, and each one surely smeared with a thousand lips.) Let the Fuel powers do what they liked—partner swapping, group orgies, whatever. She was not there to pass judgment, but a socialist girl from Sofia did not even smoke in the street, because she had been taught certain principles of behavior that did not leave her when she grew up.

"Sir Tam," she began—she remembered that he had one of those quaint British handles to his name—"it is a pleasure to see you again, but I must fly now to New York for the United Nations debate. I have no time—"

"All the time in the world, sweets, that's what I'm here for. Boy!"

Tardily the bellboy rolled up with his forklift, and that was scandalous, too: her one little zipper bag did not need a fuel-guzzling machine to carry it; she had toted it a kilometer at a time herself.

Sir Tam chuckled indulgently. "Aren't we quaint? This great, rambling old ruin—that's the Britishness of it, isn't it? We're great at backing a losing horse long past the point where anyone else would have chucked it in. Lucky for us we can afford it! Now, is there anything else you need to bring?"

"But truly, Sir Tam, a car is being sent to take me to the airport. It will be here any minute."

"Here already, sweetie. I'm it. Our Government have provided me with a Concorde Three, and I'd just rattle around in it by myself. When I heard that a friend of God Menninger's needed a lift I took the liberty of coming for you myself. You'll like it.

There's plenty of room, and we'll make New York in ninety minutes."

Scandalous, scandalous! Of course the British could afford anything, ocean of oil under the North Sea, their octopus tendrils already grabbing at the Mid-Atlantic Ridge. But morally it was so wrong.

She had no chance to refuse. Sir Tam overcame all objections, and before she knew what was happening she was lifted gently by cherry picker into—dear God!—a supersonic hydrojet.

As soon as they belted up, in deep, foam armchairs with a suction-bottomed decanter and glasses already on a little table between them, the aircraft hurled itself into the air. The acceleration was frightening. The way the ground dropped away beneath them was not to be believed. Strangely, there was less noise than she had expected, far less than the warm-up roar of a clamjet.

"How quiet," she said, leaning away from Sir Tam's casually chummy arm.

He chuckled. "That's five thousand kilometers an hour for you. We leave the sound far behind. Do you like it?"

"Oh, yes," said Nan, trying to prevent him from pouring her a drink. She failed.

"Your voice sounds more like 'oh, no.' "

"Well, yes, perhaps that is so. It is terribly wasteful of oil, Sir Tam."

"We don't burn oil, sweetie! Pure hydrogen and oxygen—have to carry them both, this far up. Not an ounce of pollution."

"But of course one burns oil, or some other fuel, to make the hydrogen." She wondered if she could keep the conversation on propellant chemistry all the way across the Atlantic, decided not, and took a new tack. "It is frightening. One can see nothing from these tiny windows."

"What is there to see? You get turned on by clouds, love?"

"I have flown the oceans many times, Sir Tam. There is always something. Sometimes icebergs. The sea itself. In a clamjet there is the excitement of the landfall as one approaches Newfoundland or Rio or the Irish Coast. But at twenty-five thousand meters there is nothing."

"I couldn't agree with you more," said Sir Tam, unstrapping

and moving closer. "If I had my way there'd be no windows in the thing at all."

Nan moistened her lips with the whiskey and said brightly, "But it is all so exciting. Could you perhaps show me around this aircraft?"

"Show you around?"

"Yes, please. It is so new to me."

"What's to see, love?" Then he shrugged. "Matter of fact, yes, there are a few features I'd like to call to your attention."

She stood up gratefully, glad to get his hand off her knee. The headaches had lessened, perhaps because now they were breathing quite pure air instead of the Glaswegian smog, but she was annoyed. He had made it clear that they were the only passengers; that was not deceitful. But she had expected at least the chaperonage of the stewardesses, and they, all three of them, had retreated to their little cubbyholes in the aft of the aircraft. The little paneled lounge was far more intimate than she liked.

But worse was in store. What she had thought was a service cubicle turned out to be a tiny, complete bedroom suite. With—could one believe it?—a *waterbed*. Easily a metric ton of profligately wasted mass! For nothing, surely, but profligately immoral purposes!

"Now there," said Sir Tam over her shoulder, "is a feature worth studying. Go ahead, Nan. Let your impulses carry you. Try it out."

"Certainly not!" She moved away from his touching hand and added formally, "Sir Tam, I must tell you that I am an engaged person. It is not correct for me to allow myself to be in a situation of this kind."

"How quaint."

"Sir Tam!" She was almost shrieking now, and furiously angry, not only with him but with herself. If she had used a tiny bit of intelligence she would have known this was coming and could have avoided it. A delicate hint that this was the wrong time. A suggestion of—what? Of a social disease, if necessary. Anything. But she was trapped, the waterbed before her, this gland case behind, already with his lips against her ear, whispering buzzingly so that her headache exploded again. Desperately she caught at a straw.

"We—we were speaking of Godfrey Menninger?"

"What?"

"Godfrey Menninger. The father of my good friend, Captain Marge Menninger. You spoke of him in the hotel."

He was silent for a moment, neither releasing her nor trying to pull her closer. "Do you know God Menninger well?"

"Only through his daughter. I was able to keep her from going to jail once."

His arm was definitely less tight. After a moment he patted her gently and stepped away. "Let's have a drink," he said, ringing for the stewardesses. The satyr's smile had been replaced by the diplomat's.

The conversation was back on its tracks again, for which Ana was intensely grateful. She even managed to return to the little cubicle with the armchairs and to persuade the stewardess to bring her a nice cup of strong *chai* instead of the whiskey Gulsmit suggested. He seemed greatly interested in the story of Margie Menninger's little episode, in every detail. Had they been fingerprinted? Was the people's magistrate a court of record, whatever that was? Had Ana spoken to anyone in the militia about the incident later on, and if so what had they said?

Such trivial things seemed to interest him, but Nan was content to go on dredging up memories for him all the way across the Atlantic, as long as it meant his keeping his hands to himself. When she was wrung dry he leaned back, nursing the new drink the stewardess had poured for him and squinting out at the blue-black and cloudless sky.

"Very interesting," he said at last. "That poor little girl. Of course, I've known her since she was tiny." It had not occurred to Ana that Margie Menninger had ever been tiny. She let it pass, and Sir Tam added, "And dear old God. Have you known him long?"

"Not in a personal sense," she said, careful not to add lying to the fault of being untruthful. "Of course he is of great importance in cultural matters. I too am deeply concerned about culture."

"Culture," repeated Sir Tam meditatively. He seemed about to produce a real smile but managed to retain the diplomatic one instead. "You are a dear, Nan," he said, and shook his wristwatch to make the red numerals blink on. "Ah, almost there," he said regretfully. "But of course you must allow me to escort you to your hotel."

The morning session of the UN was exhausting. There was no time for a real lunch because she had to post-edit the computer translations of what she had already translated once that morning before they could be printed. And the afternoon session was one long catfight.

The debate was on fishing rights for Antarctic krill. Because it was food, tempers ran high. And because sea lore is almost as old an area of human interest as eating, the translation was demanding. There were no places where she could coast, no technical words that were new-coined and common to almost all languages. Every language had developed its own words for ships, seamanship, and above all, eating, at the dawn of language itself. Only three of Nan's languages were in use—Bulgarian, English, and Russian. The Pakistanis were not involved in the debate, and there were plenty of others proficient in the Romance languages. So there were long periods when she could listen without having to speak. But there was no rest even in those periods; she needed to remember every word she could. The UN delegates had the awful habit of quoting each other at length—sometimes with approval, sometimes with a sneer, always with the risk of some tiny hairsplit that she had to get just right. Her headaches were immense.

That was, of course, the price you paid for having the two hemispheres of your brain surgically sliced apart. Not to mention the stitching back of parts of them that kept you from stumbling into things or falling down, or the DNA injections that left your neck swollen and your eyes bulging for weeks at a time and sometimes caused seizures indistinguishable from epilepsy. That had been a surprise. They hadn't told her about those things when she signed up to become a split-brain translator—not really. You never did know what pain was going to be until you had it.

What made the whole day an order of magnitude worse was that she was starved for sleep. Sir Tam had followed her to her very door and then planted a foot inside it. His hands had been all over her in the limousine all the way in from the airport. The only way she could think to get rid of him was to pretend such ex-

haustion that she could not stay awake another second, even
though it was just after lunch, New York time. And then she
found she had talked herself into it.

So she did go to sleep. And woke up before midnight with the
chance for any more sleep gone. And what was there to do with
the eleven hours before the morning session would begin?

A letter to Ahmed, of course. A few hours with English irregular verbs. Another hour or so listening to the tapes she had just
made to check her accent. But then she was tired and fretful.
What she needed most was a walk from her apartment past the
university into the fresh morning air of the park, but that was ten
thousand kilometers away in Sofia. In New York you did not go
walking in the fresh morning air. And so she had turned up for
duty in the translator's booth feeling as though a hard day's work
was already behind her, and her head throbbing and pounding in
two different rhythms, one in each temple. . . .

Her mind had wandered. She forced it back. It was Sir Tam
asking for the floor now, and she had to put his words into Bulgarian.

His face was purple-red, and he was shouting. With one half of
her brain Nan wondered at that while the other half was automatically processing his words. So much passion about such little fish!
Not even fish. They were some sort of crustacean, weren't they?
To Nan, "krill" was something that old-fashioned peasant gran-
nies stirred into their stews to give them body. It came as a
grayish-white powdery substance that you bought in jars labeled
"fish protein concentrate." You knew that it was good for you,
but you didn't like to think about what organs and oddities were
ground up to make it. In food-rich Bulgaria, nobody grew excited
about the stuff.

But Sir Tam was excited. The Fuel Bloc needed it desperately,
he shouted. Had to have it! Was entitled to it, by all the laws of
civilized humanity! The Fuel Bloc already possessed the fleets of
long-range factory ships that could seine the cold Antarctic
Ocean. He quoted *Pacem in Maris* and the British-Portuguese
Treaty of A.D. 1242. The tiny bodies of the creatures that made up
the krill, he declaimed, were absolutely essential to British agriculture, being the very best kind of fertilizer for their crops.

At which the Uruguayan delegate interrupted, snarling, "Agriculture! You are using this essential protein to feed to animals."

"Of course," Sir Tam replied stoutly. "We are not blessed with the advantages given your country, Señor Corrubias. We do not have immense plains on which our cattle can graze. In order to feed them properly, we must have imports—"

Someone in the American delegation laughed out loud, not a pleasant laugh, and the Uruguayan drummed on his desk derisively. "So it is cattle you feed, Sir Gulsmit? But we have it on the evidence of your own Ministry of Health that you give the krill to your cats and budgies! Do you then make minced kitten patties, perhaps? Or fresh chops of parrakeet?"

Sir Tam looked long-sufferingly at the president pro tem. "Sir, I must ask the courtesy of the floor."

The president was a spare Ghanaian who had not once glanced toward any speaker. He did not do so now. His eyes stayed on the letters he was signing one by one as his secretary put them before him. He said, "I would request of the delegate from Uruguay that he reserve his remarks until the delegate from the United Kingdom has concluded."

Sir Tam beamed graciously. "Thank you. In any case, I am almost finished. Of course, some part of our imports of krill does find its way into pet food, some part into protein additives for the justly famous British beef, some part into fertilizer to help us grow the vital foods that nature has otherwise denied us. Is that a matter for this body? I think not. What is of concern is the behavior of member states in their conduct of world affairs. We infringe no international treaty in continuing the long British tradition of the sea, in harvesting what is freely available to all in international waters, and of course in making suitable use of those pelagic areas which, by existing treaties freely arrived at by the member states, have long been reserved to us. But even this is not relevant to the motion before us today! That motion, I remind you, relates only to the proposal for a United Nations peacekeeping team to supervise the Antarctic fisheries. 'Peacekeeping,' my dear fellow delegates. A team to keep the peace. And therefore our position is clear. No such team is needed. The peace has been kept. There have been no incidents. There certainly will be none of our making. The United Nations has better things to do than to seek solutions for problems that do not exist."

And he sat down, managing to do so with a bow to the president pro tem, a sardonic grin for the Uruguayan, and yes, even a wink for Ana, up in the translator's booth! She shook her head in distress at this frivolous-minded person. But perhaps he was serious after all, for he was already writing something on a scrap of paper and beckoning a page, even as the Ghanaian finished signing his letters, slapped his portfolio shut, glanced at the clock, and managed not to catch the Uruguayan delegate's eye as he said, "I am informed that the address of the next delegate may occupy a substantial period of time. Since it is now four, I suggest we recess this debate until ten o'clock tomorrow morning."

A buzz rose up from the floor. Nan leaned back for a long moment, massaging her temples before she stood up and allowed herself to contemplate the next half hour: a quick meal, a bath, and then a lovely long sleep—

No. It was not to be. As she opened the door to the booth the page dashed up, out of breath, and handed her the note from Sir Tam. It said:

Absolutely essential you attend the party in the DVL, and that I have the pleasure of escorting you.

So there was no rest, no rest. She might have refused the invitation. But Sir Tam had taken the precaution of telling the head of the Bulgarian mission to the United Nations about it, and she was no sooner in her room than he was on the phone insisting she go.

She bathed quickly and dressed in what she guessed might be appropriate, then trotted back across the street from her hotel to the great quaint oblong building, so unlike its newer and fortress-like neighbors. Her head was pounding all the way. Diffidently she whispered her name to the guard at the Distinguished Visitors Lounge. He consulted a list, smiled frostily, and let her in.

What a tumult! How much smoke, and what odors of food and drinks! And there was Sir Tam, to be sure, tiny bouquet of flowers in one hand, the other hand on the shoulder of a plump, dark, grinning man whom Nan did not at once recognize but who was the very Uruguayan with whom Sir Tam had been exchanging insults an hour before.

"Nan! Ho, Nan! Over here!" He was beckoning her to him. She

could not think of a reason for refusing, and knew before it happened that Gulsmit would be *touching* her again. And it happened just that way. The flowers turned out to be a bouquet of Parma violets, outrageously out of season and, of course, for her. Gulsmit insisted on pinning the corsage on her demure bodice himself, taking much more time over it than was necessary while the others in his little conversational group jovially pretended not to notice.

It angered Nan that the Scot should put himself on such terms of evident intimacy, especially in this hyperactive atmosphere, where people who had been trading threats with each other all day were now laughing and mingling and drinking together. Not only that. Every person in this little group was from a rival bloc. What would the head of her delegation say? Sir Tam and the Saudi were Fuel. The Uruguayans were People. So were the two jolly Chinese women in their spike-heeled shoes and neo-Mao jackets of silk brocade and metal thread.

"You'll never guess, Nan," grinned Sir Tam after introducing her, "what our friends have up their sleeves for tomorrow. Tell her, Liao-tsen."

The older of the Chinese women laid her hand on Ana's arm, smiling. Clearly she had been drinking a great deal. Her consonants were fuzzy, but she said, comprehensibly enough, "The People's Republic of Bengal will put forward an emergency resolution. It is a very pretty resolution, Miss Dimitrova. All about 'the alleged multinational expedition of the Food-Exporting Powers' and their 'acts of violence against the natives of Son of Kung.'"

"Violence? What is this about violence?" demanded Nan, startled and suddenly fearful. If there was fighting on Kungson . . . if Ahmed found himself in the middle of a war . . .

"That's the funny part, dear girl," chuckled Sir Tam. "It seems your friend God's little junket has begun shooting down harmless balloonists. But not to worry. I don't think it's going to pass. It's not a party matter, is it, Señor Corrubias?"

The Uruguayan shrugged. "There has been no official consultation among the People's Republics, that is true."

"And unofficial?" Gulsmit probed.

Corrubias glanced at the elder Chinese woman, who nodded permission, and said, "I can tell you my personal opinion, and that is that the acts of violence we have heard described are not of much importance. Can one really get upset about rubber jack-o'-lanterns floating around in the sky?"

"There is also the matter of the underground race," said the Chinese woman. She took another sip of her drink, looking merrily mysterious over the top of it at Sir Tam, before going on comfortably, "But that too . . . well, a few burrows broken into, that's all. After all, how can we be sure that the creatures who inhabit them are indeed intelligent? We would not object to a Nebraska farmer, for example, opening a mole run as he plowed his corn paddies."

"One might also," said Ana boldly, surprising herself at the harshness of her voice, "speak of the crustacean race that has suffered some casualties." But Sir Tam stopped her by a gentle pressure on the shoulder. She did not protest. She had suddenly begun to fear that it was Ahmed's group that had caused those casualties, about which she knew so worryingly little.

"I would really enjoy watching you two fight it out," said Sir Tam, laughing to take the menace out of his words. But Nan wondered if he didn't really mean it. She also wondered why he was so carefully and publicly possessive of her, arm around her shoulder, hovering over her drink and refilling it from every passing tray. Surely all these foreign people would suppose they had been in bed together! She blushed at the thought. It would have been bad enough to be guilty of an immoral dalliance, like any common tart, and to have it known. But she was not even guilty! The name without the game—how awful! Why would Sir Tam go out of his way to create such an impression? Could it be that the lax morality of the Fuel people was such that he valued the appearance of sexual adventure as much as the relationship itself? Was he trying to show that he was still sexually potent? And what sort of people was she living among here?

"Please excuse me for a moment," she said, glancing about as though looking for a woman's w.c. But as soon as she was well away from Sir Tam, she circled around the white-paneled room to the buffet tables. At least she would bring up her blood sugar. Perhaps that would relieve the headaches and the exhaustion, and then she would think of a way to relieve the pressure from Sir Tam.

The table would have been lavish even in Sofia! But was it not the Tibetans who were giving this party? And why did they feel obliged to spread so wasteful a display of food? Caviar that certainly did not come from the Himalayas; delicate fruit ices that surely were unknown in their sparse, high valleys; pâtés in the original wooden boxes from France. And look what they had done! The centerpieces were carved replicas of the races of Kungson! A ballonist, half a meter thick, in butter! A crustacean carved from what looked like strawberry sherbet! A long, almost ratlike creature—was it a burrower?—made from foie gras! And there, standing next to her, was a distinguished-looking gray-haired man who was directing a pale-haired younger man to fill a plate from the display. A spoonful of the burrower, a few slices of some sort of meat, a croissant, a scoop from the balloonist to butter the roll. He caught her eye and smiled pleasantly without speaking.

It was all incredibly ostentatious. It quite took Ana's appetite away. She looked away from the food and saw Sir Tam across the room, eyes on her. Strangely, he nodded encouragement and pointed—to whom? To the graying, tall man next to her?

She looked more carefully. Had they ever met? No. But he had a face she seemed to know, from a photograph, she thought—but a photograph that had meant something to her.

She turned to speak to him, and the pale-haired man was suddenly between them, polite but at a state of readiness. For what? Did they think she was an assassin?

Then she remembered where she had seen the face. "You're Mr. Godfrey Menninger," she said.

His expression was inquiring. "Yes?"

"We've never met, but I've seen your picture in a newspaper. With your daughter. I'm Ana Dimitrova, and I met your daughter a few months ago in Sofia."

"Of course you did! The angel of rescue. It's all right, Teddy," he said to the younger man, who stepped back and began collecting silverware for Menninger's plate. "How nice to meet you at last, Ana. Margie's here somewhere. Not near the food, poor thing. She has her mother's metabolism. She can't even look at a layout like this without putting on a kilo. Let's go find her so you can say hello."

Captain Menninger was sipping her Perrier water and allowing a fifty-year-old Japanese attaché to think he was making headway against her defenses when she heard her father's voice behind her.

"Margie, dear, a surprise for you. You remember Ana Dimitrova?"

"No." Marge studied the woman carefully, not competitively but in the manner of someone trying to learn a terrain from a map. Then the card file in her head clicked over. "Yes," she corrected herself. "The Bulgarian woman. How nice to see you again."

It was not anything of the kind, and she intended the Bulgarian bint to understand that. On the other hand, Margie had no particular wish to make an enemy of her, either. There might be a time when her connection with that Pak she was screwing— Dulla? Yes. Ahmed Dulla, member of the first Peeps' expedition to Klong—could be a useful line to pursue. So she turned to the Japanese and said:

"Tetsu, I'd like you to meet Nan Dimitrova. She was such a help to me in Bulgaria. You know how foolish I am about making jokes—I just can't help this mouth of mine. It says things that get me into the most terrible trouble. And so, of course, I said something ridiculously awful. Political, you know. It could have had really sticky consequences. And along came Nan, total stranger, just a good person, and got me out of it. How is that nice young man you were with, Nan?"

"Ahmed is on Kungson," said Nan. She was unwilling to give offense, but she was not obliged to like this plump blond's nasty little put-down games.

"Is he! Why, that's a coincidence. You remember Dr. Dalehouse, of course? He's there too. Perhaps they'll meet." She saw that her father's aide had just signaled something to him and added, "Poppa, you're looking worried. Am I saying something awful again?"

Godfrey Menninger smiled. "What I'm worried about is that if I'm going to give you a lift to Boston, it's time we were on our way. You do remember you have a date at MIT tonight?"

"Oh, dear. I'd forgotten." Wholly untrue. Margie had not forgotten the time of her date, which was the following morning, and she had no doubt that her father had not either.

"Also," he went on, "you'll be sneezing and scratching if we stay here much longer. Or had you also forgotten that you are allergic to flowers?"

Margie had never in her life been allergic to anything, but she said, "You do take such good care of me, poppa. Nan, I'm sorry this was so short, but it's really nice seeing you again. And Tetsu, don't be a stranger next time you're in Houston. Stop by and say hello." The Japanese hissed and bowed. Of course, Margie reflected, she could be out of town if he ever did happen to show up in Houston. Not that it mattered. She had already accomplished her objective. Past a certain age, even going to bed with a man did not give you quite as firm a grip on his emotions as communicating the impression that you certainly would like to if you ever got the chance.

In her father's car, with the bodyguard-aide sitting in front, she said, "Now what was that all about, poppa?"

"Maybe your little Bulgarian friend isn't quite as much of a country girl as she seems. Teddy swept her as a matter of routine. There was a microphone in her corsage."

"Her? Bugged? That's a crock!"

"That's a fact," he corrected. "Maybe her delegation put it on her, who knows? That place was full of sharks. It could have been any one of them. And speaking of sharks—"

"You want to know what I picked up," she said, nodding, and told him what the Japanese had said about the Bengali resolution.

He leaned back in the seat. "Just the usual UN Mischief Night, I'd say. You turn over my garbage can, I throw a dead cat on your roof. Are they going to press it?"

"He didn't say, poppa. He didn't seem to take it very seriously."

Her father rubbed the spot below his navel thoughtfully. "Of course, with the Peeps you never know. Heir-of-Mao has an investment in Klong. The Bengalis wouldn't be starting anything they didn't clear with the Forbidden City."

Margie's hair prickled erect at the back of her neck. "Are you saying I should worry? I don't want my mission withdrawn!"

"Oh, no. No chance of that, honey. Relax, will you? You're too much like your old lady. She never did learn to swing with the action. When the PLO kidnapped you I thought she'd have a nervous breakdown."

"She was scared shitless, poppa. And you never turned a hair." Not even, she thought, when your own four-year-old daughter was bawling into the jetliner's radio.

"But I knew you were going to be all right, honey. I really did."

"Well, I'm not bringing that up again, ol' buddy." Margie folded her hands in her lap and stared out the window. Between the UN complex and the airport there was no building, no street, that Margie had not seen a dozen times before. She was not really seeing them now. But they helped spur and clarify her thoughts, the long tandem buses hobbling down the slow lanes, the apartment dwellers walking their dogs, the school kids, stores, police on their tricycles, sidewalk vendors with their handmade jewelry and pocket computers. Thomas Jefferson, as he returned to Monticello, might have looked out of his stagecoach in just the same detached but proprietary way at the slaves weeding his crops.

She said slowly, "Listen, poppa. I want to get our mission reinforced. Now."

"What's the hurry?"

"I don't know, but there's a hurry. I want it done before the Peeps and the Greasies cut us off at the roots or get enough of their own people up there to own Kungson. I want us there first and biggest, because I want it all."

"Shit, honey. Didn't they teach you about priorities at the Point? There's the krill business and the Mid-Atlantic Ridge and the Greasies threatening to raise their prices again—do you have any idea how tough all this is? I've only got one stack, and there's only room for one thing at the top of it."

"No, poppa, I don't want to be told how hard it is. Don't you understand this is a whole planet?"

"Of course I do, but—"

"No. No buts. I guess you don't really understand what it means to have a whole planet to play with. For us, poppa, all for us. To start from scratch with, to develop in a systematic manner. Find all the fossil fuels, develop them in a rational way. Locate the cities where they don't destroy arable land. Plant crops where they won't damage the soil. Develop industry where it's most convenient. Plan the population. Let it grow as it is needed, but not to where you have a surplus: good, strong, self-reliant people. American people, poppa. Maybe the place stinks now, but give it a hundred years and you'd rather be there than here, I promise. *And I want it.*"

Godfrey Menninger sighed, looking in love and some awe at the oldest and most troublesome of his children. "You're worse than your mother ever was," he said ruefully. "Well, I hear what you say. The Poles owe us one. I'll see what I can do."

TechTowTwo sprawled over the bank of the Charles River, more than twice the cubage of all the old brick buildings put together. There were no classrooms in Technology Tower Two. There was no administration, either. It was all for research, from the computer storage in the subbasements to the solar-radiation experiments that decorated the roof with saucers and bow ties.

The Massachusetts Institute of Technology had a long tradition of involvement with space exploration, going back even before there was any—or any that did not take place on a printed page. As early as the 1950s there had been a design class whose entire curriculum revolved around the creation of products for export to the inhabitants of the third planet of the star Arcturus. The fact that there was no known planet of Arcturus, let alone inhabitants of it, did not disturb either teacher or students. Techpersons were used to unhinging their imaginations on demand. In the Cambridge community that centered around MIT, Harvard, the Garden Street observatories, and all the wonderlands of Route 128 there had been designers of interstellar spacecraft before the first Sputnik went into orbit, anatomists of extraterrestrials when there was no proof of life anywhere off the surface of Earth, and specialists in interplanetary communications before anyone was on the other end of the line. Margie Menninger had taken six months of graduate studies there, dashing from Tech to Harvard. She had been careful to keep her contacts bright.

The woman Margie wanted to see was a former president of the MISFITS and thus would have been a power in the Tech world even if she had not also held the title of assistant dean of the college. She had arranged a breakfast meeting at Margie's request and had turned out five department heads on order.

The dean introduced them around the table and said, "Make it good now, Margie. Department heads aren't crazy about getting up so early in the morning."

Margie sampled her scrambled eggs. "For this kind of food, I don't blame them," she said, putting down her fork. "Let me get right to it. I have about ten minutes' worth of holos of the autochthons of Son of Kung, alias Klong. No sound. Just visible." She leaned back to the sideboard and snapped a switch, and the first of the holographic pictures condensed out of a pinkish glow. "You've probably seen most of this stuff anyway," she said. "That's a Krinpit. They are one of the three intelligent, or anyway possibly intelligent, races on Klong, and the only one of the lot that is urban. In a moment you'll see some of their buildings. They're open at the top. Evidently the Krinpit don't worry much about weather. Why they have buildings at all is anyone's guess, but they do. They would seem much the easiest of the three races to conduct trade with, but unfortunately the Peeps have a head start with them. No doubt we'll catch up."

The head of the design staff was a lean young black woman who had limited her breakfast to orange juice and black coffee and was already through with it. "Catch up at what, Captain Menninger?" she asked.

Margie took her measure and refused combat. "For openers, Dr. Ravenel, I'd like to see your people create some trade goods. For all three races. They're all going to be our customers one of these days."

The economist took his eyes off the holo of a Krinpit coracle to challenge Margie. "'Customers' implies two-way trade. What do you think these, ah, Klongans are going to have to sell us that's worth the trouble of shipping it all those light-years?"

Margie grinned. "I thought you'd never ask." She pulled an attaché case off the floor and opened it on the table in front of her, pushing the plate of eggs out of the way. "So far," she said, "we don't exactly have any *manufactured* objects. But take a look at this." She passed around several ten-centimeter squares of a filmy, resilient substance. "That's the stuff the balloonists' hydrogen sacs are made out of. It's really pretty special stuff—I mean, it holds gaseous H_2 with less than one percent leakage in a twenty-four-hour period. We could supply quite a lot of that if there was a specialty market for it."

"Don't you have to kill a balloonist to get it?"

"Good question." Margie nodded to the economist with a lying smile. "Actually, no. That is, there are other, nonsentient races with the same body structure, although this one is, I believe, from one of the sentients. How about a market? If I remember correctly, the Germans had to use the second stomach of the ox when they were building the *Hindenburg*."

"I see," said the economist gravely. "All we need to do is contact a few Zeppelin manufacturers." There was a general titter.

"I'm sure," said Margie steadily, "that you will have some better idea than that. Oh, and I ought to mention one thing. I brought my checkbook. There's a National Science Foundation grant for research and development that's waiting for someone to apply for it." And for that gift too, I thank you, poppa, she thought.

The economist had not become the head of a major department of the faculty without learning when to retreat. "I didn't mean to brush you off, Captain Menninger. This is actually a pretty exciting challenge. What else have you got for us?"

"Well, we have a number of samples that haven't been studied very carefully. Frankly, they aren't really supposed to be here. Camp Detrick doesn't know they're gone yet."

The group stirred. The dean said quickly, "Margie, I think we all get the same picture when you mention Camp Detrick. Is there anything connected with biological warfare in this?"

"Certainly not! No, believe me, that doesn't come into it at all. I sometimes go out of channels, I admit, but what do you guess they'd do to me if I broke security on something like that?"

"Then why Camp Detrick?"

"Because these are alien organisms," Margie explained. "Except for the sample of balloonist tissue, you'll notice that every item I've got here is in a double-wrapped, heat-sealed container. The outside has been acid-washed and UV-sterilized. No, wait—" she added, grinning. Everybody at the table had begun looking at their fingertips, and there was a perceptible movement away from the samples of tissue on the table. "Those balloonist samples are okay. The rest, maybe not so okay. They've been pretty carefully gone over. There don't seem to be any pathogens or allergens. But naturally you'll want to use care in handling them."

"Thanks a lot, captain," said the designer stiffly. "How can you be so sure about the tissue?"

"I ate some three days ago," she said. She had their full attention now and swept on. "I should point out that the grant naturally includes whatever you need to insure safe handling. Now, this group contains plant samples. They're photosynthetic, and their principal response is in the infrared range. Interesting for you agronomists? Right. And these over here are supposed to be art objects. They come from the Krinpit, the ones that look like squashed cockroaches. The things are supposed to 'sing.' That is, if you're a Krinpit and you rub them on your shell, they make some interesting sounds. If you don't have a chitinous shell, you can use a credit card."

The woman from design picked up one of them gingerly, peering at it through the transparent plastic. "You said you wanted us to develop some kind of trading goods?"

"I sure do." The last thing Margie pulled out of her dispatch case was a red-covered mimeographed document. The words MOST SECRET were dazzle-printed on the jacket. "As you can see, this is classified, but that's just military hang-ups. It will be turned over to the UN in about ten days anyway, or most of it will. It's the most comprehensive report we've been able to prepare on the three principal races of Klong."

All six of the faculty members at the table reached for it at once, but the design woman was fastest. "Um," she said, flipping through it. "I've got a graduate student who would eat this up. Can I show it to him?"

"Better than that. Let's leave this copy and the samples with our friends, and let's you and I go talk to him."

Fifteen minutes later Margie had succeeded in getting rid of the department head, and she and a slim, excitable young man named Walter Pinson were head to head. "Think you can handle it?" asked Margie.

"Yes! I mean, well, it's a big job—"

Margie put her hand on his arm. "I'm sure you can. I'd really appreciate it if you'd tell me how you plan to go about it, though."

Pinson thought for a moment. "Well, the first thing is to figure out what their needs are," he offered.

"That's fascinating! It must be pretty difficult. I would hardly know where to start. Offhand, I'd say their biggest need, all of them, is just staying alive. As you'll see, everything on the planet spends a lot of its time trying to eat everything else, including the other intelligent races."

"Cannibalism?"

"Well, I don't think you can call it that. They're different species. And there are a lot of other species that are trying to eat the intelligent ones."

"Predators," said Pinson, nodding. "Well, there's a starting point right there. Let's see. For the predators like the balloonists, for instance, anything that would set them on fire would help protect the sentients. Of course," he added, frowning, "we'd have to make sure that these were used only to defend the sentients against lower forms of life."

"Of course!" said Margie, shocked. "We wouldn't want to give them weapons to start a war with!" She glanced at her watch. "I've got an idea, Walter. I didn't have much of a breakfast, and it's getting on toward lunch. Why don't you and I get something to eat? There's a place I used to know when I was a graduate student. In a pretty frowsty old motel, but the food was good—if you have the time, I mean?"

"Oh, I have the time," said Pinson, looking at her appreciatively.

"It's up past Harvard Square, but we ought to be able to get a cab. And please let me—I have an expense account, and it's all your tax money anyway." As they walked toward the elevator, a mob of undergraduates flocked toward a lecture hall. Looking toward them, Margie asked, "Do you by any chance know a student named Lloyd Wensley? I think he's a freshman."

"No, I don't think so. Friend of yours?"

"Not really—or anyway, not since he was a little kid. I used to know his family. Now, about these, ah, implements for self-protection—"

Several quite pleasant hours later, Margie got into a cab outside the old motel. If the food had not been really as good as she remembered it, the rooms still came up to standard. As they approached Harvard Square she had an impulse. "Go down Mass Ave," she ordered the driver. "I want to make a little detour."

After a few blocks she directed him into a side street, and looked about.

She recognized the neighborhood. There was the supermarket. There was Giordan's Spa, and there, over the barbershop, only now it was over a hardware store, was the three-room corner apartment where she had lived with Lloyd and Lloyd Junior through the ten months that measured both her graduate year and her marriage. It was the closest Marge had ever come to motherhood, fill-in to a six-year-old for the real mother who had died when he was three. It was the closest she had ever come to wifehood, too, and closer than she would ever come again. Old Lloyd! Thirty years old when she was nineteen, and so fucking *courtly* in the Officers' Club that you'd never guess what he was like in bed. Not even if you'd tried him out a time or two, as Margie had been careful to do. Just looking up at the window of their bedroom made Marge's neck ache with the memory of being head-jammed into a corner of the bed, half choked with pillows, so Lloyd could pump himself dry as quickly as convenient. As often as convenient. When he thought convenient. You didn't ask a cuspidor for permission to spit in it, or a wife for sex. The cuspidor couldn't struggle, not if you had it jammed into position just right, and it wouldn't cry out. Neither would the wife, especially with the six-year-old stepson only marginally asleep just outside the door.

She ordered the driver on.

It would have been nice to see Lloyd Junior, all grown up. But better not. Better the way it was. She hadn't seen either of the Lloyds since the annulment, and no use pressing your luck. It had been a pretty frightening, dehumanizing experience for a young girl; how lucky she was, thought Margie, that it hadn't scarred her forever!

When she got back to her hotel there was a taped message from her father: "To hear is to obey. Catch a news broadcast."

She turned on the bedside TV while she packed, hunting for an all-news station. She was rewarded with five minutes about the latest Boston political corruption scandals, and then an in-depth interview with the Red Sox's new designated hitter. But at last there was a recap of the top international story of the day.

"In a surprise move at the United Nations this morning, the top Polish delegate, Wladislas Prczensky, announced that his government has accepted the challenge presented by the Bengali resolution. The Food powers have agreed to send out an investigatory commission with broad powers to investigate the alleged cases of brutal treatment of native races on the planet whimsically called 'Klong' or 'Son of Kung.' There will be no representatives of major powers such as the United States or the Soviet Union on the commission, which will be made up of UN peacekeeping officers from Poland itself, Brazil, Canada, Argentina, and Bulgaria."

·EIGHT·

DANNY DALEHOUSE reached out to grab the theodolite as it tipped in the soft ground. Morrissey grinned and apologized. "Must've lost my balance."

"Or else you're stoned again," said Dalehouse. He was angry—not just at Morrissey. In the candor of his heart he knew that most of his anger was at the fact that Kappelyushnikov was flying and he was not. "Anyway," he went on, "you've knocked this run in the head. Next time why don't you just go sleep it off?"

They had all been freaked out by the stuff the balloonists had sprayed on them, and from time to time, for days afterward, all of them had recurring phases of lust and euphoria. Not only were Morrissey's more intense, but Dalehouse was pretty sure the biochemist was still exposing himself. He had discovered that something in the semen or sperm of the male balloonists was highly hallucinogenic—better than that, was the long-sought-after true aphrodisiac fabled in song and story. It wasn't Morrissey's fault that his researches put him clear out of it from time to time. But he shouldn't have insisted on helping with the theodolite readings.

Far overhead Kappelyushnikov's cluster of bright yellow balloons gyrated as the pilot experimented with controlling his altitude to take advantage of the winds at various levels. When he was finished tracking them they would have basic information that could allow them to cruise the skies. Then Dalehouse's turn would come. But he was tired of waiting.

"Cappy," he said into the radio, "we've lost the readings. Might as well come on down."

Harriet was walking toward them as Kappelyushnikov's answer came through. It was in Russian; Harriet heard, and flinched irritably. That was in character. She had been a perfect bitch about the whole thing, Dalehouse thought. When they returned to normal after that first incredible trip, she had flamed at him, "Animal! Don't you know you could have got me pregnant?" It had never occurred to him to ask. Nor had it occurred to her, at the time. It was no use reminding her that she had been as eager as he. She had retreated into her hard defiant-spinster shell. And ever since, she had been ten times as upright as before and fifty times as nasty to anyone who made sexual remarks in her presence or even, as with Kappelyushnikov just now, used some perfectly justifiable bad language.

"I've got some new tapes for you," Harriet sniffed.

"Any progress?"

"Certainly there's progress, Dalehouse. There's a definite grammar. I'll brief the whole camp on it after the next meal." She glanced up at Cappy, having a last fling with his balloon as half a dozen of the Klongan gasbags soared around him, and retreated.

A definite grammar.

Well, there was no use trying to hurry Harriet. "Preliminary Studies toward a First Contact with Subtechnological Sentients" seemed very far away! Dalehouse counted up the score. It was not impressive. They had made no contact at all with the crablike things called Krinpit or with the burrowers. The gasbags had been hanging around quite a lot since the day they had showered the expedition with their milt. But they did not come close enough for the kind of contact Danny Dalehouse wanted. They bounced and swung hundreds of meters in the air most of the time, descending lower only when most of the camp was away or asleep. No doubt they had been trained to avoid ground-limited creatures through eons of predation. But it made it hard for Danny.

At least, with the gasbags in sight, rifle microphones had been able to capture quite a lot of their strident, singing dialogue—if dialogue was what it was. Harriet said she detected structure. Harriet said it was not birdsongs or cries of alarm. Harriet said she would teach him to speak to them. But what Harriet said was not always to be believed, Danny Dalehouse thought. The other thing he thought was that they needed a different translator. The split-brain operation facilitated language learning, but it had several drawbacks. It sometimes produced bad physical effects, including long-lasting pain. Once in a while it produced personality changes. And it didn't always work. A person who had no gift for languages to begin with came out of surgery still lacking the gift. In Harriet's case, Danny would have guessed all three were true.

They had transmitted all the tapes to Earth anyway. Sooner or later the big semantic computers at Johns Hopkins and Texas A&M would be checking in, and Harriet's skills, or lack of them, would stop mattering so much.

What Danny needed, or at least what Danny wanted, so badly he could taste it, was to be up there in the sky with one of the gasbags, one on one, learning a language in the good old-fashioned way. Anything else was a compromise. They'd tried everything within their resources. Free-floating instrumented balloons with sensors programmed to respond to the signatures of life; wolftraps for the Krinpit; buried microphones for the burrowers; the rifle mikes and the zoom-lens cameras for the gasbags. They had kilometers of tape, with pictures and sounds of all manner of jumping, crawling, wriggling things, and in all the endless hours hardly as much as ten minutes' worth that was any use to Danny Dalehouse.

Still, something had been accomplished. Enough for him to have composed a couple of reports to go back to Earth. Enough even for his jealous colleagues at MSU and the Double-A-L to pore over eagerly, even if not enough to satisfy Danny. It was still learning, even if much of it was negative.

The first thing to perish was the pretty fable of three independent intelligent races living in some sort of beneficent cooperation and harmony. There was no cooperation. At least, they had seen no signs of that, and many to the contrary. The burrowers seemed never to interact with the others at all. The gasbags and the Krinpit did, but not in any cooperative or harmonious way. The balloonists never touched ground, as far as Danny had seen, or at least not on purpose. There were at least a dozen species that enjoyed eating balloonists when they could catch them—sleek brown creatures that looked a little like stub-winged bats, froglike leapers, arthropods smaller than the Krinpit—not least of them, the Krinpit themselves. If a gasbag ever drifted low enough for one of them to reach it, it was dead. So the entire lives of the balloonists, from spawn to fodder, were spent in the air, and their ultimate burial was always in the digestive tract of some ground-bound race—so tawdry a fate for so pretty a species!

Kappelyushnikov was coming in low and fast, tossed by the low-level winds. He pulled the rip cord on his balloon at five meters and dropped like a stone, wriggling out of the harness to fall free. He tumbled over and over as he landed, then got up, rubbing himself, and ran to catch the deflated balloon cluster as it scudded before the breeze.

Danny winced, contemplating his own first flight. The last little bit of ballooning was going to be the hardest. He turned to help Cappy pick up the fabric, and a rifleshot next to his head made him duck and swear.

He spun around, furious. "What the hell are you up to, Morrissey?"

The biologist put the rifle at shoulder-arms and saluted the tumbling form of one of the hovering gasbags. "Just harvesting another specimen, Danny," he said cheerfully. He had judged height and wind drift with precision, and the collapsed bag was dropping almost at their feet. "Ah, shit," he said in disgust. "Another female."

"Really?" said Danny, staring at what looked like an immense erection. "Are you sure?"

"Fooled me too," Morrissey grinned. "No, the ones with the schlongs aren't the males. They aren't schlongs. I mean, they aren't penises. These folks don't make love like you and I, Danny. The females sort of squirt their eggs out to float around in the air, and then the boys come out and whack off onto them."

"When did you find all that out?" Dalehouse was annoyed; the rule of the expedition was that each of them shared discoveries as soon as made.

"When you were bugged at me for being stoned out of my

mind," Morrissey said. "I think it has to do with the way they generate their hydrogen. Solar flares seem to be involved. So when they saw our lights they thought it was a flare—and that's when they spawned. Only we happened to be underneath, and so we got sprayed with, uh, with—"

"I know what we got sprayed with," Dalehouse said.

"Yeah! You know, Danny, when I took up this career they made dissecting specimens sound pretty tacky—but every time I go near one of the males' sex glands I get high. I'm beginning to like this line of work."

"Do you have to kill them all off to do it, though? You'll chase the flock away. Then how am I going to make contact?"

Morrissey grinned. He didn't answer. He just pointed aloft. Dalehouse, in justice, had to concede the unspoken point. Whatever emotions the gasbags had, fear did not seem to be among them. Morrissey had shot down nearly a dozen of them, but ever since the first contact the swarm had almost always stayed within sight. Perhaps it was the lights that attracted them. In the permanent Klongan twilight, there was no such thing as "day." The camp had opted to create one, marked by turning on the whole bank of floodlights at an arbitrary "dawn" and turning them off again twelve clock hours later. One light always stayed on—to keep off predators, they told themselves, but in truth it was to keep out the primordially threatening dark.

Morrissey picked up the balloonist. It was still alive, its wrinkled features moving soundlessly. Once down, they never uttered a sound—because, Morrissey said, the hydrogen that gave them voice was lost when their bags were punctured. But they kept on *trying*. The first one they had shot down had lived for more than forty hours. It had crept all around the camp, dragging its gray and wrinkled bag, and it had seemed in pain all of that time. Dalehouse had been glad when it died at last, was glad now when Morrissey plunged the new one into a killer bag for return to Earth.

Kappelyushnikov limped up to them, rubbing his buttocks. "Is always a martyr, first pioneer of flight," he grumbled. "So, Danny Dalehouse. You want go up now?"

An electric shock hit Danny. "You mean *now?*"

"Sure, why not? Wind isn't bad. I go with, soon as two balloons fill."

It took longer than Dalehouse would have thought possible for the little pump to fill two batches of balloons big enough for human passengers—especially since the pump was a hastily rigged nonsparking compressor that leaked as much gas as it squeezed into the bags. Dalehouse tried to eat, tried to nap, tried to interest himself in other projects, and kept coming back to gaze at the tethered clusters of bags, quietly swelling with hydrogen, constrained by the cord netting that surrounded them.

The weather had taken a turn for the worse. Clouds covered the sky from horizon to horizon, but Kappelyushnikov was stubbornly optimistic. "Clouds will blow away. Is positive skies will be clear." When the first pinkening of sky began to show, he said decisively, "Is okay now. Strap in, Danny."

Mistrustfully, Dalehouse buckled himself into the harness. He was a taller but lighter man than the Russian, and Kappelyushnikov grumbled to himself as he valved off surplus hydrogen. "Otherwise," he explained, "you go back to state of Michigan, East Lansing, *shwoosh!* But next time, not so much wasting gas."

The harness had a quick-release latch at the shoulders, and Dalehouse touched it experimentally.

"No, no!" screamed Kappelyushnikov. "You want to pull when you are up two hundred meters, fine, pull! Is your neck. But don't waste gas for nothing." He guided Danny's hands to the two crucial cords. "Is not clamjet, you understand? Is free balloon. Clamjet uses lift to save fuel. Here is no fuel, only lift. Here you go where wind goes. You don't like direction, you find different wind. Spill water ballast, you go up. Spill *wasserstoff*, you go down."

Dalehouse wriggled in the harness. It was not going to be very much like sailplaning over the eastern shore of Lake Michigan, where there was always a west wind to bounce off the bluffs and keep a glider aloft for hours. But if the Russian could do it, he could do it. I hope, he added to himself, and said, "All right, I think I have the hang of it."

"So let's go," cried the Russian, grinning as he slipped into his own harness. He bent and picked up a fair-sized rock, gesturing to Danny to do the same. The other members of the expedition were standing back, but one of them handed Danny a rock, and at Kappelyushnikov's orders they untethered the balloons.

Kappelyushnikov danced over toward Danny like a diver stilting across a sea bottom. He came as close as he could under the bulk of their balloons, peering into his face. "You are all right?" Danny nodded. "So drop the rock and we go!" Kappelyushnikov cried. And he cast his own rock away and began to float diagonally upward.

Dalehouse took a deep breath and followed his example, watching the Russian move upward.

Nothing seemed to happen. Danny did not feel any acceleration, only that his feet seemed to have gone abruptly numb and there was no sensation of pressure on their bottoms. Because his eyes were on Kappelyushnikov he neglected to look down until he was fifty meters in the air.

They were drifting south, along the coastline. Far above them and inland, over the purple hills that marked the edge of the fern forest, the extended swarm of balloonists was grazing on whatever tiny organisms they could find floating in the sky. Below and behind was the dwindling campsite. Danny was already higher than the nose of their return rocket, the tallest object in camp. Off to his left was the sea itself, and a couple of islands in the muddy waters, covered with many-trunked trees.

He wrenched his attention away from sight-seeing; Kappelyushnikov was shouting at him. "What?" Dalehouse bellowed. The gap had widened; Cappy was now forty meters above him and moving inland, evidently in a different air layer.

"Drop . . . little . . . water!" shouted the Russian.

Dalehouse nodded and reached tentatively for the valve cord. He pulled at it with a light touch.

Nothing happened.

He pulled again, harder. Half a liter of ballast sprayed out of the tank, drenching him. Danny had not realized that the passenger was directly under the ballast tank, and gasping, he vowed to change that element of design before he went up again.

But he was flying!

Not easily. Not with grace. Not even with the clumsy control that Kappelyushnikov had taught himself. He spent the first hour chasing Cappy across the sky. It was like one of the fun-house games where you and your girl are on different rotating circles of a ride, when neither of you can take a step except to change from one spinning disk to another. Though Kappelyushnikov did all he could to make capture easy, he never caught the Russian—not that first time.

But—flying! It was exactly the dream he had always had, the dream everyone has had. The total conquest of the air. No jets. No wings. No engines. Just gently swimming through the atmospheric ocean, with no more effort than floating in a saltwater bay.

He reveled in it, and as time went on—not in the first flight or the tenth, but the supply of hydrogen was limitless, if slow in coming, and he made as many flights as he could—he began to acquire some skill.

And the problem of reaching the gasbags turned out to be no problem at all.

He didn't have to seek them out. They were far more skilled at flying than he, and they came to him, bobbing around like great jack-o'-lanterns with hideous ticklike faces, peering inquisitively into his own face, and singing, singing. Oh! how they sang.

For the next week, or what passed on Klong for a week, Dalehouse spent every minute he could in the air. The life of the camp went on almost without him. Even Kappelyushnikov was more earthbound than he. There was nothing to hold Dalehouse there, and he found himself almost a stranger when he landed, slept, relieved bladder and bowels, ate, filled his balloons, and soared again. Harriet snapped at him for demanding more than she could handle in translation. The camp commander complained bitterly at the waste of power in generating hydrogen. Jim Morrissey pleaded for time and help in collecting and studying the other species. Even Cappy was surly about the wear and tear on his balloons. Danny didn't care. In the skies of Klong he was alive. He progressed from feckless interloper to skilled aeronaut; from stranger to, almost, one of the great drifting swarm. He began to be able to exchange at least rudimentary ideas with some of the gasbags, especially the biggest of them—two meters across, with a pattern that looked almost like a tartan. Danny named him "Bonnie Prince Charlie," lacking any clue as to what the gasbag called itself. *Him*self. Danny began to think of him as almost a friend. If it had not been for his physical needs, and one other thing, Dale-house would hardly have bothered returning to the camp at all.

The one other thing was Harriet.

He could not do without her help in translation. It wasn't enough. He was convinced a lot of it was wrong. But it was all he had in the endeavor to communicate with these beautiful and monstrous creatures of the air. He raged to the rest of the en-campment and insisted on his complaints being relayed to Earth; he insulted her almost to the point of tears—from eyes that he would have sworn had never felt them before. It was not enough to suit him . . . but voyage by voyage, hour by hour, some sort of communication began to build up.

You never knew what part of your learning was going to be use-ful. Those long sessions of Chomsky and transactional grammar, the critiques of Lorenz and Dart, the semesters on territoriality and mating rites—none of them seemed very helpful in the skies of Klong. But he blessed every hour of sailplaning and every eve-ning with his local barbership quartet. The language of the gas-bags was music. Not even Mandarin made such demands on pitch and tonality as did their songs. Even before he knew any words, he found himself chiming in on their chorus, and they responded to it with, if not exactly welcome, at least curiosity. The big plaid one even learned to sing Danny Dalehouse's name—as well as he could with a sound-producing mechanism that was deficient in such basic phonemes as the fricative.

Danny learned that some of their songs were not unlike terres-trial birdcalls; there was one for food, and several for danger. There seemed to be three separate warning sounds, one for danger from the ground, and two for dangers, but evidently different kinds of dangers, from the air. One of the terms sounded almost Hawaiian, with its liquids and glottal stops; that seemed to belong to a kind of feral gasbag, a shark of the air that appeared to be their most dangerous natural enemy.

The other—Dalehouse could not be sure, and Harriet was not much help, but it appeared to relate to danger from *above* the air; and not just danger, but that kind of special macho risk-taking danger that involved mortal peril, even death, but was infinitely attractive for reasons he could not perceive. He puzzled over that for hours, making Harriet's life a living hell. On that point, no solution. But the tapes went back to Earth, and the computer matches began to come back, and Harriet was able to construct sentences for him to say. He sang, "I am friend," and, heart-stoppingly, the great crosshatched gasbag he called Charlie responded with a whole song.

"You are, you are, you are friend!" And the whole chorus joined in.

The fickle Klongan weather cooperated for eight calendar days, and then the winds began to rise and the clouds rolled in.

When the winds blew, even the gasbag swarm had trouble keeping station with each other, and Danny Dalehouse was blown all over the sky. He tried to keep the camp in range; and because he did, so did the whole swarm. But in the effort they were widely separated. When he decided to give up at last, he called good-bye and heard in response the song that seemed to mean "sky danger." Dalehouse repeated it; it seemed appropriate enough, considering the weather. But then he became conscious of a deep fluttering sound behind the whine of the winds—the sound of a helicopter.

Dalehouse abandoned the flock, climbed high enough to find a return wind, then jockeyed himself expertly down through the cross-breezes toward the camp. There it was, dropping through the frayed bottom of a cloud: the Greasy copter, with a Union Jack on its tail strut. So profligate of energy! Not only did they ship that vast mass through tachyon transit at incredible cost, but they had also shipped enough fuel to allow the pilot to take joyrides. And what was it carrying slung between its skids? Some other kind of machine! Typical Greasy oil-hoggery!

Danny swore disgustedly at the wastefulness of the Greasies. With a fraction of the kilocalories they poured out in simple inefficiency and carelessness he could have had a decent computer, Kappelyushnikov could long since have had his glider, Morrissey could have had an outboard motor for his boat and thus a nearly complete selection of marine samples by now. There was something wrong in a world that let a handful of nations burn off energy so recklessly simply because they happened to be sitting on its sources. Sure, when it was gone, they would be as threadbare as the Peruvians or the Paks, but there was no comfort in that. Their downfall would be the world's downfall. . . .

Or at least *that* world's downfall. Maybe something could be worked out for *this* one. Planning. Thought. Preparation. Control of growth so that scarce resources would not be pissed away irrevocably on foolishness. A fair division of Klong's treasures so that no nation and no individual could profit by starving others. An attempt to insure equity to all—

Dalehouse's train of thought snapped as he realized that he had been daydreaming. The winds had carried him farther than he intended, almost out over the sea. He vented hydrogen frantically and came down almost in the water, falling fast. He picked himself up and watched the ripped cases of the balloons floating out of reach in the water. Cappy would be furious.

At least he wouldn't have to carry them on what looked like a long walk back up the shore to the camp, he thought. It was some consolation, but it didn't last long. Before he was halfway back it began to rain.

And it rained. *And* it rained. It was no such ferocious, wind-slamming storm as had hit them soon after the landing, but it lasted most tediously and maddeningly long, far past the point where it was an incident, or an annoyance, to the point, and past the point, where it seemed they were all sentenced to fat, oily drops turning the ground into mud and the camp into a steam bath for all the miserable rest of their lives. There was no chance of ballooning. There were no native balloonists in sight to follow anyway. Kappelyushnikov grumpily seamed and filled new balloons in the hope of better times to come. Harriet Santori tongue-lashed everyone who came near her. Morrissey packed samples in his tent and pored over mysterious pictures and charts, coming out only to stare furiously at the rain and shake his head. Danny composed long tactran messages to SERDCOM and the Double-A-L, demanding gifts for his gasbag friends. Krivitin and Sparky Cerbo concocted some kind of witches' brew from the native berries and got terribly drunk together, and then even more terribly sick as their bodies strove to defend themselves against the alien Klongan protein traces in the popskull. They very nearly died. They surely would have, exploded Alex Woodring, shaking with anger, if they had done any such moron's trick earlier; the first total vulnerability had dwindled to reactions that no longer brought death—only protracted misery. Danny inherited the job of tending them and, at Harriet's angry insistence, of packaging samples of their various untidy emissions for Jim Morrissey to analyze.

Morrissey was crouched over his pictures and diagrams when Danny came in, and when his duty was explained to him, he flatly refused it. "Cripes, Danny, I've got no equipment for that kind of thing. Throw those samples in the crapper. I don't want them."

"Harriet says we must know how serious the poisoning is."

"We already know that, man. They got real sick. But they didn't die."

"Harriet says you can at least analyze them."

"For what? I wouldn't know what to look for."

"Harriet says—"

"Oh, screw Harriet. 'Scuse me, Danny; I didn't mean to remind you of your, uh, indiscretions. Anyway, I've got something better for us to do now that the rain's stopping."

"It hasn't stopped, Jim."

"It's slowing down. When it does stop, Boyne's going to be coming around to collect the backhoe I borrowed from him. I want to use it first."

"For what?"

"For digging up some of our light-fingered friends." He pointed straight down at the floor of the tent. "The ones that swiped Harriet's radio."

"We already tried that."

"Yes, we did. We found out that the important thing is speed. They'll close up the tunnels faster than you'd believe, so we've got to get in, get moving, and get to where they are before they have a chance to react. We'll never have a clear field to pick them up otherwise—unless," he added offhandedly, "we flooded the tunnels with cyanide first. Then we could take our time."

"Is that all you think of—killing?" Dalehouse flared.

"No, no. I wasn't suggesting it. I was *excluding* it. I know you don't like killing off our alien brothers."

Dalehouse took a deep breath. He had seen enough of the balloonists to stop thinking of them as preparations and learn to consider them, almost, as people. The burrowers were still total unknowns to him, and probably rather distasteful—he thought of termites and maggots and all sorts of vile crawling things when he thought of them—but he wasn't ready for genocide.

"So what were you suggesting?" he asked.

"I borrowed a backhoe from Boyne. I want to use it before he takes it back. The thing is, I think I know where to dig."

He gathered up a clump of the papers on the upended footlocker he was using for a desk and handed them over. The sheets on top seemed to be a map, which meant nothing to Dalehouse, but underneath was a sheaf of photographs. He recognized them; they were aerial views of the area surrounding the camp. Some he had taken himself, others were undoubtedly Kappelyushnikov's.

"There's something wrong with them," he said. "The colors look funny. Why is this part blue?"

"It's false-color photography, Danny. That batch is in the infrared; the bluer the picture, the warmer the ground. Here, see these sort of pale streaks? They're two or three degrees warmer than what's on either side of them."

Dalehouse turned the pictures about in his hands and then asked, "Why?"

"Well, see if you figure it out the same way I did. Look at the one under it, in orthodox color. You took that one. Turn it so it's oriented the same way as the false-color print—there. Do you see those clumps of orangey bushes? They seem to extend in almost straight lines. And those bright red ones? They are extensions of the same lines. The bushes are all the same plant; the difference is that the bright red ones are dead. Well, doesn't it look to you like the pale lines in the false-color pictures match up with the lines of bushes in the ortho? And I've poked a probe down along some of those lines, and guess what I found."

"Burrows?" Dalehouse hazarded.

"You're so damn smart," grumbled Morrissey. "All right, show me some real smarts. *Why* are those plants and markings related to the burrows?"

Dalehouse put down the pictures patiently. "That I don't know. But I bet you're going to tell me."

"Well, no. Not for sure. But I can make a smart guess. I'd say digging out tunnels causes some sort of chemical change in the surface. Maybe it leeches out the nutrients selectively? And those plants happen to be the kind that survive best in that kind of soil?

Or maybe the castings from the burrowers fertilize them, again selectively. Those are analogues from Earth: you can detect mole runs that way, and earthworms aerate the soil and make things grow better. This may be some wholly different process, but my bet is that that's the general idea."

He sat back on his folding campstool and regarded Danny anxiously.

Dalehouse thought for a second, listening to the dwindling plop of raindrops on the tent roof. "You tell me more than I want to know, Jim, but I think I get your drift. You want me to help you dig them up. How are we going to do that fast enough? Especially in the kind of mud there is out there?"

"That's why I borrowed Boyne's backhoe. It's been in position ever since the rain began. I think the burrowers sense ground vibrations; I wanted them to get used to its being there before we started."

"Did you tell him what you wanted it for? I got the impression they were digging burrows themselves."

"So did I, and that's why I didn't tell him. I said we needed new latrines, and by gosh, we do—sometime or other. Anyway, it's right over the best-looking patch of bushes right now, ready to go. Are you with me?"

Danny thought wistfully of his airborne friends, so much more inviting than these rats or worms. But they were out of reach for the time being . . .

"Sure," he said.

Morrissey grinned, relieved. "Well, that was the easy part. Now we come up against the tough bit: convincing Harriet to go along."

Harriet was every bit as tough as advertised. "You don't seriously *mean*," she began, "that you want to drag everybody out in a *downpour* just for the sake of digging a few *holes*?"

"Come on, Harriet," said Morrissey, trying not to explode. "The rain's almost stopped."

"And if it has, there are a *thousand* more important things to do!"

"Will be fun, Gasha," Kappelyushnikov chipped in. "Digging

for foxholes like landed oil-rich English country gentlemen! Excellent sport."

"And it isn't just a few holes," Morrissey added. "Look at the seismology traces. There are big things down there, chambers twenty meters long and more. Not just tunnels. Maybe cities."

Harriet said cuttingly, "Morrissey, if you wonder why none of us have any confidence in you, that's just the reason. You'll say any stupid thing that comes into your head. Cities! There are some indications of shafts and chambers somewhat bigger than the tunnels directly under the surface, yes. But I would not call them—"

"All right, all right. They're not cities. Maybe they aren't even villages, but they're something. At the least, they are something like breeding chambers where they keep their young. Or store their food. Or, Christ, I don't know, maybe it's where they have ballet performances or play bingo—what's the difference? Just because they're bigger, it follows that they're probably more important. It will be less likely, or at least harder, for them to seal them off."

He looked toward Alex Woodring, who coughed and said, "I think that's reasonable, Harriet. Don't you?"

She pursed her lips thoughtfully. "Reasonable? No, I certainly wouldn't call it *reasonable*. Of course, you're our leader, at least nominally, and if you think it wise for us to depart from the—"

"I do think it's a good idea, Harriet," Woodring said boldly.

"If you'll let me finish, please? I was saying, if you think we should depart from the agreement we all made that group decisions should be arrived at *unanimously*, not by a vote or some one person throwing his weight around, then I suppose I have nothing further to say."

"Gasha, dear," said Kappelyushnikov soothingly, "shut up, please? Tell us plan, Jim."

"You bet! First thing we do is open up as big a hole as we can with the backhoe. All of us are out there with shovels, and we jump in. What we want is specimens. We grab what we see. We should take them pretty much by surprise, and besides," he said, with some self-satisfaction, "two of us can carry these." He held up his camera. "They've got good bright strobes. I got that idea from Boyne when we were drinking together; I think that's what they do at the Greasies'. They go in with these things, partly to get pictures and mostly to dazzle them. While they're temporarily blinded we can grab them easily."

Dalehouse put in, "Temporarily, Jim?"

"Well," Morrissey said reluctantly, "no, I'm not real sure about that part. Their eyes are probably pretty delicate—but hell, Danny, we don't even know if they have any eyes in the first place!"

"Then how do they get dazzled?"

"All right. But still, that's the way I want to do it. And we'll take walkie-talkies. If anything, uh, goes wrong—" He hesitated and then started over. "If you should get disoriented or anything, you just dig *up*. You should be able to do that with your bare hands. If not, you just turn your walkie-talkie on. We might be unable to get voice communication from under the surface, but we know from the radio that was stolen that we can at least get carrier sound, so we'll RDF you and dig you out. That's if anything goes wrong."

Kappelyushnikov leaned forward and placed his hand on the biologist's mouth. "Dear Jim," he said, "please don't encourage us anymore, otherwise we all quit. Let's do this; no more talk."

Predictably, Harriet would have nothing to do with the venture, and she insisted that at least two of the men stay behind—"In case we have to dig you heroes out." But Sparky Cerbo volunteered to go in, and Alicia Dair claimed she could run the backhoe better than anyone else in the camp. So they had half a dozen in coveralls, head lamps, goggles, and gloves, ready to jump in when Morrissey signaled the digging to start.

He had been right about the mud; there wasn't any, except right around the main paths of the camp, where they had trodden the Klongan ground cover to death. But the soil was saturated, and the backhoe threw as much moisture as it did dirt. In less than a minute it had broken through.

Morrissey swallowed, crossed himself, and jumped into the hole. Alex Woodring followed, then Danny, then Kappelyushnikov, Di Paolo, and Sparky Cerbo.

The plan was to break up into pairs, each couple to follow one tunnel. The trouble with the plan was that it was predicated on there being more than two directions to take. There weren't. The pit they dropped into was not much more than a meter broad. It smelled damp and—and *bad*, Danny thought, like a stale cage of pet mice; and it was no more than a tunnel. Di Paolo jumped down onto Danny's ankle, and Sparky Cerbo, following, got him square in the middle of the back. They were all tangled together, cursing and grumbling, and if there was a burrower within a kilometer that didn't know they were coming, that burrower, Danny thought, would have to be dead.

"Quit screwing around!" yelled Morrissey over his shoulder. "Dalehouse! Sparky! You two follow me."

Dalehouse got himself turned around in time to see Morrissey's hips and knees, outlined against the glow from his head lamp, moving away. The cross-section of the tunnel was more oval than round, shallower than it was broad; they couldn't quite move on hands and knees, but they could scramble well enough on thighs and elbows.

"See anything?" he called ahead.

"No. Shut up. Listen." Morrissey's voice was muffled, but Dalehouse could hear it well enough. Past it and through it he thought he heard something else. What? It was faint and hard to identify—squirrellike squeals and rustlings, perhaps, and larger, deeper sounds from farther away. His own breath, the rubbing of his gear, the sounds the others made all conspired to drown it out. But there was *something*.

A bright flare made him blink. It hurt his eyes. It came from Morrissey's strobe, up ahead. All Dalehouse got of it was what trickled back, impeded by the rough dirt walls almost without reflectance. In the other direction it must have been startling. Now he was sure he heard the squirrel squeals, and they sounded anguished. As well they should, Danny realized, with a moment's empathy for the burrowers. What could light have meant to them, ever, but some predator breaking in, and death and destruction following?

He bumped into Morrissey's feet and stopped. Over his shoulder, Morrissey snarled, "The fuckers! They've blocked it."

"The tunnel?"

"Christ, yes, the tunnel! It's packed tight, too. How the hell could they do that so fast?"

Dalehouse had a moment's atavistic fear. Blocked! And in the other direction? He rolled onto his side, extinguished his light, and peered back between his feet down the tunnel. Past Sparky's crouching form he could see—he was sure he could see—the reassuring dim red glow from the Klongan sky. Even so, he could feel the muscles at the back of his neck tensed and painful with the ancient human terror of being buried alive, and he suddenly remembered that the direction they had taken was the one that went under the backhoe. What if its weight crushed the roof through and pinned them? "Ah, Jim," he called. "What do you think? Should we get back to the barn?"

Pause. Then, angrily, "Might as well. We're not doing any good here. Maybe the guys had better luck the other way."

But Cappy and the others were already outside, helping them out as they emerged. They had got only eight or nine meters into their tunnel before it was blocked; Dalehouse's group had gone more than twice as far. It came out the same in the end, though, Dalehouse reflected. Incredible that their reactions could be so fast! No doubt they had been trained into them over endless Klongan millennia. Whatever the reason, it was not going to be easy to collect a specimen, much less try to make contact. Danny thought of his airborne friends longingly; how much nicer to fly to make contact than to wiggle through the mud like a snake!

Kappelyushnikov was brushing him off, and then, more lingeringly, doing the same for Sparky Cerbo. "Dearest girl," he said, "you are disgracefully filthy! Let us all go swim in lake, take our minds off troubles."

Good-naturedly the girl moved away from his hand. "Maybe we should see what Harriet wants first," she suggested. And, sure enough, Harriet was standing at the entrance to the headquarters tent, a hundred meters away, evidently waiting for them to come to her.

As they straggled in, she looked them up and down with distaste. "A total failure, I see," she said, nodding. "Of course, that was to be expected."

"Harriet," Jim Morrissey began dangerously.

She raised her hand. "It doesn't matter. Perhaps you'll be interested in what has happened while you were gone."

"Harriet, we were only gone twenty or thirty minutes!" Morrissey exploded.

"Nevertheless. First there was a tactran signal. We're being reinforced, and so are the Peeps. Second—" She stepped aside to let them pass through into the tent. The others who had stayed behind were clustered inside, looking, Dalehouse thought, curiously self-satisfied. "I believe you wanted a specimen of those underground creatures? We found one trying to steal some of our supplies. Of course, it would have been easier if so many of you hadn't been wasting your time on foolishness, so you could have helped when we needed you—"

Kappelyushnikov bellowed, "Gasha! Get to point, right now. You caught specimen for us?"

"Of course," she said. "We put him in one of Morrissey's cages. I was quite severely scratched doing it, but that's about what you can expect when—"

They didn't let her finish; they were all inside and staring.

The stale mouse-cage smell was a thousand times stronger, almost choking Danny Dalehouse, but there it was. It was nearly two meters long, tiny eyes set close together above its snout, squeezed tight in anguish. It was squealing softly—Danny would almost have said brokenheartedly—to itself. It was gnawing at the metal bars of the cage and simultaneously scrabbling at the plastic flooring with duckfoot-shaped claws. It was covered with a sort of dun-colored down or short fur; it seemed to have at least six pairs of limbs, all stubby, all clawed, and all incredibly strong.

Whatever its teeth were made of, they were *hard*; one of the bars of the cage was almost gnawed through. And its squeals of pain never stopped.

·NINE·

THE SWARM WAS half fledglings now, tiny balloonets that had just cast off their parachuting threads of silk and now struggled bravely to keep up with the great two-meter adult spheres. In the constant chorus of the swarm, the fledglings' voices were as tiny as their gasbags. Their shrill peepings used the least possible amount of hydrogen, to preserve their precarious lift balance against the few drops in their ballast bladders.

Charlie patrolled majestically through the swarm, driving the bulk of his body reprovingly against a cluster of infant balloonets who were singing against the swarm melody, rotating his eye patches to scan the skies for *ha'aye'i*, listening to the countersongs of praise and complaint from the other adults of the swarm, and always, always, leading them as they sang. There was much praise, and much complaint. The praise he took for granted. To the complaint he attended with more care, ready either to remedy or rebuke. Three females sang despairingly of little ones who dropped their flying tails too soon, or who could not hold their hydrogen and so drifted helplessly down to the voracious world below. Another pealed a dirge of anger and sorrow, blaming the deformed fledglings on the Persons of the Middle Sun.

This was just; and Charlie led the swarm in a concurrence of sympathy and advice. "Never"—(*Never, never, never,* sang the chorus)—"never again must we breed near the New Suns."

The females chorused agreement, but some of the males sang in counterpoint, "But how can we know which is real Heaven-Danger and which is not? And where may we breed at all? The Persons of the Three Suns are under all our air!"

Charlie's answering song was serene. "I will ask my friend of the Middle Sun. He will know." (*He will know, he will know,* chorused the swarm.)

But a male sang a dire question. "And when the swarming rapture is on us, will we remember?"

"Yes," sang Charlie. "We will remember because we must." (*We must, we must.*)

That should have settled it. And yet, the song of the swarm was not at peace. Undertones buzzed and discorded against the dominant themes. Even Charlie's own song faltered now and then, and repeated itself when it should have burst into triumphant new themes. Currents were stirring under the surface of his mind. They never reached consciousness; if they had, no power could have kept him from expressing them in song. But they were there. Worries. Doubts. Puzzles. Who were these Persons of the Three Suns? Where had they come from? They seemed the same, as like as any swarms of balloonists. Yet Charlie's friend 'Anny 'Alehouse had explained that they were not the same.

First there had been the Persons of the Small Sun. They had seemed no more than another species of devouring Earth-Danger creatures in the beginning, although they had created a tiny sun almost at once. But their camp was almost at the limit of Charlie's range, and the swarm had not troubled themselves about those Persons.

Then there was the group of Charlie's friend; and almost at once, the third group, the Persons of the Big Sun. They were worrisome! Their sun was always shining brightly, brighter than the Heaven-Danger at its brightest. Since it was almost the deepest of Charlie's instincts to swarm in the direction of a bright light, it was actual pain to turn and swim away from the Big Sun. They had almost been trapped when the Persons first arrived—when all three of the parties of Persons of the Suns arrived—because each of them came roaring down through the air on a pillar of Sun-

Flame. But none had been close enough to cause them to swarm. By the time the flock had maneuvered near, the flames were gone and the lights were darkened. Then the Persons of the Big Sun had sent one of themselves up into the air in the great queer thing that fluttered and rattled; it was harder than the *ha'aye'i* Sky-Danger, and even more deadly. Something about it drew balloonists into its swinging claws, and more than a dozen of Charlie's swarm had been ripped open and gone fluttering down to ground, helpless, despairing, and silent. Now they avoided it in fear and sorrow. Two out of three of the groups of New Persons, and both to be avoided! The one because they killed, the other because they did not fly at all, were no more than any other Ground-Danger, would not have been thought to be Persons at all—

Except for 'Anny 'Alehouse.

Charlie sang of his friend, who redeemed his whole race. 'Anny 'Alehouse and his sometimes companion, 'Appy—they were Persons! They flew as Persons flew, by the majesty and the grace of the air itself. It was a sad thing that even their Middle Sun had flared like a true Heaven-Danger and caused the flock to breed poorly. But it did not occur to Charlie to blame Morrissey's flare on Dalehouse or Kappelyushnikov; it did not occur to him to think of blame at all. When Kung flared, the balloonists bred. They could not help it. They did not try. They had never developed defenses against a false flare, one lacking in the actinic radiation that helped them make their hydrogen and triggered their fertility. They had never needed any—until now. And they had no way to learn a defense.

The swarm was drifting toward a swelling cumulus cloud; Charlie swelled his singing sac and boomed out, "Hive up, my brothers!" (*Hive up, hive up,* came the answering chorus.) "Hive up, sisters and mates! Hive up, young and old! Watch for *ha'aye'i* in the wet shadows! Huddle the little ones close!"

Every member of the swarm was singing full-throatedly now as the swarm compacted, swimming into the ruddy-pink, cottony edges of the cloud. They could see each other only as ghosts, except for the oldest and biggest males, whose luminous markings gave them more visibility. But they could hear the songs, and Charlie and the other senior males patrolled the periphery of the swarm. If *ha'aye'i* were there, the males could not defend the swarm—could not even defend themselves to any purpose. But they could sing warning, and then the swarm would scatter in all directions, so that only the slowest and weakest would be caught.

Cumulus clouds formed at the top of updrafts of warm air, and the *ha'aye'i* often sought them out to supplement their comparatively weak lift. There was always a price; what the *ha'aye'i* gained in speed and control, not to mention claws and jaws, they paid for in smaller lifting bags, so that for them it was always an effort to stay in the air. The *ha'aye'i* were sharks of the air. They never slept, never stopped moving—and were always hungry.

But this time the swarm was lucky. There were no killer balloons in the cloud, and they emerged intact. Charlie trumpeted out a song of thanksgiving as the flock entered clear air again. All joined.

The swarm was drifting toward the Heat Pole. Charlie rotated his eye patches to catch clues of the movement of the air. He always knew in what direction the winds blew on each level; he was taught by the movement of cloudlets, by the fluttering of dropped fledgling silk, most of all by a lifetime of experience, so that he did not have to think of how to capture a favorable wind; he *knew*, as surely as any New Yorker hurrying down Fifth Avenue knows the number of the next cross street. He did not want to stray too far from his friend of the Middle Sun, whom he had not seen for some time. He trumpeted for the swarm to rise a hundred meters. The other males took up his song, and from all the gasbags, great and small, drops of water ballast fell. There would be no trouble replacing it for the adults, who were naturally and automatically catching and swallowing the tiny misting of dew during their passage through the clouds. The smaller ones made hard work of it. But they valiantly released swallowed gas into their bags, and the females watchfully butted the littlest ones higher. The swarm stayed together at the new level as its drift changed back in the direction of the camp of the Middle Sun.

No *ha'aye'i* in sight. Plenty of water on their skins to lick off and swallow, part to hold as ballast, part to dissociate into the oxygen they metabolized and the hydrogen that gave them lift. Charlie was well content. It was good to be a balloonist! He returned to the song of thanksgiving.

They were nearing the edges of their territory, and another swarm bobbed high above them a few kilometers away. Charlie observed them without concern. There was no rivalry between swarms. Sometimes two of them would float side by side for long periods, or even coalesce. Sometimes when two swarms were joined, individuals from one would adhere to another. No one thought anything of that. From that moment they were full members of their new swarm and joined in its songs. But it was more common that each should stay in its own unmarked but known volume of air. They grazed the pollen fields of their own home air without coveting those of their neighbors. Though after half a dozen breedings there might be no single individual still alive of the original swarm, the swarm itself would still drift placidly over the same ten thousand square kilometers of ground. One place was almost like another. Over any one of those square kilometers the sustaining air was always around them. The pollen clouds blew through them all.

Still, some parts of their range were more attractive than others. The mesa where the Persons of the Big Sun had built their shining shells and lit their blazing lamps had been one of their favorites, pollen drifting down off the hills in a pleasant stream, and few *ha'aye'i*. Charlie sang sorrowfully of his regret as he thought of it, now that they must avoid it for all time to come. The bay of the ocean-lake where 'Anny 'Alehouse lived was, on the contrary, usually to be avoided. The water evaporating from the sea meant columns of rising cloud, and killer balloons no doubt in half the columns. If any member of the swarm had chosen to question Charlie's decision to return there, it would have been quite reasonable to do so, in practical terms. But in terms of the lives of the balloonists themselves it was quite impossible. Their group decisions were never questioned. If a senior adult sang, "Do thus," it was done. Charlie was the most senior of adults, and so his song usually prevailed. Not always. Now and then another adult would sing a contrary proposal ten minutes later, but if Charlie returned to his own ten minutes after that, there was no complaint. Each of the other adults loyally picked up his song, and the swarm complied.

There was also the consideration that Charlie had brought to the swarm his friend of the Middle Sun, with his astonishing and fascinating new sounds. This was a Person! Puzzling, yes. But not like those earthbound grubbers of the Small Sun or the strange creatures of the Big Sun who flew only with the help of killing machines. As the swarm drew near the camp of the Middle Sun, all of the adults rotated their bodies so that their tiny faces, like the features of engorged ticks, looked downward, anxious to spy 'Anny or 'Appy. Even the balloonets were caught up in the happy fever of the search; and when the first of the swarm spotted Danny rising to meet them, the song of the flock became triumphant.

How strange 'Anny 'Alehouse looked this time! His lifting sac had always been disagreeably knobby and lacking in any decent coloration, but now it was swollen immensely and knobbier than ever. Charlie might not have recognized him if there had been more than one other like him in all the world to confuse him with. But it was 'Anny all the same. The swarm swallowed hydrogen and dropped to meet him, singing the song of welcome Charlie had invented for his friend.

Dalehouse was almost as overjoyed to see the swarm again as the swarm was to see Dalehouse. It had been a long time! After the storm there had been the time for cleaning up; and before they were through the second ship had dropped out of the tachyon charge state to bring them new people and a whole host of new equipment. That was fine enough, but to make them welcome and to integrate the new things into the old had taken time —more than time. Some of what they had brought had been gifts for the balloonists, and to deliver the gifts meant more load had to be lifted, which meant a bigger cluster of balloons, which meant making and filling new ones and redesigning the ballasting system to compensate. Danny was far from sure it had been worth it.

But there had also been half a kilo of microfiches from the Double-A-L, and those had been worth a lot. Professor D. Dalehouse was now a name to conjure with among xenobiologists. They had quoted his reports in every paper. And the papers themselves had given much to think of. Among the conferees at Michigan State a battle had raged. In the evolution of the balloonists, where was Darwin? When a female scattered her filamentary eggs into the air of Klong like the burst of a milkweed pod and all the males spewed sperm at once, where was the selection of the fittest? What kind of premium on strength, agility, intelligence, or sexual attraction would make each generation somehow infinitesimally more "fit" than the one before in an ontogeny where all the males spurted all their genes into a cloud of mixed female genetic material, with the wind for a mixer and random chance deciding who fathered which on whom? The balloonists kept no Leporello lists. Well any one of them might have fathered a *milletre*; but if so he never knew it.

Charlie could have settled the debate if asked. All the balloonists were sexually mature as soon as they were able to drop their spider-silk parachute threads and float free. But all balloonists were not equal in size.

The older, the bigger. The bigger, the more sperm or eggs they flung into the collective pool. Human beings, by contrast, cease to play a part in evolution before half their lives are over. Wisdom does not come at twenty-five. By the time there is a significant difference between a Da Vinci and a dolt the days of breeding are over. Selection plays no further part. Nor does it in resistance to the degenerative diseases of the old, which is why in two million years the human race has not selected against cancer, arthritis, or arteriosclerosis. Raunchy young cells have been disciplined by the stresses of fifty thousand generations. But past the breeding age the cell runs out of programming. It doesn't know what to do next. It begins to fall apart.

With the balloonists it was different. The Charlie-sized giants among them sprayed half a liter of mist-of-sperm into each receptive cloud of eggs, while the tiny first-swarm male balloonets squeezed out hardly a drop. The Charlies had proved their fitness to survive by the most conclusive of tests: they had survived.

Dalehouse was eager to try to settle questions like that as he called to Charlie and swung in to meet him, even more eager to try the new language elements the big computers on Earth had generated for him. What was occupying most of his attention, though, was his gift from Earth. Like the swarm's greeting song, it was an example of the thing his society did best. It was a weapon.

It was not entirely a free gift, Dalehouse reflected, but then there is nothing without a price. Charlie's song cost him some of his reserve of lifting gas, as the songs that were their life always cost the swarm. If they sang, they vented gas. If they vented gas, they lost lift. If they lost lift, sooner or later they drifted helplessly down to the eager mouths on the surface and were eaten. Or, almost as bad, had to live on there, helpless and voiceless, until they were able to accumulate and dissociate enough water molecules to recharge their stocks—quickly if Kung was kind enough to flare for them, painfully slowly otherwise. It was a price they paid gladly. To live was to sing; to be quiet was to be dead anyway. But in the end, for most of them, it was the price of their lives.

The price of the gift Danny Dalehouse brought was the lives of the five balloonists who had been sent back to Earth in the return capsule.

The designers at Camp Detrick had made good use of the samples. The two who were dead on arrival were dissected at once. Those were the lucky ones. The other three were studied *in vivo*. The biggest and strongest of them lasted two weeks.

The Camp Detrick experimenters also had a price to pay, because eight of them came down with the Klongan hives, and one had the severe misfortune to have his skull fill up with antigenic fluid, so that he would never again for the rest of his life stress an experimental subject. Or, indeed, hold a fork by himself. But probably the balloonists who had been his subjects would not have thought that price unfair.

Danny Dalehouse unslung the lightweight carbine from one shoulder and practiced aiming it. Its stock was metal shell, and sintered metal at that; it weighed hardly a kilogram, but half that weight was in high-velocity bullets. It was poor design. He felt sure the recoil would kick him halfway across the sky if he fired it, and anyway, what was the use of high-velocity bullets? What target was there in the Klongan air that needed that sort of impact to destroy it? But the word from Earth brought by the reinforcement party that had been labeled a UN peacekeeping committee was that it must be carried. So he carried it.

He put it back and, somewhat uncomfortably, took Charlie's gift off the other shoulder. Now, that was more like it. Somebody somewhere had understood what Charlie's people could do and what they needed in order to protect themselves against predators.

It weighed even less than the carbine, and it contained no propellants at all. Its tiny winch could be operated by the claws of a Charlie to tighten a long-lasting elastic cord. Its trigger was sized to fit a balloonist, and what it fired was a cluster of minute needles or, alternatively, a capsule of some sort of fluid. Needles were for airborne predators. The fluid, or so Danny was told, was against creatures like the crabrats, if a balloonist was forced down and needed defense; and it would only incapacitate them without killing.

It would tax all of Dalehouse's linguistics to convey any part of that to Charlie, but the way to get it done was to begin. He held the crossbow up and sang, carefully attending to the notes he had been taught by the computers at Texas A&M. "I have brought you a gift."

Charlie responded with a burst of song. Dalehouse could understand no more than a few phrases, but clearly it was a message of gratitude and polite inquiry; and anyway, the little tape recorder at his belt was getting it all down for later study.

Danny moved on to the next sentence he had been taught. "You must come with me to find a *ha'aye'i*." That was hard to sing; English does not come with glottal stops, and practicing it for an hour had left Dalehouse's throat sore. But Charlie seemed to understand, because the song of thanks changed to a thin melody of concern. Danny laughed. "Do not fear," he sang. "I will be a *ha'aye'i* to the *ha'aye'i*. We will destroy them with this gift, and the swarm will no more need to fear."

Song of confusion, with the words *the swarm* repeated over and over, not only by Charlie but by all his flock.

The hardest part of all was yet to come. "You must leave the swarm," sang Dalehouse. "They will be safe. We will return. But now just you and I must fly to seek a *ha'aye'i*."

It took time; but the message ultimately seemed to get across. It was a measure of the balloonist's trust in his friend from Earth that he was willing to embark on so fearful an adventure with him. The members of the flock *never* left it by choice. For more than an hour after they had dropped to a lower level and left the flock behind, Charlie's song was querulous and sad. And no *ha'aye'i* appeared. They left the Food Bloc camp far behind, drifting down the shore of the sea-lake and then across a neck of it to the vicinity of the Peeps' tattered colony. For some time Dale-house had been wondering if the Texas computers had really given him the right words to sing. But then Charlie's song turned to active fear. They dipped low under a bank of clouds, warm-weather cumuli that looked like female balloonists turned upside down, and from one of them dropped the predatory form of a killer.

Danny was uneasily tempted to slay this first one with his own carbine. It was frightening to see the *ha'aye'i* swoop toward them. But he wanted to demonstrate his gift to Charlie.

"Watch!" he cried, clumsily grasping the grip that had been de-signed for balloonist claws. He circled the swelling form of the airshark in the cross-haired sight, designed for balloonist eye patches, feeling the low vibrations of Charlie's muttered song of terror. At twenty meters he squeezed the trigger.

A dozen tiny metal spikes lashed out at the *ha'aye'i*, spreading like the cone of fire of a shotgun shell. One was enough. The shark's bag ripped open with a puff of moisture. The creature screamed once in pain and surprise, and then had no more breath to scream with. It dropped past them, its horrid little face writh-ing, its claws clutching uselessly toward them, meters away.

A bright trill of surprise from Charlie, and then a roaring paean of triumph. "This is a great good thing, 'Anny 'Alehouse! Will you slay all the *ha'aye'i* for us?"

"No, not I, Charlie. You will do it for yourself!" And hanging in the air, Danny showed him the clever little crank that worked the elastic cord, the simple breech that the cluster of needles dropped into. For a creature who had never used tools before, Charlie was quick to grasp the operation. Dalehouse had him fire a practice round at a cloud and then watched patiently while the balloonist painfully wound the winch for himself and loaded again.

They were no longer quite alone. Unbidden, the swarm had drifted after them and was floating half a kilometer away, all their eye patches rotated toward them, their distant song sweet and plaintive, like a puppy's lonely begging to be let in. And down below, the Peeps' camp was near; Dalehouse could see one or two upturned faces curiously staring at them. Let them look, he thought virtuously; let them see how the Food-Exporting Powers were helping the native races of Klong, if they had so little to do with their time. There were only a handful of them left of the original expedition, and their much-boasted reinforcements showed no signs of arriving.

Reinforcements. Reminded, Dalehouse began the rest of his message for Charlie. "This gift," he sang, "is yours. But we would ask a gift of you, too."

"What gift?" sang Charlie politely.

"I do not know words," sang Danny, "but soon I will show you. My swarm-mates ask you to carry some small things to other places. Some you will drop to the ground. Some you will bring back." Teaching Charlie how to point the cameras and sound-recording instruments was going to take forever, Dalehouse thought glumly; and how were they ever going to tell him where to drop the clusters of wolftrap sensors and seismic mikes? What seemed so simple on Earth was something else entirely on Klong—

"Beware, beware!" sang the distant, frantic voices of the swarm.

Tardily Danny looked around. The *ha'aye'i*'s rush caught them unaware. It came from behind and below, where Dalehouse had not thought to look. And Charlie, fondling his new toy and trying to understand what Dalehouse wanted of him, had been careless.

If it had not been for the distant shrieking of the swarm, the creature might have had them both. But Charlie spun faster than Dalehouse, and before Danny could unlimber his carbine the balloonist had shown how well he had learned his lesson by killing the killer. Either of them could have reached out and caught the long, wicked claws of the *ha'aye'i* as it fell past them; it was that close.

"Well done!" yelled Dalehouse, and Charlie pealed in rapture:

"Well, well done! How great a gift!" They rose to rejoin the swarm—

Lances of golden fire reached up faintly toward the flock from the Peeps' camp below.

"My God!" shouted Danny. "The fools are setting off fireworks!"

The rockets exploded into showers of sparks, and all through the swarm balloonists were bursting into bright hydrogen flame.

·TEN·

WHEN DULLA WAS AWAKE, which was not much of the time, he was only blurrily conscious of what was going on. At first there had been a recurrent *whick, whick* that he could not identify, and some person who seemed vaguely familiar manhandling him into whatever it was that was making the sounds. Then pain—a lot of pain. Then long periods when people were talking to him or around him. But he felt no impulse to answer. In his brief conscious times he discovered by and by that he was no longer in pain. The treatment the Greasies had given him had been unpleasant, but it seemed to have done the trick. He was alive. He was rehydrated. The swellings had gone down. He was no longer blind. He was only very weak.

When he woke up and realized that he was not only awake but actually seemed able to keep his eyes open for a while, Feng Hua-tse was standing by his cot. The Chinaman was looking very stretched out, Dulla thought with some contempt; he looked even worse than Dulla himself felt.

"You are feeling better?" Feng asked sadly.

Dulla thought it over. "Yes. I think so. What has happened?"

"I am glad you are feeling better. The long-noses brought you here from the place of your beetle friends. They said you would live, but I didn't think so. It has been a long time. Do you want to eat?"

"Yes—no," Dulla corrected himself. "I do, but not at this moment. I want the w.c. first."

"Shall I help you?"

"No. I can do it myself."

"I am glad of that, too," said Feng, who had been functioning as bedpan orderly for all the days of Ahmed Dulla's recovery and longer before that than he cared to remember. The Pakistani raised himself painfully from the inflatable cot and moved slowly toward the slit-trench latrine.

He gazed disapprovingly around the camp. One of the noises he had been hearing identified itself for him: a slapping, rasping sound that turned out to be the waterwheel. So at least there should be power. But where were the promised floodlights, the growing crops, the comforts? Where were all the people?

Feng had followed him and stood gazing mournfully as Dulla relieved himself. "Why do you stand there?" snapped Dulla, tying up his pajama cord and making hard work of it. "What has happened? Why has so little been done?"

The leader spread his hands. "What can I say? There were ten of us. Two died with you in this venture you found so necessary. One other died here. Two were so ill they had to be returned to Earth—by courtesy of the Greasies. We had no one well enough to fly the return capsule. The Italian is asleep, and the two women are gathering fuel."

"Gathering fuel! Are we become peasants again, Feng?"

The leader sighed. "I have done my best," he said. It was a sentence he had been saying over and over to himself for a long time. "Help is coming. Heir-of-Mao himself has ordered it. Two great ships, material and persons, soon—"

"Soon! And until then, what? Do we do nothing?"

"Go back to bed," said Feng wearily. "You exhaust me, Dulla. Eat if you will. There is food. The Fats gave it to us; otherwise there would be none."

"And now we are beggars," sneered Dulla. He swayed and caught hold of Feng's shoulder. "For this I studied and came all these light-years! For this I almost died! How foolish we will all look when we return in disgrace to Earth!"

Feng shook his head heavily. He disengaged the Pakistani's hand from his shoulder and stepped downwind—the man was odorously unwashed. He did not need to hear any of this. He knew it for himself. He had accepted the charity of the Fats for the food without which they all would have starved; of the Greasies for the rescue of Dulla and for the return to Earth of the sick members of the expedition—who would no doubt even now be telling their debriefers how badly Feng Hua-tse had managed the expedition with which he had been entrusted. There would be large-character posters going up in K'ushui about that even now. They would be very critical of him. When they got back to Earth —*if* they got back—the best hope he had was to become a barefoot biochemist along the Yellow River again.

Of course, if somehow they mercifully spared him until the two great ships arrived—

Ah, then! He had pored over the tactran messages and pictures yearningly. The second ship would bring not ten, not fifteen, but a majestic thirty-four new persons. An agronomist! Someone to take up Feng's own pitiful beginnings, the mushrooms he had sown, the wheat seedlings he had coaxed to sprout—the fittest of them would survive, and the fittest of their descendants would flourish. There were two more translators, both split-brained, one of them a skilled littoral pisciculturist as well. The Great Water might yet yield food they could eat. A doctor—no, Feng corrected himself, a fully schooled surgeon with a world reputation in the treatment of traumatic injuries. True, he was nearly two meters tall and black as a boy-child's hair, by his photograph. But still. Three of the new additions had had limnology crash courses, and one of them, who had once been an officer in the Red Guards, had also had three years of experience as a scout in the Gobi, and later in the Himalayas.

And the worldly goods the other ship would carry! Photovoltaic generators, capable of pouring out 230-volt a.c. in really significant quantities. Plastic to spare. Pioneering tools—axes and machetes, and a few rifles for the collection of specimens as well as for "game." Folbots. Magnesium-frame bicycles. A doubly redundant computer with no fewer than six remote-access terminals. Radio equipment. Laser equipment. Food. More food; food enough for all of them for many months . . .

It seemed a dream!

But what was not a dream was that very surely, Feng knew, among those thirty-four persons would be one who would come over to him and quietly say, "Feng Hua-tse? I am directed by Heir-of-Mao to receive your report on why your custodianship of this project has not lived up to expectations." And then would come the sweating time. There would be no excuses accepted. He would not be interested in the mushrooms that were refusing to grow or the specimens that Feng himself had painfully kept alive. He would only be interested in why three had died and two had been sent home and ten had accomplished so very little.

All this was in Feng Hua-tse's mind, but all he said was, "Go back to sleep, Dulla. I am out of patience with you."

Dulla did not go back to sleep. Anger had given him strength. What he did was wake up the Italian.

"Oh, you are alive again?" Spadetti yawned and rubbed the blue-black stubble on his chin. "We thought you were going to die," he said cheerfully. "I almost bet a day's ration on it. I would have been very angry to lose."

"I have been talking to Feng, that bungler!"

"It is not all Uazzi's fault, Dulla. We were the first. We made the mistakes that must be made so others can learn."

"I did not want to be teacher to the Fats and the Greasies! I did not want them here at all. This can be our planet, to shape as we will!"

"Yes," admitted Spadetti, "I had some such thought myself. But, *chi sa,* what can you do? Each step seemed right at the time. Even yours, to make friends with the natives—"

"Those beasts! One cannot make friends with them."

"Oh, not true, Dulla. Our rivals have succeeded. The Fats have balloonists carrying their cameras all over the planet, or so they promise on the tactran. The Greasies are teaching their moles and earthworms how to burrow under our camp and listen to what we say. Perhaps they are listening now."

"Nonsense! How stupid you are!"

"Stupid, perhaps, but no, it is not entirely nonsense," smiled the Italian, unoffended. "Perhaps I have made it a little bit of a joke, but I am not sure that I am joking. And what have we accomplished? I will be more exact, Dulla. What did you yourself accomplish, except to get two people killed, when you visited our *frutti-del-mare* friends? We failed. It is as simple as that." He yawned and scratched. "Now, Dulla, *per favore*, let me wake up by myself a little? I am not so happy with this reality around me that I want to leave my dreams so rudely."

"Drink your wine and dream then," said Dulla coldly.

"Oh, Dulla! But that is not a bad idea. If one only had a true wine instead of this filth."

"Pig," said Dulla, but softly enough that Spadetti did not have to admit he had heard it. He returned to his cot and sat heavily on the edge of it, ignoring Spadetti's soft-voiced imprecations as he tasted the jungle juice he had made for himself. Perhaps it would kill him. Why not? The smell of it kept Dulla from wanting to eat, though he knew he should; he judged he had lost ten kilos at least since landing on Son of Kung, and he could not spare very many more. He sat breathing heavily, sucking through a straw at a flask of flat, tepid water from the still. By and by he noticed that there was a plastic pouch under his bed. He upended it and covered the cot with a drift of tiny white fiche prints.

"I see you have found your love letters," called the Italian from across the tent. "Unfortunately, I cannot read your language. But she is quite a pretty girl."

Dulla ignored him. He gathered them up and carried them to the radio shack, where the only working viewer was. Spadetti had been right; they were almost all from the Bulgarian girl, and they all said much the same thing. She missed him. She thought of him. She consoled her lonely sorrow with the memory of their days together in Sofia.

But in the photographs there was Ana in Paris, Ana in London, Ana in Cairo, Ana in New York. She seemed to be having an interesting time without him.

Rich countries! At bottom, were they not all the same, whether the wealth was in fuel or in food? Wealth was wealth! A greater distance separated him from the fat Bulgarians than from—from even the Krinpit, he thought, and then realized almost at once that he was being unjust. Nan was not like that. But then, she had had the advantage of spending much of her childhood in Hyderabad.

Away from the smell of the Italian's imitation wine, Dulla realized he was hungry. He found some cracked corn and ate it while he went through Ana's letters quickly, and then, more slowly, the synoptics from Earth. Much had happened while he was out of it. The Fats had been reinforced from Earth—it was called a UN peacekeeping team, but that deceived only the most naive. The Greasies had established a satellite astronomical observatory and were monitoring changes in the radiation of Kung. There were problems with the satellite, and the results were unclear. Even so, Dulla studied the reports with fascination and envy. That should have been his own project! It was what he had trained for, all those graduate years. What a waste this expedition was! He glanced distastefully at the gaping rents in the tent, at the instruments that were scattered out to rust because there was no one to use them. So much to be done. So much that he could not think where to begin and so could do nothing.

There was a racket outside which made Dulla glance up, frowning—Feng and the Italian quarreling about something, and behind them the distant squawking of a herd of balloonists. If Heir-of-Mao had been a little more openhanded, and if Feng had been a bit less of a fool . . . then they might have had a helicopter, like the Greasies, or the wit to make balloons, like the Fats, and he too might have had the chance to fly with the flocks. That chance was lost. Even the Krinpit, whom he himself, Ahmed Dulla, had resolved to make contact with, were as strange to him as ever. It was not fair! He had taken the risk. He remembered well how he had felt as he lay helpless among the curious, jostling masses of crablike creatures. If they hadn't tried to eat the other two first, he knew he would have wound up as a meal. And for nothing. The one Krinpit they had a chance to communicate with, to keep for a specimen, Feng had allowed to be stolen by the Greasies.

There were sudden new sounds from outside, hissing white sounds that made Dulla get up and peer out of the tent. He saw flames reaching toward the sky and Feng struggling with the Italian while one of the Jamaican women swore angrily at them both.

"What is happening here?" Dulla demanded.

The Italian pushed Feng away and turned toward Dulla, his expression repentant. "Uazzi wished to greet our friends," he said, peering aloft. The rockets had climbed up into the maroon murk and exploded, and there were smaller explosions all around them. Balloonists had caught fire from the shower of sparks. "I helped him aim, but perhaps—perhaps my aim was not good," he said.

"Foolish one!" cried Dulla, almost dancing with rage. "Do you see what you have done?"

"I have burned up a few gasbags. Why not?" grumbled Spadetti.

"Not just gasbags! Rub the wine out of your eyes and look again. There! Is that a gasbag? Do you not see it is a human being hanging there, wondering why we have tried to kill him, anxious to return to his base with the Fats or the Greasies and report that the People's Republics have declared war? Another blunder! And one we may not survive."

"Peace, Dulla," panted Feng. "It does not matter if the Fats and the Greasies are angry at us now. Help is on the way."

"You are as big a fool as he! Shooting off fireworks like some farm brigade celebrating the overfulfillment of its cabbage quota!"

"I wish," said Feng, "that you had not been rescued, Dulla. There was less struggle here when you were with the Krinpit."

"And I wish," said Dulla, "that the Krinpit who tried to kill me was our leader here instead of you. He was less ugly, and less of a fool."

That Krinpit was many kilometers away, and at that moment almost as angry as Dulla. He had been driven to the brink of insanity with the infuriating attempts of the Poison Ghosts of the Fuel camp to converse with him, with hunger, and above all with the continual blinding uproar of the camp.

In the noisy, bright world of the Krinpit there was never a time of silence. But the level of sound was always manageable: sixty or seventy decibels most of the time, except for the occasional thunderclap of a storm. It almost never reached over seventy-five.

To Sharn-igon, the Fuel camp was torture. Sometimes it was quiet and dim, sometimes blindingly loud. The Krinpit had no internal-combustion engines to punish their auditory nerves. The Greasies had dozens of them. Sharn-igon had no conception of how they worked or what they were for, but he could recognize each of them when it was operating: high clatter of the drilling machine, rubbery roar of the helicopter, rattle and whine of the power saws, steady chug of the water pump. He had arrived at the camp almost blind, for the nearness of the helicopter's turbojet had affected his hearing just as staring at the uncaged sun would damage a human's eyes; the afterimage lasted for days and was still maddeningly distorting to his perceptions. He had been penned behind steel bars as soon as he arrived. However hard he gnawed and sawed, the bars of the cage would not give. As soon as he made a little scratch in one it was replaced. The Poison Ghosts troubled him endlessly, echoing his name and his sounds in a weirdly frightening way. Sharn-igon knew nothing of tape record-ing, and to hear his own sounds played back to him was as shatter-ing an experience as it would be for a human to see his own form suddenly appear before him. He had realized that the Poison Ghosts wanted to communicate with him and had understood a tiny portion of what they were trying to say. But he seldom re-plied. He had nothing to say to them.

And he was nearly starving. He survived, barely, on the little he would eat of what they put before him—mostly vegetation, of which he disdained the majority as a human being would spurn thistle and grass. His hunger was maddeningly stimulated because he could smell the tasty nearness of Ghosts Below penned near him, and even a Ghost Above now and then. But the Poison Ghosts never brought him any of these to eat. And always there was the blinding roar of noise, or the equally unpleasant silences when the camp slept and only the faint echo from tents and soft bodies kept him company. Human beings, scantily fed on bread and water in an isolation cell, with bright lights denying them sleep, go mad. Sharn-igon was not far from it.

But he clung to sanity, because he had a goal. The Poison Ghosts had killed Cheee-pruitt.

He had not learned to tell one from another in time to know which was the culprit, but that was a problem easily solved. They were all guilty. Even in his madness it was clear to him that it was proper for him to kill a great many of them to redress their guilt, but what had not become clear to him was how. The chitin of claw and shell-sword were rubbed flat and sore against the bars, and still the bars held.

When all the sounds were out he chatted with the Ghost

Above, straining longingly against the bars. "Desire to eat you," he said. If it had not been for the bars, the Ghost Above would have been easy prey. It had lost most of its gas and was crawling about the floor of a cage like his own. Its song was no more than a pathetic whisper.

"You cannot reach me," it pointed out, "unless you molt. And then I would eat you." Each spoke in its own language, but over thousands of generations all the races of Klong knew a little of the language of the others. With the Ghosts Above you could not help being exposed to their constant singing, and even the Ghosts Below could be heard chattering and whistling in their tunnels. "I have eaten several of you hard-shells," the Ghost Above wheezed faintly. "I particularly like the backlings and the first molt."

The creature was boasting, but Sharn-igon could believe the story easily enough. The balloonists fed mostly on airborne detritus, but to make their young healthy they needed more potent protein sources now and then. When the breeding time was on, the females would drop like locusts to scour the ground clean of everything they could find. Adult Krinpit in shell were too dangerous, but in molt they were fair game. Best of all was a clutch of Ghosts Below caught on their thieving raids to the surface—for Krinpit as well as balloonist. The thought made Sharn-igon's salivary glands flow.

"Hard-shell," whispered the Ghost Above, "I am dying, I think. You can eat me then if you like."

In all honesty, Sharn-igon was forced to admit, "You may be eating me before that." But then he perceived that something was strange. The Ghost Above was no longer in its cage. It was dragging slowly across the floor. "How escape?" he demanded.

"Perhaps because I am so close to death," sang the Ghost Above faintly. "The Killing Ones made a hole in my sac to let the life out of me and then closed it with a thing that stuck and clung and stung. But it has come loose, and almost all my life has spilled away, and so I was able to slide between the bars."

"Wish I could slide through bars!"

"Why do you not open the cage? You have hard things. The Killing Ones push a hard thing into a place in the cage when they want to, and it opens."

"What hard thing are you speaking of? I have worn my shell to pulp."

"No," sighed the balloonist. "Not like your shell. Wait, there is one by the door. I will show you."

Sharn-igon's conception of keys and locks was quite unlike a human's, but the Krinpit too had ways of securing one thing to another temporarily. He chattered and scratched in feverish impatience while the dying gasbag slowly dragged itself toward him, with something bright and hard in its shadowy mouth.

"Could push hard thing into place in my cage?" he wheedled.

The Ghost Above sang softly to itself for a moment. Then it pointed out, "You will eat me."

"Yes. Will. But you very close to dying anyway," Sharn-igon pointed out, and added shrewdly, "Sing very badly now."

The balloonist hissed sadly without forming words. It was true.

"If push thing in place in my cage so that I can go free," bargained Sharn-igon, "will kill some of the Poison Ghosts for you." He added honestly, "Intend to do that in any case, since they killed my he-wife."

"How many?" whispered the balloonist doubtfully.

"As many as I can," said Sharn-igon. "At least one. No, two. Two for you, and as many as I can for me."

"Three for me. The three who come to this place and cause me pain."

"All right, yes, three," cried Sharn-igon. "Anything you like! But do quickly, before Poison Ghosts come back!"

Hours later, at almost the last of his strength, Sharn-igon staggered into a Krinpit village. It was not his own. He had seen the sounds of it on the horizon for a long time, but he was so weak and filled with pain that it had taken him longer to crawl the distance than the tiniest backling. "Sharn-igon, Sharn-igon, Sharn-igon," he called as he approached the alien Krinpit. "Am not of your place. Sharn-igon, Sharn-igon!"

A gravid female scuttled past him. She moved slowly because she was near her time, but she ignored his presence.

That did not surprise Sharn-igon. It was what he had expected. Indeed, each lurching step into the alien village was harder for him than the one before, and he was a professional empathizer.

"Sharn-igon," he called bravely. "I would speak to one among you, although I am not of this place."

There was no answer, of course. It would not be easy to make contact. Each village was culturally as well as geographically isolated from every other. They did not fight. But they did not interact. If a party of Krinpit from one village chanced upon an individual or a party from another, they depersonalized each other. One Krinpit might push another from a different village out of the way. Two alien Krinpit might each take an end of a many-tree trunk that was barring their mutual way. Both would lift. Neither would address the other.

Genetically the villages were not isolated. The seedlings dropped from their he-father's backs when they were ripe to do so, wherever they might be. If they chanced to be near an alien village when they did—and if they were lucky enough to make their way to it without becoming food for a Ghost Below or any other marauder—they were accepted there as readily as any autochthon. But adults never did such a thing.

On the other hand, an adult had never found himself in Sharn-igon's position—until now.

"Sharn-igon, Sharn-igon," he called over and over, and at last a he-mother crept toward him. It did not speak directly to him, but it did not retreat, either. As it moved, it softly made the sound of its name: Tsharr-p'fleng.

"Have had good Ring-Greeting, alien brother?" Sharn-igon asked politely.

No answer, except that the sound of the stranger's name grew a trifle louder and more assured.

"Am not of this place," Sharn-igon acknowledged. "Most unpleasant for me to be here. Am aware is unpleasant also for you. However, must speak with you."

Agitatedly the other Krinpit scratched and thumped its name for a moment and then managed to speak. "Why you here, Sharn-igon?"

He collapsed on the knees of his forelegs. "Must have food," he said. The balloonist had been so very thin and frail that he made only half a meal, and of course Sharn-igon had been careful not to eat any part of the Poison Ghosts. He was not sure he had succeeded in killing all three, but two at least were certain, and the other would be a long time recovering. That settled the score for the balloonist.

But not for Cheee-pruitt.

If Sharn-igon had not been a professional empathist he could not have broken through the barriers between villages. As it was, it took much time and all of his persuasion; but at the end of it Tsharr-p'fleng helped him to a dwelling pen and ministered to his needs.

Sharn-igon devoured the crabrat they brought him while Tsharr-p'fleng engaged in agitated conversation with others of the village just outside the wall. Then they came in and ranged themselves around Sharn-igon, listening to him eat. He ignored their polite scratches of curiosity and concern until every morsel was gone. Then he pushed away the splintered carapace and spoke.

"Poison Ghosts killed my he-wife and did not eat him."

A flickering sound of disgust.

"They captured me and held me in a place without doors. They removed my backlings and took them away. I do not think they were eaten, but I have not heard them since."

Brighter sounds—disgust mixed with sympathy and anger.

"Moreover, they have also captured Ghosts Above and Ghosts Below and many of the lesser living things, and have eaten none of them. I therefore killed three of the Poison Ghosts. Intend to kill more. Are you back-mates with the Poison Ghosts?"

The he-mother rustled and spoke with contempt. "Not those! Their back-mates are the Ghosts Below."

Another said, "But Poison Ghosts have ways of killing. They have spoken to us in our language and told us to beware of them, lest they kill us."

"Beware of what? What did they tell you to do?"

"Only to refrain from harming any of them, for then they will kill all in our village."

Sharn-igon said, "The Poison Ghosts do not speak truth. Listen! They say they come from another world, like stars in sky. What are these stars?"

"They say they are like heat from sky," muttered the other.

"Have felt heat from sky. Have felt no heat from these other stars. I hear nothing from them. No matter how loud I shout, hear no echo from any of them."

"We have said these things ourselves," said Tsharr-p'fleng slowly. "But we are afraid of the Poison Ghosts. They will kill us, without eating."

"They will; it is true," said Sharn-igon. He paused. Then he went on. "Unless we kill them first. Unless all of our villages together fall upon them and kill them, without eating."

·ELEVEN·

MARGE MENNINGER'S HAIR was no longer blond. The name on her passport was not Margie Menninger. According to her travel orders, she was now a major, en route to a new duty station; and although the orders authorized a delay en route, it was unlikely that the general who signed them had contemplated that it would be spent in Paris.

In the little room of her hotel she fidgeted over the so-called croissant and what passed for orange juice, and phoned down to the concierge to see if the message she was expecting had arrived.

"I regret it, Meez Bernardi, but there is nothing," sighed the concierge. Marge took another bite of the croissant and gave it up. France was nominally part of the Food Bloc—by the skin of its teeth, and by the relabeling of Algerian wine for export—but you couldn't prove it by what they gave you for breakfast.

She was tired of this room, with its leftover smells of *khef* and sexual athletics from its previous occupants. She wanted to move around and couldn't. And while she was fretting away time in this room, the Peep ships were going through prelaunch, the training of backup crews for the next Food Bloc mission was limping along without her, and God only knew what disasters were taking place in Washington and at the UN.

She abandoned the breakfast and dressed quickly. When she

came downstairs, of course there was a message at the concierge's desk, on a flimsy blue slip of paper:

Miss Hester Bernardi will be picked up at 1500 hours for her appointment.

It had obviously been there all along. Margie did not bother to reprimand the concierge; she would take care of that at tipping time. She pushed her way out into the Rue Caumartin, deciding what to do next. Six hours to kill! And for the life of her she could not think of any productive use to make of them.

It was a warm, drizzly day. The stink of gasoline drenched the air over the Place de l'Opéra. Food Bloc or not, France was cozy with the Ay-rabs, as well as with the Peeps. That was another reason you could not trust the frogs, Margie thought darkly. One of her grandfathers had marched into this city in Wehrmacht gray, and the other, in the opposite direction a few years later, in American olive drab, and both of them had passed on to her their feelings about the French. They were inconstant allies and unreliable subjects, and the few who ever seemed to have any sense of national purpose usually wound up having their heads shaved or chopped by the many who did not. In Margie's view, the French were not a bit better than the English, the Spanish, the Italians, the Portuguese, the Asians, the Africans, the Latins—and about ninety percent of the Americans too, when you came right down to it.

But the immediate problem was not what was wrong with humanity, but what she could do with this day. There was only one answer. She could do the thing most American women came to Paris to do. She could shop.

She not only could shop, she must; it was the best way of avoiding attention. She not only must, she wanted to.

It was one of Margie's most closely guarded secrets that periodically she went on shopping binges, out of one store and into another, pricing fabric, trying on dresses, matching shoes with gowns. In her little Houston apartment there were two closets, plus half of what was meant to be a guest room, filled with her purchases. They were thrown jumbled onto shelves, pushed under a bed in their original store bags: sweaters she would never wear, material half-sewn into drapes that would never be hung. Her living room was spartan, and her bedroom was always immaculate, because you never knew who might drop in. But the secret rooms were part of the hidden personality of Margie Menninger. None of what she bought was very expensive. It was not because she was economical. She had unaccounted funds at her disposal, and the prices never mattered. But her taste was for quantity rather than quality. Periodically she would wage war against the overflow, and then for a while Goodwill and the Salvation Army would fatten off her discards. But a week later the hoard would have grown again.

Margie did not bother with the tourist traps along the Champs Élysées or with the tucked-away boutiques. Her tastes were for stores like Printemps, Uniprix, and the Galeries Lafayette. The only fly in the ointment was that she could not buy anything. She could not carry it where she was going and did not want to attract attention by leaving it, so she tried on, and she priced, and for six hours she made the lives of a score of Parisian shopgirls a living hell. That didn't bother Margie Menninger at all. By the time the taxicab picked her up at her hotel, punctually on the tick of three o'clock, her good nature was restored. She leaned back against the hard plastic seat of the cab, ready for what was to come next.

The driver stopped at the Place Vendôme long enough for another passenger to jump in. Behind tourist shades was the face of her father, which was no surprise to Margie.

"Bonjour, honey," he said. "I brought you your toy."

She took the camera he offered her and hefted it critically. It was heavier than it looked; she would have to be careful not to let anyone else pick it up.

"Don't try to take pictures with it," he said, "because it won't. Just hang it around your neck on the strap. Then, when you get where you're going"—he pushed the shutter lever, and the casing opened to reveal a dull metal object inside—"This is what you give your contact. Along with a hundred thousand petrodollars. They're in the carrying case."

"Thank you, poppa."

He twisted in the seat to look at her. "You're not going to tell your mother that I let you do this, are you?"

"Christ, no. She'd have a shit hemorrhage."

"And don't get caught," he added as an afterthought. "Your contact was one of Tam Gulsmit's best people, and he is going to be really ticked off when he finds out we turned him. How are things going at Camp Detrick?"

"Good shape, poppa. You get me the transport, I'll send some good people."

He nodded. "We've had a little lucky break," he offered. "The Peeps fired on one of our guys. No harm done, but it makes a nice incident."

"Didn't he fire back, for Christ's sake?"

"Not him! It was your old jailhouse buddy, the one from Bulgaria. As near as I can tell, he doesn't believe in the use of force. Anyway, he did exactly what I would have told him to do. He got the hell out of there and reported back to the UN peacekeeping force, and he had tapes and pictures to prove what he said." He peered out the window. They had crossed the Seine. Now they were creeping through heavy traffic in a working-class neighborhood. "This is where I get out. See you in Washington, love. And take care of yourself."

Early the next morning Margie was in Trieste. She was not Hester Bernardi anymore, but she wasn't Marge Menninger either. She was a sleepy Swiss-Italian housewife in a sweaty pantsuit, driving to the Yugoslav border in a rented Fiat electrocar with a crowd of other Sunday-morning shoppers looking for cheap vegetables and bargains in Yugoslavian kitchenware. Unlike them, she drove straight through to Zagreb, parked the car and took a bus to the capital.

When she reached Belgrade, the object her father had given her was at the bottom of a plastic shopping bag with an old sweater and a shabby pocketbook on top of it. And she had had very little sleep.

Margie could not have grown up in the household of Godfrey Menninger without learning the easy dialogue of espionage. In all the world, she was the only person with whom her father had always been open. First because she was too little to understand, and so he could speak freely in her presence. Then because she had to understand. When the PLO kidnapped her she had been terrified past the point a four-year-old can survive, and her father's patient explanations had been the only thing that let her make sense of the terror. And finally, because he trusted her to understand, always, that the grotesque and lethal things he did had a purpose. He never questioned that she shared that purpose. So she had grown up in an atmosphere of drops and liquidations and couriers and double agents, at the center of a web that stretched all around the world.

But now she was not at the center of the web; she was out where the risks were immense and the penalties drastic. She walked quickly down the busy streets, avoiding eye contact. The closet-sized shops had their doors open, and confusing smells came out of them: a knifelike aroma of roasting meat from a dressmaker's (when had she eaten last?), the sting of unwashed armpits from what seemed to be a costume-jewelry boutique. She crossed, dodging a tram, and saw the office she was looking for. The sign said Electrotek München, and it was over a sweatshop where fat, huge men in T-shirts worked at belt-driven sewing machines.

She checked her watch. There was more than an hour before her first possible contact. The man she needed to meet was a short, slim Italian who would be wearing a football blazer with the name of the Skopje team. Of course, no one like that was in sight yet—even if he turned up for the first rendezvous, which her father had warned was unlikely.

Down the block there was a cluster of roofed sheds surrounding a gabled two-story building that looked like any American suburban town's leftover railroad station. A farmers' market? It seemed to be something like that. Margie pushed her way through crowds of women in babushkas and women in minifrocks, men in blue smocks carrying crates of pink new potatoes on their shoulders, and men with a child on each hand, studying counters of chocolates and jellies. It was a satisfyingly busy mob. She was not conspicuous there.

She was, however, hungry.

Strawberries seemed to be in season. Margie bought half a kilo and a bottle of Pepsi and found a seat on a stone balustrade next to an open suitcase full of screwdrivers and cast-aluminum socket wrenches. What Margie wanted most was a hamburger, but no one seemed to be selling anything like that. But others were eating strawberries, and Margie was confident she looked like any one of them, or at least, if not like them, like some housewife who might have stopped en route to any ordinary destination to refresh herself.

At two punctually she was back in front of Electrotek München, studying a Belgrade bus guide as instructed. No short, slim Italian appeared. Twice she caught snatches of words that seemed to be in English, but when she looked up from her bus guide and glanced casually in that direction, she could not tell which of the passersby had spoken. She pitched the bus guide into a corner sewer and walked angrily away. The second appointment was not until ten o'clock at one of the big old luxury hotels, and what in God's name was she going to do until then?

She had to keep moving. It was very hard to stroll for more than seven hours, however many Camparis and soda you are willing to stop and drink. God bless, she passed something that called itself, in Cyrillic letters, an Expres-Restoran, and when she realized that it was a cafeteria, one problem at least was solved. She pointed at something that looked like roast chicken and probably was, and with the mashed potatoes and bread that went with it, at least she was full. Full of time. She emptied herself of as much of it as she could: a stroll through the botanical gardens, a long window-shopping stroll down the Boulevard Marshal Tito. And then it began to rain. She retreated into a *bioskop* and watched a Czech comedy with Serbo-Croatian subtitles until nine. The only problem was staying awake; but when she got to the hotel there was a real problem. Ghelizzi did not show up there either.

By now she was almost dizzy with fatigue, her clothes were sweaty and rain-stained, and she was sure she was beginning to smell. Poppa had not really thought these arrangements through, she thought with some bitterness. It should have occurred to him that the waiters at the hotel bar would not fail to notice a sweaty, dirty foreign woman among all their marble and their string trios. If she had been a man, it might not have mattered. A man could have been checking out the hotel whores—the skinny, dark-at-the-roots blond playing solitaire by the fireplace, the plump one with the bright red hair who had left the aperitif lounge twice in one hour, with different men, and was back again, ready for the next. Margie refused another Campari and sent the waiter for a Turkish coffee. The next appointment was not until the following afternoon, and where would she sleep?

The whores had rooms. If she had been one of them . . .

The idea did not disturb Margie in any moral way, but it took only a second for her to discard it as impractical. Even if she had a room, the waiters would surely throw her out to protect the existing monopoly the first time she looked toward one of the solitary males. They were already looking at her with interest and beginning to take the cloths off some of the tables in the farther end of the room.

Margie picked up her coffee and moved to the table of the streaked blond. She spoke to her in English, confident that in a tourist hotel the girls would be fluent in the necessary words in any major language.

"How much for all night?" she asked.

The blond looked scandalized. "For yourself? How disgusting! I could not possibly do such a thing with a woman."

"Fifty dinars."

"One hundred."

"All right, one hundred. But I have very special tastes, and you must do exactly as I ask."

The blond looked skeptical, then shrugged and signaled the waiter. "First you must buy me a real Scotch whiskey while you explain what these tastes are. Then we will see."

In the morning Margie woke up refreshed. She used the whore's tiny shower to get clean, dressed quickly and paid the woman off with a smile.

"May I ask a question?" the whore offered, counting the money.

"I can't stop you from asking."

"This thing you had me do, simply rubbing your neck each time you woke until you fell asleep again? Is that truly satisfying to you?"

"You wouldn't believe how satisfying," smiled Margie. She strolled grandly out of the hotel, nodding politely to the local police in their baggy gray uniforms open at the neck, hands on the guns in the cardboard holsters. A few blocks down the boulevard took her to the London Cafe, and there, nursing a beer at one of the indoor tables, was the slim, short Italian wearing a Skopje football cap.

She sat down and ordered a coffee, then visited the women's w.c. When she came back the Italian was gone. The bag she had left on her chair did not appear to be disturbed, but her exploring fingers told her the camera was gone, and in its place was a guide folder about the hovercraft cruise to the Iron Gorge.

She made her way back across the border the same way she had come. By the time she was in Trieste again and able to resume the identity of the Swiss-Italian housewife, she was fully restored. On the clamjet to Paris she locked herself in the toilet and studied the contents of the travel folder.

How Ghelizzi had come to be a person of trust in Sir Tam's army of spies was beyond her; he had not impressed her as being the sort of man one would repose faith in. But he had delivered the goods this time. The little device was on its way, and the complete file of secret tactran messages between Earth and the Fuel Bloc camp on Klong was in her hands in microfiche. Her father would be very proud.

·TWELVE·

WHAT ANA DIMITROVA had seen of the United States was what she had seen of most of the world: airports, hotel rooms, meeting halls, city streets. So at first she looked around with lively interest as the electrobus whined along an eight-lane superhighway toward the place she had been ordered to report to. So much open space, not even farmed! And contrarily, so many places lined up one after another as they passed through communities—places to eat, places to sleep, places to drink, places to buy gas. What prodigious devourers these Americans must be to keep them all flourishing!

More than half of her companions in the bus were Americans, and they were busy devouring, too, several smoking in flagrant disregard of the signs, a couple chewing gum, three in the back seat passing around a bottle in a brown paper bag. The army sergeant who had offered her part of a chocolate bar was now offering the Canadian agronomist woman some round hard candies with holes in them. Nan was making an effort to like the others because she surely would be seeing a lot of them in training. It wasn't easy. One by one, each of the American men had made friendly overtures to her which turned in seconds into sexual ones. Even the Vietnamese colonel, so tiny and delicate that she had sat down next to him at first, thinking he was a woman, had begun to make personal remarks in his beautiful high-pitched English. She had changed seats six times so far and now resolutely sat staring out the window even though she was no longer seeing anything. Such compulsive consumers—she could not help feeling that they seemed obliged to consume her as well.

She touched the tiny microfiche from Ahmed at the bottom of her blouse pocket. She had no reader for it, but she needed none. As always it was formal, not very rewarding, and extremely short:

> My dear Ana,
>
> I appreciate the letters you have been sending and think of you often.
>
> > With great affection,
> > Dulla

He could have spent a few P$ more, she thought resentfully, and then, as always, brought herself up sharply. Ahmed was from a poor country. Even fiched and faxed, the cost per square centimeter of a letter from Kungson to Earth was very high. (But in her own letters she had poured money out like water. (But she could not judge him; she had not had the life experience of measuring every penny. (But it was not just the economy of space and money—how much more he could have said if he had chosen, in even fewer words!—it was the economy of emotion that she begrudged.))) Three deep in parentheses, she took her mind off Dulla and resolved to think about more profitable subjects, and then realized the bus had stopped.

Three uniformed Americans had entered by the driver's seat. One of them gestured for silence and said to the bus at large, "You people are welcome, and let's see some ID."

Craning her neck, Nan could see a barricade with two other soldiers standing by it. They were not at attention, but they were watching the bus quite carefully, and she observed that what had looked like a well-clipped hedge stretching away on both sides of the barrier had barbed wire inside it. How curious. They were treating this place as though it were some sort of military installation rather than a center for preparing scientists and support personnel for a peaceful expedition to Kungson. Big-power customs were so strange to her. When the MPs came to her, she handed her passport over and smiled at the tall black one who was studying it. He returned her look impassively.

"Name?"

Of course, it was right there, next to his thumb. "Ana Elena Dimitrova."

"Place of birth?"

"My place of birth? It is Marek, Bulgaria. That is a city south of Sofia, not far from the Yugoslavian border."

"Put your thumb here, please." She pressed against the little pad he extended to her and then on a square white card, which he tucked into her passport. "Your papers will be returned to you later," he said, and then unbent. "You like to dance? There's a nice group at the club tonight. Ask for me if you don't see me. Name's Leroy."

"Thank you, Leroy."

"See you later, honey." He winked and moved along. Ana found a tissue and wiped the ink off her thumb wonderingly. These Americans were even worse than Sir Tam—not just the Americans, she corrected herself, thinking of the Vietnamese colonel and his agile, tiny hands. Would it be like this always? Would it not be even worse when she was part of the small colony on Kungson and they were all living in each other's pockets anyway?

But at least then Ahmed would be somewhere near! In the wrong encampment, yes. But she would find a way to see him. Let her just get on the same planet with him again, and they would be together! It made the whole ordeal seem worthwhile.

By the next day, not even that made it seem altogether attractive. She could not have attended Leroy's dance that night if she had wanted to. There was no time. Issue of new clothing: "You will wear these here fatigues at all times, except when instructed by your instructors." Assignment to quarters: "You will maintain cleanliness at all times. At all times all personal possessions are to be kept in your footlockers." Preliminary briefing: "You will fall out at oh six hundred hours for breakfast. From oh seven hundred to eleven hundred you will participate in your individual refresher courses of instruction in the application of your specialized skills on Klong. From twelve hundred to sixteen-thirty you will complete your survival course to teach you your survival skills for surviving in the environment of Klong. From eighteen hundred to lights out at twenty-two hundred you will conduct your personal affairs except when required to participate in additional refresher courses or survival instruction. Weekends? Who's the guy who wants to know about weekends? Oh, you. Well, there aren't any weekends here." By the time all that was finished it was nearly midnight, and then Ana dragged her suitcase to the tiny, bare room that had been assigned to her, coldly furnished like the showcase cell in a county jail, only to find out that her roommate was the Vietnamese colonel. Even here rank had its privilege. But Ana was having none of it, and so it was back to the billeting office and a good deal of argument, and by the time she was able to get to sleep in a new room with a female roommate it was nearly two.

Breakfast was discouragingly huge—eggs and sausage and cereal, and breads with jams and marmalades, and peanut butter in opened liter cans on every table—and for dessert they spent an hour receiving inoculations. None of them were painful, but from the grins and jokes of the medics Ana knew that they would be later on. And then she lined up with the other two dozen of her detachment in a wet, cold wind, and they were marched off to their various refresher courses in the application of their specialized skills. Ana's tiny group included the Canadian woman and two men unknown to her, and they wound through the camp streets, past a baseball field and a bowling alley, between barracks and anonymous buildings with armed guards patrolling before them, out into an open field half a kilometer square. In the center of it was a sort of tethered balloon shaped like a sausage, fifty meters long, with guards around the perimeter and three of them grouped before the entrance. There was a fence surrounding the whole thing, and more guards at the gate in the fence; and before any of them were permitted inside, they had to go through the same tedious business of checking IDs one more time.

Off to one side there was a tall chimney coupled to the main tent by a flexible plastic tube. The chimney roared. Though there was no smoke, the shimmering at the top showed that some very hot gases were boiling high into the air out of it. It did not seem to serve any function that Ana could guess. But then, neither did the weapons that all the permanent personnel carried. Who were they meant to be used against? What possible enemy threatened a training base for a scientific expedition which, after all, was in a sense the property of the entire world?

When she finally got through the gates and the guards, she found herself in a long, open shed covered with the opaque white plastic of the bubble. The atmosphere was damp and heavy, filled with strange smells, and the lighting was sultry red. At first she could see very little, but she was aware that people were moving about between rows of what seemed to be smaller, transparent bubbles. The lighting came from a bank of gas-glow tubes, all red, and there was not very much of it.

The guide who had brought her to this place was speaking to her. "Are you all right?"

"Yes, I think so. Why not?"

"Sometimes people can't stand the smell."

She sniffed gingerly: pepper and spice and jungle rot. "No, it is fine."

The Canadian woman said, "Everything sounds funny."

"There's positive pressure in the outer shell. Your ears probably popped a little. That's so that if there's any air leakage it will all be inward, not out, and of course the air from this chamber gets incinerated at fifteen hundred degrees as it is pumped out—maybe you saw the chimney."

"One has heard stories of dangerous diseases," Nan ventured.

"No. There aren't any. Oh, sure," the guide went on gloomily, "you can get killed around here. But that's allergies, not disease, and you've all had your shots for them. Dimitrova, you're for linguistics. You come with me; the rest of you stay right here till I get back."

He led her through the hothouselike room, past the rows of plastic bubbles. As her eyes became dark-adapted she could see that each of them contained some sort of specimen—mostly plants, and some of them were immense. One towered ten meters, nearly to the top of the shell. It looked like a giant cluster of ferns, and Ana marveled at the money that had been spent to transport that immense mass over the light-years. Apart from the outside roaring of the incinerator, the sounds of pumps, and the noises the people in the shell made, there were sounds she could not identify—a sort of faint, wailing, high-pitched song, and groaning, clattering noises. They came from where she was heading for. The guide said, "Welcome to our zoo."

And then she saw the balloonist.

She recognized it at once; there could not be another creature as strange as that anywhere in the universe! But it looked . . . damaged. It was tethered inside a cage. Its great bubble was throbbing but almost limp, sagging against the ground. She stared, fascinated, and saw that a flexible plastic coupling had been taped neatly to a hole in the gasbag, and the plastic line went to a cylinder of gas. A woman with a tape recorder was crouched by the cylinder, adjusting the gas valve as she listened to the balloonist's plaintive song.

No wonder the voice sounded so faint! He was operating at a fraction of normal pressure, far too little to let him fly, only enough to let him gasp a sobbing sort of song. The woman looked up and said, "You're Dimitrova? I'm Julia Arden, and this"—pointing at the balloonist—"is Shirley. She's singing about her childhood right now."

Ana shook hands courteously, staring at the sad, wrinkled little creature. Those sounds did not seem like language! She could not imagine understanding them, much less translating them, no matter how many times they halved her brain! She said doubtfully, "I will do my best, Mis Arden, but do you think you can really teach me to talk to that?"

"Me? Maybe not. I'll help, and so will the computers, but the one who's going to teach you is Shirley herself. She loves to sing to us. Poor thing. She doesn't have much else to do with her time, does she?"

Nan looked at the creature for a moment and then burst out, "No, but what a shame, really! Can you not see she is in pain?"

The other woman shrugged. "What do you want me to do about it?" Her tone was less hostile than defensive. "I don't suppose Shirley volunteered for this duty, but then, neither did I. Your job is learning her language, Dimitrova, and let's get on with it."

"But to see a creature in pain—"

Julia Arden laughed and then shook her head. "Sweetie, you only got here last night. Wait a day or two. Then you can talk to me about pain."

From 0700 to 1100 Ana Dimitrova stretched the muscles of her mind until she thought she would die of it, and from 1200 to 1630 she balanced the diet by doing the same to her body. Julia Arden had been right. Within forty-eight hours Ana was an expert on pain. She woke up each morning with a hazy overcast of brightness that she knew was the foretaste of migraine. She went to bed each night with so many aches, throbs, and bruises that it took all the will she had to refrain from swallowing the pills they had given her. She could not afford pills. She needed her mind alert, even while she slept, because sleeping was only another kind of study for Ana, with the taped calls of the balloonists murmuring under her pillow all night long.

The headaches, all right—they were something she was used to. Worse than that, the shots were producing their effect. Her skin was covered with little blisters and bumps, some that itched, some that were tender, some downright painful every moment of time. Not just pain. She wheezed and coughed. Her eyes ran uninterruptedly, and so did her nose. She was not alone; everyone in her group was having the same reaction to the allergy shots. If this was the prophylaxis, what could the illness itself be like? And then she saw the holos of the unfortunate Peeps who had died of their reactions before the countermeasures had been developed, and they defined for her the difference between prophylaxis and reality. It was not comforting to her. It was terrifying! How had Ahmed fared in all this? He had said nothing in his letters, but perhaps he was only being brave.

And every afternoon—feel well, feel ill, no matter—there she was out on the exercise field. Push-ups and five-hundred-meter runs, obstacle courses and rope climbing. Her hands were raw, then blistered, then calloused. Even through the coveralls her knees were scraped bloody. Everywhere on arms and legs where there was not a pimple or a blister, there was a bruise.

To be sure, she scolded herself, for all of this there was a clear purpose! Kungson was no picnic dell; it was a place of strange and perhaps lethal dangers. These measures, however brutal, were only to help her meet those dangers and conquer them. If she had not volunteered for the job, she had also not refused it when offered.

And finally, the most potent argument of all. It was the way to Ahmed. So she did her best all the time and was secretly proud of the fact that some of the others were doing less well than she. The tiny Vietnamese colonel, Nguyen Dao Tree, fell in a heap from the knotted ropes one afternoon and was taken to hospital. (He was back the next day, limping but game.) One woman, an older one, perhaps almost forty, fell flat on her face halfway up a rocky hill; she was taken away too, and she did not return.

One made quick friendships in such a place. She learned to call the colonel "Guy" and to respect his quick mind and sense of humor. She learned, too, to avoid being alone with him or with the sergeant, Sweggert—or indeed with any of the men, all of whom seemed to possess special reserves of strength when in the presence of an attractive female. Or an unattractive one. Her roommate, Corporal Elena Kristianides, was certainly not pretty, but more than once Nan staggered back to find the door locked and sounds of faint moans and giggles inside. When at last admitted, she always said forgivingly, "Please, it is all right, Kris. Do not speak of it." But it was not all right. She needed her sleep! Why didn't they need it too?

As days became weeks the fatigue lessened, the bruises healed, the reactions to the antiallergens diminished. The headaches stayed the same, but Nan was used to them, and she learned to take part in the friendly chatter in the mess hall. Always there were such stories! They were going to Kungson on a one-way trip and were expected to breed there and raise a new race of humans. They were not going to Kungson at all, but to a new planet, not yet announced or even named. They were not going into space at all. They were going to be parachuted onto the Scottish coast to commandeer the oil refineries. They were going to Antarctica, which was going to become a new Food Bloc colony, since a process had been discovered for melting the ice cap. At first Ana was frightened by such stories, then amused, then bored. She began making up stories of her own and found them as quickly passed along as any other. But some of the stories seemed true. Even some terrible ones: an unexplained accident in space that had destroyed the Peeps' resupply ships and even their tachyon-transit satellite itself. She let herself be late for dinner that night to listen to the evening news; sure enough, it was official. How terrifying! What would it mean to Ahmed? But then the news went on to say that the expeditions of the Fuel and Food blocs had offered help to the expedition of the People's Republics, and with her heart full, Ana hurried to the dining room, demanded attention, and proposed that they all sign a letter of sympathy and good wishes to their colleagues of the People's Bloc. The faces all turned to her, then whispered among themselves, half-embarrassed, but in the long run they let her write the letter, and they all signed. The next afternoon her training supervisor even excused her early to carry the document to the office of the camp commandant. He listened to her blankly, read the document three times, and then promised to send it through channels. At dinner that night she reported glowingly what had happened, but her news was drowned in other news. There were three new stories. First, that they were to receive a large shipment of new trainees the next day. Second, that a date had been set for their flight to Kungson, less than three weeks in the future. And third, contradictorily, that the whole project was about to be canceled.

Such stories! Nan stood up angrily, rapping her fork against her thick chinaware cup. "How can you all believe this nonsense?" she demanded. "How can all of these be true at once?" But not many of the others were paying attention, and she felt a tug at her elbow.

It was the colonel, who had, as he often did, squeezed in between Ana and her roommate at the table in order to try his fortunes one more time. "Sweet, beautiful Ana," he said, "don't make a fool of yourself. I know something of these stories, and they are all true."

That one of them was true was proved the next morning. Sixty-five more persons arrived at the base, and Ana knew one of them! It was the blond woman who was Godfrey Menninger's daughter.

Of course, everything was turned topsy-turvy. All of the billeting accommodations were changed to make room for the new arrivals—no, not for that reason alone, Ana realized, because most of the new ones, and quite a few of the old ones, were housed in another barracks half a kilometer away. Nan lost her WAC corporal roommate and feared at once that she would get Colonel Guy back again. But that did not happen. He went to the other barracks, and Nan was moved in with the Canadian woman, whose specialty seemed to be growing food crops in unusual circumstances. Marge Menninger caught sight of Nan in the crowd and waved to her. But they had no chance to speak—not that Ana had any particular reason to want to speak to the American, anyway—and in all the confusion, she was nearly an hour late for her morning session with the female balloonist.

The creature was no longer a specimen to Ana. She was a friend. Into the cognitive half of Ana's brain the songs of the balloonists had poured. In the first day she had learned to understand a few simple phrases, in a week to communicate abstract thoughts; now she was almost fluent. Ana had never thought of herself as having any kind of a singing voice, but the balloonist was not critical. They sang to each other for hours on end, and more and more Shirley's songs were sad and despairing, and sometimes even disconnected. She was, she told Ana, the last survivor of the dozen or more of her species who had been wrenched from Kungson and hurled to this inhospitable place. She did not expect to live much longer. She sang to Ana of the sweetness of warm pollen in a damp cloud, of the hot, stinging sadness of egg-spraying, of the communal joy of the flock in chorus. She told Ana that she would never sing in the flock again. She was thrice right. She would not have dared sing with her voice so pitifully harsh and weak because the gas pump gave her only faltering tones. She had no chance of being returned to Kungson. And she knew death was near.

Two days later she was dead. Ana arrived at the zoo to find her cage empty and Julia Arden supervising the sterilization of its parts.

"Don't take on," she advised gruffly. "You've learned all you need to know."

"It is not for the learning that I weep. It is because I have lost someone dear."

"Christ. Get out of here, Dimitrova. How did they let a jerk like you into this project in the first place? Crying over a dead fartbag and sending love letters to the Peeps—you're really out of it!"

Ana marched back to the barracks, threw herself down on her cot, and allowed herself to weep as she had not done in months—for Shirley, for Ahmed, for the world, and for herself. "Out of it" described her feelings exactly. How had everything become so hideous and complex?

That afternoon in the exercise field was an ordeal. The physical strain was no longer a real problem, but for some days now the "exercises" had taken a new turn. All of them, her own original detachment as well as the new arrivals, had been working less to strengthen their muscles and reflexes than to learn to handle unfamiliar equipment—unfamiliar to Ana, at least. She observed that all of the new people, and some of the old, had obviously had experience with it already. Such equipment! Heavy hoses like water cannon, backpack tanks and nozzles like flamethrowers, lasers, even grenade launchers. For what grotesque purpose was all this intended? Tight-lipped, Ana did as she was told. Repeatedly she found herself in difficulties and had to be bailed out by one of the others. The colonel saved her from incinerating herself with a flamethrower, and Sergeant Sweggert had to rescue her when the recoil of her water cannon knocked her off her feet.

"Please do not concern yourself," she gasped furiously, pulling herself erect and reaching once more for the hose. "I am quite all right."

"Hell you are," he said amiably. "Lean into it more, honey, you hear? It doesn't take muscle, just a little brains."

"I do not agree."

He shook his head. "Why do you get so uptight, Annie?"

"I do not like being trained in the use of weapons!"

"What weapons?" He grinned at her. "Don't you know this stuff is only to use against vermin? Colonel Menninger spelled it all out for us. We don't want to kill any sentients; that's against the law, and besides, we'll all get our asses in a crack. But all the intelligent ones got little cousins, crabrats and airsharks and things that dig around in the dirt and come out and chew your ass off. *Those* are what we're going to use this stuff for."

"In any event," said Ana, "I do not require assistance from you, sergeant—even if I believed you, or your Colonel Menninger, which I do not."

Sweggert looked past her and pursed his lips. "Hello, there, colonel," he said. "We was just talking about you."

"So I noticed," said Margie Menninger's voice. Ana turned slowly, and there she was. Looking, Ana observed without regret, quite poorly. The shots were having their way with her; her face was broken out in cerise blotches, her eyes were red and running, and her hair showed dark roots. "Get on with it, sergeant," she said. "Dimitrova, see me in my room after chow."

She turned away and raised her voice. "All right, all of you," she cried. "Get your asses down! Let's see how you crawl!"

Rebelliously Ana dropped to the ground and practiced the way of worming herself across an open field that she had learned the day before. These were infantry tactics! What nonsense for a scientific expedition! She conserved her anger carefully, and it lasted her the rest of the afternoon, through dinner, and right up to the moment she knocked on Menninger's door in that other barracks halfway across the base.

"Come in." Lt. Col. Menninger was sitting at a desk in a white, fluffy dressing gown, rimless granny glasses on her nose, a half-eaten dinner tray pushed to one side. She looked up from some papers and said, "Take a seat, Ana. Do you smoke? Would you like a drink?"

The angry fires inside Ana banked themselves. But they were still ready to blaze out. "No, thank you," she said, in general, to all.

Margie stood up and poured herself a scant shot of whiskey. She would have preferred marijuana, but she did not care to share a joint with this Bulgarian. She sipped a centimeter off the top of the drink and said, "Personal question. What have you got against Sweggert?"

"I have nothing against Sergeant Sweggert. I simply do not care to make love with him."

"What are you, Dimitrova, some maximum women's libber? You don't have to ball him on the parade ground. Just let him give you a hand when he wants to."

"Colonel Menninger," Ana said precisely, "are you ordering me to encourage his sexual overtures so that I can complete the obstacle course more readily?"

"I am not ordering you to do diddly-shit, Dimitrova. What is it with you? Sweggert comes on to everything with a hole in it. It's his nature. He comes on to me, too. I could put the son of a bitch in Leavenworth for the places his hands have been on the drill field. But I won't, because he's a good sol— Because he's essentially a good person. He'll help you if you let him. You can always tell him to fuck off later on."

"This I consider immoral, Colonel Menninger."

Margie finished her drink and poured half of another. "You're not too happy here, are you, Ana?"

"That is correct, Mis Menninger. I did not ask for this assignment."

"I did."

"Yes, no doubt, perhaps you did, but I—"

"No, that's not what I mean. I asked for it for myself, but I also asked for it for you. I picked you out by name, Ana, and it took hell's own conniving to make the Bulgarians turn you loose. They think you're pretty great at translating." She tossed down the rest of the drink and took off her glasses. "Look, Ana, I need you. This project is important to me. It should be important to you, too, if you have a spark of patriotism in your body."

"*Patriotism?*"

"Loyalty, then," said Margie impatiently. "Loyalty to our bloc. I know we come from different countries, but we stand for the same thing."

Ana found herself more puzzled than angered by this strange American. She tried to sort her feelings out and express them exactly. "Bulgaria is my home," she began. "I love my home. The Food Bloc—that is a much more abstract thing, Mis Menninger. I understand that in a world of two hundred nations there must be alliances and that one owes one's allies some sort of allegiance, or at least courtesy. But I cannot say I feel loyalty. Not to the Food Bloc."

"To the whole human race then, honey," said Margie. "Don't you see it? You just said it for yourself—a world of two hundred nations. But Klong can be a world of *one* nation! No fighting. No spies. No cloak-and-dagger shit. Who colonized America?"

"What?" It took Ana a moment to realize she was supposed to answer the question. "Why—the English? Before them, the Dutch."

"And before them maybe the Italians and Spaniards, with Columbus, and maybe, for Christ's sake, anybody you like—the Vikings, the Polynesians, the Chinese. Who knows? But the people who live in America now are the *Americans*. And that's who's going to live on Klong in another generation or two. The Klongans. Or whatever they call themselves. A single race of human beings. Never mind where they come from here! They'll be all the same, all part of the same wonderful . . . well, dream. I don't mind calling it a dream. But you and I can make it come true, Ana. We can learn how to live on Klong. We can build a world without national barriers and without the kind of senseless competition and rapacity that have ruined this one. Do you know what it means to have a whole new world to start over on?"

Ana was silent. "I—I have had some thoughts of that sort myself," she admitted.

"Of course you have. *And I want to make it happen.* I want to lay the foundations for a world society that understands planning and conservation and cooperation. Do you know how much we're putting into this? *Four ships.* Nearly ninety people. Thirty-five tons of equipment. The invasion of Europe cost less than this one launch, and believe me, everybody involved is screaming. It costs too much. It upsets the Peeps. The Greasies will raise their prices. We need the resources to solve the problems of the cities. Half the Congress would like to call it off tomorrow—"

"One has heard rumors," Ana said cautiously, "that the launch may be canceled."

Margie hesitated, and a shadow crossed her face. "No," she corrected. "That will not happen, because it is too important. But that is why I asked for you, Ana. If we can send ninety people, they must be the best ninety people there are. And you are the best translator I could find." She reached out and touched Ana's sleeve. "Do you understand?"

Ana drew away as soon as she could without giving offense, her thoughts uncertain. "Y-yes," she said unwillingly, and then, "but, on the other hand, no. What you say is most persuasive, Mis Menninger, but what has it to do with the use of flamethrowers and other weapons? Are we to build this fine monolithic world by destroying everyone else?"

"Of course not, Ana!" cried Margie, with as much shock and revulsion in her voice as she knew how to put there. "I give you my word!"

There was a silence. "I see," said Ana at last. "You give me your word."

"What else would you have me do?"

Ana said thoughtfully, "One has so little contact with the rest of the world here. I would like very much an opportunity to discuss this with others. Perhaps with my own delegation at the United Nations?"

"Why not?" exclaimed Margie. She looked thoughtful for a moment and then nodded. "I'll tell you what. As soon as training's over we're all going to get three days off. I'm going to New York myself. Come with me. We'll eat some decent food, go to a few parties. And you can talk it over with anyone you like. Agreed?"

Ana hesitated. At last, unwillingly, she said, "All right, Mis Menninger. That sounds attractive." It did not, for many reasons, but as a just person Ana had to concede that it sounded at least fair.

"Fine, honey. Now, if you don't mind, I'm overdue for a long, hot bath."

Margie locked the door behind the Bulgarian woman and ran herself a tub with some satisfaction. What the stupid prunt didn't know was that she was leaving Camp Detrick direct for the launch pad. The next chance she would have to talk anything over with anybody would be on Klong, and there let her say whatever she liked.

But Ana Dimitrova was only one problem, and maybe the easiest to solve. "One has heard rumors that the launch may be canceled" indeed! If Dimitrova had heard them, then everybody had heard them, and maybe the rumors were close to being true.

Margie allowed herself five minutes of luxurious soaking in the tub. When she got out she draped a towel around her body, not from modesty but from distaste; the shots had raised angry red welts all over her skin, and even with the ointment and the pills they itched. She did not want to be seen like that. Certainly not by the senator. It was bad advertising for the merchandise.

As she was dialing Adrian Lenz's private number she looked at herself in the mirror, frowned, and switched to voice only. "Hello, honey," she said as soon as he was on the line. "I'm sorry there's no picture, but this place doesn't have all mod. cons., and anyway"—she giggled—"I don't have any clothes on."

"Hello, Margie." Senator Lenz's voice was neutral. It was the sort of tone one uses to a brother-in-law or an airport security guard; it said, I acknowledge there is a relationship between us, but don't push it. "I assume you're calling me about your proposed new launch."

"Just 'proposed,' Adrian? You voted for it three weeks ago."

"I know my own voting record, Margie."

"Of course you do, Adrian. Listen, I didn't call you up to quarrel with you."

"No, you didn't," said the senator. "You called me up to try to keep me in line. I was pretty sure you'd call. I'm even pretty sure of what you're going to say. You're going to tell me that we've got a hell of a big investment in Klong now and if we don't nourish it the whole thing might go down the tube."

"Something like that, senator," Marge Menninger said reluctantly.

"I was sure of it. You know, we've heard those arguments before. Every time the DoD wants something outrageous they start by asking some piss-ant amount as a 'study grant.' Then a little more because the study showed some really promising idea. Then some more because, gosh, senator, we've gone this far, let's not waste it. And then, the next thing you know, we've got some stupid new missile or antiballistic defense system or nuclear bomber. Not because any sensible person wants it, but because there was no place to stop. Well, Margie, maybe this is the place to stop Klong. Three days from now there's a committee meeting. I don't know which way I'm going to vote, because I don't have all the information yet. But I'm not making any promises."

Margie kept the disappointment out of her voice, but she was less successful with the anger. "This project means a hell of a lot to me, Adrian."

"Don't you think I know it? Listen, Margie, this is an open line, but I thought you might be interested in something. I've got tomorrow's early edition of the *Herald* here, and there's a story from Peiping. 'Authoritative sources' say that repair crews at their tactran satellite have definite evidence that the explosion which destroyed the satellite and two transport ships was of suspicious origin."

"I watch the news, Adrian. I saw that. And there was another story, too, that said that dissident elements within the People's Republics were thought to be responsible."

The senator was silent. Margie would have given a lot to have seen the expression on his face just then, even at the cost of revealing the sorry condition of her own, and her hand reached out to restore the vision circuit to the call. But then the senator said, "I guess that's all we should say under the circumstances, Margie. I agree with you about one thing. You've gotten us into this pretty deep." And he broke the connection.

Margie sat thoughtfully blow-drying her hair for the next ten minutes, while her mind raced. Then she picked up the phone and dialed the orderly room. "Colonel Menninger here," she said. "Notify the training officer that I will not be present for tomorrow's formations, and have transportation ready for me at oh eight hundred. I need to go to New York."

"Yes, ma'am," said the OD. He was not surprised. All members of the project were restricted to the base, and the orders said there were no exceptions. But he knew who had written the orders.

Margie sat impatiently in the audience section of the Security Council chamber, waiting to be called. The delegation from Peru was explaining its recent vote at considerable length while the other nine members of the council waited in varying degrees of fury to explain each other's. The question seemed to have something to do with the territorial limits for fishing fleets. Normally Margie would have paid close attention, but her mind was a good many light-years away, on Klong. When the young black woman came to fetch her for her appointment she forgot about Peru before she had left the auditorium.

The woman conducted her to an inconspicuous room marked Authorized Personnel Only and held the door open for her without going, or looking, inside.

"Hello, poppa," said Margie as soon as the door was closed, turning her cheek to be kissed.

Her father did not kiss her. "You look like hell," he said, his voice flat and without affection. "What the fuck have you been teaching these 'colonists' of yours?"

Margie was caught off guard; it was not any of the questions she had expected from him, and certainly not what she had come to discuss. But she responded at once. "I've been teaching them survival tactics. Exactly what I said I was going to teach them."

"Take a look at these," he said, spreading a sheaf of holoflat pictures before her. "Art exhibits from Heir-of-Mao's private collection. Cost me quite a lot to get them."

Margie held one up, wiggling it slightly to get the effect of three-dimensional motion. "Makes me look fat," she said critically.

"These came out of the pouch of a courier in Ottawa. You recognize them, I guess. There's one of your boys throwing a grenade. And a nice shot of a flamethrower drill. And another one of a girl, I won't say who, stabbing what looks a hell of a lot like a Krinpit with what looks a hell of a lot like a sword."

"Oh, hell, poppa, that's no sword. It's just a flat, sharp knife. I got the idea from watching the stew chef opening up oysters at the Grand Central Clam Bar. And that Krinpit's only a dummy."

"Hell's shitfire, Margie! That's combat technique!"

"It's survival, dear," she corrected. "What do you think? The biggest and ugliest dangers our boys and girls are going to face are the Krinpit and the burrowers and the balloonists and, oh, yes, not to forget the Greasies and the Peeps. I'm not advocating killing, poppa, I'm just teaching them how to handle themselves if killing is going on." Her face clouded. "All the same, I wish I knew who took those pictures."

"You will," he said grimly. "But it doesn't matter; those are just copies. The Peeps have the originals, and Tam Gulsmit's probably got a set of his own by now, and the Peeps and the Greasies on Klong are going to hear about it by next week at the latest, and interexpedition friendship is over. Did you listen to the debate in the council?"

"What? Oh, sure—a little."

"You should have listened a lot. Peru has just extended its ocean borders to a thousand kilometers."

Margie squinted, perplexed. "What does that have to do with maybe some fighting on Klong?"

"Peru wouldn't do that without a lot of backing from somebody. They're nominally Food, sure, because of the anchovy catch. But they don't have a pot to piss in when the fish go deep, so they try to keep friendly with the other blocs."

"Which one?"

Her father pushed the corners of his eyes up. He did not do it because there was any risk of this supersensitive room being bugged; it was only a reflex not to speak the name of Heir-of-Mao unnecessarily.

Margie was silent for a moment while the card sorter in her brain ordered her hierarchy of priorities. She came back to Number One. "Poppa," she said, "Peru can stick their anchovies in their ear, and I'm not going to lose sleep abut which one of my people is a spy, and if we get a little scandal about combat training we'll survive it. None of it's going to matter in two or three weeks, because we'll be there, and that's what I came to see you about. Adrian Lenz is crawfishing. I need help, poppa. Don't let him cancel us out."

Her father leaned back in his chair. Margie was not used to seeing Godfrey Menninger looking old and tired, but that was how he looked now.

"Sweetie," he said heavily, "do you have any idea how much trouble we're in?"

"Of course, I do, poppa, but—"

"No, listen. I don't think you do. There's a tanker aground on Catalina Island today, with six hundred thousand tons of oil that isn't going to get to Long Beach. Wouldn't matter, normally. Southern California keeps plenty of reserves. But their reserves got diverted to your project, so they're low now. Unless they get that tanker afloat in forty-eight hours, Los Angeles is going to spend the weekend in a brownout. What do you think is going to be the public reaction to that?"

"Well, sure, a certain amount of shit is going to—"

He raised his hand. "And you saw the story in this morning's papers. The Peeps know their tactran satellite was deliberately destroyed."

"No, it wasn't! That was an accident. The bomb was just supposed to knock out the supply ship!"

"An accident in the commission of a crime becomes part of the crime, Margie."

"But they can't prove— I mean, there's no way in the world that they can pin it on me unless—"

She looked at her father. He shook his head. "The Italian isn't going to tell them anything. He's already been taken out."

So poor Guido was not going to live to spend his hundred thousand petrodollars. "He gave good value," she said. "Look what you got out of his microfiches. You have proof that the Greasies set up their base where they did because they had seismic scans to show oil under it. That's against treaty right there."

"Don't be a child, Margie. What does 'proof' have to do with it? Sir Tam and the Slopies can't prove you handed Ghelizzi the bomb, but they don't have to prove, they only have to know. And they do. Peru proves it. Not to mention a few other little news items you may not have heard about yet, like the American embassy in Buenos Aires being fire-bombed this morning. That's a little message from Sir Tam or Heir-of-Mao, I would judge. What do you suppose the next message is going to be?"

Margie realized she had been scratching her blisters and made herself take her hand away. "Oh, shit," she said glumly, and thought hard while her father waited.

But really, she reflected, the basic rules were unchanged. The equation of power was utterly clear. No nation could afford to fight any other nation in the whole world anymore. Food, Fuel, and People each owned enough muscle to smash both the others flat, and all of them knew it. Worse than that. Even the tiniest nation had a minute sliver of muscle of its own, gift of the breeder reactors and the waste reclaimers. Not enough to matter in a global sense, no. But Peru could enforce its decisions if driven to. Ecuador could kill Washington or Miami, Denmark could destroy Glasgow, Indonesia could obliterate Melbourne. Fire-bombings and riots—well, what did they matter? There was a permanent simmer of border incidents and small-scale violence. Each year, a few thousand injured, a few scores or hundreds dead. But the lid never blew off, because everybody knew what would happen.

"Poppa," she said, "you know nobody can do anything *really* serious. The balance of power prohibits it."

"Wrong! The balance of power breaks down as soon as somebody makes a mistake. The Peeps made one when they fired rockets at our gasbags on Klong. *I* made one when I let you carry that bomb to Belgrade. It's time to pull the fuses, honey."

For the first time in her adult life, Margie Menninger felt real fear. "Poppa! Are you saying you're not going to help me with Lenz?"

"I'm saying more than that, Margie. I agree with him. I'm seeing the President tomorrow, and I'm going to tell him to scrap the launch."

"*Poppa!*"

He hesitated. "Honey, maybe later. After things quiet down—"

"Later's no good! You think the Peeps aren't going to reinforce as soon as they can get another satellite up there? And the Greasies? And—"

"*It's settled, Margie.*"

She looked at him, appalled. This was the God Menninger that his whole agency knew and she had rarely seen. It wasn't her father she was looking at. It was a human being as implacable and determined as she herself had ever been, and with the accustomed support of a great deal of power to back his decisions up.

She said, "I can't change your mind." It wasn't a question, and he didn't give it an answer.

"Well," she said, "there's no reason for me to hang around here then, is there? Good-bye, poppa. Take care of yourself. I'll see you another time."

She did not look at him again as she got up, collected her brown leather officer's bag and her uniform cap, and let herself out.

If her father was as determined as she, the other side of the coin was that she was no less determined than he. She stopped in the visitors' lounge and entered a public phone booth to dial a local number.

The woman on the other end was a strikingly handsome human being, not a sex symbol but a work of art. "Why, Marjorie," she said. "I thought you were off doing spy stuff for your father or something—Marjorie! What's the matter with your face?"

Marge felt her blotched chin. "Oh, that. That's just a reaction to some shots. Can I come over to see you?"

"Of course, lover. Right now?"

"Right this second, mom." Margie hung up the phone and hurried toward the elevators. But before she entered them she stopped in a ladies' room to check her makeup.

Marge Menninger's mother lived, among other places, in the residential tower section of one of New York City's tallest and most expensive skyscrapers. It was an old-fashioned place, built when energy was cheap, so that it made economic sense at that time to economize on insulation and rely on huge inputs of BTUs all winter long and continuous air conditioning all summer. It was one of the few that had not been at least partly rebuilt when oil reached P$300 a barrel, and it would have been ruinously expensive for most tenants—even most well-to-do tenants. The condominium apartments were no more expensive to buy than any others in a good neighborhood. But if you had to ask what the maintenance costs would be, you couldn't afford them. Alicia Howe and her present husband didn't have to ask.

The butler welcomed Margie. "How nice to see you, Miss Menninger! Will you be using your room this time?"

"Afraid not, Harvey. I just want to talk to mom."

"Yes, Miss Margie. She's expecting you."

As Alicia Howe rose to be kissed, she made a quick, all-seeing inventory of her daughter. Those awful splotches on her complexion! The clothes were passable enough, as army uniforms went, and thank heaven the child had been born with her father's smiling good looks. "You could lose a couple of kilos, lover," she said.

"I will, I promise. Mom, I want you to do me a favor."

"Of course, hon."

"Poppa's being a little difficult about something, and I need to go public. I want to hold a news conference."

Alicia Howe's husband owned a lot of television: three major-city outlets and large interests in a dozen satellite networks. "I'm sure one of Harold's people can help you out," she said slowly. "Should I ask what the problem is?"

"Mom, you shouldn't even know there's a problem."

Her mother sighed. She had learned to live with God Menninger's off-the-record life while they were married, but since the divorce she had hoped to be free of it. She never talked to her ex-husband. It wasn't that she disliked him—in her heart, she still thought him the most interesting, and by a long way the sexiest, of her men. But she could not cope with the knowledge that any little slip of the tongue from him to her, and from her to anyone, might bring catastrophic consequences to the world.

"Honey, I do have to tell Harold something."

"Oh, sure, mom. But not as a problem. What I want to talk about is Kl—Jem. The planet Jem. I'm going there, mom."

"Yes, of course, you told me that. In a year or two, maybe, when things settle down—"

"I want to settle them down, mom. I want the United States to send enough muscle up there to make it fit to live in. Fit for you to visit someday, if you want to. And I want to do it now. I'm supposed to leave in eighteen days."

"Margie! Really, Margie!"

"Don't take on, will you? It's what I want."

Alicia Howe had not been able to prevail against that argument in more than a dozen years. She had no hope of prevailing against it now. The thought of her daughter flinging herself through space to some terrible place where people died disgustingly was frightening. But Margie had demonstrated a capacity for taking care of herself.

"Well," she said, "I guess I can't send you to your room. All right. You haven't told me what you want me to do."

"Ask Harold to get me onto one of his newsmaker programs. He'll know how to do it better than I can tell him. They're backing away from my planet, mom, cutting the funding, complaining about the problems. I want the public to know how important it is, and I want to be the one to tell them." She added strategically, "Poppa was right behind me on this at first, but now he's changed his mind. He wants to call the whole thing off."

"You mean you want to put the squeeze on your own father?"

"Exactly right."

Alicia Howe smiled. That part was sure to appeal to her current husband. She spread her hands resignedly and moved toward the phone. "I'll tell Harold what you want," she said.

Ana Dimitrova sat with her eyes closed in a broad, low room, elbows on a ring-shaped table, head in her hands, earphones on her head. Her lips were moving. Her head twitched from side to side as she tried to match the rhythms of the taped balloonist song that was coming over the headset. It was very difficult, in large part because it was not a balloonist's voice making the sounds. It was a Krinpit's. The tape had been made several weeks

before, when Detrick's last surviving Krinpit had had no one left
to talk to but Shirley, the one surviving balloonist.

But her name had not been Shirley. Her name, rather beautiful, had been *Mo'ahi'i Ba'alu'i*, which meant something like
Sweetly Golden Cloud-Bearer. Krinpit rasps and tympani did not
easily form the balloonist sounds. But Shirley had understood him
—no, Ana corrected herself, Mo'ahi'i Ba'alu'i had understood
him. Ana was determined to do the same, and so she played and
replayed sections of the tape:

Ma'iya'a hi'i (these creatures unlike us) *hu'u ha'iye'i* (are vicious animals).

And Cloud-Bearer's response:

Ni'u'a mali'i na'a hu'iha. (They have killed my song.)

Ana pushed the headphones off her ears and allowed herself to
rub her eyes. The headaches were very bad tonight. And this
awful room! Twenty headsets and tape-control panels before
twenty identical hard-backed chairs, all around the ring. So bleak!
So unsympathetic!

Unsympathetic? Ana clucked her lips at herself. That was one
of the English language's booby-trap words: sympathetic, *simpa-
tico*. They sounded so much alike. But they did not mean the
same thing, and it was embarrassing to a translator of Ana's skills
to fall into the blunder of confusing them. It proved she was too
tired to work anymore this night, and so she switched off the tape
decisively, hung the earphones on their hook, and stood up to go.
She intended to wish a courteous good night to those few other
eager project personnel who had shared her desire to put in over-
time at the tape ring. But there weren't any. They had all left
while she was concentrating.

It was nearly eleven o'clock! In six hours she would have to be
getting out of bed!

Hurrying down the empty company street toward her room,
Ana paused halfway, changed course, and entered the dayroom.
Really, these headaches were too bad! But there was a dispensing
machine in the dayroom, and sometimes one of the American soft
drinks containing caffeine would constrict the blood vessels and
reduce the thumping, thumping throb long enough for her to get
to sleep.

But as she dropped a dollar into the machine and waited for

the cup to fill, it seemed to her that coming here had been a mistake, after all. Such an ear-drubbing of noise! A dozen couples were dancing frenziedly to a stereo at one end of the room. At the other a young Oriental man had a guitar, and a group was singing with him, quite at cross-purposes to the music on the stereo. Quite uncaring. And even more noise came from the television alcove: a babble of excited voices, laughter. What could they be watching? She drifted closer to peer at the screen. Someone was lifting a pillowcase out of a sonic washer and exclaiming rapturously over its pristine shine. Were these people excited over a commercial?

"Oh, Nan," cried her roommate, elbowing toward her. "You missed it. She was *wonderful*."

"What? What did I miss? Who was wonderful?"

"Lieutenant Colonel Menninger. It was really super. You know," confided the woman, "I never really liked her. But tonight she was just beautiful. She was on the six o'clock news. It was just a little person-to-person interview, like a follow-up to a story about Jem. I don't know why they picked her, but I'm glad they did! She said such wonderful things! She said Jem gave hope to all the unhappy people of the world. She said it was a planet where all the old hatreds could be forgotten. A place where—what did she say?—yes, a place where each child could elect a morality and an idea, and have the space and the freedom to live his life by it!"

Ana coughed Coca-Cola in a fine spray into her cupped hand. "Colonel Menninger said that?" she gasped.

"Yes, yes, Nan, and she said it beautifully. We were all touched. Even people like Stud Sweggert and Nguyen the Tryin' were *really* moved. I mean, they even kept their hands to themselves. And the newscaster said something about sending troops to Jem, and Colonel Menninger said, 'I'm a soldier myself. Every country has soldiers like me, and every one of us prays we'll never have anything to do. But on Jem we can do something useful! Something for peace, not for destruction. Please let us do it.'— What?"

Nan had been marveling to herself in Bulgarian. "No, no, please go on," she said.

"Well. And just now they repeated parts of it on the late report, and they said the public response has been incredible. Telegrams, phone calls. To the White House and the UN and the networks—I don't know where all."

Ana forgot her headache. "Perhaps I have been doing Colonel Menninger an injustice. Truly, I am amazed."

"Well, I am too! But she made me feel really good about what we're doing, and everyone's talking about it!"

And they were. Not only in the barracks dayroom. Senator Lenz's phones were ringing, and it was constituents urging him to make sure the heroes on Jem got support. Newsrooms around the country were watching the electronic tally of calls from the public: Jem, Jem! Spot pollsters were reporting great and growing public concern. God Menninger's phone rang only once, but the person on the other end was the President of the United States. When he hung up, Menninger's face was tense and stern, but then it relaxed and he broke into a smile. "Honey," he said to empty space, "damn your black heart, you do your old man proud."

·THIRTEEN·

FOR TWENTY KILOMETERS Charlie and his flock tried to follow the little biplane as it chugged and bounced through the sky of Jem. No use. The balloonists soared high, swooped low, found winds that carried them toward the Heat Pole, but never fast enough to keep up. Charlie sang a mournful farewell song into his radio as they turned away, and the sound penetrated even the noisy rattle of the little engine inside the plane. "Too much noise," shouted Kappelyushnikov cheerfully into Danny Dalehouse's ear. "Turn off, please?"

"Let me say good-bye first." Dalehouse sang into the tiny radio, then switched it off. Far behind and half a kilometer overhead, the flock bobbed acknowledgment. Dalehouse craned his neck to see forward, but the camp of the Greasies was of course nowhere yet in sight. They were flying almost directly toward the Heat Pole—"southeast" by the convention of considering the poles of rotation as north and south, however irrelevant that was to compasses and sextants—and it was uphill almost all the way. How foolish of the Greasies to locate their camp in the least hospitable part of the planet! But who could figure why the Greasies did things?

Kappelyushnikov leaned over and slapped him on the shoulder. "You wish to puke?" he called encouragingly, pointing over the side of the cockpit. Dalehouse shook his head. "Is all right, you know," Cappy went on. "Is little rough, yes. We are fighting winds, not making love to them like in balloon. But you have truly outstanding aircraft technician in charge!"

"I'm not complaining." And in fact, he had no reason to complain. The biplane was a technological marvel on Klong—on Jem, as they were supposed to call it now, he reminded himself. At least they were flying! The Greasy camp was hard to reach any other way. There were no cars on Jem, because no roads. Only a tracked vehicle could go very far, and even the Greasies did not have them to spare. Because, in their pigheaded way, the Greasies had camped ten kilometers from the nearest usable water, boats were out. You could fly there for this semi-summit meeting that was supposed to make everyone on Jem friends again. Or you could walk. And Dalehouse spared a thought of compassion for the poor, proud, pedestrian Peeps, who were no doubt doing just that somewhere below.

So just to be flying was a triumph, although he wished Cappy had not brought up the subject of airsickness. It was not so much the motion that was bothering him as the food they had been eating. With twenty-two more mouths to feed, the old catch-as-catch-can meal style was down the drain. Unfortunately, the new people had brought their appetites, but they had forgotten to pack a chef to satisfy them. The food was unbearable. No one dared complain. The person who bitched would be the next cook.

Still, the community was growing. The third resupply ship had brought a great deal! This sputtering little two-winged airplane, folded and stacked and foolish-looking, but demonstrably workable, because it was working. The little plutonium-powered machines and instruments that had given Morrissey sensors to study the Creepies in their tunnels under the ground and Dalehouse himself radios to pass on to Charlie. A new Argus orbiter to photograph clouds and help them predict the weather. Or at least to guess at it a little more accurately.

It had even helped them in their attempts to make contact with sentients. Sort of. Charlie was delighted with his crossbow and his radio. Jim Morrissey had taken another tack. He had used the new power auger to make three widely spaced holes along a Creepy burrow. The end holes held soft charges of explosives, the center one a hose connected to the exhaust of the auger's little gasoline putt-putt. When Morrissey blew the charges he sealed both ends of that section of the tunnel, and the carbon monoxide caught four burrowers before they could dig away. By then they were no good for Dalehouse's purposes, of course, but they were a joy to Morrissey.

Even further marvels were on their way. The third resupply had brought eight metric tons of equipment, but according to the tactran messages the next would bring nearly fifty, plus maybe a hundred additional personnel. It would be a city! The summons to the meeting at the Fuel camp had not only been a welcome tour of Jem, it had been a reprieve from the tedium of erecting tents to receive the reinforcements.

What the tactran had failed to say was just what the reinforcements would be used for. They certainly needed any number of specialists they didn't have. A *real* cook. A dentist. Some better-looking women. A better translator . . . reminded, Dalehouse leaned back to see how Harriet was faring behind him.

The translator was most uncomfortably curled up in a space no more than a meter square, and studded, at that, with bolts and levers that must have been tattooing Harriet's hips and ribs indelibly. If she had been anyone else Dalehouse would have thought of some friendly, commiserating remark. For Harriet he could find none. Her eyes were closed. Her expression registered resignation to the palpable injustice of being the smallest of the three of them, and thus the one to be squeezed into the tiny rear compartment.

"Getting close," Kappelyushnikov bawled in his ear.

Dalehouse leaned forward, rubbing at the glass as though the Jemman murk were on the inside rather than all around. There was nothing but maroon cloud—

Then the stark white rim of the Heat Pole glittered through a break. And something else. The clouds themselves were clearly bright. As the biplane tunneled out of the last of the cloud bank they were leaving, Dalehouse saw the cause before him.

"Jesu Crist!" cried Kappelyushnikov. "Have they no shame?"

The light was the Oily camp. It stood out on the horizon like a bonfire, penetrating Jem's dour maroon murk with beacons, lighted windows—my God, Dalehouse marveled, even streetlamps!

It was no longer an expeditionary camp. It looked like a small town.

The vertical beacon dipped and swept across the biplane to acknowledge their approach, then courteously away so that they were not dazzled. Kappelyushnikov muttered inaudibly into his radio mouthpiece, listened for a moment, and then began to circle.

"What's the matter?" Dalehouse demanded.

"Is nothing the matter, only we are no longer in hurry," said the pilot. "Peeps will be unavoidably one hour detained, so let us study this miracle before landing on it."

A miracle it very nearly was. There were only about forty people in the Greasy camp, but they seemed to have almost that many buildings. *Buildings*, not tents or plastic huts. What had they made them out of? And what buildings! Some were barracks, some seemed individual bungalows. One looked more like a tenth-size copy of the Eiffel Tower than like a structure one could live or work in. Another was a good twenty-five meters in length. And —what was that curious, shallow, round petaled cone on the far side of the camp? It seemed to be constructed of bent strips of shiny metal arrayed around a central black cylinder. Could it be a solar generator? If so, it was almost megawatt size! And—that stubby tower with the horizontally rotating fan. Wasn't that the exhaust from an *air conditioner?*

Harriet had roused herself and was leaning forward over Dalehouse's shoulder to see. Her breath buzzed annoyingly in his ear as she said sternly, "That is a . . . *lascivious* waste!"

"Oh, yes, dear Gasha!" cried the pilot. "How wonderful would be if we, too, could afford one!"

Over the rattles and groans that came from his Krinpit escort, Ahmed Dulla heard a sputtering distant sound. "Put me down. Wait. Try to be quiet," he called peevishly in the mixture of Urdu and their own language that made communication possible between them. Or sometimes did. He lowered himself from the litter in which they had been carrying him and climbed onto a knee of a many-tree, pushing aside the pinkly glowing fronds to stare around the sky. A tiny two-winged aircraft was chuttering along just below cloud level. "So. Another triumph of technology arrives," he said.

The Krinpit, Jorrn-fteet, reared back to study him more carefully, its stubby claws waving. "Your meaning is not loud," it rattled.

"No matter. Let us move on." Dulla was in no mood for a nice chat with these grossly hypertrophied bugs, however useful they were to him. "Go carry the litter and my bag; I will walk," he ordered. "It is too steep here for riding." They were climbing from the shallow valley of the river now, up through the last of the forested slopes onto the dry highlands. The vegetation began to change from many-trees and ferns to things like succulents, stubby barrels with glowing, bright red, luminous buttons. Dulla looked at them all with distaste. Study the plants, find new products; it is in this way that my fathers became independent of the machines of the outside world. So Feng Hua-tse had advised before he left; but Dulla was an astrophysicist, not an herbal healer, and he had no intention of following the fool's instructions.

There was no overhang between him and the sky now, and he could see the little biplane circling, far off toward the bright white line of the Heat Pole. So. The Greasies had their helicopter, the Fats now had a plane, and what did the representative of the People's Republics have to take him to this meeting? A litter carried by animals that looked like squashed crustaceans. Dulla fumed. If Feng had listened to him, they would have insisted that the three-party meeting be held at their own camp. So they would have been spared this humiliation of arriving on a plastic frame carried by creatures out of some children's nonsense fable—if not the humiliation of exposing to the Fats and the Oilies the meanness of their encampment. What a disaster! And all Feng's fault, or Heir-of-Mao's. The expedition should have been properly supplied and reinforced in the first place, but leave it to the Chinamen to hoard coppers to the ruination of the project.

Without warning the Krinpit stopped, and Dulla, lost in his thoughts, almost tripped over them. "What, what?" he complained. "Why are you standing here?"

"A very loud thing moves quickly," rattled Jorrn-fteet.

"I do not hear anything." But now that he was awakened from his reverie he did see something, a swell of dust behind the hills. As he watched, a machine topped the rise, coming toward him. It was still a kilometer away, but it looked like a half-track.

"Another triumph of conspicuous waste," sneered Dulla. "How dare they come for me, as though I could not make the journey by myself?" The Krinpit rattled inquiringly, and he added, "Never mind. Put down the litter; I will carry my knapsack myself now. Hide yourselves. I do not want the Greasies to see you."

But the words conveyed no meaning to the Krinpit. A Krinpit could never hide from another Krinpit as long as they were close enough to hear each other. Dulla struggled to explain. "Go back to the place behind the hill. The Greasies will not hear you there. I will return in the space it took us to come up from the river." He was not sure they understood that, either. The Krinpit had a clear sense of time, but the vocabulary of terms to mark its units did not map well from one language based on a diurnal cycle to another which had evolved on a planet without easy temporal reference points. But they lurched away obediently, and Dulla walked steadily toward the approaching half-track.

The driver was a Kuwaiti, apparently a translator, because he greeted Dulla in flawless Urdu. "Would you like a lift?" he called. "Jump in!"

"You are very courteous," smiled Dulla. "Indeed, it is a little warm for strolling today." But it was not courtesy at all, he fumed internally, it was only more of their damnable arrogance! Ahmed Dulla was quite sure that he was the only person on Jem whose native language was Urdu, and here the Greasies had made sure they had someone who could speak to him! As though he himself were not already proficient in four other languages!

The time would come, he promised himself, when he would humble the ostentatious swine. So he rode up over the gullied hills toward the Greasy camp, chatting amiably with the Kuwaiti, remarking politely on the fine appearance of their camp, his face smiling and his heart swelling with rage.

The official host for the meeting was named Chesley Pontrefact, London-born but not of native roots that went many generations back. His skin was purplish brown and his hair white wool. Coded tactran messages had given Dulla a good deal of background on every member of the Greasy expeditions, as well as the Fats, and he knew that Pontrefact was an air vice-marshal and nominal commander of the Greasy expedition. But he also knew that real power belonged to one of the civilians from Saudi Arabia.

Pontrefact bustled about the long conference table (wood! shipped all the way from Earth!) offering drinks and smokes. "Brandy do you, Dr. Dalehouse?" he inquired solicitously. "And perhaps a Coca-Cola for you, sir? I'm afraid we don't have orange juice, but at least there's ice."

"Nothing, please," said Dulla, seething. Ice! "I suggest we begin our meeting, if that is convenient."

"Certainly, Dr. Dulla." Pontrefact sat down heavily at the head of the table and glanced inquiringly around. "Mind if I take the chair, just for form's sake?"

Dulla watched to see if any of the Fats were going to object and spoke a split second before they did. "Not at all, Marshal Pontrefact," he said warmly. "We are your guests." But one should show courtesy to guests, and what was this seating arrangement but a deliberate insult? Pontrefact at the head, two of his associates at the foot—the Kuwaiti translator and a woman who could be no one but the Saudi civilian who was the Greasies' decision maker. On one side of the table were all three of the Fats—Dalehouse, their Russian pilot, and their own translator; and on the other—only himself. How much more deliberately could they point out that he was alone and insignificant? He added diffidently, "Since we are all conversant, I believe, with English, perhaps we can dispense with the translators. It is an old saying of my people that the success of a conference is inversely proportional to the square of the number of participants."

Quickly, "I shall stay," said the Fats translator. Pontrefact raised his white-caterpillar eyebrows but said nothing; Dulla shrugged politely and gazed toward the chair, waiting for the proceedings to begin.

The Saudi whispered to the interpreter at some length. Across the table, Dalehouse hesitated, then got up to extend his hand to Dulla. "Good to see you looking fit, Ahmed," he said.

Dulla touched his hand minimally. "Thank you." He added grudgingly, "And thank you for assisting in returning me to my own camp. I have not had a chance to express my gratitude since."

"Glad to help. Anyway, it's good to see someone from your expedition—we don't see many of you, you know."

Dulla glared. Then, stiffly, "I have come a long way for this meeting. Can we not begin?"

"Oh, hell," said Pontrefact from the head of the table. "Look, mates, the whole reason for this meeting is to try to work together better. We know what a balls-up our masters have made at home. Shall we see if we can do a bit better here?"

Dulla said happily, "Please limit your observations to your own people." It was as he had suspected; the Greasies were going to insult everyone but themselves. Let this West Indian whose grandfather was a ticket collector on the London Underground make a fool of himself if he chose. Not of the People's Republics.

"But I'm in dead earnest, Dr. Dulla. We invited you here because it's clear we are all working at cross-purposes. Your own camp is in serious trouble, and we all know it. The Food people and our own lot are a bit better off, yes. But you don't have a proper doctor, do you, Dr. Dalehouse? Not to mention a few other things. And we can't be expected—that is, we don't have limitless resources either. Under the UN resolution we are all supposed to cooperate and divide the responsibilities. Particularly the science. We undertook the geology, and you can't say we haven't played fair about that. We've done a great deal."

"Indeed so," put in Kappelyushnikov blandly. "Is pure coincidence that most is in personal vicinity and relates primarily to fissionables and to salt domes."

"That is, to petroleum," Dulla agreed. "Yes, I think we are all aware of that, Marshal Pontrefact." How thoughtful of the Fats and the Greasies to begin quarreling among themselves so soon!

"Be that as it may," the chairman went on doggedly, "there's a hell of a lot to be done here, and we can't do it all. Astronomy, for instance. We did orbit a satellite observatory, but—as I am sure you know—it ran into malfunctions. Let me show you something." He got up and moved to a likris screen on the wall. When he had fiddled with it for a moment the crystals sprang into varicolored light, showing some sort of graph. "You've seen our solar generator. This shows the solar input for our power plant. As you see, there are spikes in the curve. This may not seem important to you, but our generator is a precision instrument. It isn't going to do its job properly if the solar constant isn't, well, constant."

Dulla stared in black envy at the graph. That was what he was here for, after all—because he was a specialist in stellar studies! He hardly noticed when Dalehouse put in, "If Kung is acting up, it many mean more to us than a few wiggles in your power supply."

Pontrefact nodded. "Of course it may. We notified this to Herstmonceux-Greenwich with a copy of the tape. They're quite upset about it. Kung may be a variable star."

"Hardly," sneered Dulla. "It is known that a few flares are possible."

"But it is not known how many, or how big; and that's exactly what we need to know. What, if I may say, we confidently expected to know from the astronomical researches that were meant to be conducted by your expedition, Dr. Dulla."

Dulla exploded. "But this is too much! How can one practice astrophysics when one is hungry? And whose fault is that?"

"Certainly not ours, old chap," Pontrefact said indignantly.

"But someone blew up our ships, *old chap*. Someone killed thirty-four citizens of the People's Republics, old chap!"

"But that was—" Pontrefact stopped the sentence in mid-syllable. He made a visible effort to control his temper. "Be that as it may," he got out again, "the plain fact is the work's got to be done, and someone's got to do it. You have the instruments and we don't, at least not until proper telescopes arrive from Earth. We have the manpower, and you evidently don't."

"I beg your pardon. Allow me to inform you of my academic standing. I am director of the Planetology Institute at Zulfikar Ali Bhutto University and have graduate degrees in astrophysics from—"

"But no one's disputing your degrees, dear man, only your fitness to function. Let us send our own astronomer over. Better still, let Boyne airlift your equipment here, where there's better seeing—"

"Certainly not! Not either!"

"I really don't think that's quite fair, do you? We've certainly cooperated in providing food, for instance—"

"Such food! For your people, not for ours: all flour, hardly any rice."

Dalehouse said placatingly, "We'll turn up some rice for you if that's what you like."

"How gracious of you!" Dulla sneered.

"Now, wait a minute, Dulla. We've done our best for you—and we have a couple of complaints of our own, if you want to know. Like shooting at me!"

Dulla grimaced. "That was only Hua-tse's foolishness with fireworks. The People's Republics have already expressed their regrets."

"To whom? The dead balloonists?"

"Yes," sneered Dulla with exaggerated humility, "of course, it is so; we do apologize to your close friends, the comic gasbags. And to yours too, sir, the vermin who dig in the earth and whom you find so useful!"

"If you mean the Creeps," said Pontrefact, his control of his temper wearing thin, "at least we don't use them as litter bearers."

"No! You use them to help you exploit the mineral riches! Is it not true that there has been radiation disease among them?"

"No, it isn't! At least, not here. We did use a few to dig samples for us in other areas, and yes, they did encounter some radiation, but I must say that I resent the imputation that we are exploiting the natives."

"Oh, I am sure you would not do that, Marshal Pontrefact, especially as your own ancestors must have experienced so much of that from the other side, as it were."

"Now, look here, Dulla!"

But Pontrefact was interrupted by the Saudi woman, who said: "I think we should recess for lunch. We have much to discuss, and shouting at each other will not help. Let's resolve to try to do better in the afternoon."

But the afternoon session, if quieter, did not seem very productive to Danny Dalehouse. "At least we got a decent meal out of it," he said to Kappelyushnikov outside the longhouse where they had met.

"Is as ashes in my mouth," growled the Russian. "Oh, how many nice things they have here. Not just food."

That was not to be argued. Across from the meetinghouse a new building was going up. A tracked dumpster deposited a scoop of earth into a hopper; the man running it shoved a lever forward, there was a high-pitched whine, and moments later, the sides fell away and the operator lifted out a finished panel of hard brick. The trick was in adding something to the compacted earth as a stabilizer.

"And have you seen what's up on the hill?" asked Harriet with jealousy in her tone. On the slopes above the colony there were terraced rows of green seedlings. *Green!* The Greasies were using banks of incandescent plant lights to grow Terrestrial food!

"Feel like time when I was seventeen years," said Kappelyushnikov. "Kid sailplane pilot, winner of All-Region Height and Endurance Contest, fresh from Nizhniy Tagil, walking down Kalinin-Prospekt first time in life, and oh, my God, how overwhelming was Moscow! Trams, skyscrapers, bookstores, restaurants." He pointed to the plasma column of the solar generator, with its rosette of reflectors around it. "Is daunting, dear friends. No wonder Greasies call us here to issue orders of day. They have muscle to enforce!" He shrugged, then grinned as they rounded the last barracks and saw the little landing field. "Hoy! Boyne!" he shouted. "Come say good-bye to country cousins!"

The Irish pilot hesitated, then came toward them. "Hello," he said noncommittally. "I've just been putting our friend Dulla on a jeep on his way home."

"He didn't seem in a very good mood," Dalehouse observed.

The pilot grinned. "His feelings were hurt, I'd say. He didn't want us to see that he was using Krinpit transportation to get here. You didn't know that? They came up the river by boat, and then the Krips carried him up eight or ten kilometers until we picked him up."

Harriet said spitefully, "He might have been in a better mood if you hadn't gone out of your way to insult him, Dalehouse."

"Me? How?"

"He thought you were making a joke about the fact that so few of the Peeps have survived. His face went all tight."

Dalehouse protested. "I didn't mean anything like that. He's such a thorny son of a bitch."

"Forget," advised Kappelyushnikov. "He is such close friend of cockroaches, let them worry about his feelings."

"Well, I don't understand that either, Cappy. The Krinpit almost killed him."

"Then how is possible they become native bearers for fine Pakistani sahib as he daringly marches through jungle?"

"I can explain that," Boyne said gloomily, "although I can't say I like it. That first Krinpit you and I carried here, Dalehouse, the one that calls itself Sharn-igon? It's mad at all human beings. Apparently its girlfriend, or actually I think it was a boyfriend, died from the first contact with the Peeps, and it just wants to get even. Only its idea of getting even seems to be to make as much trouble for as many human beings as it can. It's raised a hell of a fuss with the Krips near here; we can't make any contact with them at all. I guess it thinks the Peeps are pretty well screwed, so it's willing to help them screw the rest of us. Looks damn bad for the future, if you ask me."

He was walking along with them toward the airstrip, but his manner seemed reserved; he made no eye contact with any of them, and what he said was more of a monologue than a conversation.

Kappelyushnikov said placatingly, "Hey, Boyne, you pissed about something?"

"Me? Why should I be?" But Boyne still did not look at him.

Kappelyushnikov glanced at the others, then back to the pilot. "Hey, Boyne," he wheedled. "We two are members of great interstellar brotherhood of pilotry, should not be pissed at each other."

"Look, it's not you personally," said Boyne angrily. "I got my ass eaten out for lending you chaps the backhoe, not to mention talking a little more openly than I was supposed to about what we were doing here."

"But we're all in this together," Dalehouse put in. "It's like Pontrefact said at the meeting. We're supposed to share information."

"Oh, Ponty's got the right idea, but that's supposed to go both ways. You didn't see fit to mention some of your own little deeds, did you? Like arming the balloonists against the Krinpit?"

"We didn't! I mean, that's my own department, Boyne. We've given them a few simple weapons to protect themselves against the *ha'aye'i*, that's all."

"Well, they've been using them against everything they can

catch. Not to mention that business with the Peeps' supply ship."

"That was an accident!" Dalehouse said.

"Sure it was. Same as it's an accident that your plane—" He hesitated, then closed his mouth.

"Come on, Boyne, what are you trying to say?" Dalehouse demanded.

"Nothing. Forget it." Boyne glanced back toward the camp, then said rapidly, "Look, this peace conference was a bust, right? Nothing got settled. And the way things are going—well, I've got a bad feeling. The local Krips are gassing our Creepies in their burrows every once in a while—that's Peeps' doing, I suppose. The Peep ship gets blown up; you say it's an accident, but the gen says CIA. You're giving the Loonies weapons. And your plane—well, shit, man," he said, glaring at Kappelyushnikov. "I've got eyes. So right now I don't feel like having a heart-to-heart, all right? Maybe some other time. So, so long, and have a nice flight home." He nodded briskly and turned back to the Greasy base.

Kappelyushnikov broodingly watched him go. "I too have bad feeling," he said. "About dear friend and fellow pilot Boyne, too. Questions I would like to ask, but this is not good time."

"I'd like to know more about what they're using the Creepies for," Dalehouse agreed. "And frankly, that bit about our being responsible for the Peeps' accident is beginning to get under my skin. Do you think there's any possibility it could be true?"

Cappy regarded him thoughtfully. "You are very nice person, Danny," he said sadly. "Perhaps you do not wonder enough. Like, do you wonder why Greasies have landing strip when gillicopter lands anywhere?"

"That hadn't occurred to me," Dalehouse admitted.

"Occurred to me," said the Russian. "Just like occurred to Boyne to wonder why strange little hatch dear Gasha rode on is in our plane. You and Gasha look at it, you say, 'Oh, what a nuisance. Cannot understand purpose.' But when pilot looks at it, Boyne or me, we say at once, 'Oh, how strange that aircraft designed for peaceful exploration has built-in bomb bay.'"

Thirty meters below the airstrip, Mother dr'Shee woke with the smell of cyanide in her splayed nose, too faint to be dangerous, too strong to ignore. The Shelled Devils were at it again.

She yipped peremptorily for the brood-member on duty. It turned out to be t'Weechr, the runt of the litter and the one the others saddled with the least attractive jobs—including, she realized justly, attending to the wants of the Mother when she first woke up. There were only seven in this present brood of hers, and all of them male, and none of them the size or the strength or the wit of their father. It was a loose and unsettling time, and it spoiled her temper.

"Food," she ordered harshly. "And drink. And someone to groom me while I am waiting."

T'Weechr said humbly, "There is no one but me, Brood Mother. I will be quick with the food and groom you while you eat."

"And why is there no one?"

"The New Devils are teaching, Brood Mother. All are commanded to be present."

"Tssheee." If dr'Shee had been a human, the sound would have been a grunt, written "Humph" for convenience's sake. But she was not actually displeased, merely fretful; and when t'Weechr returned it was not only with tubers and a shell of water, but there were even some fresh leaves and fruits from Above.

"Taken or given?" she demanded, sniffing them suspiciously.

"These were gifts of the New Devils, Brood Mother," the youth apologized.

"Tssheee." They were, however, tasty, and she was hungry. She defecated neatly into the shell when she was finished, and t'Weechr folded it closed.

"Is there any other service, Brood Mother?" he asked, licking a final strand of her fur into neatness.

"No. Be gone." He touched noses and wriggled away to deliver the package to the rotting rooms. The next brood would mix it with the planting mud and plaster it into the ceilings of the farm tunnels when they prepared the next crops. By then it would be well aged, and of great value in growing the tubers.

Runt or not, t'Weechr was a good child. She would miss him when the litter matured and scattered. And that time was not far off. At every awakening now, her dugs had been smaller and harder. The breeding males knew it, and every time she left her nest they wriggled close to touch her, nose to anus, testing to see how near she was to courtship. Only yesterday the male with the scarred leg had said, half-jesting, "What would you like next time, dr'Shee? Krinpit shell? A live Flying Devil? The head of a New Devil?"

"Your own head," she had said, half-irritated, half-flirtatious. He had snorted laughter through the spreading folds of his nose and crept away, but he would be back. It was not an unpleasing thought. Dr'Shee's brood-sister had mated with that one, two litters ago. A fine brood, three females! And the sister had said he was indefatigable at rut. Well. A proper courtship was a proper courtship, but she could not help hoping that he might turn out to be the male with the finest gift to lay before her.

Faint and distant vibrations in the earth set her whiskers to quivering. That was the New Devils, too. Time was when such tremors had meant only a particularly violent thunderstorm Above, or perhaps the crash of a falling many-tree. Now the New Devils scraped and shoved hillocks and boulders around at will, and the earth was no longer easy to her senses. As she moved around her chamber, sniffing and touching to make sure everything was in its place, it was touch and smell and taste that principally guided her. Sometimes her males had plastered bits of fungus and vegetation into the walls along with the secretions that made their tunnels hard and waterproof, and from the plant decay there was some faint glow. Dr'Shee appreciated the light but did not need it. For her people, eyes were almost a handicap, especially on their infrequent dashes to the Surface, when only the densest of clouds and worst of storms dimmed Kung's radiance enough for them to bear.

"Greeting, dr'Shee."

She sniffed in startlement and then recognized the female at the entrance to her chamber. "How are you, qr'Tshew? Come in, come in."

The other female entered, and dr'Shee said at once, "I will send for food."

"I have eaten," said qr'Tshew politely. "What lovely courtship gifts." She fondled dr'Shee's collection. Six breedings, six fine gifts: a hard thing stolen from the New Devils that no one understood; the leg of a crabrat—that had been her first gift, and the least worthy, but in some ways the most satisfying of her courtship gifts; even the claws of a balloonist. Every one had been stolen from the Surface itself, at great risk, and delivered to her at a cost. Few males survived more than two or three mad, half-blind dashes to the Surface to steal courtship gifts. The enemies were everywhere.

Manners satisfied, qr'Tshew came to the point. "The father of my last brood has died of a bad breathing," she said. "Also three young of other mothers."

"What a pity," said dr'Shee. She was not referring to the male, of course; once a male had achieved breeding he was done, for that female. But to have young die of the cyanide gas!

"I fear for our way of life," said qr'Tshew primly. "Since the New Devils came, our litters have not been the same."

"I have had the same thought," dr'Shee admitted. "I have spoken of it to my sisters."

"And I to mine. I and my sisters have thought something we wish to share. Our young are being taught things by the New Devils. Dr'Shee, shouldn't we mothers learn what the litters are learning?"

"But they are learning ways of bringing death! You and I are mothers, qr'Tshew!" Dr'Shee was shocked.

"The Krinpit bring death to us, do they not? The broods in the upper galleries have blocked off the tunnels where the bad air came from, but is it not certain that the Shelled Devils will break through again and more bad air will come?"

"I cannot bring death, except of course for food."

"Then let us eat them, shells and all," said qr'Tshew grimly. "Touch closely, dr'Shee. There is a story—" She hesitated. "I do not know how true it is. It came from a Krinpit and might as well have come from a Flying Devil." That was an old saying to indicate dubiousness, but in this case, dr'Shee realized, it was actually true. "This Shelled Devil taunted one of my sister's brood by saying that New Devils had destroyed an entire city of our race. He said the New Devils thought of us as vermin and would not rest until we were all gone. That is why they have given the Krinpit the bad air."

"But the New Devils are teaching our litters how to destroy Krinpit."

"The next part of the story is puzzling, but I think it is so. The

Shelled Devil says that there are three kinds of New Devils. One kind destroyed the city. Another kind gave them the bad air with which they harm us here. And the kind that teaches our litters is a third kind. They have destroyed Flying Devils and Krinpit, as well as persons of the two other kinds of their own race. But they do not destroy us."

Dr'Shee thrashed her long, supple body in agitation. "But that is not true!" she cried. "They have taken several litters from their classes to some other place, and only a few have returned. And they have been weak and slow, and speak of their brood-mates dying!"

"My sisters and I have heard this also," agreed qr'Tshew.

"Tssheee!" The petaled folds of dr'Shee's nose were rippling furiously. "It feels," she said at length, "as though the teaching of bringing death is not a bad thing. If we bring death to the Krinpit, then they will not be able to bring more bad air to us. If we help our New Devils to bring death to the others, then they will not be able to aid the Krinpit or the Flying Devils against us."

"I have had this same thought, dr'Shee."

"I have a further thought, qr'Tshew. Once we have brought death to these others, perhaps we can then bring death to our own New Devils."

"And then our litters will be ours again, dr'Shee!"

"And our burrows will be safe and dark. Yes! Do not go away, qr'Tshew. I will summon t'Weechr and he will begin to teach us these lessons!"

·FOURTEEN·

EVEN IN JEM's favorable conditions—air denser, gravity less than Earth—there was a peremptory equation of lift. Danny Dalehouse could carry whatever he liked simply by adding balloons to his cluster. Charlie had no such power. He could carry what he could carry, and there was an end to it. To carry any of Dalehouse's gifts meant sacrificing ballast and therefore mobility. To carry them all was impossible. When Dalehouse scolded him for giving the cross-bow to a flock-mate—at a time when the *ha'aye'i* seemed every-where!—Charlie sang placatingly, "But I must keep the speaker-to-air! I cannot have both, cannot have both."

"And if you are killed by a *ha'aye'i*, what good will the radio do you?" But Charlie didn't even seem to understand the question. He and the flock were singing a sort of rhapsody about the speaker-to-air and how it enriched their chorus; and Dalehouse abandoned the effort.

Charlie's possession of the radio wasn't all good. It meant that Dalehouse could really keep in contact with the flock from the ground as long as they stayed in line of sight or somewhere near it, and that fact had not escaped Major Santangelo, the new camp commandant. It was getting less easy to escape into the air. At the same time, it was getting less attractive to stay in the camp. Santangelo had established command at once. He had proved it by sending Harriet and Alex Woodring off to try to make contact with a distant tribe of burrowers, hopefully uncontaminated by contact with the Greasies. And the camp was being run along increasingly strict military lines.

Dalehouse broke through the flock's song. "I must return. Four more flocks of our people are joining us, and I wish to be there when they arrive."

"We will come with you, we will come with you—"

"No, you won't," he contradicted. "Too many *ha'aye'i* near the camp." That was the truth, and that, too, was a consequence of the "gifts" he had given them. Since the Oilies had found out that Santangelo's "scientific instruments" were being used by the balloonists to keep tabs on what was going on in their camp they had taken to shooting down every balloonist that came within a kilometer of them. So balloonists were growing locally scarce, and the predators hungry.

"Fly by the Wet Valleys," he commanded. "Learn if our people are well there."

"No need," sang Charlie. "See the wings of your friend 'Appy coming from there even now!" And back behind the shoreline, there it was, Cappy's little biplane coming back from visiting the outpost, circling in for a landing.

"Then good-bye," sang Dalehouse, and expertly vented hydrogen until he came down to the level of the onshore winds that carried him back to the camp.

He was getting really good at ballooning, and he was smiling as he drifted down over the commandant's pet project, the little mud fort on the shore, and dropped to earth on the first bluff. He gathered up the deflated balloons, slung their loose-netted bulk over his shoulder, and walked happily enough up to the hydrogen shed.

That was the end of happiness. Half the camp was gathered around Kappelyushnikov and Santangelo, farther up the hill. Jim Morrissey and half a dozen others were coming toward him, their faces grim. Dalehouse caught Morrissey's arm as he passed. "What's the matter?" he demanded.

Morrissey paused. "Trouble, Danny. Something's happened to the outcamp. Harriet, Woodring, Dugachenko—they're missing. Cappy says the camp's been ripped apart, and they're gone."

"Harriet?"

"All of them, damn it! And there's blood and Krinpit tracks all over the place. Let go, we've got to get down to Castle Santangelo —in case they invade by sea, I guess. Anyway, you'd better get up there and see what your orders are."

Orders! How like an army officer to overreact and start issuing orders in all directions! Dalehouse let them go past and walked belligerently up to the group around Santangelo and the pilot. Someone was saying, "—I didn't know there were any Krinpit in the Wet Valleys."

"If you were in Beverly Hills you wouldn't know there were any rattlesnakes in California, either, but if you wandered around Hollywood Hills they'd bite your ass off. That's enough for arguing," the major said. "Those of you with assigned defense posts, get to them. We've got four ships coming in in the next twenty hours. It'd be a good time for anybody to catch us off guard, and we're not going to be caught. Move it!"

Dalehouse, who had been given no assigned defense post, was not anxious to get one. He moved away briskly with the others as the group broke up, circling around the outskirts to approach the communications shack.

Inside, the comm team on duty was watching a continually shifting display of moving symbols against a green grid of coordinate lines: the four resupply ships, already in orbit around Jem, making their final course corrections before dropping down to the surface. Dalehouse had expected Kappelyushnikov to show up there, and he did, moments after Dalehouse himself.

"Ah, Danny," he said dismally, "you have good taste for finding nice place to fuck off. Wait one while I see if asshole traffic controller has accidentally got ships in right orbit." He peered into the screen, grumbled at the crew on duty, then shrugged and returned to Dalehouse. "Is on course," he reported. "Now question is, is course right? We find out. Poor Gasha!"

"Are you sure she's dead?"

"Have not seen corpus delicti, no. But Danny, there was very much blood, two liters at least."

"But you didn't see the bodies."

"No, Danny, did not. Saw blood. Saw tents chopped up to fine Venetian lace, clothes all over, food, radio smashed, little scratchy bug-tracks everywhere I looked. No bodies. So I yelled some, listened, poked into bushes. Then came home. So poor Gasha, not to mention poor Alexei and poor Gregor."

Danny shook his head wonderingly. "The Krinpit are damn noisy beasts. I don't see how they could catch the camp by surprise, and if they weren't surprised they should've been able to take care of themselves. Santangelo made them carry guns."

Kappelyushnikov shrugged. "You want to, I fly you there and you study scene of crime for yourself. Right now, excuse. First ship is about to come out of orbit, and I must keep controller up to personal high standard of accuracy."

Half the personnel in the first ship were a combat team—a fact which would have come as a distinctly unpleasant shock to Dalehouse at one time but now seemed less so. While they were still in orbit, the Vietnamese colonel commanding them had been briefed by radio, and the squad formed up outside the ship as they debarked, and immediately drew weapons and trotted to reinforce the perimeter guards. The second ship was also mostly military, but among the faces was one Dalehouse recognized. It took him a moment to make the connection, but then it was clear: the Bulgarian girl who had interceded for him and Marge Menninger in Sofia. He called to her and waved; she looked startled, then smiled —rather attractively, he thought—and called a greeting.

That was as far as it went just then, for by that time the new colonel had conferred with Major Santangelo, and the whole camp was mobilized. The Vietnamese—his name was Tree—commandeered Kappelyushnikov and the airplane, and they were gone for more than two hours, orbiting the camp in widening circles, first at high altitude, then nearly brushing the tops of the trees. All the tents had to come down. By the time the third rocket landed the tents were up again, now lined up six to a row, four rows paralleling each other, in what had become a company street. At each corner of the encampment pits were dug, and out of the third ship came machine guns and flamethrowers to go into them, while the few rankless nonspecialists who had not been tapped for unloading, tent detail, or pit digging had been set to pounding steel stakes into the ground ten meters outside the limits of the camp. Among the third ship's cargo were two huge reels of barbed wire, and by the time the last ship began its drop they had been strung along the stakes.

For once the Jemman skies were almost clear as the fourth ship came into sight high over the far horizon of the ocean-lake. First there was a broad, bright, meteoritic splash of light as the ablative entry shields soaked up the worst of the excess energy and spilled it away in incandescent shards. Then the ship itself was in naked-eye range, falling free for a moment. A quick blue-white jet flare made a course correction. Then the trigger parachute came free, pulling the three main chutes after it. The ship seemed to hang almost motionless in the ruddy air; but slowly, slowly it grew larger until it was almost overhead, two hundred meters up. Then the chutes were jettisoned and the ship lowered itself, on its blinding, ear-destroying rockets, to the beach.

Dalehouse had seen, he counted, five of those landings now, not including the one he himself had been in. They were all almost miraculous to watch. And they were all different. The ships themselves were different. Of the new four, only one was the tall, silver shape of his own ship. The other three were squat double cones, ten meters from rounded top to rounded bottom as they crouched on their landing struts, nearly twenty meters across at their widest.

The first person out of the ship was Marge Menninger.

It was not a surprise. The surprising part was that she hadn't come earlier. Dalehouse realized he had been half-expecting her on every ship that landed. She looked tired, disheveled, and harried, and obviously she had been sleeping in her olive-drab fatigues for all of the transit-time week. But she also looked pretty good to Dalehouse. The female members of the Food Bloc party had not been chosen for their sexuality. Apart from a rare occasional grapple with someone he didn't really like very much—sometimes impelled by tickling one of the balloonists into parting with a few sprays of joy-juice, sometimes by nothing more than boredom—Dalehouse's sex life had been sparse, joyless, and dull. Margie reminded him of better times.

Margie had also come up in the world since Sofia; the insignia on her collar tabs were no longer captain's bars but full colonel's eagles, and as she moved aside to let the rest of the troops debark, Colonel Tree and Major Santangelo were already beginning to report to her. She listened attentively while her eyes were taking inventory of the camp, the defense perimeter, and the progress of the debarkation. Then she began speaking in short, quick sentences. Dalehouse was not close enough to hear the words, but there was no doubt that the sentences were orders. Tree argued about something. Good-humoredly, Margie slipped her arm around his shoulder while she answered, then patted his bottom as he moved off, scowling, to do as he was told. She and Santangelo moved up toward the command center, still talking; and Dalehouse began to revise his notions of what to expect from seeing Margie Menninger again.

But as they approached where he was standing, she caught sight of him and threw out her arms. "Hey, Dan! Beautiful to see you!" She kissed him enthusiastically. "You're looking real fine, you know? Or as close to fine as you can in this light."

"You, too," he said. "And congratulations."

"On what, being here? Oh, you mean the eagles. Well, they had to give me that to handle Guy Tree. Dimitrova ought to be around somewhere. Have you seen her? Now if we could only get the Pak to come for a visit, we could all have a nice time talking over good old days in the Bulgarian slammer."

"Colonel Menninger—"

"All right, major, I'm coming. Stay loose, Dan. We've got catching up to do."

He stared after her. In the old Rotsy days in college, before he had dropped out as it became clear that nobody would ever need to fight wars anymore, colonels had seemed quite different. It wasn't just that she was female. And pretty, and young. Colonels had seemed to have more on their minds than Margie Menninger did—especially colonels coming into a situation where the panic button had been so recently pressed.

A husky man in a sergeant's uniform was speaking to him. "You Dr. Dalehouse? There's mail for you at the library."

"Oh, sure. Thanks." Dalehouse took note of the fact that the sergeant's expression was both surprised and a little amused, but he understood both reactions. "Nice kid, the colonel," he said benevolently. He didn't wait for an answer.

Most of the "mail" was from Michigan State and the Double-A-L, but one of the letters was a surprise. It was from Polly! So

long ago, so far away, Dalehouse had almost forgotten he had ever
had a wife. He could think of no reason why she would be writing
him. Nearly everyone in the first two parties had also received
mail, and the lines at the viewers were discouraging. Dalehouse
put the collection of fiches in his pocket and headed for Kappelyushnikov's private store of goodies in the hydrogen shed. The
pilot had long since scrounged the things he deemed essential to
the good life on Jem, and among them was his own microfiche
viewer. With considerable curiosity, Dalehouse slid his ex-wife's
letter into position.

Dear Daniel:

I don't know if you knew that Grandfather Medway died
last summer. When his will was probated it turned out he
left the Grand Haven house to us. I guess he just never got
around to changing the will after our divorce.

It isn't worth a whole lot, but of course it's worth something—the lawyer says its assessed value is $43,500. I'm a lit-
tle embarrassed about this. I have this strong feeling that
says you're going to say you'll waive your share. Well, if
that's really what you want I'd appreciate it if you'd sign a
release for me and have it notarized—is there anybody there
who's a notary? Otherwise, will you tell me what you'd like
to do?

We are all well, Daniel, in spite of everything. Detroit
had another blackout last week, and the rioting and looting
were pretty bad, and the new emergency surtaxes are going
to be hard to handle. Not to mention the heatless days and
the moratorium on daytime TV and the scary news about
international politics. Most people seem to think it's because of what's going on up where you are—but that's not
your fault, is it? I remember you with a lot of affection,
Daniel, and hope you do me.

Pauline

Sitting on the edge of Kappelyushnikov's personal cot, Dalehouse put the viewer down thoughtfully. The Grand Haven
house. It was really only a bungalow, at least fifty years old and
only sketchily modernized. But he and Polly had spent their honeymoon in it, in a snowy January with the wind whipping up over
the bluff from Lake Michigan all day and all night. Of course she

could have the house. Somebody in the camp could probably no-
tarize a quitclaim, at least legally enough to satisfy some up-
country surrogate court.

He stretched out on the cot, thinking about his ex-wife and her
letter. News from Earth had not seemed either very interesting or
very relevant, and Dalehouse had spent a lot more time thinking
about the balloonists and the complications of life on Jem than
about the brief paragraphs on the camp wall newspaper. But Polly
made it sound serious. Riots, looting, blackouts, heatless days! He
decided he would have to talk to some of the new people as soon
as they quit bustling around and getting settled. That Bulgarian
girl, for instance. She could fill him in on what was really happening back home, and, besides, she was a pretty nice person. He lay
drowsily trying to decide whether it was better to do that now or
to keep on enjoying the private space to think his own thoughts.

The decision was taken out of his hands. "Hello, Dr. Dalehouse," came Ana Dimitrova's voice. "Mr. Kappelyushnikov said
you'd be here. But I must confess I was not sure he was in earnest."

Dalehouse opened his eyes and sat up as Cappy and the girl
stooped through the entrance to the shed. The pilot's expression
made it clear that, whatever he had told the girl, he had hoped
there would be no one there, but he rallied and said, "Ah,
Anyushka, you must learn to trust me. Here is old friend to see
you, Danny."

Dalehouse accepted the formal handshake she offered. She had
a nice smile, he observed. In fact, if she had not chosen to wear
her hair pulled severely back and avoid the use of makeup, she
could have been quite attractive.

"I was hoping to get a chance to talk to you, Miss Dimitrova."

"Heavens, Ana, please. Old cellmates must not be formal with
each other."

"But on other hand," said the pilot, "must not impose on dear
Danny, who is no doubt hungry and must get to mess hall at once
or risk missing excellent dog-meat-and-slime meal."

"Nice try, Cappy," Dalehouse acknowledged. "No, I'm not
hungry. How are things on Earth, Ana? I've just been hearing
some bad stories."

Her expression clouded. "If the stories you have heard have

been of violence and disaster, then, yes, that is how things are. Just before we left the television news spoke of martial law in the city of Los Angeles, and also in several cities of Europe. And there was some sinking of an Australian naval vessel off the coast of Peru."

"Dear God."

"Oh, there is much more than that, Dr. Dalehouse—Dan. But we have brought all the recent newspapers, as well as tapes of television programs—it is really quite an extensive library, I understand. I believe there are more than twenty thousand books in microfiche, at Colonel Menninger's express orders."

"Twenty thousand books?" Dalehouse shook his head. "You know, I never thought of her as a reader."

Ana smiled and sat cross-legged on the floor before him. "Please, let us be comfortable. I too am sometimes astonished at Colonel Menninger." She hesitated, then said, "She is not, however, always to be relied on. I had expected some time to consult with my government before coming here, on her promise. But it did not happen. None of us were allowed to leave the camp until we were flown to the launching point. Perhaps it was because she did not want to risk exposing us to the unstable conditions we might have found."

"As bad as that?"

"Worse," growled Kappelyushnikov. "You see, Danny? We should be grateful to be here on safe tropical-paradise planet like Jem, where only once in a while isolated party gets wiped out by giant cockroaches."

"That's another thing," said Danny. "Marge Menninger doesn't seem particularly worried, after the flap yesterday."

"No reason to worry, dear Danny. I and little Vietnamese colonel have scoured every centimeter from ten klicks in all directions, using magnetometer, IR scanners, and good piloting eyes. Is no metal thing bigger than breadbasket anywhere around, I promise, and not more than three, maybe six, creatures larger than crabrat. So sleep safely tonight, Danny. In own bed," he added pointedly, and did not need to add "soon."

Nan was quicker than he. "That is good advice, Cappy," she said, standing up. "I think I will take it for myself."

"I will escort you," rumbled Kappelyushnikov. "No, do not disturb self, Danny. I see you are quite tired."

Ana sighed. "Gospodin Kappelyushnikov," she scolded, "apart from the fact that I am tired and quite disoriented from all these new experiences, you and I have barely met. I do hope that we will be friends. Please don't make that difficult by behaving like some Cossack with a peasant maid."

Cappy looked abashed, then angry. Then he grinned. "Anyushka, you are fine Slavic girl. Yes, we will be friends at once. Later on, perhaps more—but," he added hastily, "only in proper Soviet style, no premature touching, all right? Now let us all three stroll through pleasant Jemman murk to your tent."

Ana laughed and slapped him on the shoulder. "Russian bear! Come, then." She led the way outside and stood for a moment, glancing around at the quieting camp. The floodlights that marked official "day" were out, but Kung was clear and ruddy in the sky overhead. "I do not know if I can get used to a world where it is never night," she complained.

"Is severe handicap for certain purposes, yes," Kappelyushnikov agreed. They climbed the bluff and walked along it toward the female tent area. At the very edge, surrounded by a border of rounded stones in lieu of a lawn, was a tent larger than the others. It already had a flat rock before it stenciled *Col. M. Menninger, Commanding.*

"Margie's doing herself well," Dalehouse commented.

"Is privilege of rank," said Kappelyushnikov, but he was staring down the beach at the four new ships, one tall and slim, three squat, resting on their landing struts.

"That's strange, isn't it?" Dalehouse said. "Those three are quite unlike the others."

Cappy glanced at him. "You are truly observant, Danny." But his tone was strange.

"All right, Cappy. What's the secret?"

"Secret? Simple pilot is not told secrets. But I have eyes, and I can make conjectures."

"Come on, Cappy. You're going to tell us your conjecture sooner or later. Why not do it now?"

"Two conjectures," he corrected. "First, observe shape of three new spacecraft. Imagine sliced in half, forming two little cones each. Then imagine all six cones set on base around perimeter of camp, and the glass removed from those long, narrow ports that are so unnecessary for navigation of space. What have we then?"

"Upside-down cones with unglazed long, narrow ports," Dalehouse guessed.

"Yes, exactly. Only when installed on defense perimeter we have other name for them. We call them 'machine-gun emplacements.'" He sighed. "I think is triumph of two-faced engineering design, not accident, that this is so."

"But one can scarcely believe that," objected Ana. "This is, after all, a peaceable exploration party, not an invading army!"

"Yes, also exactly. Is only coincidence that so many members of peaceable exploration party are also soldiers."

Both Dalehouse and the girl were silent, studying the landed spaceships. "I would like not to believe you," said Ana at last. "But perhaps—"

"Wait a minute!" Dalehouse interrupted. "Those three ships—they don't have any return stage! That's why they're so short!"

Kappelyushnikov nodded. "And that is second conjecture," he added heavily. "Only is not really conjecture. Library of twenty thousand books is not light reading for weekend. Spacecraft that come apart to make forts are not for round trip. Vessels without return-capsule capability are not accident. Total of sum is clear. For many of us, is not intended we ever go back to dear old planet Earth."

Getting into the Jemman sky again the next day was a victory for Dalehouse, and he did not know how many more of those victories he would have. The day had begun unpromisingly. As soon as the "morning" lights were on he had found a mini-memo on the bench inside his tent door to let him know that, as from 0800 hours that standard day, he was to consider himself under military discipline with the assimilated rank of captain. On the way to breakfast he had passed an orderly carrying two covered trays into Margie's tent. An orderly! Not even the late Harriet Santori had gone that far. And on the way back past the tent, the Vietnamese colonel had been coming out.

Who Marge Menninger kept in her bed was no concern of his, and all this other military Mickey Mouse was irrelevant to his purpose on Jem. All the same, Dalehouse was not enjoying his flight as much as usual that day.

For one thing, Charlie and his flock were nowhere around—partly because Major Santangelo had insisted they overfly some of the other parts of Jem to bring back intelligence. Mostly because Dalehouse himself was reluctant to have them there, with so many *ha'aye'i* waiting in the clouds to prey on them. At least he had insisted they stay a full two kilometers away from the Greasy camp; maybe that was enough for safety. Meanwhile, Dalehouse had his lightweight carbine with him, and he was hoping to take out at least a couple of the *ha'aye'i* before Charlie drifted back. There was already one balloonist in the camp as a sort of combination convalescent and pet, waiting for his *ha'aye'i*-ripped gasbag to mend enough for flight. Dalehouse didn't want Charlie to join him.

Trying to look appetizing, he drifted under the base of a low cumulus humilis. It was exactly the sort of place the airsharks chose for hiding. But if there was one in the cloud it wasn't hungry just then.

He vented gas and dropped away from the cloud as the updraft began to suck him toward it; if there were *ha'aye'i*, he wanted to meet them in clear air, not where they could be upon him before he could shoot. A return flow carried him back toward the camp, and he looked down from half a kilometer on a busy scene. About twenty people were still unloading the new ships. Others were clearing brush and forest to widen the perimeter around the camp, and up past the camp toward the hills, in a natural meadow of thorn-bearing ground vines, a tiny tractor was plowing furrows. That was new! The tractor must have come out of one of the ships, and the furrows looked exactly as though someone was planning to farm.

That was reasonable enough, and even good news—certainly they could use fresh vegetables, and if the Greasies could grow them so could the Fats. But something about it troubled Dalehouse. He couldn't put his finger on it; something about using soldiers to farm? Forced labor on land?

He dismissed the thought; he was getting too low.

He vented some ballast, and the water sluiced down on the newly plowed land like a toy-scale rain shower. The thing that was tickling his memory was beginning to be annoying. For some reason, it reminded him of his undergraduate anthropology professor, a gentle and undemanding man a lot like Alex Woodring—

Like Alex Woodring, who was dead. Along with Gasha and the Bulgarian corporal he had never really come to know.

He was having none but depressing thoughts. His reserves of hydrogen and ballast were getting a little low, and evidently the *ha'aye'i* had learned to distinguish between a balloonist and a human being swinging from a netted cluster of bags. They were not to be tricked this day. Reluctantly he swung back over the beach, vented gas, and dropped to the pebbly sand.

By the time he had picked up and stowed the deflated balloons Margie Menninger was approaching, along with the woman sergeant who was her orderly. "Nice flying, Danny," she said. "Looks like fun. Will you take me up with you sometime?"

He stood regarding her for a moment. She really looked very pretty, even in the maroon Kung-light that darkened her lips and hid the gold of her hair. Her fatigues were new and sharply pressed, and her short hairdo flopped becomingly as she moved. "Any time you say, Marge. Or is it 'colonel'?"

She laughed. "All you brand-new officers are the same, very rank conscious. We're off duty right now, Danny, so it's Marge. You'll learn."

"I'm not sure I want to learn how to be a soldier."

"Oh, you'll catch on," she promised. "Tinka, take the point. Let's go for a walk, shall we?"

The sergeant moved out ahead of them, trotting to the barbed-wire enclosure. The troops in the pit at the corner lifted a section of the wire aside so the three of them could pass through; the sergeant in charge gave Margie a soft salute, and she nodded pleasantly back.

"If a person went swimming in this water," she said, "would she find herself being eaten up by something?"

"Not so far. We do it all the time."

"Looks pretty tempting. Care to join me?"

Dalehouse shook his head, not in negation but in wonder. "Margie, you're something. I thought colonels had to keep busy, especially when they think their troops need armed guards and barbed-wire fences day and night."

"Dear Danny," she said good-naturedly, "I haven't been a colonel very long, but I taught the theory of it to a couple thousand plebes at the Point. I think I have a pretty good grasp of the basic principles. A colonel doesn't have to do much; she just has to see that everybody else gets everything done. I already put in four hours of pretty solid work this morning."

"Yes, I saw Colonel Tree coming out of your tent."

She looked at him thoughtfully. She didn't comment but went on, "As to your other point, the perimeter watch is SOP from now on, but there are patrols in the woods and aerial reconnaissance every hour, and besides, Tinka's a qualified expert with all hand weapons. I think you'll be all right."

"I wasn't worried about my personal safety."

"No, you weren't. You were worried about the troops under my command, and on their behalf I thank you for your concern." She grinned and patted his arm. "Hold on a minute." She fished a cigarette case out of her pocket, ducked behind him to get out of the wind, and expertly lit up. She inhaled deeply and held it, passing him the joint. When she exhaled, she called to the sergeant, "Tinka!"

"Yes'm."

"Next batch of dope you clean for us, save the seeds. Let's see if we can grow the little buggers here."

"Yes'm."

Danny took a long hit, beginning to relax. Being with Margie Menninger was never dull, at least. As he slowly exhaled he looked her over in some admiration. She had adjusted at once to the heat, the disconcertingly low gravity, the thick air that had troubled them all for weeks. She was some kind of woman.

By the time they had finished passing the joint back and forth they were out of sight of the perimeter guard where the beach widened under a high, bare bluff. Margie stopped, looking around. "Seems as good as any," she commented. "Tinka, take your position."

"Yes'm." The sergeant scrambled agilely up the side of the bluff to the top, and Margie shucked her fatigues. She wore nothing underneath. "If you're coming, come. If not, stay and help Tinka keep watch." And she splashed into the water.

Dope, company, or whatever, Dalehouse was feeling better than he had all day. He laughed out loud, then skinned out of his own clothes and joined her.

Ten minutes later they were both back on the beach, lying not very comfortably on their clothes, waiting to dry.

"Ouch," said Margie. "If I ever get any extra people for punishment detail, I think I'll see if they can get the rocks out of this sand."

"You get used to it."

"Only if I have to, Danny. I'm going to make this a nice camp if I can—good duty. For instance, you know what we're going to have tonight?"

He rolled his head to look at her. "What?"

"The first official Jemman Food-Exporting Bloc encampment dance."

"A *dance?*"

She grinned. "See what I mean? Those turkeys who were running this place never thought of that. But there's nothing to it: spread out some flats on the dirt, put a few tapes in the machine, and there you are. Saturday night special. Best thing in the world for morale."

"You are probably about the US Army's best colonel for having fun," Dalehouse said.

"For all the rest of being a colonel, too, Danny. Don't you forget it."

"Well, I won't, Margie. I believe it. Only it's kind of hard to remember under the, ah, present circumstances."

"Well, I'll put my clothes back on if it'll help you concentrate. This isn't just fun and games. I wanted to talk to you."

"About what?"

"Whatever you want to tell me. How you think things are going. What isn't being done that ought to be. What you've learned being here that I haven't found out yet."

He propped himself up on an elbow to look at her. She returned his gaze serenely, scratching her bare abdomen just above the pubic hair. "Well," he said, "I guess you've seen all the reports about making contact with the sentients."

"Memorized them, Danny. I even saw some of the sentients at

Detrick, but they weren't in very good condition. Especially the Creepie."

"The burrower? We haven't had very good luck with them."

"Piss-poor, I'd say."

"Well—yes, that's fair. But we did get about ten specimens, two of them alive. And Morrissey has a whole report on them not transmitted yet. He says they're farmers—from underneath, which is kind of an interesting idea. They plant some kind of tubers in the roofs of their tunnels. He was planning to talk to that expert you were supposed to bring—I don't know her name."

"Sondra Leckler? She didn't come, Danny. I had her scratched."

"Why?"

"Political. She's Canadian." She looked at him thoughtfully. "Does that fact mean anything to you?"

"Not a thing."

"No, I didn't think so. Canada voted for Peru's thousand-mile limit in the UN. That's cozying with the Peeps, right there. And everybody knows Canada's got the hots for the Greasies because of their goddam Athabasca tar sands. They're politically unreliable right now, Danny. There were four Canadians scheduled for this shipment, and I scratched all their asses right off."

"That sounds pretty paranoid," he commented.

"No, realistic. I've got no time to teach you the facts of life, Danny. What else? I don't mean about the burrowers."

He regarded her thoughtfully. She lay on her back, hands behind her head, comfortable in her nudity as she squinted toward the glowing red Kung. For a slightly plump girl her waist curved beautifully into her hips, and her breasts were rounded even while she lay flat on her back. But under that blond hair was a brain Dalehouse did not fully understand.

He dropped back and said, "Well, there's the balloonists. I know the most about them. Our regular flock is off toward the Heat Pole, but there's another one out over the water. They're basically territorial, but—"

"You were at the Greasy camp awhile ago, weren't you?"

"Yeah. When we were still on visiting terms. Is that what you want me to tell you about?"

"Among other things."

"All right. They've got a hell of a lot of stuff we don't, Margie." He described the machine that molded building blocks, the plasma generator, the farm, the air conditioning, the *ice.*

"Sounds pretty nice," she commented. "We'll have all that stuff too, Danny, I promise you. Did you see a plane and four gliders?"

"No. There was an airstrip—Cappy commented on it; it didn't make sense, with just a helicopter. But they didn't have a plane then."

"They do now. I thought they'd sneaked a reinforcement in that you didn't catch. Did you know about the base on Farside?"

"*Farside?* You mean the dark half of Jem? What the hell would anyone want there?"

"That's what I need to find out. But they've got it. Why do you think I stayed four extra orbits before I came down? I made damn sure I photomapped and radar-surveyed everything I could; I know every satellite around Jem, I know every spot on the surface that's using energy, and I don't like all of what I know. The Farside base was a real shock. Did you see any children in the Greasy camp?"

"Children? Hell, no! Why would—"

"Well, I think they're moving whole families in, Danny, which seems to indicate they've got more than an exploring expedition in mind."

"How could you tell whether they had children from space?"

"No way, Danny. I didn't say the orbital reconnaissance was the *only* way I knew what was going on with the Greasies. One other thing. No, two. Have they got a baseball field?"

"Baseball?" He was sitting up now, staring at her. "What the hell would they do with a baseball field? Cricket, maybe, and no doubt football, but—"

"That's a break," she said, without explaining. "Last question. Did you happen to run into a fellow named Tamil?"

"I don't think so." Dalehouse thought hard. "Wait a minute. Short fellow with a shaved head? Chess player?"

"I don't know. He's an Indonesian."

"Well, I'm not sure, but I think there was a petrochemist with a name like that. I didn't talk to him. I don't think he spoke English."

"Pity." Margie ruminated for a moment, then sat up, shading her eyes. "Are those your balloonists out there?"

As Dalehouse turned to look, Margie was standing, taking a few steps toward the shore, and what he looked at was not the sky but her. The artist Hogarth had said that the most beautiful line in nature was the curve of a woman's back, and Margie, silhouetted against the ruddy sky, was a fine figure of a woman. Half-amused, Dalehouse realized by the stirrings in his groin that he was beginning to display interest. But only beginning. The stimulus was that beautiful and remembered butt; the suppressant was the things she said. He would be some little while figuring out just how it was he did feel about Margie Menninger.

Then he got his eyes past her and forgot the stirrings. "There are *ha'aye'i* out there!" he said furiously.

"What'ys?"

"They're predators. That's not our regular flock; they just drifted in, because of the lights, most likely. And those clouds are full of *ha'aye'i!*" The flock was close enough to be heard now, singing loudly, only a few hundred meters away. And far beyond and above them three slimmer shapes were swooping toward them.

"That's a what-you-call-it there? Jesus! Look at that mother," she cried, as the first of the airsharks expertly ripped at the bag of a huge female, slipped past, turned end-for-end, and reversed itself. It came back ten meters lower to catch the deflated balloonist as it fell, braying its death song. "That's a fucking *Immelmann* that thing just did! Nobody's done that since World War One!"

"This isn't a performance, damn it! They're dying!" Two more of the predators had struck, and two more balloonists were caught farther down the shore. But at least it was not Charlie's flock. None of those victims were friends. "See that stuff coming out of the female?" he asked. "Those are her eggs. They're long spider-silk kind of things. They'll float around forever, but they won't be fertilized because none of the males have—"

"Fuck her eggs, little buddy. I'm rooting for the shark! What a killing machine! Shit, Danny, I can see why things are going badly here. You people picked the wrong allies. We ought to team up with the sharks!"

Dalehouse was scandalized. "They're animals! They're not even intelligent!"

"Show me a professor," she said, "and I'll show you a fart-brain. How intelligent do you have to be to fight?"

"Christ. The balloonists are our friends. We've got them doing surveillance for us. The *ha'aye'i* would never do that. Now you want us to line up with their natural enemies?"

"Well, I can see there might be problems." She stared wistfully at the *ha'aye'i*, which had ripped away the inedible bag and was now feasting on the soft parts of its still-living prey. "Too bad," she said philosophically. She stepped back toward Danny, still watching the spectacle, and took his hand. "You're really sure about this? There's no way to persuade our gooks to get along with the sharks?"

"No way at all! Even if you could somehow reach the *ha'aye'i* to explain what you wanted. The *ha'aye'i* don't even sing. That's the whole meaning of life to balloonists. They could never deal with creatures that didn't sing."

"Oh?" Margie looked at him thoughtfully. Then she released his hand and sat down again, leaning back on her arms and looking up at him. "Tell me, Danny, would you like to make me sing?"

He stared at her. Why, she was sexually excited by watching the slaughter!

He glanced at the top of the bluff, where the back of the head of the orderly was motionless in sight. "Maybe we'd better be getting back," he said.

"What's the matter, sweetie? Don't like having an audience? Tinka won't bother us."

"I don't care about her."

"Then what?" she asked cheerfully. "Hey, I bet I can guess. You're hassled about the colonel."

"Tree? He's got nothing to do with me."

"Aw, come off it, sweets." She patted the ground beside her. After a moment, he sat down, not very close. "You think I've been getting it on with old Nguyen the Tryin'."

"No. I don't think it, I know it."

"And suppose I have?"

"Your business," he said promptly. "I'm not saying it isn't. Maybe I've got some sexist-pig notions, but—"

"But no maybe. You fucking well do, Danny-boy." She was smiling without softness now.

He shrugged. "Let's go back, colonel."

"Let's stay here. And," she said, "I've got the rank on you, and when a colonel says 'let's' to a captain, what it means is *do it*."

There was no more stirring in Dalehouse's groin; he was both angry and amused at his own anger. He said, "Let's get this straight. Are you ordering me to fuck you?"

"No. Not at the moment, dear boy." She grinned. "I hardly ever order officers to fuck me. Only enlisted men, and very seldom them, because it's bad for discipline."

"Are you saying the colonel ordered you to fuck him?"

"Danny dear," she said patiently, "first, he couldn't—I've got the rank. Second, he wouldn't have had to. I'd fuck Guy any time. For any reason. Because he's technically my superior officer and I don't want to rub in the fact that I'm the one who's commanding. Because it'd make things go smoother on the mission. Because it's interesting to get it on with somebody half my size. I'd fuck a Krinpit if it would help the war effort, only I don't know how we'd bring up the kids. But," she said, "a girl's entitled to a certain amount of non-goal-oriented recreation, too, and Danny, I really have the fondest memories of you from last year in Bulgaria."

Fully relaxed, she rummaged under her for her clothes and pulled out another joint.

Dalehouse watched her lighting it. Her body was tanned over every inch—no bikini marks—and looking a lot better than the fishbelly white that came after a while on Jem. She scratched between the crease that hid her navel and her pale pubic hair, exhaled peacefully, and passed him the joint. The thing was, Dalehouse conceded to himself, that he really had the fondest memories of her last year in Bulgaria, too, and it did not seem to matter that he also had some bad memories.

"You know the thing that gets me about you?" he asked. "You make me laugh about a hundred different ways. Lean over this way, will you?"

When they had used each other up, they rested for a moment.

Then Margie jumped up and dashed into the water again. Dale-house followed; they splashed and roared; and as they came out he was astonished to discover that suddenly he didn't feel quite used up anymore. But Margie was calling up the bluff, "Tinka! Time hack!"

"Thirteen twenty hours, ma'am!"

Margie slipped into her fatigues quickly and leaned over to kiss Dalehouse as he was standing with one leg in his pants. "Time to get back. I've got a busy afternoon before the dance, and Danny, I'd appreciate it if you'd do something for me."

"What's that?"

"Teach Tinka how to do that balloon thing this afternoon."

"Why?"

"I want her to run an errand for me. It's important."

He considered. "I can get her started, anyway. But I don't know if she can learn it all in a few hours."

"She learns fast, I promise. Come on—I'll race you back!"

They ran the hundred meters. Marge got off first, but by the time the outpost was in sight Dalehouse had caught up with her. As he passed she reached out and took his hand and pulled him back to a walk. "Thanks for the exercise," she panted.

"Which exercise—swimming, running, or fucking?"

"All of them, dear Danny." She breathed hard, and then, just before they got within earshot of the perimeter guards she halted him. "One thing I ought to mention to you," she said.

"What's that?"

"I just want to set the record straight. With Nguyen Tree I'm fucking. With you I was making love."

Twelve on perimeter guard, two in sick bay, three in the comm shack, and eight more on the other twenty-four-hour details that always had to be manned: that left over a hundred and twenty people in the Food camp, and nearly every one of them was at the dance. Marge congratulated herself as she flung through a hora. It was a big success. When the dance ended and the rhythm changed to something Latin, she shook off the three men who came toward her. "I've got to sit this one out and catch my breath," she said. "After the next number I make my little speech. Then you're all on."

She retreated behind the little stand and sat cross-legged on the ground, breathing deeply. Marge Menninger's parents had endowed her with good genes, and she had taken care of the equipment; after a long day and a solid hour's dancing she was not tired and her wits were all about her. And the day had been not only long but good. She had got the camp over their scare about the loss of the three people by treating it as if it didn't matter. She had brought them all together in the dance. She had laid the groundwork for Tinka's little mission, organized an effective perimeter guard, broken the back of the job of unloading and stowing cargo, and begun six other tasks equally important. And she had got it on with Dan Dalehouse, on terms of her own making but obviously acceptable to him. That was a personal matter, but not unimportant. Marge was careful to keep an eye on long-range prospects. And as a possible permanent future pair, if permanent pairing turned out to be the way things were going to go on Jem, Dalehouse was the best bet she had yet identified.

It was Marge Menninger's conviction, recent but certain, that this job was what she had been born for. The important thing was to do it the right way, which was her own way, which had to be laid out from day one. No false starts. A happy camp—plenty of work to keep them busy and plenty of time to enjoy themselves. And a productive camp. Jem belonged to her and hers, and now they had it.

While she was waiting for the cha-cha to end she considered the next day. Ship One would be empty, and a team could be started on separating the two halves and moving them into position in the perimeter. Dalehouse or Kappelyushnikov—which? the Russian, she decided—Kappelyushnikov could be briefed on Tinka's mission, or at least enough of it so that he could escort her partway to the Greasy camp. A work team could be organized to start putting up poles for the farm plot. She would meet and learn to know at least six of the advance party; in two weeks, she should know everything she had to know about everyone in the camp. Orders would be cut naming Guy Tree as her G-1 and Santangelo as G-2. The others she would wait on; there might be people she hadn't met yet who should have the jobs. And, if things went well, during the three hours she allowed herself for a midday break, she would go for a walk in the woods. If you could call them woods. They needed to be dealt with too: Knock down some of those skungy ferns, scoop out some farm ponds to drain that soggy swamp. It would work—all they needed was a couple of bulldozers. Which reminded her that she needed at least to make a first approximation of a requisition list for the next shipment from Earth. That couldn't wait. With all the fuss the civilians were kicking up, Marge Menninger wasn't sure how many more shipments there would be. She already knew a number of goodies she wanted, but the old-timers would probably think of more. So she would need to talk to some of the old-timers. Morrissey, Krivitin, Kappelyushnikov—she would fill in the others later.

The smell of pot from beyond the stand pleased her. She thought of lighting up before getting up to make her speech—it was another way of showing her personal style. But it had been less than half an hour since the last one, and Marge knew her tolerances exactly; it might make her fuzzy.

The cha-cha ended, and the girl at the tape machine, looking toward Margie, switched it off. Marge nodded and climbed the stand.

The laughter and buzz dwindled as the hundred-odd people turned to face her. She smiled out at them for a moment, waiting for silence. They looked exactly like the plebes at West Point had looked, exactly like the audience in the Senate hearing room, like every audience she had ever faced. Marge was in touch with her audiences; she could always make them like her, and for that reason she liked them.

"Welcome to the first weekly Food Bloc Expedition Saturday Night Dance. I'm Colonel Marjorie Menninger, USA, and I'm your camp commander. Some of us already know each other pretty well by now. The rest of us are going to get to know each other very well very soon, because when you come right down to it we don't have much choice, do we? I'm not worried about that, and I hope you're not. We are a pretty select bunch." She allowed her gaze to drift past the audience to the edge of the lighted area, where two of her grunts were holding another while he vomited, and added, "Although you might not know that at first." A small laugh, but genuine. "So let's start getting to know each other. Guy? Saint? Where are you?" She introduced Tree and Santangelo as they stood forth. "Now Vince Cudahy—are you there?

Vince is a mathematician, but he's also our chaplain. He used to teach at Fordham, but he's agreed to be nondenominational for the purposes of this mission. So if any of you want to get married, Vince is authorized to do it." Small chuckle. "He's a little old-fashioned, so he'd prefer it if you're of different sexes." Somewhat larger laugh, but a little questioning note in it. "And in case you do," she went on, "or even if you don't, you ought to meet Chiche Arkashvili. Cheech? There she is, our medical officer. Try not to get sick over the next twenty-four hours, because she's still setting up. But then she'll be ready for business, and back home in Ordzhonikidze her specialty was obstetrics." No laugh at all this time. She hadn't expected one. She gave them a moment to draw the logical conclusion and then pressed it home. "As you can see, we're planning a permanent base, and I'm planning to make this the best duty any of you have ever had so that a lot of you will want to re-up and stay here. And if you do—and if any of you take seriously what I've just been talking about and decide to settle down and have a family on Jem, I'm offering a special prize. A thousand petrobucks for the first baby born in our camp— provided you name it Marjorie, after me." She waited a beat and added, "Two thousand if it's a boy." She got the laugh she wanted and closed it out. "Now on with the dance." And as the music started she jumped off the platform, grabbed the first man in reach, and started them all going.

For the next half-hour Marge Menninger played hostess, at which she was very, very good. She danced with the men who didn't much dance, kept the music going, made sure the drinks kept coming. What she wanted was for everybody to have a good time. The next day was time enough for them to start thinking about permanent colonies and how much choice they would be likely to have about extending their stay. When chance permitted she got a word in with the people who had known what she was going to say, asking how they thought it had gone. It had seemed to go well. It made her feel good, and she found she was really enjoying the party. She drank with the drinkers, smoked with the dopers, and danced with everyone. It was safe enough now. When the time came to shut the dance down Tinka would let her know, and meanwhile Tinka would keep an eye on her colonel.

Coming back from the brand-new latrine, Marge paused to enjoy the sight of her people having fun. It was going to be all right! They really were a good bunch, hand-selected, fit, well trained. Whatever she had said to anyone else, in a secret, inside part of her heart Marge had felt a small but unsettling fear that her first really independent command might take qualities she hadn't known she would need. So far, not. So far, everything was going precisely as she had planned, according to the priorities she had laid out in her own mind. Priority 1, safeguard the integrity of the unit. And it was safeguarded; she could see the perimeter guards in regular patrol, a little disgruntled at missing the dance but carrying out their orders meticulously. Priority 2, accomplish the mission assigned. And that was well on the way. Priority 3, subject to accomplishing 1 and 2, make it a busy and happy camp. And that looked good, too.

She walked around the outskirts of the dance, nodding and smiling, not quite ready to get back on the floor. Tinka appeared beside her, one hand on her government-issue pouch, looking questioningly at her. Marge shook her head. She didn't need another joint just then. She was feeling happy and relaxed, but just the littlest bit light-headed. Part of it was the smarmy heat and the peculiar instability that came from weighing only about three-quarters what she had been used to for ten years. But she was feeling a little edgy, too, and checking dates in her mind, she thought she knew why. When she came near the medical officer she said in her ear, "Got your freezers going for the sperm and ovum bank yet, doc? Because I think I'm getting ready to make a donation."

"Noon tomorrow we'll be ready," Chiche Arkashvili promised. "But the way the boys and girls have been disappearing into the bushes, I don't know if we'll need it."

"Better to have it and not need it than need it and not have it. If I could, I'd—"

She stopped. "What would you do, colonel?"

"Forget it. Don't let me keep you from urgent business," said Marge amiably, and watched the doctor go on toward the latrine. If she could, she'd get a whole stock of frozen sperm and ova from Earth, because the bigger the gene pool you started with, the better the chances you'd have a healthy, stable population in another two or three generations. But she was not quite ready to put that request in her next letter to Santa Claus. She would have quite enough trouble with the items she was already determined to requisition, and from Christ's own number of light-years away her powers of argument were limited.

A few meters away the Bulgarian girl was in some sort of altercation with Stud Sweggert, the sergeant Marge had put onto the first of her ships. Normally she wouldn't have interfered, but there was something she wanted from Dimitrova.

"Tinka," she said softly over her shoulder.

"Yes'm."

"Stay with." Marge went up to the arguing couple, who stopped as she came close. "Sorry to break this up," she said.

Dimitrova glared at her. Feisty little prunt; it crossed Marge's mind that her first impulses about Ana Dimitrova might have been best, but it was not a useful thought anymore. She discarded it.

"There is nothing to break up, colonel," the girl said. "The sergeant wished to show me something I did not want to see."

"I bet he did, honey," Marge smiled. "Will you excuse us a second, sergeant?" And, when he was out of earshot, she asked, "How is your Indonesian, Dimitrova?"

"Indonesian? It is not one of my four-oh languages, but I believe I could translate a document satisfactorily."

"I don't want a document translated. I want to know how to say, 'Good morning. Where is the baseball park?' "

"What?"

"Shit, lady! Just tell us how to say it."

Ana hesitated and then, with some disdain, said, *"Selamat pagi, dimana lapangan baseball?"*

"Um." Marge rehearsed it to herself for a moment, glancing at Tinka. The orderly shrugged. "Well, write it down for me. Now, how do you say, 'Have you a map?' "

"Saudara punja peta?"

"Got that?" asked Marge, looking at the orderly. "Not sure? All right, Dimitrova, take Tinka to my office and write it out for her. Make sure she gets it right." For a moment she thought the Bulgarian might object, but then she nodded and the two of them started away.

Sergeant Sweggert was still standing there, three meters away, watching her with calm interest. Margie laughed. "What are you doing, sergeant—waiting to ask me for a dance? Or do you want to show me that little thing you were so anxious to drag out for Dimitrova?"

"Hell, colonel. You've got me all wrong."

"I bet I do. Sweggert," she said good-naturedly, "you're not a bad guy, but it's against my policy to, ah, fraternize with enlisted men. Except in an emergency, of course. And what you've got to show has been widely seen already, I guarantee you."

"Ah, no, colonel! It was educational. They got a tame gasbag here, and it's real interesting."

"Yeah?" She looked at him more closely, and from the way he stood, the way his head sank into his shoulders, she realized that the man was pretty full of something. But he was also RA, and whether they chose to call the present time night or day, as a practical matter Kung made it pretty close to broad daylight. "I'll take a look," she decided. She followed him behind the cook-tent, and there was one of the balloonists, clinging to a rope and singing softly and mournfully to itself. It was much bigger than the female she had seen at Camp Detrick, but obviously in some sort of trouble.

"What's it saying?" she demanded.

The sergeant said with a straight face, "I really don't know, ma'am. You want to hold him a minute? Just pull down on the rope."

Margie looked at him thoughtfully for a moment, but he was right—it was interesting. She pulled on the rope. "Damn thing's strong," she complained. "Hey, Sweggert! What are you doing?"

He had leaned down and pulled something out from under a tarpaulin. "Just a strobe light, ma'am."

"And what are you going to do with it?"

"Well," he said cunningly, "I haven't never seen it, but the guys say if you give one of these things a flash it's real interesting."

She looked from him to the sad, wrinkled face of the balloonist, and back. "Sergeant," she said grimly, "it damn well better be or I'll have your ass on toast. Flash your fucking strobe."

"Is that an order, ma'am?"

"Flash it!" she snarled. "Or—"

And then he did.

·FIFTEEN·

AFTER FOUR DAYS of trying, Ana was finally granted permission to use the radio for a call to the People's camp. When the communications clerk signaled *go*, she leaned forward and spoke in Urdu into the microphone. "This is Ana Dimitrova calling from the camp of the Food-Exporting Bloc. I wish to speak to Ahmed Dulla, please."

The comm clerk switched off the microphone and said, "Now you wait. It usually takes about ten minutes for a return message."

"Message? Can I not speak directly to Dr. Dulla?"

"Not with the Peeps, honey. We transmit a message, they transmit an answer. If they feel like it."

"How very queer. Well, thank you, I will wait outside." As she left she added, "Please call me when the answer comes."

"Count on it, sweets."

What a nuisance, she thought crossly, sitting lotus-legged in the warm electric-heater glow from Kung overhead. Still—ten minutes! She had waited much longer than ten minutes to hear Ahmed's voice. And at least his plight could no longer be as serious as she had feared at first. The word was out in the camp that the People's Republics, through what superhuman exertions one could hardly imagine, had succeeded in reestablishing communication with their outpost on Jem. A ship had landed—a small one, to be sure, but at least they were no longer helplessly dependent on the other colonies for the means to survive. How that must have angered Dulla!

Around her the camp was very busy. Nearly a hectare had been cleared and seeded on the slopes above, and the stanchions were in place for the lights that would make the seeds grow. Power would be next, and that was already being attended to. The Food Bloc at last had its own solar-power plant in process of assembly, and meanwhile there was a nuclear-fueled steam plant already in operation—small, expensive, but reliable.

Ana was the best of the three translators in the camp and, since the disappearance of Harriet Santori, the only one who seemed capable of picking up the fine structure of an only partly understood language. Her Krinpit was quite imperfect, and there seemed little chance to practice it. For the burrowers she had spent much time with this James Morrissey, who seemed to have taken them as his personal reason for existence; but none of it had come to much. The microphones he insinuated so gently into the tunnels sometimes picked up a scrap or two of squealing, chittering, half-muffled sounds; but evidently the burrowers detected them at once and avoided them—when they didn't steal them. More than once Morrissey had pulled out a probe and found the working head neatly disconnected.

But with the balloonists she had become almost fluent. She had worked closely with Professor Dalehouse, so far only by radio; the intriguing but frightening prospect of soaring with him under a cluster of bags of hydrogen was for some indeterminate time in the future. Then the Russian pilot, Kappelyushnikov, had taken off with Colonel Menninger's orderly and a cluster of hydrogen tanks on some foolish, secretive errand, and she had been ordered off the radio until further notice. Instead she was assigned to clerical work in the tiny hospital, where there was no clerical work to speak of, since it had as yet no real patients.

But. Regardless. No matter what the small frustrations and annoyances, was she not on Jem, only a matter of a few score kilometers at most from Ahmed? Not to mention the dizzying excitement of being on Jem at all. Another planet! Circling another star! So far from home that not even the sun itself could be found in the ruddy Jemman sky! She had not yet dared to go out into the jungle (though others had, and returned safe and excited at the strangenesses they had seen). She had not even swum in that great lake, or sea, so temptingly near; she had not thought to bring a bathing suit, had not yet found time to make one, and certainly would not follow the custom of those others who frolicked in nothing at all along the beach. Just now she could see a batch of them splashing and shouting. They were supposed to be working on the hydroplanes that were being assembled at the water's edge, but their thoughts, she would warrant, were far less on transportation than on the animal joy of the beach.

Not, she thought justly, that that in itself was wrong; why should they not? It was not Ana's concern if other persons had moral standards different from her own, so long as they did not try to inflict them on her. And splashing would in fact be great fun in this muggy heat—

"Dimitrova!" She jumped up and ran inside the tent for her answer, but it was only:

"Ahmed Dulla is not available at present. The message will be given to him."

In English. And English with a very bad accent, at that; whatever Heir-of-Mao had sent, it was not good translators. She thanked the comm clerk, concealing her disappointment, and strolled toward the perimeter. Off duty, not time to eat, too early to sleep; what should she do since she could not do the thing she wanted most?

Really, it was too disappointing! Where could he be?

She was annoyed to discover that she was beginning another headache. How infuriating! For some reason she had not had very many in her first days on Jem—perhaps because everything was so intensely exciting that she had no time to think of headaches. She did not want one now. Ana was an industrious person by nature, and it occurred to her that idleness was not likely to prevent the headache, but only to make it worse. What to do? If she only had a proper costume, how agreeable it would be to help the boatbuilders on the beach. Or to climb the slope and assist in planting —but no, at the moment they were only plowing, and she did not know how to run the tractor. The power plant? She knew nothing of it, of course, but she had sturdy limbs and a willingness to use her muscles. Why not?

Unfortunately, as she approached she discovered that one of the noncoms working on the project was Sergeant Sweggert.

She changed course and walked briskly away.

She had avoided Sweggert since the night she had come back with the colonel's orderly and found the two of them in rut, out in the open for all to see! Of course, no other had seen. Nan had turned away at once, sweating with embarrassment, and there had been no one else, or all the camp would have been talking of it. Tinka would not speak, Sweggert would perhaps not dare to, and the colonel—well, Ana did not have the delusion that she understood the colonel. But Colonel Marge Menninger she had not been able to avoid, and the woman had said nothing of the incident, had in fact showed no signs that it had ever taken place. That bleached American, copulating with a man whose name she perhaps did not even know! No, that was unfair; they knew each other. But certainly not socially. Oh, yes, to be sure, she would blame it on the aphrodisiac effect of the—the mist, she put it to herself, that the wounded balloonist emitted. One had heard all about that by now. Still, how appallingly lewd! Not to say—what was the word?—"tacky."

Ana found herself at a guard post in the perimeter fence, and at once it became clear what she wished to do. "I am going for a walk," she told the corporal in charge, who shrugged and watched impassively as Ana squeezed between the strands of the barbed wire.

In a few steps she was out of sight of the camp.

If she could not see Ahmed, at least she could see Jem. She pushed through the violet-oily growth, here all flickering with blue-green lights, and paused to listen: tiny skittering sounds from the underbrush, the rustle of the plants in the wind. There was no wildlife here that would harm her, she had been assured. Because of the presence of the camp, there were not many animals at all. Some had been frightened away, some poisoned away; where the garbage details had brought a day's collection of slops into the woods and buried them, you could see the ferns withered, the crabgrass ground cover dry. Terrestrial biochemistry was as hostile to Jemman as the other way around, but the Jemmans had not had a Camp Detrick to make them salves and injections against the rot.

But what was left—how fascinating and how strange! Forests of plants like ferns, but fruiting and with woody stems; succulents almost like bamboo (the hollow stems would make good structural materials, and Ana's thrifty soul instructed her to tell the colonel not to waste precious iron on tent stakes anymore); vines like grapes, with hard seeds no doubt meant to be spread in the excrement of small animals (if any survived in this part of the forest); and the mangrovelike giants called "many-trees," a dozen or more trunks linking together at the crown, which made a canopy over her.

She stopped and looked around. There was no question of getting lost, she reassured herself, as long as she kept the red-glinting water in sight on her left. At any time she could simply climb down to it and return along the beach.

And there was no question of being tired here, either, when one climbed so lightly over fallen logs and rocks. It was an excellent time for taking a nature stroll, she thought, squirming between the trunks of a many-tree that glittered blue-green in firefly beads —if only her head did not hurt so.

In front of her was a lump of fungus, gray-pink and without lights of its own. It looked quite like a brain, she thought. In fact, rather like her own. Since the brain splitting had been done under local anesthesia she had seen every step, sometimes in the mirror overhead, sometimes in the closed-circuit likris screen. That was how her brain had seemed to her, quite remote and unfeeling. Even when the sharp hooked blade had halved it in one smooth motion, it had been hard to connect that sight with the insistent dragging pressure that was all she felt. . . . Later, when they were reconnecting some of the necessary nerves, she suddenly felt the reality of it. She would have been ill except for the surgeon's motherly scorn. "A great strong girl like you!" she had laughed. "No. Nonsense! You will not vomit." And Nan had not. . . .

What was that noise?

It sounded like distant sticks rattling against hollow logs and someone moaning. It was the sort of sound she had heard before, on tapes at Camp Detrick. The crustaceans, yes! But perhaps not the social race. Perhaps those wild and surely dangerous ones that had been only rumored—

The human voice that came from behind her was severe.

"Is it sensible for you to be alone here, Ana?"

In Urdu! With that stern compassion she had heard so often! She knew before she turned that it was Ahmed.

An hour later, a kilometer away, she lay in his arms, unwilling to move lest she wake him. The Krinpit's sound was always audible, sometimes near, sometimes moving farther away; she smiled to herself as she thought that the creature had surely been near while they were making love. No matter. It was not a matter for shame, what she would proclaim anywhere. It was not at all like that American bleached blond, because—well, of course, because it was with Ahmed.

He twitched, snorted, and woke up. "Ah, Ana! Then I did not dream this!"

"No, Ahmed." She hesitated and then said in a softer voice, "But I have had that dream many times. . . . No! Not so quickly again, please, dear Ahmed—or yes, whenever you like; but first let me look at you." She shook her head and scolded, "You are so thin! Have you been ill?"

The black-bead eyes were opaque. "Ill? Yes, sometimes. Also sometimes starving."

"Starving! How terrible! But—but—"

"But why starve? That is simple to answer. Because your people shot down our transports."

"But that is quite impossible!"

"It is not impossible," he contradicted, "because it happened. Food for many days, scientific instruments, two ships—and thirty-four human beings, Ana."

"It must have been an accident."

"You are naive." He got up angrily, pulling his clothes together. "I do not blame you, Ana. But those crimes are a fact, and I must blame someone." He disappeared behind a many-tree, and after a moment she could hear the splashing of his urine against the bole.

And also another sound: the Krinpit's rattle and moan, growing close again. If only she had had more time with the tapes at Detrick! But even so, she could distinguish a pattern that was repeated over and over. *Sssharrn—*, and then two quick notes: *eye-gone.*

She called weakly, "Ahmed?" and heard his laugh.

"Ah, Ana, does my friend frighten you? He will not harm us. We are not good for him to eat."

"I did not know you had such friends."

"Well, perhaps I have not. No. We are not friends. But as I am the enemy of his enemies, we are allies at least. Come along, Sharn-igon," he said, like a householder strolling a puppy, and came back into view.

Scuttling lopsidedly behind him was a great nightmare creature, rattling and moaning. Ana had never been so close to an adult, live Krinpit, had never quite realized their size and the loudness of their sounds. It did not have a crab's claws. It had jointed limbs that waved above it, two that tapered to curved points like a cat's claw, two that ended in fistlike masses of shell.

It paused, seeming to regard Nan, although as far as she could tell it had no eyes. And among the sounds, she recognized words in Urdu! Syllable by syllable, it scratched and grumbled out a sentence.

"Is this one to die?"

"No, no!" said Ahmed quickly. "She is—" He hesitated, then emitted sounds in the Krinpit language. Perhaps it was his accent, but Ana could not understand a word. "I have told him you are my he-wife," he explained.

"He-wife?"

"They have a very rich sexual life," he said.

"Please, Ahmed. I am not ready for a joking little chat. The Krinpit said 'to die,' and what does it mean?"

"Naive Ana," he said again, looking at her thoughtfully. Then he shrugged. He did not reply, but he unwrapped a ruddy-brown leaf from an object he had been carrying. It was a flat metal blade, broader at the end, the edge razor-sharp. The hilt was sized to fit a man's hand, and the whole thing half a meter long.

"Ahmed! Is that a sword?"

"A machete. But you are right; it is a sword also now."

"Ahmed," she said, her heart pounding harder than the throbbing in her head, "some days ago three persons from the Food camp were killed. I have thought it was an accident, but now I am not sure. Shall I ask you if you know anything of this?"

"Ask what you like, woman."

"Tell me!"

He thrust the machete into the loamy ground. "All right, if you will have it so, I will tell you. No. I did not kill those Fats. But yes, I know of their death. I do not mourn them, I hope many more will die. And if it is necessary for me to kill a few, I shall not shrink from it!"

"But—but— But Ahmed," she babbled, "dear, gentle Ahmed, this is murder! Worse than murder, it is an act of war! Suppose the Food Bloc retaliates? Suppose our homelands do not accept this as a mere struggle far away, but themselves retaliate on each other? Suppose—"

"Have done with your supposing!" he shouted. "What can they do to retaliate? Bomb Pakistan? Let them! Let them destroy Hyderabad and Multan, let them bomb Karachi, let them wipe out all the cities and burn the whole coast. You have been there, Ana. How much of Pakistan can be destroyed? What bombs can blast through mountains? The people will survive. The leeches that flock to the cities to beg, the government parasites— yes, the intellectuals, the proud bloodsuckers like you and me— what do I care if they all die? The people in the valleys will live!"

She was silent, frightened, searching for words that might sway him and finding none. "Ah," he said in disgust, "what is the sense of this? But do not be angry with me."

"Angry? That is not what I feel," she said miserably.

"Then what? Hatred? Fear? Ana, what are we to do? Let them starve us? We have one small ship to save us, and what have the Fats and the Greasies? Navies! And if the fighting spreads—" He hesitated and then burst out, "Let it! Let all the rich ones kill each other. What do we care? Remember, six out of ten human beings on Earth are ours! If there is war on Earth—if only a million survive, then six hundred thousand of them will be citizens of the People's Republics. And here—"

She shook her head, almost weeping. "And here? Sixty percent too?"

"No. More. On Son of Kung—if anyone survives—one hundred percent ours."

·SIXTEEN·

THE RAINS were all around, squall clouds driving toward them, squall clouds already past them, up toward the Heat Pole, where the raindrops fell a kilometer or two and then evaporated, never striking the hot, salt ground. The flock was spread out over a kilometer of sky, and grumbling in dissonant chords.

"Have patience," Charlie scolded them. "We must stay, must stay."

And they echoed, "We must stay," but it was poorly sung.

No matter. Charlie had promised his two-legged friend that they would stay on station, waiting to observe certain strange and incomprehensible events, and the flock would do as he vowed.

Still, it was uncomfortable to him, like an itch or a sunburn to a human being, to have the swarm in such disarray. The place he had promised to watch was upwind of the camp of the Big Sun. It did not do to come too close to that. Many of his flock, and even more of other flocks, had been punctured or burned by the far-striking missiles of that camp, and so he had to try to keep the flock from drifting toward it, seeking every counterflowing gust, and still avoid the squalls as much as possible. Dalehouse had told him that it would be difficult. But he had also said it was important.

Charlie rotated his eye patches over the entire horizon. No sign of the aircraft he had been told to expect. But he did see a vagrant drift of thistledown and spinner silk moving across the hills below. A crosscurrent! He sang his flock together and vented gas.

The swarm followed, dropping into a level where the wind took them away from the rain to a likely-looking area of updraft. They followed well, everything considered. Expertly he guided them under the base of a fair-weather cumulus, and they rose with the drift.

The song of the swarm became contented. It was at the top of these invisible pillars of rising air that the best feeding was found: pollen and butterfly-seed capsules, the small, soft creatures that filled the same ecological niche that insects did on Earth, dried salt particles from the wavelets of landlocked seas, and even tinier things. A flock at feed was queer-looking, with every fin and frill extended to trap whatever touched it. It was also at risk, or once would have been. It was a favorite time for the *ha'aye'i* to knife in, slashing every bag they passed and tearing the life out of the victims before the helpless gaze of their flock-mates. Helpless no more! Charlie sang a boastful song of his great friend Danny Dalehouse, who had given them the far-striking weapons that drove the *ha'aye'i* a hundred clouds away. Or sometimes did. Now each male and some of the females in his own flock had the weapons, and the *ha'aye'i* had come to recognize Charlie's swarm and avoid it.

Although, in truth, it was no longer as tempting to the predators as it had once been. So few were left! Once there had been hundreds, now fewer than a score.

There was still no aircraft on the horizon, nothing happening on the mesa upwind of the camp of the Big Sun. Charlie relaxed and fed with his swarm, and as he ate he became more mellow. He led the flock in gentle songs of childhood and joy.

There had been a time when Charlie was a tiny pip-sized pod, pumping mightily to bulge the creases out of his little gasbag but still tied to the ragged end of his sailing ribbon and to the winds that bore it where they liked. Gusts blew. Air-to-air lightning spat all around him. Because he had no real control over his altitude he was sometimes tossed up through the tops of towering convection clouds, with the dull red sun hot on his tiny balloon and actual stars shining through the murky sky; other times he was so low that he brushed hills and fern trees, and shelled or furred creatures clutched after him as he spun by. Eighty out of a hundred of his brood-mates died then, in one of those ways or in some other. Ten more died almost as soon as their drift-ribbons fell away, when they were tasty hors d'oeuvres for the *ha'aye'i*, or sometimes for the protein-hungry adults of another chance-met flock. Or even of their own. Only a few out of each hundred survived to reproduce. And then there were still the *ha'aye'i*. And the storms. And the clutching beasts from below.

But still—to be a balloonist! To soar and to sing! Above all, to share the chorused flocklore that united them every one, from the tiniest pod to the leaky, old, slow giants that even the *ha'aye'i* scorned. Charlie's song was triumphant, and all the flock around him stopped their greedy gobbling to join in the harmony.

Still his eye patches rotated watchfully toward the mesa; but still there was no sign of the airplane or of the New Friend he had been told would rise from the spot. And they were drifting with the cloud, away from the camp of the Big Sun.

Many of the flock were sated now, softly singing their private courtesy songs of thanksgiving. They were a fine flock, although, Charlie admitted, very few in number.

He sang to them, "Stop feeding, stop feeding! We must go!"

"Go where, go where?" grumbled a chorus of the slower and hungrier ones, and an individual song sounded above the choir.

Faintly: "I must eat more. I die." That was the old female, Blue-Rose Glow. Her bag had been meanly seared when half the flock was set aflame.

"Not now, not now," sang Charlie commandingly. "Follow!" And he sang the new song, the duty song he had learned from his friend Danny Dalehouse. It was no longer enough to float and sing and replenish hydrogen and breed. Not anymore. Station must be kept and the mesa observed. And the camp of the Big Sun must be avoided, and the *ha'aye'i* guarded against, and the swarm kept together; so many imperatives, both the new and the old! And so he led them through their slow, bobbing dance, crisscross with the winds.

For a long time he led them, watching ceaselessly as he had promised. Even so, it was not he who first saw the thing. From far behind, old Blue-Rose Glow sang feebly, "There is a new Sky-Danger."

"Catch up, catch up!" he commanded. "You sing poorly." It was not sung in unkindness but only because it was true.

"I leak," she apologized. "Nevertheless it is there, almost in reach of the Earth-Dangers, far away."

He rotated his eye patches and rose to another air current. There it was. "I see the Sky-Danger," he sang, and the rest of the flock confirmed. It was not a *ha'aye'i*. It was the hard mechanical thing from the camp of the Middle Sun, as he had been told. In it, he knew, was the Other Friend who had sometimes soared with Danny Dalehouse, and also the New Friend he had not yet seen.

It was all as had been said by Danny Dalehouse. The biplane slunk in at treetop level and set itself down on the dry mesa a dozen kilometers upwind of the Greasy camp. While the swarm watched, Kappelyushnikov and a female person emerged and began to fill a net of balloons out of tiny tanks.

When the New Friend's cluster began to swell and she rose gently from the ground, the aircraft took off again, turned quickly, and slipped back down the slope toward the distant ocean-lake. The New Friend rose into the prevailing poleward wind and drifted directly toward the camp of the Big Sun.

Charlie dared come no closer, but he saw her venting gas as she approached the camp. She tumbled into the underbrush somewhere nearby; and it was all as had been foretold.

"The thing is done," Charlie caroled triumphantly.

"And what now?" asked the swarm, milling around him, staring after the New Friend as she fell.

"I will ask the air," he sang. His little insect legs fumbled at the switch of the hard, shiny speaker-to-air Danny Dalehouse had given him. He sang a questioning greeting to his friend.

He tried twice, listening between times as Dalehouse had taught him. There was no answer, only an unpleasant hissing song of static and distant storms.

"We must go near to the camp of the Middle Sun," he announced. "The speaker-to-air cannot sing so far." His skilled eyes read the signs of the clouds and the fern tops far below, seeking the currents he wanted. It was too bad that Dalehouse could so seldom soar with the flock these days because of the hated *ha'aye'i* of his own kind, but Charlie knew that once they were in line of sight the speaker-to-air would bring his song.

"Follow!" he sang. He swarmed the flock around him. They dropped, all fourteen of them, through a fast-moving layer of stratus cloud into the backflow near the surface.

When they emerged, old Blue-Rose Glow was gone, the leaks in her bag finally too great to allow her to remain airborne. So was the young female called Shrill-Squeal, nowhere in sight, even her song no longer audible.

By the time they approached the camp of the Middle Sun and Charlie began to sing through the radio to Dalehouse, there were only twelve left in the flock.

Marge Menninger looked up as Kappelyushnikov came in from the orderly room, closing the flap to her private office behind him. "Any word?" she asked.

"Danny has had radio from gasbag, yes. Your friend was seen to descend near Greasies, all in order."

"How long ago?"

"With gasbags, who can say? Perhaps some hours. Not long after I departed spy-drop scene."

"All right. Thanks." After he left, Marge started to call the communications tent, then decided against it. If the Greasies radioed that they had rescued Tinka, blown helplessly off course, the communications clerk would let her know. And he hadn't. So the Greasies were playing it covert and slick, and what was Tinka up against in their camp? Had they figured out that she really wasn't there by accident? Could she . . . ? Were they . . . ? Wasn't it . . . ? Questions multiplied themselves in Margie's mind endlessly, and there was no straightforward way of getting answers. You could get your ass lost in those swamps of contingencies and subjunctives.

That was not the way Marge Menninger ran her life. She made a decision. In one hour exactly she would have the comm clerk radio a query to the Greasies, and until then she would put it out of her mind. Meanwhile, lunch was fifty minutes away, and what to use that time for?

The fifteen notes she had made to herself on this morning's calendar had all been checked off. All current projects were on schedule, or close enough. Everyone had been assigned tasks. The first hectare of wheat was in the ground, sixteen different strains competing to see which would thrive best. The perimeter defenses were in order. Three turrets still sat on the beach, ready to be put where needed when she wanted to expand the perimeter or establish another post. She looked at the 1:1000 map, two meters long and a meter high, that covered almost all of one wall of her office. That was something! It showed every feature within a kilometer of where she sat—seven creeks or rivers, a dozen hills, two capes, several bays. Grid references were not enough, they needed names. What better way to name them than to let individual members of the camp pick them? She would organize a drawing; each winner could name something, and that would give them something to do. She called in her temporary orderly and dictated a short memo for the bulletin board. "Check it with the communications section," she finished. "Make sure we list all the features worth naming."

"Yes'm. Colonel? Sergeant Sweggert wants to see you. Says it's not urgent."

Margie wrote *Sweggert* on her calendar. "I'll let you know." Then she put Sweggert out of her mind, too. She had not yet decided what to do about Sweggert. She had a wide variety of options, from laughing it off to court-martialing him for rape. Which she elected would depend a lot on how Sweggert conducted himself. So far he had had the smarts to keep a low profile around her.

On the other hand, she thought, her authority to court-martial anybody for anything rested on the military chain of command, which extended up from her through the tactran link to higher authority on Earth. And who was to say how long Earth would give a shit about backing her up? Or about whether the colony lived or died? The news from home was bad, so bad that she had not passed all of it on to the camp. The tactran message acknowledging her shopping list had advised that it was touch and go whether she would get everything she had asked for. And requests for further supplies after that shipment were, quote, to be evaluated in terms of conditions at the time of receipt of requisition, unquote.

It was what she had expected. But it was sobering.

On her pad for the afternoon she made two notes: *Medic.— bank okay? Food—6 mos. estimate firm? Stretch 1 yr w rationing?*

It was a damn nuisance that the agronomists all seemed to be Canadian! Margie needed some smart and private help—smart, because how they managed their crops was quite likely to be life-and-death for the colony; private, because she didn't want the colony to know that just yet. If she got everything on her shopping list she would have plenty of seed stock. But who knew whether she had the ones that would grow best?

Dismiss that thought, too.

Forty minutes left.

She unlocked the private drawer of her desk and lit a joint. Assume the shopping list all gets delivered. There was enough on it for pretty fair margin against most kinds of disasters, she thought, and there was no sense worrying until she had to.

The requisition list included a good chunk of personal things for Margie herself: clothes, cosmetics, microfiche sewing patterns. With the patterns there would be enough variety in styles to suit everyone in the camp, male or female, for a good long time, assuming they found some way of producing fabrics to make the patterns on. It would be nice to have some pretty clothes. She was already beginning to feel the absence of Sakowitz, Marks and Sparks, Sears, and Two Guys. One day, maybe, she thought, drawing a deep hit. Not Sakowitz, no. But maybe a few boutiques. Maybe some of the people in the camp had sewing or tailoring skills, and maybe it was about time she started locating them. She flipped the calendar ahead a few pages and made a note on a virgin page. That Bulgarian prunt was the kind of girly-girl who would like to sew, possibly even as much as Margie did herself; she had been pretty morose after her long walk in the countryside, but she did her work and might need something to occupy her mind. It didn't seem that she wanted a man for that purpose; at least, she had thoroughly discouraged Guy Tree and Cappy and Sweggert . . .

Sweggert.

"Jack, send the sergeant in," she called.

"Yes'm. He's gone back to the perimeter, but I'll get him."

As she leaned back, marshalling her thoughts about Sweggert, the handset buzzed; it was the communications clerk. "Colonel? I was just talking to the Greasies about Sergeant Pellatinka."

"I didn't tell you to ask them."

"No'm. But I kept sending on her frequency like you ordered, and their radioman cut in to ask if we had lost her. So I said she didn't answer. So they said they'd send out a party to look for her."

Margie sat back and took a thoughtful drag on the joint. According to the balloonists, there was no way the Greasies couldn't have seen her come down. So now they were overtly lying.

Sergeant Sweggert shared a number of traits with Marge Menninger. One of them was that he was willing to go to a lot of trouble to get things right, and then if he saw a chance for improvement he was willing to do whatever it took to make them righter. When he perceived that moving the Number Three machine-gun emplacement two meters toward the lake would improve the field of fire, he moved it. Or his squad did. The fact that it took five hours of backbreaking work did not affect his decision. He lent a hand to put the HMG on its tripod and swung it to check the field. "Fucking lousy," he told the crew, "but we'll leave it for now. Get that ammo restowed."

He crouched behind the gun, swiveling it through full traverse. It was an act that gave him pleasure. As far as the shore of the lake on the extreme left and the beginning of the fern forest on the right, there was no way that any sizable creature could approach without being a clear target for the gunner. The claymores and smoke bombs were emplaced and fused, and his command-post detonating radio was keyed to each of them. The floodlights were in position, with quadruple redundancy. At any given moment only a quarter of them were lit, searching the entire area around the perimeter. Every hour that quarter went off and the next quarter came on so that any burned-out bulbs or wiring deficiencies would distribute themselves equally and could be fixed in the downtime. In actual combat, of course, they would all be on. Most would be shot out, but not in time to let anyone cross that perimeter. Not alive.

Although, he admitted to himself as he climbed out of the dome, the chances that anyone would try a straightforward frontal attack were very small. Maybe an attack from the sky. Maybe by long-range rocket fire. Maybe not at all. This whole fucking shoot-up was crazy, if you asked Sergeant Sweggert. What the fuck was there to fight about in this asshole place without a bar or a town or even, for God's sake, a decent tree or field? If you had asked him, that was what he would have said, in total sincerity, but it would not have stopped him from fighting for it.

And inside he was swearing. The colonel wouldn't have kept him waiting like this a week ago. If she was going to shaft him, what was she waiting for? . . . "Sarge." He looked up. "They're calling you from the orderly room." He turned idly and saw the corporal waving.

"Aggie, take over," he ordered. "If I come back and that ammo isn't restowed, it's all your asses."

He strolled back toward the HQ tent and walked in. Marge Menninger was eating out of a mess kit, reading from a small-screen viewer. She didn't look up. "The perimeter's looking good, Sweggert," she said. "Got that machine gun back in place?"

"Yes'm. Colonel? There's a bunch of gasbags around, and that one we been using is about used up. We'll be relieved in a couple of minutes. Can we get a fix from the new ones?"

She put down her spoon and looked at him. After a moment, she said, "Just who do you mean by 'we,' soldier?"

"Oh, no, ma'am!" Jesus, she was touchy! He knew he was close to trouble. "I don't mean nothing, ma'am, just that the detail's been working hard and they need a little break. We'll—they'll come out of it in an hour, and the relief'll be there anyway."

She studied him for a moment. "That's four-oh, Sweggert, but only half the detail. Keep the rest sober."

"Sure thing, colonel. Thank you, colonel." He got out of there as fast as he could. Shit, he should've been more careful, knowing how she felt and all. Not that she was all wrong. If he hadn't been drunk he wouldn't have done it. But, shit! It was worth it. Remembering the way she had been with a skin full of the balloonist mist, his groin grew heavy.

When he got back to the detail he looked at them with some disapproval. Corporal Kristianides was skinny and had sideburns all down her cheeks, but she was the best he had to pick from. "Aggie, take Peterson and four others; you're on duty till the relief shows up. Kris, you and the rest come along with me. We're gonna take ourselves a jizzum break. Anybody don't want to come, switch with somebody don't want to stay. Let's move it."

The balloonists were out over the ocean-lake now, half a kilometer away and low. Sweggert marched his dozen troops across the camp to the empty tents at the end of the company street; he would do it in the open if he had to, but damned if he wouldn't take a little privacy when he could get it. The tethered balloonist, further than ever from recuperating, had been moved there days since, along with the strobe light.

Sweggert stopped, swearing. Nan Dimitrova and Dalehouse were talking to the balloonist, and only a few meters away the Russian pilot, Kappelyushnikov, was complaining about something to Colonel Tree. Privacy, *shit*. But it didn't matter; he had Colonel Menninger's permission, and she was the one who counted. He retrieved the strobe and pointed it toward the hovering swarm.

Predictably, Dalehouse butted in. "What do you think you're doing, Sweggert?"

Sweggert took time to aim the strobe and flash it to bring them in before he answered. "Gonna have a little fun. The colonel said it was okay."

"Hell she did! Anyway—"

"Anyway," Sweggert interrupted, "why don't you go check with her if you don't believe me? Would you move a little, sir? You're getting between them and the light."

Ana Dimitrova laid her hand on Dalehouse's arm to keep him from replying. "It is not fun for the balloonists, Sergeant Sweggert. To experience sexual climax is very painful and debilitating. As you can see, this one is seriously affected. It may die."

"What a way to go, hey, Ana?" Sweggert grinned. "Take it up with the colonel—hey, Dalehouse! What are you doing?"

Dalehouse had switched on his radio and was singing softly into it. Colonel Tree, beginning to pay attention, walked toward them, and Sweggert turned to him. "Colonel! We have Colonel Menninger's permission to get the Loonies in for a fix, and this guy's telling them to screw off!"

Tree stopped with his hands clasped behind his back and nodded gravely. "A dilemma," he said in his soft child's voice. "It will be quite interesting to see what they do."

What they were doing was spreading themselves all over the sky, some dropping lower to catch the onshore breeze, others hesitating. They were singing loudly and discordantly, and the sounds came distantly from the sky and tinnily from the radio in Dalehouse's hand. Sweggert stood rock-still, controlling the rage that was building up in him. Fucking Cong! When you had the CO's permission, that was all you were supposed to need! Why wouldn't Tree back him up?

"Gimme that," he growled, reaching out for Dalehouse's radio.

But Dalehouse's expression had changed. "Hold it," he snapped, and sang a quick phrase into the radio. The answer came back as a cascade of musical phrases; Dalehouse looked startled and Ana Dimitrova gasped, her hand to her lips. "Tree," he said, "according to Charlie, there's some Krinpit down the beach, and they're eating a couple of people."

"But Krinpit do not eat human beings," objected Colonel Tree, and Sweggert chimed in:

"There's nobody down there. Nobody's gone through the perimeter all day."

Dalehouse repeated his question into the radio and shrugged. "That's what he says. He could be wrong about the eating part, I guess—he doesn't have a very clear concept of killing, except to eat."

Sweggert put down the strobe. "We better tell the colonel," he said.

Colonel Tree said, "That's correct. You do so, Dalehouse. Sergeant, form your squad on the beach in thirty seconds, full combat gear. We're going to see what's happening."

Half an hour later Marge Menninger herself, with thirty armed grunts behind her, met the first party coming back along the beach. There were no casualties, or at least none from the Food Bloc, but they were carrying two people. One was in a sort of sling made from two jackets knotted together, the other on Sergeant Sweggert's shoulder, fireman-carry. They were both dead. When Sweggert put his burden down it was obvious why he had been easy to carry. Both legs were missing, and so was part of his head.

The other body was less mutilated, so that Marge Menninger recognized her at once.

It was Tinka.

Marge stood numbly while Sweggert made his report. No Krinpit in sight; they had got away, so far that they couldn't even be heard. Both people were dead when they got there, but recently; the bodies were still warm. For that matter, they were still warm now. And the man had had a packet in a waterproof wrapping inside his shirt. Margie accepted it and tore it open. Microfiches—scores of them. The man's ID card, which showed that he was the Indonesian Tinka had gone to contact. A pair of child-sized spectacles—flat glass, not optically ground. Why glasses? For that matter, how had the two got here? Had they been caught as spies and then somehow escaped? And how had they come the long distance from the Greasy camp to the beach where they died?

By the time they got back to the base, she had an answer to at least part of the question, because Dalehouse reported that the balloonists had spotted something farther down the beach that looked like the remains of a deflated rubber boat. She swung the tiny glasses from their elastic band as she listened, nodding, taking in all of it as information to process, not quite ready to take in the information of Tinka's death as a pain to feel.

She looked down at the glasses. They were now almost opaque.

"That's interesting," she said in a voice that was very nearly normal. "They must be photosensitive glass. Like indoor-outdoor sunglasses." She glanced up at the sullen red coal of Kung overhead. "Only what in the world would anybody want with them on Jem?"

·SEVENTEEN·

SIX KILOMETERS down the shoreline from where he had slain the Poison Ghosts, Sharn-igon paused in his flight to scratch out a shallow pit under a bluff. He needed to hide because he needed to rest.

Digging was always dangerous for a Krinpit because of the Ghosts Below. But here it was unlikely they would be near—too close to the water. They did not like to risk their tunnels flooding. And the many-tree on the bluff above him was a good sign. The roots of the many-tree were distasteful to them.

As he settled himself in, Sharn-igon wondered briefly what had become of his cobelligerent, the Poison Ghost Dulla. He did not feel concern, as one might for a fellow being. He did not think of Dulla in that way. Dulla was a weapon, a tool, without "being-ness." After they had slain the Poison Ghosts Dulla called "Greas-ies," they had both fled, and of course Dulla had fled faster and farther. Sharn-igon did not think of that as a betrayal. If he had been the nimble one and Dulla the slow-moving, he would certainly have done the same. Dulla's utility as a tool lay in his speed and in the way he was able to speak words to other Poison Ghosts that caused them to hesitate, to be uncertain, while Sharn-igon had time to come in upon them and kill. It was so very easy to kill Poison Ghosts! A few slashes, a blow with the club-claw—it took no more than that. Sometimes they had weapons, and Sharn-igon had learned to respect some of those weapons. But the two on the beach had had so little—a bright-sounding popgun whose tiny bullets bounced off his shell, a thing that squirted some sort of foul, stinging smell that made him feel queer and unpleasant for a moment but did not slow him in the kill. Such as they he could kill with or without his tool, the Poison Ghost Dulla.

He switched his carapace back and forth to wedge himself deeper in his pit and rested, his hearing receptors watchful toward the water, his feelers drilled deep into the soil to listen for vibrations from any approaching Ghosts Below. It was the burrowers he feared, more than any danger from the water or the beach.

Of course, in normal circumstances an adult Krinpit in shell was a match for a dozen of the Ghosts Below—as long as he could stay on the surface, or at least in sound of it. In the open, Ghosts Below seemed deaf, running almost at random. But these were not normal circumstances. Sharn-igon was not only weary; he felt sick. He felt irritable, tense, bloated—ready, he would have said to his he-wife (but Cheee-pruitt was months dead, his carapace dry), to stridulate and jump out of his shell. But it was not the right time for that. He was not due for many months yet, so it couldn't be normal pre-molt tension.

Abruptly his sphincter loosened. He regurgitated everything he had eaten in a great flood—meat of deafworm, scraps of chitin of crabrat, half-digested fruits and fungi and leaves.

Vomiting left him weak but calm. After resting for a moment, he covered the mess over and then methodically began to clean his shell. No doubt the Poison Ghosts were taking revenge for being killed on the beach. It had to be their scraps of flesh still caught in Sharn-igon's chelae that were making him ill. That—and the inner sickness that had claimed him when the Poison Ghosts first came to his city and began the remorseless chain of circumstance that had taken all joy from his life.

Krinpit did not cry. They had no tear ducts; they had no eyes to have tear ducts in. They did have the emotion of sorrow, and no culture-driven taboos against expressing it in their own way. That way was stillness. A quiet Krinpit—or as close to quiet as a Krinpit could get—was a weeping Krinpit.

For most of an hour, once he had polished the last dried particle of alien blood off his tympanum, Sharn-igon was nearly sound-less: a rasp of claw against carapace, an occasional respiring moan, little else.

Unbidden, sounds of happier times echoed in his mind. He heard Cheee-pruitt again, and the little female—what was her name?—whom they had impregnated and who bore their young. She had been a dulcet creature. She had had almost a personality of her own, along with the bittersweet appeal of any mated fe-male, her young growing and eating inside her until too much was destroyed and she died, and the brood polished her carapace clean and emerged to the loud, exciting world of their wife-father's back.

But everything was changed now.

It was all the fault of the Poison Ghosts! Ever since the first of them had arrived and Cheee-pruitt—dear, lost Cheee-pruitt—had had the unwisdom to try to eat it, Sharn-igon's world had fallen apart. Not just Cheee-pruitt, all of it. The Krinpit he had mobi-lized against the Poison Ghosts Dulla called Greasies had been punished severely. His own village-mates had been attacked from the air in reprisal, and so many of them were dead. And how many had he succeeded in killing in return? A few. Hardly any. The two on the beach, the handful that he and Dulla had sur-prised at the outpost—not enough! And all of Dulla's plans had come to little: the Krinpit village nearest to the Fats had wavered and wobbled, promised to join in an attack and withdrawn the promise; and meanwhile all he and Dulla could do was skulk around like crabrats, looking for strays to attack and finding none. Until the two came out of their sinking vessel—

There was a sound from the water.

Sharn-igon froze. It was not possible for him to be wholly silent while he breathed at all, but he did his best.

He listened out of his shallow cave and heard a small, almost inaudible, blurred echo from the water. A coracle. And in it what seemed to be a Poison Ghost.

Another to kill? It was approaching. Sharn-igon thrust himself out of the cave and reared up to defend himself; and then he heard his own name shouted across the beach: "Sharn-igon!" And then those barbarous sounds that were the name of his mistrusted ally, or his truced foe: "OCK-med doo-LAH."

He scuttled across the sand, half to greet Dulla, half still ready to kill, as Dulla yelled and pleaded. "Hurry! The Fats will be searching this whole coast. We must get out!"

With Sharn-igon aboard, the coracle rode very low in the water. It could not easily sink. Its cellular shell entrapped too much air for that. But it could swamp.

Crossing Broad Water it often did, and then both of them splashed and bailed and kept a watchful eye or ear for Ghosts Above until they could get under weigh again. The little sail helped them when the wind blew fair, but there was no keel. When the wind shifted, the sail had to come down and they had to paddle. It seemed to take forever; and Sharn-igon felt increasingly ill; and at every stroke or splash the grim recriminations continued.

"But for you, my he-wife would still be alive."

"You are foolish, Sharn-igon. He tried to kill us; it is not our fault he died of it."

"And my village was attacked, and another village destroyed entirely, and I myself am ill."

"Speak of something else, Sharn-igon. Speak of the promises your Krinpit made to join in the attack on the Fats and how they broke them."

"I will speak of my sorrow and my anger, Ahmed Dulla."

"Then speak also of mine! We too have suffered in fighting with you against the common enemy."

"Suffered?"

"Yes, suffered! Before my radio was destroyed—by you, Sharn-igon, by your clumsiness!—I could hear no voice from my camp. They may be dead, all of them!"

"How many, Ahmed Dulla?"

"A dozen or more!"

"A dozen or more of you have then died. Of us, how many? Of persons, two hundred. Of females, forty. Of backlings and infants—"

But it was not until they had crossed Broad Water and Sharn-igon heard the silence from his city that he perceived the immensity of the tragedy. There was no originated sound! There were only echoes—and what echoes!

Always before, when he crossed Broad Water, the city had presented a bustling, beautiful sound. Not this time. He heard nothing. Nothing! No drone of immature males at the waterfront shredding the fish catch. No songs from the mold-eaters on the Great White Way. No hammering of stakes to build new palisades on the made land on the point. He heard the echo of his own sounds faintly returning to him and recognized the shadowy outline of the mooring rocks, a few sheds, one or two boats, some structures half destroyed, a litter of empty carapaces. Nothing else.

The city was dead.

The Poison Ghost Dulla chattered worriedly to him, and Sharn-igon made out the words. "Another attack! The place is empty. The Greasies must have come back to finish the job."

He could not reply. Stillness overcame him, a great, mourning silence so deep that even the Poison Ghost turned toward him in wonder. "Are you ill? What is happening?"

With great effort Sharn-igon scratched the words out on his tympanum. "You have killed my city and all my back-mates."

"We? Certainly not! It could not have been the People's Republics; we have not the strength anymore. It must have been the Greasies."

"Against whom you vowed to protect us!" roared Sharn-igon. He rose on hind legs to tower over Dulla, and the Poison Ghost cringed in fear. But Sharn-igon did not attack. He threw himself forward, out of the coracle, with a broad *splat* that sent the waves dancing. The water was shallow here. Sharn-igon managed to keep some of his hind feet on the oozy bottom, while enough of his breathing pores were above the surface to keep him from drowning. He charged up the shoreline, scattering the littered water in a V of foam.

The tragedy made him still again, at every step and at each fresh echo. Dead! All dead. The streets empty except for abandoned carapaces, already dry. The shops untended. The homes deserted. Not a living male, not a female, not even any scrambling, chittering young.

Dulla waded through the stink of dead and floating marine animals, towing the coracle and staring about. "What a horror!" he exclaimed. "We are brothers now more than ever, Sharn-igon."

"All of my brothers are dead."

"What? Well, yes. But we must be as brothers, to take revenge! We must be allies against the Greasies and the Fats."

Sharn-igon reared up, trapping him against the wall of a ruined shed. "I now need new allies, Ahmed Dulla," he ground out, falling upon him. In the last moment Dulla saw what was to happen and tried to escape. But it was too late; his quickness was not enough when he dodged from the snatching claws only to take the full force of the murderous club of chitin that stove his head in.

When he was quite sure Dulla was dead, Sharn-igon staggered away, blundering through the dried shells that had once been friends, to rest creakily against the wall of a shop he had once known.

He took little satisfaction in the death of one more Poison Ghost. He did not even mourn any longer for the death of his city. A nearer pain touched him. His joints were aching, his body felt bloated, his carapace seemed to be sundering at the seams. It was not his time. But there was no doubt about it. Alone in the open tomb that had once been his home, with no one to care for him while he was helpless, he was beginning to molt.

·EIGHTEEN·

AT 0130 HOURS, Major Santangelo, along with the pilot-engineer who had brought in the third ship, reported in.

"Some good news, Margie. There's a coal outcropping in the Bad Hills, two kilometers up. Plus we can burn wood and biomass, and Richy here says we can make a steam boiler with plates from one of the landing craft. If your turbine arrives, that means we can drive the generator up to full capacity, fifty kilowatts, without using up our fuel reserves."

"When?"

Santangelo looked at the engineer. "Ten days? Call it two weeks."

"Call it one week," Margie snapped. "What about alcohol?"

"Well, Morrissey's got a kind of a yeast—something like a yeast —anyway, he's getting fermentation. Should be putting the first batch through the solar still tomorrow. You can probably smell it."

"Saint, I can *taste* it. I need that alcohol to stretch out the airplane fuel!"

"I'll goose him along," Santangelo promised.

"Do it," said Margie. When they were gone she picked up the handset and called the radio shack. "Any ETA yet?"

"No, ma'am. They're still in orbit, figuring a minimum-energy descent." She hung up. At least the resupply ship was in orbit around Jem, not light-years away. But that last little step was a killer. The captain had radioed that his maneuvering reserve was low and he was waiting for the most favorable approach. That might be days! Worse than that. If the Cape had launched them without plenty of reserve, that meant things were seriously wrong at the Cape. Even wronger than the coded tactrans from Earth had indicated, and that was wrong enough.

She looked at her watch: 0145. "Send in Dr. Arkashvili," she called, and the medic came in on cue, bearing a cup of steaming black coffee.

"Medical supplies, Margie. But a little sleep would do you more good."

Marge sniffed the aluminum cup rapturously and took a scalding sip. "I wish they'd land," she said fretfully. Among the goodies on her shopping list were coffee beans, or seeds, or whatever it took to try to grow coffee for themselves. Otherwise the next couple of years, anyway, might be coffee-free. Of course, the Greasies probably had some growing already, to make that vile stuff they handed out in the little brass pots, but they weren't likely to give any away. They weren't giving anything away now, not even information over the radio; and the Peeps simply were not answering at all.

At least the camp was gratifyingly healthy, according to the medic's report. The antiallergens were standing up well, and there was nothing else in the Jemman environment to make a human being sick. A few headaches, probably from the climate and from the switch to a twenty-four-hour day; some dentistry; an appendix that needed watching; a request for a vasectomy—

"No," said Margie sharply. "Don't do any vasectomies. Or laparoscopies, either."

The doctor looked thoughtful. "You're going to have some knocked-up personnel."

"You're supposed to be able to handle that, right? Anyway, give them the pill, diaphragms, condoms—anything reversible or temporary. I get along fine with an IUD, and I can always take it out if I want to have a baby."

"Which you might?"

"Which all of us females may damn well have to, Cheech.

That's an order: everybody capable of breeding *stays* capable. How's the baby bank?"

"Coming along fine. I've got twenty-eight ova in cryonic hold, and about a hundred sperm samples."

"Good, Cheech, but not good enough. I want a hundred percent compliance with that. If anything happens to anybody, I don't want his genes lost. Or hers. They don't take up much space, do they? Then I want, let's say, four samples from each, and—what are you grinning about?"

The medic said, "Well, it's just that a couple of the ova turned out to be prefertilized. They're fine. They'll keep in the deep-freeze indefinitely, but whenever you want them reimplanted we won't have to go to the bother of getting them started."

"Hum." Margie scratched thoughtfully. "I'm almost sorry you took the sample; we could start having kids any time now. Who were they? Come on, Cheech, none of this medical confidentiality; I'm your commanding officer."

"Well, one was Ana Dimitrova."

"No shit! Whose kid?"

"You can ask her if you want to. I didn't."

Marge shook her head wonderingly. "I would have guessed her about last," she said. "And the other one? Now, wait a minute! It couldn't be me! The IUD—"

"The IUD doesn't keep an ovum from getting fertilized; it only prevents it taking root and developing."

Margie sat back and stared at the doctor. "I'll be damned," she said.

Nguyen Dao Tree was ten minutes late for his 0200 appointment, and he arrived sleepy-eyed and irritable. "This twenty-four-hour day of yours is not comfortable, Margie," he complained.

"You're not the one to bitch, Guy. I took the midnight-to-eight myself. If you'd spend your sleeping time sleeping instead of tom-catting around with every woman in the camp—"

"As to that, Marjorie," he said, "I much preferred when you and I slept on the same schedule."

"Yeah. Well. Maybe we'll have to do something about that, Guy, but right now we're late for inspection." She swallowed the last of her coffee, now cold but still delicious, and led the way.

Complaints aside, the three-shift day was working well. On the plus side, the perimeter was well guarded, the hectarage under cultivation was growing by nearly two thousand square meters every day, the each-one-teach-one training schedule Santangelo had set up so that the skills of the community were shared among several persons (what if Chiche Arkashvili died? or their one and only surviving agronomist?) was on track. On the minus, aerial surveillance showed large numbers of Krinpit roaming around the woods, coffee was not the only food item to be running low, and the resupply ship still could not give a firm landing time.

Marie allowed one hour of each day for her inspection, and she used every minute of it. No white-glove chickenshit. The inspection was rough and dirty; if everybody was doing their job and the jobs were being done, that was it. Her Bastogne grandfather had not cared if the troops were shaved, only if they could fight. And Margie had learned the skills appropriate to a fortress under siege.

That was what they were. No one had attacked the perimeter, not even a wandering Krinpit. But they were isolated in a world of enemies. From spy satellites and balloonists, from the breaking of codes and from what little could be gleaned from their infrequent radio contacts, above all from the contents of the Indonesian's pouch, Margie had formed a pretty good idea of what the Greasies were up to. Or had been up to a few weeks earlier. They had occupied the Peeps' camp; they had requisitioned quantities and varieties of personnel and equipment that made her drool. Even her letter to Santa Claus (who might or might not be hanging in orbit, waiting to come down her chimney) had not been so greedy. They had subdued the local autochthons, apparently by killing off all the nearby Krinpit and shooting down any balloonist who came near. Their burrowers they seemed to have tamed. And they were using them for minerals exploration, because it seemed the Greasies had perched themselves on a Kuwait of oil and a Scranton of other fossil fuels. They had devised an enzyme, or possibly it was a hormone—the information had been unclear—which took Krinpit out of action as effectively as 2, 4-D had dried up the jungles of Vietnam, by causing them to molt. They had acquired something from their Creepies that let them make building materials out of dirt, as the burrowers themselves hardened the interior surfaces of their tunnels. They had—Christ, what had they not done! If only her father had listened to her and given her the support she demanded, how gladly and competently she could have done the same!

Not that she had done badly. But for Marge Menninger there was no such thing as second best, and the Greasies at that moment controlled the entire planet. Barring the dozen hectares her colony sat on, it was all theirs. Their aircraft roamed it at will, so the spy satellites said. They had three separate colonies now, counting the one that had once belonged to the probably no longer surviving Peeps. And apart from the rare occasions when she dared send Kappelyushnikov on a quick survey flight (what would she do if there were some unexplained "accident" to her one and only aircraft?), she was blind except for what the satellites and the few living balloonists could tell. She had even grounded Danny Dalehouse. Not only because of the risk to him—but that was a reason in itself, she admitted privately; she did not want him killed—but because the electricity that made his hydrogen was better used for floodlights to protect the camp and make the crops grow. Also she had apprenticed him to the agronomist, along with Morrissey and the Bulgarian girl—wait a minute, she thought to herself; Dalehouse and Dimitrova? Maybe so. Probably not. They had been friendly, but not *that* friendly. But then who?

For that matter, she thought, looking at Guy Tree as he chattered away about contingency plans in the event of a major Krinpit attack, who was the father of her own sort-of child? Dalehouse? Tree? That son of a bitch Sweggert, with his cute little tricks? They were the most likely candidates, but which?

In other times, one part of Marge Menninger would have contemplated with sardonic amusement that other part of Marge Menninger which really, dammit!, wanted to *know*. At present she had no room for that sort of amusement in her mind. The thought of mentioning to Nguyen Tree that the two of them might be in the process of becoming somewhat delayed parents crossed her mind just long enough for her to dismiss it. It promised some good comedy, but it also promised complications she did not want to handle. First things first.

"Are there any archers in the camp?" she asked.

Tree stopped in the middle of explaining his proposal for arming a couple of canoes. "What?"

"People who know how to shoot a bow and arrow, dammit. We must have some. I'd like to organize a contest, part of the sports program."

"Very likely so, Marjorie. I don't believe there are any bows and arrows, however."

"If they know how to shoot them, they know how to make them, don't they? Or anyway, it'll be in the microfiches. Get started on that, please, Guy. We'll give prizes. Coffee, cigarettes. I'll donate a bottle of Scotch." The thought that had crossed her mind as he spoke of how he planned to mount a light machine gun in a canoe was that the supplies of ammunition for the guns would not last forever, either, but she wasn't ready to say that even to her second in command.

Tree looked puzzled, but paused to make a note in his book. "It would be a useful skill for hunting, I suppose."

Margie nodded without replying. Hunting what? Every animal they had seen on the surface of the planet was well enough armored to laugh off any homemade bow—a conspicuous blunder on the part of evolution in this place, she was convinced. But she let it go.

As they were inspecting the power plant a messenger from the communications shack trotted up. "Ship's on its way in, colonel," she reported, panting. "They've already retrofired. We ought to see them in a couple of minutes."

"Thank God," said Margie. "Put it on the PA. Guy, get twenty grunts for unloading. Tell Major Arkashvili to stand by in case they land rough."

They didn't land rough. But they didn't land right, either. The drogue chute deployed handsomely, the craft came swinging down on its cluster of three big chutes they jettisoned on schedule, and it came in on its rockets. But it never made it to the beach where the others had landed. It came in almost a kilometer short and dropped into the jungle and out of sight.

The good part was that no one was hurt. The fifteen persons on board all came into the camp on their own power; and twelve of them were both young and female. God had answered Margie's prayer that far, at least. The bad part was that everything on the ship had to be manhandled over eight hundred meters of bad terrain, through jungle and over half a dozen ravines. No matter. They were there. And as Margie scanned the bill of lading she began to relax. It was all there, every last thing she had asked for, and more besides. Seeds and hand tools, weapons and training manuals. It was not enough—there was no such thing as enough—but it was all she had hoped.

First priority was to get everything movable inside the perimeter of the camp. That meant organizing working parties and armed guards to go with them. No Krinpit had been spotted near the landing site, but the woods were full of them. It wasn't until the first detachments began straggling back with cases of food and boxes of microfiches, folded bicycles and crates of electronic parts, that Margie relaxed long enough to greet the new arrivals. She shook each hand, spoke each name, and turned them over to Santangelo for assignment to quarters. A short black major hung behind. "I've got something for you, colonel," he said, patting a dispatch case. "In private, if you please, ma'am."

"Come ahead. Vandemeer, is it?" He nodded politely and followed her into her office, where he placed his dispatch case on her desk.

"This is it, ma'am," he said, unsnapping the case.

It was not a dispatch case. When he had undone the snaps the side peeled back and revealed a microprocessor with a liquid-crystal panel. He touched one of the buttons and it sprang into light, displaying a row of close-typed symbols.

"There's your guidance, ma'am. There are twelve satellite busters in orbit, and these are the controls."

Margie touched it. A warm feeling grew in the pit of her stomach and spread, an almost sexual excitement. "You're checked out on this, Vandemeer? Can you locate the Greasies' satellites?"

"Yes, ma'am. We've got acquisition and lock on four of theirs, including their main tactran receiver. Also the Peeps; they have two, but they don't seem to be active." He expertly punched a combination into the processor, and the colors of the symbols changed. "Green lights are ours. Red are Peeps. Yellow are Oilies. The lines that are still white are standby. If anything else comes within two million klicks the guidance system will track and identify it, and one of the spare birds will lock on."

The warmth was spreading. That had been the biggest and

most important item on Margie's Christmas list, and the one she had been least sure of getting. Now the sons of bitches survived at her pleasure!

"Thanks, major," she said. "I want you to show me how to work this thing, and from then on I want it in your possession or mine, twelve hours a day each, until further notice."

"Yes, ma'am," he said unemotionally. "And I have something your father asked me to hand to you personally."

It was a letter, not a microfiche. A paper letter, in an envelope with her name on it in Godfrey Menninger's own handwriting. "Thanks, major," she said again. "Go get settled in, and take the controller with you." As he turned, she added, "Major? Are things pretty bad at home?"

He paused, looking at her. "Pretty bad," he said. "Yes, I would say that, colonel. They're pretty bad."

Margie stood holding the letter for a moment. Then she jammed it in her pocket and went out to see how the unloading was coming along, because she wasn't quite ready to get the uncensored word on how bad "pretty bad" was.

Putting it away did not let her forget it was there. While she was chewing Sergeant Sweggert out for talking up two of the new girls when he should have been shifting cargo, she was fingering it. When she was breaking up an argument over what had become of a case of flashlights—"Jesus, colonel, I just put them down for a second; I thought one of the other guys took them!"—her hand returned to it. When the mess tent called a halt for breakfast, she could resist no longer, and she took her tray and her letter back into her office and ate while she read.

Marge, honey,

You've got it all, everything on the list. But there's no more where that came from. The Greasies have ordered our rigs off the Mid-Atlantic Ridge. It's a bluff. We're calling it. But every drop of booster fuel is now sequestered for missiles until they back down—and then there's Peru. The Peeps have flanged up a phoney "election," and we're not going to sit still for it. So we'll be at full military alert for months to come, maybe longer than that.

You're on your own, honey. Figure at least a year. And it may be more than that, because the president's being threatened with impeachment, maybe worse—there was an assassination attempt with two National Guard tanks last week. I told him what to do. Declare martial law. Send Congress home. Crack down all around. But he's a politician. He thinks he can ride it out. If he does, that means the rest of his term he'll be trying to score brownie points with the voters, and that means cutting back a lot of important programs.

And one of them might be you, honey.

I wouldn't be telling you this if I didn't think you could handle it. But it looks as if you'll have to.

That was all, not even a signature. Margie sat with the letter in her hands and minutes later noticed that she had forgotten to finish her breakfast.

She no longer wanted it, but neither would she waste food—especially not now. She forced herself to eat it all, and it wasn't until she had swallowed every scrap that she realized the sound of the camp had changed. Something was wrong.

While Sergeant Sweggert was eating he heard two sounds, not very near and not very loud. They sounded like shots. No one else in the mess tent seemed to have heard anything. He scraped the plate of its canned ham and dehydrated eggs, picked up the big chunk of bread, and strolled toward the entrance, still chewing.

There was a third shot.

This time there was no mistake. Some dumb son of a bitch was playing with his piece. You couldn't blame him—if Sweggert got a Krinpit in his sights he would have been tempted to blow it away, too. But three shots was wasting ammunition. He speeded up and headed toward the perimeter. As he rounded the cook tent he saw a dozen people standing around the uphill emplacement peering up the trail toward the spot where the resupply ship had landed. Others were converging on the post, and by the time he reached it there were twenty, all talking at once.

The shots had come from the trail. "Who's out there?" he demanded, grabbing Corporal Kristianides by the shoulder.

"Aggie and two grunts. They decided to get another load in before they bucked the chow line. Lieutenant Macklin just took a patrol up after them."

"So sit down and shut up till they get back," Sweggert ordered; but it was an order he didn't want to follow himself. It wasn't like Aggie to shoot up the jungle. The crowd was getting bigger; Colonel Tree came trotting up, looking like a little China doll, then half a dozen from the mess tent, then the colonel herself. Ten people were talking at once, until the colonel snarled, "All of you, at ease! Here comes Macklin. Let's see what he has to say."

But Macklin didn't have to say a word. He came stepping along the worn place that had become their path, carbine at port arms, looking both ways into the jungle. As he got closer they could see that the two men behind him were carrying someone, and the last soldier was backing toward them, carrying her weapon as Macklin carried his.

What they were bringing in was a body. It was female, and that was all you could say. The face was unrecognizable. When they dropped her down, it was plain that not only the face had been attacked. One arm was shredded up to the shoulder, and there was a bullet hole between her breasts.

"Krinpit," snapped Major Santangelo.

"Krinpit don't have guns," said Colonel Menninger, tight-lipped. "Maybe Krinpit, but they had company. Tree! Check the perimeter. I want every weapon manned and a reserve at every point. Santangelo, fall the off-duty troops in. Give Sweggert and me two hundred meters, then follow us. Sweggert, take three people, and you and I are going to take the point."

"Yes'm." He spun around, took Corporal Kristianides's gas-operated recoilless away from her, and picked three from his squad at random while Colonel Menninger was listening to Lieutenant Macklin's report. He had got only about halfway up the trail, where he found the casualty and a couple of spilled and ransacked cases of supplies. Where the other two were he didn't know. He had come back for reinforcements. Marge Menninger listened to no more. She turned him over to Major Santangelo and signaled Sweggert to move in.

At twenty-second intervals they dogged it across the open space that was the field of fire, reforming under the arch of a many-tree. As Sweggert waited for the others, he could hear the rattle and moan of some shelled creatures, but not very near. The next man in heard it too and turned a questioning face to Sweggert, mouthing the word *Krinpit*. Sweggert nodded savagely and motioned silence. When Colonel Menninger crossed the field of fire, she trotted ten meters past them, then dropped to a knee and looked around warily before raising a hand and ordering them in.

Fucking hairy, thought Sweggert. It was like that bitch to pick him for something like this! She'd had it in for him ever since he had it in her. He hand-signaled the rest of the patrol to move up one at a time, two on one side of the trail and the other with him and the colonel on the other, and when they had made their run he waited ten seconds and then sprinted to drop down beside the colonel. "That's where they got her," he breathed, pointing ahead on the trail, where half a case of fluorescent tubes lay crunched and scattered on the ground.

"I see that, sergeant! Keep moving, I don't want Santangelo running up my ass."

"Yes'm." He stooped low, dodging through the underbrush, and flopped down. The distant Krinpit rattle was still audible, but not closer. The patrol leapfrogged through the jungle until the bulk of the resupply ship loomed ahead, with its tramped-down clearing before it. He waved to catch Colonel Menninger's eye, then pointed to the top of a many-tree. She nodded, and when his turn came again he raced for the nearest of its trunks, slung his GORR over his shoulder, and started up the clump of growth. It was not much like climbing a real tree; it was easier. The flat, arched branches were like a series of steps, and the stalactitic growths that hung down between them made good handholds. The problem was that it was hard to see. Sweggert had to change position twice before he could get a clear view of the rocket.

What he saw was the base of the ship, and right in front of it the bodies of the other two grunts. They had been savagely mutilated. There was no sign of Krinpit, and the sounds he had heard seemed to have gone farther away.

Sergeant Sweggert began to feel a little better. Why the fuck should he worry about Krinpit? They were noisy bastards; there was no way one of them could get within twenty meters with him hearing it. And then the GORR would take care of it. Of course, he speculated, maybe they weren't alone. Maybe there were a couple of Greasies with them. But what did that matter? Greasies were Greasies—they were spics, Ay-rabs, or limeys—and the day hadn't come when he worried about meeting one of them in the woods. He pushed his cap back and settled down. If anything showed up in that clearing he would blow its ass off, and meanwhile he had the entertaining spectacle of Margie Menninger silently worming her way forward on the ground, almost right under him. Off to the other side of the trail somebody else was moving, equally silently; he swiveled the GORR to sight in on it, but as the figure slid between bushes he saw that it was one of his own patrol. He returned the gun and slowly centered it on Marge Menninger, moving the cross hairs in the reticle down from the base of her skull to her hips. Wouldn't it be nice, he speculated, if he could give her one she'd never forget, right up the old—

The faintest of sounds behind him made him freeze.

A little too late, he comprehended a mistake in his thinking. Krinpit and human beings were not the only creatures on Jem. As he started to turn he saw a skinny, stretched-out creature, longer than he was tall, climbing toward him with at least half a dozen legs, while others held what looked like some kind of a gun. The damn thing was wearing sunglasses, he thought with surprise, trying to bring the GORR around. He was too slow. He never heard the shot that went through his head.

Marge Menninger was the first one back into the camp. She didn't wait for the cleanup; once they knew what they were looking for, the forty armed troops scoured the area. All they got was three of the burrowers, but one of them was the one who had killed Sergeant Sweggert. You were always a lucky son of a bitch, she thought; now you don't have to worry about a court-martial for rape anymore. She collared a passing man and sent him running toward the communications tent, and before she was in her office she heard the announcement coming over the PA: "Major Vandemeer! Report to the colonel on the double!"

She met him at the door. Good man, he was trotting over half-dressed, but he had the case with him. "Open it up," she snarled. "They're arming the Creepies against us, guns and glasses. That's what Tinka was trying to get back to tell me. Move it, man!"

"Yes'm." But even the stolid Major Vandemeer fumbled as he undid the snaps. "Ready, ma'am," he reported, fingers poised.

The red fury in her mind was balanced by the warmth spreading at the base of her belly. She scratched vigorously and snapped, "Take 'em out!"

"Who, ma'am?"

"The Greasies! Bust their birds, all of them!" She watched the complicated ritual and then frowned. "While you're at it, take the Peeps' out too."

·NINETEEN·

GODFREY MENNINGER woke up wondering who was shaking the foot of his bed.

No one was. He was alone in his room, exactly like a hundred thousand Holiday Inn or Howard Johnson's Motor Lodge rooms all over the world. There was the phone on a nightstand beside the bed, the TV set staring grayly across at him from the long desk-plus-chest-plus-luggage-rack that stood against the wall. The phone was almost the only visible element that made it different, for it was a push-button jobber with colored lights flickering across its face. The other element of strangeness was harder to see. The drapes over one wall covered an immense likris display panel, not a window. There was no point in having a window. He was two hundred meters under the earth.

It was 6:22 on the clock.

Menninger had left orders to be awakened at seven. Therefore it was not a call that had awakened him. Therefore there were only a couple of other possibilities, and none of them were attractive. God Menninger considered picking up the phone or switching on the TV or pulling back the drapes over the likris situation screen, any of which would have told him at once what was happening. He decided against doing so. If it had posed an immediate threat he would have been notified at once. Margie's disciplined and hierarchical approach to problem solving had not been taught at West Point; it had come to her on her father's knee. If she was good at putting unwanted thoughts out of her mind, he was superb. He dismissed the question, slipped into his brocaded robe, went into the bathroom, and made himself a cup of instant coffee with tap water.

God Menninger's waking-up minutes were precious to him. He was of the opinion that both his marriages had failed because he had been unable to make either wife understand that he was never, not ever, to be spoken to for at least half an hour after waking. That was coffee time and summoning-up-strength time and remembering-what-he-had-to-do time. Conversation destroyed it. A weakness of Godfrey Menninger's character was that he was apt to destroy anyone who infringed on it.

The coffee was at just the right temperature, and he drank it like medicine, swallow by swallow, until it was down. Then he threw off the robe, sat cross-legged on the bed in the half-lotus position, let his body go calm, and began to say his mantra.

Godfrey Menninger had never really understood what happened among his neurons and synapses when he practiced transcendental meditation, nor had he ever really tried. It did not seem to do any harm of any kind, except to cost him some twenty-four hundred seconds out of every twenty-four hours. He seldom discussed it with anyone else and therefore did not have to defend it. And it seemed to work. Work how? Do what? He could not exactly have said. When he did it he felt more confident and more relaxed about his confidence. That was not a bad return on the investment of less than three percent of his time. As he sat, his body withdrawing from him, the reiterated *ta-lenn, ta-lenn* of the mantra becoming a sort of drapery of sound that surrounded him without being present, his whole brain became a receptor. It contributed nothing. It only perceived. On the inside of his eyelids he saw faces and shapes that melted into each other. Some were beautiful and some gargoyles. Some were etched in the sharpest of drypoint lines. Some seemed to be beaten out of gold. They held no emotional content for him. The demon snarls did not frighten. The loveliness did not attract. They were only there. Wispy chains of words floated past his consciousness like snatches of conversation from the next table at a restaurant. They spoke of ultimata and megatonnages and a remembered caress and the need for a haircut, but there were no imperatives in them anywhere. The circulating memory that pumped them past his mind sucked them away again without residue.

More than two thousand kilometers away and half a kilometer down, inside a submarine belonging to the Fuel Bloc, a vice admiral in the Libyan navy was programming The One That Had His Name on It. Menninger did not know it. His thoughts floated free into infinity in all directions, but all directions lay within that inner space of his mind. He could not have done anything useful about it if he had known.

The bed moved again.

It was not an earthquake. There were no earthquakes in West Virginia, he thought, bringing himself up out of reverie, getting ready to open his eyes. It was sharper than an earthquake would have been, more quick and trivial than the slow battering of a crustal slip. It was not particularly strong, and if he had still been asleep it might not even have awakened him. But it was something. And then the lights flickered.

Two hundred meters down in the side of a West Virginia mountain, the lights were not meant to flicker. A ^{239}Pu megawatt generating plant, vented through a kilometer of piping to emerge on the other side of the hill, was immune to most external events. Lightning bolts lid not strike transformers underground. Winds could not tear loose a line, since there were no lines in the open air. And then, tardily, the flickering colors on the base of the telephone all went out. A single red light flared, and the buzzer sounded. He picked up the phone and said, "Menninger."

"Three missiles came in, sir—near misses. There's no structural damage. Point of origin backtracks probably to near Sinkiang province. The city of Wheeling is out."

"I'll be there in a minute," he said. He was still coming up from his meditation, and so he did not look at his own situation panel, but he also did not stop to shower or shave. He rubbed deodorant on his armpits—French whore's bath, but good enough —ran a brush over his hair, pulled on his coveralls and shoes, and walked briskly down the placid, beige-carpeted corridor to his command room.

The situation map was alight from end to end.

"Here's your coffee," said General Weinenstat. That was all she said. She knew his ways. He took the cup without looking at her, because his eyes were on the board. It displayed a Mercator projection of the earth in outline. Within it, bright red stars were targets taken out. Bright blue stars were also targets taken out, but on the wrong side: that was Washington and Leningrad and Buenos Aires and Hanoi and Chicago and San Francisco. Broken red profiles in the ocean areas of the map were enemy missile-launching vessels destroyed. There were more than a hundred of them. But there were also nearly sixty broken blue ones. Pulsating targets, red and blue, were major concentrations not yet destroyed. There were relatively few of them. The number decreased as he watched. Kansas City, Tientsin, Cairo, and the whole urban complex around Frankfurt ceased to exist.

The second cup of coffee was not medicine but comfort. He took a sip of it and then asked, "What's their remaining second-strike capability?"

"Marginal, Godfrey. Maybe one hundred missiles operational within the next twenty-four hours, but we're cutting that down all the time. We have almost eighty. And only two of our hardened installations are scratched."

"Local damage?"

"Well—there are a lot of casualties. Otherwise, not bad. Surface contamination is within acceptable limits—inside shielded vehicles, anyway." She signaled an orderly for a coffee refill and added, "Too early to tell about long-lived isotope capture, but most of the Corn Belt looks okay. So's Mexico and the Pacific Northwest. We did lose the Imperial Valley."

"So we're not bad for now."

"I would say so, yes, God."

"For the next twenty-four hours. Then they can start to redeploy." She nodded. It was a known fact that every major country had squirreled away missiles and components. They were not at ten-minute command like the ones in the silos or on the subs. They could not be launched by pushing a button. But they could not be taken out at long range, either, since you didn't know where they were hidden. He added, "And we can't look for them, because the satellite busters have half-blinded us."

"We've all-blinded them, Godfrey. They don't have an eye in orbit."

"Yes, yes, I understand," he said testily. "We've won the exchange. The damn fools. Well, let's get to work."

Menninger's "work" was not directly related to the exchange of missiles that was remodeling the surface of the earth to a facsimile of hell. That was not his responsibility. It was only a precursor, like a friend's retiring to the bathroom to fit in her diaphragm while he slouched, waiting, on the edge of the bed. She would not need his advice or his help at that stage, and neither would the Chiefs of Staff while the actual fire fight was going on. His involvement would be central immediately thereafter.

Meanwhile, one of the damn fools had finished the programming and was trying to round up enough of a crew for the launch. It wasn't easy. The neutron bomb had done just what ERW weapons were supposed to do—penetrated the carelessly scant meters of water and the 'steel tube of his submarine and knocked out most of the crew. The Libyan vice admiral himself had taken nearly five thousand rads. He knew he had only hours to live, but with any luck his target would have less than that.

Three hours' sleep was not enough. Menninger knew that he was quick-tempered and a little fuzzy, but he had trained his people to know that too, and they made allowances.

At five-minute intervals the map disappeared and the likris screen sequenced itself through a round of ten-second displays: profiles of industrial capacity destroyed and remaining, curves of casualties, histograms of combat-effectiveness estimates. In the Ops Room next to God Menninger's command post, more than fifty persons were working on overdrive to correct and update those figures. Menninger hardly glanced at them. His concerns were political and organizational. Rose Weinenstat was on the scrambler to the Combined Chiefs every few minutes, not so much to give information or to get it as to keep them aware, every minute, that the most powerful unofficial figure in government had his eye on them all the time. His three chief civilian liaisons were in touch with state governments and government agencies, and Menninger himself spoke, one after another, with cabinet officers, key senators, and a few governors—when they could be found. It was all US, not Fats; the rest of the Food Bloc was in touch through the filter of the Alliance Room, and when one of them demanded his personal attention it was an intrusion.

"He isn't satisfied with me," General Weinenstat reported. "Maybe you should give him a minute, Godfrey."

"Shit." Menninger put down his pen at the exact place on a remobilization order where he stopped reading and nodded for her to switch over.

The face on his phone screen was that of Marshal Bressarion of the Red Army, but the voice was his translator's. "The marshal," she said, sounding tinny through the scrambler, "does not question that you and the Combined Chiefs are acting under the President's orders, but he wishes to know just who the President is. We are aware that Washington is no more, and that Strongboxes One and Two have been penetrated."

"The present President," said Menninger, patiently restraining his irritation, "is Henry Moncas, who was Speaker of the House of Representatives. The succession is as provided in our basic law, the Constitution of the United States."

"Yes, of course," said the translator after Bressarion had listened and then barked something in Russian, "but the marshal has been unable to reach him for confirmation."

"There have been communications problems," Menninger agreed. He looked past the phone, where Rose Weinenstat was shaping the words "in transit" with her lips. "Also," he added, "I am informed the President is in the process of moving to a fully secure location. As the marshal will realize, that requires a communications lid."

The marshal listened impatiently and then spoke for some seconds in rapid-fire Russian. The translator sounded a good deal more uptight as she said, "We quite understand, but there is some question of lines of authority, and the marshal would appreciate hearing from him directly as soon—hello? Hello?"

His image faded. General Weinenstat said apologetically, "I thought it was a good time to develop transmission difficulties."

"Good thinking. Where is the son of a bitch, by the way?"

"Henry? Oh, he's safe and sound, Godfrey. He's been ordering you to report to him for the last hour or so."

"Um." Menninger thought for a moment. "Tell you what.

Send out a radiation-safe team to escort him here so I can report. Don't take no for an answer. Tell him he'll be safer here than in his own hole." He picked up the pencil, scratching the pit of his stomach. Which was complaining. He wanted orange juice to build up his blood sugar, a stack of flapjacks to give a foundation for the next cup of coffee, and that cup of coffee. He wanted his breakfast, and he was aware that he was cranky because he was hungry. "Then we'll see who's President," he added, to the air.

On the edge of the Bahía de Campeche the Libyan vice admiral had got his crew together and his submarine up to two hundred meters, running straight and level. None of them were functioning well, with prodromal diarrhea and vomiting often enough so that the whole ship smelled like a latrine, but they could serve. For a while, at least. They did. Libya's naval doctrine called for one big missile instead of a few dozen little ones. As this one big one broke the surface of the gulf it was immediately captured by a dozen radars. The scared but as yet untouched tourists on their lanais in Mérida saw bright, bad flashes out west, over the water, as a Cuban cruiser locked in and fired ABMs. None of them caught it. It was a cruise missile, not ballistic, easy to identify but hard to predict as it drove itself north-northwest toward the Florida panhandle. A dozen times defensive weapons clawed at it as it crossed the coast, and then it was lost to view. There were plenty of installations along the way charged with the duty of detecting and destroying just such a weapon, but none that were functioning anymore.

The latest picture from Margie showed her with one foot on the shell of a dead Krinpit, looking tired and flushed and happy. It was as good a picture of his daughter as God had had since her bearskin-rug days, and he had it blown into a hard print for his wallet. General Weinenstat looked at it carefully and passed it back to him. "She's a credit to you, God," she said.

He looked at it for a moment and put it away. "Yeah. I hope she got her stuff. Can you imagine her mother? I told her Margie wanted some dress patterns, and she wanted me to put in about a thousand meters of fabric."

"Well, if you'd left her raising to her mother she wouldn't be getting the kind of efficiency ratings you've been showing me."

"I suppose not." The latest one had been nothing but praise, or at least up to the psychologist's report:

Latent hostility toward men due to early marital trauma and mild inverse-Oedipal effect. Well compensated. Does not affect performance of duties.

I really hope that's so, thought Godfrey Menninger. Rose Weinenstat looked at him carefully. "You're not worrying about her, are you? Because there's no need—wait a minute." General Weinenstat touched the thing in her ear that looked like, but wasn't, a hearing aid. Her expression turned somber.

"What is it?"

She turned off the communicator. "Henry Moncas. His shelter took a direct hit. They're trying to find out who's President now."

"Shit!" Godfrey Menninger stared at the remains of his breakfast for a moment and saw none of it. "Oh, shit," he said again. "It looks bad, Rosie. The worst part is we never had a choice!"

General Weinenstat started to speak, then changed her mind.

"What? What were you going to say, Rosie?"

She shrugged. "No good second-guessing, is it?"

He pounced on her words. "About what? Come on, Rosie!"

"Well—maybe moving into Canada—"

"Yeah. That was a mistake, all right. I'll give you that. But not ours! The Greasies knew we couldn't let them move troops into Manitoba. That was Tam Gulsmit's mistake! Same with the Peeps. Once we were engaged we had to take Lop Nor out— quick, clean, minimum casualties. They should've accepted it instead of retaliating—"

But he could hear voices within him denying it, speaking in the tones of Tam Gulsmit and Heir-of-Mao. "We were safe moving troops in to protect the tar sands, because we knew you couldn't afford to invade." "You shouldn't have bombed Lop Nor. You should have known we would have to retaliate." The voices within God Menninger's mind were the only voices they would ever have again. Heir-of-Mao lay with eyes bulging and tongue protruding from his lips, dead in the deep shelter under Peking, and the atoms that had once been Gulsmit's body were falling out from the column of fire over Clydeside.

The Libyan missile had bypassed Atlanta and Asheville and

Johnson City, matching their terrains against the profiles imprinted in its memory. The safety interlocks on its thermonuclear
charge were falling away one by one as its tiny, paranoid brain
began to recognize its nearness to the thing it was unleashed to
destroy.

"It's bad, Rosie," said Godfrey Menninger at last, rising to return to his desk. Maybe he should have let Margie's mother have
the raising of her. Then Margie would probably have had a husband and a couple of kids by now. And perhaps—perhaps the
world would have been a different place. He wondered if he
would ever hear from her again. "Rosie," he said, "check Houston. See if the communication links with Jem are holding up.
With the other colonies, too, of course."

"Right now, Godfrey? Give me ten minutes; I've got a call
coming in from the DoD."

"Ten minutes is fine," he said; but before the ten minutes was
up he was dead.

·TWENTY·

THE CORACLE first appeared between showers, far out over the water. In the pit beside Ana Dimitrova, Corporal Kristianides—no, Lieutenant Kristianides now, she corrected herself—stood up and turned the field glasses on it.

"Krinpit," she said. "Son of a bitch. Lay your gun on it, Nan, but don't fire unless I tell you to."

Unnecessary order! Not for worlds would she have fired. Not until she saw for herself that there were only Krinpit in the boat, and not Ahmed Dulla. Perhaps not even then, for this insanity of guns and shooting was awful even to play at. She had not yet had to fire at a living being, was far from sure that she could, and had said as much; but no one wanted to hear. But the good thing about her machine gun was that it had a telescopic sight, and she was glad enough to aim it.

The coracle disappeared into a squall, but not before she had seen that there was no human being in it, though it was large enough for several.

When it appeared again it was larger and nearer, and she could see that the single Krinpit was working furiously to keep it bailed and the trapezoidal sail intact, and paddling to bring it straight into the camp. By then everyone had seen, and at least a dozen weapons were pointed at it. Over the PA system Guy Tree's voice shrilled an order to hold fire. Down on the beach Marge Menninger stood, a GORR under her arm, oblivious of the rain that soaked her. Ana wiped the wet off her sight as carefully as she had been taught and looked again. She had no skill at recognizing individual Krinpit by sight, but this one did not look familiar.

Disappointment of a hope. But what a foolish hope, she scolded herself. How improbable that Ahmed would once again miraculously appear. And even if he had, who was this Ahmed who had taken her and used her and left her again? He was not the person of Sofia, she thought gloomily, and roused herself and tried to think more constructively.

It was a failure. There was so little to think constructively about! The world she had left was blowing itself up, and the world she had come to seemed determined to do the same. What went on in the secret conferences among Marge Menninger and her warrior knights in the headquarters shed she did not know, nor wish to. But it might well be the death of all of them.

The Krinpit was in the shallows now. It raised itself and splashed over the side, and the coracle bobbled away as it lurched ashore. It seemed to be in bad shape. It staggered in a half-circle on the shore and then fell to the ground with a painful crash as Colonel Menninger and half a dozen of her warriors formed a wary perimeter around it.

Perhaps they would kill it, she thought. Well, let them. Everyone else was standing and staring, but Ana's attention wandered— until one of the riflemen came running toward her.

"Dimitrova, front and center!" he was calling. "It's the one that speaks Pak! Colonel wants you to come translate!"

When Ana Dimitrova was nineteen years old, precocious senior at the University of Sofia, candidate for the callosectomy that would forever sunder the two halves of her brain and lead to a distinguished career in translation, she had watched a film on the subject. It was not her choice. They would not accept her application without it. The first part was quite tedious, though instructive, as it described the anatomy of that senseless and defenseless kilogram of pinky-gray jelly that mediated and transformed and commanded all the senses and defenses of the body. Before her very eyes a surgeon took a human brain in his hands and peeled away tissue to expose that great suety bridge that connected the two halves and that, in her, she would ask someone to sever. There was a long explanation, quite hard to follow, of how nerves crossed, so that the right half of the brain seemed to take responsibility for the left half of the body, and vice versa: strange quirk of anatomy! She saw how the nerves carrying visual impressions intersected at the optic chiasma, but not completely—as though prankish evolution had tired of the joke and decided not to finish it. All that part of the film was difficult to absorb, as well as unsettling to look at. But then there were some comic parts. Each half of the brain commanded its own network of afferent and efferent nerves. The efferent nerves, the ones that directed action, were spared in the resection or reconnected afterwards, which was why the split-brain people were able to walk without stumbling. Most of the time. The afferent nerves, the ones that accepted sensory impressions from the world, were kept apart. So each half of the brain could receive and process and store its own information, not shared with the other. That was why translation became easy.

But.

But some kinds of afferent input were not value-free. They produced glandular responses. They caused emotions. This was where the comic part came in. The film showed a woman, one of the earliest volunteers for the surgery. She had an earplug in one ear and was reading from a prepared text. The voice-over narration explained what she was doing: delivering a translated talk to a mathematical congress. But while one half of her brain was reading and translating and speaking, the other half was listening to the words coming in over the earplug; and those words were the filthiest of scatological jokes. The woman began to stammer and falter, and over her face spread the rosiest of blushes, though the operating half of her brain had not an idea in the world why. Blushes. Stammers. Headaches. Depression. They were the symptoms of leakage from one half to the other. The scar tissue that blocked the flow of impulses through the corpus callosum let each half of the brain work efficiently on its own. But feelings seeped through. All the time Ana Dimitrova was translating for Colonel Menninger she could feel them pounding at her—

"He says that as the People's Republics are no longer a force, he wishes to help us against the Fuel Bloc."

"Fucking great. What's he going to do, scratch them to death with his sharp little feet?"

—and the headache was the worst she had ever had: sickening, sandbag blows at the base of her skull. She felt nauseated and was not helped by the Krinpit.

Sharn-igon was repulsively ill. Even the dull, recurrent rasp of his name—Sharn-igon, Sharn-igon—was badly played, like a defective radio. His carapace was a sickly yellow instead of the rich mahogany it had been. It was cracked and seamed. At the edges of it, where undershell joined the massive armor of the top, seams did not quite join, and a thin, foul liquid oozed out.

"He has molted," she explained to the colonel, "and feels he is about to molt again. Perhaps it is because of the chemicals the Fuel people used against them."

"You don't look so fucking great yourself, Dimitrova."

"I am quite capable of continuing, Colonel Menninger." All the same, she moved away from the Krinpit. The exudations of his shell had darkened the sand around him, and the smell was like rancid fat. Moving did not help. The headache, and the pain behind it, grew with every moment.

Marge Menninger ran her hands through her wet hair, pulling it back so that her ears were exposed. She looked almost like a little girl as she said, "What do you think, Guy? Have we got ourselves a real blood-hungry tiger?"

Colonel Tree said, "One does not refuse an ally, Marge. But the Greasies would eat these jokers up."

"So what is he saying exactly, Dimitrova? That he'll tell all his Crawly friends to attack the Greasy camp if we want them to?"

"Something like that, yes. What he says," she added, "is not always easy to understand, Colonel Menninger. He speaks a little Urdu, but not much, and he speaks it *very* badly. Besides, his mind wanders. It is a personal matter with him, to kill. He does not care who. Sometimes he says he wants to kill *me*."

Menninger looked appraisingly at the Krinpit. "I don't think he's in shape to do much killing."

"Must one be well for that?" Ana flared. "I am sick in my heart from talk of killing, and from killing itself! It is a wicked insanity to kill when so few persons are still alive."

"As to that," said Margie mildly, raising her hand to stop Guy

Tree from exploding, "we'll talk another time. You look like shit, Dimitrova. Go get some sleep."

"Thank you, Colonel Menninger," Ana said stiffly, hating her, perhaps hating even more the look of compassion in Margie's eyes. How dare the bloody trollop feel pity!

Ana stalked off to her tent. It was raining hard again, and lightning lashed over the water. She hardly felt it. At every step the throbbing in her head punished her, and she knew that behind the headache a greater pain was scratching to come out. Pity was the solvent that would melt the dam and let it through, and she wanted to be by herself when that happened. She stooped into the tent without a word to the woman who shared it with her, removed only her shoes and slacks, and buried herself under the covers.

Almost at once she began to weep.

Ana made no sound, did not shake, did not thrash about. It was only the ragged unevenness of her breathing that made the black girl in the other cot rise up on one elbow to look toward her; but Ana did not speak, and after a moment her roommate went back to sleep. Ana did not. Not for an hour and more. She wept silently for a long time, helpless to contain the pain any longer. Hopes gone, pleasures denied, dreams melted away. She had held off accepting the thing that the Krinpit had said almost in his first sentence, but now it could not be denied. There was no longer a reason for her to be on Jem. There was hardly even a reason to live. Ahmed was dead.

She woke to the loud, incongruous sound of dance music.

The storm of silent weeping had cleared her mind, and the deep and dreamless sleep that followed had begun the healing. Ana was quite composed as she bathed sparingly in the shower at the end of the tent line, brushed her hair dry, and dressed. The music was, of course, that other of Marge Menninger's eccentricities, the Saturday night dance. How very strange she was! But her strangeness was not all unwelcome. One of the fruits of it had been the patterns and fabric that had come in the last ship. Ana chose to put on a simple blouse and skirt, not elaborate, but not purely utilitarian either. She was a very long way from dancing. But she would not spoil the pleasure of those who enjoyed it.

She cut past the generator, where the Krinpit was rumbling hollowly as it scratched through the clumps of burnable vegetation for something to eat, a guard with a GORR trailing its every step, and visited the fringe of the dance area long enough to get something to eat from the buffet. (Of course, she had slept through two meals.) When men asked her to dance she smiled and thanked them as she shook her head. The rain had stopped, and sullen Kung glowed redly overhead. She took a plate of cheese and biscuits and slipped away. Not that there was far to go. No one walked in the woods anymore these days. They lived and ate and slept in a space one could run across in three minutes. But all who could be there were at the dance, and down by the beach were only the perimeter guards. She sat down with her back against one of the machine-gun turrets and finished her meal. Then she put her plate down beside her, pulled her knees up to her chin, and sat staring at the purple-red waves.

Ahmed was dead.

It was not much comfort to tell herself that her dreams had been foolish to begin with, that Ahmed had never taken her as seriously as she had taken him. Nevertheless, it was true, and Ana Dimitrova was a practical person. She had learned the trick of dissecting pain into its parts. That she would never see him again, touch his strong and supple body, lie beside him while he slept—that was purest pain, and there was no help for it. But that she would never marry him and bear his children and grow old by his side—that was only a spoiled fantasy. It had never been real. That loss could not hurt her now, because it was of something she had never owned; and so her pain was diminished by half.

(But, oh, how that half still ached!)

She wept gently and openly for a moment, then sighed and rubbed the tears away. What she had lost, she told herself, she had lost long ago. From the moment Ahmed came to Jem, he had become a different person. In any event, it was over. She had a life to make for herself, and the materials to make it from were all in this camp; there was nothing else anywhere. You should dance, she scolded herself. You should go up where they are laughing and singing and drinking.

Plainly and simply, she did not want to. It was not merely that she didn't want to dance, not yet. It was more deep and damaging than that. Ana, translating for the Krinpit, had heard enough of what was going on in the minds of Marge Menninger and Nguyen Tree and the other hawks who directed the fate of the camp. So much madness in so few minds! They were determined to carry on a war, even here, even after Earth had blown itself into misery! And yet there they all were, smiling and bobbing around the floor. Her own brain had been divided by a surgeon's knife. What had divided theirs, so that they could plot genocide in an afternoon and drink and cavort and play their sexual games at night? How Ahmed would scowl at them!

But Ahmed was dead.

She took a deep breath and decided not to cry again.

She stood up and stretched her cramped limbs. The Krinpit was lurching slowly down toward the water for a drink after his unappetizing meal, the soldier wandering after. She did not particularly want to be near him, but she needed to rinse her plate—either that or carry it back to the cook tent, which was too near the dance floor. She kept her distance, paralleling his scuttling path, and then she heard someone call her name.

It was the Russian pilot, Kappelyushnikov, sitting cross-legged at a gun pit and talking to Danny Dalehouse, on duty inside it. Why not? Ana changed course to approach them and wished them a good evening.

"Is truly good, Anyushka? But Danny Dalehouse has told me of death of Ahmed Dulla. I am deeply sympathetic for you."

There it was, the first time someone had spoken of it to her. She discovered that it was not impossible for her to respond.

"Thank you, Visha," she said steadily. "What, have you become a monk that you do not dance tonight?"

"Is no one I care to dance with," he said gloomily. "Also have been having most interesting discussion with Danny on subject of slavery."

"And what have you concluded, then, Danny?" she asked brightly. "Are we all slaves to your mistress, the beautiful blond colonel?"

He did not answer directly, but chose to be placating. "I know you're upset, Ana. I'm sorry, too."

"Upset?" She nodded judiciously, looking down into the pit at him. "Yes, perhaps. I must assume that my home has been destroyed—yours, too, I suppose. But you are braver than I. I am not brave; I become upset. It upsets me that what has happened on Earth is now to happen again, here. It upsets me that my—that my friend is dead. It upsets me that the colonel intends to kill a great many more persons. Can you imagine? She proposes to tunnel under the Fuel camp and explode a nuclear bomb, and that upsets me."

Why are you doing this? she asked herself; but she knew that she could not accept more sympathy without crying, and she was not ready to cry before these men. At least she had diverted them. Dalehouse was frowning.

"We don't have any nuclear weapons," he objected.

"Softheaded person!" she scoffed. "Your mistress has what she wants to have. I should not be astonished if she had a fleet of submarines or a division of tanks. She wears weapons as she wears that cheap perfume. The smell of them is always around her."

"No," he said doggedly, peering up at her, "you're wrong about the nuclear weapons. She couldn't conceal that from us. And she's not my mistress."

"Do not flatter yourself that I care. She may have her sexual excesses with whomever she likes, and so may you."

Kappelyushnikov coughed. "I think," he said, "dance has suddenly become more attractive."

As he stood up, Ana put her hand on his arm. "I am driving you away. Please forgive me."

"No, no, Anyushka. Are difficult times for all, nothing to forgive." He patted her hand, then grinned and kissed it. "As to myself," he said, "I see beautiful blond colonel roaming about alone, and perhaps she wishes to dance or otherwise relate to some new person, such as I. Also do not care for cheap perfume worn by big cockroach. You do not yourself desire to dance? Or otherwise relate? No. Then stay with friend Danny."

They watched him walk steadily toward Marge Menninger, strolling past her checkpoints. They heard her laugh as Cappy spoke to her; then he shrugged and moved on toward the dance floor.

The Krinpit, in his random stagger around the beach, was coming closer. It was true that the stench of his exudations was strong. So was the sighing, droning sound of his presence. Ana listened, then said gloomily, "This one is muttering about his love now," she said. "It was killed somehow, I cannot tell how. I think Ahmed had something to do with it, and it is for that that it is determined to kill human beings. But it had become Ahmed's ally! Dan, is not that lunacy? It is as though killing has become an end in itself. It no longer matters who is killed or for what possible gain the killing is done. Only the killing itself matters."

Dalehouse stood up in his shallow rifle pit, looking up the hill toward the dancers. "She's coming this way," he said. "Listen, before she gets here. About her being my mistress—"

"Please, Danny. I spoke without thinking and because I am, yes, upset. It is not a time to worry about personal matters."

Clearly he was not satisfied and would have pursued the subject, but Margie was now too close. She paused to light a cigarette, studying the Krinpit and its guard, now a model of military deportment, his recoilless at port arms as the colonel approached. Then she came smiling over to Danny and Nan. "Getting it on, are you?" she said amiably. "When was the last time you checked your earphones, Danny?"

Guiltily Dalehouse clapped the phone to one ear. He had been neglecting the buried microphone probes, which were supposed to warn of burrowers digging toward him under the ground. There was no sound. "Sorry, Margie," he said.

She shook her head. "When you're on duty, that's *colonel*. And when I say frog, you hop. Now that that's understood," she said, smiling sunnily, "would either of you folks like a hit before we talk some business?"

"I am not in the habit of using narcotics," Ana said.

"Pity. Danny?" She watched while Dalehouse filled his lungs, and as she took the stick back from him, she said, "I want you to draft your gasbag friend. One hundred and—" She glanced at her wristwatch. "One hundred and eight hours from now, give or take a little, we're going to hit the Greasy camp, and he's going to be our air arm."

Dalehouse coughed and spluttered. "He—he can't—"

"Take your time, Danny," she encouraged. "While you're getting your breath, just listen for a moment. Storm's over. Looks like we've got maybe five or six good days. I'm taking fifteen front-line effectives, plus you, Danny. We'll mop up that camp without breathing hard. Only I don't want to take a plane, and I don't want you or Cappy floating around up there where they can see you, and that leaves Charlie."

"Charlie can't fight!"

"Well," she said reasonably, "come to that, I don't figure you for your real Geronimo trained killer, either. But I don't expect it of you. You communicate. Charlie observes. The Greasies won't pay any attention to one more fartbag hanging around—"

"Bullshit they won't! They've been shooting balloonists down all along."

"Danny," she said, "I'm not asking your advice. I'm giving you an order." She dragged on the joint, down to the last centimeter, and then carefully rubbed it out and pocketed it before exhaling. "You see," she said, "the Greasies are going to come to the same conclusions I did, only it'll take them a little longer. One of us has to run things. The only way to do that is to knock the other out. All Charlie has to do is hang in there with his radio and keep us posted if they send up a plane or put some people out in the woods. I'll bring the company up overland. But we're naked without air cover. We need to know when to get out of sight. That's easy enough for him, right?"

"Well, sure. But—shit, Margie. He's almost the last survivor. It's a lot to ask—"

"But I'm not asking, Danny. You keep making that same mistake. I'm ordering. If he doesn't, he'll make a nice flame." She scratched under her belt, regarding him amiably. "So after the dance I break the news to the camp, and tomorrow this time we're on our way."

"To atom-bomb the Fuel Bloc," said Ana bitterly.

Marge Menninger's face froze. After a moment she said, "I guess I'll let that pass, Dimitrova. I didn't specifically order you to keep your mouth shut. But I won't let it pass again. What you hear when you're translating is *classified*."

"Holy Christ," Dalehouse said. "You really have a nuclear bomb?"

"Bet your ass, Danny. You've got a piece of it right there in your ground mikes."

"Where? You mean the plutonium power-packs? That's no

good, Margie—colonel, I mean. There's not enough of them. Even if there were, you couldn't flange them together to make a bomb."

"Wrong and wrong, Danny. Takes eighteen hundred grams and a bit to fission. I have a little over six thousand grams, all tidied away in the stores marked 'fuel replacements.' All this was planned a long time ago, and they'll fit together because some pretty high-powered weapons people designed them to do that before the first ship took off. Oh, it's not one of your hundred-megaton jobs. Maybe not even a kiloton, because I don't have containment to keep the parts together very long. But I don't want a big one. I don't want to wipe out the Greasy camps, I want to own them. I want to take out their ammunition and their food stores, and I know just the place to put baby for that. Then they can beg."

She looked serene and innocent as she said it, and Dalehouse responded with shocked disbelief. "That's—that's unprovoked aggression! A stab in the back!"

"Wrong, Dalehouse. That's preemption. The Greasies don't have a choice, either. They just haven't figured it out yet."

"Bullshit! It's what the Japanese did at Pearl Harbor all over again!"

She opened her eyes wide. "Sure, why not? There was nothing wrong with Pearl Harbor, except they fucked it up. If they'd gone on to take out the carrier fleet and follow up with a landing, history would be a lot different. You'd be saying 'Pearl Harbor' the way you say 'Normandy' now, only you'd be saying it in Japanese."

She seemed quite pleased with herself, but then she hesitated. She sought a dry place on the ground and sat down before adding, "But I will admit to you two dear old friends from Bulgaria that right now I'm scared and tired and not what you'd call real happy with the way things are going. I—what's the matter with that thing?"

The Krinpit was staggering closer to them, moaning and stridulating. Ana listened. "He is quite hard to follow. He is speaking of Poison Ghosts and Ghosts Above—that is, of ourselves and of balloonists. He seems to have us confused in his mind."

"All enemies look alike after a while, I guess. Tell him to back away. I don't like the way he smells."

"Yes, Colonel Menninger." But before Ana could summon up the commands in Krinpit-Urdu, Margie stopped her again.

"Wait a minute. What was that?" There had been a voice on the PA system along with the blare of dance music.

"I couldn't make it out," said Dalehouse, "but I do hear something. Out in the woods. Or in the air—"

Then the dance music abruptly died, and a scared voice replaced it. "Colonel Menninger! All personnel! Aircraft approaching!"

The sounds were clear now, two sets of them: the whickering putt-putt of a helicopter, and a quicker, higher sound. The dancers scattered.

Over the trees two shapes appeared. Neither was moving very fast, but they came without warning: the Fuel helicopter and a stub-winged STOL plane, one they had not seen in the air before. They did not come in peace. Soldiers strapped to the pods of the helicopter were firing incendiary rockets while wing-mounted machine guns on the STOL strafed the camp. The fixed-wing plane made a roaring run that took it out over the water; then it rose, turned, and dived in again. On its second pass the guns did not fire, but four tiny rockets leaped out from under the wing, streaked into the store shed, and set fire to a row of tents.

The Greasies had not been so slow after all.

Here and there, around the camp and inside it, perimeter guards and the more quick-witted of the dancers were beginning to return the fire. Margie jumped to her feet and began to run toward the nearest rocket launcher, and then, on its third pass, the stub-winged plane swerved toward her. It was using both machine guns and a flamethrower now. As the bullets stitched toward her, Margie dodged and fell, almost beside the Krinpit; and the creature rose up high above her. It launched itself, two hundred kilograms of half-molted body, on top of Marge Menninger.

Sharn-igon knew that this would be his last molt, terribly premature, agonizing, fruitless. He would never experience the satisfying itch of his new carapace as it hardened and stretched over the soft inner pulp, never feel the sexual stirring of the newly shelled and embark on the quick conquest of a female with a he-mate. As the Poison Ghosts Above zoomed in toward the camp, he tried to warn these new allies. But they were deaf to the brilliant sounds from over the trees, deaf to his warnings.

The pain was too much.

It had been his intention to assist them in killing each other to the maximum extent possible, and then to kill the survivors himself. But perhaps he had done all the assisting he would ever do. The agony of his new shell, already beginning to crack again, tormented his thoughts. The blinding sounds of the aircraft and the explosions dazed him.

There was only one Poison Ghost left that he could kill. It would have to be enough. He raised himself on his pitifully soft-shelled limbs, leaned forward, and crashed down on top of her just as the soft, deadly tongue of the flamethrower licked at them both.

By then the whole camp was firing at the aircraft—or that much of it that was still able to fire. But the planes were out of reach. They hung out over the water, a kilometer and more away, the helicopter dancing lightly, the STOL turning in small circles, and did not return to the attack.

The next assault came from another place.

A scream from one of the machine-gun pits, and the two soldiers in it were down, ripped to shreds. Out of the pit came a long, limber, black shape wearing tiny goggles and racing on its dozen limbs to the nearest knot of humans; and another behind him, and another.

The burrowers managed to kill more than ten of the survivors. But that was all. Even with the sunglasses they were no match for trained human soldiers on the surface of the planet. If the planes had continued their attack—but they didn't. The human defenders quickly rallied, and at the end there were fifty burrowers stretched out on the ground, soiling the sand with their watery black blood. No more came because there were no more in the nest to come. That burrow had been wiped out.

Dan Dalehouse stood peering out over the sea while one of Cheech Arkashvili's assistants bandaged a deep gash on his arm.

The planes were gone. In the middle of everything, they had quietly flown down the coastline and away.

"And why didn't they finish us off?" he asked.

There was no answer.

·TWENTY-ONE·

By THE TIME they found Margie Menninger, still alive, the fight was long over and the camp was almost functioning again.

She had lain under the dead and stinking Krinpit for more than two hours, stunned, half-suffocated, unable to shift the gross dead weight on top of her, her limbs twisted painfully but unhurt. Like the djinn in the bottle, at first she would have given a king's ransom to her rescuer. When they finally heard her sand-gagged attempts at a bellow and dug her out, what she wanted to give was death.

They helped her a few steps away, with their heads averted from the stink. She gagged and swore at them, and when they tried to help her stand she collapsed and vomited into the sand again. The doctor came running, but a doctor wasn't what Marge needed. What she needed was to get the cesspool stench of the Krinpit off her and out of her nostrils. She let Cheech strip off her coveralls and assist her to the edge of the water, and then she splashed around until the smell was gone and she could walk again. Limpingly, yes. But under her own power. Wearing a bra and bikini panties, with her gun belt over her shoulder, she walked up the shore past the dead Krinpit, seared into a sort of omelette of meat and shell, until someone came up with a terrycloth robe. She was giving orders as she walked.

Why had they stopped?

The camp had been at their mercy. With great precision they had knocked out the heavy weapons on the first pass. There was not a rocket launcher or a machine gun untouched—nothing but hand weapons. Of the hundred eight persons in the Food camp, twenty-two were dead, nearly fifty were wounded or burned. The planes had been unscathed. The burrowers had been wiped out entirely, but if the planes had finished their work first, the burrowers would have had an easy time with the survivors. Why? The timing had been exact. As soon as the planes had stopped shooting, the burrowers came out. That could not have been a coincidence, and the goggles the burrowers wore were proof that the Greasies had prepared them for the job. But then they hadn't followed through.

Why not?

But thank God for poppa and his parting gift! A metric ton of ammunition had been blown up, but there were metric tons left untouched by virtue of the spare supplies in the final ship. Tents burned and food was destroyed. But there was more. If Cappy's airplane had been stitched across by machine-gun fire, there were spare parts to fix it. And that greatest of gifts, the six kilograms of ^{239}Pu in its carefully crafted sheaths—that was still intact. The dead were irreplaceable, of course. Worse still were the casualties, because some of them were not merely a loss but a debit. Nguyen Dao Tree, who had lost a leg and a lot of blood to go with it; six persons badly burned, two others with serious abdominal wounds—a whole cluster of damages for Cheech Arkashvili to try to repair. For each one of the worst off, there was the cost of an able-bodied person to tend him. There was no tent still standing big enough to hold them all, and so Cheech had put them onto cots dragged out of the damaged tents, out in the open. Some of the bedding was scorched, and if it began to rain again they would be in trouble. But for now they were as well off as they were likely to be, Margie thought as she moved among them.

One of them got up as Margie approached: Lieutenant Kristianides, one whole side of her body in gauze and antiburn dressing. But functioning. "Colonel," she said. "I had to leave the radio—"

Marge glanced at the doctor, who shook her head. "Get back in bed, Kris. Tell me about it later."

"No, I'm all right. When they shot the tent up I ran out. But I left the tape going. I was getting their chatter, only it was in all different languages."

"Thanks. Now get back in bed," Marge ordered, and looked around. "Dalehouse, front and center!" she called. "Check the radio shack. If the tape's still working, give me a yell."

He didn't look too good himself, she thought as he put down the tray of dressings and headed up the hill without a word—but then, none of them did. Especially herself. Margie's own tent had been totaled, and she was wearing fatigues belonging to a woman who would never again need them—not unfair, but she had been a taller and fatter woman than Marge Menninger.

When Dalehouse called her, she had forgotten about the tapes. But she went up to the shack, which was unburned and not really harmed except for bullet holes, commandeering Ana Dimitrova on the way. The tape was voice-actuated, and Dalehouse had already found the right place to begin. Ana put on the earphones and began to translate.

"First one of the pilots says, 'On target,' and the base acknowledges. Then there are some carrier noises, as though they were going to transmit and changed their minds, and then the base says, 'Suspend operations at once. Do not attack.' And one of the pilots, I think it is the Egyptian, says in a different Arab dialect, 'Strike already in progress. We have taken out their weapons dump. Body count around twenty-five.' Then there is some mumbling that I cannot make out, as though they are talking at the base with the transmitter on but not close enough to pick it up. And then the base says, 'Urgent. Suspend operations immediately.' And then the other pilot, the Irishman, says they are observing from over the water, waiting for instructions, and then the base orders them to return without further attack. That is all there is on the tape until they get landing instructions later on."

"That's it?" Margie asked.

"As I have said, colonel, yes. There is nothing else."

"Now, why would they change their minds in the middle?" Margie asked. Neither Dalehouse nor Dimitrova offered an answer. She hadn't expected one. It didn't matter. The Greasies had declared war, and if they backed out in the middle of it that was their problem, not hers. She would not back out. To Marge Menninger, the attack on her base—*her* base!—answered all questions right there. *Why* didn't really matter. The only question was *how*—how to carry the fight to them, and win it.

"Can you dig with that shoulder?" she asked Dalehouse.

"I guess so. It's not bleeding."

"Then go help Kappelyushnikov dig graves. Dimitrova, you're a radio operator now. No transmissions. Just listen. If the Greasies say anything, I want to hear about it right away."

She left them and headed for the surviving latrine. She didn't particularly need to go to the bathroom; she just wanted to be alone for a moment to clarify her thoughts. She ranked her way to the head of the line, closed the door, and sat there smoking a cigarette and staring into space.

There was no question in her mind that she could win this war, because she had some powerful cards to play. The plutonium store was one of them. The other was Major Vandemeer's little dispatch case. There were still four birds in orbit; one could hit the Greasy main camp, and another their Farside base, anytime she gave the order—and that would be that.

The trouble was, she didn't want to destroy the Greasy facilities. She wanted to acquire them. The birds and the bomb were overkill, like trying to take care of a mosquito with a mortar.

No. It would have to be a straight overland operation. Maybe the plutonium, if it could be placed exactly right. Not the missiles. It was a pity the Greasies had launched their preemptive strike before she was quite ready to launch hers. But not a disaster. The worst thing about the raid was that her cadre of effectives had been seriously reduced. How was she going to mount her retaliatory strike without grunts?

Marge Menninger had just taken the only decision that gave the human race a future on Jem, even though she didn't know it.

"The only good thing about all this," Dalehouse said to Kappelyushnikov, "is that most of the casualties were military. At least now we can get on with the real business of the expedition."

Kappelyushnikov grunted and threw a few more spadefuls of dirt before he answered. "Of course, is so," he said, pausing and wiping sweat off his face. "Only one question. What is real business of expedition?"

"To survive! And to preserve. God knows what's happening on Earth. We may be all that's left of the human race, and if anything's going to be left of, what, maybe five thousand years of science and literature and music and art, it's here."

"Very discouraging amount of responsibility for two gravediggers," Kappelyushnikov commented. "You are of course right, Danny. We have saying in Soviet Union: longest journey begins with single step. What step do we take now?"

"Well—"

"No, wait, was rhetorical question. First step is apparent. Have finished covering up graves of now absent friends, so you, Danny, please step up to colonel's headquarters and report burial services can begin."

He jammed his spade into the dirt and sat down, looking more despondent than Dalehouse had ever seen him.

Dalehouse said, "All right. We're all pretty tired and shook up, I guess."

The pilot shook his head, then looked up and grinned. "Am not only tired, dear Danny, am also very Russian. Heavy load to carry. We have other saying in Soviet Union: in thousand years, what difference will it make? But now I tell you the truth, Danny. All sayings are bullshit. I know what we do, you and I and all of us. We do the best we can. Is not much, but is all there is."

Dalehouse laid down his spade and trudged up the hill to the headquarters shack, thinking hard. A heavy responsibility! When you looked at it carefully, there was no way to preserve everything; so much that was irreplaceable would inevitably be lost—probably already was lost. There was not much chance that the Arc de Triomphe and the British Museum and the Parthenon had all survived, not to mention some billions of fairly irreplaceable human beings. It was hard for Danny to accept that he would never again see a ballet or listen to a concert. Or fly in a clamjet or drink in a revolving restaurant on top of a skyscraper. So much was gone forever! And so much more would inevitably vanish as they tried to rebuild. . . .

Yet there was one great asset not yet destroyed: hope. They could survive. They could rebuild. They could even rebuild in a better way, learning from the mistakes of the past, on this virgin planet—

There was a knot of people gathering around the headquarters shack, and Marge Menninger, with a couple of her aides, was trotting up to join them. Dalehouse hurried his pace and arrived in time to hear Ana saying, "This message just came in, Colonel Menninger. I will play the tape for you."

"Do it," snapped Marge, out of breath and exhausted. Dalehouse moved closer to her. She seemed near to collapse. But as the tape player hummed and scratched, she pulled herself together and stood listening intently.

Danny recognized the voice. It was the black air vice-marshal, Pontrefact; and what he said did not take very long.

"This is an official message on behalf of the Fuel Exporting Powers to the Food camp. We offer an immediate and permanent armistice. We propose that you remain within twenty kilometers of your camp, in the direction toward ours, and we will observe the same limits from ours. We request an answer within one hour."

There was a pause, as though he was shuffling papers in his hand, and then the rich Jamaican tones began again.

"As you are aware, our air strike against your camp was provoked by your destruction of our satellites. It was ordered only after full exploration of all alternatives. Our intention was to wipe your base out completely. However, as you are also aware, we terminated the strike after inflicting relatively minor damage on your base. The reason for this decision is the reason for this offer of armistice now.

"Our star, Kung, is unstable. It is about to flare.

"We have been aware for some time that its radiation level has been fluctuating. Within the past twenty-four hours it has become more extreme. While the air strike was in progress we received information from our astrophysicists that a major flare will occur in the near future. We do not have an exact time. Our understanding is that it may occur as early as forty-eight hours from now, and almost surely within the next two weeks. If you accept our offer of armistice, we will transmit all technical data at once, and your people can make their own judgments."

The voice hesitated, then resumed in a less formal way. "We have no knowledge of conditions on Earth at present and suppose you have none as well. But it is clear that for all practical purposes we on Jem are alone in the universe at this time. We think we will need all the resources we have to prepare our camp for this flare. If we continue to fight, we suppose we will all die. I do not propose that we work together. But I propose that we stop fighting, at least until this crisis is past." Another pause. Then: "Please respond within an hour. God help us all."

Margie closed her eyes for a moment while everyone waited. Then she opened them again and said, "Call them back, Dimitrova. Tell them we accept their offer, ask for their technical data at once, and say we will be in contact again when we have something to say. Folks, the war is over."

Ten minutes later, the whole camp knew it. Margie had gone on the public-address system, played the tape from Marshal Pontrefact, and broken the news of the disaster and the truce. She had called a general meeting for 0300 hours, about ninety minutes from then, and ordered Alexis Harcourt, the nearest thing they had left to an astronomer, to go over the data from the Greasies and report before that time. Then she turned to Danny Dalehouse and said, "I don't have a bed anymore, but I need about an hour's sleep real bad."

"There's a spare in my tent."

"I was hoping you'd ask." She peered up toward the sullen glow in the clouds where Kung was hiding and shook her head. "It's been a son of a bitch of a day," she said as they picked their way toward the tent row. "And it's not over yet. Know what I'm going to do at the meeting?"

"Am I supposed to guess?"

"No way, Danny. You'd never make it. I'm going to announce the impending retirement of Colonel Marjorie Menninger from active service."

"*What?*"

"Pick your teeth up, Danny, and don't just stand there," she advised, tugging him along. "We're going to convert this place to civilian government, effective as soon as the emergency is over. Or maybe before. I don't care. Maybe all you guys who're bitching about the army way of doing things are right. I have to say that my way hasn't been working out too well, everything considered.

So I think we're going to need elections for a new government, and if you want my advice you'll run."

"For what? Why me? Margie, you get me all mixed up!"

"Why you? Because you're practically the only original settler left, you know that? Just you and Cappy. Because nobody hates your guts. Because you're the only person in the camp who has the age and experience to handle the job of running things and who isn't a soldier. Don't let me pressure you. It's your decision. But you've got my vote. If," she added in a different tone, "anything we decide makes any difference at all now."

They were at his tent, and Marge paused at the flap, staring up at the sky. "Oh, shit," she said, "it's beginning to rain." It was—big drops, with promise of more behind them.

"The casualties!" he said.

"Yeah. We're going to have to get them under cover. And that's a pity, Danny, because I was kind of hoping we could catch us a little R and R before the meeting."

In spite of everything, Danny could not help himself. He laughed out loud. "Marjorie Menninger, you are some kind of strange. Get in there and get some sleep." But before she turned, he put his arms around her for a moment. "I never would have thought it of you," he said. "What converted you to civilian values?"

"Who's converted?" Then she said, "Well, maybe it was that fucking Krinpit. If it hadn't been for him, you'd've been burying me a little while ago, too. I didn't trust him, either, but he gave his silly life to save me."

With so few of them left, they didn't really need the PA system to cope with the fifty-five or sixty persons listening, but they hooked in one speaker for the benefit of the casualties who were well enough to hear, in their tents down the hill. The rest sat or stood on the wet planks of the dance floor in the sullen, steady rain while Marge Menninger spoke to them from the little dais. She turned the stage over to Harcourt.

He said, "A lot of the data from the Greasies isn't astronomy, it's geology. They've done a lot of digging. They say there seem to be flare episodes every twenty or thirty years. There's no set pattern, but by the amount of ash and char, they think your av-

erage flare involves about a seventy-five percent increase in radiation spread out over a period of a week or more. That's enough to
kill us. Partly heat. Mostly ionizing radiation.

"Now, when does it happen? Their best guess is ten days,—give
or take ten days." There was a murmur from the audience, and
he nodded. "Sorry about that, but I don't have the training to
make it any closer than they do; in fact, I'm only taking their
word. The picture I get is of slowly increasing heat over a period
of a couple of weeks. I think we've been having that, and maybe
it's why the weather has been so lousy. Then the flare. Surface
temperature goes up to maybe three-fifty degrees. That's Kelvin—
say, somewhere between where we are now and the boiling point of
water. I don't *think* it goes over that, not for very long, anyway.
But there are peak flares, and they're like striking a match. If anything can burn, it will. Apparently the forests burn, but maybe
not right away—they'd probably have to dry out first. Then the
flare recedes, the temperature comes down, the air drops out moisture, and you get rain to put out the fires. Probably a hell of a lot
of rain, over a period of weeks or months. Then you're back to
normal."

"Only dead," somebody called out from the audience. Harcourt
spread his hands defensively.

"Maybe not. If you're in shelter, you might survive." He started
to continue, then stopped himself. Margie came up beside him.

"You don't sound too confident."

"I'm not. The—ah, the geological record doesn't inspire much
confidence. The Greasies took cores from more than a hundred
different sites, and they all showed the same pattern—recurring
char and soil, back thousands of years."

Dalehouse stood up. "Alex," he called, "why hasn't it killed off
everything on the surface of Jem long ago?"

"You're asking for a guess? I guess it has. At least all the vegetation. It burns off, then regrows from roots, most likely. Seeds
probably would survive, though. And those drenching rains after
each flare would give the new growth a good start in fertile soil—
the char's great fertilizer; primitive man used to slash and burn to
get his farms started, back on Earth. I don't know about the animals. I'd guess the Creepies would be all right in their tunnels if
they didn't starve to death waiting for new growth to live on.

Probably a lot of them do. Maybe the same for the Krinpit, because it would take a lot to kill them off. They don't have to worry about being blinded by the radiation, because they don't have any eyes to begin with. And those shells are pretty good armor for their vital organs. Probably get a lot of mutations, but in the long run that's as much good as it is bad for the race."

"What about Charlie?"

"I don't know. That's harder. I guess a really good flare might wipe out damn near all the adults. But that's when they spawn, and the spawn might survive—also, no doubt, with a lot of mutations. I'd say evolution moves pretty fast here."

"Well, look," Margie cut in, "if all these things can survive, why can't we?"

Harcourt shrugged. "They're adapted, we're not. Besides, I'm talking about *races* surviving, not individuals. Maybe as few as one percent live through it. Maybe less." He looked around the audience. "One percent of us leaves how many?" he asked.

"Yeah," Margie said slowly. "Well, I think we get the picture. We need to get under something big enough to stop both heat and radiation, and we need to do it in a hurry. Got any ideas on what we can make a roof out of?"

Harcourt hesitated. "Not a clue," he confessed. "Certainly the tents won't do it. Oh, and I should mention the winds. They probably get pretty fierce, with all that insolation. So anything we did build would have to stand up to maybe two-hundred-kilometer-an-hour hurricanes. Maybe more. I, uh, I thought for a minute of using the Creepies' tunnels, and that might work—for some of us, anyway. But I doubt more than ten percent of us would live through maybe two or three weeks underground without very good ventilation and certainly without air conditioning—and that air down there is going to get *hot*."

There was a silence while everyone considered possibilities. Then Kappelyushnikov came forward. "Is one thing we can do," he announced. "Not many of us. Maybe fifteen, twenty. Can get in return capsule and go into orbit."

"It's just as hot there," Marge Menninger protested.

Cappy shook his head. "Is only radiation. Steel hull reflects ninety-nine percent, maybe. Anyway, plenty. Only problem—who decides which twenty lucky people go up?"

Marge Menninger thought for a moment, then said, "No, that's a last ditch, Cappy. There's another problem with it: what do those lucky fellows do when they come down again? There aren't enough of us left now. I don't think twenty would be enough to survive. If we went up—strike that; I'm not saying I would be one of the 'we.' If anyone went up, it'd be just as smart to keep on going. Try to get back to Earth. Maybe go to one of the other colonies. The chances would be as good as coming back here when the whole planet's fried."

Harcourt nodded but corrected her automatically. "Not the whole planet."

"What?"

"Well, only half the planet. Our half. The part that faces Kung. The far side probably wouldn't even notice there was a flare going on. That's no good for us," he went on quickly, "because we can't live there; we don't have time to build an airtight heated dome and move everything— What's the matter?"

Margie had burst out laughing. "Son of a bitch," she said. "Shows how wrong you can be when you start trying to trust people. Those bastard Greasies aren't giving us a square count! They didn't stop fighting because they wanted to make peace. They stopped because we were as good as dead anyway!"

"But—but so are they—"

"Wrong! Because they *have* a Farside base!" She shook her head ruefully. "Folks," she said, "I was going to make a real magnolious announcement about turning the reins over to civilian government, only now I think that's going to have to wait. We've got a military job to do first. When this side of the planet goes, they've got that snug little nest on the side that never gets radiation from Kung anyway, and they couldn't care less if the son of a bitch blows up. That's going to be a nice place to be. And we're going to take it away from them."

·TWENTY-TWO·

THESE WERE THE mesas and canyons of the high desert. Danny Dalehouse had flown over them in less than an hour and seen them only as quaint patterns in an unimportant carpet beneath. Marching over them was something else. Kappelyushnikov ferried them in as close as he dared, three at a time, once four, with the little biplane desperately slow to wallow off the ground. He made more than a dozen round trips and saved them a hundred kilometers of cutting through jungle. Even so, it was a three-day march, and every step hard work.

Nevertheless, Dalehouse had not felt as well in weeks. In spite of bone-bruising fatigue. In spite of the star that might explode at any moment. In spite of the fact that Marge Menninger's shopping list had overlooked a supply of spare hiking boots, and so he limped on a right foot that was a mass of blisters. He was not the unluckiest. Three of the effectives had been unable to go on at all. "We'll come back for you," Margie had promised; but Dalehouse thought she lied, and he could see in the eyes of the casualties that they were certain of it.

And still he would have sung as he marched, if he'd had breath enough for it.

It had been raining on and off for nearly forty hours—mean, wind-driven rain that kept them sodden in the steamy heat even when it let up, and chilled when it drenched them. That didn't matter, either. It was regrettable, because it meant that Charlie and the two remaining members of his flock could not keep in touch with them visually. (He had had to take the radio away from the balloonist before they left—far too easy for the Greasies to intercept.) Whenever the clouds lightened, Dalehouse searched the sky for his friend. He never saw him, never heard his song, but he knew he was up there somewhere. It wasn't serious. The weather that kept Charlie from scouting danger for them kept the Greasies from providing it.

There were twelve of them still toiling toward the Greasy camp. They had left the rest of the survivors—the highly impermanent survivors, if this expedition didn't do what it was supposed to—back at the base with orders to look as though they were twice as numerous as they were. Margie herself had transmitted the last message to the Greasies: "We are beginning construction of underground shelters. When the flare is over we can discuss a permanent peace. Meanwhile, if you approach we will shoot on sight." Then she pulled the plug on the radio and crawled into Cappy's plane for the last ferry trip.

They had less than ten kilometers to go—a three hour stroll under good conditions, but it would take them all of a day. It was scramble down one side of a ravine and crawl up the other, peer over the top of a crest and scuttle down its other face. And it was not just the terrain. They were all heavily loaded. Food, water, weapons, equipment. Everything they would need they had to carry on their backs.

The red cylinders marked "Fuel Elements—Replacement" were the worst. Each cylinder contained hundreds of the tiny clad needles and weighed more than a kilogram. Twelve of them made a heavy load.

At first they took turns carrying the puzzle pieces that would unite to form a nuclear bomb. One of the tricks was to make sure they didn't unite prematurely, and at every stop Lieutenant Kristianides supervised the stacking of knapsacks so that no two bomb loads were within a meter of each other. The chance was very small that they could in fact be dropped, kicked, or jostled into a configuration of critical mass. Making that happen on purpose when desired had been a serious challenge for some of the best munitions experts on Earth; for that purpose they carried another twenty kilos of highly sophisticated casing and trigger. Without that there was no real danger—or so Marge assured them all. But they were careful anyway, because in their guts none of them believed the assurance. Perhaps not even Marge.

At the end of the first march Margie had gone through the party, checking loads. When she came to Ana Dimitrova, sitting hugging her knees next to Danny Dalehouse, she said softly, "Are you sterile?"

"What? Really! What a question!" But then Margie shook her head.

"Sorry, I'm just tired. I should have remembered you aren't." And she grinned and winked at both Dalehouse and Ana; but when they picked up packs again Nan's load was changed to water flasks, and limping old Marguerite Moseler was carrying the fuel rods.

Margie looked terrible, and at every stop she seemed to look worse. Her plumpness was long gone. The bone structure of her face showed for the first time in years, and her voice was a rasp. More than that, her complexion was awful. When the Krinpit had buried her for two hours, its molting juices overrode her defenses. A day later she had broken out in great purplish blotches and a skin discoloration like sunburn. She said it did not hurt; there, too, Dalehouse thought she lied.

But he thought she was telling the truth about one very important thing, and perhaps that was the reason he could not repress a feeling of cheer. The bomb they were carrying would not be used.

He had been the one to propose it, and she had accepted the idea at once. "Of course," she said. "I don't want to destroy their camp. I want it, all of it—not only for us, but for the future of the human race on Jem. The bomb's best use is as a threat, and that's what we'll use it for."

He said as much to Ana at their last halt before coming in sight of the Greasy base. "She's planning for future generations. At least she thinks it's worth keeping your chromosomes intact."

"Of course," said Ana, surprised. "I have that confidence too." And so, Danny Dalehouse was discovering, did he. Bad as things were, he had hope. It carried him through that last belly-crawl, three hundred meters in the drenching rain, into the muddy cave that was their point of entrance for the burrower tunnels under the Greasy base. It sustained him while Major Vandemeer and Kris Kristianides painfully and gingerly assembled the parts of the detonator and fitted the fuel rods into it. It survived after Margie and Vandemeer and two others wriggled their way into the abandoned courses and disappeared from sight. The part of his life, of all their lives, that they were living through at that moment was misery and fear. Maybe worse than that, it was self-reproach; they were doing something that Dalehouse could not think of as noble or even tolerable. It was a holdup. Armed robbery. No better than a mugging. But it would be *over*. And a better time would come! And that hope kept him going for two full hours after Margie and the others had crawled away. Until Kris Kristianides, looking scared and harried, checked her watch and said, "That's it. From now on, everybody stay inside. Face the wall. Hands over your eyes. When the fireball comes, *don't look up*. Wait ten minutes at least. I've got goggles. I'll tell you when you—"

Then they drowned her out, Dalehouse first and loudest. "She's going to do it! But she promised—"

"Shit, Dalehouse, she couldn't keep that promise! The Greasies would think it was a bluff. She's going to take out their arms and food just like we planned, and then we'll move in and wipe them up."

"What insanity!" cried Ana. "There'll be nothing there! The fallout will kill us if we go into the camp."

"Maybe. I've got a counter; we'll check everything out. The important thing's the planes. If we get them we can get to their base on Farside." She hesitated. She had been carefully rehearsed in all this and had carried the secret with her for more than a day. But she had dreaded this moment. If it had not been for her burns, she would have been in the warrens with the colonel and the major, and a lot happier there than she was here. "Anyway," she finished, "there's nothing we can do about it now. She'll blow the bomb in the next ten minutes. Get your faces down!"

And then, at last, hope was dead.

For the Brood Mother, too, all hope was gone. Blind and alone she moved slowly down through the tunnels to the only place left for her to be.

The thirty-meter level was for pups and outcasts. It was a place to play growing-up games or, at the end of all games, a place to die. Mother dr'Shee had never been there before. She had been a biddable pup, trained early to responsibility. As a tiny thing she had found it tingly-thrilling to listen to the stories of the half-growns, shivering in delight as she groped for the teat in her nurse's sheltering silk. But she had never explored the adventurous levels for herself. Not once. She had known that the time would come soon enough when, at the end of her life, she would drag herself down to see those old, unvisited levels and die.

In that she had been partly wrong. It was time to die, and she was there. But she could not see.

With dignity the Brood Mother raised her forebody to its fullest stretch and called, "Is anyone near?"

There was no reply. No sound. No scent except the stale, spoiled smell of elders long dead. She tried again, not because she had any hope of being answered, but for the sake of being methodical. "Person or pup, can anyone hear my voice?"

Nothing. If there had been an answer, it could only have been one of the wild young males who roamed the upper corridors, seeking only to kill. But there was not even that.

So another of her senses had become useless to her. Hearing meant nothing when there was nothing to hear.

It was a pity she was blind, but she bore no malice toward the Two-Legs who had burned out her eyes with their stroboscopic lights. She had in any case revenged herself upon a number of them in advance—for poisoning her tunnels, for abducting her young, for perverting the brood into new and vile practices. Most of all for coming to disturb her life in the first place. She had fought against it all, against the Two-Legs and sometimes against members of her own brood turned against her by the new ways of the Two-Legs. And now the tunnels were empty, and she was blind. *Tssheee!* It would have been less—less *final* to be here and alone if she could have seen at least an occasional phosphorescent glimmer of fungus or decay. What was left of her senses? Taste no longer mattered. There was little to eat. Smell was unrewarding, with neither males nor pups to nuzzle. She could still feel the powdery dust floor beneath her, the curving wall at her side.

Dr'Shee took comfort from being tightly enclosed, as she had been through all the happiest parts of her life . . .

Which was now over.

She stretched and sighed a feline, purring sound of despair. She was beginning to be very hungry. The Two-Legs had ruined most of the food stores when they poisoned the tunnels to get at her and her few surviving allies. But the tunnels stretched ten kilometers in all directions. Somewhere there would be something, in this immense engineered warren that had been her world. She did not seriously think of seeking it. A Brood Mother did not debase herself to prolong a life that was over.

Woomp—

The tunnel around her moved. It was not a shake or a tremor, but a deliberate and almost peristaltic movement. Mother dr'Shee had never before experienced such a thing. Burrows sometimes crumbled, Krinpit invaded them, the rains might wash through a roof. But for all the earth to move? Such a thing could not happen! For the Brood Mother such an event was exactly as disquieting as it would have been for a fish to scull its tail and yet not move, or for a human being to feel the air about him turn glassy and shatter.

And then, from thirty meters above and more than a kilometer away, she heard the sound that followed. It was more than a sound; it was a pressure in the air that stung her ears and left them filled with a distant, discordant chatter, like the peeping of a hungry litter. But there were no pups to cry for her, ever again.

For some reason Margie's right knee was only scraped and sore, while the left one was bloodily gouged, the leg of the coverall worn through, the skin itself long since rubbed away. It was harder and harder for her to keep up with the two ahead of her. God had not intended her to crawl through tunnels ninety centimeters high for hours on end. . . . Which God she meant was not quite clear. To spare her knee she tried for a while a three-legged gait, putting a little weight on her left toes, the rest on right leg and hands. That was a bummer. She wound up with the worst cramp she had ever had in the calf of her leg. She had to stop and press it out while Vandemeer behind her almost caught up and the two ahead kept on going. So then she speeded her pace and ripped the knee still more.

She paused and glanced at her watch. Still more than a quarter of an hour before the device would go off. Before that the two grenades they had left at bends in the tunnels would bring down enough dirt to tamp the explosion; and they were a good kilometer away by now. Probably far enough for survival, if not comfort. "Take ten," she shouted. She rolled over and rested her limbs, breathing hard of the stale and tainted air. Funnily, it was not really dark in the tunnels. That she had not expected. Once her eyes had adjusted, she could see little will-o'-the-wisp lights, so faint and pale that they hardly had color at all. Swamp gas, foxfire, Wilis—whatever they were, they were welcome.

She heard a quick, quiet scuffle down the tunnel behind her, then a *thwuck*.

Then silence again.

"Van?" she called. "Major Vandemeer?"

The dirt walls swallowed her words, and there was no reply. Painfully she rolled herself over, turned herself around, and crawled back.

The mouse-droppings odor was very strong. She touched the switch of her little helmet light and saw that the major was dead. One of the burrowers had been here, and the dart that protruded from Vandemeer's face proved it.

"Shit," whispered Margie, and then belatedly lifted her head and drew her pistol. The light showed nothing for sure down the crooked, uneven tunnel—was that a glint of something? a reflection from an eye? She fired twice.

When she looked again there was nothing there. But every few meters there were little side passages and bays, and a dozen Creepies could be waiting there for her to turn her head.

She almost raised her voice to call the others back but stopped herself as she was opening her mouth. For what? They could not bring the major's body back. Doubled over as it was—he seemed to have been turning when he was shot—he almost blocked the tunnel. Maybe that was the last service he could render his cause—to slow down pursuit.

There was a better way. She had two grenades left. She pulled one off her belt, set it to ten clicks, turned around, and scuttled as rapidly as she could after the others. When she had counted a hundred seconds, she dropped, locked her hands over the back of her neck, and waited for the distant, muffled thud that told her she had dropped a part of the tunnel roof down to bury the major.

When the grenade went off, it occurred to her that it was strange she had not caught up with the others. "Sam! Chotnik! Sound off!" she cried. They didn't answer; they hadn't heard her order to stop. She left the helmet light on and hurried after them, the pain in her knee no longer signifying. When the red numerals on her watch told her it was time for the nuclear blast, she still had not caught up.

She rolled over on her back again. For this blast it did not matter whether she protected her neck. She would be killed or she would not, and the only factor that mattered was whether there was enough earth between her and the explosion. There should be. When the impellers drove the sets of plutonium needles in to mesh with each other, there would be a nuclear blast. But not a big one. They would not stay in contact more than a few microseconds. If she had placed them right, they would expend their force up through the roof of the tunnel, carrying the Greasies' arms stores with them, and not much else. If she had placed them right. She was far less sure of that than she had pretended to Vandemeer and the others. The maps that Tinka and the Indonesian had given their lives to get to her were extremely complete and clear. But reading them in the open air was one thing; trying to follow them as you crawled from level to level underground was something quite different. She was not even sure that they had followed the same route on the way out as going in. They should have drawn a silken cord after them or broken off bits of gingerbread cookies for a trace—

At that moment the explosion occurred. Right on time. And she was still alive.

It was not even frightening. It was, she thought, as it would have been in her mother's womb if her mother had fallen. Some external event had taken place. But here in the tunnel she moved with the ground, and even the sound of the explosion was too huge and slow to be frightening.

So that part of the plan, at least, had worked. Now, if Kris could rally the patrol to the attack— If they remembered their radiation ponchos and the wind was not too unfavorable— If the Greasies did not pull themselves together fast enough to resist— If the bomb had been in the right place after all— There were too many ifs. Her place was with her troops, not here.

A sighing, slithering sound a few meters behind her caught her attention. She turned the headlamp toward it and saw that a section of the roof had collapsed into the tunnel.

Shaken loose by the nuclear blast? Maybe. More likely not. Creepies had been known to try to trap a foe by plugging tunnels before. She was terribly easy to find and follow, with the trail of blood from her knee.

It was time to get out of there. Doggedly detaching herself from the pain and from the fear that one of them was silently creeping up behind her, she resumed her crawl.

In ten meters her head struck dirt.

She turned on the light again. It was fresh dirt. The burrowers had closed both ends of the tunnel. She whirled quickly. Nothing moved behind her. She was alone.

Margie Menninger said to the wall, "The most basic human fear is of being buried alive." She waited for a moment, as though hoping someone would answer. Then she pulled out her pistol with one hand and reached for her entrenching tool with the other. It wasn't there. Then she remembered she had left it where they assembled the bomb.

Fingers then.

She dropped the pistol and tore at the dirt plug with her bare hands. Furiously. Then in terror. At last because there was nothing else for her to do.

From horizon to horizon, as far as Charlie could see, there was a solid undercast of clouds, and taller ones poked up all around. The storm was weakening off toward the ocean, but here, somewhere above the Greasy camp, it had been hours since he had seen the ground at all, days since he had last seen the little party of his friend 'Anny. And it was impossible to stay on station! At all levels up to ten thousand meters and more the wind was strong and solidly toward the Heat Pole, and it dragged him remorselessly away. Charlie could read the fraying of the anvil-shaped

tops of the cumulonimbus; it showed that at fifteen thousand meters there was a return flow. But he and the two females of his
flock who survived were worn and tired. They had lost much lift.
It took them forever to reach those lofty levels.

As they labored upward a new flock came sailing down from the
Pole, and Charlie led his tiny fragment to join it, eager for a new
audience for his songs about the new friends from Earth, hungry
to hear songs he had not heard before. It had been long and long
since he had joined in a proper eisteddfod, and his soul ached for
it. The new flock was small, fewer than sixty adults, but there
were voices in it he had never heard, and he sang greeting toward
them with joy.

White light lashed across them.

The flare caught them all by surprise. Charlie was one of the
fortunate ones. He was facing away from the blast, and so he was
not blinded at once. He saw the high cirrus starkly outlined, blue-
white against the sullen, crimson Jemman sky, saw the shapes of
the new flock picked out in brighter, sharper colors than he had
ever seen. Minutes later he heard the sound, and behind him
and below a new thundercloud boiled up out of the undercast.

Chorus of welcome became a dirge of pain and fear. Charlie
could only reply with a lifting song. The seniors of the new flock
took it up, and the swarm dropped ballast, belched swallowed hydrogen into their sacs, and rose. A few did not. They were not
merely blind; they were in too great pain to respond.

Although they were far from the blast, when the winds struck,
the swarm was thrown helter-skelter across the sky. Charlie had
never felt such gusts before. Always in other storms there had
been warning—gathering clouds and the deadly play of lightning
to tell them it was time to swallow hydrogen and ride out the
storm, or soar to escape above it. This time there was no warning
and no escape. His feeding flaps and winglets felt as though they
were being torn out at the roots. Captive of the huge sail of his
surface, he was thrown through the new flock, caroming off their
seniors, cannoning balloonets out of the way.

And then, without warning, he felt the familiar creeping tension of the surface of his gas sac and recognized the sweet, stinging odor of the females. Estrus, swarming time, time to breed!

The spinnerets of the females were working furiously now,

spraying threadlike ova and pheronomes into the air. All around the swarm, the air was fragrant with the demand to breed. For Charlie, and for all the males, there was no question about what to do next: hive up, spray milt, soar back and forth through the stinging mist while their teats elongated, convulsed, spread their seed. The skins of their air sacs tightened, drawing the features of their tiny faces into caricatures. Behind the expressions that looked like pain was pain. The overtures to sex were no joy to Charlie. They were like being locked in an Iron Maiden with acid-tipped spikes. Only the relief that came when the semen squirted out made the pain end.

But it was wrong, wrong!

Charlie sang out his question and his fear, and the new flock sang with him. What breeding was this, with the flare coming from the enemy ground and not the sky? What was this heat that smote them like a fist, following on the thunder and the wild gales? Charlie could see that in the turbulence most of the silk-lings had been missed by the milt. They were all over the sky. Within his own body he could feel it was wrong. Where was the bubbling of hydrogen to replenish his sac, radiation-stung out of his body fluids? And what—what was this monstrous, bubbling cloud that was growing so fast it was drawing them all toward it?

And that was the question that answered all the others and put an end to questions forever for Charlie as the searing heat of the nuclear cloud burned out his eye patches, cracked his gas sac, touched off the hydrogen that spilled out, and ended his songs for always.

·TWENTY-THREE·

As NUCLEAR EXPLOSIONS went, it was inconsiderable. Less than a kiloton, it would hardly have been noticed in the multimegaton blasts that had scoured the surface of Earth. When the imploding grenades forced the bright plutonium needles out of their sheaths to mate, they were in contact for only a few microseconds before their own immense reaction drove them apart.

But by then the explosion had occurred. The needles, the shell, the walls of the tunnel around them had been vaporized to a hot gas, billions of atmospheres of pressure, irresistibly determined to escape. It escaped. Within a few thousandths of a second it had formed its pipsqueak fireball, fifty meters across, racing upward at five hundred kilometers an hour, brighter than Kung, brighter than Earth's sun, brighter than hundreds of them put together. The fireball grew and soared, first bright red with its burden of nitric acid, then whitening and losing its brightness as it began to cool.

Even through closed eyes that stark flare was visible to the people huddled in the cave, and the shock front that swept over them shook the cave and their bodies. The noise was immense. After it, over the echoes, Kris Kristianides was shouting, "Stay down! Don't open your eyes! Wait!" For nearly ten minutes she kept them there, and then, slowly, she peered through half-closed lids and the dark goggles and announced they could get up.

Tentatively they poked their heads over the ridge. Squinting, they saw what Marge Menninger had done.

The nuclear cloud boiled tall through the layers of stratus. It had punched its own hole in the rain clouds, but its mushroom top was out of sight. Nearer, the Greasy camp seemed hardly touched: a shed blown over, a couple of tents burning, people moving dazedly around.

"She—she missed the base!" cried Kris, and Danny Dalehouse could not tell whether her tone was angry or glad. But what she said was true. The bottom of the blast was half a kilometer away from the camp toward the Heat Pole. Marge had got herself lost. The half of the blast that went into explosive pressure had wasted itself on the sand and succulents of the steppe.

But the third that went into heat had done better. The nearest persons in the Greasy camp were staggering around, blind and in agony. No one had given them goggles. No one had warned them not to look toward the blast.

"Check your pieces," Kristianides ordered. She had taken the goggles off, and under them her eyes were red. But her voice was determined. "Put on your cloaks. Let's go. We're moving in."

Dalehouse stood up and pulled the plastic poncho over his head like an automaton. (Would that really protect against any fallout at all?) He picked up his recoilless and slapped a cartridge into the breech. (Why am I doing this?) He started off with the others in a ragged line of skirmish, all nine of them walking slowly toward the Fuel base.

At every step he was telling himself that it was wrong. Wrong tactically: the nuclear blast had knocked out no more than a few unfortunates, and they were likely to get their heads blown off by the survivors. Wrong strategically: they should never have allowed themselves to get into this position. And wrong, most wrong of all, morally. What kind of world were they fighting for when they killed people without warning?

Dalehouse looked uneasily back and forth at the others in the line. All were staring straight ahead at the Fuel camp. Didn't any of them feel the way he did?

He stopped in his tracks. "Kris," he said, "I don't want to do this."

She turned slowly so that the muzzle of her gun covered him. "Move your ass, Dalehouse."

"No, wait, Kris. Let's—"

She said tightly, "I was expecting that from you. We're going in there. All of us. Colonel Menninger set this up, and I'm not going to let it go to waste. Now move it."

The others had stopped to look at them. None of them spoke; they only waited while Dalehouse watched the barrel of the GORR come into line with the bridge of his nose. He sighed deeply and said, "No, Kris." And then he stood there as her expression changed and hardened and he realized that, yes, she was going to pull the trigger—

"Put down your rifle, lieutenant," Ana called.

She was behind Kris and a little to one side, and she had her own gun pointed firmly at the lieutenant's back. "I do not wish to kill," she said, "but I, too, do not want to attack this camp."

Dalehouse didn't wait to see what would happen. He stepped forward and took the GORR from Kristianides's hands. He threw it back over the crest of the hill they had just crossed and then followed it with his own. After a second Ana did the same, and so, one by one, did the others.

"You fucking fools!" Kris raged. "They'll shoot you down like rats!"

Dalehouse did not answer. He stared toward the Greasy camp, where a few persons who were not blind or incapacitated had begun to appear. They had weapons, and they were gazing at the drama on the hill.

Dalehouse raised his hands over his head and began to walk steadily toward them. Out of the corner of his eye he saw Ana doing the same thing. Maybe Kris was right. Maybe one of those armed people kneeling in the shelter of a smoldering tent would begin to shoot. But it was out of his hands. Whatever guilt there was, it would not anymore belong to him; and for the first time in months he felt at peace.

·TWENTY-FOUR·

AND SO, AT THE LAST, what can one say of them? What is to be said of Marjorie Menninger and Danny Dalehouse and Ana Dimitrova—and of Charlie and Ahmed Dulla, or of Sharn-igon and Mother dr'Shee? They did what they could. More often than not, they did what they thought they should. And what can be said of them is what can be said of all persons, human and otherwise, at the end: they died. Some survived the fighting. Some survived the flare. But in the long run there are no survivors.

There are only replacements. And time passes, and generations come and go.

And then, what can one say of that beautiful and powerful woman named Muskrat Greencloud An-Guyen?

One can say that she bears the traces of Margie and Nan and some of the others. Some through the passage of chains of DNA, some only because of what they did or who they were. She never knew any of them, of course, because they are all six generations dead; she is a replacement.

Like all of us, she is not a single person. She wears three personas, or six, or a hundred if you count the subjective memories and stereotypes other persons carry around that bear the label "Muskie An-Guyen." To a former lover, she is the sweetly sweaty companion of a weekend at Lake Hell. To her grandchildren, she is the docent who leads them through the museums and the zoo. To your average registered Republicate lot-caster of the Boyne-Feng Metropolitan Area, she is the selection judge who supervises the machineries of government. Or, actually, of nongovernment. Muskie is one hundred percent solidly behind the Six Precepts of the Jemman Republics, and *No strong central government* is the last and maybe most important of them. "Government" is a dead wickedness to Muskie, burned out in the Blast and starved in the Desperation. It has been gone from Jem this century and a half. No one wants to see that pawkish horror back, least of all Muskie. It is as obsolete as armies and indolence and waste. Muskie will keep it so, if it demands her last drop of blood as well as the utmost sacrifices by her militia volunteers and gift acceptors.

But to see who Muskie is, let us look at the three principal faces she wears to show the sultry and satisfied world of Jem.

The first of these is Muskie the nurturer. She provides more than a tenth of the food for Boyne-Feng, and nearly all of it that comes from underground. She does not do it by herself, of course. See her as she stands in the gallery gate. The morning shift is coming on duty. The bad old days of "owners" died when government did. Muskie is not an owner. She is only one among equals. But she is a special one.

You might think she looks like a Virginia planter overseeing slaves, or perhaps like a Shensi landlord accepting squeeze from the tenant farmers in her paddies. This would be deceiving. There is no ownership. There is not even any compulsion. The tokens the Krinpit laborers give her one by one as they scuttle past to the underground farms are not extorted. They are gifts. They are freely given. If Muskie is not pleased with the gift of one of them, she does not reproach him or order him to give more. She simply refuses it. Then the Krinpit chooses to go back to his village, where he may freely starve. A meter or two past Muskie's station the Creepie overseers spray the Krinpit with anti-allergen lacquer. No force is employed here, either. If the Krinpit do not choose to make gifts to the overseers, they need not turn back. The overseers will then choose not to spray them. The Krinpit will then itch or molt or die as a consequence of exposure to the terraborn crops they handle. It is the Krinpits' right to choose this if they wish. There is absolutely no compulsion, by anyone, of anyone, at any time. That is part of the Six Precepts.

The Krinpit know this and rejoice in their freedom—not to mention rejoicing in the radios, the gaily raucous drums and zithers, the chemical intoxicants, beads and metal tools that they prize. These are freely given to them when they freely give up the tokens that Muskie has freely given to them at the end of each voluntary work shift. The Creepies also know that this is true. They are also grateful, especially for the Two-Legs' improvements on their savage old burrows, and they freely assist the stronger, bigger Krinpit laborers by instructing them in where to plant the floor crops of mushrooms and the roof crops of potato and yam. They too now rejoice in the possession of beads, devices, and intoxicants their rude progenitors never knew. The balloonists know it—what fun they have with their taped music and their repeated orgasms! And, of course, Muskrat Greencloud An-Guyen knows it really well. She has everything she wants. Perhaps the best part of what she has is the certain knowledge that the Six Precepts are always followed, and so justice is always served, and everybody else on Jem—and that means everybody, Krip or balloonist, stranger or son—has everything, too. Though not usually as much of everything as she.

Then there is Muskie the civil volunteer. Not merely a discussant or a participator, like everyone else. She is a selection judge who gives freely of her time to serve the whole community, even at holidays.

She leaves the agricultural galleries and goes aboveground into the warm, bright dome of Fat City. Muskie is still a sturdily beautiful woman. She is tanned by the ultraviolet lights of the pool-grotto, tall, solid rather than plump; she weighs sixty standard kilos, but she has a fifty-centimeter waist, and her lovers prefer her to partners half her age. Eyes follow her as she comes smiling into Remembrance Hall, removes her slacks and slicks for comfort, gives Ring-Greeting to all, and reclines on a foam couch. "I would like to begin," she says sunnily. The other six volunteer selection judges agree that they, too, would like to discuss the issues of the day.

Most of the issues are routine, and consensus appears at once. (They are all saving themselves for the big one.) From his place under the bust of Mother Kristianides, wide-browed and serene as she looks down on them, Roanoke t'Schreiber describes the progress in cleaning up Lake Hell. All the city's sewage is being pumped there. The native aquatic life is being satisfactorily killed off, since *Escherichia coli* is antibiotic against most forms of Jemman life. "Another two million bowel movements and we'll have it sparkly clean," he comments. Sod House Flareborn looks up from inspecting her ten-centimeter fingernails to wonder if the militia should be freely given extra tokens, since so many of them have unfortunately (though voluntarily) given up their lives in the exploration of additional Creepie burrows and the liberation of distant camps of Krinpit. All agree that this seems desirable. The woman in militia fatigues who has been hovering by the door leaves with a smile of satisfaction.

Then Muskie's face clouds and she observes, "I have heard that there has been another tactran from Alphabase."

There is silence in the chamber. This is the issue that holds the seeds of dissent, and even change. No one really wants to get into it. All the judges stir uncomfortably on the couches under the busts of the ancestors, each waiting for the others to speak.

At last t'Schreiber offers an opinion. "I, for one, think it was unwise of our predecessors to attempt to resume space exploration. They freely gave much value to put new tactran satellites in orbit. What have we gained? Sorrow and confusion." He lists the contacts made: a garble that *might* have been from the Martian colony; pitiful pleas for help from old Earth itself; a dozen cocky messages from the base at Alpha Centauri suggesting an attempt at an actual flight to and from Jem. From the rest of the universe, nothing.

Muskie waits uncomfortably, shifting position and scratching just above the plaque of her string bikini. Then she says, "I wonder if we should answer messages from Alphabase anymore."

No one responds.

Therefore it is agreed; and the judges turn to speaking of the gratifying growth in human population—from one hundred eighty survivors to eighteen hundred in the third generation, and now nearly a quarter of a million in the sixth. There is no longer a fear that humanity might not survive. On Jem Man flourishes.

This reminds Muskie that her newest baby is about ready to be born. She speaks softly into her telephone to the hospital. The mare is in the delivery room even at that moment. But the news is bad. The baby was born dead.

"I blame myself," says Muskie to the doctor remorsefully. "Sarah Glowbag—was that her name?"

"Mary Glowbag," the doctor corrects her.

"Yes, Mary. She was nearly sixty years old. I should have invited a younger mare to brood my baby."

"Don't let it spoil your day," consoles the doctor. "One must expect a failure now and then. Nearly all of your children have lived, and remember, you have three others in the oven right now."

"You're very kind." Muskie hangs up with a smile. But the news has upset her—and just at Christmas, too. "I would like to leave now," she tells the other judges, and of course they also wish to close the discussion and return to their homes.

And then there is Muskrat the mother, the honored one at the head of her family.

This is no small part of her. Her family is huge. Forty-four living children, the dozen oldest long since having made her a multiple grandmother, the three youngest still unborn in the borrowed wombs of other women. (She reminds herself to make a voluntary gift to Sarah, or Mary, Glowbag for her kindness in carrying her most recent implanted ovum to term. Not as large as usual, of course; after all, the child had been born dead.) At Christmas all of them will come to give her Ring-Greeting, and she looks forward to the day with pleasure.

But not all of a family's concerns are pleasurable. As she walks across the pleasant gardens toward the place where she sleeps and keeps her belongings, a short, pale youth pushes toward her through the shrubs. He is d'Dalehouse Dolphin An-Guyen, and he is one of her sons. He has been running. He is breathing hard. Muskie sighs and says, "How nice of you to hurry to give me Ring-Greeting, Dolph."

He stops and blinks at the pretty Christmas many-tree in the

center of the garden, with its ring-shaped lights and yellow Star of
Earth at the top. Obviously he has forgotten about the holiday.
Muskie sighs again. "Merry Christmas anyway, Dolph. I know
you're going to reproach me some more. Sit down and catch your
breath first."

They sit on a pressed creepystone bench under a grape arbor. (A
few raisins had survived the flare-storm under a bunk in that Outpost of the People. From the six germinable seeds that were found
in them had come all the wine on Jem, and this arbor.)

Muskie does not look at her son. She knows that in spite of his
faults, he is too well brought up to begin before she has given him
encouragement, and she wants him to feel the peace of this place.
All around the garden are the statues of the First Generation, the
eighteen Mothers in gold, the fifty-two Mares in crystal, the
eighty-nine Fathers in granite quarried from the cliffs under the
Heat Pole. (The twenty-one survivors who contributed no genes
to the pool, even by cloning, have statues too, but they are ranged
outside the park. None of them were even mares.) There are further distinctions in the statues. The eighty-one survivors who returned from Farside have their names picked out in frost-etched
silver. The thirty-two who survived in the burrows under the Outpost of Food when the flare caught them before the ferrying to
Farside was complete are marked in ruby. And the sixty-seven
others—few of them viable—who survived the flare in caves, under
machines, inside space capsules, or wherever they could hide from
the rage of the star are marked in orange chrysolite, the color of
flame. That was six generations back. Muskie could have been descended from 2^6 of them, more than a third, but actually only
eleven are truly her ancestors, with considerable overlap. (For instance, she is quintuply each descended from Marjorie Menninger,
Ana Dimitrova, Nguyen Tree, and Firstborn McKenzie, the tiny
phocomelic child born to the one woman who survived both the
nuclear bombing of the Outpost of Fuel and the flare. She lived
only long enough to bear her damaged child, but the child was
marvelously fertile.)

When Muskie feels that this holy place has done all it can for
her son, she scratches below the waistband of her slacks and says,
"All right, Dolph, you may as well say it."

He cannot wait to get the words out, he is so impatient. "All right, I'll say it! You've made a mistake, Mother Muskie. We can't say no to Alphabase!"

" 'Can't'?"

He is doggedly stubborn. Even ferocious. "Yes, that's what I said, *can't*. It's a crime against the human race! Jem's rotting away before your eyes, Mother Muskie. This is the best chance we've ever had to get things going again. They've got high-energy technology on Alphabase! Do you know what it means, what they're suggesting? They're able to put ten tons standard into the tachyon charge state—we couldn't do that to save our lives."

"Dear Dolph," she begins, sweetly reasonable, "we have more pressing problems right here on Jem. Do you know how many wild flocks of Loons there are? Krips who still wallow in savagery? Creepies unreached and unbenefited. We have a duty—"

"We have a duty to humanity!" he cries.

"Yes. Certainly! And we are carrying it out. Our ancestors gave their lives to save us, and we are true to the Six Precepts. There is no tyrannical government, no coercion, no contending nationalities here. We haven't raped Jem, we've wooed it. We live off renewable resources, while the Alphs are back to industry and all the evils of technology."

"Dear God," he shouts, "*resources?* The quarter-million of us don't begin to scratch the surface of them! Do you know that fossil fuel is *forming* faster than we use it?"

"Good! Proper! That makes it renewable. But be reasonable, Dolph dear. Why spoil everyone's happiness by striving for something foolish? Suppose everyone wanted to do what you say. Who would mine these fossil fuels?"

"Krips. Creeps. People. Machines! I don't care. If they don't want to, they should be ordered to!"

Muskrat is shaken. "You have spoiled my Christmas," she says sorrowfully, and walks away. What a shame! A foolishly stubborn boy and an incompetent mare, and her whole holiday was ruined before it had rightly begun. Dolph is her favorite son, or often is. She admires his tiny, quick body and his bright mind. But what rot, really! What a bore! Why can't he accept paradise like everyone else and be happy in it?

Dolph's holiday is spoiled, too, and he sits on the creepystone bench so angry and frustrated that he does not even hear the carols beginning.

> A'es'e fi'eles,
> lae'i 'riumphan'es.

If only she could be made to understand! The winning of Jem had cost so much in blood and pain. Not just in that first terrible year. Over and over again, every time Kung had flared in those first decades. There had been eight flares since the days of the ancestors, and only the last two or three had been fairly painless. Plenty of warning. A frenzied rush to ionproof the domes and hustle essential perishables inside. A week of confinement while the star raged, a year or so of one or another kind of scarcity until the planet replenished itself. But that left half a dozen sieges of misery, the first worst, but all of them catastrophic. Was all that to go for nothing?

> Veni'e d'oremus,
> 'Ominum.

A Creepie overseer darts whickering past him toward the many-tree, followed by four noisy Krinpit gardeners in their bright red and green Ring-Greeting coats of lacquer. He becomes aware of the choir belatedly.

> —save us all from Sa'an's power
> When we were gone as'ray—

Hell of a season of joy this is, he thinks to himself. Season of suicide! Time of deciding to die on the vine while all the rest of the galaxy goes on to who knows what triumphs of technology and adventure! Glumness battles Christmas inside him. Gradually glumness loses. He remembers what the Creepie had been carrying—palely glowing ultraviolet strobes—and decides to stroll over to the Christmas many-tree.

The Krinpit are pushing away benches and picnic tables to make room, moaning and clattering to themselves; they finish and scuttle away. The Creepie positions his strobes and waits for orders. On the tree itself, the tethered balloonists are singing their little hearts out.

Schlaf im heilige ruhe,
Schlaf im heilige ruh'.

All around the tree young people like him are removing their clothes and slipping in between the gaily decorated trunks. "Time to start!" they cry; and the Loons begin the jolly, lively "Good King Wenceslas." Obediently the Creepie touches off the strobes. The Loons gasp and continue to sing and begin to emit their milt, and all under the lovely tree the couples link in the traditional Rings.

And Dolph can stand it no longer. Gloom loses. Christmas wins. He flings off his clothing and plunges into the trunks of the many-tree. Why fight Utopia? he thinks to himself. And so in that moment he completes the process of growing up. And begins the process of dying. Which is much the same thing.